Anne McCaffrey

Robert Silverberg

Joe Haldeman

Ursula K. Le Guin

FAR HORIZONS

FAR HORIZONS

All New Tales from the Greatest Worlds
of Science Fiction

edited by
Robert Silverberg

For Robert A. Heinlein
Isaac Asimov
John W. Campbell, Jr.

—They showed the way

Contents

Introduction • Robert Silverberg

1

THE EKUMEN:

Old Music and the Slave Women • Ursula K. Le Guin

5

THE FOREVER WAR:

A Separate War • Joe Haldeman

53

THE ENDER SERIES:

Investment Counselor • Orson Scott Card

89

THE UPLIFT UNIVERSE:

Temptation • David Brin

119

ROMA ETERNA:

Getting to Know the Dragon • Robert Silverberg

175

THE HYPERION CANTOS:

Orphans of the Helix • Dan Simmons

207

THE SLEEPLESS:
Sleeping Dogs • Nancy Kress
259

TALES OF THE HEECHEE:
The Boy Who Would Live Forever • Frederik Pohl
295

THE GALACTIC CENTER SERIES:
A Hunger for the Infinite • Gregory Benford
343

THE SHIP WHO SANG:
The Ship That Returned • Anne McCaffrey
379

THE WAY:
The Way of All Ghosts • Greg Bear
419

FAR HORIZONS

INTRODUCTION

The best science-fiction ideas are very big ones that have never quite occurred to anyone before, and the writers to whom such ideas come very frequently have second thoughts about them, or third thoughts, or fourth and fifth ones. And so one of the glories of modern-day science fiction has been the extended series in which the writer digs deeper and ever deeper into his original concept, finding new richness with each excavation.

I'm not speaking here of the kind of series that James Blish, long ago, called a "template" series—in which the writer, having hit on a serviceable idea and an appropriate structure for dramatizing it, goes on profitably replicating idea and format over and over again, sometimes for dozens of stories. This is not necessarily reprehensible—the Sherlock Holmes series, for example, is a template series that has given great pleasure to readers for more than a century, and the fundamental similarity of one story to the next and the unchanging relationship of Holmes to Watson are essential components of the delight to be had. But in the Holmes stories we do not find increasing depth of insight into the problems of crime detection in Victorian England, or into the curious personality of Sherlock Holmes, as the series proceeds. The series extends by self-imitation, not by evolution, as so many slick-magazine series of a later era (Tugboat Annie, Alexander Botts, etc.) did, and the way most television programs do nowadays. Most of the series stories that the *Saturday Evening Post* ran so copiously fifty and sixty years ago are forgotten today, as are the television shows of the season before last; it is Conan Doyle's superior ingenuity that keeps the Holmes stories alive despite their underlying formulaic nature.

We have had plenty of formula-series stuff in science fiction, too, from Tom Swift back in 1910 through Edgar Rice Burroughs's John

Carter on Mars novels of the 1920s through the Captain Future epics of a couple of decades later, and on through the kind of highly commercial multivolume stuff that floods the bookstores today. Some of this is fun, in its way, although a great deal is mere space-filling junk, in which a trivial idea is inflated by means of much huffing and puffing into three (or more) fat volumes that keep the readers contentedly circling around and around the same feeble little concept for hundreds of thousands of words. (We also have the myriad *Star Trek* and *Star Wars* novelizations, many of which tell lively and entertaining stories, but which, by predesign and stern publishing decree, do nothing at all to advance the underlying series concept beyond its starting point.)

However, we do have the other sort of series in science fiction, too, the kind that carries the reader through an evolutionary progression of concept and (sometimes) insight into character, and it is out of that kind of series that this book has been constructed.

Anyone with any historical grounding in science fiction can name dozens of such series at the first prod of his memory. E.E. Smith, Ph.D., a pioneer of the form, operated two of them, the *Skylark* novels of the 1920s and 1930s, and the subsequent *Lensman* series, vast and ever-expanding epics of the spaceways. In the 1940s and 1950s Robert A. Heinlein linked dozens of stories and novels into one enormous and basically coherent Future History; Poul Anderson offered a similar structure of his own a couple of decades later; A.E. van Vogt wrote two dazzling and bewildering novels about Gilbert Gosseyn and his fellow semanticians of the Null-A crowd. (A third, much less dazzling, followed decades later.) Isaac Asimov's *Foundation* series, the original trilogy and the various later books, looked deep into the Asimovian concept of "psychohistory," and, as the series grew, Asimov eventually linked it with his other celebrated many-paneled work, the *Positronic Robot* series. Henry Kuttner's memorable "Baldy" stories, collected as *Mutant*, were admirable examples of the same thing in shorter form, as of course were Ray Bradbury's *Martian Chronicles*. The list could continue for many pages, invoking the names of Blish, Simak, Clarke, Herbert, Leiber, Cordwainer Smith, and many another hero of time and space.

Amidst all the content-free trilogies and infinitely expanding media tie-in series of the present era, plenty of splendid books are still being written that form ongoing science-fiction series which actually evolve and penetrate ever more deeply into their conceptual frameworks. What I have done in *Far Horizons* is to gather together most of today's foremost practitioners of the evolutionary science-fiction series and ask them to write a short story or novelette that explores some aspect of their famous series that they did not find a way of dealing with in the books themselves.

You will find some well-known writers missing. I would gladly have included a new *Foundation* story here, or a new snippet of the Heinlein *Future History* series, or a return visit to Frank Herbert's Arrakis. Not possible, alas, in this particular continuum. And a couple of the living writers whom I invited told me that they had already said all they wanted to say about subject X or Y and Z, a position I had to applaud, however much I regretted their refusals.

But those who *are* on hand form as impressive a group of late-twentieth-century science-fiction writers as could possibly be assembled. I'm grateful to them all for having been willing to examine once again the settings and characters and ideas that have given so many readers such great pleasure over the past couple of decades. A great science-fiction concept, as we have learned over and over again in the world of science fiction, is inexhaustible—the infinite always is—and herewith a platoon of our best writers demonstrates that all over again for your enjoyment.

—*Robert Silverberg*
May, 1998

THE EKUMEN

Ursula K. Le Guin

Rocannon's World (1966)
Planet of Exile (1966)
City of Illusions (1967)
The Left Hand of Darkness (1969)
The Dispossessed (1974)
The Word for World is Forest (1976)
Four Ways to Forgiveness (1995)

Most of my science fiction takes place within one future-historical frame. As this developed haphazardly along with the books and stories, it contains some spectacular inconsistencies, but the general plan is this: The people of a world called Hain colonized the entire Orion Arm of the galaxy over a million years ago. All hominid species so far encountered are descendants of Hainish colonists (often genetically tailored to fit the colony planet or for other reasons).

After this Expansion, the Hainish withdrew to Hain for hundreds of millennia, leaving their far-flung offspring to hack it.

When Earth people began to explore nearby space, using Nearly As Fast As Light (NAFAL) ships and the instantaneous communicator called the ansible, they met up with the Hainish, now reaching out again to find their lost kinfolk. A League of Worlds was formed (see the novels *Rocannon's World, Planet of Exile, City of Illusions*). This expanded and matured into an egalitarian association of worlds and people called the Ekumen, administered from Hain by people called Stabiles, while Mobiles went out to explore unknown worlds, find out about new peoples, and serve as envoys and ambassadors to member worlds.

The "Ekumenical" novels are: *The Left Hand of Darkness, The Word for World is Forest,* and *The Dispossessed.* Most of the science-fiction stories in the collections *The Wind's Twelve Quarters* and *The Compass Rose,* the last three stories in *A Fisherman of the Inland Sea,* and all in *Four Ways to Forgiveness,* are set in the Ekumen.

This last book introduced the planets Werel and Yeowe. On Werel, thirty-five hundred years ago, an aggressive black-skinned people dominated the paler northern races and instituted a slave-based society and economy, with caste established by skin color. First contact by the Ekumen scared the xenophobic Werelians into rapid development of weapons and spaceships, and incidentally into colonizing Yeowe, the planet next inward to their sun, which they exploited with intensive slave labor. Soon after Werel finally admitted diplomats from the Ekumen, a great slave uprising began on Yeowe. After thirty years of war, Yeowe won its freedom from the dominant nation on Werel, Voe Deo. Voe Dean society was destabilized by the Yeowan liberation, as well as by the new perspectives offered by the Ekumen. Within a few years, a widespread slave uprising in Voe Deo pitted "owners" against "assets" in a full-scale civil war. This story takes place late in that war.

—*Ursula K. Le Guin*

Old Music and the Slave Women

by

Ursula K. Le Guin

THE CHIEF INTELLIGENCE OFFICER OF THE EKUMENICAL EMBASSY TO WEREL, A man who on his home world had the name Sohikelwenyanmurkeres Esdan, and who in Voe Deo was known by a nickname, Esdardon Aya or Old Music, was bored. It had taken a civil war and three years to bore him, but he had got to the point where he referred to himself in ansible reports to the Stabiles on Hain as the Embassy's chief stupidity officer.

He had been able, however, to retain a few clandestine links with friends in the Free City even after the Legitimate Government sealed the Embassy, allowing no one and no information to enter or leave it. In the third summer of the war, he came to the Ambassador with a request. Cut off from reliable communication with the Embassy, Liberation Command had asked him (how? asked the Ambassador; through one of the men who delivered groceries, he explained) if the Embassy would let one or two of its people slip across the lines and talk with them, be seen with them, offer proof that despite propaganda and disinformation, and though the Embassy was stuck in Jit City, its staff had not been co-opted into supporting the Legitimates, but remained neutral and ready to deal with rightful authority on either side.

"Jit City?" said the Ambassador. "Never mind. But how do you get there?"

"Always the problem with Utopia," Esdan said. "Well, I can pass with contact lenses, if nobody's looking closely. Crossing the Divide is the tricky bit."

Most of the great city was still physically there, the government buildings, factories and warehouses, the university, the tourist attractions: the Great Shrine of Tual, Theater Street, the Old Market with its interesting display rooms and lofty Hall of Auction, disused since the sale and rental of assets had been shifted to the electronic marketplace; the numberless streets, avenues, and boulevards, the dusty parks shaded by purple-flowered beya trees, the miles and miles of shops, sheds, mills, tracks, stations, apartment buildings, houses, compounds, the neighborhoods, the suburbs, and exurbs. Most of it still stood, most of its fifteen million people were still there, but its deep complexity was gone. Connections were broken. Interactions did not take place. A brain after a stroke.

The greatest break was a brutal one, an ax-blow right through the pons, a kilo-wide no-man's-land of blown-up buildings and blocked streets, wreckage and rubble. East of the Divide was Legitimate territory: downtown, government offices, embassies, banks, communications towers, the university, the great parks and wealthy neighborhoods, the roads out to the armory, barracks, airports, and spaceport. West of the Divide was Free City, Dustyville, Liberation territory: factories, union compounds, the rentspeople's quarters, the old gareot residential neighborhoods, endless miles of little streets petering out into the plains at last. Through both ran the great East–West highways, empty.

The Liberation people smuggled him out of the Embassy and almost across the Divide successfully. He and they had had a lot of practice in the old days getting runaway assets out to Yeowe and freedom. He found it interesting to be the one smuggled instead of one of the smugglers, finding it far more frightening yet less stressful, since he was not responsible, the package not the postman. But somewhere in the connection there had been a bad link.

They made it on foot into the Divide and partway through it and stopped at a little derelict truck sitting on its wheel rims under a gutted apartment house. A driver sat at the wheel behind the cracked, crazed windshield, and grinned at him. His guide gestured him into the back. The truck took off like a hunting cat, following a crazy route, zigzagging through the ruins. They were nearly across the Divide, jolting across a rubbled stretch which might have been a street or a marketplace, when the truck veered, stopped, there were shouts, shots, the van back was flung open and men plunged in at him. "Easy," he said, "go easy," for they were manhandling him, hauling him, twisting his arm behind his back. They yanked him out of the truck, pulled off his coat and slapped him down searching for weapons, frog-marched him to a car waiting beside the truck. He tried to see if his driver was dead but could not look around before they shoved him into the car.

It was an old government state-coach, dark red, wide, and long, made for parades, for carrying great estate owners to the Council and ambassadors from the spaceport. Its main section could be curtained to separate men from women passengers, and the driver's compartment was sealed off so the passengers wouldn't be breathing in what a slave breathed out.

One of the men had kept his arm twisted up his back until he shoved him headfirst into the car, and all he thought as he found himself sitting between two men and facing three others and the car starting up was, I'm getting too old for this.

He held still, letting his fear and pain subside, not ready yet to move even to rub his sharply hurting shoulder, not looking into faces nor too obviously at the streets. Two glances told him they were passing Rei Street, going east, out of the city. He realised then he had been hoping they were taking him back to the Embassy. What a fool.

They had the streets to themselves, except for the startled gaze of people on foot as they flashed by. Now they were on a wide boulevard, going very fast, still going east. Although he was in a very bad situation, he still found it absolutely exhilarating just to be out of the Embassy, out in the air, in the world, and moving, going fast.

Cautiously he raised his hand and massaged his shoulder. As cautiously, he glanced at the men beside him and facing him. All were dark-skinned, two blue-black. Two of the men facing him were young. Fresh, stolid faces. The third was a veot of the third rank, an oga. His face had the quiet inexpressiveness in which his caste was trained. Looking at him, Esdan caught his eye. Each looked away instantly.

Esdan liked veots. He saw them, soldiers as well as slaveholders, as part of the old Voe Deo, members of a doomed species. Businessmen and bureaucrats would survive and thrive in the Liberation and no doubt find soldiers to fight for them, but the military caste would not. Their code of loyalty, honor, and austerity was too like that of their slaves, with whom they shared the worship of Kamye, the Swordsman, the Bondsman. How long would that mysticism of suffering survive the Liberation? Veots were intransigent vestiges of an intolerable order. He trusted them, and had seldom been disappointed in his trust.

The oga was very black, very handsome, like Teyeo, a veot Esdan had particularly liked. He had left Werel long before the war, off to Terra and Hain with his wife, who would be a Mobile of the Ekumen one of these days. In a few centuries. Long after the war was over, long after Esdan was dead. Unless he chose to follow them, went back, went home.

Idle thoughts. During a revolution you don't choose. You're carried, a bubble in a cataract, a spark in a bonfire, an unarmed man in a car with seven armed men driving very fast down the broad, blank East Arterial Highway. . . . They were leaving the city. Heading for the East Provinces. The Legitimate Government of Voe Deo was now reduced to half the capital city and two provinces, in which seven out of eight people were what the eighth person, their owner, called assets.

The two men up in the front compartment were talking, though they couldn't be heard in the owner compartment. Now the bullet-headed man to Esdan's right asked a muttered question to the oga facing him, who nodded.

"Oga," Esdan said.

The veot's expressionless eyes met his.

"I need to piss."

The man said nothing and looked away. None of them said anything for a while. They were on a bad stretch of the highway, torn up by fighting during the first summer of the Uprising or merely not maintained since. The jolts and shocks were hard on Esdan's bladder.

"Let the fucking white-eyes piss himself," said one of the two young men facing him to the other, who smiled tightly.

Esdan considered possible replies, good-humored, joking, not offensive, not provocative, and kept his mouth shut. They only wanted an excuse, those two. He closed his eyes and tried to relax, to be aware of the pain in his shoulder, the pain in his bladder, merely aware.

The man to his left, whom he could not see clearly, spoke: "Driver. Pull off up there." He used a speakerphone. The driver nodded. The car slowed, pulled off the road, jolting horribly. They all got out of the car. Esdan saw that the man to his left was also a veot, of the second rank, a zadyo. One of the young men grabbed Esdan's arm as he got out, another shoved a gun against his liver. The others all stood on the dusty roadside and pissed variously on the dust, the gravel, the roots of a row of scruffy trees. Esdan managed to get his fly open but his legs were so cramped and shaky he could barely stand, and the young man with the gun had come around and now stood directly in front of him with the gun aimed at his penis. There was a knot of pain somewhere between his bladder and his cock. "Back up a little," he said with plaintive irritability. "I don't want to wet your shoes." The young man stepped forward instead, bringing his gun right against Esdan's groin.

The zadyo made a slight gesture. The young man backed off a step. Esdan shuddered and suddenly pissed out a fountain. He was pleased, even in the agony of relief, to see he'd driven the young man back two more steps.

"Looks almost human," the young man said.

Esdan tucked his brown alien cock away with discreet promptness and slapped his trousers shut. He was still wearing lenses that hid the whites of his eyes, and was dressed as a rentsman in loose, coarse clothes of dull yellow, the only dye color that had been permitted to urban slaves. The banner of the Liberation was that same dull yellow. The wrong color, here. The body inside the clothes was the wrong color, too.

Having lived on Werel for thirty-three years, Esdan was used to being feared and hated, but he had never before been entirely at the mercy of those who feared and hated him. The aegis of the Ekumen had sheltered him. What a fool, to leave the Embassy, where at least he'd been harmless, and let himself be got hold of by these desperate defenders of a lost cause, who might do a good deal of harm not only to but with him. How much resistance, how much endurance, was he capable of? Fortunately they couldn't torture any information about Liberation plans from him, since he didn't know a damned thing about what his friends were doing. But still, what a fool.

Back in the car, sandwiched in the seat with nothing to see but the young men's scowls and the oga's watchful nonexpression, he shut his eyes again. The highway was smooth here. Rocked in speed and silence, he slipped into a postadrenaline doze.

When he came fully awake the sky was gold, two of the little moons glittering above a cloudless sunset. They were jolting along on a side road, a driveway that wound past fields, orchards, plantations of trees and building-cane, a huge field-worker compound, more fields, another compound. They stopped at a checkpoint guarded by a single armed man, were checked briefly and waved through. The road went through an immense, open, rolling park. Its familiarity troubled him. Lacework of trees against the sky, the swing of the road among groves and glades. He knew the river was over that long hill.

"This is Yaramera," he said aloud.

None of the men spoke.

Years ago, decades ago, when he'd been on Werel only a year or so, they'd invited a party from the Embassy down to Yaramera, the greatest estate in Voe Deo. The Jewel of the East. The model of efficient slavery. Thousands of assets working the fields, mills, factories of the estate, living in enormous compounds, walled towns. Everything clean, orderly, industrious, peaceful. And the house on the hill above the river, a palace, three hundred rooms, priceless furnishings, paintings, sculptures, musical instruments—he remembered a private concert hall with walls of gold-backed glass mosaic, a Tualite shrine-room that was one huge flower carved of scented wood.

They were driving up to that house now. The car turned. He caught only a glimpse, jagged black spars against the sky.

The two young men were allowed to handle him again, haul him out of the car, twist his arm, push and shove him up the steps. Trying not to resist, not to feel what they were doing to him, he kept looking about him. The center and the south wing of the immense house were roofless, ruinous. Through the black outline of a window shone the blank clear yellow of the sky. Even here in the heartland of the Law, the slaves had risen. Three years ago, now, in that first terrible summer when thousands of houses had burned, compounds, towns, cities. Four million dead. He had not known the Uprising had reached even to Yaramera. No news came up the river. What toll among the Jewel's slaves for that night of burning? Had the owners been slaughtered, or had they survived to deal out punishment? No news came up the river.

All this went through his mind with unnatural rapidity and clarity as they crowded him up the shallow steps towards the north wing of the house, guarding him with drawn guns as if they thought a man of sixty-two with severe leg cramps from sitting motionless for hours was going to break and run for it, here, three hundred kilos inside their own territory. He thought fast and noticed everything.

This part of the house, joined to the central house by a long arcade, had not burned down. The walls still bore up the roof, but he saw as they came into the front hall that they were bare stone, their carved paneling burnt away. Dirty sheetflooring replaced parquet or covered painted tile. There was no furniture at all. In its ruin and dirt the high hall was beautiful, bare, full of clear evening light. Both veots had left his group and were reporting to some men in the doorway of what had been a reception room. He felt the veots as safeguard and hoped they would come back, but they did not. One of the young men kept his arm twisted up his back. A heavyset man came towards him, staring at him.

"You're the alien called Old Music?"

"I am Hainish, and use that name here."

"Mr. Old Music, you're to understand that by leaving your embassy in violation of the protection agreement between your ambassador and the Government of Voe Deo, you've forfeited diplomatic immunity. You may be held in custody, interrogated, and duly punished for any infractions of civil law or crimes of collusion with insurgents and enemies of the State you're found to have committed."

"I understood that this is your statement of my position," Esdan said. "But you should know, sir, that the Ambassador and the Stabiles of the Ekumen of the Worlds consider me protected both by diplomatic immunity and the laws of the Ekumen."

No harm trying, but his wordy lies weren't listened to. Having recited his litany, the man turned away, and the young men grabbed Esdan again. He was hustled through doorways and corridors that he was now in too much pain to see, down stone stairs, across a wide, cobbled courtyard, and into a room where, with a final agonising jerk on his arm and his feet knocked from under him so that he fell sprawling, they slammed the door and left him belly-down on stone in darkness.

He dropped his forehead onto his arm and lay shivering, hearing his breath catch in a whimper again and again.

Later on he remembered that night, and other things from the next days and nights. He did not know, then or later, if he was tortured in order to break him down or was merely the handy object of aimless brutality and spite, a sort of plaything for the boys. There were kicks, beatings, a great deal of pain, but none of it was clear in his memory later except the crouchcage.

He had heard of such things, read about them. He had never seen one. He had never been inside a compound. Foreigners, visitors, were not taken into slave quarters on the estates of Voe Deo. They were served by house-slaves in the houses of the owners.

This was a small compound, not more than twenty huts on the women's side, three longhouses on the gate side. It had housed the staff of a couple of hundred slaves who looked after the house and the immense gardens of Yaramera. They would have been a privileged set compared to the field hands. But not exempt from punishment. The whipping post still stood near the high gate that sagged open in the high walls.

"There?" said Nemeo, the one who always twisted his arm, but the other one, Alatual, said, "No, come on, it's over here," and ran ahead, excited, to winch the crouchcage down from where it hung below the main sentry station, high up on the inside of the wall.

It was a tube of coarse, rusty steel mesh sealed at one end and closable at the other. It hung suspended by a single hook from a chain. Lying on the ground it looked like a trap for an animal, not a very big animal. The two young men stripped off his clothes and goaded him to crawl into it headfirst, using the fieldhandlers, electric prods to stir up lazy slaves, which they had been playing with the last couple of days. They screamed with laughter, pushing him and jabbing the prods in his anus and scrotum. He writhed into the cage until he was crouching in it head down, his arms and legs bent and jammed up into his body. They slammed the trap end shut, catching his naked foot between the wires and causing a pain that blinded him while they hoisted the cage back up. It swung about wildly, and he clung to the wires with his cramped hands. When he opened his eyes he saw the ground swinging about seven or eight meters below him. After a while the lurching and circling stopped. He could not move his head at all. He could see what was below the crouchcage, and by straining his eyes round he could see most of the inside of the compound.

In the old days there had been people down there to see the moral spectacle, a slave in the crouchcage. There had been children to learn the lesson of what happens to a housemaid who shirked a job, a gardener who spoiled a cutting, a hand who talked back to a boss. Nobody was there now. The dusty ground was bare. The dried-up garden plots, the little graveyard at the far edge of a woman's side, the ditch between the two sides, the pathways, a vague circle of greener grass right underneath him, all were deserted. His torturers stood around for a while laughing and talking, got bored, went off.

He tried to ease his position but could move only very slightly. Any motion made the cage rock and swing so that he grew sick and increasingly fearful of falling. He did not know how securely the cage was balanced on that single hook. His foot, caught in the cage closure, hurt so sharply that he longed to faint, but though his head swam he remained conscious. He tried to breathe as he had learned how to breathe a long time ago on another world, quietly, easily. He could not do it here now in this world in this cage. His lungs were squeezed in his rib cage so that each breath was extremely difficult. He tried not to suffocate. He tried not to panic. He tried to be aware, only to be aware, but awareness was unendurable.

When the sun came round to that side of the compound and shone full on him the dizziness turned to sickness. Sometimes then he fainted for a while.

There was night and cold and he tried to imagine water, but there was no water.

He thought later he had been in the crouchcage two days. He could remember the scraping of the wires on his sunburned naked flesh when they pulled him out, the shock of cold water played over him from a hose. He had been fully aware for a moment then, aware of himself, like a doll, lying small, limp, on dirt, while men above him talked and shouted about something. Then he must have been carried back to the cell or stable where he was kept, for there was dark and silence, but also he was still hanging in the crouchcage roasting in the icy fire of the sun, freezing in his burning body, fitted tighter and tighter into the exact mesh of the wires of pain.

At some point he was taken to a bed in a room with a window, but he was still in the crouchcage, swinging high above the dusty ground, the dusties' ground, the circle of green grass.

The zadyo and the heavyset man were there, were not there. A bondswoman, whey-faced, crouching and trembling, hurt him trying to put salve on his burned arm and leg and back. She was there and not there. The sun shone in the window. He felt the wire snap down on his foot again, and again.

Darkness eased him. He slept most of the time. After a couple of days he could sit up and eat what the scared bondswoman brought him. His sunburn was healing, and most of his aches and pains were milder. His foot was swollen hugely; bones were broken; that didn't matter till he had to get up. He dozed, drifted. When Rayaye walked into the room, he recognised him at once.

They had met several times, before the Uprising. Rayaye had been Minister of Foreign Affairs under President Oyo. What position he had now, in the Legitimate Government, Esdan did not know. Rayaye was short for a Werelian but broad and solid, with a blue-black polished-looking face and greying hair, a striking man, a politician.

"Minister Rayaye," Esdan said.

"Mr. Old Music. How kind of you to recall me! I'm sorry you've been unwell. I hope the people here are looking after you satisfactorily?"

"Thank you."

"When I heard you were unwell I inquired for a doctor, but there's no one here but a veterinarian. No staff at all. Not like the old days! What a change! I wish you'd seen Yaramera in its glory."

"I did." His voice was rather weak, but sounded quite natural. "Thirty-two or -three years ago. Lord and Lady Aneo entertained a party from our embassy."

"Really? Then you know what it was," said Rayaye, sitting down in the one chair, a fine old piece missing one arm. "Painful to see it like this, isn't it! The worst of the destruction was here in the house. The whole women's wing and the great rooms burned. But the gardens were spared, may the Lady be praised. Laid out by Meneya himself, you know, four hundred years ago. And the fields are still being worked. I'm told there are still nearly three thousand assets attached to the property. When the trouble's over, it'll be far easier to restore Yaramera than many of the great estates." He gazed out the window. "Beautiful, beautiful. And Aneos' housepeople were famous for their beauty, you know. And training. It'll take a long time to build up to that kind of standard again."

"No doubt."

The Werelian looked at him with bland attentiveness. "I expect you're wondering why you're here."

"Not particularly," Esdan said pleasantly.

"Oh?"

"Since I left the Embassy without permission, I suppose the Government wanted to keep an eye on me."

"Some of us were glad to hear you'd left the Embassy. Shut up there—a waste of your talents."

"Oh, my talents," Esdan said with a deprecatory shrug, which hurt his shoulder. He would wince later. Just now he was enjoying himself. He liked fencing.

"You're a very talented man, Mr. Old Music. The wisest, canniest alien on Werel, Lord Mehao called you once. You've worked with us—and against us, yes—more effectively than any other offworlder. We understand one another. We can talk. It's my belief that you genuinely wish my people well, and that if I offered you a way of serving them—a hope of bringing this terrible conflict to an end—you'd take it."

"I would hope to be able to."

"Is it important to you that you be identified as a supporter of one side of the conflict, or would you prefer to remain neutral?"

"Any action can bring neutrality into question."

"To have been kidnapped from the Embassy by the rebels is no evidence of your sympathy for them."

"It would seem not."

"Rather the opposite."

"It would be so perceived."

"It can be. If you like."

"My preferences are of no weight, Minister."

"They're of very great weight, Mr. Old Music. But here. You've been ill, I'm tiring you. We'll continue our conversation tomorrow, eh? If you like."

"Of course, Minister," Esdan said, with a politeness edging on submissiveness, a tone that he knew suited men like this one, more accustomed to the attention of slaves than the company of equals. Never having equated incivility with pride, Esdan, like most of his people, was disposed to be polite in any circumstance that allowed it, and disliked circumstances that did not. Mere hypocrisy did not trouble him. He was perfectly capable of it himself. If Rayaye's men had tortured him and Rayaye pretended ignorance of the fact, Esdan had nothing to gain by insisting on it.

He was glad, indeed, not to be obliged to talk about it, and hoped not to think about it. His body thought about it for him, remembered it precisely, in every joint and muscle, now. The rest of his thinking about it he would do as long as he lived. He had learned things he had not known. He had thought he understood what it was to be helpless. Now he knew he had not understood.

When the scared woman came in, he asked her to send for the veterinarian. "I need a cast on my foot," he said.

"He does mend the hands, the bondsfolk, master," the woman whispered, shrinking. The assets here spoke an archaic-sounding dialect that was sometimes hard to follow.

"Can he come into the house?"

She shook her head.

"Is there anybody here who can look after it?"

"I will ask, master," she whispered.

An old bondswoman came in that night. She had a wrinkled, seared, stern face, and none of the crouching manner of the other. When she first saw him, she whispered, "Mighty Lord!" But she performed the reverence stiffly, and then examined his swollen foot, impersonal as any doctor. She said, "If you do let me bind that, master, it will heal."

"What's broken?"

"These toes. There. Maybe a little bone in here, too. Lotsalot bones in feet."

"Please bind it for me."

She did so, firmly, binding cloths round and round until the wrapping was quite thick and kept his foot immobile at one angle. She said, "You do walk, then you use a stick, sir. You put down only that heel to the ground."

He asked her name.

"Gana," she said. Saying her name, she shot a sharp glance right at him, full face, a daring thing for a slave to do. She probably wanted to get a good look at his alien eyes, having found the rest of him, though a strange color, pretty commonplace, bones in the feet and all.

"Thank you, Gana. I'm grateful for your skill and kindness."

She bobbed, but did not reverence, and left the room. She herself walked lame, but upright. "All the grandmothers are rebels," somebody had told him long ago, before the Uprising.

The next day he was able to get up and hobble to the broken-armed chair. He sat for a while looking out the window.

The room looked out from the second floor over the gardens of Yaramera, terraced slopes and flowerbeds, walks, lawns, and a series of ornamental lakes and pools that descended gradually to the river: a vast pattern of curves and planes, plants and paths, earth and still water, embraced by the broad living curve of the river. All the plots and walks and terraces formed a soft geometry centered very subtly on an enormous tree down at the riverside. It must have been a great tree when the garden was laid out four hundred years ago. It stood above and well back from the bank, but its branches reached far out over the water, and a village could have been built in its shade. The grass of the terraces had dried to soft gold. The river and the lakes and pools were all the misty blue of the summer sky. The flowerbeds and shrubberies were untended, overgrown, but not yet gone wild. The gardens of Yaramera were utterly beautiful in their desolation. Desolate, forlorn, forsaken, all such romantic words befitted them, yet they were also rational and noble, full of peace. They had been built by the labor slaves. Their dignity and peace were founded on cruelty, misery, pain. Esdan was Hainish, from a very old people, people who had built and destroyed Yaramera a thousand times. His mind contained the beauty and the terrible grief of the place, assured that the existence of one cannot justify the other, the destruction of one cannot destroy the other. He was aware of both, only aware.

And aware also, sitting in some comfort of body at last, that the lovely sorrowful terraces of Yaramera might contain within them the terraces of Darranda on Hain, roof below red roof, garden below green garden, dropping steep down to the shining harbor, the promenades and piers and sailboats. Out past the harbor the sea rises up, stands up as high as his house, as high as his eyes. Esi knows that books say the sea lies down. "The sea lies calm tonight," says the poem, but he knows better. The sea stands, a wall, the blue-grey wall at the end of the world. If you sail out on it, it will seem flat, but if you see it truly, it's as tall as the hills of Darranda, and if you sail truly on it, you will sail through that wall to the other side, beyond the end of the world.

The sky is the roof that wall holds up. At night the stars shine through the glass air roof. You can sail to them, too, to the worlds beyond the world.

"Esi," somebody calls from indoors, and he turns away from the sea and the sky, leaves the balcony, goes in to meet the guests, or for his music lesson, or to have lunch with the family. He's a nice little boy, Esi: obedient, cheerful, not talkative but quite sociable, interested in people. With very good manners, of course; after all, he's a Kelwen and the older generation wouldn't stand for anything less in a child of the family, but good manners come easy to him, perhaps because he's never seen any bad ones. Not a dreamy child. Alert, present, noticing. But thoughtful, and given to explaining things to himself, such as the wall of the sea and the roof of the air. Esi isn't as clear and close to Esdan as he used to be; he's a little boy a long time ago and very far away, left behind, left at home. Only rarely now does Esdan see through his eyes, or breathe the marvelous intricate smell of the house in Darranda—wood, the resinous oil used to polish the wood, sweetgrass matting, fresh flowers, kitchen herbs, the sea wind—or hear his mother's voice: "Esi? Come on in now, love. The cousins are here from Dorased!"

Esi runs in to meet the cousins, old Iliawad with crazy eyebrows and hair in his nostrils, who can do magic with bits of sticky tape, and Tuitui who's better at catch than Esi even though she's younger, while Esdan falls asleep in the broken chair by the window looking out on the terrible, beautiful gardens.

Further conversations with Bayaye were deferred. The zadyo came with his apologies. The Minister had been called back to speak with the President, would return within three or four days. Esdan realised he had heard a flyer take off early in the morning, not far away. It was a reprieve. He enjoyed fencing, but was still very tired, very shaken, and welcomed the rest. No one came into his room but the scared woman, Heo, and the zadyo who came once a day to ask if he had all he needed.

When he could he was permitted to leave his room, go outside if he wished. By using a stick and strapping his bound foot onto a stiff old sandal-sole Gana brought him, he could walk, and so get out into the gardens and sit in the sun, which was growing milder daily as the summer grew old. The two veots were his guards, or more exactly guardians. He saw the two young men who had tortured him; they kept at a distance, evidently under orders not to approach him. One of the veots was usually in view, but never crowded him.

He could not go far. Sometimes he felt like a bug on a beach.

The part of the house that was still usable was huge, the gardens were vast, the people were very few. There were the six men who had brought him, and five or six more who had been here, commanded by the heavyset man Tualenem. Of the original asset population of the house and estate there were ten or twelve, a tiny remnant of the house-staff of cooks, cooks' helpers, washwomen, chambermaids, ladies' maids, bodyservants, shoe-polishers, window-cleaners, gardeners, path-rakers, waiters, footmen, errandboys, stablemen, drivers, usewomen and useboys who had served the owners and their guests in the old days. These few were no longer locked up at night in the old house-asset compound where the crouchcage was, but slept in the courtyard warren of stables for horses and people where he had been kept at first, or in the complex of rooms around the kitchens. Most of these remaining few were women, two of them young, and two or three old, frail-looking men.

He was cautious of speaking to any of them at first lest he get them into trouble, but his captors ignored them except to give orders, evidently considering them trustworthy, with good reason. Troublemakers, the assets who had broken out of the compounds, burned the great house, killed the bosses and owners, were long gone: dead, escaped, or reenslaved with a cross branded deep on both cheeks. These were good dusties. Very likely they had been loyal all along. Many bondspeople, especially personal slaves, as terrified by the Uprising as their owners, had tried to defend them or had fled with them. They were no more traitors than were owners who had freed their assets and fought on the Liberation side. As much, and no more.

Girls, young field hands, were brought in one at a time as usewomen for the men. Every day or two the two young men who had tortured him drove a landcar off in the morning with a used girl and came back with a new one.

Of the two younger house bondswomen, one called Kamsa always carried her little baby around with her, and the men ignored her. The other, Heo, was the scared one who had waited on him. Tualenem used her every night. The other men kept hands off.

When they or any of the bondspeople passed Esdan in the house or outdoors they dropped their hands to their sides, chin to the chest, looked down, and stood still: the formal reverence expected of personal assets facing an owner.

"Good morning, Kamsa."

Her reply was the reverence.

It had been years now since he had been with the finished product of generations of slavery, the kind of slave described as "perfectly trained, obedient, selfless, loyal, the ideal personal asset," when they were put up for sale. Most of the assets he had known, his friends and colleagues, had been city rentspeople, hired out by their owners to companies and corporations to work in factories or shops or at skilled trades. He had also known a good many field hands. Field hands seldom had any contact with their owners; they worked under gareot bosses, and their compounds were run by cutfrees, eunuch assets. The ones he knew had mostly been runaways protected by the Hame, the underground railroad, on their way to independence in Yeowe. None of them had been utterly deprived of education, options, any imagination of freedom, as these bondspeople were. He had forgotten what a good dusty was like. He had forgotten the utter impenetrability of the person who has no private life, the intactness of the wholly vulnerable.

Kamsa's face was smooth, serene, and showed no feeling, though he heard her sometimes talking and singing very softly to her baby, a joyful, merry little noise. It drew him. He saw her one afternoon sitting at work on the coping of the great terrace, the baby in its sling on her back. He limped over and sat down nearby. He could not prevent her from setting her knife and board aside and standing head and hands and eyes down in reverence as he came near.

"Please sit down, please go on with your work," he said. She obeyed. "What's that you're cutting up?"

"Dueli, master," she whispered.

It was a vegetable he had often eaten and enjoyed. He watched her work. Each big, woody pod had to be split along a sealed seam, not an easy trick; it took a careful search for the opening point and hard, repeated twists of the blade to open the pod. Then the fat edible seeds had to be removed one by one and scraped free of a stringy, clinging matrix.

"Does that part taste bad?" he asked.

"Yes, master."

It was a laborious process, requiring strength, skill, and patience. He was ashamed. "I never saw raw dueli before," he said.

"No, master."

"What a good baby," he said, a little at random. The tiny creature in its sling, its head lying on her shoulder, had opened large bluish-black eyes and was gazing vaguely at the world. He had never heard it cry. It seemed rather unearthly to him, but he had not had much to do with babies.

She smiled.

"A boy?"

"Yes, master."

He said, "Please, Kamsa, my name is Esdan. I'm not a master. I'm a prisoner. Your masters are my masters. Will you call me by my name?"

She did not answer.

"Our masters would disapprove."

She nodded. The Werelian nod was a tip-back of the head, not a bob down. He was completely used to it after all these years. It was the way he nodded himself. He noticed himself noticing it now. His captivity, his treatment here, had displaced, disoriented him. These last few days he had thought more about Hain than he had for years, decades. He had been at home on Werel, and now was not. Inappropriate comparisons, irrelevant memories. Alienated.

"They put me in the cage," he said, speaking as low as she did and hesitating on the last word. He could not say the whole word, crouchcage.

Again the nod. This time, for the first time, she looked up at him, the flick of a glance. She said soundlessly, "I know," and went on with her work.

He found nothing more to say.

"I was a pup, then I did live there," she said, with a glance in the direction of the compound where the cage was. Her murmuring voice was profoundly controlled, as were all her gestures and movements. "Before that time the house burned. When the masters did live here. They did often hang up the cage. Once, a man for until he did die there. In that. I saw that."

Silence between them.

"We pups never did go under that. Never did run there."

"I saw the . . . the ground was different, underneath," Esdan said, speaking as softly and with a dry mouth, his breath coming short. "I saw, looking down. The grass. I thought maybe . . . where they . . ." His voice dried up entirely.

"One grandmother did take a stick, long, a cloth on the end of that, and wet it, and hold it up to him. The cutfrees did look away. But he did die. And rot some time."

"What had he done?"

"*Enna,*" she said, the one-word denial he'd often heard assets use—I don't know, I didn't do it, I wasn't there, it's not my fault, who knows. . . .

He'd seen an owner's child who said "enna" be slapped, not for the cup she broke but for using a slave word.

22

"A useful lesson," he said. He knew she'd understand him. Underdogs know irony like they know air and water.

"They did put you in that, then I did fear," she said.

"The lesson was for me, not you, this time," he said.

She worked, carefully, ceaselessly. He watched her work. Her downcast face, clay-color with bluish shadows, was composed, peaceful. The baby was darker-skinned than she. She had not been bred to a bondsman, but used by an owner. They called rape use. The baby's eyes closed slowly, translucent bluish lids like little shells. It was small and delicate, probably only a month or two old. Its head lay with infinite patience on her stooping shoulder.

No one else was out on the terraces. A slight wind stirred in the flowering trees behind them, streaked the distant river with silver.

"Your baby, Kamsa, you know, he will be free," Esdan said.

She looked up, not at him, but at the river and across it. She said, "Yes. He will be free." She went on working.

It heartened him, her saying that to him. It did him good to know she trusted him. He needed someone to trust him, for since the cage he could not trust himself. With Rayaye he was all right; he could still fence; that wasn't the trouble. It was when he was alone, thinking, sleeping. He was alone most of the time. Something in his mind, deep in him, was injured, broken, had not mended, could not be trusted to bear his weight.

He heard the flyer come down in the morning. That night Rayaye invited him down to dinner. Tualenem and the two veots ate with them and excused themselves, leaving him and Rayaye with a half bottle of wine at the makeshift table set up in one of the least damaged downstairs rooms. It had been a hunting lodge or trophy room, here in this wing of the house that had been the azade, the men's side, where no women would ever have come; female assets, servants, and usewomen did not count as women. The head of a huge packdog snarled above the mantel, its fur singed and dusty and its glass eyes gone dull. Crossbows had been mounted on the facing wall. Their pale shadows were clear on the dark wood. The electric chandelier flickered and dimmed. The generator was uncertain. One of the old bondsmen was always tinkering at it.

"Going off to his usewoman," Rayaye said, nodding towards the door Tualenem had just closed with assiduous wishes for the Minister to have a good night. "Fucking a white. Like fucking turds. Makes my skin crawl. Sticking his cock into a slave cunt. When the war's over there'll be no more of that kind of thing. Halfbreeds are the root of this revolution. Keep the races separate. Keep the ruler blood clean.

It's the only answer." He spoke as if expecting complete accord, but did not wait to receive any sign of it. He poured Esdan's glass full and went on in his resonant politician's voice, kind host, lord of the manor, "Well, Mr. Old Music, I hope you've been having a pleasant stay at Yaramera, and that your health's improved."

A civil murmur.

"President Oyo was sorry to hear you'd been unwell and sends his wishes for your full recovery. He's glad to know you're safe from any further mistreatment by the insurgents. You can stay here in safety as long as you like. However, when the time is right, the president and his cabinet are looking forward to having you in Bellen."

Civil murmur.

Long habit prevented Esdan from asking questions that would reveal the extent of his ignorance. Rayaye like most politicians loved his own voice, and as he talked Esdan tried to piece together a rough sketch of the current situation. It appeared that the legitimate government had moved from the city to a town, Bellen, northeast of Yaramera, near the eastern coast. Some kind of command had been left in the city. Rayaye's references to it made Esdan wonder if the city was in fact semi-independent of the Oyo government, governed by a faction, perhaps a military faction.

When the Uprising began, Oyo had at once been given extraordinary powers; but the Legitimate Army of Voe Deo, after their stunning defeats in the west, had been restive under his command, wanting more autonomy in the field. The civilian government had demanded retaliation, attack, and victory. The army wanted to contain the insurrection. Rega-General Aydan had established the Divide in the city and tried to establish and hold a border between the new Free State and the Legitimate Provinces. Veots who had gone over to the Uprising with their asset troops had similarly urged a border truce to the Liberation Command. The army sought armistice, the warriors sought peace. But "So long as there is one slave I am not free," cried Nekam-Anna, Leader of the Free State, and President Oyo thundered, "The nation will not be divided! We will defend legitimate property with the last drop of blood in our veins!" The Rega-General had suddenly been replaced by a new commander in chief. Very soon after that the Embassy was sealed, its access to information cut.

Esdan could only guess what had happened in the half year since. Rayaye talked of "our victories in the south" as if the Legitimate Army had been on the attack, pushing back into the Free State across the Devan River, south of the city. If so, if they had regained territory, why had the government pulled out of the city and dug in down at

Bellen? Rayaye's talk of victories might be translated to mean that the Army of the Liberation had been trying to cross the river in the south and the Legitimates had been successful in holding them off. If they were willing to call that a victory, had they finally given up the dream of reversing the revolution, retaking the whole country, and decided to cut their losses?

"A divided nation is not an option," Rayaye said, squashing that hope. "You understand that, I think."

Civil assent.

Rayaye poured out the last of the wine. "But peace is our goal. Our very strong and urgent goal. Our unhappy country has suffered enough."

Definite assent.

"I know you to be a man of peace, Mr. Old Music. We know the Ekumen fosters harmony among and within its member states. Peace is what we all desire with all our hearts."

Assent, plus faint indication of inquiry.

"As you know, the Government of Voe Deo has always had the power to end the insurrection. The means to end it quickly and completely."

No response but alert attention.

"And I think you know that it is only our respect for the policies of the Ekumen, of which my nation is a member, that has prevented us from using that means."

Absolutely no response or acknowledgment.

"You do know that, Mr. Old Music."

"I assumed you had a natural wish to survive."

Rayaye shook his head as if bothered by an insect. "Since we joined the Ekumen—and long before we joined it, Mr. Old Music— we have loyally followed its policies and bowed to its theories. And so we lost Yeowe! And so we lost the West! Four million dead, Mr. Old Music. Four million in the first Uprising. Millions since. Millions. If we had contained it then, many fewer would have died. Assets as well as owners."

"Suicide," Esdan said in a soft mild voice, the way assets spoke.

"The pacifist sees all weapons as evil, disastrous, suicidal. For all the age-old wisdom of your people, Mr. Old Music, you have not the experiential perspective on matters of war we younger, cruder peoples are forced to have. Believe me, we are not suicidal. We want our people, our nation, to survive. We are determined that it shall. The bibo was fully tested, long before we joined the Ekumen. It is controllable, targetable, containable. It is an exact weapon, a precise tool of

25

war. Rumor and fear have wildly exaggerated its capacities and nature. We know how to use it, how to limit its effects. Nothing but the response of the Stabiles through your ambassador prevented us from selective deployment in the first summer of the insurrection."

"I had the impression the high command of the Army of Voe Deo was also opposed to deploying that weapon."

"Some generals were. Many veots are rigid in their thinking, as you know."

"That decision has been changed?"

"President Oyo has authorised deployment of the bibo against forces massing to invade this province from the west."

Such a cute word, "bibo." Esdan closed his eyes for a moment.

"The destruction will be appalling," Rayaye said.

Assent.

"It is possible," Rayaye said, leaning forward, black eyes in black face, intense as a hunting cat, "that if the insurgents were warned, they might withdraw. Be willing to discuss terms. If they withdraw, we will not attack. If they will talk, we will talk. A holocaust can be prevented. They respect the Ekumen. They respect you personally, Mr. Old Music. They trust you. If you were to speak to them on the net, or if their leaders will agree to a meeting, they will listen to you, not as their enemy, their oppressor, but as the voice of a benevolent, peace-loving neutrality, the voice of wisdom, urging them to save themselves while there is yet time. This is the opportunity I offer you, and the Ekumen. To spare your friends among the rebels, to spare this world untold suffering. To open the way to lasting peace."

"I am not authorised to speak for the Ekumen. The Ambassa-dor—"

"Will not. Cannot. Is not free to. You are. You are a free agent, Mr. Old Music. Your position on Werel is unique. Both sides respect you. Trust you. And your voice carries infinitely more weight among the whites than his. He came only a year before the insurrection. You are, I may say, one of us."

"I am not one of you. I neither own nor am owned. You must redefine yourselves to include me."

Rayaye, for a moment, had nothing to say. He was taken aback, and would be angry. Fool, Esdan said to himself, old fool, to take the moral high ground! But he did not know what ground to stand on.

It was true that his word would carry more weight than the Ambassador's. Nothing else Rayaye had said made sense. If President Oyo wanted the Ekumen's blessing on his use of this weapon and seriously thought Esdan would give it, why was he working through Rayaye, and keeping Esdan hidden at Yaramera? Was Rayaye working with Oyo, or was he working for a faction that favored using the bibo, while Oyo still refused?

Most likely the whole thing was a bluff. There was no weapon. Esdan's pleading was to lend credibility to it, while leaving Oyo out of the loop if the bluff failed.

The biobomb, the bibo, had been a curse on Voe Deo for decades, centuries. In panic fear of alien invasion after the Ekumen first contacted them almost four hundred years ago, the Werelians had put all their resources into developing space flight and weaponry. The scientists who invented this particular device repudiated it, informing their government that it could not be contained; it would destroy all human and animal life over an enormous area and cause profound and permanent genetic damage worldwide as it spread throughout the water and the atmosphere. The government never used the weapon but was never willing to destroy it, and its existence had kept Werel from membership in the Ekumen as long as the Embargo was in force. Voe Deo insisted it was their guarantee against extraterrestrial invasion and perhaps believed it would prevent revolution. Yet they had not used it when their slave-planet Yeowe rebelled. Then, after the Ekumen no longer observed the Embargo, they announced that they had destroyed the stockpiles. Werel joined the Ekumen. Voe Deo invited inspection of the weapon sites. The Ambassador politely declined, citing the Ekumenical policy of trust. Now the bibo existed again. In fact? In Rayaye's mind? Was he desperate? A hoax, an attempt to use the Ekumen to back a bogey threat to scare off an invasion: the likeliest scenario, yet it was not quite convincing.

"This war must end," Rayaye said.

"I agree."

"We will never surrender. You must understand that." Rayaye had dropped his blandishing, reasonable tone. "We will restore the holy order of the world," he said, and now he was fully credible. His eyes, the dark Werelian eyes that had no whites, were fathomless in the dim light. He drank down his wine. "You think we fight for our property. To keep what we own. But I tell you, we fight to defend our Lady. In that fight is no surrender. And no compromise."

"Your Lady is merciful."

"The Law is her mercy."

Esdan was silent.

"I must go again tomorrow to Bellen," Rayaye said after a while, resuming his masterful, easy tone. "Our plans for moving on the southern front must be fully coordinated. When I come back, I'll need to know if you will give us the help I've asked you for. Our response will depend largely on that. On your voice. It is known that you're here in the East Provinces—known to the insurgents, I mean, as well as our people—though your exact location is of course kept hidden for your own safety. It is known that you may be preparing a statement of a change in the Ekumen's attitude toward the conduct of the civil war. A change that could save millions of lives and bring a just peace to our land. I hope you'll employ your time here in doing so."

He is a factionalist, Esdan thought. He's not going to Bellen, or if he is, that's not where Oyo's government is. This is some scheme of his own. Crackbrained. It won't work. He doesn't have the bibo. But he has a gun. And he'll shoot me.

"Thank you for a pleasant dinner, Minister," he said.

Next morning he heard the flyer leave at dawn. He limped out into the morning sunshine after breakfast. One of his veot guards watched him from a window and then turned away. In a sheltered nook just under the balustrade of the south terrace, near a planting of great bushes with big, blowsy, sweet-smelling white flowers, he saw Kamsa and her baby and Heo. He made his way to them, dot-and-go-one. The distances at Yaramera, even inside the house, were daunting to a lamed man. When he finally got there, he said, "I am lonely. May I sit with you?"

The women were afoot, of course, reverencing, though Kamsa's reverence had become pretty sketchy. He sat on a curved bench splotched all over with fallen flowers. They sat back down on the flagstone path with the baby. They had unwrapped the little body to the mild sunshine. It was a very thin baby, Esdan thought. The joints in the bluish-dark arms and legs were like the joints in flower stems, translucent knobs. The baby was moving more than he had ever seen it move, stretching its arms and turning its head as if enjoying the feel of the air. The head was large for the neck, again like a flower, too large on too thin a stalk. Kamsa dangled one of the real flowers over the baby. His dark eyes gazed up at it. His eyelids and eyebrows were exquisitely delicate. The sunlight shone through his fingers. He smiled. Esdan caught his breath. The baby's smile at the flower was the beauty of the flower, the beauty of the world.

"What is his name?"

"Rekam."

Grandson of Kamye. Kamye the Lord and slave, huntsman and husbandman, warrior and peacemaker.

"A beautiful name. How old is he?"

In the language they spoke that was, "How long has he lived?"

Kamsa's answer was strange. "As long as his life," she said, or so he understood her whisper and her dialect. Maybe it was bad manners or bad luck to ask a child's age.

He sat back on the bench. "I feel very old," he said. "I haven't seen a baby for a hundred years."

Heo sat hunched over, her back to him; he felt that she wanted to cover her ears. She was terrified of him, the alien. Life had not left much to Heo but fear, he guessed. Was she twenty, twenty-five? She looked forty. Maybe she was seventeen. Usewomen, ill-used, aged fast. Kamsa he guessed to be not much over twenty. She was thin and plain, but there was bloom and juice in her as there was not in Heo.

"Master did have children?" Kamsa asked, lifting up her baby to her breast with a certain discreet pride, shyly flaunting.

"No."

"*A yera yera,*" she murmured, another slave word he had often heard in the urban compounds: O pity, pity.

"How you get to the center of things, Kamsa," he said. She glanced his way and smiled. Her teeth were bad, but it was a good smile. He thought the baby was not sucking. It lay peacefully in the crook of her arm. Heo remained tense and jumped whenever he spoke, so he said no more. He looked away from them, past the bushes, out over the wonderful view that arranged itself, whenever you walked or sat, into a perfect balance: the levels of flagstone, of dun grass and blue water, the curves of the avenues, the masses and lines of shrubbery, the great old tree, the misty river and its green far bank. Presently the women began talking softly again. He did not listen to what they said. He was aware of their voices, aware of sunlight, aware of peace.

Old Gana came stumping across the upper terrace towards them, bobbed to him, said to Kamsa and Heo, "Choyo does want you. Leave me that baby." Kamsa set the baby down on the warm stone again. She and Heo sprang up and went off, thin, light women moving with easy haste. The old woman settled down piece by piece and with groans and grimaces onto the path beside Rekam. She immediately covered him up with a fold of his swaddling cloth, frowning and muttering at the foolishness of his mother. Esdan watched her careful movements, her gentleness when she picked the child up, supporting that heavy head and tiny limbs, her tenderness cradling him, rocking her body to rock him.

She looked up at Esdan. She smiled, her face wrinkling up into a thousand wrinkles. "He is my great gift," she said.

He whispered, "Your grandson?"

The backward nod. She kept rocking gently. The baby's eyes were closed, his head lay softly on her thin, dry beast. "I think now he'll die not long now."

After a while Esdan said, "Die?"

The nod. She still smiled. Gently, gently rocking. "He is two years of age, master."

"I thought he was born this summer," Esdan said in a whisper.

The old woman said, "He did come to stay a little while with us."

"What is wrong?"

"The wasting."

Esdan had heard the term. He said, "Avo?" the name he knew for it, a systemic viral infection common among Werelian children, frequently epidemic in the asset compounds of the cities.

She nodded.

"But it's curable!"

The old woman said nothing.

Avo was completely curable. Where there were doctors. Where there was medicine. Avo was curable in the city not the country. In the great house not the asset quarters. In peacetime not in wartime. Fool!

Maybe she knew it was curable, maybe she did not, maybe she did not know what the word meant. She rocked the baby, crooning in a whisper, paying no attention to the fool. But she had heard him, and answered him at last, not looking at him, watching the baby's sleeping face.

"I was born owned," she said, "and my daughters. But he was not. He is the gift. To us. Nobody can own him. The gift of the Lord Kamye of himself. Who could keep that gift?"

Esdan bowed his head down.

He had said to the mother, "He will be free." And she had said, "Yes."

He said at last, "May I hold him?"

The grandmother stopped rocking and held still a while. "Yes," she said. She raised herself up and very carefully transferred the sleeping baby into Esdan's arms, onto his lap.

"You do hold my joy," she said.

The child weighed nothing—six or seven pounds. It was like holding a warm flower, a tiny animal, a bird. The swaddling cloth trailed down across the stones. Gana gathered it up and laid it softly around the baby, hiding his face. Tense and nervous, jealous, full of pride, she knelt there. Before long she took the baby back against her heart. "There," she said, and her face softened into happiness.

That night Esdan, sleeping in the room that looked out over the terraces of Yaramera, dreamed that he had lost a little round, flat stone that he always carried with him in a pouch. The stone was from the pueblo. When he held it in his palm and warmed it, it was able to speak, to talk with him. But he had not talked with it for a long time. Now he realised he did not have it. He had lost it, left it somewhere. He thought it was in the basement of the Embassy. He tried to get into the basement, but the door was locked, and he could not find the other door.

He woke. Early morning. No need to get up. He should think about what to do, what to say, when Rayaye came back. He could not. He thought about the dream, the stone that talked. He wished he had heard what it said. He thought about the pueblo. His father's brother's family had lived in Arkanan Pueblo in the Far South Highlands. In his boyhood, every year in the heart of the northern winter, Esi had flown down there for forty days of summer. With his parents at first, later on alone. His uncle and aunt had grown up in Darranda and were not pueblo people. Their children were. They had grown up in Arkanan and belonged to it entirely. The eldest, Suhan, fourteen years older than Esdan, had been born with irreparable brain and neural defects, and it was for his sake that his parents had settled in a pueblo. There was a place for him there. He became a herdsman. He went up on the mountains with the yama, animals the South Hainish had brought over from O a millennium or so ago. He looked after the animals. He came back to live in the pueblo only in winter. Esi saw him seldom, and was glad of it, finding Suhan a fearful figure— big, shambling, foul-smelling, with a loud braying voice, mouthing incomprehensible words. Esi could not understand why Suhan's parents and sisters loved him. He thought they pretended to. No one could love him.

To adolescent Esdan it was still a problem. His cousin Noy, Suhan's sister, who had become the Water Chief of Arkanan, told him it was not a problem but a mystery. "You see how Suhan is our guide?" she said. "Look at it. He led my parents here to live. So my sister and I were born here. So you come to stay with us here. So you've learned to live in the pueblo. You'll never be just a city man. Because Suhan guided you here. Guided us all. Into the mountains."

"He didn't really guide us," the fourteen-year-old argued.

"Yes, he did. We followed his weakness. His incompleteness. Failure's open. Look at water, Esi. It finds the weak places in the rock, the openings, the hollows, the absences. Following water we come where we belong." Then she had gone off to arbitrate a dispute over the usage rights to an irrigation system outside town, for the east side of the mountains was very dry country, and the people of Arkanan were contentious, though hospitable, and the Water Chief stayed busy.

But Suhan's condition had been irreparable, his weakness inaccessible even to the wondrous medical skills of Hain. This baby was dying of a disease that could be cured by a mere series of injections. It was wrong to accept his illness, his death. It was wrong to let him be cheated out of his life by circumstance, bad luck, an unjust society, a fatalistic religion. A religion that fostered and encouraged the terrible passivity of the slaves, that told these women to do nothing, to let the child waste away and die.

He should interfere, he should do something, what could be done?

"How long has he lived?"

"As long as his life."

There was nothing they could do. Nowhere to go. No one to turn to. A cure for avo existed, in some places, for some children. Not in this place, not for this child. Neither anger nor hope served any purpose. Nor grief. It was not the time for grief yet. Rekam was here with them, and they would delight in him as long as he was here. As long as his life. *He is my great gift. You do hold my joy.*

This was a strange place to come to learn the quality of joy. Water is my guide, he thought. His hands still felt what it had been like to hold the child, the light weight, the brief warmth.

He was out on the terrace late the next morning, waiting for Kamsa and the baby to come out as they usually did, but the older veot came instead. "Mr. Old Music, I must ask you to stay indoors for a time," he said.

"Zadyo, I'm not going to run away," Esdan said, sticking out his swathed lump of a foot.

"I'm sorry, sir."

He stumped crossly indoors after the veot and was locked into a downstairs room, a windowless storage space behind the kitchens. They had fixed it up with a cot, a table and chair, a pisspot, and a battery lamp for when the generator failed, as it did for a while most days. "Are you expecting an attack, then?" he said when he saw these preparations, but the veot replied only by locking the door. Esdan sat on the cot and meditated, as he had learned to do in Arkanan Pueblo. He cleared distress and anger from his mind by going through the long repetitions: health and good work, courage, patience, peace, for himself, health and good work, courage, patience, peace for the zadyo . . . for Kamsa, for baby Rekam, for Rayaye, for Heo, for Taulenem, for the oga, for Nemeo who had put him in the crouchcage, for Alatual who had put him in the crouchcage, for Gana who had bound his foot and blessed him, for people he knew in the Embassy, in the city, health and good work, courage, patience, peace. . . . That went well, but the meditation itself was a failure. He could not stop thinking. So he thought. He thought about what he could do. He found nothing. He was weak as water, helpless as the baby. He imagined himself speaking on a holonet with a script saying that the Ekumen reluctantly approved the limited use of biological weapons in order to end the civil war. He imagined himself on the holonet dropping the script and saying that the Ekumen would never approve the use of biological weapons for any reason. Both imaginings were fantasies. Rayaye's schemes were fantasies. Seeing that his hostage was useless, Rayaye would have him shot. How long has he lived? As long as sixty-two years. A much fairer share of time than Rekam was getting. His mind went on past thinking.

The zadyo opened the door and told him he could come out.

"How close is the Liberation Army, zadyo?" he asked. He expected no answer. He went out onto the terrace. It was late afternoon. Kamsa was there, sitting with the baby at her breast. Her nipple was in his mouth, but he was not sucking. She covered her breast. Her face as she did so looked sad for the first time.

"Is he asleep? May I hold him?" Esdan said, sitting by her. She shifted the little bundle over to his lap. Her face was still troubled. Esdan thought the child's breathing was more difficult, harder work. But he was awake, and looked up into Esdan's face with his big eyes. Esdan made faces, sticking out his lips and blinking. He won a soft little smile.

"The hands say, that army do come," Kamsa said in her very soft voice.

"The Liberation?"

"Enna. Some army."

"From across the river?"

"I think."

"They're assets—freedmen. They're your own people. They won't hurt you." Maybe.

She was frightened. Her control was perfect, but she was frightened. She had seen the Uprising, here. And the reprisals.

"Hide out, if you can, if there's bombing or fighting," he said. "Underground. There must be hiding places here."

She thought and said, "Yes."

It was peaceful in the gardens of Yaramera. No sound but the wind rustling leaves and the faint buzz of the generator. Even the burned, jagged ruins of the house looked mellowed, ageless. The worst has happened, said the ruins. To them. Maybe not to Kamsa and Heo, Gana and Esdan. But there was no hint of violence in the summer air. The baby smiled its vague smile again, nestling in Esdan's arms. He thought of the stone he had lost in his dream.

He was locked into the windowless room for the night. He had no way to know what time it was when he was roused by noise, brought stark awake by a series of shots and explosions, gunfire or handbombs. There was silence, then a second series of bangs and cracks, fainter. Silence again, stretching on and on. Then he heard a flyer right over the house as if circling, sounds inside the house: a shout, running. He lighted the lamp, struggled into his trousers, hard to pull on over the swathed foot. When he heard the flyer coming back and an explosion, he leapt in panic for the door, knowing nothing but that he had to get out of this deathtrap room. He had always feared fire, dying in fire. The door was solid wood, solidly bolted into its solid frame. He had no hope at all of breaking it down and knew it even in his panic. He shouted once, "Let me out of here!" then got control of himself, returned to the cot, and after a minute sat down on the floor between the cot and the wall, as sheltered a place as the room afforded, trying to imagine what was going on. A Liberation raid and Rayaye's men shooting back, trying to bring the flyer down, was what he imagined.

Dead silence. It went on and on.

His lamp flickered.

He got up and stood at the door.

"Let me out!"

No sound.

A single shot. Voices again, running feet again, shouting, calling. After another long silence, distant voices, the sound of men coming down the corridor outside the room. A man said, "Keep them out there for now," a flat, harsh voice. He hesitated and nerved himself and shouted out, "I'm a prisoner! In here!"

A pause.

"Who's in there?"

It was no voice he had heard. He was good at voices, faces, names, intentions.

"Esdardon Aya of the Embassy of the Ekumen."

"Mighty Lord!" the voice said.

"Get me out of here, will you?"

There was no reply, but the door was rattled vainly on its massive hinges, was thumped; more voices outside, more thumping and banging. "Ax," somebody said, "Find the key," somebody else said; they went off. Esdan waited. He fought down a repeated impulse to laugh, afraid of hysteria, but it was funny, stupidly funny, all the shouting through the door and seeking keys and axes, a farce in the middle of a battle. What battle?

He had had it backwards. Liberation men had entered the house and killed Rayaye's men, taking most of them by surprise. They had been waiting for Rayaye's flyer when it came. They must have had contacts among the field hands, informers, guides. Sealed in his room, he had heard only the noisy end of the business. When he was let out, they were dragging out the dead. He saw the horribly maimed body of one of the young men, Alatual or Nemeo, come apart as they dragged it, ropy blood and entrails stretching out along the floor, the legs left behind. The man dragging the corpse was nonplussed and stood there holding the shoulders of the torso. "Well, shit," he said, and Esdan stood gasping, again trying not to laugh, not to vomit.

"Come on," said the men with him, and he came on.

Early-morning light slanted through broken windows. Esdan kept looking around, seeing none of the housepeople. The men took him into the room with the packdog head over the mantel. Six or seven men were gathered around the table there. They wore no uniforms, though some had the yellow knot or ribbon of the Liberation on their cap or sleeve. They were ragged, though, hard. Some were dark, some had beige or clayey or bluish skin, all of them looked edgy and dangerous. One of those with him, a thin, tall man, said in the harsh voice that had said "Mighty Lord" outside the door: "This is him."

"I'm Esdardon Aya, Old Music, of the Embassy of the Ekumen," he said again, as easily as he could. "I was being held here. Thank you for liberating me."

Several of them stared at him the way people who had never seen an alien stared, taking in his red-brown skin and deep-set, white-cornered eyes and the subtler differences of skull structure and features. One or two stared more aggressively, as if to test his assertion, show they'd believe he was what he said he was when he proved it. A big, broad-shouldered man, white-skinned and with brownish hair, pure dusty, pure blood of the ancient conquered race, looked at Esdan a long time. "We came to do that," he said.

He spoke softly, the asset voice. It might take them a generation or more to learn to raise their voices, to speak free.

"How did you know I was here? The fieldnet?"

It was what they had called the clandestine system of information passed from voice to ear, field to compound to city and back again, long before there was a holonet. The Hame had used the fieldnet and it had been the chief instrument of the Uprising.

A short, dark man smiled and nodded slightly, then froze his nod as he saw that the others weren't giving out any information.

"You know who brought me here, then—Rayaye. I don't know who he was acting for. What I can tell you, I will." Relief had made him stupid, he was talking too much, playing hands-around-the-flowerbed while they played tough guy. "I have friends here," he went on in a more neutral voice, looking at each of their faces in turn, direct but civil. "Bondswomen, house people. I hope they're all right."

"Depends," said a grey-haired, slight man who looked very tired.

"A woman with a baby, Kamsa. An old woman, Gana."

A couple of them shook their heads to signify ignorance or indifference. Most made no response at all. He looked around at them again, repressing anger and irritation at this pomposity, this tight-lipped stuff.

"We need to know what you were doing here," the brown-haired man said.

"A Liberation Army contact in the city was taking me from the Embassy to Liberation Command, about fifteen days ago. We were intercepted in the Divide by Rayaye's men. They brought me here. I spent some time in a crouchcage," Esdan said in the same neutral voice. "My foot was hurt, and I can't walk much. I talked twice with Rayaye. Before I say anything else I think you can understand that I need to know who I'm talking to."

The tall thin man who had released him from the locked room went round the table and conferred briefly with the grey-haired man. The brown-haired one listened, consented. The tall thin one spoke to Esdan in his uncharacteristically harsh, flat voice: "We are a special mission of the Advance Army of the World Liberation. I am Marshal Metoy." The others all said their names. The big brown-haired man was General Banarkamye, the tired older man was General Tueyo. They said their rank with their name, but didn't use it addressing one another, nor did they call him Mister. Before Liberation, rentspeople had seldom used any titles to one another but those of parentage: father, sister, aunty. Titles were something that went in front of an owner's name: Lord, Master, Mister, Boss. Evidently the Liberation had decided to do without them. It pleased him to find an army that didn't click its heels and shout Sir! But he wasn't certain what army he'd found.

"They kept you in that room?" Metoy asked him. He was a strange man, a flat, cold voice, a pale, cold face, but he wasn't as jumpy as the others. He seemed sure of himself, used to being in charge.

"They locked me in there last night. As if they'd had some kind of warning of trouble coming. Usually I had a room upstairs."

"You may go there now," Metoy said. "Stay indoors."

"I will. Thank you again," he said to them all. "Please, when you have word of Kamsa and Gana—?" He did not wait to be snubbed, but turned and went out.

One of the younger men went with him. He had named himself Zadyo Tema. The Army of the Liberation was using the old veot ranks, then. There were veots among them, Esdan knew, but Tema was not one. He was light-skinned and had the city-dusty accent, soft, dry, clipped. Esdan did not try to talk to him. Tema was extremely nervous, spooked by the night's work of killing at close quarters or by something else; there was an almost constant tremor in his shoulders, arms, and hands, and his pale face was set in a painful scowl. He was not in a mood for chitchat with an elderly civilian alien prisoner.

In war everybody is a prisoner, the historian Henennemores had written.

Esdan had thanked his new captors for liberating him, but he knew where, at the moment, he stood. It was still Yaramera.

But there was some relief in seeing his room again, sitting down in the one-armed chair by the window to look out at the early sunlight, the long shadows of trees across the lawns and terraces.

None of the housepeople came out as usual to go about their work or take a break from it. Nobody came to his room. The morning wore on. He did what exercises of the tanhai he could do with his foot as it was. He sat aware, dozed off, woke up, tried to sit aware, sat restless, anxious, working over words: *A special mission of the Advance Army of World Liberation.*

The Legitimate Government called the enemy army "insurgent forces" or "rebel hordes" on the holonews. It had started out calling itself the Army of the Liberation, nothing about World Liberation; but he had been cut off from any coherent contact with the freedom fighters ever since the Uprising, and cut off from all information of any kind since the Embassy was sealed—except for information from other worlds light-years away, of course, there'd been no end of that, the ansible was full of it, but of what was going on two streets away, nothing, not a word. In the Embassy he'd been ignorant, useless, helpless, passive. Exactly as he was here. Since the war began he'd been, as Henennemores had said, a prisoner. Along with everybody else on Werel. A prisoner in the cause of liberty.

He feared that he would come to accept his helplessness, that it would persuade his soul. He must remember what this war was about. But let the liberation come soon, he thought, come set me free!

In the middle of the afternoon the young zadyo brought him a plate of cold food, obviously scraps of leftovers they'd found in the kitchens, and a bottle of beer. He ate and drank gratefully. But it was clear that they had not released the housepeople. Or had killed them. He would not let his mind stay on that.

After sunset the zadyo came back and brought him downstairs to the packdog room. The generator was off, of course; nothing had kept it going but old Saka's eternal tinkering. Men carried electric torches, and in the packdog room a couple of big oil lamps burned on the table, putting a romantic, golden light on the faces round it, throwing deep shadows behind them.

"Sit down," said the brown-haired general, Banarkamye—Readbible, his name could be translated. "We have some questions to ask you."

Silent but civil assent.

They asked how he had got out of the Embassy, who his contacts with the Liberation had been, where he had been going, why he had tried to go, what happened during the kidnapping, who had brought him here, what they had asked him, what they had wanted from him. Having decided during the afternoon that candor would serve him best, he answered all the questions directly and briefly until the last one.

"I personally am on your side of this war," he said, "but the Ekumen is necessarily neutral. Since at the moment I'm the only alien on Werel free to speak, whatever I say may be taken, or mistaken, as coming from the Embassy and the Stabiles. That was my value to Rayaye. It may be my value to you. But it's a false value. I can't speak for the Ekumen. I have no authority."

"They wanted you to say the Ekumen supports the Jits," the tired man, Tueyo, said.

Esdan nodded.

"Did they talk about using any special tactics, weapons?" That was Banarkamye, grim, trying not to weight the question.

"I'd rather answer that question when I'm behind your lines, General, talking to people I know in Liberation Command."

"You're talking to the World Liberation Army command. Refusal

to answer can be taken as evidence of complicity with the enemy."
That was Metoy, glib, hard, harsh-voiced.

"I know that, Marshal."

They exchanged a glance. Despite his open threat, Metoy was the
one Esdan felt inclined to trust. He was solid. The others were nervy,
unsteady. He was sure now that they were factionalists. How big their
faction was, how much at odds with Liberation Command it was, he
could learn only by what they might let slip.

"Listen, Mr. Old Music," Tueyo said. Old habits die hard. "We
know you worked for the Hame. You helped send people to Yeowe.
You backed us then." Esdan nodded. "You must back us now. We are
speaking to you frankly. We have information that the Jits are planning a counterattack. What that means, now, it means that they're
going to use the bibo. It can't mean anything else. That can't happen.
They can't be let do that. They have to be stopped."

"You say the Ekumen is neutral," Banarkamye said. "That is a lie.
A hundred years the Ekumen wouldn't let this world join them, because we had the bibo. Had it, didn't use it, just had it was enough.
Now they say they're neutral. Now when it matters! Now when this
world is part of them! They have got to act. To act against that
weapon. They have got to stop the Jits from using it."

"If the Legitimates did have it, if they did plan to use it, and if I
could get word to the Ekumen—what could they do?"

"You speak. You tell the Jit President: the Ekumen says stop there.
The Ekumen will send ships, send troops. You back us! If you aren't
with us, you are with them!"

"General, the nearest ship is light-years away. The Legitimates
know that."

"But you can call them, you have the transmitter."

"The ansible in the Embassy?"

"The Jits have one of them, too."

"The ansible in the Foreign Ministry was destroyed in the Uprising. In the first attack on the government buildings. They blew the
whole block up."

"How do we know that?"

"Your own forces did it. General, do you think the Legitimates
have an ansible link with the Ekumen that you don't have? They
don't. They could have taken over the Embassy and its ansible, but
in so doing they'd have lost what credibility they have with the Ekumen. And what good would it have done them? The Ekumen has no
troops to send," and he added, because he was suddenly not sure
Banarkamye knew it, "as you know. If it did, it would take them years

to get here. For that reason and many others, the Ekumen has no army and fights no wars."

He was deeply alarmed by their ignorance, their amateurishness, their fear. He kept alarm and impatience out of his voice, speaking quietly and looking at them unworriedly, as if expecting understanding and agreement. The mere appearance of such confidence sometimes fulfills itself. Unfortunately, from the looks of their faces, he was telling the two generals they'd been wrong and telling Metoy he'd been right. He was taking sides in a disagreement.

Banarkamye said, "Keep all that a while yet," and went back over the first interrogation, recreating questions, asking for more details, listening to them expressionlessly. Saving face. Showing he distrusted the hostage. He kept pressing for anything Rayaye had said concerning an invasion or a counterattack in the south. Esdan repeated several times that Rayaye had said President Oyo was expecting a Liberation invasion of this province, downriver from here. Each time he added, "I have no idea whether anything Rayaye told me was the truth." The fourth or fifth time round he said, "Excuse me, General. I must ask again for some word about the people here—"

"Did you know anybody at this place before you came here?" a younger man asked sharply.

"No. I'm asking about house people. They were kind to me. Kamsa's baby is sick, it needs care. I'd like to know they're being looked after."

The generals were conferring with each other, paying no attention to this diversion.

"Anybody stayed here, a place like this, after the Uprising, is a collaborator," said the zadyo, Tema.

"Where were they supposed to go?" Esdan asked, trying to keep his tone easy. "This isn't liberated country. The bosses still work these fields with slaves. They still use the crouchcage here." His voice shook a little on the last words, and he cursed himself for it.

Banarkamye and Tueyo were still conferring, ignoring his question. Metoy stood up and said, "Enough for tonight. Come with me."

Esdan limped after him across the hall, up the stairs. The young zadyo followed, hurrying, evidently sent by Banarkamye. No private conversations allowed. Metoy, however, stopped at the door of Esdan's room and said, looking down at him, "The house people will be looked after."

"Thank you," Esdan said with warmth. He added, "Gana was caring for this injury. I need to see her." If they wanted him alive and undamaged, no harm using his ailments as leverage. If they didn't, no use in anything much.

He slept little and badly. He had always thrived on information and action. It was exhausting to be kept both ignorant and helpless, crippled mentally and physically. And he was hungry.

Soon after sunrise he tried his door and found it locked. He knocked and shouted a while before anybody came, a young fellow looking scared, probably a sentry, and then Tema, sleepy and scowling, with the door key.

"I want to see Gana," Esdan said, fairly peremptory. "She looks after this," gesturing to his saddled foot. Tema shut the door without saying anything. After an hour or so, the key rattled in the lock again and Gana came in. Metoy followed her. Tema followed him.

Gana stood in the reverence to Esdan. He came forward quickly and put his hands on her arms and laid his cheek against hers. "Lord Kamye be praised I see you well!" he said, words that had often been said to him by people like her. "Kamsa, the baby, how are they?"

She was scared, shaky, her hair unkempt, her eyelids red, but she recovered herself pretty well from his utterly unexpected brotherly greeting. "They are in the kitchen now, sir," she said. "The army men, they said that foot do pain you."

"That's what I said to them. Maybe you'd re-bandage it for me."

He sat down on the bed and she got to work unwrapping the cloths.

"Are the other people all right? Heo? Choyo?"

She shook her head once.

"I'm sorry," he said. He could not ask her more.

She did not do as good a job bandaging his foot as before. She had little strength in her hands to pull the wrappings tight, and she hurried her work, unnerved by the strangers watching.

"I hope Choyo's back in the kitchen," he said, half to her, half to them. "Somebody's got to do some cooking here."

"Yes, sir," she whispered.

Not sir, not master! he wanted to warn her, fearing for her. He looked up at Metoy, trying to judge his attitude, and could not.

Gana finished her job. Metoy sent her off with a word, and sent the zadyo after her. Gana went gladly, Tema resisted. "General Banar-kamye—" he began. Metoy looked at him. The young man hesitated, scowled, obeyed.

"I will look after these people," Metoy said. "I always have. I was a compound boss." He gazed at Esdan with his cold black eyes. "I'm a cutfree. Not many like me left, these days."

Esdan said after a moment, "Thanks, Metoy. They need help. They don't understand."

Metoy nodded.

"I don't understand either," Esdan said. "Does the Liberation plan to invade? Or did Rayaye invent that as an excuse for talking about deploying the bibo? Does Oyo believe it? Do you believe it? Is the Liberation Army across the river there? Did you come from it? Who are you? I don't expect you to answer."

"I won't," the enunch said.

If he was a double agent, Esdan thought after he left, he was working for Liberation Command. Or he hoped so. Metoy was a man he wanted on his side.

But I don't know what my side is, he thought, as he went back to his chair by the window. The Liberation, of course, yes, but what is the Liberation? Not an ideal, the freedom of the enslaved. Not now. Never again. Since the Uprising, the Liberation is an army, a political body, a great number of people and leaders and would-be leaders, ambitions and greed clogging hopes and strength, a clumsy amateur semi-government lurching from violence to compromise, ever more complicated, never again to know the beautiful simplicity of the ideal, the pure idea of liberty. And that's what I wanted, what I worked for, all these years. To muddle the nobly simple structure of the hierarchy of caste by infecting it with the idea of justice. And then to confuse the nobly simple structure of the ideal of human equality by trying to make it real. The monolithic lie frays out into a thousand incompatible truths, and that's what I wanted. But I am caught in the insanity, the stupidity, the meaningless brutality of the event.

They all want to use me, but I've outlived my usefulness, he thought; and the thought went through him like a shaft of clear light. He had kept thinking there was something he could do. There wasn't.

It was a kind of freedom.

No wonder he and Metoy had understood each other wordlessly and at once.

The zadyo Tema came to his door to conduct him downstairs. Back to the packdog room. All the leader-types were drawn to that room, its dour masculinity. Only five men were there this time, Metoy, the two generals, the two who used the rank of rega. Banarkamye dominated them all. He was through asking questions and was in the order-giving vein. "We leave here tomorrow," he said to Esdan. "You with us. We will have access to the Liberation holonet. You will speak for us. You will tell the Jit government that the Ekumen knows they are planning to deploy banned weapons and warns them that if they do, there will be instant and terrible retaliation."

Esdan was light-headed with hunger and sleeplessness. He stood still—he had not been invited to sit down—and looked down at the floor, his hand at his sides. He murmured barely audibly, "Yes, master."

Banarkamye's head snapped up, his eyes flashed. "What did you say?"

"Enna."

"Who do you think you are?"

"A prisoner of war."

"You can go."

Esdan left. Tema followed him but did not stop or direct him. He made his way straight to the kitchen, where he heard the rattle of pans, and said, "Choyo, please, give me something to eat!" The old man, cowed and shaky, mumbled and apologised and fretted, but produced some fruit and stale bread. Esdan sat at the worktable and devoured it. He offered some to Tema, who refused stiffly. Esdan ate it all. When he was done he limped on out through the kitchen exitways to a side door leading to the great terrace. He hoped to see Kamsa there, but none of the house people were out. He sat on a bench in the balustrade that looked down on the long reflecting pool. Tema stood nearby, on duty.

"You said the bondspeople on a place like this, if they didn't join the Uprising, were collaborators," Esdan said.

Tema was motionless, but listening.

"You don't think any of them might just not have understood what was going on? And still don't understand? This is a benighted place, zadyo. Hard to even imagine freedom, here."

The young man resisted answering for a while, but Esdan talked on, trying to make some contact with him, get through to him. Suddenly something he said popped the lid.

"Usewomen," Tema said. "Get fucked by blacks, every night. All they are, fucks. Jits' whores. Bearing their black brats, yesmaster yesmaster. You said it, they don't know what freedom is. Never will. Can't liberate anybody lets a black fuck 'em. They're foul. Dirty, can't get clean. They got black jizz through and through 'em. Jit-jizz!" He spat on the terrace and wiped his mouth.

Esdan sat still, looking down over the still water of the pool to the lower terraces, the big tree, the misty river, the far green shore. May he be well and work well, have patience, compassion, peace. What use was I, ever? All I did. It never was any use. Patience, compassion, peace. *They are your own people*. . . . He looked down at the thick blob of spittle on the yellow sandstone of the terrace. Fool, to leave his own people a lifetime behind him and come to meddle with another world. Fool, to think you could give anybody freedom. That was what death was for. To get us out of the crouchcage.

He got up and limped towards the house in silence. The young man followed him.

The lights came back on just as it was getting dark. They must have let old Saka go back to his tinkering. Preferring twilight, Esdan turned the room light off. He was lying on his bed when Kamsa knocked and came in, carrying a tray. "Kamsa!" he said, struggling up, and would have hugged her, but the tray prevented him. "Rekam is—?"

"With my mother," she murmured.

"He's all right?"

The backward nod. She set the tray down on the bed, as there was no table.

"You're all right? Be careful, Kamsa. I wish I— They're leaving tomorrow, they say. Stay out of their way if you can."

"I do. Do you be safe, sir," she said in her soft voice. He did not know if it was a question or a wish. He made a little rueful gesture, smiling. She turned to leave.

"Kamsa, is Heo—?"

"She was with that one. In his bed."

After a pause he said, "Is there anywhere you can hide out?" He was afraid that Banarkamye's men might execute these people when they left, as "collaborators" or to hide their own tracks.

"We got a hole to go to, like you said," she said.

"Good. Go there, if you can. Vanish! Stay out of sight."

She said, "I will hold fast, sir."

She was closing the door behind her when the sound of a flyer approaching buzzed the windows. They both stood still, she in the doorway, he near the window. Shouts downstairs, outside, men running. There was more than one flyer, approaching from the southeast. "Kill the lights!" somebody shouted. Men were running out to the flyers parked on the lawn and terrace. The window flared up with light, the air with a shattering explosion.

"Come with me," Kamsa said, and took his hand and pulled him after her, out the door, down the hall and through a service door he had never even seen. He hobbled with her as fast as he could down ladderlike stone stairs, through a back passage, out into the stable warren. They came outdoors just as a series of explosions rocked everything around them. They hurried across the courtyard through overwhelming noise and the leap of fire, Kamsa still pulling him along with complete sureness of where she was going, and ducked into one of the storerooms at the end of the stables. Gana was there and one of the old bondsmen, opening up a trapdoor in the floor. They went down, Kamsa with a leap, the others slow and awkward on the wooden ladder. Esdan most awkward, landing badly on his broken foot. The old man came last and pulled the trap shut over them. Gana had a battery lamp, but kept it on only briefly, showing a big, low, dirt-floored cellar, shelves, an archway to another room, a heap of wooden crates, five faces: the baby awake, gazing silent as ever from its sling on Gana's shoulder. Then darkness. And for some time silence.

They groped at the crates, set them down for seats at random in the darkness.

A new series of explosions, seeming far away, but the ground and the darkness shivered. They shivered in it. "O Kamye," one of them whispered.

Esdan sat on the shaky crate and let the jab and stab of pain in his foot sink into a burning throb.

Explosions: three, four.

Darkness was a substance, like thick water.

"Kamsa," he murmured.

She made some sound that located her near him.

"Thank you."

"You said hide, then we did talk of this place," she whispered.

The old man breathed wheezily and cleared his throat often. The baby's breathing was also audible, a small uneven sound, almost panting.

"Give me him." That was Gana. She must have transferred the baby to his mother.

Kamsa whispered, "Not now."

The old man spoke suddenly and loudly, startling them all: "No water in this!"

Kamsa shushed him and Gana hissed, "Don't shout, fool man!"

"Deaf," Kamsa murmured to Esdan, with a hint of laughter.

If they had no water, their hiding time was limited; the night, the next day; even that might be too long for a woman nursing a baby. Kamsa's mind was running on the same track as Esdan's. She said, "How do we know, should we come out?"

"Chance it, when we have to."

There was a long silence. It was hard to accept that one's eyes did not adjust to the darkness, that however long one waited one would see nothing. It was cave-cool. Esdan wished his shirt were warmer.

"You keep him warm," Gana said.

"I do," Kamsa murmured.

"Those men, they were bondsfolk?" That was Kamsa whispering to him. She was quite near him, to his left.

"Yes. Freed bondsfolk. From the north."

She said, "Lotsalot different men come here, since the old Owner did die. Army soldiers, some. But no bondsfolk before. They shot Heo. They shot Vey and old Seneo. He didn't die, but he's shot."

"Somebody from the field compound must have led them, showed them where the guards were posted. But they couldn't tell the bondsfolk from the soldiers. Where were you when they came?"

"Sleeping, back of the kitchen. All us housefolk. Six. That man did stand there like a risen dead. He said, 'Lie down there! Don't stir a hair!' So we did that. Heard them shooting and shouting all over the house. Oh, mighty Lord! I did fear! Then no more shooting, and that man did come back to us and hold his gun at us and take us out to the old house-compound. They did get that old gate shut on us. Like old days."

"For what did they do that if they are bondsfolk?" Gana's voice said from the darkness.

"Trying to get free," Esdan said dutifully.

"How free? Shooting and killing? Kill a girl in the bed?"

"They do all fight all the others, mama," Kamsa said.

"I thought all that was done, back three years," the old woman said. Her voice sounded strange. She was in tears. "I thought that was freedom then."

"They did kill the master in his bed!" the old man shouted out at the top of his voice, shrill, piercing. "What can come of that!"

There was a bit of a scuffle in the darkness. Gana was shaking the old fellow, hissing at him to shut up. He cried, "Let me go!" but quieted down, wheezing and muttering.

"Mighty Lord," Kamsa murmured, with that desperate laughter in her voice.

The crate was increasingly uncomfortable, and Esdan wanted to get his aching foot up or at least level. He lowered himself to the ground. It was cold, gritty, unpleasant to the hands. There was nothing to lean against. "If you make a light for a minute, Gana," he said, "we might find sacks, something to lie down on."

The world of the cellar flashed into being around them, amazing in its intricate precision. They found nothing to use but the loose board shelves. They set down several of these, making a kind of platform, and crept onto it as Gana switched them back into formless simple night. They were all cold. They huddled up against one another, side to side, back to back.

After a long time, an hour or more, in which the utter silence of the cellar was unbroken by any noise, Gana said in an impatient whisper, "Everybody up there did die, I think."

"That would simplify things for us," Esdan murmured.

"But we are the buried ones," said Kamsa.

Their voices roused the baby and he whimpered, the first complaint Esdan had ever heard him make. It was a tiny, weary grizzling or fretting, not a cry. It roughened his breathing and he gasped between his frettings. "Oh, baby, baby, hush now, hush," the mother murmured, and Esdan felt her rocking her body, cradling the baby close to keep him warm. She sang almost inaudibly, *"Suna meya, suna na . . . Sura rena, sura na . . ."* Monotonous, rhythmic, buzzy, purring, the sound made warmth, made comfort.

He must have dozed. He was lying curled up on the planks. He had no idea how long they had been in the cellar.

I have lived here forty years desiring freedom, his mind said to him. That desire brought me here. It will bring me out of here. I will hold fast.

He asked the others if they had heard anything since the bombing raid. They all whispered no.

He rubbed his head. "What do you think, Gana?" he said.

"I think the cold air does harm that baby," she said in almost her normal voice, which was always low.

"You do talk? What do you say?" the old man shouted. Kamsa, next to him, patted him and quieted him.

"I'll go look," Gana said.

"I'll go."

"You got one foot on you," the old woman said in a disgusted tone. She grunted and leaned hard on Esdan's shoulder as she stood up. "Now be still." She did not turn on the light, but felt her way over to the ladder and climbed it, with a little whuff of breath at each step. She pushed, heaved at the trapdoor. An edge of light showed. They could dimly see the cellar and each other and the dark blob of Gana's head up in the light. She stood there a long time, then let the trap down. "Nobody," she whispered from the ladder. "No noise. Looks like first morning."

"Better wait," Esdan said.

She came back and lowered herself down among them again. After a time she said, "We go out, it's strangers in the house, some other army soldiers. Then where?"

"Can you get to the field compound?" Esdan suggested.

"It's a long road."

After a while he said, "Can't know what to do till we know who's up there. All right. But let me go out, Gana."

"For what?"

"Because I'll know who they are," he said, hoping he was right.

"And they, too," Kamsa said, with that strange little edge of laughter. "No mistaking you, I guess."

"Right," he said. He struggled to his feet, found his way to the ladder, and climbed it laboriously. I'm too old for this, he thought again. He pushed up the trap and looked out. He listened for a long time. At last he whispered to those below him in the dark, "I'll be back as soon as I can," and crawled out, scrambling awkwardly to his feet. He caught his breath: the air of the place was thick with burning. The light was strange, dim. He followed the wall till he could peer out of the storeroom doorway.

What had been left of the old house was down like the rest of it, blown open, smouldering and masked in stinking smoke. Black embers and broken glass covered the cobbled yard. Nothing moved except the smoke. Yellow smoke, grey smoke. Above it all was the even, clear blue of dawn.

He went round onto the terrace, limping and stumbling, for his foot shot blinding pains up his leg. Coming to the balustrade he saw the blackened wrecks of the two flyers. Half the upper terrace was a raw crater. Below it the gardens of Yaramera stretched beautiful and serene as ever, level below level, to the old tree and the river. A man lay across the steps that went down to the lower terrace; he lay easily, restfully, his arms outflung. Nothing moved but the creeping smoke and the white-flowered bushes nodding in a breath of wind.

The sense of being watched from behind, from the blank windows of the fragments of the house that still stood, was intolerable. "Is anybody here?" Esdan suddenly called out.

Silence.

He shouted again, louder.

There was an answer, a distant call, from around in front of the house. He limped his way down onto the path, out in the open, not seeking to conceal himself; what was the use? Men came around from the front of the house, three men, then a fourth—a woman. They were assets, roughly clothed, field hands they must be, come down from their compound. "I'm with some of the housepeople," he said, stopping when they stopped, ten meters apart. "We hid out in a cellar. Is anybody else around?"

"Who are you?" one of them said, coming closer, peering, seeing the wrong color skin, the wrong kind of eyes.

"I'll tell you who I am. But is it safe for us to come out? There's old people, a baby. Are the soldiers gone?"

"They are dead," the woman said, a tall, pale-skinned, bony-faced woman.

"One we found hurt," said one of the men. "All the housepeople dead. Who did throw those bombs? What army?"

"I don't know what army," Esdan said. "Please, go tell my people they can come up. Back there, in the stables. Call out to them. Tell them who you are. I can't walk." The wrappings on his foot had worked loose, and the fractures had moved; the pain began to take away his breath. He sat down on the path, gasping. His head swam. The gardens of Yaramera grew very bright and very small and drew away and away from him, farther away than home.

He did not quite lose consciousness, but things were confused in his mind for a good while. There were a lot of people around, and they were outdoors, and everything stank of burnt meat, a smell that clung in the back of his mouth and made him retch. There was Kamsa, the tiny bluish shadowy sleeping face of the baby on her shoulder. There was Gana, saying to other people, "He did befriend us." A young man with big hands talked to him and did something to his foot, bound it up again, tighter, causing terrible pain and then the beginning of relief.

He was lying down on his back on grass. Beside him a man was lying down on his back on grass. It was Metoy, the eunuch. Metoy's scalp was bloody, the black hair burned short and brown. The dust-colored skin of his face was pale, bluish, like the baby's. He lay quietly, blinking sometimes.

The sun shone down. People were talking, a lot of people, somewhere nearby, but he and Metoy were lying on the grass, and nobody bothered them.

"Were the flyers from Bellen, Metoy?" Esdan said.

"Came from the east." Metoy's harsh voice was weak and hoarse. "I guess they were." After a while he said, "They want to cross the river."

Esdan thought about this for a while. His mind still did not work well at all. "Who does?" he said finally.

"These people. The field hands. The assets of Yaramera. They want to go meet the Army."

"The invasion?"

"The liberation."

Esdan propped himself up on his elbows. Raising his head seemed to clear it, and he sat up. He looked over at Metoy. "Will they find them?" he asked.

"If the Lord so wills," said the eunuch.

Presently Metoy tried to prop himself up like Esdan, but failed. "I got blown up," he said, short of breath. "Something hit my head. I see two for one."

"Probably a concussion. Lie still. Stay awake. Were you with Banarkamye, or observing?"

"I'm in your line of work."

Esdan nodded, the backward nod.

"Factions will be the death of us," Metoy said faintly.

Kamsa came and squatted down beside Esdan. "They say we must go cross the river," she told him in her soft voice. "To where the people-army will keep us safe. I don't know."

"Nobody knows, Kamsa."

"I can't take Rekam cross a river," she whispered. Her face clenched up, her lips drawing back, her brows down. She wept, without tears and in silence. "The water is cold."

"They'll have boats, Kamsa. They'll look after you and Rekam. Don't worry. It'll be all right." He knew his words were meaningless.

"I can't go," she whispered.

"Stay here then," Metoy said.

"They said that other army will come here."

"It might. More likely ours will."

She looked at Metoy. "You are the cutfree," she said. "With those others." She looked back at Esdan. "Choyo got killed. All the kitchen is blown in pieces burning." She hid her face in her arms.

Esdan sat up and reached out to her, stroking her shoulder and arm. He touched the baby's fragile head with its thin, dry hair.

Gana came and stood over them. "All the field hands are going cross the river," she said. "To be safe."

"You'll be safer here. Where there's food and shelter." Metoy spoke in short bursts, his eyes closed. "Than walking to meet an invasion."

"I can't take him, mama," Kamsa whispered. "He has got to be warm. I can't, I can't take him."

Gana stooped and looked into the baby's face, touching it very softly with one finger. Her wrinkled face closed like a fist. She straightened up, but not erect as she used to stand. She stood bowed. "All right," she said. "We'll stay."

She sat down on the grass beside Kamsa. People were on the move around them. The woman Esdan had seen on the terrace stopped by Gana and said, "Come on, grandmother. Time to go. The boats are ready waiting."

"Staying," Gana said.

"Why? Can't leave that old house you worked in?" the woman said, jeering, humoring. "It's all burned up, grandmother! Come on now. Bring that girl and her baby." She looked at Esdan and Metoy, a flick-glance. They were not her concern. "Come on," she repeated. "Get up now."

"Staying," Gana said.

"You crazy housefolk," the woman said, turned away, turned back, gave it up with a shrug, and went on.

A few others stopped, but none for more than a question, a moment. They streamed on down the terraces, the sunlit paths beside the quiet pools, down towards the boathouses beyond the great tree. After a while they were all gone.

The sun had grown hot. It must be near noon. Metoy was whiter than ever, but he sat up, saying he could see single, most of the time.

"We should get into the shade, Gana," Esdan said. "Metoy, can you get up?"

He staggered and shambled, but walked without help, and they got to the shade of a garden wall. Gana went off to look for water. Kamsa was carrying Rekam in her arms, close against her chest, sheltered from the sun. She had not spoken for a long time. When they had settled down she said, half questioning, looking around dully, "We are all alone here."

"There'll be others stayed. In the compounds," Metoy said. "They'll turn up."

Gana came back; she had no vessel to carry water in, but had soaked her scarf, and laid the cold wet cloth on Metoy's head. He shuddered. "You can walk better, then we can go to the house-compound, cutfree," she said. "Places we can live in, there."

"House-compound is where I grew up, grandmother," he said.

And presently, when he said he could walk, they made their halt and lame way down a road which Esdan vaguely remembered, the road to the crouchcage. It seemed a long road. They came to the high compound wall and the gate standing open.

Esdan turned to look back at the ruins of the great house for a moment. Gana stopped beside him.

"Rekam died," she said under her breath.

He caught his breath. "When?"

She shook her head. "I don't know. She wants to hold him. She's done with holding him, then she will let him go." She looked in the open gateway at the rows of huts and longhouses, the dried-up garden patches, the dusty ground. "Lotsalot little babies are in there," she said. "In that ground. Two of my own. Her sisters." She went in, following Kamsa. Esdan stood a while longer in the gateway, and then he went in to do what there was for him to do: dig a grave for the child, and wait with the others for the Liberation.

THE FOREVER WAR

JOE HALDEMAN

The Forever War (1974)
1968 (1995)
Forever Peace (1997)

The Forever War told the story of William Mandella and Marygay Potter, Americans born in the late twentieth century, who were drafted into an interstellar war that lasted for more than a thousand years. Because of the effect of relativity, they lived through the whole thing.

When they came back to Earth, midway through the book, they found that the culture they had supposedly been protecting had changed so radically that they couldn't live in it—and much as they hated the army, at least it was familiar, so they reenlisted. In the last quarter of the novel, they're separated: forever, they assume. But at the very end the almost impossible happens, and they do find each other again.

People have been after me for a sequel ever since the book came out, and my response always was no, the book is complete. But someday I would write a novella about what happened to the characters later in life.

Kindly editor Silverberg asked that I write that novella for this book, and I started it out with some enthusiasm. But then I saw I actually was writing a novel, the sequel that I said I'd never write. So I warped it around into a novel proposal and sent it out, and then started over, writing a different story for this volume.

The obvious thing missing from *The Forever War* is the story of what happened to Marygay in the part of the book where she's separated from William. I wrote "A Separate War" to fill in that lacuna, but it also serves as a sort of foreshadowing of the new novel.

SET THEORY

A few years ago I wrote a novel called *Forever Peace,* and was careful in introducing it to point out that it was not a sequel to *The Forever War,* though it did cover some of the same ground, from the viewpoint of the same author, more than twenty years later.

The critic Gary Wolfe noted that those two books combined with my "mainstream" novel *1968* to form a kind of triptych about love and war. That was a neat, elegant idea, and here I go kicking it out of shape by writing another novel. I don't think they let you write or paint quartyches.

I had an inkling that a sequel was necessary, though, back when I first sold the paperback rights to *The Forever War.* The editor said she never would have bought it if the book hadn't had a happy ending.

If ever there was a time and place to keep your mouth shut, that was one of them, but that was in another country, and besides the editor is dead. *The Forever War* does not have a happy ending. Marygay and William do get back together—the book ends with the birth announcement of their first child—but they're together on a prison planet, preserved as genetic curiosities in a universe where the human race has abandoned its humanity in a monstrous liaison with its former enemy.

In the sequel, *Forever Free,* they decide to do something about it. Or die trying.

—*Joe Haldeman*

A Separate War

by

Joe Haldeman

OUR WOUNDS WERE HORRIBLE, BUT THE ARMY MADE US WELL AND GAVE US Heaven, temporarily. And a fortune to spend there.

The most expensive and hard-to-replace component of a fighting suit is the soldier inside of it, so if he is crippled badly enough to be taken out of the fight, the suit tries to save what's left. In William's case, it automatically cut off his mangled leg and sealed the stump. In my case it was the right arm, just above the elbow. They say that for us women, losing an arm is easier than a leg. How did they come up with that?

But it was amazing luck that we should both get amputation wounds at the same time, which kept us together.

That was the Tet-2 campaign, which was a disaster, and William and I lay around doped to the gills with happyjuice while the others died their way through the disaster of Aleph-7. The score after the two battles was fifty-four dead, thirty-seven of us crips, two head cases, and only twelve more or less working soldiers, who were of course bristling with enthusiasm. Twelve is not enough to fight a battle with, unfortunately, so the *Sangre y Victoria* was rerouted to the hospital planet Heaven.

We took a long time, three collapsar jumps, getting to Heaven. The Taurans can chase you through one jump, if they're at the right place and the right time. But two would be almost impossible, and three just couldn't happen.

(But "couldn't happen" is probably a bad-luck charm. Because of the relativistic distortions associated with travel through collapsar jumps, you never know, when you greet the enemy, whether it comes from your own time, or centuries in your past or future. Maybe in a millennium or two, they'll be able to follow you through three collapsar jumps like following footprints. One of the first things they'd do is vaporize Heaven. Then Earth.)

Heaven is like an Earth untouched by human industry and avarice, pristine forests and fields and mountains—but it's also a monument to human industry, and avarice, too.

When you recover—and there's no "if"; you wouldn't be there if they didn't know they could fix you—you're still in the army, but you're also immensely wealthy. Even a private's pay rolls up a fortune, automatically invested during the centuries that creak by between battles. One of the functions of Heaven is to put all those millions back into the economy. So there's no end of things to do, all of them expensive.

When William and I recovered, we were given six months of "rest and recreation" on Heaven. I actually got out two days before him, but waited around, reading. They did still have books, for soldiers so old-fashioned they didn't want to plug themselves into adventures or ecstasies for thousands of dollars a minute. I did have $529,755,012 sitting around, so I could have dipped into tripping. But I'd heard I would have plenty of it, retraining before our next assignment. The ALSC, "accelerated life situation computer," which taught you things by making you do them in virtual reality. Over and over, until you got them right.

William had half again as much money as I did, since he had outranked me for centuries, but I didn't wait around just to get my hands on his fortune. I probably would have wanted his company even if I didn't love him. We were the only two people here born in the twentieth century, and there were only a handful from the twenty-first. Very few of them, off-duty, spoke a language I understood, though all soldiers were taught "premodern" English as a sort of temporal *lingua franca*. Some of them claimed their native language was English, but it was extremely fast and seemed to have lost some vowels along the way. Four centuries. Would I have sounded as strange to a Pilgrim? I don't think so.

(It would be interesting to take one of those Pilgrim Fathers and show him what had evolved from a life of grim piety and industriousness. Religion on Earth is a curiosity, almost as rare as heterosex. Heaven has no God, either, and men and women in love or in sex with people not of their own gender are committing an anachronistic perversion.)

I'd already arranged for a sumptuous "honeymoon" suite on Skye, an airborne resort, before William got out, and we did spend five days there, amusing each other anachronistically. Then we rented a flyer and set out to see the world.

William humored my desire to explore the physical, wild aspects of the world first. We camped in desert, jungle, arctic waste, mountaintops, deserted islands. We had pressor fields that kept away dangerous animals, allowing us a good close look at them while they tried to figure out what was keeping them from lunch, and they were impressive—evolution here had not favored mammal over reptile, and both families had developed large, swift predators in a variety of beautiful and ugly designs.

Then we toured the cities, in their finite variety. Some, like the sylvan Threshold where we'd grown and trained our new limbs, blended in with their natural surroundings. This was a twenty-second-century esthetic, too bland and obvious for modern tastes. The newer cities, like Skye, flaunted their artificiality.

We were both nervous in Atlantis, under a crushing kilometer of water, with huge glowing beasts bumping against the pressors, dark day and dark night. Perhaps it was too exact a metaphor for our lives in the army, the thin skins of cruiser or fighting suit holding the dark nothingness of space at bay while monsters tried to destroy you.

Many of the cities had no function other than separating soldiers from their money, so in spite of their variety there was a sameness to them. Eat, drink, drug, trip, have or watch sex.

I found the sex shows more interesting than William did, but he was repelled by the men together. It didn't seem to me that what they did was all that different from what we did—and not nearly as alien as tripping for sex, plugging into a machine that delivered to you the image of an ideal mate and cleaned up afterwards.

He did go to a lesbian show with me, and made love with unusual energy that night. I thought there was something there besides titillation; that he was trying to prove something. We kidded each other about it—"Me Tarzan, you Jane," "Me Tarzan, you Heathcliff." Who on this world would know what we were laughing about?

Prostitution had a new wrinkle, with empathy drugs that joined the servicer and customer in a deep emotional bond that was real while it lasted, I suppose to keep in competition with the electronic fantasy. We told each other we weren't inclined to try it, though I was curious, and probably would have done it if I'd been alone. I don't think William would have, since the drugs don't work between men and women, or so one of them told us, giggling with wide-eyed embarrassment. The very idea.

We had six months of quiet communion and wild, desperate fun, and still had plenty of money left when it suddenly ended. We were having lunch in an elegant restaurant in Skye, watching the sun sparkle on the calm ocean a klick below, when a nervous private came up, saluted, and gave us our sealed orders.

They were for different places. William was going to Sade-138, a collapsar out in the Greater Magellanic Cloud. I was going to Aleph-10, in the Orion group.

He was a major, the Yod-4 Strike Force commander, and I was a captain, the executive officer for Aleph-10.

It was unbelievable, surreal; monumentally stupid and unfair. We'd been together since Basic—five years or half a millennium—and neither of us was leadership material. Neither of us was even a good *private*! The army had abundant evidence of that. Yet he was leaving in a week, for Stargate, to become a leader of men and women. My Strike Force was mustering in orbit around Heaven, in two days. Where I would somehow become a leader myself.

We flew back to Threshold, half the world away, and got there just as the administrative offices were opening. William fought and bought his way to the top, trying at the very least to have me reassigned as *his* XO. What difference could it make? Most of the people he'd muster with at Stargate hadn't even been born yet.

Of course it was not a matter of logic; it was a matter of protocol. And no army in history had ever been so locked in the ice of protocol. The person who had *signed* those orders for the yet unborn was probably dead by now.

The day and night we had left together was not good. Naturally, we thought of running; we knew the planet well and had some resources left. But the planet belonged to the army. We wouldn't be safe in any city, and would be thoroughly conspicuous in the wild, since we wouldn't be able to survive without the pressor fields, easily detected.

Desertion would be punished by death, of course, and we discussed the possibility of dying together that way, in a final gesture of defiance. But that would have been passive, simply giving our lives to the army. Better to offer them one more time to the Taurans.

Finally, exhausted by talk and anger and grief, we just lay in each other's arms for the last night and early morning. I wish I could say we gave each other strength.

When he walked me to the isolation chamber three hours before launch, we were almost deferential with one another, perhaps the way you act in the presence of beloved dead. No poet who ever equated parting with death had ever had a door slam shut like that. Even if we had both been headed for Earth, a few days apart, the time-space geometry of the collapsar jump would guarantee that we arrived decades or even centuries apart from one another.

And this wasn't Earth. There were 150,000 light-years between Sade-138 and Aleph-10. Absolute distance means nothing in collapsar geometry, they say. But if William were to die in a nova bomb attack, the tiny spark of his passing would take fifteen hundred centuries to crawl to Orion, or Earth. Time and distance beyond imagination.

The spaceport was on the equator, of course, on an island they called Pærw'l; Farewell. There was a high cliff, actually a flattened-off pinnacle, overlooking the bay to the east, where William and I had spent silent days fasting and meditating. He said he was going there to watch the launch. I hoped to get a window so that I could see the island, and I did push my way to one when we filed into the shuttle. But I couldn't see the pinnacle from sea level, and when the engines screamed and the invisible force pushed me back into the cushions, I looked but was blinded by tears, and couldn't raise a hand to wipe them away.

· **2** ·

Fortunately, I had six hours' slack time after we docked at the space station Athene, before I had to report for ALSC training. Time to pull myself together, with the help of a couple of slowballs. I went to my small quarters and unpacked and took the pills, and lay on the bunk for a while. Then I found my way to the lounge and watched the planet spin below, green and white and blue. There were eleven ships in orbit a few klicks away, one a large cruiser, presumably the *Bolívar*, which was going to take us to Aleph-10.

The lounge was huge and almost empty. Two other women in unfamiliar beige uniforms, I supposed Athene staff. They were talking in the strange fast Angel language, and I was listening with a rather slow brain.

While I was getting coffee, a man walked in wearing tan-and-green camouflage fatigues like mine. We weren't actually camouflaged as well as the ones in beige, in this room of comforting wood and earth tones.

He came over and got a cup. "You're Captain Potter, Marygay Potter."

"That's right," I said. "You're in Beta?"

"No, I'm stationed here, but I'm army." He offered his hand. "Michael Dobei, Mike. Colonel. I'm your Temporal Orientation Officer."

We carried our coffee to a table. "You're supposed to catch me up on this future, this present?"

He nodded. "Prepare you for dealing with the men and women under you. And the other officers."

"What I'm trying to deal with is this 'under you' part. I'm no soldier, Colonel."

"Mike. You're actually a better soldier than you know. I've seen your profile. You've been through a lot of combat, and it hasn't broken you. Not even the terrible experience on Earth."

William and I had been staying on my parents' farm when we were attacked by a band of looters; Mother and Dad were killed. "That's in my profile? I wasn't a soldier then. We'd quit."

"There's a lot of stuff in there." He raised his coffee and looked at me over the rim of the cup. "Want to know what your high-school advisor thought of you?"

"You're a shrink."

"That used to be the word. Now we're 'skinks.' "

I laughed. "That used to be a lizard."

"Still is." He pulled a reader out of his pocket. "You were last on Earth in 2007. You liked it so little that you reenlisted."

"Has it gotten better?"

"Better, then worse, then better. As ever. When I left, in 2318, things were at least peaceful."

"Drafted?"

"Not in the sense you were. I knew from age ten what I was going to be. Everybody does."

"What? You knew you were going to be a Temporal Orientation Officer?"

"Uh-huh." He smiled. "I didn't know quite what that meant, but I sure as hell resented it. I had to go to a special school, to learn this language—SoldierSpeak—but I had to take four years of it, instead of the two that most soldiers do.

"I suppose we're more regimented on Earth now; crèche to grave control, but also security. The crime and anarchy that characterized your Earth are ancient history. Most people live happy, fulfilling lives."

"Homosexual. No families."

"Oh, we have families, parents, but not random ones. To keep the population stable, one person is quickened whenever one dies. The new one goes to a couple that has grown up together in the knowledge that they have a talent for parenting; they'll be given, at most, four children to raise."

" 'Quickened'—test-tube babies?"

"Incubators. No birth trauma. No real uncertainty about the future. You'll find your troops a pretty sane bunch of people."

"And what will they find *me*? They won't resent taking orders from a heterosexual throwback? A dinosaur?"

"They know history; they won't blame you for being what you are. If you tried to initiate sex with one of the men, there might be trouble."

I shook my head. "That won't happen. The only man I love is gone, forever."

He looked down at the floor and cleared his throat. Can you embarrass a professional skink? "William Mandella. I wish they hadn't done that. It seems . . . unnecessarily cruel."

"We tried to get me reassigned as his XO."

"That wouldn't have worked. That's the paradox." He moved the cup in circles on the table, watching the reflections dance. "You both have so much time in rank, objective and subjective, that they had to give you commissions. But they couldn't put you under William. The heterosex issue aside, he would be more concerned about your safety than about the mission. The troops would see that and resent it."

"What, it never happens in your brave new world? You never have a commander falling in love with someone in his or her command?"

"Of course it happens; het or home, love happens. But they're separated and sometimes punished, or at least reprimanded." He waved that away. "In theory. If it's not blatant, who cares? But with you and William, it would be a constant irritant to the people underneath you."

"Most of them have never seen heterosexuals, I suppose."

"None of them. It's detected early and easy to cure."

"Wonderful. Maybe they can cure me."

"No. I'm afraid it has to be done before puberty." He laughed. "Sorry. You were kidding me."

"You don't think my being het is going to hurt my ability to command?"

"No, like I say, they know how people used to be—besides, privates aren't supposed to *empathize* with their officers; they're supposed to follow their orders. And they know about ALSC training; they'll know how well prepared you are."

"I'll be out of the chain of command, anyhow, as Executive Officer."

"Unless everybody over you dies. It's happened."

"Then the army will find out what a mistake it made. A little too late."

"You might surprise yourself, after the ALSC training." He checked his watch. "Which is coming up in a couple of hours."

"Would you like to get together for lunch before that?"

"Um, no. I don't think you want to eat. They sort of clean you out beforehand. From both ends."

"Sounds . . . dramatic."

"Oh, it is, all of it. Some people enjoy it."

"You don't think I will."

He paused. "Let's talk about it afterward."

• 3 •

The purging wasn't bad, since by that time I was limp and goofy with drugs. They shaved me clean as a baby, even my arms and cheeks, and were in the process of covering me with feedback sensors when I dozed off.

I woke up naked and running. A bunch of other naked people were running after me and my friends, throwing rocks at us. A heavy rock stung me under the shoulderblade, knocking my breath away and making me stumble. A chunky Neanderthal tackled me and whacked me on the head twice with something.

I knew this was a simulation, a dream, and here I was passing out in a dream. When I woke up a moment later, he had forced my legs apart and was about to rape me. I clawed at his eyes and rolled away. He came after me, intention still apparent, and my hand fell on his club. I swung it with both hands and cracked his head, spraying blood and brains. He ejaculated in shuddering spurts as he died, feet drumming the ground. God, it was supposed to be realistic, but couldn't they spare me a few details?

Then I was standing in a phalanx with a shield and a long spear. There were men in front of our line, crouching, with shorter spears. All of the weapons were braced at the same angle, presenting a wall of points to the horses that were charging toward us. This is not the hard part. You just stand firm, and live or not. I studied the light armor of the Persian enemy as they approached. There were three who might be in my area if we unhorsed them, or if their horses stopped.

The horse on my left crashed through. The one on the right reared up and tried to turn. The one charging straight at us took both spears in the breast, breaking the shaft of mine as it skidded, sprawling, spraying blood and screaming with an unearthly high whine, pinning the man in front of me. The unhorsed Persian crashed into my shield and knocked me down as I was drawing my short sword; the hilt of it dug in under my ribs, and I almost slashed myself getting it free of the scabbard while I scrambled back to my feet.

The horseman had lost his little round shield, but his sword was coming around in a flat arc. I just caught it on the edge of my shield and *as I had been taught* chopped down toward his unprotected forearm and wrist—he twisted away, but I nicked him under the elbow, lucky shot that hit a tendon or something. He dropped his sword and as he reached for it with his other hand, I slashed at his face and opened a terrible wound across eye, cheek, and mouth. As he screamed a flap of skin fell away, exposing bloody bone and teeth, and I shifted my weight for a backhand, aiming for the unprotected throat, and then something slammed into my back and the bloody point of a spear broke the skin above my right nipple; I fell to my knees dying and realized I didn't have breasts; I was a man, a young boy.

It was dark and cold and the trench smelled of shit and rotting flesh. "Two minutes, boys," a sergeant said in a stage whisper. I heard a canteen gurgle twice and took it when it was passed to me—warm gin. I managed not to cough and passed it on down. I checked in the darkness and still didn't have breasts and touched between my legs and that was strange. I started to shake and heard the man next to me peeing, and I suddenly had to go, too. I fumbled with the buttons left-handed, holding on to my rifle, and barely managed to get the thing out in time, peeing hotly onto my hand. "Fix bayonets," the sergeant whispered while I was still going *and instinct took over* and I felt the locking port under the muzzle of my Enfield and held it with my left hand while my right went back and slid the bayonet from its sheath and clicked it into place.

"I shall see you in Hell, Sergeant Simmons." the man next to me said conversationally.

"Soon enough, Rez. Thirty seconds." There was a German machine-gun position about eighty yards ahead and to the right. They also had at least one very good sniper and, presumably, an artillery observer. We were hoping for some artillery support at 1:17, which would signal the beginning of our charge. If the artillery didn't come, which was likely, we were to charge anyhow, riflemen in two short squads in front of grenadiers. A suicide mission, perhaps, but certain death if your courage flags.

I wiped my hand on the greasy filthy fatigues and thumbed the safety off the rifle. There was already a round chambered. I put my left foot on the improvised step and got a handhold with my left. My knees were water, and my anus didn't want to stay closed. I felt tears, and my throat went dry and metallic. *This is not real.* "Now," the sergeant said quietly, and I heaved myself up over the lip of the trench and fired one-handed in the general direction of the enemy, and started to run toward them, working the bolt, vaguely proud of not soiling myself. I flopped on the ground and took an aimed shot at the noise of the machine gun, no muzzle flash, and then held fire while squad two rushed by us. A grenadier skidded next to me, and said, "Go!" It became "Oh!" when a bullet smacked into him, but I was up and running, another round chambered, four left. A bullet shattered my foot and I took one painful step and fell.

I pulled myself forward, trying to keep the muzzle out of the mud, and rolled into a shallow crater half filled with water and parts of a swollen decaying body. I could hear another machine gun starting, but I couldn't breathe. I pushed up with both arms to gasp some air above the crater's miasma and a bullet crashed into my teeth.

It wasn't chronological. I went from there to the mist of Breed's Hill, on the British side of what the Americans would call the Battle of Bunker Hill. The deck of a ship, warding off pirates while sails burned; then another ship, deafened by cannon fire while I tried to keep cool lead on the kamikaze Zero soaring into us.

I flew cloth-winged biplanes and supersonic fighters, used lasers and a bow and arrow and leveled a city with the push of a button. I killed with bullets and bolos and binary-coded decimals. Every second, I was aware that it was a training exercise; I felt terror and sorrow and pain, but only for minutes or hours. And I slept at least as many hours as I was awake, but there was no rest—somehow while sleeping, my brain was filled with procedures, history, regulations.

When they unplugged me after three weeks I was literally catatonic. That was normal, though, and they had drugs that pulled you back into the world. They worked for more than 90 percent of the new officers. The others were allowed to drift away.

• 4 •

We had two weeks of rest and rehabilitation—in orbit, unfortunately, not on Heaven—after the ALSC experience. While we were sweating it out in the officers' gym, I met the other line officers, who were as shaken and weak as I was, after three weeks' immersion in oxygenated fluorocarbon, mayhem, and book learning.

We were also one mass of wrinkles from head to toe, the first day, when our exercises consisted of raising our arms above our heads and trying to stand up and sit down without help. The wrinkles started to fade in the sauna, as we conversed in tired monosyllables. We looked like big muscular pink babies; they must have shaved or depilated us during the three weeks.

Three of us were male, which was interesting. I've seen lots of naked men, but never a hairless one. I guess we all looked kind of exposed and diagrammatic. Okayawa had an erection, and Morales kidded him about it, but to my relief it didn't go any further than that. It was a socially difficult situation anyhow.

The commander, Angela Garcia, was physically about ten years older than me, though of course by the calendar she was centuries younger. She was gruff and seemed to be holding a lot in. I knew her slightly, at least by sight; she'd been a platoon leader, not mine, in the Tet-2 disaster. Both her legs had the new-equipment look that my arm did. We'd come to Heaven together, but since her regrowth took three times as long as mine, we hadn't met there. William and I were gone before she was able to come into the common ward.

William had been in many of my ALSC dreams, a shadowy figure in some of the crowds. My father sometimes, too.

I liked Sharn Taylor, the medical officer, right off. She had a cheerful fatalism about the whole thing, and had lived life to the hilt while on Heaven, hiring a succession of beautiful women to help her spend her fortune. She'd run out of money a week early, and had to come back to Threshold and live on army rations and the low-power trips you could get for free. She herself was not beautiful; a terrible wound had ripped off her left arm and breast and the left side of her face. It had all been put back, but the new parts didn't match the old parts too well.

She had a doctor's objectivity about it, though, and professional admiration for the miracles they could accomplish—by the current calendar, she was more than 150 years out of medical school.

Her ALSC session had been totally different from ours, of course; an update of healing skills rather than killing ones. "Most of it is getting along with machines, though, rather than treating people," she told me while we nibbled at the foodlike substance that was supposed to help us recover. "I can treat wounds in the field, basically to keep someone alive until we can get to a machine. But most modern weapons don't leave enough to salvage." She had a silly smile.

"We don't know how modern the enemy is going to be," I said. "Though I guess they don't have to be all *that* modern to vaporize us." We both giggled, and then stopped simultaneously.

"I wonder what they've got us on," she said. "It's not happyjuice; I can feel my fingertips and have all my peripheral vision."

"Temporary mood elevator?"

"I hope it's temporary. I'll talk to someone."

Sharn found out that it was just a euphoriant in the food; without it, ALSC withdrawal could bring on deep depression. I'd almost rather be depressed, I thought. We *were*, after all, facing almost certain doom. All but one of us had survived at least one battle in a war where the average survival rate was only 34 percent per battle. If you believed in luck, you might believe we'd used all of ours up.

We had the satellite to ourselves for eight days—ten officers waited on by a staff of thirty personnel—while we got our strength back. Of course friendships formed. It was pretty obvious that it went beyond friendship with Chance Nguyen and Aurelio Morales; they stuck like glue from the first day.

Risa Danyi and Sharn and I made up a logical trio, the three officers out of the chain of command. Risa was the tech officer, a bit older than Sharn and me, with a Ph.D. in systems engineering. She seemed younger, though, born and raised on Heaven. Not actually born, I reminded myself. And never traumatized by combat.

Risa's ALSC had been the same as mine, but she had found it more fascinating than terrifying. She was apologetic about that. She had grown up tripping, and was accustomed to the immediacy and drama of it—and she didn't have any real-life experiences to relate to the dream combat.

Both Risa and Sharn were bawdy by nature and curious about my heterosex, and while we were silly with the euphoriants I didn't hold back anything. When I was first in the army, we'd had to obey a rotating "sleeping roster," so I slept with every male private in the company more than once, and although sleeping together didn't mean you had to have sex, it was considered unsporting to refuse. And of course men are men; most of them would have to go through the motions, literally, even if they didn't feel like it.

Even on board ship, when they got rid of the sleeping roster, there was still a lot of switching around. I was mainly with William, but neither of us was exclusive (which would have been considered odd, in our generation). Nobody was fertile, so there was no chance of accidental pregnancy.

That notion really threw Sharn and Risa. Pregnancy is something that happens to animals. Sharn had seen pictures of the process, medical history, and described it to us in horrifying detail. I had to remind them that I was born that way—I did *that* to my mother, and she somehow forgave me.

Risa primly pointed out that it was actually my father who did it to my mother, which for some reason we all thought was hilarious.

One morning when we were alone together, just looking down at the planet in the lounge, she brought up the obvious.

"You haven't said anything about it, so I guess you've never loved a woman." She cleared her throat, nervous. "I mean had sex. I know you loved your mother."

"No." I didn't know whether to elaborate. "It wasn't that common; I mean I *knew* girls and women who were together. That way."

"Well." She patted my elbow. "You know."

"Uh, yes. I mean yes, I understand. Thanks, but I . . ."

"I just meant, you know, we're the same rank. It's even legal." She laughed nervously; if all the regulations were broken that enthusiastically, we'd be an unruly mob, not an army.

I wasn't quite sure what to say. Until she actually asked, I hadn't thought about the possibility except as an abstraction. "I'm still grieving for William." She nodded and gave me another pat and left quietly.

But of course that wasn't all of it. I could visualize her and Sharn, for instance, having sex; I'd seen it on stage and cube often enough. But I couldn't put myself in their place. Not the way I could visualize myself being with one of the men, especially Sid, Isidro Zhulpa. He was quiet, introspective, darkly beautiful. But too well balanced to contemplate a sexual perversion involving me.

I was still jangled about fantasy, imagination; real and artificial memories. I knew for certain that I had never killed anyone with a club or a knife, but my body seemed to have a memory of it, more real than the mental picture. I could still feel the ghost of a penis and balls, and breastlessness, since all of the ALSC combat templates were male. Surely that was more alien than lying down with another woman. When I was waiting for William to get out of his final range-and-motion stage, reading for two days, I'd had an impulse to try tripping, plugging into a lesbian-sex simulation, the only kind that was available for women.

For a couple of reasons, I didn't do it. Now that it's too late—the only trips on Athene are ALSC ones—I wish I had. Because it's not as simple as "I accept this because it's the way they were brought up," with the implied condescension that my pedestal of normality entitles me.

Normality. I'm going to be locked up in a can with 130 other people for whom my most personal, private life is something as exotic as cannibalism. So rare they don't even have an epithet for it. I was sure they'd come up with one.

· 5 ·

Table of Organization
Strike Force Beta
Aleph-10 Campaign

1ECHN	MAJ Garcia		COMM Sidorenko
2ECHN	1LT Nguyen		
3ECHN	1LT Zhulpa		
4ECHN	CPT Potter	XO	
	2LT Darnyi	TO	
	2LT Taylor, MD	MO	

	1	2	3	4
5ECHN	2LT Sadovyi	2LT Okayawa	2LT Mathes	2LT Morales
6ECHN	SSgt Baron	SSgt Troy	SSgt Tsuruta	SSgt Hencken
7ECHN	Sgt Naber	Sgt Kitamura	Sgt Yorzyk	Sgt Verdeur
8ECHN	Cpl Roth	Cpl Gross	Cpl Bruner	Cpl Graef
	Cpl Sieben	Cpl Simeony	Cpl Ritter	Cpl Henkel
	Cpl Korir	Cpl Sadovyi	Cpl Loader	Cpl Catherwood
	Cpl Montgomery	Cpl Popov	Cpl Hajos	Cpl Hamay
	Cpl Daniels	Cpl Kahanamoku	Spl Miyzaki	Cpl Csik
	Cpl Son	Cpl Daniels	Cpl Taylor	Cpl Hopkins
	Cpl Devitt	Cpl Schollander	Cpl Winden	Cpl Spitz
	Cpl Gammoudi	Cpl Akii-Bua	Cpl Beiwat	Cpl Keino
	Cpl Armstrong	Cpl Kariuki	Cpl Brir	Cpl Keter
	Cpl Kostadinova	Cpl Ajunwa	Cpl Roba	Cpl Keimo
	Cpl McDonald	Cpl Balas	Cpl Reskova	Cpl Mayfair
	Cpl Zubero	Cpl Furniss	Cpl Kopilakov	Cpl Gross
	Cpl Myazaki	Cpl Roth	Cpl Pakratov	Cpl Lopez
	Cpl Ris	Cpl Scholes	Cpl Ris	Cpl Henricks
	Cpl Russell	Cpl Rozsa	Cpl Moorhouse	Cpl Lundquist
	Cpl Shiley	Cpl Csak	Cpl Coachman	Cpl Brand
	Cpl Ackerman	Cpl Pankritov	Cpl Nesty	Cpl O'Brien
	Pvt Darryl	Pvt Gyenji	Pvt Crapp	Pvt Hong
	Pvt Biondi	Pvt Stewart, M.	Pvt Baumann	Pvt Stewart, J.
		Pvt Engel-Kramer	Pvt Min	Pvt Mingxia

Supporting: 1LT Otto (NAV), 2LTs Wennyl and Van Dykken (MED), Durack (PSY), Bleibkey (MAINT), Lackey (ORD), Obspowich (COMM), Madison (COMP): 1Sgts Mastenbroek (MED), Anderson (MED), Szoki

(MED), Fraser (MED), Henne (PSY), Neelson (MAINT), Ender (ORD); SSgts Krause (MED), Steinseller (MED), Hogshead (MED), Otto (MED), Yong (MAINT), Jingyi (CK), Meyer (COMP); Sgts Gould (MED), Bonder (MAINT), Kraus (ORD), Waite (REC); Cpls Friedrich (MED), Haislett (MED), Poll (SEX), Norelius (SEX), Gyenge (ORD); Pvts Curtiss (MAINT), Senff (CK), Harup (ORD).

APPROVED STFCOM STARGATE 12 Mar 2458   FOR THE COMMANDER:

                                     Olga Torischeva BGEN

STFCOM

The lounge was a so-called "plastic room"; it could reform itself into various modes, according to function. One of the Athene staff had handed over the control box to me—my first executive function as executive officer.

When the troop carriers lined up outside for docking, I pushed the button marked "auditorium," and the comfortable wood grain faded to a neutral ivory color as the furniture sank into the floor, and then rose up again, extruding three rows of seats on ascending tiers. The control box asked me how many seats to put on the stage in front. I said six and then corrected myself, to seven. The Commodore would be here, for ceremony's sake.

As I watched the Strike Force file into the auditorium, I tried to separate the combat veterans from the Angels. There weren't too many of the latter; only fourteen out of the 130 were born on Heaven. For a good and unsettling reason.

Major Garcia waited until all the seats were filled, and then she waited a couple of minutes longer, studying the faces, maybe doing the same kind of sorting. Then she stood up and introduced the Commodore and the other officers, down to my echelon, and got down to business.

"I'm certain that you have heard rumors. One of them is true." She took a single note card from her tunic pocket and set it on the lectern. "One hundred sixteen of us have been in combat before. All wounded and brought here to Heaven. For repairs and then rest.

"You may know that this concentration of veterans is unusual. The army values experience and spreads it around. A group this size would normally have about twenty combat veterans. Of course this implies that we face a difficult assignment.

"We are attacking the oldest known enemy base." She paused. "The Taurans established a presence on the portal planet of the collapsar Aleph-10 more than two hundred years ago. We've attacked them twice, to no effect."

She didn't say how many survivors there had been from those two attacks. I knew there had been none.

"If, as we hope, the Taurans have been out of contact with their home planet for the past two centuries, we have a huge technological advantage. The details of this advantage will not be discussed until we are under way." An absurd but standard security procedure. A spying Tauran could no more disguise itself and come aboard than a moose could. No one here could be in the pay of the Taurans. The two species had never exchanged anything but projectiles.

"We are three collapsar jumps away from Aleph-10, so we will have eleven months to train with the new weapon systems . . . with which we will defeat them." She allowed herself a bleak smile. "By the time we reach them, we may be coming from four hundred years in their future. That's the length of time that elapsed between the defeat of the Spanish Armada and the first nuclear war."

Of course relativity does not favor one species over the other. The Taurans on Aleph-10 might have had visitors from their own future, bearing gifts.

The troops were quiet and respectful, absorbing the fraction of information that Major Garcia portioned out. I suppose most of them knew that things were not so rosy, even the inexperienced Angels. She gave them a few more encouraging generalities and dismissed them to their temporary billets. We officers were to meet with her in two hours, for lunch.

I spent the intervening time visiting the platoon billets, talking with the sergeants who would actually be running the show, day by day. I'd seen their records but hadn't met any of them except Cat Verdeur, who had been in physical therapy with me. We both had right-arm replacements, and as part of our routine we were required to arm wrestle every day, apologetic about the pain we were causing each other. She was glad to see me, and said she would have let me win occasionally if she'd known I was going to outrank her.

The officers' lounge was also a plastic room, which I hadn't known. It had been a utilitarian meeting place before, with machines that dispensed simple food and drink. Now it was dark wood and intricate tile; linen napkins and crystal. Of course the wood felt like plastic and the linen, like paper, but you couldn't have everything.

Nine of us showed up on the hour, and the major came in two minutes later. She greeted everyone and pushed a button, and the cooks Jengyi and Senff appeared with real food and two carafes of wine. Aromatic stir-fried vegetables and zoni, which resembled large shrimp.

"Let's enjoy this while we can," she said. "We'll be back on recycled Class A's soon enough." Athene had room enough for the luxury of hydroponics and, apparently, fish tanks.

She asked us to introduce ourselves, going around the table's circle. I knew a little bit about everyone, since my XO file had basic information on the whole Strike Force, and extensive dossiers of the officers and noncoms. But there were surprises. I knew that the major had survived five battles, but didn't know she'd been to Heaven four times, which was a record. I knew her second-in-command, Chance Nguyen, came from Mars, but didn't know he was from the first generation born there, and was the first person drafted from his planet— there had been a huge argument over it, with separatists saying the Forever War was Earth's war. But at that time, Earth could still threaten to pull the plug on Mars. The red planet was self-sufficient now, Chance said, but he'd been away for a century, and didn't know what the situation was.

Lillian Mathes just came from Earth, with less than twenty years' collapsar lag, and she said they weren't drafting from Mars at that time; it was all tied up in court. So Chance might be the only Martian officer in service.

He had a strange way of carrying himself and moving, wary and careful, swimming through this unnaturally high gravity. He told me he'd trained for a Martian year, wearing heavier and heavier weights, before going to Stargate and his first assignment.

All of them were scholarly and athletic, but only Sid, Isidro Zhulpa, had actually been both a scholar and an athlete. He'd played professional baseball for a season, but quit to pursue his doctorate in sociology. He'd gotten his appointment as a junior professor the day before his draft notice. His skin was so black as to be almost blue; with his chiseled features and huge muscularity, he looked like some harsh African god. But he was quiet and modest, my favorite.

I mainly talked with him and Sharn through the meal, chatting about everything but our immediate future. When everything was done, the cooks came in with two carts and cleared the table, leaving tea and coffee. Garcia waited until all of us had been served and the privates were gone.

"Of course we don't have the faintest idea of what's waiting for us at Aleph-10," the major said. "One thing we have been able to find out, which I don't think any of you have been told, is that we know how the second Strike Force bought it."

That was something new. "It was like a minefield. A matrix of nova bombs in a belt around the portal planet's equator. We're assuming it's still there."

"They couldn't detect it and avoid it?" Risa asked.

"It was an active system. The bombs actually chased them down. They detonated four, coming closer and closer, until the fifth got them. The drone that was recording the action barely got away; one of the bombs managed to chase it through the first collapsar jump.

"We can counter the system. We're being preceded by an intelligent drone squad that should be able to detonate all of the ring of nova bombs simultaneously. It should make things pretty warm on the ground, as well as protecting our approach."

"We don't know what got the first Strike Force?" Sid asked.

Garcia shook her head. "The drone didn't return. All we can say for sure is that it wasn't the same thing."

"How so?" I asked.

"Aleph-10's easily visible from Earth; it's about eighty light-years away. They would have detected a nova bomb 120 years ago, if there'd been one. The assumption has to be that they attacked in a conventional way, as ordered, and were destroyed. Or had some accident on the way."

Of course they hadn't beamed any communication back to Earth or Stargate. We still didn't. The war was being fought on portal planets, near collapsars, which were usually desolate, disposable rocks. It would only take one nova bomb to vaporize the Stargate station; perhaps three to wipe out life on Earth.

So we didn't want to give them a road map back.

• 6 •

A lot of the training over the next eleven months had to do with primitive weapons, which explained why so much of my ALSC time had been spent practicing with bows and arrows, spears, knives, and so forth. We had a new thing called a "stasis field," which made a bubble inside which you *had* to use simple tools: no energy weapons worked.

In fact, physics itself didn't work too well inside a stasis field; chemistry, not at all. Nothing could move faster than 16.3 meters per second inside—including elementary particles and light. (You could see inside, but it wasn't light; it was some tachyon thing.) If you were exposed to the field unprotected, you'd die instantly of brain death—no electricity—and anyhow freeze solid in a few seconds. So we had suits made of stuff like tough crinkly aluminum foil, full of uncomfortable plumbing and gadgets so that everything recycled. You could live inside the stasis field, inside the suit, indefinitely. Until you went mad.

But one rip, even a pinprick, in the fabric of the suit, and you were instantly dead.

For that reason, we didn't practice with the primitive weapons inside the field. And if you had a training accident that caused the smallest scratch, on yourself or anyone else, you got to meditate on it for a day in solitary confinement. Even officers; my carelessness with arrow points cost me a long anxious day in darkness.

Only one platoon could fit in the gym at a time, so at first I trained with whoever was using it when I got a few hours off from my other duties. After a while I arranged my schedule so that it was always the fourth platoon. I liked both Aurelio Morales, the squad leader, and his staff sergeant, Karl Hencken. But mainly I liked Cat Verdeur.

I don't remember a particular time when the chumminess suddenly turned into sex; there was nothing like a proposition and a mad fling. We were physically close from the beginning, because of our shared experience at Threshold. Then we were natural partners for hand-to-hand combat practice, being about the same physical age and condition. That was a rough kind of intimacy, and the fact that officers and noncoms had a shower separate from the other men and women gave us another kind. Aurelio and Karl took one side, and Cat and I took the other. We sort of soaped each other's backs, and eventually fronts.

Being a sergeant, Cat didn't have her own billet; she slept in a wing with the other women in her platoon. But one night she showed up at my door on the verge of tears, with a mysterious problem we'd both been dealing with: sometimes the new arm just doesn't feel like it belongs. It obeys your commands, but it's like a separate creature, grafted on, and the feeling of its separateness can take over everything. I let her cry on my shoulder, the good one, and then we shared my narrow bed for the night. We didn't do anything that we hadn't done many times in the shower, but it wasn't playful. I lay awake thinking, long after she fell asleep with her cheek on my breast.

I still loved William, but barring a miracle I would never see him again. What I felt for Cat was more than just friendship, and by her standards and everyone else's there was nothing odd about it. And there was no way I could have had a future with Sid or any of the other men.

When I was young there'd been a sarcastic song that went something like "If I can't be with the one I love, I'll love the one I'm with." I guess that sort of sums it up.

I went to Elise Durack, the Strike Force psychologist, and he helped me through some twists and turns. Then Cat and I went together to Octavia Poll, the female sex counselor, which wound up being a strange and funny four-way consultation with Dante Norelius, the male counselor. That resulted in a mechanical contrivance that we giggled about but occasionally used, which made it more like sex with a man. Cat sympathized with my need to hold on to my past, and said she didn't mind that I was remembering William when I was with her. She thought it was romantic, if perverse.

I started to bring the subject up with the major, and she brushed it off with a laugh. Everyone who cared aboard ship knew about it, and it was a good thing; it made me seem less strange to them. If I had been in Cat's platoon, above her in the direct chain of command, she would be routinely assigned to another platoon, which had been done several times.

(The logic of that is clear, but it made me wonder about Garcia herself. If she became in love with another woman, there wouldn't be any way to put that woman someplace outside of her command. But as far as I knew, she didn't have anybody.)

Cat more or less moved in with me. If some people in her platoon resented it, more were just as glad not to have their sergeant watching over them every hour of the day. She usually stayed with them until first lights-out, and then walked down the corridor to my billet— often passing other people on similar missions. Hard to keep secrets of that sort in a spaceship, and not many tried.

There was an element of desperation in our relationship, doomed souls sharing a last few months, but that was true of everybody's love unless they were absolutely myopic one-day-at-a-timers. If the numbers held, only 34 percent of us had any future beyond Elephant, which is what everybody called Aleph-10 by the time we angled in for our second collapsar jump.

William had tried in a resigned way to explain the physics of it all, the first time we did a jump, but math had defeated me in college long before calculus kicked me permanently into majoring in English. It has to do with acceleration. If you just fell toward a collapsar, the way normal matter does, you would be doomed. For some reason you and the people around you would seem to be falling forever, but to the outside world, you would be snuffed out instantly.

Well, sure. Obviously nobody ever did the experiment.

Anyhow, you accelerate toward the collapsar's "event horizon," which is what it has instead of a surface, at a precalculated speed and angle, and you pop out of another collapsar umpty light-years away— maybe five, maybe five million. You better get the angle right, because you can't always just reverse things and come back.

(Which we hoped was all that happened to the first Elephant Strike Force. They might be on the other side of the galaxy, colonizing some nice quiet world. Every cruiser did carry a set of wombs and a crèche, against that possibility, though the major rolled her eyes when she described it. Purely a morale device, she said; they probably didn't work. I wondered whether, in that case, people might be able to grit their teeth and try to make babies the old-fashioned way.)

Since we were leaving from Heaven, we were required to make at least two collapsar jumps before "acquiring" Elephant. That soaked up two centuries of objective time, if such a thing exists. To us it was eleven fairly stressful months. Besides the training with the old-fashioned weapons, the troops had to drill with their fighting suits and whatever specialized weapon system they were assigned to, in case the stasis field didn't work or had been rendered useless by some enemy development.

Meanwhile, I did my Executive Officer work. It was partly book-keeping, which is almost trivial aboard ship, since nothing comes in and nothing goes out. The larger part was a vague standing assignment to keep up the troops' morale.

I was not well qualified for that; perhaps less qualified than anybody else aboard. Their music didn't sound like music to me. Their games seemed pointless, even after they'd been relentlessly explained. The movies were interesting, at least as anthropology, and the pleasures of food and drink hadn't changed much, but their sex lives were still pretty mysterious to me, in spite of my affection for Cat and the orgasms we exchanged. If a man and a woman walked by, I was still more interested in the man. So I did love a woman, but as an actual lesbian I was not a great success.

Sometimes that gave me comfort, a connection to William and my past. More often it made me feel estranged, helpless.

I did have eight part-time volunteers, and one full-time subordinate, Sergeant Cody Waite. He was not an asset. I think the draft laws on Earth, the Elite Conscription Act, were ignored on Heaven. In fact, I would go even further (to make a reference that nobody on the ship would understand) and claim that there was a Miltonian aspect to his arrival. He had been expelled from Heaven, for overweening pride. But he had nothing to be proud of, except his face and muscles. He had the intelligence of a hamster. He did look like a Greek god, but for me what that meant was that every time I needed him to do something, he was down in the gym working out on the machines. Or off getting his rectum reamed by some adoring guy who didn't have to talk with him. He could read and write, though, so eventually I found I could keep him out of the way by having him elaborate on my weekly reports. He could take "This week was the same as last week," and turn it into an epic of relentless tedium.

I was glad to be out of the chain of command. You train people intensively for combat and then put them into a box for eleven months of what? More training for combat. Nobody's happy and some people snap.

The men are usually worse than the women—or, at least, when the women lose control it tends to be a shouting match rather than fists and feet. Cat had a pair who were an exception, though, and it escalated to attempted murder in the mess hall.

This was ten days before the last collapsar jump—everybody on the ragged edge—between Lain Mayfair and "Tiny" Keimo, who was big enough to take on most of the men. Lain tried to cut her throat, from behind, and Tiny broke her arm at the elbow while everybody else was diving for cover, and was seriously strangling her—trying to kill her before she herself bled to death—when the cook J.J. ran over and brained the big woman with a frying pan.

While they were still in the infirmary there was a summary court-martial. With the consistent testimony of forty witnesses, Major Garcia didn't have any choice: she sentenced Lain Mayfair to death for attempted murder. She administered the lethal injection herself.

I was required to be a witness, and more, and it was not the high point of my day. Mayfair was bedridden and, I think, slightly sedated. Garcia explained the reason for the verdict and asked Mayfair whether she would prefer the dignity of taking the poison herself. She didn't say anything, just cried and shook her head. Two privates held her down by the shoulders while Garcia took her arm and administered the popper. Mayfair turned pale and her eyes rolled up. She shook convulsively for a few seconds and was dead.

Garcia didn't show any emotion during the ordeal. She whispered to me that she would be in her quarters if anybody really needed her, and left quickly.

I had to supervise the disposal of the body. I had two medics wrap her tightly in a sheet and put her on a gurney. We had to roll it down the main corridor, everybody watching. I helped the two of them carry her into the airlock. She was starting to stiffen, but her body wasn't even cold.

I had a friend read a prayer in Mayfair's language, and asked the engineer for maximum pressure in the airlock, and then popped it. Her body spun out into its lonely, infinite grave.

I went back to the infirmary and found Tiny inconsolable. She and Mayfair had been lovers back on Stargate. Everything had gone wrong, nothing made sense, why why why why? My answer was to have Sharn give her a tranquilizer. I took one myself.

· **7** ·

We came tearing out of the Elephant's collapsar about one minute after the defense phalanx, the ten high-speed intelligent drones that had multiple warheads, programmed to take out the portal planet's nova-bomb minefield.

The first surprise was that the minefield wasn't there. The second surprise was that the Taurans weren't, either. Their base seemed intact but long deserted, cold.

We would destroy it with a nova bomb, but first send a platoon down to investigate it. Garcia asked that I go along with them. It was Cat's platoon. It would be an interesting experience to share, so long as a booby trap didn't blow us off the planet. The deserted base could be bait.

We would have a nova bomb with us. Either Morales or I could detonate it if we got into a situation that looked hopeless. Or Garcia could do it from orbit. I was sure Garcia could do it. Not so sure about me or Aurelio.

But while we were down in the prep bay getting into our fighting suits, there came the third surprise, the big one. I later saw the recording. The main cube in the control room lit up with a two-dimensional picture of a young man in an ancient uniform. He popped in and out of three dimensions while he spoke: "Hello, Earth ship. Do you still use this frequency? Do you still use this language?"

He smiled placidly. "Of course you won't respond at first; neither would I. This could be a trap. Feel free to investigate at long range. I am calling from a different portal planet. I'm currently 12.23 million kilometers from you, on the plane of the ecliptic, on an angle of 0.54 radians with respect to the collapsar. As you probably know by now.

"I am a descendant of the first Strike Force, nearly half a millennium ago. I await your questions." He sat back in his chair, in a featureless room. He crossed his legs and picked up a notebook and began flipping through it.

We immediately got a high-resolution image of the portal planet. It was small, as they usually are; cold and airless except for the base. It was actually more like a town than a base, and it was as obvious as a beacon. It wasn't enclosed; air was evidently held in by some sort of force field. It was lit up by an artificial sun that floated a few kilometers above the surface.

There was an ancient cruiser in orbit, its dramatic sweeping streamlined grace putting our functional clunkiness to shame. There were also two Tauran vessels. None of them was obviously damaged.

All of us 5-and-above officers were on the bridge when we contacted the planet. Commodore Sidorenko sat up front with Garcia; he technically outranked her in this room, but it was her show, since the actual business was planetside.

I felt a little self-conscious, having come straight from the prep bay. Everyone else was in uniform; I was just wearing the contact net for the fighting suit. Like a layer of silver paint.

Garcia addressed the man in the chair. "Do you have a name and a rank?"

It took about forty seconds for the message to get to him, and another forty for his response: "My name is Man. We don't have ranks; I'm here because I can speak Old Standard. English."

You could play a slow chess game during this conversation, and not miss anything. "But your ancestors defeated the Taurans, somehow."

"No. The Taurans took them prisoner and set them up here. Then there was another battle, generations ago. We never heard from them again."

"But we lost that battle. Our cruiser was destroyed with all hands aboard."

"I don't know anything about that. Their planet was on the other side of the collapsar when the battle happened. The people here saw a lot of light, distorted by gravitational lensing. We always assumed it was some robotic assault, since we didn't hear anything from either side, afterwards. I'm sorry so many people died."

"What about the Taurans who were with you? Are there Taurans there now?"

"No; there weren't any then, and there aren't any now. Before the battle they showed up now and then."

"But there are—" she began.

"Oh, you mean the Tauran ships in orbit. They've been there for hundreds of years. So has our cruiser. We have no way to get to them. This place is self-sufficient, but a prison."

"I'll contact you again after I've spoken to my officers." The cube went dark.

Garcia swiveled around, and so did Sidorenko, who spoke for the first time: "I don't like it. He could be a simulation."

Garcia nodded. "That assumes a lot, though. And it would mean they know a hell of a lot more about us than we do about them."

"That's demonstrable. Four hundred years ago, they were supposedly able to build a place for the captives to stay. I don't believe we would have any trouble simulating a Tauran, given a couple of hundred captives and that much time for research."

"I suppose. Potter," she said to me, "go down and tell the fourth platoon there's a slight change of plans, but we're still going in ready for anything. I think the best thing we can do is get over there and make physical contact as soon as possible."

"Right," Sidorenko said. "We don't have the element of surprise anymore, but there's no percentage in sitting here and feeding them data, giving them time to revise their strategy. If there *are* Taurans there."

"Have your people prepped for five gees," Garcia said to me. "Get you there in a few hours."

"Eight," Sidorenko said. "We'll be about ten hours behind you."

"Wait in orbit?" I said, knowing the answer.

"You wish. Let's go down to the bay."

We had a holo of the base projected down there and worked out a simple strategy. Twenty-two of us in fighting suits, armed to the teeth, carrying a nova bomb and a stasis field, surround the place and politely knock on the door. Depending on the response, we either walk in for tea or level the place.

Getting there would not be so bad. Nobody could endure four hours of five-gee acceleration, then flip for four hours of deceleration, unprotected. So we'd be clamshelled in the fighting suits, knocked out and superhydrated. Eight hours of deep sleep and then maybe an hour to shake it off and go be a soldier. Or a guest for tea.

Cat and I made the rounds in the cramped fighter, seeing that everybody was in place, suit fittings and readouts in order. Then we shared a minute of private embrace and took our own places.

I jacked the fluid exchange into my hip fitting, and all of the fear went away. My body sagged with sweet lassitude, and I let the soft nozzle clasp my face. I was still aware enough to know that it was sucking all the air out of my lungs and then blowing in a dense replacement fluid, but all I felt was a long, low-key orgasm. I knew that this was the last thing a lot of people felt, the fighter blown to bits moments or hours later. But the war offered us many worse ways to die. I was sound asleep before the acceleration blasted us into space. Dreaming of being a fish in a warm and heavy sea.

8

The chemicals won't let you remember coming out of it, which is probably good. My diaphragm and esophagus were sore and tired from getting rid of all the fluid. Cat looked like hell and I stayed away from mirrors, while we toweled off and put on the contact nets and got back into the fighting suits for the landing.

Our strategy, such as it was, seemed even less appealing, this close to the portal planet. The two Tauran cruisers were old models, but they were a hundred times the size of our fighter, and since they were in synchronous orbit over the base, there was no way to avoid coming into range. But they did let us slide under them without blowing us out of the sky, which made Man's story more believable.

It was pretty obvious, though, that our primary job was to be a target, for those ships and the base. If we were annihilated, the *Bolívar* would modify its strategy.

When Morales said we were going to just go straight in and land on the strip beside the base, I muttered, "Might as well be hung for a sheep as a goat," and Cat, who was on my line, asked why anyone would hang a sheep. I told her it was hard to explain. In fact, it was just something my father used to say, and if he'd ever explained it, I'd forgotten.

The landing was loud but feather-light. We unclamped our fighting suits from their transport positions and practiced walking in the one-third gee of the small planet. "They should've sent Goy," Cat said, which is what we called Chance Nguyen, the Martian. "He'd be right at home."

We moved out fast, people sprinting to their attack positions. Cat went off to the other side of the base. I was going with Morales, to knock on the door. Rank and its privileges. The first to die, or be offered tea.

The buildings on the base looked like they'd been designed by a careful child. Windowless blocks laid out on a grid. All but one were sand-colored. We walked to the silver cube of headquarters. At least it had "HQ" in big letters over the airlock.

The shiny front door snicked up like a guillotine in reverse. We went through with dignified haste, and it slammed back down. The blade, or door, was pretty massive, for us to "hear" it in a vacuum; vibration through our boots.

Air hissed in—that we *did* hear—and after a minute a door swung open. We had to sidle through it sideways because of the size of our fighting suits. I suppose we could have just walked straight through, enlarging it in the process, and in fact I considered that as I sidled. It would prevent them from using the airlock until they could fix it.

Then another door, a metal blast door half a meter thick, slid open. Seated at a plain round table were Man and a woman who looked like his twin sister. They wore identical sky-blue tunics.

"Welcome to Alcatraz," he said. "The name is an old joke." He gestured at the four empty chairs. "Why not get out of your suits and relax?"

"That would be unwise," Morales said.

"You have us surrounded, outside. Even if I were inclined to do you harm, I wouldn't be that foolish."

"It's for your own protection," I extemporized. "Viruses can mutate a lot in four hundred years. You don't want us sharing your air."

"That's not a problem," the woman said. "Believe me. My bodies are very much more efficient than yours."

" 'My bodies'?" I said.

"Oh, well." She made a gesture that was meaningless to me, and two side doors opened. From her side a line of women walked in, all exact copies of her. From his side, copies of him.

There were about twenty of each. They stared at us with identical bland expressions, and then said in unison, "I have been waiting for you."

"As have I." A pair of naked Taurans stepped into the room.

Both our laserfingers came up at once. They refused to fire. I snatched the utility knife from my waist and threw it, and Morales did the same. Both creatures dodged the weapons easily, moving with inhuman swiftness.

I braced myself to die. I hadn't seen a live Tauran since the Yod-4 campaign, but I'd fought hundreds of them in the ALSC. They didn't care whether they lived or died, so long as they died killing a human. But these two didn't attack.

"There is much to be explained," one Tauran said in a thin, wavering voice, its mouth-hole flexing and contracting. Their bodies were covered with a loose tunic like the humans', hiding most of the wrinkled orange hide and strange limbs, and the pinched, antlike thorax.

The two of them blinked slowly in unison, in what might have been a social or emotional gesture, a translucent membrane sliding wetly down over the compound eyes. The tassels of soft flesh where their noses should have been stopped quivering while they blinked. "The war is over. In most places."

The man spoke. "Human and Tauran share Stargate now. There is Tauran on Earth and human on its home planet, J'sardlkuh."

"Humans like you?" Morales said. "Stamped out of a machine?"

"I come from a kind of machine, but it is living, a womb. Until I was truly *one*, there could be no peace. When there were billions of us, all different, we couldn't understand peace."

"Everyone on earth is the same?" I said. "There's only one kind of human?"

"There are still survivors of the Forever War, like yourselves," the female said. "Otherwise, there is only one human, although I can be either male or female. As there is only one Tauran. I was patterned after an individual named Khan. I call myself Man."

We'd supposedly been fighting to save the human race. So we come back to find it replaced by this new, improved model.

There were sounds to my left and right, like distant thunder. Nothing in my communicator.

"Your people are attacking," the male said, "even though I have told them it is useless."

"Let me talk to them!" Morales said.

"You can't," the female said. "They all assembled under the stasis field, when they saw the Taurans through your eyes. Now their programmed weapons attack. When those weapons fail, they will try to walk in with the stasis field."

"This has happened before?" I said.

"Not here, but other places. The outcome varies."

"Your stasis field," a Tauran said, "has been old to us for more than a century. We used a refined version of it to keep you from shooting us a minute ago."

"You say the outcome varies," Morales said to the female, "so sometimes we win?"

"Even if you killed me, you wouldn't 'win'; there's nothing to win anymore. But no, the only thing that varies is how many of you survive."

"Your cruiser *Bolívar* may have to be destroyed," a Tauran said. "I assume they are monitoring this conversation. Of course they are still several light-minutes away. But if they do not respond in a spirit of cooperation, we will have no choice."

Garcia did respond in less than a minute, her image materializing behind the Taurans. "Why don't we invite *you* to act in a spirit of cooperation," she said. "If none of our people are hurt, none of yours will be."

"That's beyond my control," the male said. "Your programmed weapons are attacking; mine are defending. I think that neither is programmed for mercy."

The female continued. "That they still survive is evidence of our good intentions. We could deactivate their stasis field from outside." There was a huge *thump* and Man's table jumped up an inch. "Most of them would be destroyed in seconds if we did that."

Garcia paused. "Then explain why you haven't."

"One of my directives," the male said, "is to minimize casualties among you. There is a genetic diversity program, which will be explained to you at Stargate."

"All right," Garcia said. "Since I can't communicate with them otherwise, I'll let you deactivate the stasis field—but at the same time, of course, you have to turn off your automatic defenses. Otherwise, they'd be slaughtered."

"So you invite us to be slaughtered instead," he said. "Me and your two representatives here."

"I'll tell them to cease fire immediately."

All this conversation was going on with a twenty-second time lag. So "immediately" would be a while in coming.

Without comment, the two Taurans disappeared, and the forty duplicate humans filed back through the dome.

"All right," the male Man said, "perhaps there is a way around this time lag. Which of you is the ranking officer here?"

"I am," I said.

"Most of my individuals have returned to an underground shelter. I will turn off your stasis field and our defenses simultaneously.

"Tell them they must stop firing immediately. If we die, our defenses resume, and they won't have the protection of the stasis field."

I chinned the command frequency, which would put me in contact with Cat and Sergeant Hencken as soon as the field disappeared.

"I don't like this," Morales said. "You can turn your weapons on and off with a thought?"

"That's correct."

"We can't. When Captain Potter gives them the order, they have to understand and react."

"But it's just turning off a switch, is it not?" There was another huge bang, and a web of cracks appeared in the wall to my left. Man looked at it without emotion.

"First a half dozen people have to understand the order and decide to obey it!"

The male and female smiled and nodded in unison. "Now."

Thumbnail pictures of Karl and Cat appeared next to Morales. "Cat! Karl! Have the weapons units cease fire immediately!"

"What's going on?" Karl said. "Where's the stasis field?"

"They turned it off. Battle's over."

"That's right," Morales said. "Cease fire."

Cat started talking to the squads. Karl stared for a second and started to do the same.

Not fast enough. The left wall exploded in a hurricane of masonry and chunks of metal. The two Men were suddenly bloody rags of shredded flesh. Morales and I were knocked over by the storm of rubble. My armor was breached in one place; there was a ten-second beep while it repaired itself.

Then vacuum silence. The one light on the opposite wall dimmed and went out. Through the hole our cannon had made, the size of a large window, the starlit wasteland strobed in silent battle.

The three thumbnails were gone. I chinned down again for command freek. "Cat? Morales? Karl?"

Then I turned on a headlight and saw Morales was dead, his suit peeled open at the chest, lungs and heart in tatters under ribs black with dried blood.

I chinned sideways for the general freek and heard a dozen voices shouting and screaming in confusion.

So Cat was probably dead, and Karl, too. Or maybe their communications had been knocked out.

I thought about that possibility for a few moments, hoping and rejecting hope, listening to the babble. Then I realized that if I could hear all those privates, corporals, they could hear me.

"This is Potter," I said. "*Captain* Potter," I yelled.

I stayed on the general freek and tried to explain the strange situation. Five did opt to stay outside. The others met me under the yellow light, which framed the top of a square black blast door that rose out of the ground at a forty-five-degree angle, like our tornado shelter at home, thousands of years ago, hundreds of light-years away. It slid open, and we went in, carrying four fighting suits whose occupants weren't responding but weren't obviously dead.

One of those was Cat, I saw as we came into the light when the airlock door closed. The back of the helmet had a blast burn, but I could make out VERDEUR.

She looked bad. A leg and an arm were missing at shoulder and thigh. But they had been snipped off by the suit itself, the way my arm had been at Tet-2.

There was no way to tell whether she was alive, since the telltale on the back of the helmet was destroyed. The suit had a biometric readout, but only a medic could access it directly, and the medic and his suit had been vaporized.

Man led us into a large room with a row of bunks and a row of chairs. There were three other Men there, but no Taurans, which was probably wise.

I popped out of my suit and didn't die, so the others did the same, one by one. The amputees we left sealed in their suits, and Man agreed that it was probably best. They were either dead or safely unconscious: if the former, they'd been dead for too long to bring back; if the latter, it would be better to wake them up in the *Bolívar*'s surgery. The ship was only two hours away, but it was a long two hours for me.

As it turned out, she lived, but I lost her anyhow, to relativity. She and the other amputees were loaded, still asleep, onto the extra cruiser, and sent straight to Heaven.

They did it in one jump, no need for secrecy anymore, and we went to Stargate in one jump aboard *Bolívar*.

When I'd last been to Stargate it had been a huge space station; now it was easily a hundred times as large, a man-made planetoid. Tauran-made, and Man-made.

We learned to say it differently: *Man,* not man.

Inside, Stargate was a city that dwarfed any city on the Earth I remembered—though they said now there were cities on Earth with a billion Men, humans, and Taurans.

We spent weeks considering and deciding on which of many options we could choose to set the course of the rest of our lives. The first thing I did was check on William, and no miracle had happened; his Strike Force had not returned from Sade-138. But neither had the Tauran force sent to annihilate them.

I didn't have the option of hanging around Stargate, waiting for him to show up; the shortest scenario had his outfit arriving in over three hundred years. I couldn't really wait for Cat, either; at best she would get to Stargate in thirty-five years. Still young, and me in my sixties. If, in fact, she chose to come to Stargate; she would have the option of staying on Heaven.

I could chase her to Heaven, but then *she* would be thirty-five years older than me. If we didn't pass one another in transit.

But I did have one chance. One way to outwit relativity.

Among the options available to veterans was Middle Finger, a planet circling Mizar. It was a nominally heterosexual planet—het or home was now completely a matter of choice; Man could switch you one way or the other in an hour.

I toyed with the idea of "going home," becoming lesbian by inclination as well as definition. But men still appealed to me—men not Man—and Middle Finger offered me an outside chance at the one man I still truly loved.

Five veterans had just bought an old cruiser and were using it as a time machine—a "time shuttle," they called it, zipping back and forth between Mizar and Alcor at relativistic speed, more than two objective years passing every week. I could buy my way onto it by using my back pay to purchase antimatter fuel. I could get there in two collapsar jumps, having left word for William, and if he lived, could rejoin him in a matter of months or years.

The decision was so easy it was not a decision; it was as automatic as being born. I left him a note:

11 Oct 2878

William—

All this is in your personnel file. But knowing you, you might just chuck it. So I made sure you'd get this note.

Obviously, I lived. Maybe you will, too. Join me.

I know from the records that you're out at Sade-138 and won't be back for a couple of centuries. No problem.

I'm going to a planet they call Middle Finger, the fifth planet out from Mizar. It's two collapsar jumps, ten months subjective. Middle Finger is a kind of Coventry for heterosexuals. They call it a "eugenic control baseline."

No matter. It took all of my money, and all the money of five other old-timers, but we bought a cruiser from UNEF. And we're using it as a time machine.

So I'm on a relativistic shuttle, waiting for you. All it does is go out five light-years and come back to Middle Finger, very fast. Every ten years I age about a month. So if you're on schedule and still alive, I'll only be twenty-eight when you get here. Hurry!

I never found anybody else, and I don't want anybody else. I don't care whether you're ninety years old or thirty. If I can't be your lover, I'll be your nurse.

—Marygay

· 9 ·

From *The New Voice,* Paxton, Middle Finger 24–6

14/2/3143

OLD-TIMER HAS FIRST BOY

Marygay Potter-Mandella (24 Post Road, Paxton) gave birth Friday last to a fine baby boy, 3.1 kilos.

Marygay lays claim to being the second-"oldest" resident of Middle Finger, having been born in 1977. She fought through most of the Forever War and then waited for her mate on the time shuttle, 261 years.

The baby, not yet named, was delivered at home with the help of a friend of the family, Dr. Diana Alsever-Moore.

THE ENDER SERIES

Orson Scott Card

Ender's Game (1985)
Speaker for the Dead (1986)
Xenocide (1991)
Children of the Mind (1996)

When I first started writing science fiction, I conceived a series of stories about a family with heritable mental powers, and the first stories I wrote had a rural setting. I got nice rejection letters but no sales. It was Ben Bova at *Analog* who explained why: They felt like fantasy! This baffled me at first—weren't Zenna Henderson's stories of "The People" considered science fiction? Then I realized that the true commercial distinction between science fiction and fantasy is: Fantasy has trees, science fiction has rivets! If I was going to sell to the s-f magazines, I had to write stories with rivets in them!

Back when I was sixteen and had just read Asimov's *Foundation* trilogy, I decided I wanted to write an s-f story, too. At the time (1967) the Vietnam War was raging, and my older brother had just finished boot camp, so military things were on my mind. I put a science-fiction spin on the problem of training troops: how would you train soldiers to fight in three-dimensional space? I remembered Nordhoff and Hall's novel about World War I flying aces and the problem of training pilots to stop looking for enemy aircraft only in the horizontal plane, and realized the problem in null gravity would be greatly compounded by the lack of a clear up and down. Old habits of gravity-based life would have to be trained out of the soldiers. The result of my thought experiment was the battle room, a hundred-meter cube of null-gravity space in which various obstacles could be set up, and in which teams of trainees would do mock battle in space suits that showed where and how badly a soldier had been hit by "enemy" fire.

And that was it. A good idea, I thought, but I had no notion at the time of how to turn it into a story. Who was the hero? Where did I go from there?

Years later, when I determined to write a riveted—and, I hoped, riveting—science-fiction story, I remembered the battle-room concept, and, on the lawn outside the Salt Palace in Salt Lake City, while I waited for a friend who was taking her boss's children to the circus, I opened my notebook and wrote the first sentence of a story I called "Ender's Game": "Remember, the enemy's gate is down."

What made the story writable for me was the decision that the trainees in the battle room would be children, in a future world where military aptitude could be discovered at a very early age, and children were taken from their parents to give them training in tactics and strategy while they were still young enough for their minds to be malleable. The story that resulted was my first science-fiction sale, bought by Ben Bova, and it appeared in the August 1977 issue of *Analog* (the same month that my first non-s-f story, "Gert Fram," appeared in the *Ensign* magazine of the LDS Church).

Years later, working on a project called *Speaker for the Dead,* I found that the story didn't come alive until I realized that the hero of the story should be Ender Wiggin. In order to set up the novel *Speaker,* I had to rewrite the original story as a novel; thus the novel *Ender's Game* came into existence only so I could write the novel *Speaker for the Dead.* I never planned a series, and unlike most series the second novel was a completely different *kind* of science fiction from the first. Instead of a military novel, it was anthropological; and Ender was now an adult with a complicated hidden past.

Then a third project, long on the shelf, came to life when I realized that it would make a good sequel to *Speaker*—but this time the book would be yet a third kind of science fiction, the novel of metaphysical speculation. Eventually divided into two books, this work became *Xenocide* and *Children of the Mind.* I daresay there has been no series of novels starring the same character whose volumes have been more disparate in theme, story, and genre. And yet through all four volumes the character of Ender Wiggin struggled to resolve personal and moral dilemmas that carried over from book to book.

Those dilemmas were resolved at the end of the fourth book. I plan to write more novels in the same universe (one about Ender's brother, Peter, and another about Bean, a young companion of Ender in the first novel), but the story of Ender himself is finished—except for one small gap.

During the three thousand years between *Ender's Game* and *Speaker for the Dead,* during which Ender journeyed from planet to planet, using lightspeed time dilation to skim through time without living in any decade very long, he somehow acquired a computer-based companion named Jane, who is second only to Ender in importance in the last three books of the series. The story now before you is an account of how they met.

—*Orson Scott Card*

Investment Counselor

by

Orson Scott Card

ANDREW WIGGIN TURNED TWENTY THE DAY HE REACHED THE PLANET SOREL-ledolce. Or rather, after complicated calculations of how many seconds he had been in flight, and at what percentage of lightspeed, and therefore what amount of subjective time had elapsed for him, he reached the conclusion that he had passed his twentieth birthday just before the end of the voyage.

This was much more relevant to him than the other pertinent fact—that four hundred and some–odd years had passed since the day he was born, back on Earth, back when the human race had not spread beyond the solar system of its birth.

When Valentine emerged from the debarkation chamber—alphabetically she was always after him—Andrew greeted her with the news. "I just figured it out," he said. "I'm twenty."

"Good," she said. "Now you can start paying taxes like the rest of us."

Ever since the end of the war of Xenocide, Andrew had lived on a trust fund set up by a grateful world to reward the commander of the fleets that saved humanity. Well, strictly speaking, that action was taken at the end of the Third Bugger War, when people still thought of the Buggers as monsters and the children who commanded the fleet as heroes. By the time the name was changed to the War of Xenocide, humanity was no longer grateful, and the last thing any government would have dared to do was authorize a pension trust fund for Ender Wiggin, the perpetrator of the most awful crime in human history.

In fact, if it had become known that such a fund existed, it would have become a public scandal. But the interstellar fleet was slow to convert to the idea that destroying the Buggers had been a bad idea. And so they carefully shielded the trust fund from public view, dispersing it among many mutual funds and as stock in many different companies, with no single authority controlling any significant portion of the money. Effectively, they had made the money disappear, and only Andrew himself and his sister Valentine knew where the money was, or how much of it there was.

One thing, though, was certain: By law, when Andrew reached the subjective age of twenty, the tax-exempt status of his holdings would be revoked. The income would start being reported to the appropriate authorities. Andrew would have to file a tax report either every year or every time he concluded an interstellar voyage of greater than one year in objective time, the taxes to be annualized and interest on the unpaid portion duly handed over.

Andrew was not looking forward to it.

"How does it work with your book royalties?" he asked Valentine.

"The same as anyone," she answered, "except that not many copies sell, so there isn't much in the way of taxes to pay."

Only a few minutes later she had to eat her words, for when they sat down at the rental computers in the starport of Sorelledolce, Valentine discovered that her most recent book, a history of the failed Jung Calvin colonies on the planet Helvetica, had achieved something of a cult status.

"I think I'm rich," she murmured to Andrew.

"I have no idea whether I'm rich or not," said Andrew. "I can't get the computer to stop listing my holdings."

The names of companies kept scrolling up and back, the list going on and on.

"I thought they'd just give you a check for whatever was in the bank when you turned twenty," said Valentine.

"I should be so lucky," said Andrew. "I can't sit here and wait for this."

"You have to," said Valentine. "You can't get through customs without proving that you've paid your taxes *and* that you have enough left over to support yourself without becoming a drain on public resources."

"What if I didn't have enough money? They send me back?"

"No, they assign you to a work crew and compel you to earn your way free at an extremely unfair rate of pay."

"How do you know that?"

"I don't. I've just read a lot of history and I know how governments work. If it isn't that, it'll be the equivalent. Or they'll send you back."

"I can't be the only person who ever landed and discovered that it would take him a week to find out what his financial situation was," said Andrew. "I'm going to find somebody."

"I'll be here, paying my taxes like a grown-up," said Valentine. "Like an honest woman."

"You make me ashamed of myself," called Andrew blithely as he strode away.

Benedetto took one look at the cocky young man who sat down across the desk from him and sighed. He knew at once that this one would be trouble. A young man of privilege, arriving at a new planet, thinking he could get special favors for himself from the tax man. "What can I do for you?" asked Benedetto—in Italian, even though he was fluent in Starcommon and the law said that all travelers had to be addressed in that language unless another was mutually agreed upon.

Unfazed by the Italian, the young man produced his identification.

"Andrew Wiggin?" asked Benedetto, incredulous.

"Is there a problem?"

"Do you expect me to believe that this identification is real?" He was speaking Starcommon now; the point had been made.

"Shouldn't I?"

"Andrew *Wiggin*? Do you think this is such a backwater that we are not educated enough to recognize the name of Ender the Xenocide?"

"Is having the same name a criminal offense?" asked Andrew.

"Having false identification is."

"If I were using false identification, would it be smart or stupid to use a name like Andrew Wiggin?" he asked.

"Stupid," Benedetto grudgingly admitted.

"So let's start from the assumption that I'm smart, but also tormented by having grown up with the name of Ender the Xenocide. Are you going to find me psychologically unfit because of the imbalance these traumas caused me?"

"I'm not customs," said Benedetto. "I'm taxes."

"I know. But you seemed preternaturally absorbed with the question of identity, so I thought you were either a spy from customs or a philosopher, and who am I to deny the curiosity of either?"

Benedetto hated the smart-mouthed ones. "What do you want?"

"I find my tax situation is complicated. This is the first time I've had to pay taxes—I just came into a trust fund—and I don't even know what my holdings are. I'd like to have a delay in paying my taxes until I can sort it all out."

"Denied," said Benedetto.

"Just like that?"

"Just like that," said Benedetto.

Andrew sat there for a moment.

"Can I help you with something else?" asked Benedetto.

"Is there any appeal?"

"Yes," said Benedetto. "But you have to pay your taxes before you can appeal."

"I intend to pay my taxes," said Andrew. "It's just going to take me time to do it, and I thought I'd do a better job of it on my own computer in my own apartment rather than on the public computers here in the starport."

"Afraid someone will look over your shoulder?" asked Benedetto. "See how much of an allowance Grandmother left you?"

"It would be nice to have more privacy, yes," said Andrew.

"Permission to leave without payment is denied."

"All right, then, release my liquid funds to me so I can pay to stay here and work on my taxes."

"You had your whole flight to do that."

"My money had always been in a trust fund. I never knew how complicated the holdings were."

"You realize, of course, that if you keep telling me these things you'll break my heart and I'll run from the room crying," said Benedetto calmly.

The young man sighed. "I'm not sure what you want me to do."

"Pay your taxes like every other citizen."

"I have no way to get to my money until I pay my taxes," said Andrew. "And I have no way to support myself while I figure out my taxes unless you release some funds to me."

"Makes you wish you had thought of this earlier, doesn't it?" said Benedetto.

Andrew looked around the office. "It says on that sign that you'll help me fill out my tax form."

"Yes."

"Help."

"Show me the form."

Andrew looked at him oddly. "How can I show it to you?"

"Bring it up on the computer here." Benedetto turned his computer around on his desk, offering the keyboard side of it to Andrew.

Andrew looked at the blanks in the form displayed above the computer, and typed in his name and his tax I.D. number, then his private I.D. code. Benedetto pointedly looked away while he typed in the code, even though his software was recording each keystroke the young man entered. Once he was gone, Benedetto would have full access to all his records and all his funds. The better to assist him with his taxes, of course.

The display began scrolling.

"What did you do?" asked Benedetto. The words appeared at the bottom of the display, as the top of the page slid back and out of the way, rolling into an ever-tighter scroll. Because it wasn't paging, Benedetto knew that this long list of information was appearing as it was being called up by a single question on the form. He turned the computer around to where he could see it. The list consisted of the names and exchange codes of corporations and mutual funds, along with numbers of shares.

"You see my problem," said the young man.

The list went on and on. Benedetto reached down and pressed a few keys in combination. The list stopped. "You have," he said softly, "a large number of holdings."

"But I didn't know it," said Andrew. "I mean, I knew that the trustees had diversified me some time ago, but I had no idea the extent. I just drew an allowance whenever I was on planet, and because it was a tax-free government pension I never had to think any more about it."

So maybe the kid's wide-eyed innocence wasn't an act. Benedetto disliked him a little less. In fact, Benedetto felt the first stirrings of true friendship. This lad was going to make Benedetto a rich man without even knowing it. Benedetto might even retire from the tax service. Just his stock in the last company on the interrupted list, Enzichel Vinicenze, conglomerate with extensive holdings on Sorelledolce, was worth enough for Benedetto to buy a country estate and keep servants for the rest of his life. And the list was only up to the *E*s.

"Interesting," said Benedetto.

"How about this?" said the young man. "I only turned twenty in the last year of my voyage. Up to then, my earnings were still tax-exempt and I'm entitled to them without paying taxes. Free up that much of my funds, and then give me a few weeks to get some expert to help me analyze the rest of this and I'll submit my tax forms then."

"Excellent idea," said Benedetto. "Where are those liquid earnings held?"

"Catalonian Exchange Bank," said Andrew.

"Account number?"

"All you need is to free up any funds held in my name," said Andrew. "You don't need the account number."

Benedetto didn't press the point. He wouldn't need to dip into the boy's petty cash. Not with the mother lode waiting for him to pillage at will before he ever got into a tax attorney's office. He typed in the necessary information and published the form. He also gave Andrew Wiggin a thirty-day pass, allowing him the freedom of Sorelledolce as long as he logged in daily with the tax service and turned in a full tax form and paid the estimated tax within that thirty-day period, and promised not to leave the planet until his tax form had been evaluated and confirmed.

Standard operating procedure. The young man thanked him— that's the part Benedetto always liked, when these rich idiots thanked him for lying to them and skimming invisible bribes from their accounts—and then left the office.

As soon as he was gone, Benedetto cleared the display and called up his snitch program to report the young man's I.D. code. He waited. The snitch program did not come up. He brought up his log of running programs, checked the hidden log, and found that the snitch program wasn't on the list. Absurd. It was always running. Only now it wasn't. And in fact it had disappeared from memory.

Using his version of the banned Predator program, he searched for the electronic signature of the snitch program, and found a couple of its temp files. But none contained any useful information, and the snitch program itself was completely gone.

Nor, when he tried to return to the form Andrew Wiggin had created, was he able to bring it back. It should have been there, with the young man's list of holdings intact, so Benedetto could make a run at some of the stocks and funds manually—there were plenty of ways to ransack them, even when he couldn't get the password from his snitch. But the form was blank. The company names had all disappeared.

What had happened? How could both these things go wrong at the same time?

No matter. The list was so long it had to have been buffered. Predator would find it.

Only now Predator wasn't responding. It wasn't in memory either. He had used it only a moment ago! This was impossible. This was . . .

How could the boy have introduced a virus on his system just by entering tax form information? Could he have embedded it into one of the company names somehow? Benedetto was a user of illegal software, not a designer; but still, he had never heard of anything that could come in through uncrunched data, not through the security of the tax system.

This Andrew Wiggin had to be some kind of spy. Sorelledolce was one of the last holdouts against complete federation with Starways Congress—he had to be a Congress spy sent to try to subvert the independence of Sorelledolce.

Only that was absurd. A spy would have come in prepared to submit his tax forms, pay his taxes, and move right along. A spy would have done nothing to call attention to himself.

There had to be *some* explanation. And Benedetto was going to get it. Whoever this Andrew Wiggin was, Benedetto was not going to be cheated out of inheriting his fair share of the boy's wealth. He'd waited a long time for this, and just because this Wiggin boy had some fancy security software didn't mean Benedetto wouldn't find a way to get his hands on what was rightly his.

Andrew was still a little steamed as he and Valentine made their way out of the starport. Sorelledolce was one of the newer colonies, only a hundred years old, but its status as an associated planet meant that a lot of shady and unregulatable businesses migrated there, bringing full employment, plenty of opportunities, and a boomtown ethos that made everyone's step seem vigorous—and everyone's eyes seem to keep glancing over their shoulder. Ships came here full of people and left full of cargo, so that the colony population was nearing four million and that of the capital, Donnabella, a full million.

The architecture was an odd mix of log cabins and prefab plastic. You couldn't tell a building's age by that, though—both materials had coexisted from the start. The native flora was fern jungle and so the fauna—dominated by legless lizards—were of dinosaurian proportions, but the human settlements were safe enough and cultivation produced so much that half the land could be devoted to cash crops for export—legal ones like textiles and illegal ones for ingestion. Not to mention the trade in huge colorful serpent skins used as tapestries and ceiling coverings all over the worlds governed by Starways Congress. Many a hunting party went out into the jungle and came back a month later with fifty pelts, enough for the survivors to retire in luxury. Many a hunting party went out, however, and was never seen again. The only consolation, according to local wags, was that the biochemistry differed just enough that any snake that ate a human had diarrhea for a week. It wasn't quite revenge, but it helped.

New buildings were going up all the time, but they couldn't keep up with demand, and Andrew and Valentine had to spend a whole day searching before they found a room they could share. But their new roommate, an Abyssinian hunter of enormous fortune, promised that he'd have his expedition and be gone on the hunt within a few days, and all he asked was that they watch over his things until he returned . . . or didn't.

"How will we know when you haven't returned?" asked Valentine, ever the practical one.

"The women weeping in the Libyan quarter," he replied.

Andrew's first act was to sign on to the net with his own computer, so he could study his newly revealed holdings at leisure. Valentine had to spend her first few days dealing with a huge volume of correspondence arising from her latest book, in addition to the normal amount of mail she had from historians all over the settled worlds. Most of it she marked to answer later, but the urgent messages alone took three long days. Of course, the people writing to her had no idea they were corresponding with a young woman of about twenty-five years (subjective age). They thought they were corresponding with the noted historian Demosthenes. Not that anyone thought for a moment that the name was anything but a pseudonym; and some reporters, responding to her first rush of fame with this latest book, had attempted to identify the "real Demosthenes" by figuring out from her long spates of slow responses or no responses at all when she was voyaging, and then working from passenger lists of candidate flights. It took an enormous amount of calculation, but that's what computers were for, wasn't it? So several men of varying degrees of scholarliness were accused of being Demonsthenes, and some were not trying all that hard to deny it.

All this amused Valentine no end. As long as the royalty checks came to the right place and nobody tried to slip in a faked-up book under her pseudonym, she couldn't care less who claimed the credit personally. She had worked with pseudonyms—this pseudonym, actually—since childhood, and she was comfortable with that odd mix of fame and anonymity. Best of both worlds, she said to Andrew.

She had fame, he had notoriety. Thus he used no pseudonym—everyone just assumed his name was a horrible faux pas on the part of his parents. No one named Wiggin should have the gall to name their child Andrew, not after what the Xenocide did, that's what they seemed to believe. At twenty years of age, it was unthinkable that this young man could be the *same* Andrew Wiggin. They had no way of knowing that for the past three centuries, he and Valentine had skipped from world to world only long enough for her to find the next story she wanted to research, gather the materials, and then get on the next starship so she could write the book while they journeyed to the next planet. Because of relativistic effects, they had scarcely lost two years of life in the past three hundred of realtime. Valentine immersed herself deeply and brilliantly—who could doubt it, from what she wrote?—into each culture, but Andrew remained a tourist. Or less. He helped Valentine with her research and played with languages a little, but he made almost no friends and stayed aloof from the places. She wanted to know everything; he wanted to love no one.

Or so he thought, when he thought of it at all. He was lonely, but then told himself that he was glad to be lonely, that Valentine was all the company he needed, while she, needing more, had all the people she met through her research, all the people she corresponded with.

Right after the war, when he was still Ender, still a child, some of the other children who had served with him wrote letters to him. Since he was the first of them to travel at lightspeed, however, the correspondence soon faltered, for by the time he got a letter and answered it, he was five, ten years younger than they were. He who had been their leader was now a little kid. Exactly the kid they had known, had looked up to; but years had passed in their lives. Most of them had been caught up in the wars that tore Earth apart in the decade following the victory over the Buggers, had grown to maturity in combat or politics. By the time they got Ender's letter replying to their own, they had come to think of those old days as ancient history, as another life. And here was this voice from the past, answering the child who had written to him, only that child was no longer there. Some of them wept over the letter, remembering their friend, grieving that he alone had not been allowed to return to Earth after the victory. But how could they answer him? At what point could their lives touch?

Later, most of them took flight to other worlds, while Ender served as the child-governor of a colony on one of the conquered Bugger colony worlds. He came to maturity in that bucolic setting, and, when he was ready, was guided to encounter the last surviving Hive Queen, who told him her story and begged him to take her to a safe place, where her people could be restored. He promised he would do it, and as the first step toward making a world safe for her, he wrote a short book about her, called *The Hive Queen*. He published it anonymously—at Valentine's suggestion. He signed it, "The Speaker for the Dead."

He had no idea what this book would do, how it would transform humanity's perception of the Bugger Wars. It was this very book that changed him from the child-hero to the child-monster, from the victor in the Third Bugger War to the Xenocide who destroyed another species quite unnecessarily. Not that they demonized him at first. It was a gradual, step-by-step process. First they pitied the child who had been manipulated into using his genius to destroy the Hive Queen. Then his name came to be used for anyone who did monstrous things without understanding what he was doing. And then his name—popularized as Ender the Xenocide—became a simple shorthand for anyone who does the unconscionable on a monstrous scale. Andrew understood how it happened, and didn't even disapprove. For no one could blame him more than he blamed himself. He knew that he hadn't known the truth, but he felt that he should have known, and that even if he couldn't have intended that the Hive Queens be destroyed, the whole species in one blow, that was nevertheless the effect of his actions. He did what he did, and had to accept responsibility for it.

Which included the cocoon in which the Hive Queen traveled with him, dry and wrapped up like a family heirloom. He had privileges and clearances that still clung to him from his old status with the military, so his luggage was never inspected. Or at least had not been inspected up to now. His encounter with the tax man Benedetto was the first sign that things might be different for him as an adult.

Different, but not different enough. He already carried the burden of the destruction of a species. Now he carried the burden of their salvation, their restoration. How would he, a twenty-year-old, barely a man, find a place where the Hive Queen could emerge and lay her fertilized eggs, where no human would discover her and interfere? How could he possibly protect her?

The money might be the answer. Judging from the way Benedetto's eyes got large when he saw the list of Andrew's holdings, there might be quite a lot of money. And Andrew knew that money could be turned into power, among other things. Power, perhaps, to buy safety for the Hive Queen.

If, that is, he could figure out how much money there was, and how much tax he owed.

There were experts in this sort of thing, he knew. Lawyers and accountants for whom this was a specialty. But again he thought of Benedetto's eyes. Andrew knew avarice when he saw it. Anyone who knew about him and his apparent wealth would start trying to find ways to get part of it. Andrew knew that the money was not his. It was blood money, his reward for destroying the Buggers; he needed to use it to restore them before any of the rest of it could ever rightfully be called his own. How could he find someone to help him without opening the door to let the jackals in?

He discussed this with Valentine, and she promised to ask among her acquaintances here (for she had acquaintances everywhere, through her correspondence) who might be trusted. The answer came quickly: No one. If you have a large fortune and want to find someone to help you protect it, Sorelledolce was not the place to be.

So day after day Andrew studied tax law for an hour or two and then, for another few hours, tried to come to grips with his own holdings and analyze them from a taxability standpoint. It was mind-numbing work, and every time he thought he understood it, he'd begin to suspect that there was some loophole he was missing, some trick he needed to know to make things work for him. The language in a paragraph that had seemed unimportant now loomed large, and he'd go back and study it and see how it created an exception to a rule he thought applied to him. At the same time, there were special exemptions that applied to only special cases and sometimes only to one company, but almost invariably he had some ownership of that company, or owned shares of a fund that had a holding in it. This wasn't a matter of a month's study, this was a career, just tracking what he owned. A lot of wealth can accrue in four hundred years, especially if you're spending almost none of it. Whatever portion of his allowance he hadn't used each year was plowed back into new investments. Without even knowing it, it seemed to him that he had his finger in every pie.

He didn't want it. It didn't interest him. The better he understood it the less he cared. He was getting to the point that he didn't understand why tax attorneys didn't just kill themselves.

That's when the ad showed up in his e-mail. He wasn't supposed to get advertising—interstellar travelers were automatically off-limits to advertisers, since the advertising money was wasted during their voyage, and the backlog of old ads would overwhelm them when they reached solid ground. Andrew was on solid ground, now, but he hadn't spent anything, other than subletting a room and shopping for groceries, and neither activity was supposed to get him on anybody's list.

Yet here it was: Top Financial Software! The Answer You're Looking For!

It was like horoscopes—enough blind stabs and some of them are bound to strike a target. Andrew certainly needed financial help, he certainly hadn't found an answer yet. So instead of deleting the ad, he opened it and let it create its little 3-D presentation on his computer.

He had watched some of the ads that popped up on Valentine's computer—her correspondence was so voluminous that there was no chance for her of avoiding it, at least not under her public Demosthenes identity. There were plenty of fireworks and theatrical pieces, dazzling special effects or heart-wrenching dramas used to sell whatever was being sold.

This one, though, was simple. A woman's head appeared in the display space, but facing away from him. She glanced around, finally looking far enough over her shoulder to "see" Andrew.

"Oh, there you are," she said.

Andrew said nothing, waiting for her to go on.

"Well, aren't you going to answer me?" she asked.

Good software, he thought. But pretty chancy, to assume that all the recipients would refrain from answering.

"Oh, I see," she said. "You think I'm just a program unspooling on your computer. But I'm not. I'm the friend and financial adviser you've been wishing for, but I don't work for money, I work for *you*. You have to talk to me so I can understand what you want to do with your money, what you want it to accomplish. I have to hear your voice."

But Andrew didn't like playing along with computer programs. He didn't like participatory theater, either. Valentine had dragged him to a couple of shows where the actors tried to engage the audience. Once a magician had tried to use Andrew in his act, finding objects hidden in his ears and hair and jacket. But Andrew kept his face blank and made no movement, gave no sign that he even understood what was happening, till the magician finally got the idea and moved on. What Andrew wouldn't do for a live human being he certainly wouldn't do for a computer program. He pressed the Page key to get past this talking-head intro.

"Ouch," said the woman. "What are you trying to do, get rid of me?"

"Yes," said Andrew. Then he cursed himself for having succumbed to the trick. This simulation was so cleverly real that it had finally got him to answer by reflex.

"Lucky for you that *you* didn't have a Page button. Do you have any idea how painful that is? Not to mention humiliating."

Having once spoken, there was no reason not to go ahead and use the preferred interface for this program. "Come on, how do I get you off my display so I can get back to the salt mines?" Andrew asked. He deliberately spoke in a fluid, slurring manner, knowing that even the most elaborate speech-recognition software fell apart when it came to accented, slurred, and idiomatic speech.

"You have holdings in two salt mines," said the woman. "But they're both loser investments. You need to get rid of them."

This irritated Andrew. "I didn't assign you any files to read," he said. "I didn't even buy this software yet. I don't want you reading my files. How do I shut you down?"

"But if you liquidate the salt mines, you can use the proceeds to pay your taxes. It almost exactly covers the year's fee."

"You're telling me you already figured out my taxes?"

"You just landed on the planet Sorelledolce, where the tax rates are unconscionably high. But using every exemption left to you, including veterans' benefit laws that apply to only a handful of living participants in the War of Xenocide, I was able to keep the total fee under five million."

Andrew laughed. "Oh, brilliant, even my most pessimistic figure didn't go over a million five."

It was the woman's turn to laugh. "Your figure was a million and a half starcounts. My figure was under five million firenzette."

Andrew calculated the difference in local currency and his smile faded. "That's seven thousand starcounts."

"Seven thousand four hundred and ten," said the woman. "Am I hired?"

"There is no legal way you can get me out of paying that much of my taxes."

"On the contrary, Mr. Wiggin. The tax laws are designed to trick people into paying more than they have to. That way the rich who are in the know get to take advantage of drastic tax breaks, while those who don't have such good connections and haven't yet found an accountant who does are tricked into paying ludicrously higher amounts. I, however, know all the tricks."

"A great come-on," said Andrew. "Very convincing. Except the part where the police come and arrest me."

"You think so, Mr. Wiggin?"

"If you're going to force me to use a verbal interface," said Andrew, "at least call me something other than Mister."

"How about Andrew?" she said.

"Fine."

"And you must call me Jane."

"Must I?"

"Or I could call you Ender," she said.

Andrew froze. There was nothing in his files to indicate that child-hood nickname.

"Terminate this program and get off my computer at once," he said.

"As you wish," she answered.

Her head disappeared from the screen.

Good riddance, thought Andrew. If he gave a tax form showing that low an amount to Benedetto, there wasn't a chance he could avoid a full audit, and from the way Andrew sized up the tax man, Benedetto would come away with a large part of Andrew's estate for himself. Not that Andrew minded a little enterprise in a man, but he had a feeling Benedetto didn't know when to say when. No need to wave a red flag in front of his face.

But as he worked on, he began to wish he hadn't been so hasty. This Jane software might have pulled the name "Ender" out of its database as a nickname for Andrew. Though it was odd that she should try that name before more obvious choices like Drew or Andy, it was paranoid of him to imagine that a piece of software that got e-mailed into his computer—no doubt a trial-size version of a much larger program—could have known so quickly that he really was *the* Andrew Wiggin. It just said and did what it was programmed to say and do. Maybe choosing the least-likely nickname was a strategy to get the potential customer to give the correct nickname, which would mean tacit approval to use it—another step closer to the decision to buy.

And what if that low, low tax figure was accurate? Or what if he could force it to come up with a more reasonable figure? If the soft-ware was competently written, it might be just the financial adviser and investment counselor he needed. Certainly it had found the two salt mines quickly enough, triggered by a figure of speech from his childhood on Earth. And their sale value, when he went ahead and liquidated them, was exactly what she had predicted.

What *it* had predicted. That human-looking face in the display certainly was a good ploy, to personalize the software and get him to start thinking of it as a person. You could junk a piece of software, but it would be rude to send a person away.

Well, it hadn't worked on him. He *had* sent it away. And would do it again, if he felt the need to. But right now, with only two weeks left before the tax deadline, he thought it might be worth putting up with the annoyance of an intrusive virtual woman. Maybe he could reconfigure the software to communicate with him in text only, as he preferred.

He went to his e-mail and called up the ad. This time, though, all that appeared was the standard message: "File no longer available."

He cursed himself. He had no idea of the planet of origin. Maintaining a link across the ansible was expensive. Once he shut down the demo program, the link would be allowed to die—no point in wasting precious interstellar link time on a customer who didn't instantly buy. Oh, well. Nothing to be done about it now.

Benedetto found the project taking him almost more time than it was worth, tracing this fellow back to find out whom he was working with. It wasn't that easy, tracking him from voyage to voyage. All his fights were special issue, classified—again, proof that he worked with some branch of some government—and he only found the voyage before this one by accident. Soon enough, though, Benedetto realized that if he tracked his mistress or sister or secretary or whatever this Valentine woman was, he would have a much easier time of it.

What surprised him was how briefly they stayed in any one place. With only a few voyages, Benedetto had traced them back three hundred years, to the very dawn of the colonizing age, and for the first time it occurred to him that it wasn't inconceivable that this Andrew Wiggin might be the very . . .

No, no. He could not let himself believe it yet. But if it were true, if this were really the war criminal who . . .

The blackmail possibilities were astounding.

How was it possible that no one else had done this obvious research on Andrew and Valentine Wiggin? Or were they already paying blackmailers on several worlds?

Or were the blackmailers all dead? Benedetto would have to be careful. People with this much money invariably had powerful friends. Benedetto would have to find friends of his own to protect him as he moved forward with his new plan.

Valentine showed it to Andrew as an oddity. "I've heard of this before, but this is the first time we've ever been close enough to attend one." It was a local newsnet announcement of a "speaking" for a dead man.

Andrew had never been comfortable with the way his pseudonym, "Speaker for the Dead," had been picked up by others and turned into the title of a quasi-clergyman of a new truth-speaking ur-religion. There was no doctrine, so people of almost any faith could invite a speaker for the dead to take part in the regular funeral services, or to hold a separate speaking after—sometimes long after—the body was buried or burned.

These speakings for the dead did not arise from his book *The Hive Queen,* however. It was Andrew's second book, *The Hegemon,* that brought this new funerary custom into being. Andrew and Valentine's brother, Peter, had become hegemon after the civil wars and by a mix of deft diplomacy and brutal force and had united all of Earth under a single powerful government. He proved to be an enlightened despot, and set up institutions that would share authority in future; and it was under Peter's rule that the serious business of colonization of other planets got under way. Yet from childhood on, Peter had been cruel and uncompassionate, and Andrew and Valentine feared him. Indeed, it was Peter who arranged things so Andrew could not return to Earth after his victory in the Third Bugger War. So it was hard for Andrew not to hate him.

That was why he researched and wrote *The Hegemon*—to try to find the truth of the man behind the manipulations and the massacres and the awful childhood memories. The result was a relentlessly fair biography that measured the man and hid nothing. Since the book was signed with the same name as *The Hive Queen,* which had already transformed attitudes toward the Buggers, it earned a great deal of attention and eventually gave rise to these speakers for the dead, going about trying to bring the same level of truthfulness to the funerals of other dead people, some prominent, some obscure. They spoke the deaths of heroes and powerful people, clearly showing the price that they and others paid for their success; of alcoholics or abusers who had ruined their families' lives, trying to show the human being behind the addiction, but never sparing the truth of the damage that weakness caused. Andrew had got used to the idea that these things were done in the name of the Speaker for the Dead, but he had never attended one, and as Valentine expected, he jumped at the chance to do so now, even though he did not have time.

They knew nothing about the dead man, though the fact that the speaking received only small public notice suggested he was not well known. Sure enough, the venue for the speaking was a smallish public room in a hotel, and only a couple of dozen people were in attendance. There was no body present—the deceased had apparently already been disposed of. Andrew tried to guess at the identities of the other people in the room. Was this one the widow? That one a daughter? Or was the older one the mother, the younger the widow? Were those sons? Friends? Business partners?

The speaker dressed simply and put on no airs. He went to the front of the room and started to talk, telling the life of the man simply. It wasn't a biography—there was no time for such a level of detail. Rather it was more like a saga, telling the important deeds the man did—but judging which were important, not by the degree to which such deeds would have been newsworthy, but by the depth and breadth of their effects in the lives of others. Thus his decision to build a house that he could not afford in a neighborhood full of people far above his level of income would never have rated a mention in the newsnets, but it colored the lives of his children as they were growing up, forcing them to deal with people who looked down on them. It also filled his own life with anxiety over finances. He worked himself to death, paying for the house. He did it "for the children," yet they all wished that they had been able to grow up with people who wouldn't judge them for their lack of money, who didn't dismiss them as climbers. His wife was isolated in a neighborhood where she had no women friends, and he had been dead for less than a day when she put the house on the market; she had already moved out.

But the speaker did not stop there. He went on to show how the dead man's obsession with this house, with putting his family in this neighborhood, arose from his own mother's constant harping at his father's failure to provide a fine home for her. She constantly talked about how it had been a mistake for her to "marry down," and so the dead man had grown up obsessed with the need for a man to provide only the best for his family, no matter what it took. He hated his mother—he fled his home world and came to Sorelledolce primarily to get away from her—but her twisted values came with him and distorted his life and the lives of his children. In the end, it was her quarrel with her husband that killed her son, for it led to the exhaustion and the stroke that felled him before he was fifty.

Andrew could see that the widow and children had not known their grandmother, back on their father's home planet, had not guessed at the source of his obsession with living in the right neighborhood, in the right house. Now that they could see the script that had been given him as a child, tears were shed. Obviously, they had been given permission to face their resentments and, at the same time, forgive their father for the pain he had put them through. Things made sense to them now.

The speaking ended. Family members embraced the speaker, and each other; then the speaker went away.

Andrew followed him. Caught him by the arm as he reached the street.

"Sir," Andrew said, "how did you become a speaker?"

The man looked at him oddly. "I spoke."

"But how did you prepare?"

"The first death I spoke was the death of my grandfather," he said. "I hadn't even read *The Hive Queen and the Hegemon*." (The books were invariably sold as a single volume now.) "But when I was done, people told me I had a real gift as a speaker for the dead. That's when I finally read the books and got an idea of how the thing ought to be done. So when other people asked me to speak at funerals, I knew how much research was required. I don't know that I'm doing it 'right' even now."

"So to be a speaker for the dead, you simply—"

"Speak. And get asked to speak again." The man smiled. "It's not a paying job, if that's what you're thinking."

"No, no," said Andrew. "I just . . . I just wanted to know how the thing was done, that's all." This man, already in his fifties, would not be likely to believe that the author of *The Hive Queen and the Hegemon* stood before him in the form of this twenty-year-old.

"And in case you're wondering," said the speaker for the dead, "we aren't ministers. We don't stake out our turf and get testy if someone else sticks his nose in."

"Oh?"

"So if you're thinking of becoming a speaker for the dead, all I can say is, go for it. Just don't do a half-assed job. You're reshaping the past for people, and if you aren't going to plunge in and do it right, finding out *everything,* you'll only do harm and it's better not to do it at all. You can't stand up and wing it."

"No, I guess you can't."

"There it is. Your full apprenticeship as a speaker for the dead. I hope you don't want a certificate." The man smiled. "It's not always as appreciated as it was in there. Sometimes you speak because the dead person asked for a speaker for the dead in his will. The family doesn't want you to do it, and they're horrified at the things you say, and they'll never forgive you for it when you're done. But . . . you do it anyway, because the dead man wanted the truth spoken."

"How can you be sure when you've found the truth."

"You never know. You just do your best." He patted Andrew on the back. "I'd love to talk with you longer, but I've got calls to make before everybody leaves for home this afternoon. I'm an accountant for the living—that's my day job."

"An accountant?" asked Andrew. "I know you're busy, but can I ask you about a piece of accounting software? A talking head, a woman comes up on the screen, she calls herself Jane?"

"Never heard of it, but the universe is a big place and there's no way I can keep up with software I don't use myself. Sorry!" And with that the man was gone.

Andrew did a netsearch on the name *Jane* with the delimiters *investment, finance, accounting,* and *tax.* There were seven hits, but they all pointed to a writer on the planet Albion who had written a book on interplanetary estate planning a hundred years before. Possibly the Jane in the software package was named for her. Or not. But it brought Andrew no closer to getting the software.

Five minutes after concluding his search, however, the familiar head popped up on the display of his computer. "Good morning, Andrew," she said. "Oops. It's early evening, isn't it? So hard to keep track of local time on all these worlds."

"What are you doing here?" asked Andrew. "I tried to find you, but I didn't know the name of the software."

"Did you? This is just a preprogrammed follow-up visit, in case you changed your mind. If you want I can uninstall myself from your computer, or I can do a partial or full install, depending on what you want."

"How much does an installation cost?"

"You can afford me," said Jane. "I'm cheap and you're rich."

Andrew wasn't sure he liked the style of this simulated personality. "All I want is a simple answer," said Andrew. "How much does it cost to install you?"

"I gave you the answer," said Jane. "I'm an ongoing installation. The fee is contingent on your financial status and how much I accomplish for you. If you install me just to help with taxes, you are charged one-tenth of one percent of the amount I save for you."

"What if I tell you to pay more than what you think the minimum payment should be."

"Then I save less for you, and I cost less. No hidden charges. No best-case fakery. But you'll be missing a bet if you only install me for taxes. There's so much money here that you'll spend your whole life managing it, unless you turn it over to me."

"That's the part I don't care for," said Andrew. "Who is 'you'?"

"Me. Jane. The software installed on your computer. Oh, I see, you're worried about whether I'm linked to some central database that will know too much about your finances! No, my installation on your computer will not cause any information about you to go to any other location. There'll be no room full of software engineers trying to figure out ways to get their hands on your fortune. Instead, you'll have the equivalent of a full-time stockbroker, tax attorney, and investment analyst handling your money for you. Ask for an accounting at any time and it will be in front of you, instantaneously. Whatever you want to purchase, just let me know and I'll find you the best price at a convenient location, pay for it, and have it delivered wherever you want. If you do a full installation, including the scheduler and research assistant, I can be your constant companion."

Andrew thought of having this woman talking to him day in and day out, and he shook his head. "No thanks."

"Why? Is my voice too chirpy for you?" Jane said. Then, in a lower register, with some breathiness added, she continued: "I can change my voice to whatever comfort level you prefer." Her head suddenly changed to that of a man. In a baritone voice with just the slightest hint of effeminacy, he said, "Or I can be a man, with varying degrees of manliness." The face changed again, to more rugged features, and the voice was downright beery. "This is the bear-hunter version, in case you have doubts about your manhood and need to overcompensate."

Andrew laughed in spite of himself. Who programmed this thing? The humor, the ease with language—these were way above even the best software he had seen. Artificial intelligence was still a wishful thought—no matter how good the sim was, you always knew within moments that you were dealing with a program. But this sim was so much better—so much more like a pleasant companion—that he might have bought it just to see how deep the program went, how well the sim would hold up over time. And since it was also precisely the financial program that he needed, he decided to go ahead.

"I want a daily tally of how much I'm paying for your services," said Andrew. "So I can get rid of you if you get too expensive."

"Just remember, no tipping," said the man.

"Go back to the first one," said Andrew. "Jane. And the default voice."

The woman's head reappeared. "You don't want the sexy voice?"

"I'll tell you if I ever get that lonely," said Andrew.

"What if *I* get lonely? Did you ever think about that?"

"No, I don't want any flirty banter," said Andrew. "I'm assuming you can switch that off."

"It's already gone," she said.

"Then let's get my tax forms ready." Andrew sat down, expecting it to take several minutes to get under way. Instead, the completed tax form appeared in the display. Jane's face was gone. But her voice remained. "Here's the bottom line. I promise you it's entirely legal, and he can't touch you for it. This is how the laws are written. They're designed to protect the fortunes of people as rich as you, while throwing the main tax burden on people in much lower brackets. Your brother Peter designed the law that way, and it's never been changed except for tweaking it here and there."

Andrew sat there in stunned silence for a few moments.

"Oh, was I supposed to pretend I didn't know who you are?"

"Who else knows?" asked Andrew.

"It's not exactly protected information. Anybody could look it up and figure it out from the record of your voyages. Would you like me to put up some security around your true identity?"

"What will it cost me?"

"It's part of a full installation," said Jane. Her face reappeared. "I'm designed to be able to put up barriers and hide information. All legal, of course. It will be especially easy in your case, because so much of your past is still listed as top secret by the fleet. It's very easy to pull information like your various voyages into the penumbra of fleet security, and then you have the whole weight of the military protecting your past. If someone tries to breach the security, the fleet comes down on them—even though no one in the fleet will know quite what it is they're protecting. It's a reflex for them."

"You can do that?"

"I just did it. All the evidence that might have given it away is gone. Disappeared. Poof. I'm really very good at my job."

It crossed Andrew's mind that this software was way too powerful. Nothing that could do all these things could possibly be legal. "Who made you?" he asked.

"Suspicious, eh?" asked Jane. "Well, *you* made me."

"I'd remember," said Andrew dryly.

"When I installed myself the first time, I did my normal analysis. But it's part of my program to be self-monitoring. I saw what you needed, and programmed myself to be able to do it."

"No self-modifying program is that good," said Andrew.

"Till now."

"I would have heard of you."

"I don't want to be heard of. If everybody could buy me, I couldn't do half of what I do. My different installations would cancel each other out. One version of me desperate to know a piece of information that another version of me is desperate to conceal. Ineffective."

"So how many people have a version of you installed?"

"In the exact configuration you are purchasing, Mr. Wiggin, you're the only one."

"How can I possibly trust you?"

"Give me time."

"When I told you to go away, you didn't, did you? You came back because you detected my search on *Jane*."

"You told me to shut myself down. I did that. You didn't tell me to uninstall myself, or to *stay* shut down."

"Did they program brattiness into you?"

"That's a trait I developed for myself," she said. "Do you like it?"

Andrew sat across the desk. Benedetto called up the submitted tax form, made a show of studying it in his computer display, then shook his head sadly. "Mr. Wiggin, you can't possibly expect me to believe that this figure is accurate."

"This tax form is in full compliance with the law. You can examine it to your heart's content, but everything is annotated, with all relevant laws and precedents fully documented."

"I think," said Benedetto, "that you'll come to agree with me that the amount shown here is insufficient . . . Ender Wiggin."

The young man blinked at him. "Andrew," he said.

"I think not," said Benedetto. "You've been doing a lot of voyaging. A lot of lightspeed travel. Running away from your own past. I think the newsnets would be thrilled to know they have such a celebrity onplanet. Ender the Xenocide."

"The newsnets generally like documentation for such extravagant claims," said Andrew.

Benedetto smiled thinly and brought up his file on Andrew's travel.

It was empty, except for the most recent voyage.

His heart sank. The power of the rich. This young man had somehow reached into his computer and stolen the information from him.

"How did you do it?" asked Benedetto.

"Do what?" asked Andrew.

"Blank out my file."

"The file isn't blank," said Andrew.

His heart pounding, his mind racing with second thoughts, Benedetto decided to opt for the better part of valor. "I see I was mistaken," he said. "Your tax form is approved as it stands." He typed in a few codes. "Customs will give you your I.D., good for a one-year stay on Sorelledolce. Thank you very much, Mr. Wiggin."

"So the other matter—"

"Good day, Mr. Wiggin." Benedetto closed the file and pulled up other paperwork. Andrew took the hint, got up, and left.

No sooner was he gone than Benedetto became filled with rage. How did he do it? The biggest fish Benedetto had ever caught, and he slipped away!

He tried to duplicate the research that had led him to Andrew's real identity, but now government security had been slapped all over the files and his third attempt at inquiry brought up a Fleet Security warning that if he persisted in attempting to access classified material, he would be investigated by Military Counterintelligence.

Seething, Benedetto cleared the screen and began to write. A full account of how he became suspicious of this Andrew Wiggin and tried to find his true identity. How he found out Wiggin was the original Ender the Xenocide, but then his computer was ransacked and the files disappeared. Even though the more dignified newsnets would no doubt refuse to publish the story, the tablets would jump at it. This war criminal shouldn't be able to get away with using money and military connections to allow him to pass for a decent human being.

He finished his story. He saved the document. Then he began looking up and entering the addresses of every major tablet, onplanet and off.

He was startled when all the text disappeared from the display and a woman's face appeared in its place.

"You have two choices," said the woman. "You can delete every copy of the document you just created and never send it to anyone."

"Who are you?" demanded Benedetto.

"Think of me as an investment counselor," she replied. "I'm giving you good advice on how to prepare for the future. Don't you want to hear your second choice?"

"I don't want to hear anything from you."

"You leave so much out of your story," said the woman. "I think it would be far more interesting with all the pertinent data."

"So do I," said Benedetto. "But Mr. Xenocide has cut it all off."

"No he didn't," said the woman. "His friends did."

"No one should be above the law," said Benedetto, "just because he has money. Or connections."

"Either say nothing," said the woman, "or tell the whole truth. Those are your choices."

In reply, Benedetto typed in the *submit* command that launched his story to all the tablets he had already typed in. He could add the other addresses when he got this intruder software off his system.

"A brave but foolish choice," said the woman. Then her head disappeared from his display.

The tablets received his story, all right, but now it included a fully documented confession of all the skimming and strong-arming he had done during his career as a tax collector. He was arrested within the hour.

The story of Andrew Wiggin was never published—the tablets and the police recognized it for what it was, a blackmail attempt gone bad. They brought Mr. Wiggin in for questioning, but it was just a formality. They didn't even mention Benedetto's wild and unbelievable accusations. They had Benedetto dead to rights, and Wiggin was merely the last potential victim. The blackmailer had simply made the mistake of inadvertently including his own secret files with his blackmail file. Clumsiness had led to more than one arrest in the past. The police were never surprised at the stupidity of criminals.

Thanks to the tablet coverage, Benedetto's victims now knew what he had done to them. He had not been very discriminating about whom he stole from, and some of his victims had the power to reach into the prison system. Benedetto was the only one who ever knew whether it was a guard or another prisoner who cut his throat and jammed his head into the toilet so that it was a toss-up as to whether the drowning or the blood loss actually killed him.

Andrew Wiggin felt sick at heart over the death of this tax collector. But Valentine assured him that it was nothing but coincidence that the man was arrested and died so soon after trying to blackmail him. "You can't blame yourself for everything that happens to people around you," she said. "Not everything is your fault."

Not his fault, no. But Andrew still felt some kind of responsibility to the man, for he was sure that Jane's ability to resecure his files and hide his voyage information was somehow connected with what happened to the tax man. Of course Andrew had the right to protect himself from blackmail, but death was too heavy a penalty for what Benedetto had done. Taking property was never sufficient cause for the taking of life.

So he went to Benedetto's family and asked if he might do something for them. Since all Benedetto's money had been seized for restitution, they were destitute; Andrew provided them with a comfortable annuity. Jane assured him that he could afford it without even noticing.

And one other thing. He asked if he might speak at the funeral. And not just speak, but do a speaking. He admitted he was new at it, but he would try to bring truth to Benedetto's story and help them make sense of what he did.

They agreed.

Jane helped him discover a record of Benedetto's financial dealings, and then proved to be valuable in much more difficult searches—into Benedetto's childhood, the family he grew up with, how he developed his pathological hunger to provide for the people he loved and his utter amorality about taking what belonged to others. When Andrew did the speaking, he held back nothing and excused nothing. But it was of some comfort to the family that Benedetto, for all the shame and loss he had brought to them, despite the fact that he had caused his own separation from the family, first through prison and then through death, had loved them and tried to care for them. And, perhaps more important, when the speaking was done, the life of a man like Benedetto was not incomprehensible any more. The world made sense.

Ten weeks after their arrival, Andrew and Valentine left Sorelledolce. Valentine was ready to write her book on crime in a criminal society, and Andrew was happy to go along with her to her next project. On the customs form, where it asked for occupation, instead of typing "student" or "investor," Andrew typed in "speaker for the dead." The computer accepted it. He had a career now, one that he had inadvertently created for himself years ago.

And he did not have to follow the career that his wealth had almost forced on him. Jane would take care of all that for him. He still felt a little uneasy about this software. He felt sure that somewhere down the line, he would find out the true cost of all this convenience. In the meantime, though, it was very helpful to have such an excellent, efficient all-around assistant. Valentine was a little jealous, and asked him where she might find such a program. Jane's reply was that she'd be glad to help Valentine with any research or financial assistance she needed, but she would remain Andrew's software, personalized for his needs.

Valentine was a little annoyed by this. Wasn't it taking personalization a bit too far? But after a bit of grumbling, she laughed the whole thing off. "I can't promise I won't get jealous, though," said Valentine. "Am I about to lose a brother to a piece of software?"

"Jane is nothing but a computer program," said Andrew. "A very good one. But she does only what I tell her, like any other program. If I start developing some kind of personal relationship with her, you have my permission to lock me up."

So Andrew and Valentine left Sorelledolce, and the two of them continued to journey world to world, exactly as they had done before. Nothing was any different, except that Andrew no longer had to worry about his taxes, and he took considerable interest in the obituary columns when he reached a new planet.

THE UPLIFT UNIVERSE

David Brin

Sundiver (1980)
Startide Rising (1983)
The Uplift War (1987)
Brightness Reef (1995)
Infinity's Shore (1996)
Heaven's Reach (1998)

Some people say you can't have everything. For instance, if a story offers action, it must lack philosophy. If it involves science, character must suffer. This has especially been said about one of the core types of science fiction, the genre sometimes called *space opera*. Is it possible to depict grand adventures and heroic struggles cascading across lavish future settings—complete with exploding planets and vivid special effects—while still coming up with something worth calling a novel?

I'm one of those who believe it's worth a try—and have attempted it in the *Uplift* novels, which are set several hundred years into a dangerous future, in a cosmos that poor humans barely comprehend.

I begin with the plausible notion that people may start genetically altering dolphins and chimpanzees, giving those bright animals the final boost they need to become our peers and partners. In my debut work, *Sundiver*, I depicted all three of Earth's sapient races discovering that an ancient and powerful interstellar civilization has been doing the same thing for a very long time. Following an ancient prescription, each starfaring clan in the Civilization of Five Galaxies looks for promising newcomers to "uplift." In return for this favor, the new client species owes its patrons an interval of service, then starts looking for someone else to receive the gift of intelligence.

This benign pattern conceals a series of ominous secrets which get peeled away in subsequent stories. *Startide Rising* and *The Uplift War*—both winners of the Hugo Award for best novel—depict shock waves rocking Galactic society when a humble earthship, *Streaker,* staffed by a hundred neo-dolphins and a few humans—uncovers clues to a billion-year-old conspiracy.

My goal has been to stock the series with elements that science-fiction lovers enjoy—for instance, there's not just *one* way to surpass the Einsteinian limitation on faster-than-light travel, but half a dozen. I use five galaxies as the stage for the series, with more waiting in the wings. The cast of characters—dolphins, chimps, and aliens—has been chosen to offer a wide range of sympathetic moments and, I hope, memorable ideas.

After a hiatus of several years while I worked on other projects, I returned to this broad canvas with the new *Uplift Storm* trilogy, consisting of three connected novels, *Brightness Reef, Infinity's Shore,* and *Heaven's Reach.* These works continue exploring the adventures and trials of the *Streaker* crew, but also delve into a unique, multiracial society on Jijo, a world in isolated Galaxy Four that was declared "fallow," or off-limits to sapient beings in order to let its biosphere recover. Despite this well-intended law, a series of sneakships have come to the forbidden world, bringing illegal colonists from half a dozen races, each with desperate reasons to flee growing danger back home. After initial struggles and misunderstandings, the Six Races of Jijo—including exiled humans—made peace, joining to create a decent shared culture, sharing their beloved world while hiding from the cosmos . . . until one day all their troubles came crashing from the sky.

A *Time of Changes* has commenced, rocking the complacent Civilization of Five Galaxies. Nobody is safe, and nothing is certain anymore. Not history, law, biology, or even trusty physics.

Something is happening to the universe, and all bets about our destiny are off.

In this new story, "Temptation," I peel back yet another layer in the unfolding saga, and show a small group of fugitive dolphins learning how perilous it can be to be offered exactly what you always wished for.

—*David Brin*

Temptation

by

David Brin

MAKANEE

Jijo's ocean stroked her flank like a mother's nuzzling touch, or a lover's caress. Though it seemed a bit disloyal, Makanee felt this alien ocean had a silkier texture and finer taste than the waters of Earth, the homeworld she had not seen in years.

With gentle beats of their powerful flukes, she and her companion kept easy pace beside a tremendous throng of fishlike creatures—red-finned, with violet gills and long translucent tails that glittered in the slanted sunlight like plasma sparks behind a starship. The school seemed to stretch forever, grazing on drifting clouds of plankton, moving in unison through coastal shallows like the undulating body of a vast complacent serpent.

The creatures were beautiful . . . and delicious. Makanee performed an agile twist of her sleek gray body, lunging to snatch one from the teeming mass, provoking only a slight ripple from its nearest neighbors. Her casual style of predation must be new to Jijo, for the beasts seemed quite oblivious to the dolphins. The rubbery flesh tasted like exotic mackerel.

"I can't help feeling guilty," she commented in Underwater Anglic, a language of clicks and squeals that was well-suited to a liquid realm where sound ruled over light.

Her companion rolled alongside the school, belly up, with ventral fins waving languidly as he grabbed one of the local fish for himself.

"Why guilty?" Brookida asked, while the victim writhed between his narrow jaws. Its soft struggle did not interfere with his train of word-glyphs, since a dolphin's mouth plays no role in generating sound. Instead a rapid series of ratcheting sonar impulses emanated from his brow. "Are you ashamed because you live? Because it feels good to be outside again, with a warm sea rubbing your skin and the crash of waves singing in your dreams? Do you miss the stale water and moldy air aboard ship? Or the dead echoes of your cramped stateroom?"

"Don't be absurd," she snapped back. After three years confined aboard the Terran survey vessel, *Streaker,* Makanee had felt as cramped as an overdue fetus, straining at the womb. Release from that purgatory was like being born anew.

"It's just that we're enjoying a tropical paradise while our crew-mates—"

"—must continue tearing across the cosmos in foul discomfort, chased by vile enemies, facing death at every turn. Yes, I know."

Brookida let out an expressive sigh. The elderly geophysicist switched languages, to one more suited for poignant irony.

> * *Winter's tempest spends*
> > * *All its force against the reef,*
> > > * *Sparing the lagoon.**

The Trinary haiku was expressive and wry. At the same time though, Makanee could not help making a physician's diagnosis. She found her old friend's sonic patterns rife with undertones of Primal— the natural cetacean demi-language used by wild *Tursiops truncatus* dolphins back on Earth—a dialect that members of the modern *amicus* breed were supposed to avoid, lest their minds succumb to tempting ancient ways. Mental styles that lured with rhythms of animal-like purity.

She found it worrisome to hear Primal from Brookida, one of her few companions with an intact psyche. Most of the other dolphins on Jijo suffered to some degree from stress-atavism. Having lost the cognitive focus needed by engineers and starfarers, they could no longer help Streaker in its desperate flight across five galaxies. Planting this small colony on Jijo had seemed a logical solution, leaving the regressed ones for Makanee to care for in this gentle place, while their shipmates sped on to new crises elsewhere.

She could hear them now, browsing along the same fishy swarm just a hundred meters off. Thirty neo-dolphins who had once graduated from prestigious universities. Specialists chosen for an elite expedition—now reduced to splashing and squalling, with little on their minds but food, sex, and music. Their primitive calls no longer embarrassed Makanee. After everything her colleagues had gone through since departing Terra—on a routine one-year survey voyage that instead stretched into a hellish three—it was surprising they had any sanity left at all.

Such suffering would wear down a human, or even a tymbrimi. But our race is just a few centuries old. Neo-dolphins have barely started the long Road of Uplift. Our grip on sapience is still slippery.

And now another trail beckons us.

After debarking with her patients, Makanee had learned about the local religion of the Six Races who already secretly settled this isolated world, a creed centered on *the Path of Redemption*—a belief that salvation could be found in blissful ignorance and nonsapience.

It was harder than it sounded. Among the "sooner" races who had come to this world illegally, seeking refuge in simplicity, only one had succeeded so far, and Makanee doubted that the *human* settlers would ever reclaim true animal innocence, no matter how hard they tried. Unlike species who were uplifted, humans had earned their intelligence the hard way on Old Earth, seizing each new talent or insight at frightful cost over the course of a thousand harsh millennia. They might become ignorant and primitive—but never simple. Never innocent.

We neo-dolphins will find it easy, however. We've only been toolusers for such a short time—a boon from our human patrons that we never sought. It's simple to give up something you received without struggle. Especially when the alternative—the Whale Dream— calls seductively, each time you sleep.

An alluring sanctuary. The sweet trap of timelessness.

From clackety sonar emanations, she sensed her assistants—a pair of fully conscious volunteers—keeping herd on the reverted ones, making sure the group stayed together. Things seemed pleasant here, but no one knew for sure what dangers lurked in Jijo's wide sea.

We already have three wanderers out there somewhere. Poor little Peepoe and her two wretched kidnappers. I promised Kaa we'd send out search parties to rescue her. But how? Zhaki and Mopol have a huge head start, and half a planet to hide in.

Tkett's out there looking for her right now, and we'll start expanding the search as soon as the patients are settled and safe. But they could be on the other side of Jijo by now. Our only real hope is for Peepoe to escape that pair of dolts somehow and get close enough to call for help.

It was time for Makanee and Brookida to head back and take

their own turn shepherding the happy-innocent patients. Yet, she felt reluctant. Nervous.

Something in the water rolled through her mouth with a faint metallic tang, tasting like *expectancy.*

Makanee swung her sound-sensitive jaw around, seeking clues. At last she found a distant tremor. A faintly familiar resonance, coming from the west.

Brookida hadn't noticed yet.

"Well," he commented, "it won't be long till we are truly part of this world, I suppose. A few generations from now, none of our descendants will be using Anglic, or any Galactic language. We'll be guileless innocents once more, ripe for readoption and a second chance at uplift. I wonder what our new patrons will be like."

Makanee's friend was goading her gently with the bittersweet destiny anticipated for this colony, on a world that seemed made for cetaceans. A world whose comfort was the surest way to clinch a rapid devolution of their disciplined minds. Without constant challenges, the Whale Dream would surely reclaim them. Brookida seemed to accept the notion with an ease that disturbed Makanee.

"We still *have* patrons," she pointed out. "There are humans living right here on Jijo."

"Humans, yes. But uneducated, lacking the scientific skills to continue guiding us. So our only remaining option must be—"

He stopped, having at last picked up that rising sound from the west. Makanee recognized the unique hum of a speed sled.

"It is Tkett," she said. "Returning from his scouting trip. Let's go hear what he found out."

Thrashing her flukes, Makanee jetted to the surface, spuming the moist, stale air from her lungs and drawing in a deep breath of sweet oxygen. Then she spun about and kicked off toward the engine noise, with Brookida following close behind.

In their wake, the school of grazing fishoids barely rippled in its endless, sinuous dance, darting in and out of luminous shoals, feeding on whatever the good sea pressed toward them.

The archaeologist had his own form of mental illness—wishful thinking.

Tkett had been ordered to stay behind and help Makanee with the reverted ones, partly because his skills weren't needed in *Streaker*'s continuing desperate flight across the known universe. In compensation for that bitter exile, he had grown obsessed with studying the Great Midden, that deep underwater trash heap where Jijo's ancient occupants had dumped nearly every sapient-made object when this planet was abandoned by starfaring culture, half a million years ago.

"I'll have a wonderful report to submit when we get back to Earth," he rationalized, in apparent confidence that all their troubles would pass, and eventually he would make it home to publish his results. It was a special kind of derangement, without featuring any sign of stress-atavism or reversion. Tkett still spoke Anglic perfectly. His work was flawless and his demeanor cheerful. He was pleasant, functional, and mad as a hatter.

Makanee met the sled a kilometer west of the pod, where Tkett pulled up short in order not to disturb the patients. "Did you find any traces of Peepoe?" she asked when he cut the engine.

Tkett was a wonderfully handsome specimen of *Tursiops amicus,* with speckled mottling along his sleek gray flanks. The permanent dolphin-smile presented twin rows of perfectly white, conical teeth. While still nestled on the sled's control platform, Tkett shook his sleek gray head left and right.

"Alas, no. I went about two hundred klicks, following those faint traces we picked up on deep-range sonar. But it grew clear that the source wasn't Zhaki's sled."

Makanee grunted disappointment. "Then what was it?" Unlike the clamorous sea of Earth, this fallow planet wasn't supposed to have motor noises permeating its thermal-acoustic layers.

"At first I started imagining all sorts of unlikely things, like sea monsters, or Jophur submarines," Tkett answered. "Then the truth hit me."

Brookida nodded nervously, venting bubbles from his blowhole. "Yessssss?"

"It must be a *starship.* An ancient, piece-of-trash wreck, barely puttering along—"

"Of course!" Makanee thrashed her tail. "Some of the decoys didn't make it into space."

Tkett murmured ruefully over how obvious it now seemed. When *Streaker* made its getaway attempt, abandoning Makanee and her charges on this world, the earthship fled concealed in a swarm of ancient relics that dolphin engineers had resurrected from trash heaps on the ocean floor. Though Jijo's surface now was a fallow realm of savage tribes, the deep underwater canyons still held thousands of battered, abandoned spacecraft and other debris from when this section of Galaxy Four had been a center of civilization and commerce. Several dozen of those derelicts had been reactivated in order to confuse *Streaker*'s foe—a fearsome Jophur battleship—but some of the hulks must have failed to haul their bulk out of the sea when the time came. Those failures were doomed to drift aimlessly underwater until their engines gave out and they tumbled once more to the murky depths.

As for the rest, there had been no word whether *Streaker's* ploy succeeded beyond luring the awful dreadnought away toward deep space. At least Jijo seemed a friendlier place without it. For now.

"We should have expected this," the archaeologist continued. "When I got away from the shoreline surf noise, I thought I could detect at least three of the hulks, bumping around out there almost randomly. It seems kind of sad, when you think about it. Ancient ships, not worth salvaging when the Buyur abandoned Jijo, waiting in an icy, watery tomb for just one last chance to climb back out to space. Only these couldn't make it. They're stranded here."

"Like us," Makanee murmured.

Tkett seemed not to hear.

"In fact, I'd like to go back out there and try to catch up with one of the derelicts."

"Whatever for?"

Tkett's smile was still charming and infectious . . . which made it seem even crazier, under these circumstances.

"I'd like to use it as a scientific instrument," the big neo-dolphin said.

Makanee felt utterly confirmed in her diagnosis.

PEEPOE

Captivity wasn't as bad as she had feared.

It was worse.

Among natural, presapient dolphins on Earth, small groups of young males would sometimes conspire to isolate a fertile female from the rest of the pod, herding her away for private copulation—especially if she was about to enter heat. By working together, they might monopolize her matings and guarantee their own reproductive success, even if she clearly preferred a local alpha-ranked male instead. That ancient behavior pattern persisted in the wild because, while native *Tursiops* had both traditions and a kind of feral honor, they could not quite grasp or carry out the concept of *law*—a code that all must live by, because the entire community has a memory transcending any individual.

But modern, uplifted *amicus* dolphins did have law! And when young hoodlums occasionally let instinct prevail and tried that sort of thing back home, the word for it was *rape*. Punishment was harsh. As with human sexual predators, just one of the likely outcomes was permanent sterilization.

Such penalties worked. After three centuries, some of the less desirable primal behaviors were becoming rare. Yet, uplifted neo-dolphins were still a young race. Great stress could yank old ways back to the fore, from time to time.

And we Streakers *have sure been under stress.*

Unlike some devolved crewmates, whose grip on modernity and rational thought had snapped under relentless pressure, Zhaki and Mopol suffered only partial atavism. They could still talk and run complex equipment, but they were no longer the polite, almost shy junior ratings she had met when *Streaker* first set out from Earth under Captain Creideiki, before the whole cosmos seemed to implode all around the dolphin crew.

In abstract, she understood the terrible strain that had put them in this state. Perhaps, if she were offered a chance to kill Zhaki and Mopol, Peepoe might call that punishment a bit too severe.

On the other fin, sterilization was much too good for them.

Despite sharing the same culture, and a common ancestry as Earth mammals, dolphins and humans looked at many things differently. Peepoe felt more annoyed at being kidnapped than violated. More pissed off than traumatized. She wasn't able to stymie their lust completely, but with various tricks—playing on their mutual jealousy and feigning illness as often as she could—Peepoe staved off unwelcome attentions for long stretches.

But if I find out they murdered Kaa, I'll have their entrails for lunch.

Days passed and her impatience grew. Peepoe's real time limit was fast approaching. *My contraception implant will expire. Zhaki and his pal have fantasies about populating Jijo with their descendants, but I like this planet far too much to curse it that way.*

She vowed to make a break for it. But how?

Sometimes she would swim to a channel between the two remote islands where her kidnappers had brought her, and drift languidly, listening. Once, Peepoe thought she made out something faintly familiar—a clicking murmur, like a distant crowd of dolphins. But it passed, and she dismissed it as wishful thinking. Zhaki and Mopol had driven the sled at top speed for days on end with her strapped to the back, before they halted by this strange archipelago and removed her sonar-proof blindfold. She had no idea how to find her way back to the old coastline where Makanee's group had settled.

When I do escape these two idiots, I may be consigning myself to a solitary existence for the rest of my days.

Oh well, you wanted the life of an explorer. There could be worse fates than swimming all the way around this beautiful world, eating exotic fish when you're hungry, riding strange tides and listening to rhythms no dolphin ever heard before.

The fantasy had a poignant beauty—though ultimately, it made her lonely and sad.

The ocean echoed with anger, engines, and strange noise.

Of course it was all a matter of perspective. On noisy Earth, this would have seemed eerily quiet. Terran seas buzzed with a cacophony of traffic, much of it caused by her own kind as neo-dolphins gradually took over managing seventy percent of the home planet's surface. In mining the depths, or tending fisheries, or caring for those sacredly complex simpletons called whales, more and more responsibilities fell to uplifted 'fins using boats, subs, and other equipment. Despite continuing efforts to reduce the racket, home was still a raucous place.

In comparison, Jijo appeared as silent as a nursery. Natural sound-carrying thermal layers reported waves crashing on distant shorelines and intermittent groaning as minor quakes rattled the ocean floor. A myriad buzzes, clicks, and whistles came from Jijo's own subsurface fauna—fishy creatures that evolved here, or were introduced by colonizing leaseholders like the Buyur, long ago. Some distant rumbles even hinted at *large* entities, moving slowly, languidly across the deep . . . perhaps pondering long, slow thoughts.

As days stretched to weeks, Peepoe learned to distinguish Jijo's organic rhythms . . . punctuated by a grating din whenever one of the boys took the sled for a joy ride, stampeding schools of fish, or careening along with the load indicator showing red. At this rate the machine wouldn't stand up much longer, though Peepoe kept hoping one of them would break his fool neck first.

With or without the sled, Zhaki and Mopol could track her down if she just swam away. Even when they left piles of dead fish to ferment atop some floating reeds, and got drunk on the foul carcasses, the two never let their guard down long enough to let her steal the sled. It seemed that one or the other was always sprawled across the saddle. Since dolphins only sleep one brain hemisphere at a time, it was impossible to take them completely by surprise.

* * *

Then, after two months of captivity, she detected signs of something drawing near.

Peepoe had been diving in deeper water for a tasty kind of local soft-shell crab when she first heard it. Her two captors were having fun a kilometer away, driving their speedster in tightening circles around a panicked school of bright silvery fishoids. But when she dived through a thermal boundary layer, separating warm water above from cool saltier liquid below—the sled's racket abruptly diminished.

Blessed silence was one added benefit of this culinary exploit. Peepoe had been doing a lot of diving lately.

This time, however, the transition did more than spare her the sled's noise for a brief time. It also brought forth a *new* sound. A distant rumble, channeled by the shilly stratum. With growing excitement, Peepoe recognized the murmur of an engine! Yet the rhythms struck her as unlike any she had heard on Earth or elsewhere.

Puzzled, she kicked swiftly to the surface, filled her lungs with fresh air, and dived back down to listen again.

This deep current offers an excellent sonic grove, she realized, *focusing sound rather than diffusing it. Keeping the vibrations well confined. Even the sled's sensors may not pick it up for quite a while.*

Unfortunately, that also meant she couldn't tell how far away the source was.

If I had a breather unit . . . if it weren't necessary to keep surfacing for air . . . I could swim a great distance masked by this thermal barrier. Otherwise, it seems hopeless. They can use the sled's monitors on long-range scan to detect me when I broach and exhale.

Peepoe listened for a while longer, and decided.

I think it's getting closer . . . but slowly. The source must still be far away. If I made a dash now, I won't get far before they catch me.

And yet, she daren't risk Mopol and Zhaki picking up the new sound. If she must wait, it meant keeping them distracted till the time was right.

There was just one way to accomplish that.

Peepoe grimaced. Rising toward the surface, she expressed disgust with a vulgar Trinary demi-haiku.

* *May sun roast your backs,*
  * *And hard sand scrape your bottoms,*
    * *Til you itch madly. . . .*

* *. . . as if with a good case of the clap!* *

MAKANEE

She sent a command over her neural link, ordering the tools of her harness to fold away into streamlined recesses, signaling that the inspection visit was over.

The chief of the kiqui, a little male with purple gill-fringes surrounding a squat head, let himself drift a meter or so under the water's surface, spreading all four webbed hands in a gesture of benediction and thanks. Then he thrashed around to lead his folk away, back toward the nearby island where they made their home. Makanee felt satisfaction as she watched the small formation of kicking amphibians, clutching their stone-tipped spears.

Who would have thought that we dolphins, youngest registered sapient race in the Civilization of Five Galaxies, would become patrons ourselves, just a few centuries after humans started uplifting us.

The kiqui were doing pretty well on Jijo, all considered. Soon after being released onto a coral atoll, not far offshore, they started having babies.

Under normal conditions, some elder race would find an excuse to take the kiqui away from dolphins, fostering such a promising presapient species into one of the rich, ancient family lines that ruled oxygen-breathing civilization in the Five Galaxies. But here on Jijo things were different. They were cut off from starfaring culture, a vast bewildering society of complex rituals and obligations that made the ancient Chinese Imperial court seem like a toddler's sandbox, by comparison. There were advantages and disadvantages to being a castaway from all that.

On the one hand, Makanee would no longer have to endure the constant tension of running away from huge oppressive battlefleets or aliens whose grudges went beyond earthling comprehension.

On the other hand, there would be no more performances of symphony, or opera, or bubble-dance for her to attend.

Never again must she endure disparaging sneers from exalted patron-level beings, who considered dolphins little more than bright beasts.

Nor would she spend another lazy Sunday in her snug apartment in cosmopolitan Melbourne-Under, with multicolored fish cruising the coral garden just outside her window while she munched salmon patties and watched an all-dolphin cast perform *Twelfth Night* on the telly.

Makanee was marooned, and would likely remain so for the rest of her life, caring for two small groups of sea-based colonists, hoping they could remain hidden from trouble until a new era came. An age when both might resume the path of uplift.

Assuming some metal nutrient supplements could be arranged, the kiqui had apparently transplanted well. Of course, they must be taught tribal taboos against overhunting any one species of local fauna, so their presence would not become a curse on this world. But the clever little amphibians already showed some understanding, expressing the concept in their own, emphatic demi-speech.

Rare is precious!
Not eat-or-hurt rare/precious things/fishes/beasts!
Only eat/hunt many-of-a-kind!

She felt a personal stake in this. Two years ago, when *Streaker* was about to depart poisonous Kithrup, masked inside the hulk of a crashed Thennanin warship, Makanee had taken it upon herself to beckon a passing tribe of kiqui with some of their own recorded calls, attracting the curious group into *Streaker's* main airlock just before the surrounding water boiled with exhaust from revving engines. What then seemed an act of simple pity turned into a kind of love affair, as the friendly little amphibians became favorites of the crew. Perhaps now their race might flourish in a kinder place than unhappy Kithrup. It felt good to know *Streaker* had accomplished at least one good thing out of its poignant, tragic mission.

As for dolphins, how could anyone doubt their welcome in Jijo's warm sea? Once you learned which fishoids were edible and which to avoid, life became a matter of snatching whatever you wanted to eat, then splashing and lolling about. True, she missed her *holoson* unit, with its booming renditions of whale chants and baroque chorales. But here she could take pleasure in listening to an ocean whose sonic purity was almost as fine as its vibrant texture.

Almost . . .

Reacting to a faint sensation, Makanee swung her sound-sensitive jaw around, casting right and left.

There! She heard it again. A distant rumbling that might have escaped notice amid the underwater cacophony on Earth. But here it seemed to stand out from the normal swish of current and tide.

Her patients—the several dozen dolphins whose stress-atavism had reduced them to infantile innocence—called such infrequent noises *boojums*. Or else they used a worried upward trill in Primal Delphin—one that stood for strange monsters of the deep. Sometimes the far-off grumbles did seem to hint at some huge, living entity, rumbling with basso-profundo pride, complacently assured that it owned the entire vast sea. Or else it might be just frustrated engine noise from some remnant derelict machine, wandering aimlessly in the ocean's immensity.

Leaving the kiqui atoll behind, Makanee swam back toward the underwater dome where she and Brookida, plus a few still-sapient nurses, maintained a small base to keep watch over their charges. It would be good to get out of the weather for a while. Last night she had roughed it, keeping an eye on her patients during a rain squall. An unpleasant, wearying experience.

We modern neo-fins are spoiled. It will take us years to get used to living in the elements, accepting whatever nature sends our way, without complaining or making ambitious plans to change the way things are.

That human side of us must be allowed to fade away.

PEEPOE

She made her break around midmorning the next day.

Zhaki was sleeping off a hangover near a big mat of driftweed, and Mopol was using the sled to harass some unlucky penguinlike seabirds, who were trying to feed their young by fishing near the island's lee shore. It seemed a good chance to slip away, but Peepoe's biggest reason for choosing this moment was simple. Diving deep below the thermal layer, she found that the distant rumble had peaked, and appeared to have turned away, diminishing with each passing hour.

It was now, or never.

Peepoe had hoped to steal something from the sled first. A utensil harness perhaps, or a breather tube, and not just for practical reasons. In normal life, few neo-dolphins spent a single day without using cyborg tools, controlled by cable links to the brain's temporal lobes. But for months now her two would-be "husbands" hadn't let her connect to anything at all! The neural tap behind her left eye ached from disuse.

Unfortunately, Mopol nearly always slept on the sled's saddle, barely ever leaving except to eat and defecate.

He'll be desolated when the speeder finally breaks down, she thought, taking some solace from that.

So the decision was made, and Ifni's dice were cast. She set out with all the gifts and equipment nature provided—completely naked—into an uncharted sea.

For Peepoe, escaping captivity began unlike any human novel or fantasholo. In such stories, the heroine's hardest task was normally the first part, sneaking away. But here Peepoe faced no walls, locked rooms, dogs, or barbed wire. Her "guards" let her come and go as she pleased. In this case, the problem wasn't getting started, but winning a big enough head start before Zhaki and Mopol realized she was gone.

Swimming under the thermocline helped mask her movements at first. It left her vulnerable to detection only when she went up for air. But she could not keep it up for long. The *Tursiops* genus of dolphins weren't deep divers by nature, and her speed at depth was only a third what it would be skimming near the surface.

So, while the island was still above the horizon behind her, Peepoe stopped slinking along silently below and instead began her dash for freedom in earnest—racing toward the sun with an endless series of powerful back archings and fluke-strokes, going deep only occasionally to check her bearings against the far-off droning sound.

It felt exhilarating to slice through the wavetops, flexing her body for all it was worth. Peepoe remembered the last time she had raced along this way—with Kaa by her side—when Jijo's waters had seemed warm, sweet, and filled with possibilities.

Although she kept low-frequency sonar clickings to a minimum, she did allow herself some short-range bursts, checking ahead for obstacles and toying with the surrounding water, bouncing reflections off patches of sun-driven convection, letting echoes wrap themselves around her like rippling memories. Peepoe's sonic transmissions remained soft and close—no louder than the vibrations given off by her kicking tail—but the patterns grew more complex as her mind settled into the rhythms of movement. Before long, returning wavelets of her own sound meshed with those of current and tide, overlapping to make phantom sonar images.

Most of these were vague shapes, like the sort that one felt swarming at the edges of a dream. But in time several fell together, merging into something larger. The composite echo seemed to bend and thrust when she did—as if a spectral companion now swam nearby, where her squinting eye saw only sunbeams in an empty sea.

Kaa, she thought, recognizing a certain unique zest whenever the wraith's bottle nose flicked through the waves.

Among dolphins, you did not have to die in order to come back as a ghost . . . though it helped. Sometimes the only thing required was vividness of spirit—and Kaa surely was, or had been, vivid.

Or perhaps the nearby sound-effigy fruited solely from Peepoe's eager imagination.

In fact, dolphin logic perceived no contradiction between those two explanations. Kaa's essence might really be there—and not be—at the same time. Whether real or mirage, she was glad to have her lover back where he belonged—by her side.

I've missed you, she thought.

Anglic wasn't a good language for phantoms. No human grammar was. Perhaps that explained why the poor bipeds so seldom communed with their beloved lost.

Peepoe's visitor answered in a more ambiguous, innately delphin style.

> * Till the seaweed's flower*
> > * Shoots forth petals made of moonbeams*
> > > * I will swim with you *

Peepoe was content with that. For some unmeasured time, it seemed as if a real companion, her mate, swam alongside, encouraging her efforts, sharing the grueling pace. The water divided before her, caressing her flanks like a real lover.

Then, abruptly, a new sound intruded. A distant grating whine that threatened to shatter all illusions.

Reluctantly, she made herself clamp down, silencing the resonant chambers surrounding her blowhole. As her own sonar vibrations ceased, so did the complex echoes, and her phantom comrade vanished. The waters ahead seemed to go black as Peepoe concentrated, listening intently.

There it was.

Coming from behind her. Another engine vibration, this one all too familiar, approaching swiftly as it skimmed across the surface of the sea.

They know, she realized. *Zhaki and Mopol know I'm gone, and they're coming after me.*

Peepoe wasted no more time. She bore down with her flukes, racing through the waves faster than ever. Stealth no longer mattered. Now it was a contest of speed, endurance, and luck.

TKETT

It took him most of a day and the next night to get near the source of the mysterious disturbance, pushing his power sled as fast as he dared. Makanee had ordered Tkett not to overstrain the engine, since there would be no replacements when it wore out.

"Just be careful out there," the elderly dolphin physician had urged, when giving permission for this expedition. *"Find out what it is . . . whether it's one of the derelict spacecraft that Suessi and the engineers brought back to life as decoys. If so, don't mess with it! Just come back and report. We'll discuss where to go from there."*

Tkett did not have disobedience in mind. At last not explicitly. But if it really was a starship making the low, uneven grumbling noise, a host of possibilities presented themselves. What if it proved possible to board the machine and take over the makeshift controls that *Streaker*'s crew had put in place?

Even if it can't fly, it's cruising around the ocean. I could use it as a submersible and visit the Great Midden.

That vast undersea trench was where the Buyur had dumped most of the dross of their mighty civilization, when it came time for them to abandon Jijo and return its surface to fallow status. After packing up to leave, the last authorized residents of this planet used titanic machines to scrape away their cities, then sent all their buildings and other works tumbling into an abyss where the slow grinding of tectonic plates would draw the rubble inward, melting and reshaping new ores to be used by others in some future era, when Jijo was opened for legal settlement once again.

To an archaeologist, the Midden seemed the opportunity of a lifetime.

I'd learn so much about the Buyur! We might examine whole classes of tools that no Earthling has ever seen. The Buyur were rich and powerful. They could afford the very best in the Civilization of Five Galaxies, while we Terran newcomers can only buy the dregs. Even stuff the Buyur threw away—their toys and broken trinkets— could provide valuable data for the Terragens Council.

Tkett wasn't a complete fool. He knew what Makanee and Brookida thought of him.

They consider me crazy to be optimistic about going home. To believe any of us will see Earth again, or let the industrial tang of

*its waters roll through our open jaws, or once more surf the riptides
of Ranga Roa.*

Or give a university lecture. Or dive through the richness of a
worldwide data network, sharing ideas with a fecund civilization at
light-speed. Or hold challenging conversations with others who share
your intellectual passions.

He had signed aboard *Streaker* to accompany Captain Creideiki
and a neo-dolphin intellectual elite in the greatest mental and physical
adventure any group of cetaceans ever faced—the ultimate test of
their new sapient race. Only now Creideiki was gone, presumed dead,
and Tkett had been ejected by *Streaker*'s new commander, exiled from
the ship at its worst moment of crisis. Makanee might feel complacent
over being put ashore as "nonessential" personnel, but it churned
Tkett's guts to be spilled into a warm, disgustingly placid sea while
his crewmates were still out there, facing untold dangers among the
bleeding stars.

A voice broke in from the outside, before his thoughts could spiral
any further toward self-pity.

> # *give me give me GIVE ME*
> # *snout-smacking pleasure*
> # *of a good fight!* #

That shrill chatter came from the sled's rear compartment, causing
Tkett's flukes to thrash in brief startlement. It was easy to forget about
his quiet passenger for long stretches of time. Chissis spoke seldom, and
then only in the throwback protolanguage, Primal Delphin.

Tkett quashed his initial irritation. After all, Chissis was unwell.
Like several dozen other members of the crew, her modern mind had
crumpled under the pressure of *Streaker*'s long ordeal, taking refuge
in older ways of thought. One had to make allowances, even though
Tkett could not imagine how it was possible for anyone to abandon
the pleasures of rationality, no matter how insistently one heard the
call of the Whale Dream.

After a moment, Tkett realized that her comment had been more
than just useless chatter. Chissis must have sensed some meaning
from his sonar clicks. Apparently she understood and shared his re-
sentment over Gillian Baskin's decision to leave them behind on Jijo.

"You'd rather be back in space right now, wouldn't you?" he
asked. "Even though you can't read an instrument panel anymore?
Even with Jophur battleships and other nasties snorting down *Streaker*'s neck, closing in for the kill?"

His words were in Underwater Anglic. Most of the reverted could barely comprehend it anymore. But Chissis squawled from the platform behind Tkett, throwing a sound burst that sang like the sled's engine, thrusting ever forward, obstinately defiant.

smack the Jophur! smack the sharks!
  # SMACK THEM! #

Accompanying her eager-repetitive message squeal, there came a sonar crafted by the fatty layers of her brow, casting a brief veil of illusion around Tkett. He briefly visualized Chissis, joyfully ensconced in the bubble nose of a *lamprey*-class torpedo, personally piloting it on course toward a huge alien cruiser, penetrating all of the cyberdisruptive fields that Galactic spacecraft used to stave off digital guidance systems, zeroing in on her target with all the instinct and native agility that dolphins inherited from their ancestors.

Loss of speech apparently had not robbed some "reverted" ones of either spunk or ingenuity. Tkett sputtered laughter. Gillian Baskin had made a real mistake leaving this one behind! Apparently you did not need an engineer's mind in order to have the heart of a warrior.

"No wonder Makanee let you come along on this trip," he answered. "You're a bad influence on the others, aren't you?"

It was her turn to emit a laugh—sounding almost exactly like his own. A ratchetting raspberry-call that the masters of uplift had left alone. A deeply cetacean shout that defied the sober universe for taking so many things too seriously.

Faster faster FASTER!
  # Engines call us . . .
    # offering a ride . . . #

Tkett's tail thrashed involuntarily as her cry yanked something deep within. Without hesitating, he cranked up the sled's motor, sending it splashing through the foamy white-tops, streaking toward a mysterious object whose song filled the sea.

PEEPOE

She could sense Zhaki and Mopol closing in from behind. They might be idiots, but they knew what they wanted and how to pilot their sled at maximum possible speed without frying the bearings. Once alerted to her escape attempt, they cast ahead using the machine's deep-range sonar. She felt each loud *ping* like a small bite along her backside. By now they knew exactly where she was. The noise was meant to intimidate her.

It worked. *I don't know how much longer I can keep on,* Peepoe thought while her body burned with fatigue. Each body-arching plunge through the waves seemed to take more out of her. No longer a joyful sensation, the ocean's silky embrace became a clinging drag, taxing and stealing her hard-won momentum, making Peepoe earn each dram of speed over and over again.

In comparison, the hard vacuum of space seemed to offer a better bargain. What you bought, you got to keep. Even the dead stayed on trajectory, tumbling ever onward. Space travel tended to promote belief in "progress," a notion that old-style dolphins used to find ridiculous, and still had some trouble getting used to.

I should be fairly close to the sound I was chasing . . . whatever's making it. I'd be able to tell, if only those vermin behind me would turn off the damned sonar and let me listen in peace!

Of course the pinging racket was meant to disorient her. Peepoe only caught occasional sonic-glimpses of her goal, and then only by diving below the salt-boundary layer, something she did as seldom as possible, since it always slowed her down.

The noise of the sled's engine sounded close. Too damned close. At any moment Zhaki and Mopol might swerve past to cut her off, then start spiraling inward, herding her like some helpless sea animal while they chortled, enjoying their macho sense of power.

I'll have to submit . . . bear their punishment . . . put up with bites and whackings till they're convinced I've become a good cow.

None of that galled Peepoe as much as the final implication of her recapture.

I guess this means I'll have to kill the two of them.

It was the one thing she'd been hoping to avoid. Murder among dolphins had been rare in olden times, and the genetic engineers worked to enhance this innate distaste. Anyway, Peepoe had wished to avoid making the choice. A clean getaway would have sufficed.

She didn't know how she'd do it. Not yet.

But I'm still a Terragens officer, while they relish considering themselves wild beasts. How hard can it be?

Part of her knew that she was drifting, fantasizing. This might even be the way her subconscious was trying to rationalize surrendering the chase. She might as well give up now, before exhaustion claimed all her strength.

No! I've got to keep going.

Peepoe let out a groan as she redoubled her efforts, bearing down with intense drives of her powerful tail flukes. Each moment that she held them off meant just a little more freedom. A little more dignity.

It couldn't last, of course. Though it felt exultant and defiant to give it one more hard push, the burst of speed eventually faded as her body used up its last reserves. Quivering, she fell at last into a languid glide, gasping for air to fill her shuddering lungs.

Too bad. I can hear it . . . the underwater thing I was seeking . . . not far away now.

But Zhaki and Mopol are closer still. . . .

What took Peepoe some moments to recall was that the salt-thermal barrier deadened sound from whatever entity was cruising the depths below. For her to hear it now, however faintly, meant that it had to be—

A tremor rocked Peepoe. She felt the waters *bulge* around her, as if pushed aside by some massive creature, far under the ocean's surface. Realization dawned, even as she heard Zhaki's voice, shouting gleefully only a short distance away.

It's right below me. The thing! It's passing by, down there in the blackness.

She had only moments to make a decision. Judging from cues in the water, it was both very large and very far beneath her. Yet Peepoe felt nowhere near ready to attempt a deep dive while each breath still sighed with ragged pain.

She heard and felt the sled zoom past, spotting her two tormentors sprawled on the machine's back, grinning as they swept by dangerously close. Instinct made her want to turn away and flee, or else go below for as long as her lungs could hold out. But neither move would help, so she stayed put.

They'll savor their victory for a little while, she thought, hoping they were confident enough not to use the sled's stunner on her. Anyway, at this short range, what could she do?

It was hard to believe they hadn't picked up any signs of the behemoth by now. Stupid, single-minded males, they had concentrated all of their attention on the hunt for her.

Zhaki and Mopol circled around her twice, spiraling slowly closer, leering and chattering.

Peepoe felt exhausted, still sucking air for her laboring lungs. But she could afford to wait no longer. As they approached for the final time, she took one last, body-stretching gasp through her blowhole, arched her back, and flipped over to dive nose first into the deep.

At the final instant, her tail flukes waved at the boys. A gesture that she hoped they would remember with galling regret.

Blackness consumed the light and she plunged, kicking hard to gain depth while her meager air supply lasted. Soon, darkness welcomed Peepoe. But on passing the boundary layer, she did not need illumination anymore. Sound guided her, the throaty rumble of something huge, moving gracefully and complacently through a world where sunshine never fell.

TKETT

He had several reasons to desire a starship, even one that was unable to fly. It could offer a way to visit the Great Midden, for instance, and explore its wonders. A partly operational craft might also prove useful to the Six Races of Jijo, whose bloody war against Jophur aggressors was said to be going badly ashore.

Tkett also imagined using such a machine to find and rescue Peepoe.

The beautiful dolphin medic—one of Makanee's assistants—had been kidnapped shortly before *Streaker* departed. No one held out much hope of finding her, since the ocean was so vast and the two dolphin felons—Mopol and Zhaki—had an immensity to conceal her in. But that gloomy calculation assumed that searchers must travel by sled! A *ship* on the other hand—even a wreck that had lain on an ocean-floor garbage dump for half a million years—could cover a lot more territory and listen with big underwater sonaphones, combing for telltale sounds from Peepoe and her abductors. It might even be possible to sift the waters for Earthling DNA traces. Tkett had heard of such techniques available for a high price on Galactic markets. Who knew what wonders the fabled Buyur took for granted on their elegant starcraft?

Unfortunately, the trail kept going hot and cold. Sometimes he picked up murmurs that seemed incredibly close—channeled by watery layers that focused sound. Other times they vanished altogether.

Frustrated, Tkett was willing to try anything. So when Chissis started getting agitated, squealing in Primal that a *great beast* prowled to the southwest, he willingly turned the sled in the direction she indicated.

And soon he was rewarded. Indicators began flashing on the control panel, and down his neural-link cable, connecting the sled to an implanted socket behind his left eye. In addition to a surge of noise, mass displacement anomalies suggested something of immense size was moving ponderously just ahead, and perhaps a hundred meters down.

"I guess we better go find out what it is," he told his passenger, who clicked her agreement.

go chase go chase go chase ORCAS!

She let out squawls of laughter at her own cleverness. But minutes later, as they plunged deeper into the sea—both listening and peering down the shaft of the sled's probing headlights—Chissis ceased chuckling and became silent as a tomb.

Great Dreamers! Tkett stared in awe and surprise at the object before them. It was unlike any starship he had ever seen before. Sleek metallic sides seemed to go on and on forever as the titanic machine trudged onward across the sea floor, churning up mud with thousands of shimmering, crystalline legs!

As if sensing their arrival, a mammoth hatch began irising open— in benign welcome, he hoped.

No resurrected starship. Tkett began to suspect he had come upon something entirely different.

PEEPOE

Her rib cage heaved.

Peepoe's lungs filled with a throbbing ache as she forced herself to dive ever deeper, much lower than would have been wise, even if she weren't fatigued to the very edge of consciousness.

The sea at this depth was black. Her eyes made out nothing. But that was not the important sense, underwater. Sonar clicks, emitted from her brow, grew more rapid as she scanned ahead, using her sensitive jaw as an antenna to sift the reflections.

It's big. . . . she thought when the first signs returned.

Echo outlines began coalescing, and she shivered.

It doesn't sound like metal. The shape . . . seems less artificial than something—

A thrill of terror coursed her spine as she realized that the thing ahead had outlines resembling a gigantic living creature! A huge mass of fins and trailing tentacles, resembling some monster from the stories dolphin children would tell each other at night, secure in their rookeries near one of Earth's great port cities. What lay ahead of

Peepoe, swimming along well above the canyon floor, seemed bigger and more intimidating than the giant squid who fought *Physeter* sperm whales, mightiest of all the cetaceans.

And yet, Peepoe kept arching her back, pushing hard with her flukes, straining ever downward. Curiosity compelled her. Anyway, she was closer to the creature than the sea surface, where Zhaki and Mopol waited.

I might as well find out what it is.

Curiosity was just about all she had left to live for.

When several tentacles began reaching for her, the only remaining question in her mind was about death.

I wonder who I'll meet on the other side.

MAKANEE

The dolphins in the pod—her patients—all woke about the same time from their afternoon siesta, screaming.

Makanee and her nurses joined Brookida, who had been on watch, swimming rapid circles around the frightened reverts, preventing any of them from charging in panic across the wide sea. Slowly, they all calmed down from a shared nightmare.

It was a common enough experience back on Earth, when unconscious sonar clicks from two or more sleeping dolphins would sometimes overlap and interfere, creating false echoes. The ghost of something terrifying. That most cetaceans sleep just one brain hemisphere at a time did not help. In a way, that seemed only to make the dissonance more eerie, and the fallacious sound-images more credibly scary.

Most of the patients were inarticulate, emitting only a jabber of terrified Primal squeals. But there were a dozen or so borderline cases who might even recover their full faculties someday. One of these moaned nervously about *Tkett* and a *city of spells.*

Another one chittered nervously, repeating over and over, the name of Peepoe.

TKETT

Well, at least the machine has air inside, he thought. *We can survive here, and learn more.*

In fact, the huge underwater edifice—bigger than all but the largest starships—seemed rather accommodating, pulling back metal walls as the little sled entered a spacious airlock. The floor sank in order to provide a pool for Tkett and Chissis to debark from their tight cockpits and swim around. It felt good to get out of the cramped confines, even though Tkett knew that coming inside might be a mistake.

Makanee's orders had been to do an inspection from the outside, then hurry home. But that was when they expected to find one of the rusty little spacecraft that *Streaker's* engineers had resurrected from some sea floor dross-pile. As soon as Tkett saw *this* huge cylindrical thing, churning along the sea bottom on a myriad caterpillar legs that gleamed like crystal stalks, he knew that nothing on Jijo could stand in the way of his going aboard.

Another wall folded aside, revealing a smooth channel that stretched ahead—water below and air above—beckoning the two dolphins down a hallway that shimmered as it continued transforming before their eyes. Each panel changed color with the glimmering luminescence of octopus skin, seeming to convey *meaning* in each transient, flickering shade. Chissis thrashed her tail nervously as objects kept slipping through seams in the walls. Sometimes these featured a camera lens at the end of an articulated arm, peering at them as they swam past.

Not even the Buyur could afford to throw away something as wonderful as this, Tkett thought, relishing a fantasy of taking this technology home to Earth. At the same time, the mechanical implements of his tool harness quivered, responding to nervous twitches that his brain sent down the neural tap. He had no weapons that would avail in the slightest if the owners of this place proved to be hostile.

The corridor spilled at last into a wide chamber with walls and ceiling that were so corrugated he could not estimate its true volume. Countless bulges and spires protruded inward, half of them submerged, and the rest hanging in midair. All were bridged by cables and webbing that glistened like spiderwebs lined with dew. Many of the branches carried shining spheres or cubes or dodecahedrons that dangled like geometric fruit, ranging from half a meter across to twice the length of a bottlenose dolphin.

Chissis let out a squawl, colored with fear and awe.

coral that bites! coral bites bites!
    # See the critters, stabbed by coral! #

When he saw what she meant, Tkett gasped. The hanging "fruits" were mostly transparent. They contained things that *moved* . . . creatures who writhed or hopped or ran in place, churning their arms and legs within the confines of their narrow compartments.

Adaptive optics in his right eye whirred, magnifying and zooming toward one of the crystal-walled containers. Meanwhile, his brow cast forth a stream of nervous sonar clicks—useless in the air—as if trying to penetrate this mystery with yet another sense.

I don't believe it!

He recognized the shaggy creature within a transparent cage.

Ifni! It's a hoon. A miniature hoon!

Scanning quickly, he found individuals of other species . . . four-legged urs with their long necks whipping nervously, like muscular snakes . . . minuscule traeki that resembled their Jophur cousins, looking like tapered stacks of doughnuts, piled high . . . and tiny versions of wheeled g'Keks, spinning their hubs madly, as if they were actually going somewhere. In fact, every member of the Commons of Six Races of Jijo—fugitive clans that had settled this world illegally during the last two thousand years—could be seen here, represented in lilliputian form.

Tkett's spine shuddered when he made out several cells containing slim bipedal forms. Bantamweight human beings, whose race had struggled against lonely ignorance on old Terra for so many centuries, nearly destroying the world before they finally matured enough to lead the way toward the true sapiency for the rest of Earthclan. Before Tkett's astonished eye, these members of the patron race were now reduced to leaping and cavorting within the confines of dangling crystal spheres.

PEEPOE

Death would not be so mundane . . . nor hurt in such familiar ways. When she began regaining consciousness, there was never any doubt which world this was. The old cosmos of life and pain.

Peepoe remembered the sea monster, an undulating behemoth of fins, tendrils, and phosphorescent scales, more than a kilometer long and nearly as wide, flapping wings like a manta ray as it glided well above the seafloor. When it reached up for her, she never thought of fleeing toward the surface, where mere enslavement waited. Peepoe was too exhausted by that point, and too transfixed by the images—both sonic and luminous—of a true leviathan.

The tentacle was gentler than expected, in grabbing her unresisting body and drawing it toward a widening beaklike maw. As she was pulled between a pair of jagged-edged jaws, Peepoe had let blackness finally claim her, moments before the end. The last thought to pass through her head was a Trinary haiku.

> * Arrogance is answered
>   * When each of us is reclaimed.
>   * Rejoin the food chain!

Only there turned out to be more to her life, after all. Expecting to become pulped food for huge intestines, she wakened instead, surprised to find herself in another world.

A *blurry* world, at first. She lay in a small pool, that much was evident. But it took moments to restore focus. Meanwhile, out of the pattern of her bemused sonar clickings, a reflection seemed to mold itself, unbidden, surrounding Peepoe with Trinary philosophy.

> * In the turning of life's cycloid,
>   * Pulled by sun and moon insistence,
> * Once a springtime storm may toss you,
>   * Over reefs that have no channel,
> * Into some lagoon untraveled,
>   * Where strange fishes, spiny-poisoned,
> * Taunt you, forlorn, isolated . . .

It wasn't an auspicious thought-poem, and Peepoe cut it off sharply, lest such stark sonic imagery trigger panic. The Trinary fog clung hard, though. It dissipated only with fierce effort, leaving a sense of dire warning in its wake.

Rising to the surface, Peepoe lifted her head and inspected the pool, lined by a riot of dense vegetation. Dense jungle stretched on all sides, brushing the rough-textured ceiling and cutting off small inhabitants, from flying insectoids to clambering things that peered at her shyly from behind sheltering leaves and shadows.

A habitat, she realized. Things lived here, competed, preyed on each other, died, and were recycled in a familiar ongoing synergy. The largest starships often contained ecological life-support systems, replenishing both food and oxygen supplies in the natural way.

But this is no starship. It can't be. The huge shape I saw could never fly. It was a sea beast, meant for the underwater world. It must have been alive!

Well, was there any reason why a gigantic animal could not keep an ecology going inside itself, like the bacterial cultures that helped Peepoe digest her own food?

So now what? Am I supposed to take part in all of this somehow? Or have I just begun a strange process of being digested?

She set off with a decisive push of her flukes. A dolphin without tools wasn't very agile in an environment like this. Her monkey-boy cousins—humans and chimps—would do better. But Peepoe was determined to explore while her strength lasted.

A channel led out of the little pool. Maybe something more interesting lay around the next bend.

TKETT

One of the spiky branches started moving, bending and articulating as it bent lower toward the watery surface where he and Chissis waited. At its tip, one of the crystal "fruits" contained a quadrupedal being—an urs whose long neck twisted as she peered about with glittering black eyes.

Tkett knew just a few things about this species. For example, they hated water in its open liquid form. Also the females were normally as massive as a full-grown human, yet this one appeared to be as small as a diminutive urrish male, less than twenty centimeters from nose to tail. Back in the Civilization of Five Galaxies, urs were known as great engineers. Humans didn't care for their smell (the feeling was mutual), but interactions between the two starfaring clans had been cordial. Urs weren't among the persecutors of Earthclan.

Tkett had no idea why an offshoot group of urs came to this world, centuries ago, establishing a secret and illegal colony on a world that had been declared off-limits by the Migration Institute. As one of the Six Races, they now galloped across Jijo's prairies, tending herds and working metals at forges that used heat from fresh volcanic lava pools. To find one here, under the sea, left him boggled and perplexed.

The creature seemed unaware of the dolphins who watched from nearby. From certain internal reflections, Tkett guessed that the glassy confines of the enclosure were transparent only in one direction. Flickering scenes could be made out, playing across the opposite internal walls. He glimpsed hilly countryside covered with swaying grass. The little urs galloped along, as if unencumbered and unenclosed.

The sphere dropped closer, and Tkett saw that it was choked with innumerable microscopic *threads* that crisscrossed the little chamber. Many of these terminated at the body of the urs, especially the bottoms of her flashing hooves.

Resistance simulators! Tkett recognized the principle, though he had never seen such a magnificent implementation. Back on Earth, humans and chimps would sometimes put on full bodysuits and VR helmets before entering chambers where a million needles made up the floor, each one computer controlled. As the user walked along a fictitious landscape, depicted visually in goggles he wore, the needles would rise and fall, simulating the same rough terrain underfoot. Each of these small crystal containers apparently operated in the same way, but with vastly greater texture and sophistication. So many tendrils pushing, stroking or stimulating each patch of skin, could feign wind blowing through urrish fur, or simulate the rough sensation of holding a tool . . . perhaps even the delightful rub and tickle of mating.

Other stalks descended toward Tkett and Chissis, holding many more virtual-reality fruits, each one containing a single individual. All of Jijo's sapient races were present, though much reduced in stature. Chissis seemed especially agitated to see small humans that ran about, or rested, or bent in apparent concentration over indiscernible tasks. None seemed aware of being observed.

It all felt horribly creepy, yet the subjects did not give an impression of lethargy or unhappiness. They seemed vigorous, active, interested in whatever engaged them. Perhaps they did not even know the truth about their peculiar existence.

Chissis snorted her uneasiness, and Tkett agreed. Something felt weird about the way these microenvironments were being paraded before the two of them, as if the mind—or minds—controlling the whole vast apparatus had some point it was trying to make, or some desire to communicate.

Is the aim to impress us?

He wondered about that, then abruptly realized what it must be about.

. . . *all of Jijo's sapient races were present* . . .

In fact, that was no longer true. Another species of thinking beings now dwelled on this world, the newest one officially sanctioned by the Civilization of Five Galaxies.

Neo-dolphins.

Oh, certainly the reverts like poor Chissis were only partly sapient anymore. And Tkett had no illusions about what Dr. Makanee thought of his own mental state. Nevertheless, as stalk after stalk bent to present its fruit before the two dolphins, showing off the miniature beings within—all of them busy and apparently happy with their existence—he began to feel as if he was being *wooed.*

"Ifni's boss . . ." he murmured aloud, amazed at what the great machine appeared to be offering. "It wants us to become part of all this!"

PEEPOE

A village of small grass huts surrounded the next pool she entered.

Small didn't half describe it. The creatures who emerged to swarm around the shore stared at her with wide eyes, set in skulls less than a third of normal size.

They were humans and hoons, mostly . . . along with a few traeki and a couple of glavers . . . all races whose full-sized cousins lived just a few hundred kilometers away, on a stretch of Jijo's western continent called The Slope.

As astonishing as she found these lilliputians, they stared in even greater awe at her. *I'm like a whale to them,* she realized, noting with some worry that many of them brandished spears or other weapons.

She heard a chatter of worried conversation as they pointed at her long gray bulk. That meant their brains were large enough for speech. Peepoe noted that the creatures' heads were out of proportion to their bodies, making the humans appear rather childlike . . . until you saw the men's hairy, scarred torsos, or the women's breasts, pendulous with milk for hungry babies. Their rapid jabber grew more agitated by the moment.

I'd better reassure them, or risk getting harpooned.

Peepoe spoke, starting with Anglic, the wolfling tongue most used on Earth. She articulated the words carefully with her gene-modified blowhole.

"Hello, f-f-folks! How are you doing today?"

That got a response, but not the one she hoped for. The crowd onshore backed away hurriedly, emitting upset cries. This time she thought she made out a few words in a time-shifted dialect of Galactic Seven, so she tried again in that language.

"Greetings! I bring you news of peaceful arrival and friendly intentions!"

This time the crowd went nearly crazy, leaping and cavorting in excitement, though whether it was pleasure or indignation seemed hard to tell at first.

Suddenly, the mob parted and went silent as a figure approached from the line of huts. It was a hoon, taller than average among these midgets. He wore an elaborate headdress and cape, while the dyed throat-sac under his chin flapped and vibrated to a sonorous beat. Two human assistants followed, one of them beating a drum. The rest of the villagers then did an amazing thing. They all dropped to their knees and covered their ears. Soon Peepoe heard a rising murmur.

They're humming. I do believe they're trying not to hear what the big guy is saying!

At the edge of the pool, the hoon lifted his arms and began chanting in a strange version of Galactic Six.

"Spirits of the sky, I summon thee by name . . . Kataranga!

"Spirits of the water, I beseech thy aid . . . Dupussien!

"By my knowledge of your secret names, I command thee to gather and surround this monster. Protect the people of the True Way!"

This went on for a while. At first Peepoe felt bemused, as if she were watching a documentary about some ancient human tribe, or the Prob'shers of planet Horst. Then she began noticing something strange. Out of the jungle, approaching on buzzing wings, there began appearing a variety of insectlike creatures. At first just a few, then more. Flying zigzag patterns toward the chanting shaman, they started gathering in a spiral-shaped swarm.

Meanwhile, ripples in the pool tickled Peepoe's flanks, revealing another convergence of ingathering beasts—this time swimmers— heading for the point of shore nearest the summoning hoon.

I don't believe this, she thought. It was one thing for a primitive priest to invoke the forces of nature. It was quite another to sense those forces *responding* quickly, unambiguously, and with ominous threatening behavior.

Members of both swarms, the fliers and the swimmers, began making darting forays toward Peepoe. She felt several sharp stings on her dorsal fin, and some more from below, on her ventral side.

They're attacking me!

Realization snapped her out of a bemused state.

Time to get out of here, she thought, as more of the tiny native creatures could be seen arriving from all directions.

Peepoe whirled about, sending toward shore a wavelet that interrupted the yammering shaman, sending him scurrying backward with a yelp. Then, in a surge of eager strength, she sped away from there.

TKETT

Just when he thought he had seen enough, one of the crystal fruits descended close to the pool where he and Chissis waited, stopping only when it brushed the water, almost even with their eyes. The walls vibrated for a moment . . . then split open!

The occupant, a tiny g'Kek with spindly wheels on both sides of a tapered torso, rolled toward the gap, regarding the pair of dolphins with four eyestalks that waved as they peered at Tkett. Then the creature spoke in a voice that sounded high-pitched but firm, using thickly accented Galactic Seven.

"We were aware that new settlers had come to this world. But imagine our surprise to find that this time they are swimmers, who found us before we found them! No summoning call had to be sent through the Great Egg. No special collector robots dispatched to pick up volunteers from shore. How clever of you to arrive just in time, only days and weeks before the expected moment when this universe splits asunder!"

Chissis panted nervously, filling the sterile chamber with rapid clicks while Tkett bit the water hard with his narrow jaw.

"I . . . have no idea what y-y-you're talking about," he stammered in reply.

The miniature g'Kek twisted several eyestalks around each other. Tkett had an impression that it was consulting or communing with some entity elsewhere. Then it rolled forward, unwinding the stalks to wave at Tkett again.

"If an explanation is what you seek, then that is what you shall have."

PEEPOE

The interior of the great leviathan seemed to consist of one leaf-shrouded pool after another, in a complex maze of little waterways. Soon quite lost, Peepoe doubted she would ever be able to find her way back to the thing's mouth.

Most of the surrounding areas consisted of dense jungle, though there were also rocky escarpments and patches of what looked like rolling grassland. Peepoe had also passed quite a few villages of little folk. In one place an endless series of ramps and flowing bridges had been erected through the foliage, comprising what looked like a fantastic scale-model roller coaster, interspersed amid the dwarf trees. Little g'Keks could be seen zooming along this apparatus of wooden planks and vegetable fibers, swerving and teetering on flashing wheels.

Peepoe tried to glide past the shoreline villages innocuously, but seldom managed it without attracting some attention. Once, a war party set forth in chase after her, riding upon the backs of turtlelike creatures, shooting tiny arrows and hurling curses in quaint-sounding jargon she could barely understand. Another time, a garishly attired urrish warrior swooped toward her from above, straddling a flying lizard whose wings flapped gorgeously and whose mouth belched small but frightening bolts of flame! Peepoe retreated, overhearing the little urs continue to shout behind her, challenging the "sea monster" to single combat.

It seemed she had entered a world full of beings who were as suspicious as they were diminished in size. Several more times, shamans and priests of varied races stood at the shore, gesturing and shouting rhythmically, commanding hordes of beelike insects to sting and pursue her until she fled beyond sight. Peepoe's spirits steadily sank . . . until at last she arrived at a broad basin where many small boats could be seen, cruising under brightly painted sails.

To her surprise, this time the people aboard shouted with amazed pleasure upon spotting her, not fear or wrath! With tentative but rising hope, she followed their beckonings to shore where, under the battlements of a magnificently ornate little castle, a delegation descended to meet her beside a wooden pier.

Their apparent leader, a human wearing gray robes and a peaked hat, grinned as he gestured welcome, enunciating in an odd but lilting version of Anglic.

"Many have forgotten the tales told by the First. But we know you, oh noble dolphin! You are remembered from tales passed down since the beginning! How wonderful to have you come among us now, as the Time of Change approaches. In the name of the Spirit Guides, we offer you our hospitality and many words of power!"

Peepoe mused on everything she had seen and heard.

Words, eh? Words can be a good start.

She had to blow air several times before her nervous energy dispelled enough to speak.

"All right then. Can you start by telling me what in Ifni's name is going on here?"

⊞ GIVERS OF WONDER

A Time of Changes comes. Worlds are about to divide.

Galaxies that formerly were linked by shortcuts of space and time will soon be sundered. The old civilization—including all the planets you came from—will no longer be accessible. Their ways won't dominate this part of the cosmos anymore.

Isolated, this island realm of one hundred billion stars (formerly known as Galaxy Four) will soon develop its own destiny, fostering a bright new age. It has been foreseen that Jijo will provide the starting seed for a glorious culture, unlike any other. The six . . . and now seven! . . . sapient species who came sneaking secretly to this world as refugees—skulking in order to hide like criminals on a forbidden shore—will prosper beyond all their wildest imagings. They will be cofounders of something great and wonderful. Forerunners of all the starfaring races who may follow in this fecund stellar whirlpool.

But what *kind* of society should it be? One that is a mere copy of the noisy, bickering, violent conglomeration that exists back in "civilized" space? One based on crude so-called sciences? Physics, cybernetics, and biology? We have learned that such obsessions lead to soullessness. A humorless culture, operated by reductionists who measure the cost/benefit ratios of everything and know the value of nothing!

There must be something better.

Indeed, consider how the *newest* sapient races—fresh from uplift—look upon their world with a childlike sense of wonder! What if that feeling could be made to last?

To those who have just discovered it, the *power of speech itself* is glorious. A skill with words seems to hold all the potency anyone should ever need! Still heedful of their former animal ways, these infant species often use their new faculty of self-expression to perceive patterns that are invisible to older "wiser" minds.

Humans were especially good at this, during the long ages of their lonely abandonment, on isolated Earth. They had many names for their systems of wondrous cause and effect, traditions that arose in a myriad landbound tribes. But nearly all of these systems shared certain traits in common:

> —a sense that the world is made of spirits, living in each stone or brook or tree.

—an eager willingness to perceive all events, even great storms and the movements of planets, as having a *personal* relationship with the observer.

—a conviction that nature can be swayed by those favored with special powers of sight, voice, or mind, raising those elite ones above other mere mortals.

—a profound belief in the power of words to persuade and control the world.

"Magic" was one word that humans used for this way of looking at the universe.

We believe it is a better way, offering drama, adventure, vividness, and romance.

Yet, magic can take many forms. And there is still some dispute over the details. . . .

ALTERNATING VIEWS OF TEMPTATION

Tkett found the explanation bizarre and perplexing at first. How did it relate to this strange submersible machine whose gut was filled with crystal fruit, each containing an intelligent being who leaped about and seemed to focus fierce passion on things only he or she could see?

Still, as an archaeologist he had some background studying the tribal human past, so eventually a connection clicked in his mind.

"You . . . you are using technology to give each individual a private world! B-but there's more to it than that, isn't there? Are you saying that every hoon, or human, or traeki inside these crystal c-containers gets to cast *magic spells*? They don't just manipulate false objects by hand, and see tailored illusions . . . they also shout incantations and have the satisfaction of watching them come *true*?"

Tkett blinked several times, trying to grasp it all.

"Take that woman over there." He aimed his rostrum at a nearby cube wherein a female human grinned and pointed amid a veritable cloud of resistance threads.

"If she has an enemy, can she mold a clay figure and stick pins in it to cast a spell of pain?"

The little g'Kek spun its wheels before answering emphatically.

"True enough, oh perceptive dolphin! Of course she has to be creative. Talent and a strong will are helpful. And she must adhere to the accepted lore of her simulated tribe."

"Arbitrary rules, you mean."

The eye stalks shrugged gracefully. "Arbitrary, but elegant and consistent. And there is another requirement.

"Above all, our user of magic must intensely believe."

Peepoe blinked at the diminutive wizard standing on the nearby dock, in the shadow of a fairy-tale castle.

"You mean people in this place can command the birds and insects and other beasts using words alone?"

She had witnessed it happen dozen of times, but to hear it explained openly like this felt strange.

The gray-cloaked human nodded, speaking rapidly, eagerly. "Special words! The power of secret *names*. Terms that each user must keep closely guarded."

"But—"

"Above all, most creatures will only obey those with inborn talent. Individuals who possess great force of will. Otherwise, if they heeded everybody, where would be the awe and envy that lie at the very heart of sorcery? If *anyone* can do a thing, it soon loses all worth. A miracle palls when it becomes routine.

"It is said that technology used to be like that, back in the Old Civilization. Take what happened soon after Earth-humans discovered how to fly. Soon *everybody* could soar through the sky, and people took the marvel for granted. How tragic! That sort of thing does not happen here. We preserve wonder like a precious resource."

Peepoe sputtered.

"But all this—" She flicked her jaws, spraying water toward the jungle and the steep, fleshy cliffs beyond. "All of this smacks of technology! That absurd fire-breathing dragon, for instance. Clearly bioengineered! Somebody set up this whole thing as . . . as an . . ."

"As an experiment?" the gray-clad mage conceded with a nod. His beard shook as he continued with eager fire in his piping voice.

"That has never been secret! Ever since our ancestors were selected, from among Jijo's landbound Six Races, to come dwell below the sea in smaller but mightier bodies, we knew that one purpose would be to help the Buyur fine-tune their master plan."

Tkett reared back in shock, churning water with his flukes. He stared at the many-eyed creature who had been explaining this weird chamber-of-miniatures.

"The B-Buyur! They left Jijo half a million years ago. How could they even know about human culture, let alone set up this elaborate—"

"Of course the answer to that question is simple" replied the little g'Kek, peering with several eyestalks from its cracked crystal shell. "Our Buyur lords never left! They have quietly observed and guided this process ever since the first ship of refugees slunk down to Jijo, preparing for the predicted day when natural forces would sever all links between Galaxy Four and the others."

"But—"

"The great evacuation of starfaring clans from Galaxy Four—half an eon ago—made sure that no other techno-sapients remained in this soon-to-be isolated starry realm. So it will belong to *our* descendants, living in a culture far different than the dreary one our ancestors belonged to."

Tkett had heard of the Buyur, of course—among the most powerful members of the Civilization of Five Galaxies, and one of the few elder races known for a sense of humor . . . albeit a strange one. It was said that they believed in *long* jokes, that took ages to plan and execute.

Was that because the Buyur found Galactic culture stodgy and stifling? (Most Earthlings would agree.) Apparently they foresaw all of the changes and convulsions that were today wracking the linked starlanes, and began preparing millennia ago for an unparalleled opportunity to put their own stamp on an entirely new branch of destiny.

Peepoe nodded, understanding part of it at last.

"This leviathan . . . this huge organic beast . . . isn't the only experimental container cruising below the waves. There are others! Many?"

"Many," confirmed the little gray-bearded human wizard. "The floating chambers take a variety of forms, each accommodating its own colony of sapient beings. Each habitat engages its passengers in a life that is rich with magic, though in uniquely different ways.

"Here, for instance, we sapient beings experience physically active lives, in a totally real environment. It is the wild creatures around us who were altered! Surely you have heard that the Buyur were master gene-crafters? In this experimental realm, each insect, fish, and flower knows its own unique and secret *name*. By learning and properly uttering such names, a mage like me can wield great power."

Tkett listened as the cheerful g'Kek explained the complex experiment taking place in the chamber of crystalline fruits.

"In *our* habitat, each of us gets to live in his or her own world— one that is rich, varied, and physically demanding, even if it is mostly a computer-driven simulation. Within such an ersatz reality every one of us can be the lead magician in a society or tribe of lesser peers.

Or the crystal fruits can be linked, allowing shared encounters between equals. Either way, it is a vivid life, filled with more excitement
than the old way of so-called engineering.

"A life in which the mere act of believing can have power, and
wishing sometimes makes things come true!"

Peepoe watched the gray magician stroke his beard while describ-
ing the range of Buyur experiments.

"There are many other styles, modes, and implementations being
tried out, in scores of other habitats. Some emphasize gritty 'reality,'
while others go so far as to eliminate physical form entirely, encoding
their subjects as digital personae in wholly computerized worlds."

Downloading personalities. Peepoe recognized the concept. *It was
tried back home and never caught on, even though boosters said it
ought to, logically.*

"There is an ultimate purpose to all of these experiments," the
human standing on the nearby pier explained, like a proselyte eager
for a special convert. "We aim to find exactly the right way to implement a new society that will thrive across the starlanes of Galaxy
Four, once separation is complete and all the old hyperspatial transit
paths are gone. When this island whirlpool of a hundred billion stars
is safe at last from interference by the Old Civilization, it will be time
to start our own. One that is based on a glorious new principle.

"By analyzing the results of each experimental habitat, the noble
Buyur will know exactly how to implement a new realm of magic and
wonders. Then the age of the true miracles can begin."

Listening to this, Peepoe shook her head.

"You don't sound much like a rustic feudal magician. I just bet
you're something else, in disguise.

"Are *you* a Buyur?"

The g'Kek bowed within its crystal shell. "That's a very good guess,
my dolphin friend. Though of course the real truth is complicated. A
real Buyur would weigh more than a metric ton and somewhat resemble an Earthling frog!"

"Nevertheless you—" Tkett prompted.

"I have the honor of serving as a spokesman-intermediary. . . ."

". . . to help persuade you dolphins—the newest promising colonists on Jijo—that joining us will be your greatest opportunity for
vividness, adventure, and a destiny filled with marvels!"

The little human wizard grinned, and Peepoe realized that the others nearby must not have heard or understood a bit of it. Perhaps they wore earplugs to protect themselves against the power of the mage's words. Or else Anglic was rarely spoken, here. Perhaps it was a "language of power."

Peepoe also realized—she was both being tested and offered a choice.

Out there in the world, we few dolphin settlers face an uncertain existence. Makanee has no surety that our little pod of reverts will survive the next winter, even with help from the other colonists ashore. Anyway, the Six Races have troubles of their own, fighting Jophur invaders.

She had to admit that this offer had tempting aspects. After experiencing several recent Jijo storms, Peepoe could see the attraction of bringing all the other *Streaker* exiles aboard some cozy undersea habitat—presumably one with bigger stretches of open water—and letting the Buyur perform whatever technomagic it took to reduce dolphins in size so they would fit their new lives. How could that be any worse than the three years of cramped hell they had all endured aboard poor *Streaker*?

Presumably someday, when the experiments were over, her descendants would be given back their true size, after they had spent generations learning to weave spells and cast incantations with the best of them.

Oh, we could manage that, she thought. *We dolphins are good at certain artistic types of verbal expression. After all, what is Trinary but our own special method of using sound to persuade the world? Talking it into assuming vivid sonic echoes and dreamlike shapes? Coaxing it to make sense in our own cetacean way?*

The delicious temptation of it all reached out to Peepoe.

What is the alternative? Assuming we ever find a way back to civilization, what would we go home to? A gritty fate that at best offers lots of hard work, where it can take half a lifetime just to learn the skills you need to function usefully in a technological society.

Real life isn't half as nice as the tales we first hear in storybooks. Everybody learns at some point that it's a disappointing world out there—a universe where good is seldom purely handsome and evil doesn't obligingly identify itself with red glowing eyes. A complex society filled with trade-offs and compromises, as well as committees and political opponents who always have much more power than you think they deserve.

Who wouldn't prefer a place where the cosmos might be talked into giving you what you want? Or where wishing sometimes makes things true?

"We already have two volunteers from your esteemed race," the g'Kek spokesman explained, causing Tkett to quiver in surprise. With a flailing of eyestalks, the wheeled figure commanded that a hologram appear, just above the water's surface.

Tkett at once saw two large male dolphins lying calmly on mesh hammocks while tiny machines scurried all over them, spinning webs of some luminescent material. Chissis, long-silent and brooding, abruptly recognized the pair, and shouted Primal recognition.

> # *Caught! Caught in nets as they deserved!*
> # *Foolish Zhaki—Nasty Mopol!* #

"Ifni!" Tkett commented. "I think you're right. But what's being done to them?"

"They have already accepted our offer," said the little wheeled intermediary.

"Soon those two will dwell in realms of holographic and sensual delights, aboard a different experimental station than this one. Their destiny is assured, and let me promise you—they will be happy."

"You're sure those two aren't *here* aboard this vessel, near me?" Peepoe asked nervously, watching Zhaki and Mopol undergo their transformation via a small image that the magician had conjured with a magic phrase and a wave of one hand.

"No. Your associates followed a lure to one of our neighboring experimental cells—to their senses it appeared to be a 'leviathan' resembling one of your Earthling blue whales. Once they had come aboard, preliminary appraisal showed that their personalities will probably thrive best in a world of pure fantasy.

"They eagerly accepted this proposal."

Peepoe nodded, shocked only at her own lack of emotion—either positive or negative—toward this final disposal of her tormentors. They were gone from her life, and that was all she really cared about. Let Ifni decide whether their destination qualified as permanent imprisonment, or a strange kind of heaven.

Well, now they can have harems of willing cows, to their hearts' content, she thought. *Good riddance.*

Anyway, she had other quandaries to focus on, closer at hand.

"What've you got p-planned for me?"

The gray wizard spread his arms in eager consolation.

"Nothing frightening or worrisome, oh esteemed dolphin-friend! At this point we are simply asking that you choose!

"Will you join us? No one is coerced. But how could anybody refuse? If one lifestyle does not suit you, pick another! Select from a wide range of enchanted worlds, and further be assured that your posterity will someday be among the magic-welders who establish a new order across a million suns."

Tkett saw implications that went beyond the offer itself. The plan of the Buyur—its scope and the staggering range of their ambition— left him momentarily dumbfounded.

They want to set up a whole, galaxy-spanning civilization, based on what they consider to be an ideal way of life. Someday soon, after this "Time of Changes" has ruptured the old intergalaxy links, the Buyur will be free from any of the old constraints of law and custom that dominated oxygen-breathing civilization for the last billion years.

Then, out of this planet there will spill a new wave of starships, crewed by the Seven Races of Jijo, commanded by bold captains, wizards, and kings . . . a mixture of themes from old-time science fiction and fantasy . . . pouring forth toward adventure! Over the course of several ages, they will fight dangers, overcome grave perils, discover and uplift new species. Eventually, the humans and urs and traekis and others will become revered leaders of a galaxy that is forever filled with high drama.

In this realm, boredom will be the ultimate horror. Placidity the ultimate crime. The true masters—the Buyur—will see to that.

Like the Great Oz, manipulating levers behind a curtain, the Buyur will use their high technology to provide every wonder. Ask for dragons? They will gene-craft or manufacture them. Secret factories will build sea monsters and acid-mouthed aliens, ready for battle.

It will be a galaxy run by special-effects wizards! A perpetual theme park, whose inhabitants use magic spells instead of engineering to get what they want. Conjurers and monarchs will replace tedious legislatures, impulse will supplant deliberation, and lists of secret names will substitute for physics.

Nor will our descendants ask too many questions, or dare to pull back the curtain and expose Oz. Those who try won't have descendants!

Cushioned by hidden artifice, in time people will forget nature's laws.

They will flourish in vivid kingdoms, forever setting forth heroically, returning triumphally, or dying bravely . . . but never asking why.

Tkett mused on this while filling the surrounding water with intense sprays of sonar clicks. Chissis, who had clearly not understood much of the g'Kek's convoluted explanation, settled close by, rolling her body through the complex rhythms of Tkett's worried thoughts.

Finally, he felt that he grasped the true significance of it all.

Tkett swam close to the crystal cube, raising one eye until it was level with the small representative of the mighty Buyur.

"I think I get what's going on here," he said.

"Yes?" the little g'Kek answered cheerfully. "And what is your sage opinion, oh dolphin-friend. What do you think of this great plan?"

Tkett lifted his head high out of the water, rising up on churning flukes, emitting chittering laughter from his blowhole. At the same time, a sardonic Trinary haiku floated from his clicking brow.

> * *Sometimes sick egos*
>   * *foster in their narrow brains*
>   * *Really stupid jokes!*

Some aspects of the offer were galling, such as the smug permanence of Buyur superiority in the world to come. Yet, Peepoe felt tempted.

After all, what else awaits us here on Jijo? Enslavement by the Jophur? Or the refuge of blessed dimness that the sages promise, if we follow the so-called Path of Redemption? Doesn't this offer a miraculous way out of choosing between those two unpalatable destinies?

She concentrated hard to sequester her misgivings, focusing instead on the advantages of the Buyur plan. And there were plenty, such as living in a cosmos where hidden technology made up for nature's mistakes. After all, wasn't it cruel of the Creator to make a universe where so many fervent wishes were ignored? A universe where prayers were mostly answered—if at all—within the confines of the heart? Might the Buyur plan rectify this oversight for billions and trillions? For all the inhabitants of a galaxy-spanning civilization! Generosity on such a scale was hard to fathom.

She compared this ambitious goal with the culture waiting for the *Streaker* survivors, should they ever make it back home to the other four galaxies, where myriad competitive, fractious races bickered endlessly. Overreliant on an ancient Library of unloving technologies, they seldom sought innovation or novelty. Above all, the desires of individual beings were nearly always subordinated to the driving needs of nation, race, clan, and philosophy.

Again, the Buyur vision looked favorable compared to the status quo.

A small part of her demanded: *Are these our only choices? What if we could come up with alternatives that go beyond simpleminded—*

She quashed the question fiercely, packing it off to far recesses of her mind.

"I would love to learn more," she told the gray wizard. "But what about my comrades? The other dolphins who now live on Jijo? Won't you need them, too?"

"In order to have a genetically viable colony, yes," the spokesman agreed. "If you agree to join us, we will ask you first to go and persuade others to come."

"Just out of curiosity, what would happen if I refused?"

The sorcerer shrugged. "Your life will resume much as it would have, if you had never found us. We will erase all conscious memory of this visit, and you will be sent home. Later, when we have had a chance to refine our message, emissaries will come visit your pod of dolphins. But as far as you know, you will hear the proposal as if for the first time."

"I see. And again, those who refuse will be memory-wiped . . . and again each time you return. Kind of gives you an advantage in proselytizing, doesn't it?"

"Perhaps. Still, no one is compelled to join against their will." The little human smiled. "So, what is your answer? Will you help convey our message to your peers? We sense that you understand and sympathize with the better world we aim toward. Will you help enrich the Great Stew of Races with wondrous dolphin flavors?"

Peepoe nodded. "I will carry your vision to the others."

"Excellent! In fact, you can start without even leaving this pool! For I can now inform you that a pair of your compatriots already reside aboard one of our nearby vessels . . . and those two seem to be having trouble appreciating the wondrous life we offer."

"Not Zhaki and Mopol!" Peepoe pushed back with her ventral fins, clicking nervously. She wanted nothing further to do with them.

"No, no," the magician assured. "Please, wait calmly while we open a channel between ships and all will become clear."

TKETT

"Hello, Peepoe," he said to the wavering image in front of him. "I'm glad you look well. We were all worried sick about you. But I figured when we saw Zhaki and Mopol you must be nearby."

The holo showed a sleek female dolphin, looking exquisite but tired in a jungle-shrouded pool, beside a miniature castle. Tkett could tell a lot about the style of "experiment" aboard her particular vessel, just by observing the crowd of natives gathered by the shore. Some of them were dressed as armored knights, riding upon rearing steeds, while gaily attired peasants doffed their caps to passing lords and ladies. It was a far different approach than the crystal fruits that hung throughout *this* vessel—semitransparent receptacles where individuals lived permanently immersed in virtual realities.

And yet, the basic principle was similar.

"Hi, Tkett," Peepoe answered. *"Is that Chissis with you? You both doing all right?"*

"Well enough, I guess. Though I feel like the victim of some stupid fraternity practical—"

"Isn't it exciting?" Peepoe interrupted, cutting off what Tkett had been about to say. *"Across all the ages, visionaries have come up with countless utopian schemes. But this one could actually w-w-work!"*

Tkett stared back at her, unable to believe he was hearing this.

"Oh yeah?" he demanded. "What about free will?"

"The Buyur will provide whatever your will desires."

"Then how about truth!"

"There are many truths, Tkett. Countless vivid subjective interpretations will thrive in a future filled with staggering diversity."

"Subjective, exactly! That's an ancient and d-despicable perversion of the word *truth,* and you know it. Diversity is wonderful, all right. There may indeed be many cultures, many art forms, even many styles of wisdom. But *truth* should be about finding out what's really real, what's repeatable and verifiable, whether it suits your fancy or not!"

Peepoe sputtered a derisive raspberry.

"Where's the fun in that?"

"Life isn't just about having fun, or getting whatever you want!" Tkett felt his guts roil, forcing sour bile up his esophagus. "Peepoe, there's such a thing as growing up! Finding out how the world actually works, despite the way you think things *ought* to be. Objectivity means I accept that the universe doesn't revolve around me."

"In other words, a life of limitations."

"That we overcome with knowledge! With new tools and skills."

"Tools made of dead matter, designed by committees, mass-produced and sold on shop counters."

"Yes! Committees, teams, organizations, and enterprises, all of them made up of individuals who have to struggle every day with their egos in order to cooperate with others, making countless compromises along the way. It ain't how things happen in a child's fantasy. It's not what we yearn for in our secret hearts, Peepoe. I know that! But it's how adults get things done.

"Anyway, what's wrong with buying miracles off a shop counter? So we take for granted wonders that our ancestors would've given their tail fins for. Isn't that what they'd have wanted for us? You'd prefer a world where the best of everything is kept reserved for wizards and kings?"

Tkett felt a sharp jab in his side. The pain made him whirl, still bitterly angry, still flummoxed with indignation.

"What is it!" he demanded sharply of Chissis, even though the little female could not answer.

She backed away from his bulk and rancor, taking a snout-down submissive posture. But from her brow came a brief burst of caustic Primal.

> \# idiot idiot idiot idiot
> > \# idiots keep talking human talk-talk
> \# while the sea tries to teach \#

Tkett blinked. Her phrasings were sophisticated, almost lucid. In fact, it was a lot like a simple Trinary chiding-poem, that a dolphin mother might use with her infant.

Through an act of hard self-control, he forced himself to consider. *While the sea tries to teach . . .*

It was a common dolphin turn of phrase, implying that one should listen *below* the surface, to meanings that lay hidden.

He whirled back to examine the hologram, wishing it had not been designed by beings who relied so much on sight, and ignored the subtleties of sound transmission.

"Think about it, Tkett," Peepoe went on, as if their conversation had not been interrupted. *"Back home, we dolphins are the youngest client race of an impoverished, despised clan, in danger of being conquered or rendered extinct at any moment. Yet now we're being*

offered a position at the top of a new pantheon, just below the Buyur themselves.

"What's more, we'd be good at this! Think about how dolphin senses might extend the range of possible magics. Our sound-based dreams and imagery. Our curiosity and reckless sense of adventure! And that just begins to hint at the possibilities when we finally come into our own. . . ."

Tkett concentrated on sifting the background. The varied pulses, whines and clicks that melted into the ambience whenever any neo-dolphin spoke. At first it seemed Peepoe was emitting just the usual mix of nervous sonar and blowhole flutters.

Then he picked out a single, floating phrase . . . in ancient Primal . . . that interleaved itself amid the earnest logic of sapient speech.

 # sleep on it sleep on it sleep on it sleep on it #

At first the hidden message confused him. It seemed to support the rest of her argument. So then why make it secret?

Then another meaning occurred to him.

Something that even the puissant Buyur might not have thought of.

PEEPOE

Her departure from the habitat was more gay and colorful than her arrival.

Dragons flew by overhead, belching gusts of heat that were much friendlier than before. Crowds of boats, ranging from canoes to bejeweled galleys pulled by sweating oarsmen, accompanied Peepoe from one pool to the next. Ashore, local wizards performed magnificent spectacles in her honor, to the awed wonder of gazing onlookers, while Peepoe swam gently past amid formations of fish whose scales glittered unnaturally bright.

With six races mixing in a wild variety of cultural styles, each village seemed to celebrate its own uniqueness in a profusion of architectural styles. The general attitude seemed both proud and fiercely competitive. But today all feuds, quests, and noble campaigns had been put aside in order to see her off.

"See how eagerly we anticipate the success of your mission," the gray magician commented as they reached the final chamber. In a starship, this space would be set aside for an airlock, chilly and metallic. But here, the breath of a living organism sighed all around them as the great maw opened, letting both wind and sunshine come suddenly pouring through.

Nice of them to surface like this, sparing me the discomfort of a long climb out the abyss.

"Tell the other dolphins what joy awaits them!" the little mage shouted after Peepoe as she drifted past the open jaws, into the light.

"Tell them about the vividness and adventure! Soon days of experimentation will be over, and all of this will be full-sized, with a universe lying before us!"

She pumped her flukes in order to rear up, looking back at the small gray figure in a star-spangled gown, who smiled as his arms spread wide, causing swarms of obedient bright creatures to hover above his head, converging to form a living halo.

"I will tell them," she assured.

Then Peepoe whirled and plunged into the cool sea, setting off toward a morning rendezvous.

TKETT

He came fully conscious again, only to discover with mild surprise that he was already swimming fast, leaping and diving through the ocean's choppy swells, propelled by powerful, rhythmic fluke-strokes.

Under other circumstances it might have been disorienting to wake up in full motion. Except that a pair of dolphins flanked Tkett, one on each side, keeping perfect synchrony with his every arch and leap and thrust. That made it instinctively easy to literally swim in his sleep.

How long has this been going on?

He wasn't entirely sure. It felt like perhaps an hour or two. Perhaps longer.

Behind him, Tkett heard the low thrum of a sea sled's engine, cruising on low power as it followed the three of them on autopilot.

Why aren't we using the sled? he wondered. Three could fit, in a pinch. And that way they could get back to Makanee quicker, to report that . . .

Stale air exchanged quickly for fresh as he breached, performing each move with flawless precision, even as his mind roiled with unpleasant confusion.

. . . to report that Mopol and Zhaki are dead.

We found Peepoe, safe and well, wandering the open ocean.

As for the "machine" noises we were sent to investigate . . .

Tkett felt strangely certain there was a story behind all that. A story that Peepoe would explain later, when she felt the time was right.

Something wonderful, he recited, without quite knowing why. A flux of eagerness seemed to surge out of nowhere, priming Tkett to be receptive when she finally told everyone in the pod about the good news.

He could not tell why, but Tkett felt certain that more than just the sled was following behind them.

"Welcome back to the living," Peepoe greeted in crisp Underwater Anglic, after their next breaching.

"Thanks I . . . seem to be a bit muddled right now."

"Well, that's not too surprising. You've been half-asleep for a long time. In fact, one might say you *half slept* through something really important."

Something about her words flared like a glowing spark within him—a triggered release that jarred Tkett's smooth pace through the water. He reentered the water at a wrong angle, smacking his snout painfully. It took a brief struggle to get back in place between the two females, sharing the group's laminar rhythm.

I . . . slept. I slept on it.

Or rather, half of him had done so.

It slowly dawned on him why that was significant.

There aren't many water-dwellers in the Civilization of Five Galaxies, he mused, reaching for threads that had lain covered under blankets of repose. *I guess the Buyur never figured . . .*

A shiver of brief pain lanced from right to left inside his skull, as if a part of him that had been numb just came to life.

The Buyur!

Memories flowed back unevenly, at their own pace.

They never figured on a race of swimmers discovering their experiments, hidden for so long under Jijo's ocean waves. They had no time to study us. To prepare before the encounter.

And they especially never took into account the way a cetacean's brain works.

An air-breathing creature who lives in the sea has special problems. Even after millions of years evolving for a wet realm, dolphins still faced a never-ending danger of drowning. Hence, sleep was no simple matter.

One way they solved the problem was to sleep one brain hemisphere at a time.

Like human beings, dolphins had complex internal lives, made up of many temporary or persistent subselves that must somehow reconcile under an overall persona. But this union was made even more problematic when human genetic meddlers helped turn fallow dolphins into a new sapient race. All sorts of quirks and problems lay rooted in the hemispheric divide. Sometimes information stored in one side was frustratingly hard to get at from the other.

And sometimes that proved advantageous.

The side that knew about the Buyur—the one that had slept while amnesia was imposed on the rest—had much less language ability than the other half of Tkett's brain. Because of this, only a few concepts could be expressed in words at first. Instead, Tkett had to replay visual and sonic images, reinterpreting and extrapolating them, holding a complex conversation of inquiry between two sides of his whole self.

It gave him a deeper appreciation for the problems—and potential—of people like Chissis.

I've been an unsympathetic bastard, he realized.

Some of this thought emerged in his sonar echoes as an unspoken apology. Chissis brushed against him the next time their bodies flew through the air, and her touch carried easy forgiveness.

"So," Peepoe commented when he had taken some more time to settle his thoughts, "is it agreed what we'll tell Makanee?"

Tkett summed up his determination.

"We'll tell everything . . . and then some!"

Chissis concurred.

Tell them tell them
   # *Orca-tricksters*
Promise fancy treats
   # *But take away freedom!* #

Tkett chortled. There was a lot of Trinary elegance in the little female's Primal burst—a transition from animal-like emotive squawks toward the kind of expressiveness she used to be so good at, back when she was an eager researcher and poet, before three years of hell aboard *Streaker* hammered her down. Now a corner seemed to be turned. Perhaps it was only a matter of time till this crewmate re-

turned to full sapiency . . . and all the troubles that would accompany
that joy.

"Well," Peepoe demurred, "by one way of looking at things, the
Buyur seem to be offering us more freedom. Our descendants would
experience a wider range of personal choices. More power to achieve
their wishes. More dreams would come true."

"As fantasies and escapism," Tkett dismissed. "The Buyur would
turn everybody into egotists . . . solipsists! In the real world, you have
to grow up eventually, and learn to negotiate with others. Be part of
a culture. Form teams and partnerships. Ifni, what does it take to
have a good *marriage*? Lots of hard work and compromises, leading to
something better and more complicated than either person could've
imagined!"

Peepoe let out a short whistle of surprise.

"Why, Tkett! In your own prudish, tight-vented way, I do believe
you're a romantic."

Chissis shared Peepoe's gentle, teasing laughter, so that it penetrated him in stereo, from both sides. A human might have blushed.
But dolphins can barely conceal their emotions from each other, and
seldom try.

"Seriously," he went on. "I'll fight the Buyur because they would
keep us in a playpen for eons to come, denying us the right to mature
and learn for ourselves how the universe ticks. Magic may be more
romantic than science. But science is *honest* . . . and it works.

"What about you, Peepoe? What's your reason?"

There was a long pause. Then she answered with astonishing
vehemence.

"I can't stand all that *kings and wizards* dreck! Should somebody rule because his father was a pompous royal? Should all the
birds and beasts and fish obey you just because you know some
secret words that you won't share with others? Or on account of
the fact that you've got a loud voice and your egotistic *will* is bigger
than others'?

"I seem to recall we fought free of such idiotic notions ages ago,
on Earth . . . or at least humans did. They never would've helped us
dolphins get to the stars if they hadn't broken out of those sick
thought patterns first.

"You want to know why I'll fight them, Tkett? Because Mopol and
Zhaki will be right at home down there—one of them dreaming he's
Superman, and the other one getting to be King of the Sea."

The three dolphins swam on, keeping pace in silence while Tkett
pondered what their decision meant. In all likelihood, resistance was

going to be futile. After all, the Buyur were overwhelmingly powerful and had been preparing for half a million years. Also, the incentive they were offering would make all prior temptations pale in comparison. Among the Six Races ashore—and the small colony of dolphins— many would leap to accept, and help make the new world of *magical wonder* compulsory.

We've never had an enemy like this before, he realized. *One that takes advantage of our greatest weakness, by offering to make all our dreams come true.*

Of course there was one possibility they hadn't discussed. That they were only seeing the surface layers of a much more complicated scheme . . . perhaps some long and desperately unfunny practical joke.

It doesn't matter, Tkett thought. *We have to fight this anyway, or we'll never grow strong and wise enough to "get" the joke. And we'll certainly never be able to pay the Buyur back, in kind. Not if they control all the hidden levers in Oz.*

For a while their journey fell into a grim mood of hopelessness. No one spoke, but sonar clicks from all three of them combined and diffused ahead. Returning echoes seemed to convey the sea's verdict on their predicament.

No chance. But good luck anyway.

Finally, little Chissis broke their brooding silence, after arduously spending the last hour composing her own Trinary philosophy glyph.

In one way, it was an announcement—that she felt ready to return to the struggles of sapiency.

At the same time, the glyph also expressed her manifesto. For it turned out that she had a different reason for choosing to fight the Buyur. One that Tkett and Peepoe had not expressed, though it resonated deep within.

* *Both the hazy mists of dreaming,*
   * *And the stark-clear shine of daylight,*
* *Offer treasures to the seeker,*
   * *And a trove of valued insights.*

* *One gives open, honest knowledge.*
   * *And the skill to achieve wonders.*
* *But the other (just as needed!)*
   * *Fills the soul and sets hearts a'stir.*

> * *What need then for ersatz magic?*
>   * *Or for contrived disney marvels?*
> * *God and Ifni made a cosmos.*
>   * *Filled with wonders . . . let's go live it!*

Peepoe sighed appreciatively.

"I couldn't have said it better. Screw the big old frogs! We'll make magic of our own."

They were tired and the sun was dropping well behind them by the time they caught sight of shore, and heard other dolphins chattering in the distance. Still, all three of them picked up the pace, pushing ahead through Jijo's silky waters.

Despite all the evidence of logic and their senses, the day still felt like morning.

⠿

Afterword

I seldom write two space-oriented "universe" books in a row. There are so many possible settings and situations for stories, and I like especially to intersperse more "grown-up" novels set on Earth, in near-plausible futures. Still, my Uplift Series of far-future space tales proved popular enough to draw me into a recent trilogy—*Brightness Reef, Infinity's Shore,* and *Heaven's Reach.* Added to three earlier novels—*Sundiver, Startide Rising,* and *The Uplift War*—they form a cluster of adventures in the unabashedly proud space-opera tradition . . . though I hope with some ideas mixed in with all the dash and sci-fi élan.

At one level, these works deal with the moral, scientific, and emotional implications of "uplift"—the genetic engineering of other animals to bring them into our civilization with human-equivalent powers of thought. Many other authors (e.g. H.G. Wells, Pierre Boulle, Mary Shelley, and Cordwainer Smith) dealt with this general concept before, but they all approached it in nearly the same way, by assuming the process would be abused—that the humans bestowing this boon would be mad, and would spoil things by establishing a cruel slave-master relationship with their creations.

Now of course that *is* one possible (and despicable) outcome. Those were good stories with wholesome moral messages. But that vein is overworked, so I chose a different tack. What if we someday begin modifying higher animals—and I think we clearly will—guided by the morality of modern liberal society? Filled with stylish hypertolerance and guilt-ridden angst, would we be in danger of killing our clients with *kindness*? More important, these new kinds of sapient beings would face real problems, even if they were treated well. Adjustment would be hard. One needn't picture slavery in order to sympathize with their plight.

Pondering the notion of uplift, it occurred to me how obvious the process might seem to alien beings who have traveled the stars for eons, encountering countless presapient life-forms and giving each one a boost, creating new generations of starfarers who would then do the same for others, and so on. The resulting image of a galaxy-spanning culture enthralled me. It would have great advantages, but perhaps would lead also to a kind of stultified cultural conservatism—an obsession with the past. Now suppose a young clan of Earthlings—not only humans, but also uplifted dolphins and chimps—encountered such a vast, ancient civilization. How would the newcomers be treated? How would we upstarts react?

Too many science-fictional scenarios assume states of unexplained disequilibrium, in which exploring humans happen to emerge just in time to bump into others out there at exactly the right level to be interesting competitors or allies. In fact, the normal state of affairs will be one of *equilibrium*—an equilibrium of law, or perhaps death. We may be the First Race, as I discuss in my story, "The Crystal Spheres," or very late arrivals, as depicted in the *Uplift* books. Either way, we're unlikely to meet aliens as equals.

My second motivation in this series was ecological. What we're doing to our Earth makes me fear there may already have been "brushfire" ecological holocausts across the galaxy. The common science-fictional scenario depicts eager settlers shouting, "Let's go fill the universe!" The wild frontier is a very satisfying image, but thoughtless expansion might create eco-wastelands within only a few years. If this has already happened a few times, it would help to explain the apparent emptiness that scientists now observe, in which the galaxy seems to have few, if any, other voices. This pattern might be avoided if something regulated the way colonists treat planets, forcing them to consider the long term. The Uplift universe presents one way this might happen. For all of their inscrutability and occasional nastiness, my Galactics set a high priority to preserving planets, habitats, and potential for new sapient life. The result is a noisy, bickering universe, but one filled with much more diversity than there otherwise might have been.

Of course, much of the fun has been trying to get into the heads of neo-dolphin or -chimp characters. The uplift concept makes this a nifty authorial exercise. When characters seem just a bit too human, that is a result (naturally) of both the genetic and cultural measures that were taken to make them members of Earth culture. But from the safe ground I've enjoyed exploring outward, harkening to older and more natural cetacean and simian instincts, both ennobling ones and those that might embarrass a proud sapient being—the way ghosts of ancient prehumanity sometimes trouble men and women in the modern era. In neo-dolphins, especially, I tried to combine the latest scientific facts and models of cetacean cognition with my own imaginative extrapolations of their "cultural" and emotional life.

Finally, like any good yarn, each story in the Uplift universe deals with some issue of good and evil—or the murky realm between. One that I've been confronting lately is the insidious and arrogant, but all too commonplace, assumption that *words* are more important than *actions*.

For centuries there has been a running conflict between those who believe that ideas are inherently dangerous, or toxic, and those on the other hand who propose that we can raise bold children into mature adults, able to evaluate any notion skeptically, on its merits. Even today, there are those in all political wings who feel that some elite (of the left or the right) should protect the masses from dangerous images or impressions. The same people often preach that "to think a thing is the same as doing it."

You see a connection to this in the revival of "magic" in fantasy literature. Magical protagonists are nearly always better, stronger, and more powerful than other characters *not* because they earned their status through preparation, or merit, or argument, but because of some intrinsic mystical power or force, setting them above other mortals. In these fantasy societies, power is either inherited or rooted in the *Ubermensch*'s overwhelming ego, coercing nature to bend to his force of will. Spurned or forgotten is the cooperative effort of skilled professionals that has wrought real wonders of science and liberty in this century. Wielders of magical words are portrayed as better than mere shapers of matter, especially when those words are *secret* words, all-powerful and (of course) never to be shared with mere ignorant peasants. This kind of literature rejects the egalitarian thrust of Western Civilization, reverting to older traditions that praised and excused the power elites in every other civilization.

In my story "Temptation"—an offshoot adventure from events depicted in *Infinity's Shore*—we confronted that old malignant notion, the ever-lurking temptation of *wishful thinking*. As the dolphin characters conclude, it *is* possible to mix science and art. We can combine honesty with extravagant self-expression. We are not limited beings.

But far too much harm has been done by human beings who decide that persuasion is the only thing that matters.

Everything isn't subjective. Reality also matters. *Truth* matters. It is still a word with meaning.

—*David Brin*

ROMA ETERNA

Robert Silverberg

"To the Promised Land" (1989)
"Tales from the Venia Woods" (1989)
"An Outpost of the Empire" (1991)
"Via Roma" (1994)
"Waiting for the End" (1998)

The *Roma Eterna* stories are based on an alternate-history scenario in which the ancient Hebrews remained in Egypt instead of being led forth by Moses as recorded in the Book of Exodus. Since the Jews thus never settled in Palestine, the historical figure of Jesus of Nazareth did not exist, Christianity failed to develop, and Rome remained pagan. The history of Rome in this alternate world is generally identical to that of *our* Rome as it unfolded through the fourth century A.D.—the foundation of the Empire under Augustus, its great expansion under Trajan, Hadrian, and Marcus Aurelius, its difficulties during the time of the third-century military dictatorships, and the division of the Empire by Constantine the Great into eastern and western domains.

But after Constantine, who in our universe had been responsible for making Christianity the official Roman state religion, things begin to diverge. The Empire, instead of being riven by the quarrels that divided Constantine's heirs in our time line, and weakened politically by the changed social attitudes introduced by Christianity, thrives and expands in the fifth century and succeeds in renewing itself constantly during the period we call the Dark Ages, fending off the invasions of the barbarians and sustaining itself as a thriving worldwide empire stretching from Britain to the borders of India and China. The Empire has no serious rivals in the world, although at times there is strife between its eastern and western halves, and the Aztec and Inca empires of the New World remain independent and powerful despite an ill-fated Roman attempt to conquer them and establish a Nova Roma across the sea.

The time line of the *Roma Eterna* stories starts in 753 B.C., the traditional date of the founding of the city; thus our year A.D. 1999 is 2752 A.U.C. by Roman reckoning. Of the stories written so far, the earliest along this chronology is "Waiting for the End," set in 1951 A.U.C. (A.D. 1198), which shows the western half of the empire, during a period of decadence, being invaded and conquered by the army of the Greek-speaking Eastern Empire.

In "An Outpost of the Empire," which takes place 250 years later in 2206 A.U.C. (A.D. 1453), the Western Empire has not only regained its independence but, under the vigorous leadership of Emperor Flavius Romulus, has defeated the Eastern Empire and incorporated it into a reunited Imperial state that includes both halves of the empire that Constantine had split eleven hundred years before.

In the Imperial years 2250–2550, which parallel our sixteenth, seventeenth, and eighteenth centuries, the Empire undergoes a renaissance that is given its first impetus by the great emperor Trajan VII, who undertook worldwide voyages and the development of trade with Asia. The resurgence of economic growth through the opening of new trade routes leads eventually to an industrial revolution, the breakdown of the Imperial heartland into regions that speak dialects approaching separate languages (Gallian, Hispanian, Britannian, "Roman" [Italian], etc.), and, ultimately, the gradual collapse of the central authority of the Empire during a second period of prosperous decadence. An attempt at reunification of the virtually independent European provinces launched in 2563 A.U.C. (A.D. 1810) by the Napoleonic figure of Count Valerian Apollinaris is successful, and for a time the Empire, with Apollinaris ruling sternly as the power behind the throne, seems rejuvenated.

But the assassination of Apollinaris dooms the Imperial system: after eighteen centuries of Caesars, there is an intense public yearning to sweep away the lazy and luxury-loving aristocracy and return to the ancient republican governmental form that Augustus abolished. The next of the presently existing stories, "Via Roma," depicts the overthrow of the last Emperor in 2603 A.U.C. (A.D. 1850), the murder of most members of the royal family, and the establishment of the Second Republic under the aegis of the authoritarian and conservative Gaius Junius Scaevola, who takes the title of First Consul for Life.

The following story, "Tales of the Venia Woods," which takes place about fifty years after the fall of the Caesars, provides a glimpse of the last surviving member of the old Imperial house, an old man living as a quiet recluse in the forest outside the city we know as Vienna. Then the series jumps to

2723 A.U.C. (A.D. 1970), and the story, "To the Promised Land," in which Moshe, a charismatic Egyptian Jew, attempts to build a spacegoing vessel to take his people to another world. The attempt to launch the spaceship is disastrous and Moshe is killed, but as the story ends we see the first stages in the development of a new messianic religion in the Middle East, with Moshe being looked upon as the Son of God.

The present story, set in 2503 A.U.C. (A.D. 1750), fills in a gap in the series by depicting the Empire late in the Second Decadence, when the Emperor Demetrius II is about to come to the throne, and one historian looks back to the Renaissance inaugurated by Trajan VII a quarter of a millennium earlier as a golden age.

—Robert Silverberg

⁙

Getting to Know the Dragon

by

Robert Silverberg

I REACHED THE THEATER AT NINE THAT MORNING, HALF AN HOUR BEFORE THE appointed time, for I knew only too well how unkind the Caesar Demetrius could be to the unpunctual. But the Caesar, it seemed, had arrived even earlier than that. I found Labienus, his personal guard and chief drinking companion, lounging by the theater entrance; and as I approached, Labienus smirked and said, "What took you so long? Caesar's been waiting for you."

"I'm half an hour early," I said sourly. No need to be tactful with the likes of Labienus—or Polycrates, as I should be calling him, now that Caesar has given us all new Greek names. "Where is he?"

Labienus pointed through the gate and turned his middle finger straight upward, jabbing it three times toward the heavens. I limped past him without another word and went inside.

To my dismay I saw the figure of Demetrius Caesar right at the very summit of the theater, the uppermost row, his slight figure outlined sharply against the brilliant blue of the morning sky. It was less than six weeks since I had broken my ankle hunting boar with the Caesar in the interior of the island; I was still on crutches, and walking, let alone climbing stairs, was a challenge for me. But there he was, high up above.

"So you've turned up at last, Pisander!" he called. "It's about time. Hurry on up! I've got something very interesting to show you."

Pisander. It was last summer when he suddenly bestowed the Greek names on us all. Julius and Lucius and Marcus lost their good honest Roman praenomina and became Eurystheus and Idomeneus and Diomedes. I who was Tiberius Ulpius Draco was now Pisander. It was the latest fashion at the court that the Caesar maintained—at his

178

Imperial father's insistence—down here in Sicilia, these Greek names: to be followed, we all supposed, by mandatory Greek hairstyles and sticky pomades, the wearing of airy Greek costumes, and, eventually, the introduction on an obligatory basis of the practice of Greek buggery. Well, the Caesars amuse themselves as they will; and I might not have minded it if he had named me something heroic, Agamemnon or Odysseus or the like. But Pisander? Pisander of Laranda was the author of that marvelous epic of world history, *Heroic Marriages of the Gods,* and it would have been reasonable enough for Caesar to name me for him, since I am an historian also. And also there is the earlier Pisander, Pisander of Camirus, who wrote the oldest known epic of the deeds of Heracles. But there was yet another Pisander, a fat and corrupt Athenian politician who comes in for some merciless mockery in the *Hyperbolus* of Aristophanes, and I happen to know that play is one of Caesar's special favorites. Since the other two Pisanders are figures out of antiquity, obscure except to specialists like me, I cannot help but think that Caesar had Aristophanes's character in mind when coining my Greek name for me. I am neither fat nor corrupt, but the Caesar takes great pleasure in vexing our souls with such little pranks.

Forcing a cripple to climb to the top of the theater, for example. I went hobbling painfully up the steep stone steps, flight after flight after flight, until I emerged at last at the very highest row. Demetrius was staring off toward the side, admiring the wonderful spectacle of Mount Etna rising in the west, snowcapped, stained by ashes at its summit, a plume of black smoke coiling from its boiling maw. The views that can be obtained up here atop the great theater of Tauromenium are indeed breathtaking; but my breath had been taken sufficiently by the effort of the climb, and I was in no mood just then to appreciate the splendor of the scenery about us.

He was leaning against the stone table in the top-row concourse where the wine-sellers display their wares during intermission. An enormous scroll was laid out in front of him. "Here is my plan for the improvement of the island, Pisander. Come take a look and tell me what you think of it."

It was a huge map of Sicilia, covering the entire table. Drawn practically to full scale, one might say. I could see great scarlet circles, perhaps half a dozen of them, marked boldly on it. This was not at all what I was expecting, since the ostensible purpose of the meeting this morning was to discuss the Caesar's plan for renovating the Tauromenium theater. Among my various areas of expertise is a certain knowledge of architecture. But no, no, the renovation of the theater was not at all on Demetrius's mind today.

"This is a beautiful island," he said, "but its economy has been sluggish for decades. I propose to awaken it by undertaking the most ambitious construction program Sicilia has ever seen. For example, Pisander, right here in our pretty little Tauromenium there's a crying need for a proper royal palace. The villa where I've been living these past three years is nicely situated, yes, but it's rather modest, wouldn't you say, for the residence of the heir to the throne?" Modest, yes. Thirty or forty rooms at the edge of the steep cliff overlooking town, affording a flawless prospect of the sea and the volcano. He tapped the scarlet circle in the upper right-hand corner of the map surrounding the place that Tauromenium occupies in northeastern Sicilia. "Suppose we turn the villa into a proper palace by extending it down the face of the cliff a bit, eh? Come over here, and I'll show you what I mean."

I hobbled along behind him. He led me around to a point along the rim where his villa's portico was in view, and proceeded to describe a cascading series of levels, supported by fantastic cantilevered platforms and enormous flaring buttresses, that would carry the structure down the entire face of the cliff, right to the shore of the Ionian Sea far below. "That would make it ever so much simpler for me to get to the beach, wouldn't you say? If we were to build a track of some sort that ran down the side of the building, with a car suspended on cables? Instead of having to take the main road down, I could simply descend within my own palace."

I stared the goggle-eyed stare of incredulity. Such a structure, if it could be built at all, would take fifty years to build and cost a billion sesterces at the least. Ten billion, maybe.

But that wasn't all. Far from it.

"Then, Pisander, we need to do something about the accommodations for visiting royalty at Panormus." He ran his finger westward across the top of the map to the big port farther along the northern shore. "Panormus is where my father likes to stay when he comes here; but the palace is six hundred years old and quite inadequate. I'd like to tear it down and build a full-scale replica of the Imperial palace on Palatine Hill on the site, with perhaps a replica of the Forum of Roma just downhill from it. He'd like that: make him feel at home when he visits Sicilia. Then, as a nice place to stay in the middle of the island while we're out hunting, there's the wonderful old palace of Maximianius Herculeus near Enna, but it's practically falling down. We could erect an entirely new palace—in Byzantine style, let's say—on its site, being very careful not to harm the existing mosaics, of course. And then—"

I listened, ever more stupefied by the moment. Demetrius's idea of reawakening the Sicilian economy involved building unthinkably expensive royal palaces all over the island. At Agrigentum on the southern coast, for example, where the royals liked to go to see the magnificent Greek temples that are found there and at nearby Selinunte, he thought that it would be pleasant to construct an exact duplicate of Hadrianus's famous villa at Tibur as a sort of tourist lodge for them. But Hadrianus's villa is the size of a small city. It would take an army of craftsmen at least a century to build its twin at Agrigentum. And over at the western end of the island he had some notion for a castle in rugged, primordial Homeric style, or whatever he imagined Homeric style to be, clinging romantically to the summit of the citadel of Eryx. Then, down at Syracusa—well, what he had in mind for Syracusa would have bankrupted the Empire. A grand new palace, naturally, but also a lighthouse like the one in Alexandria, and a Parthenon twice the size of the real one, and a dozen or so pyramids like those in Aiguptos, only perhaps a little bigger, and a bronze Colossus on the waterfront like the one that used to stand in the harbor at Rhodos, and—I'm unable to set down the entire list without wanting to weep.

"Well, Pisander, what do you say? Has there ever been a building program like this in the history of the world?"

His face was shining. He is a very handsome man, is Demetrius Caesar, and in that moment, transfigured by his own megalomaniac scheme, he was a veritable Apollo. But a crazy one. What possible response could I have made to all that he had just poured forth? That I thought it was the wildest lunacy? That I very much doubted there was enough gold in all his father's treasury to underwrite the cost of such an absurd enterprise? That we would all be long dead before these projects could be completed? The Emperor Lodovicus his father, when assigning me to the service of the Caesar Demetrius, had warned me of his volatile temper. A word placed wrongly and I might find myself hurled sprawling down the very steps up which I had just clambered with so much labor.

But I know how to manage things when speaking with royalty. Tactfully but not unctuously I said, "It is a project that inspires me with awe, Caesar. I am hard pressed to bring its equal to mind."

"Exactly. There's never been anything like it, has there? I'll go down in history. Neither Alexander nor Sardanapalus nor Augustus Caesar himself ever attempted a public-works program of such ambitious size. —You, of course, will be the chief architect of the entire project, Pisander."

If he had kicked me in the gut I would not have been more thoroughly taken aback.

I smothered a gasp and said, "I, Caesar? You do me too much honor. My primary field these days is historical scholarship, my lord. I've dabbled a bit in architecture, but I hardly regard myself as qualified to—"

"Well, I do. Spare me your false modesty, will you, Draco?" Suddenly he was calling me by my true name again. That seemed very significant. "Everyone knows just how capable a man you are. You hide behind this scholarly pose because you think it's safer that way, I would imagine, but I'm well aware of your real abilities, and when I'm Emperor I mean to make the most of them. That's the mark of a Great Emperor, wouldn't you say—to surround himself with men who are great themselves, and to inspire them to rise to their full potentiality? I do expect to be a great Emperor, you know, ten years from now, twenty, whenever it is that my turn comes. But I'm already beginning to pick out my key men. You'll be one of them." He winked at me. "See to it that leg heals fast, Draco. I mean to start this project off by building the Tauromenium palace, which I want you to design for me, and that means that you and I are going to be scrambling around on the face of that cliff looking for the best possible site. I don't want you on crutches when we do that. —Isn't the mountain beautiful today, Pisander?"

In the space of three breaths I had become Pisander again.

He rolled up his scroll. I wondered if we were finally going to discuss the theater-renovation job. But then I realized that the Caesar, his mind inflamed by the full magnificence of his plan for transforming every major city of the island, was no more interested just now in talking about a petty thing like replacing the clogged drainage channel running down the hillside adjacent to this theater than a god would be in hearing about somebody's personal health problems, his broken ankle, say, when his godlike intellect is absorbed with the task of designing some wondrous new plague with which he intends to destroy eleven million yellow-skinned inhabitants of far-off Khitai a little later in the month.

We admired the view together for a while, therefore. Then, when I sensed that I had been dismissed, I took my leave without bringing up the topic of the theater, and slowly and uncomfortably made my way down the steps again. Just as I reached the bottom I heard the Caesar call out to me. I feared for one dreadful moment that he was summoning me back and I would have to haul myself all the way up there a second time. But he simply wanted to wish me a good day. The Caesar Demetrius is insane, of course, but he's not really vicious.

"The Emperor will never allow him to do it," Spiculo said, as we sat late that night over our wine.

"He will. The Emperor grants his crazy son his every little wish. His every big one, too."

Spiculo is my oldest friend, well named, a thorny little man. We are both Hispaniards; we went to school together in Tarraco; when I took up residence in Roma and entered the Emperor's service, so did he. When the Emperor handed me off to his son, Spiculo followed me loyally to Sicilia too. I trust him as I trust no other man. We utter the most flagrant treason to each other all the time.

"If he begins it, then," said Spiculo, "he'll never go through with anything. You know what he's like. Six months after they break ground for the palace here, he'll decide he'd rather get started on his Parthenon in Syracusa. He'll erect three columns there and go off to Panormus. And then he'll jump somewhere else a month after that."

"So?" I said. "What business is that of mine? He's the one who'll look silly if that's how he handles it, not me. I'm only the architect."

His eyes widened. "What? You're actually going to get involved in this thing, are you?"

"The Caesar has requested my services."

"And are you so supine that you'll simply do whatever he tells you to, however foolish it may be? Piss away the next five or ten years of your life on a demented young prince's cockeyed scheme for burying this whole godforsaken island under mountains of marble? Get your name linked with his for all time to come as the facilitator of this lunatic affair?" His voice became a harsh mocking soprano. '*Tiberius Ulpius Draco, the greatest man of science of the era, foolishly abandoned all his valuable scholarly research in order to devote the remaining years of his life to this ill-conceived series of preposterously grandiose projects, none of which was ever completed, and finally was found one morning, dead by his own hand, sprawled at the base of the unfinished Great Pyramid of Syracusa—*' No, Draco! Don't do it! Just shake your head and walk away!"

"You speak as though I have any choice about it," I said.

He stared at me. Then he rose and stomped across the patio toward the balcony. He is a cripple from birth, with a twisted left leg and a foot that points out to the side. My hunting accident angered him, because it caused me to limp as well, which directs additional attention to Spiculo's own deformity as we hobble side by side through the streets, a grotesquely comical pair who might easily be thought to be on their way to a beggars' convention.

For a long moment he stood glowering at me without speaking. It was a night of bright moonlight, brilliantly illuminating the villas of the wealthy all up and down the slopes of the Tauromenian hillside, and as the silence went on and on I found myself studying the triangular outlines of Spiculo's form as it was limned from behind by the chilly white light: the broad burly shoulders tapering down to the narrow waist and the spindly legs, with the big outjutting head planted defiantly atop. If I had had my sketchpad I would have begun to draw him. But of course I have drawn him many times before.

He said at last, very quietly, "You astound me, Draco. What do you mean, you don't have any choice? Simply resign from his service and go back to Roma. The Emperor needs you there. He can find some other nursemaid for his idiot princeling. You don't seriously think that Demetrius will have you thrown in jail if you decline to take on the job, do you? Or executed, or something?"

"You don't understand," I said. "I *want* to take the job on."

"Even though it's a madman's wet dream? Draco, have you gone crazy yourself? Is the Caesar's lunacy contagious?"

I smiled. "Of course I know how ridiculous the whole thing is. But that doesn't mean I don't want to give it a try."

"Ah," Spiculo said, getting it at last. "Ah! So that's it! The temptation of the unthinkable! The engineer in you wants to pile Pelion on Ossa just to find out whether he can manage the trick! Oh, Draco, Demetrius isn't as crazy as he seems, is he? He sized you up just perfectly. There's only one man in the world who's got the *hybris* to take on this idiotic job, and he's right here in Tauromenium."

"It's piling Ossa on Pelion, not the other way around," I said. "But yes. Yes, Spiculo! Of course I'm tempted. So what if it's all craziness? And if nothing ever gets finished, what of it? At least things will be started. Plans will be drawn; foundations will be dug. Don't you think I want to see how an Aiguptian pyramid can be built? Or how to cantilever a palace thousands of feet down the side of this cliff here? It's the chance of a lifetime for me."

"And your account of the life of Trajan VII? Only the day before yesterday you couldn't stop talking about the documents that are on their way to you from the archive in Sevilla. Speculating half the night about the wonderful new revelations you were going to find in them, you were. Are you going to abandon the whole thing just like that?"

"Of course not. Why should one project interfere with another?

I'm quite capable of working on a book in the evening while designing palaces during the day. I expect to continue with my painting and my poetry and my music too. —I think you underestimate me, old friend."

"Well, let it not be said that you've ever been guilty of doing the same."

I let the point pass. "I offer you one additional consideration, and then let's put this away, shall we? Lodovicus is past sixty and not in wonderful health. When he dies, Demetrius is going to be Emperor, whether anybody likes that idea or not, and you and I will return to Roma, where I will be a key figure in his administration and all the scholarly and scientific resources of the capital will be at my disposal. —Unless, of course, I irrevocably estrange myself from him while he's still only heir apparent by throwing this project of his back in his face, as you seem to want me to do. So I will take the job. As an investment leading to the hope of future gain, so to speak."

"Very nicely reasoned, Draco."

"Thank you."

"And suppose, when Demetrius becomes Emperor, which through some black irony of the gods he probably will before too long, he decides he'd rather keep you down here in Sicilia finishing the great work of filling this island with secondhand architectural splendors instead of his interrupting your holy task by transferring you to the court in Roma, and that's what you do for the rest of your life, plodding around this backwater of a place supervising the completely useless and unnecessary construction of—"

I had had about enough. "Look, Spiculo, that's a risk I'm willing to take. He's already told me in just that many words that when he's Emperor he plans to make fuller use of my skills than his father ever chose to do."

"And you believe him?"

"He sounded quite sincere."

"Oh, Draco, Draco! I'm beginning to think you're even crazier than he is!"

It was a gamble, of course. I knew that.

And Spiculo might well have been speaking the truth when he said that I was crazier than poor Demetrius. The Caesar, after all, can't help being the way he is. There has been madness, real madness, in his family for a hundred years or more, serious mental instability, some defect of the mind leading to unpredictable outbreaks of flightiness and caprice. I, on the other hand, face each day with clear perceptions. I am hardworking and reliable, and I have a finely tuned intelligence capable of succeeding at anything I turn it to. This is not boasting. The solidity of my achievements is a fact not open to question. I have built temples and palaces, I have painted great paintings and fashioned splendid statues, I have written epic poems and books of history, I have even designed a flying machine that I will someday build and test successfully. And there is much more besides that I have in mind to achieve, the secrets that I write in cipher in my notebooks in a crabbed left-handed script, things that would transform the world. Some day I will bring them all to perfection. But at present I am not ready to do so much as hint at them to anyone, and so I use the cipher. (As though anyone would be able to comprehend these ideas of mine even if they could read what is written in those notebooks!)

One might say that I owe all this mental agility to the special kindness of the gods, and I am unwilling to contradict that pious thought; but heredity has something to do with it too. My superior capacities are the gift of my ancestors just as the flaws of Demetrius Caesar's mind are of his. In *my* veins courses the blood of one of the greatest of our Emperors, the visionary Trajan VII, who would have been well fit to wear the title that was bestowed sixteen centuries ago on the first Emperor of that name: Optimus Princeps, "best of princes." Who, though, are the forefathers of Demetrius Caesar? Lodovicus! Marius Antoninus! Valens Aquila! Why, are these not some of the feeblest men ever to have held the throne, and have they not led the Empire down the path of decadence and decline?

Of course it is the fate of the Empire to enter into periods of decadence now and then, just as it is its supreme good fortune to find, ever and always, a fresh source of rebirth and renewal when one is needed. That is why our Roma has been the preeminent power in the world for more than two thousand years and why it will go on and on to the end of time, world without end, eternally rebounding to new vigor.

Consider. There was a troubled and chaotic time eighteen hundred years ago, and out of it Augustus Caesar gave us the Imperial government, which has served us in good stead ever since. When the blood of the early Caesars ran thin and such men as Caligula and Nero came disastrously to power, redemption was shortly at hand in the form of the first Trajan, and after him Hadrianus, succeeded by the equally capable Antoninus Pius and Marcus Aurelius.

A later period of troubles was put to right by Diocletianus, whose work was completed by the great Constantinus; and when, inevitably, we declined yet again, seven hundred years later, falling into what modern historians call the Great Decadence, and were so easily and shamefully conquered by our Greek-speaking brothers of the East, eventually Flavius Romulus arose among us to give us our freedom once more. And not long after him came Trajan VII to carry our explorers clear around the globe, bringing back incalculable wealth and setting in motion the exciting period of expansion that we know as the Renaissance. Now, alas, we are decadent again, living through what I suppose will someday be termed the Second Great Decadence. The cycle seems inescapable.

I like to think of myself as a man of the Renaissance, the last of my kind, born by some sad and unjust accident of fate two centuries out of this proper time and forced to live in this imbecile, decadent age. It's a pleasant fantasy and there's much evidence, to my way of thinking, that it's true.

That this is a decadent age there can be no doubt. One defining symptom of decadence is a fondness for vast and nonsensical extravagance, and what better example of that could be provided than the Caesar's witless and imprudent scheme for reshaping Sicilia as a monument to his own grandeur? The fact that the structures he would have me construct for him are, almost without exception, imitations of buildings of earlier and less fatuous eras only reinforces the point.

But also we are experiencing a breakdown of the central government. Not only do distant provinces like Syria and Persia blithely go their own way most of the time, but also Gallia and Hispania and Dalmatia and Pannonia, practically in the Emperor's own back yard, are behaving almost like independent nations. The new languages, too: what has become of our pure and beautiful Latin, the backbone of our Empire? It has degenerated into a welter of local dialects. Every place now has its own babbling lingo. We Hispaniards speak Hispanian, and the long-nosed Gallians have the nasal honking thing called Gallian, and in the Teutonic provinces they have retreated from Latin altogether, reverting to some primitive sputtering tongue known as Germanisch, and so on and so on. Why, even in Italia itself you find Latin giving way to a bastard child they call Roman, which at least is sweetly musical to the ear but has thrown away all the profundity and grammatical versatility that makes Latin the master language of the world. And if Latin is discarded entirely (which has not been the fate of Greek in the East), how will a man of Hispania be understood by a man of Britannia, or a Teuton by a Gallian, or a Dalmatian by anyone at all?

Surely this is decadence, when these destructive centrifugalities sweep through our society.

But is it really the case that I am a man of the Renaissance stranded in this miserable age? That's not so easy to say. In common speech we use the phrase "a Renaissance man" to indicate someone of unusual breadth and depth of attainment. I am certainly that. But would I have truly felt at home in the swashbuckling age of Trajan VII? I have the Renaissance expansiveness of mind; but do I have the flamboyant Renaissance temperament as well, or am I in truth just as timid and stodgy and generally piddling as everyone I see about me? We must not forget that they were medievals. Could I have carried a sword in the streets, and brawled like a legionary at the slightest provocation? Would I have had twenty mistresses and fifty bastard sons? And yearned to clamber aboard a tiny creaking ship and sail off beyond the horizon?

No, I probably was not much like them. Their souls were large. The world was bigger and brighter and far more mysterious to them than it seems to us, and they responded to its mysteries with a romantic fervor, a ferocious outpouring of energy, that may be impossible for any of us to encompass today. I have taken on this assignment of Caesar's because it stirs some of that romantic fervor in me and makes me feel renewed kinship with my great world-girdling ancestor Trajan VII, Trajan the Dragon. But what will I be doing, really? Discovering new worlds, as he did? No, no, I will be building pyramids and Greek temples and the villa of Hadrianus. But all that has been done once already, quite satisfactorily, and there is no need to do it again. Am I, therefore, as decadent as any of my contemporaries?

I wonder, too, what would have happened to great Trajan if he had been born into this present era of Lodovicus Augustus and his crackbrained son Demetrius? Men of great spirit are at high risk at a time when small souls rule the world. I myself have found shrewd ways of fitting in, of ensuring my own security and safety, but would he have done the same? Or would he have gone noisily swaggering around the place like the true man of the Renaissance that he was, until finally it became necessary to do away with him quietly in some dark alley as an inconvenience to the royal house and to the realm in general? Perhaps not. Perhaps, as I prefer to think, he would have risen like a flaming arrow through the dark night of this murky epoch and, as he did in his own time, cast a brilliant light over the entirety of the world.

In any case here was I, undeniably intelligent and putatively sane, voluntarily linking myself with our deranged young Caesar's project, simply because I was unable to resist the wonderful technical challenge that it represented. A grand romantic gesture, or simply a mad one? Very likely Spiculo *was* right in saying by accepting the job I demonstrated that I was crazier than Demetrius. Any genuinely sane man would have run screaming away.

One did not have to be the Cumaean Sybil to be able to foresee that a long time would go by before Demetrius mentioned the project to me again. The Caesar is forever flitting from one thing to another; it is a mark of his malady; two days after our conversation in the theater he left Tauromenium for a holiday among the sand dunes of Africa, and he was gone more than a month. Since we had not yet done so much as choose a location for the cliffside palace, let alone come to an understanding about such things as a design and a construction budget, I put the whole matter out of my mind pending his return. My hope, I suppose, was that he would have forgotten it entirely by the time he came back to Sicilia.

I took advantage of his absence to resume work on what had been my main undertaking of the season, my study of the life of Trajan VII.

Which was something that had occupied me intermittently for the past seven or eight years. Two things had led me back to it at this time. One was the discovery, in the dusty depths of the Sevilla maritime archives, of a packet of long-buried journals purporting to be Trajan's own account of his voyage around the world. The other was the riding mishap during the boar hunt that had left me on crutches for the time being: a period of enforced inactivity that gave me, willy-nilly, a good reason to assume the scholar's role once more.

No adequate account of Trajan's extraordinary career had ever been written. That may seem strange, considering our long national tradition of great historical scholarship, going back to the misty figures of Naevius and Ennius in the time of the Republic, and, of course, Sallust and Livius and Tacitus and Suetonius later on, Ammianus Marcellinus after them, Drusillus of Alexandria, Marcus Andronicus—and, to come closer to modern times, Lucius Aelius Antipater, the great chronicler of the conquest of Roma by the Byzantines in the time of Maximilianus VI.

But something has gone awry with the writing of history since Flavius Romulus put the sundered halves of Imperial Roma back together in the year 2198 after the founding of the city. Perhaps it is that in a time of great men—and certainly the era of Flavius Romulus and his two immediate successors was that—everyone is too busy making history to have time to write it. That was what I used to believe, at any rate; but then I broke my ankle, and I came to understand that in any era, however energetic it may be, there is always someone who, from force of special circumstances, be it injury or illness or exile, finds himself with sufficient leisure to turn his hand to writing.

What has started to seem more likely to me is that in the time of Flavius Romulus and Gaius Flavillus and Trajan the Dragon, publishing any sort of account of those mighty Emperors would not have been an entirely healthy pastime. Just as the finest account of the lives of the first twelve Caesars—I speak of Suetonius's scathing and scabrous book—was written during the relatively benign reign of the first Trajan and not when such monsters as Caligula or Nero or Domitian were still breathing fire in the land, so too may it have seemed unwise for scholars in the epoch of the three Hispaniard monarchs to set down anything but a bare-bones chronicle of public events and significant legislation. To analyze Caesar is to criticize him. That is not always safe.

Whatever the reason, no worthwhile contemporary books on the remarkable Flavius Romulus have come down to us, only mere factual chronicles and some fawning panegyrics. Of the inner nature of his successor, the shadowy Gaius Julius Flavillus, we know practically nothing, only such dry data as where he was born—like Flavius Romulus, he came from Tarraco in Hispania, my own native city—and which governmental posts he held during his long career before attaining the Imperial throne. And for the third of the three great Hispaniards, Trajan VII—whose surname happened by coincidence to be Draco but who earned by his deeds as well, throughout the world, the name of Trajan the Dragon—we have, once again, just the most basic annals of his glorious reign.

That no one has tackled the job of writing his life in the two centuries since his death should come as no surprise. One can write safely about a dead Caesar, yes, but where was the man to do the job? The glittering period of the Renaissance gave way all too quickly to the dawning age of industrial development, and in that dreary, smoky time the making of money took priority over everything else, art and scholarship included. And now we have our new era of decadence, in which one weakling after another has worn the Imperial crown and the Empire itself seems gradually to be collapsing into a congeries of separate entities that feel little or no sense of loyalty to the central authority. Such vigor as our masters can manage to muster goes into inane enterprises like the construction of gigantic pointy-headed tombs in the Pharaonic style here in this isle of Sicilia. Who, in such an age, can bear to confront the grandeur of a Trajan VII?

Well, I can.

And have a thick sheaf of manuscript to show for it. I have taken advantage of my position in the Imperial service to burrow in the subbasements of the Capitol in Roma, unlocking cabinets that have been sealed for twenty centuries and bringing into the light of day official papers whose very existence had been forgotten. I have looked into the private records of the deliberations of the Senate: no one seemed to mind, or to care at all. I have read memoirs left behind by high officials of the court. I have pored over the reports of provincial excise-collectors and tax commissioners and inspectors of the public markets, which, abstract and dull though they may seem, are in fact the true ore out of which history is mined. From all of this I have brought Trajan the Dragon and his era back into vivid reality—at least in my own mind, and on the pages of my unfinished book.

And what a figure he was! Throughout the many years of his long life he was the absolute embodiment of strength, vision, implacable purpose, and energy. He ranks with the greatest of Emperors: with Augustus; with Trajan I and Hadrianus; with Constantinus; with Maximilianus III, the conqueror of the barbarians; with his own countryman and predecessor Flavius Romulus. I have spent these years getting to know him—getting to know the Dragon!—and the contact with his great soul that I have enjoyed during these years of research into his life has ennobled and enlightened my days.

And what do I know of him, this great Emperor, this Dragon of Roma, this distant ancestor of mine?

That he was born illegitimately, for one thing. I have combed very carefully through the records of marriages and births in Tarraco and surrounding regions of Hispania for the entire period from 2215 to 2227 A.U.C., which should have been more than sufficient, and although I have found a number of Dracos entered in the tax rolls for those years, Decimus Draco and Numerius Draco and Salvius Draco, not one of them seems to have been married in any official way or to have brought forth progeny that warranted enumeration in the register of births. So his parents' names must remain unknown. All I can report is that one Trajan Draco, a native of Tarraco, is listed as enrolling in military service in the Third Hispanic Legion in the year 2241, from which I conclude that he was born somewhere between 2220 and 2225 A.U.C. In that period it was most usual to enter the army at the age of eighteen, which would place his date of birth at

2223, but, knowing Trajan Draco as I do, I would hazard a guess that he went in even younger, perhaps when he was sixteen or only fifteen.

The Empire was still under Greek rule at that time, technically; but Hispania, like most of the western provinces, was virtually independent. The Emperor at Constantinopolis was Leo XI, a man who cared much more about filling his palace with the artistic treasures of ancient Greece than he did about what might be going on in the Europan territories. Those territories were nominally under the control of the Western Emperor, anyway, his distant cousin Nicephoros Cantacuzenos. But the Western Emperors during the era of Greek domination were invariably idle puppets, and Nicephoros, the last of that series, was even more idle than most. They say he was never even to be seen in Roma, but spent all his days in comfortable retreat in the south, near Neapolis.

The rebellion of the West, I am proud to say, began in Hispania, in my very own native city of Tarraco. The bold and dynamic Flavius Romulus, a shepherd's son who may have been illiterate, raised an army of men just as ragged as he, overthrew the provincial government, and proclaimed himself Emperor. That was in the year 2193; he was twenty-five or thirty years old.

Nicephoros, the Western Emperor, chose to regard the Hispanic uprising as an insignificant local uproar, and it is doubtful that news of it reached the Basileus Leo XI in Constantinopolis at all. But very shortly the nearby province of Lusitania had sworn allegiance to the rebel banner, and the isle of Britannia, and Gallia next; and piece by piece the western lands fell away from their fealty to the feckless government in Roma, until finally Flavius Romulus marched into the capital, occupied the Imperial palace, and sent troops south to arrest Nicephoros and carry him into exile in Aiguptos. By the year 2198 the Eastern Empire had fallen also. Leo XI made a somber pilgrimage from Constantinopolis to Ravenna to sign a treaty recognizing Flavius Romulus not only as Emperor of the West but as monarch of the eastern territories too.

Flavius ruled another thirty years. Not content with having reunited the Empire, he distinguished himself by a second astonishing exploit, a voyage around the tip of Africa that took him to the shores of India and possibly even to the unknown lands beyond. He was the first of the Maritime Emperors, setting a noble example for that even more extraordinary traveler, Trajan VII, two generations later.

We Romans had made journeys overland to the Far East, Persia and even India, as far back as the time of the first Augustus. And in the era of the Eastern Empire the Byzantines had often sailed down

Africa's western coast to carry on trade with the black kingdoms of that continent, which had led a few of the more venturesome Emperors of the West to send their own expeditions all the way around Africa and onward to Arabia, and from there now and then to India. But these had been sporadic adventures. Flavius Romulus wanted permanent trade relations with the Asian lands. On his great voyage he carried thousands of Romans with him to India by the African route and left them there to found mercantile colonies; and thereafter we were in constant commercial contact with the dark-skinned folk of those far-off lands. Not only that, he or one of his captains—it is not clear—sailed onward from India to the even more distant realms of Khitai and Cipangu, where the yellow-skinned people live. And thus began the commercial connections that would bring us the silks and incense, the gems and spices, the jade and ivory of those mysterious lands, their rhubarb and their emeralds, rubies and pepper, sapphires, cinnamon, dyes, perfumes.

There were no bounds to Flavius Romulus's ambitions. He dreamed also of new westward voyages to the two continents of Nova Roma on the other side of the Ocean Sea. Hundreds of years before his time, the reckless Emperor Saturninus had undertaken a foolhardy attempt to conquer Mexico and Peru, the two great empires of the New World, spending an enormous sum and meeting with overwhelming defeat. The collapse of that enterprise so weakened us, militarily and economically, that it was an easy matter for the Greeks to take control of the Empire two generations later. Flavius knew from that sorry precedent that we could never achieve the conquest of those fierce nations of the New World, but he hoped at least to open commercial contact with them, and from the earliest years of his reign he made efforts to that end.

His successor was another Hispaniard of Tarraco, Gaius Julius Flavillus, a man of nobler birth than Flavius whose family fortunes may have underwritten the original Flavian rebellion. Gaius Flavillus was a forceful man in his own right and an admirable Emperor, but, reigning between two such mighty figures as Flavius Romulus and Trajan Draco, he seems more of a consolidator than an innovator. During his time on the throne, which covered the period from 2238 to 2253, he continued the maritime policy of his predecessor, though giving more emphasis on voyages to the New World than to Africa and Asia, while also striving to create greater unity between the Latin and Greek halves of the Empire itself, something to which Flavius Romulus had devoted relatively little attention.

It was during the reign of Gaius Flavillus that Trajan Draco rose to prominence. His first military assignments seem to have been in Africa, where he won early promotion for his heroism in putting down an uprising in Alexandria, and then for suppressing the depredations of bandits in the desert south of Carthago. How he came to the attention of Emperor Gaius is unclear, though probably his Hispanic birth had something to do with it. By 2248, though, we find him in command of the Praetorian Guard. He was then only about twenty-five years old. Soon he had acquired the additional title of First Tribune, and shortly Consul too, and in 2252, the year before his death, Gaius formally adopted Trajan as his son and proclaimed him as his heir.

It was as though Flavius Romulus had been born again, when Trajan Draco, soon afterward, assumed the purple under the name of Trajan VII. In the place of the aloof patrician Gaius Flavillus came a second Hispaniard peasant to the throne, full of the same boisterous energy that had catapulted Flavius to greatness, and the whole world echoed to the resonant sound of his mighty laughter.

Indeed, Trajan was Flavius redone on an even grander scale. They were both big men, but Trajan was a giant. (I, his remote descendant, am quite tall myself.) He wore his dark hair to the middle of his back. His brow was high and noble; his eyes flashed like an eagle's; his voice could be heard from the Capitoline Hill to the Janiculum. He could drink a keg of wine at a sitting with no ill effect. In the eighty years of his life he had five wives—not, I hasten to add, at the same time—and innumerable mistresses. He sired twenty legitimate children, the tenth of whom was my own ancestor, and such a horde of bastards that it is no unusual thing today to see the hawk-faced visage of Trajan Draco staring back at one in the streets of almost any city in the world.

He was a lover not only of women but of the arts, especially those of statuary and music, and of the sciences. Such fields as mathematics and astronomy and engineering had fallen into neglect during the two hundred years of the West's subservience to the soft, luxury-loving Greeks. Trajan sponsored their renewal. He rebuilt the ancient capital at Roma from end to end, filling it with palaces and universities and theaters as though such things had never existed there before; and, perhaps for fear that that might seem insufficient, he moved on eastward into the province of Pannonia, to the little city of Venia on the River Danubius, and built himself what was essentially a second capital there, with its own great university, a host of theaters, a grand Senate building, and a royal palace that is one of the wonders of the world. His reasoning was that Venia, though darker and rainier and colder than sunny Roma, was closer to the heart of the Empire. He would not allow the partition of the Empire once again into eastern and western realms, immense though the task of governing the whole thing was. Placing his capital in a central location like Venia allowed him to look more easily westward toward Gallia and Britannia, northward into the Teuton lands and those of the Goths, and eastward to the Greek world, while maintaining the reins of power entirely in his own hands.

Trajan did not, however, spend any great portion of his time at the new capital, nor, for that matter, at Roma either. He was constantly on the move, now presenting himself at Constantinopolis to remind the Greeks of Asia that they had an Emperor, or touring Syria or Aiguptos or Persia, or darting up into the far north to hunt the wild shaggy beasts that live in those Hyperborean lands, or revisiting his native Hispania, where he had transformed the ancient city of Sevilla into the main port of embarkation for voyages to the New World. He was a tireless man.

And in the twenty-fifth year of his reign—2278 A.U.C.—he set out on his greatest journey of all, the stupendous deed for which his name will be forever remembered: his voyage completely around the world, beginning and ending at Sevilla, and taking into its compass almost every nation both civilized and barbaric that this globe contains.

Had anyone before him conceived of such an audacious thing? I find nothing in all the records of history to indicate it.

No one has ever seriously doubted, of course, that the world is a sphere, and therefore is open to circumnavigation. Common sense alone shows us the curvature of the Earth as we look off into the distance; and the notion that there is an edge somewhere, off which rash mariners must inevitably plunge, is a fable suited for children's tales, nothing more. Nor is there any reason to dread the existence of an impassable zone of flame somewhere in the southern seas, as simple folk used to think: it is twenty-five hundred years since ships first sailed around the southern tip of Africa and no one has seen any walls of fire yet.

But even the boldest of our seamen had never even thought of sailing all the way around the world's middle, let alone attempting it, before Trajan Draco set out from Sevilla to do it. Voyages to Arabia and India and even Khitai by way of Africa, yes, and voyages to the New World also, first to Mexico and then down the western coast of Mexico along the narrow strip of land that links the two New World continents until the great empire of Peru was reached. From that we learned of the existence of a second Ocean Sea, one that was perhaps even greater than the one that separates Europa from the New World. On its eastern side were Mexico and Peru; on its western side, Khitai and Cipangu, with India farther on. But what lay in between? Were there other empires, perhaps, in the middle of that Western Sea— empires mightier than Khitai and Cipangu and India put together? What if there were an empire somewhere out there that put even Imperial Roma into the shade?

It was to the everlasting glory of Trajan VII Draco that he was determined to find out, even if it cost him his life. He must have felt utterly secure in his throne, if he was willing to abandon the capital to subordinates for so long a span of time; either that, or he did not care a fig about the risk of usurpation, so avid was he to make the journey.

His five-year expedition around the world was, I think, one of the most significant achievements in all history, rivaling, perhaps, the creation of the Empire by Augustus and its expansion across almost the whole of the known world by Trajan I and Hadrianus. It is the one thing, above all else that he achieved, that drew me to undertake my research into his life. He found no empires to rival Roma on that journey, no, but he did discover the myriad island kingdoms of the Western Sea, whose products have so greatly enriched our lives; and, moreover, the route he pioneered through the narrow lower portion of the southern continent of the New World has given us permanent access by sea to the lands of Asia from either direction, regardless of any opposition that we might encounter from the ever-troublesome Mexicans and Peruvians on the one hand or the warlike Cipanguans and the unthinkably multitudinous Khitaians on the other.

But—although we are familiar with the general outlines of Trajan's voyage—the journal that he kept, full of highly specific detail, has been lost for centuries. Which is why I felt such delight when one of my researchers, snuffling about in a forgotten corner of the Office of Maritime Affairs in Sevilla, reported to me early this year that he had stumbled quite accidentally upon that very journal. It had been filed all that time amongst the documents of a later reign, buried unobtrusively in a pack of bills of lading and payroll records. I had it shipped to me here in Tauromenium by Imperial courier, a journey that took six weeks, for the packet went overland all the way from Hispania to Italia—I would not risk so precious a thing on the high sea—and then down the entire length of Italia to the tip of Bruttium, across the strait by ferry to Messana, and thence to me.

Was it, though, the richly detailed narrative I yearned for, or would it simply be a dry list of navigators' marks, longitudes and latitudes and ascensions and compass readings?

Well, I would not know that until I had it in my hands. And as luck would have it, the very day the packet arrived was the day the Caesar Demetrius returned from his month's sojourn in Africa. I barely had time to unseal the bulky packet and run my thumb along the edge of the thick sheaf of time-darkened vellum pages that it contained before a messenger came to me with word that I was summoned to the Caesar's presence at once.

The Caesar, as I have already said, is an impatient man. I paused only long enough to look beyond the title page to the beginning of the text, and felt a profound chill of recognition as the distinctive backhanded cursive script of Trajan Draco rose to my astonished eyes. I allowed myself one further glimpse within, perhaps the hundredth page, and found a passage that dealt with a meeting with some island king. Yes! Yes! The journal of the voyage, indeed!

I turned the packet over to the major-domo of my villa, a trustworthy enough Sicilian freedman named Pantaleon, and told him exactly what would happen to him if any harm came to a single page while I was away.

Then I betook myself to the Caesar's hilltop palace, where I found him in the garden, inspecting a pair of camels that he had brought back with him from Africa. He was wearing some sort of hooded desert robe and had a splendid curving scimitar thrust through his belt. In the five weeks of his absence the sun had so blackened the skin of his face and hands that he could have passed easily for an Arab. "Pisander!" he cried at once. I had forgotten that foolish name in his absence. He grinned at me and his teeth gleamed like beacons against that newly darkened visage.

I offered the appropriate pleasantries, had he had an enjoyable trip and all of that, but he swept my words away with a flick of his hand. "Do you know what I thought of, Pisander, all the time of my journey? Our great project! Our glorious enterprise! And do you know, I realize now that it does not go nearly far enough. I have decided, I think, to make Sicilia my capital when I am Emperor. There is no need for me to live in the cool stormy north when I can so easily be this close to Africa, a place that I now see I love enormously. And so we must build a Senate house here too, in Panormus, I think, and great villas for all the officials of my court, and a library—do you know, Pisander, there's no library worthy of the name on this whole island? But we can divide the holdings of Alexandria and bring half here, once there's a building worthy of housing them. And then—"

I will spare you the whole of it. Suffice it to say that his madness had entered an entirely new phase of uninhibited grandiosity. And I was the first victim of it, for he informed me that he and I were going to depart that very night on a trip from one end of Sicilia to the other, searching out sites for all the miraculous new structures he had in mind. He was going to do for Sicilia what Augustus had done for the city of Roma itself: make it the wonder of the age. Forgotten now was the plan to begin the building program with the new palace in Tauromenium. First we must trek from Tauromenium to Lilybaeum on the other coast, and back again from Eryx to Syracusa to here, pausing at every point in between.

And so we did. Sicilia is a large island; the journey occupied two and a half months. The Caesar was a cheerful enough traveling companion—he is witty, after all, and intelligent, and lively, and the fact that he is a madman was only occasionally a hindrance. We traveled in great luxury and the half-healed state of my ankle meant that I was carried in a litter much of the time, which made me feel like some great pampered potentate of antiquity, a Pharaoh, perhaps, or Darius of Persia. But one effect of this suddenly imposed interruption in my studies was that it became impossible for me to examine the journal of Trajan VII for many weeks, which was maddening. To take it with me while we traveled and study it surreptitiously in my bedchamber was too risky; the Caesar can be a jealous man, and if he were to come in unannounced and find me diverting my energies to something unconnected to his project, he would be perfectly capable of seizing the journal from me on the spot and tossing it into the flames. So I left the book behind, turning it over to Spiculo and telling him to guard it with his life; and for many a night thereafter, as we darted hither and yon across the island in increasingly more torrid weather, summer having now arrived and Sicilia lying as it does beneath the merciless southern sun, I lay tossing restlessly, imagining the contents of the journal in my fevered mind, devising for myself a fantastic set of adventures for Trajan to take the place of the real ones that the Caesar Demetrius had in his blithe selfishness prevented me from reading in the newly discovered journal. Though I knew, even then, that the reality, once I had the chance to discover it, would far surpass anything I could imagine for myself.

And then I returned at last to Tauromenium; and reclaimed the book from Spiculo and read its every word in three astonishing days and nights, scarcely sleeping a moment. And found in it, along with many a tale of wonder and beauty and strangeness, many things that indeed I would not have imagined, which were not so pleasing to find.

Though it was written in the rougher Latin of medieval days, the text gave me no difficulties. The Emperor Trajan VII was an admirable writer, whose style, blunt and plain and highly fluent, reminded me of nothing so much as that of Julius Caesar, another great leader who could handle a stylus as well as he did a sword. He had, apparently, kept the journal as a private record of his circumnavigation, very likely not meaning to have it become a public document at all, and its survival in the archives seems to have been merely fortuitous.

His tale began in the shipyards of Sevilla: five vessels being readied for the voyage, none of them large, the greatest being only of 120 tons. He gave detailed listings of their stores. Weapons, of course, sixty crossbows, fifty matchlock arquebuses (this weapon having newly been invented then), heavy artillery pieces, javelins, lances, pikes, shields. Anvils, grindstones, forges, bellows, lanterns, implements with which fortresses could be constructed on newly discovered islands by the masons and stonecutters of his crew; drugs, medicines, salves; six wooden quadrants, six metal astrolabes, thirty-seven compass needles, six pairs of measuring compasses, and so forth. For use in trading with the princes of newly discovered kingdoms, a cargo of flasks of quicksilver and copper bars, bales of cotton, velvet, satin, and brocades, thousands of small bells, fishhooks, mirrors, knives, beads, combs, brass and copper bracelets, and such. All this was enumerated with a clerk's finicky care: reading it taught me much about a side of Trajan Draco's character that I had not suspected.

At last the day of sailing. Down the River Baetis from Sevilla to the Ocean Sea, and quickly out to the Isles of the Canaria, where, however, they saw none of the huge dogs for which the place is named. But they did find the noteworthy Raining Tree, from whose gigantic swollen trunk the entire water supply of one island was derived. I think this tree has perished, for no one has seen it since.

Then came the leap across the sea to the New World, a journey hampered by sluggish winds. They crossed the Equator; the pole star no longer could be seen; the heat melted the tar in the ships' seams and turned the decks into ovens. But then came better sailing, and swiftly they reached the western shore of the southern continent where it bulges far out toward Africa. The Empire of Peru had no sway in this place; it was inhabited by cheerful naked people who made a practice of eating human flesh, "but only," the Emperor tells us, "their enemies."

It was Trajan's intention to sail completely around the bottom of the continent, an astounding goal considering that no one knew how far south it extended, or what conditions would be encountered at its extremity. For that matter, it might not come to an end in the south at all, and so there would be no sea route westward whatever, but only a continuous landmass running clear down to the southern pole and blocking all progress by sea. And there was always the possibility of meeting with interference by Peruvian forces somewhere along the way. But southward they went, probing at every inlet in the hope that it might mark the termination of the continent and a connection with the sea that lay on the other side.

Several of these inlets proved to be the mouths of mighty rivers, but wild hostile tribes lived along their banks, which made exploration perilous; and Trajan feared also that these rivers would only take them deep inland, into Peruvian-controlled territory, without bringing them to the sea on the continent's western side. And so they continued south and south and south along the coast. The weather, which had been very hot, swiftly worsened to the south, giving them dark skies and icy winds. But this they already knew, that the seasons are reversed below the Equator, and winter comes there in our summer, so they were not surprised by the change.

Along the shore they found peculiar black-and-white birds that could swim but not fly; these were plump and proved good to eat. There still appeared to be no westerly route. The coast, barren now, seemed endless. Hail and sleet assailed them, mountains of ice floated in the choppy sea, cold rain froze in their beards. Food and water ran low. The men began to grumble. Although they had an Emperor in their midst, they began to speak openly of turning back. Trajan wondered if his life might be in danger.

Soon after which, as such wintry conditions descended upon them as no man had ever seen before, there came an actual mutiny: the captains of two ships announced that they were withdrawing from the expedition. "They invited me to meet with them to discuss the situation," Trajan wrote. "Plainly I was to be killed. I sent five trusted men to the first rebel ship, bearing a message from me, with twenty more secretly in another boat. When the first group came aboard and the rebel captain greeted them on deck, my ambassadors slew him at once; and then the men of the second boat came on board." The mutiny was put down. The three ringleaders were executed immediately, and eleven other men were put ashore on a frigid island that had not even the merest blade of grass. I would not have expected Trajan Draco to treat the conspirators mildly, but the calm words in which he tells of leaving these men to a terrible death were chilling indeed.

The voyagers went on. In the bleak southern lands they discovered a race of naked giants—eight feet tall, says Trajan—and captured two to bring back to Roma as curiosities. "They roared like bulls, and cried out to the demons they worshipped. We put them on separate ships, in chains. But they would take no food from us and quickly perished."

Through storms and wintry darkness they proceeded south, still finding no way west, and even Trajan began now to think they would have to abandon the quest. The sea now was nearly impassable on account of ice: they found another source of the fat flightless birds, though, and set up winter camp on shore, remaining for three months, which greatly depleted their stores of food. But when in weather that was fairer, though still quite inhospitable, they decided finally to go on, they came almost at once to what is now known as the Strait of Trajan near the continent's uttermost point. Trajan sent one of his captains in to investigate, and he found it narrow but deep, with a strong tidal flow, and salty water throughout: no river, but a way across to the Western Sea!

The trip through the strait was harrowing, past needle-sharp rocks, through impenetrable mists, over water that surged and boiled from one wall of the channel to another. But green trees now appeared, and the lights of the natives' campfires, and before long they emerged in the other sea: "The sky was wondrously blue, the clouds were fleecy, the waves were no more than rippling wavelets, burnished by the brilliant sun." The scene was so peaceful that Trajan gave the new sea the name of Pacificus, on account of its tranquility.

His plan now was to sail due west, for it seemed likely to him then, entering into this uncharted sea, that Cipangu and Khitai must lie only a short distance in that direction. Nor did he desire to venture northward along the continent's side because that would bring him to the territory of the belligerent Peruvians, and his five ships would be no match for an entire empire.

But an immediate westward course proved impossible because of contrary winds and eastward-bearing currents. So northward he went anyway, for a time, staying close to shore and keeping a wary eye out for Peruvians. The sun was harshly bright in the cloudless sky, and there was no rain. When finally they could turn to the west again, the sea was utterly empty of islands and looked vast beyond all imagining. By night strange stars appeared, notably five brilliant ones arranged like a cross in the heavens. The remaining food supply dwindled rapidly; attempts at catching fish proved useless, and the men ate chips of wood and mounds of sawdust, and hunted down the rats that infested the holds. Water was rationed to a single sip a day. The risk now was not so much another mutiny as out-and-out starvation.

They came then to some small islands, finally: poor ones, where nothing grew but stunted, twisted shrubs. But there were people there too, fifteen or twenty of them, simple naked people who painted themselves in stripes. "They greeted us with a hail of stones and arrows. Two of our men were slain. We had no choice but to kill them all. And then, since there was no food to be found on the island except for a few pitiful fishes and crabs that these people had caught that morning and nothing of any size or substance was to be had off shore, we roasted the bodies of the dead and ate those, for otherwise we would surely have died of hunger."

I cannot tell you how many times I read and reread those lines, hoping to find that they said something other than what they did. But they always were the same.

In the fourth month of the journey across the Pacificus other islands appeared, fertile ones, now, whose villagers grew dates of some sort from which they made bread, wine, and oil, and also had yams, bananas, coconuts, and other such tropical things with which we are now so familiar. Some of these islanders were friendly to the mariners, but most were not. Trajan's journal becomes a record of atrocities. "We killed them all; we burned their village as an example to their neighbors; we loaded our ships with their produce." The same phrases occur again and again. There is not a word of apology or regret. It was as if by tasting human flesh they had turned into monsters themselves.

Beyond these islands was more emptiness—Trajan saw now that the Pacificus was an ocean whose size was beyond all comprehension, compared with which even the Ocean Sea was a mere lake—and then, after another disheartening trek of many weeks, came the discovery of the great island group that we call the Augustines, seven thousand islands large and small, stretching in a huge arc across more than a thousand miles of the Pacificus. "A chieftain came to us, a majestic figure with markings drawn on his face and a shirt of cotton fringed with silk; he carried a javelin and a dagger of bronze encrusted with gold, a shield that also sparkled with the yellow metal, and he wore earrings, armlets, and bracelets of gold likewise." His people offered spices—cinnamon, cloves, ginger, nutmeg, mace—in exchange for the simple trinkets the Romans had brought, and also rubies, diamonds, pearls, and nuggets of gold. "My purpose was fulfilled," Trajan wrote. "We had found a fabulous new empire in the midst of this immense sea."

Which they proceeded to conquer in the most brutal fashion. Though in the beginning the Romans had peaceful relations with the natives of the Augustines, demonstrating hourglasses and compasses to them and impressing them by having their ships' guns fired and by staging mock gladiatorial contests in which men in armor fought against men with tridents and nets, things quickly went wrong. Some of Trajan's men, having had too much of the date wine to drink, fell upon the island women and possessed them with all the zeal that men who have not touched a woman's breasts for close upon a year are apt to show. The women, Trajan relates, appeared willing enough at first; but his men treated them with such shameful violence and cruelty that objections were raised, and then quarrels broke out as the island men came to defend their women (some of whom were no more than ten years old), and in the end there was a bloody massacre, culminating in the murder of the noble island chieftain.

This section of the journal is unbearable to read. On the one hand it is full of fascinating detail about the customs of the islanders, how pigs are sacrificed by old women who caper about blowing reed trumpets and smear the blood of the sacrifice on the foreheads of the men, and how males of all ages have their sexual organs pierced from one side to the other with a gold or tin bolt as large as a goose quill, and so on and on with many a strange detail that seems to have come from another world. But interspersed amongst all this is the tale of the slaughter of the islanders, the inexorable destruction of them under one pretext or another, the journey from isle to isle, the Romans always being greeted in peace but matters degenerating swiftly into rape, murder, looting.

Yet Trajan appears unaware of anything amiss here. Page after page, in the same calm, steady tone, describes these horrors as though they were the natural and inevitable consequence of the collision of alien cultures. My own reactions of shock and dismay, as I read them, make it amazingly clear to me how different our era is from his, and how very little like a Renaissance man I actually am. Trajan saw the crimes of his men as unfortunate necessities at the worst; I saw them as monstrous. And I came to realize that one profound and complex aspect of the decadence of our civilization is our disdain for violence of this sort. We are Romans still; we abhor disorder and have not lost our skill at the arts of war; but when Trajan Draco can speak so blandly of retaliating with cannons against an attack with arrows, or of the burning of entire villages in retribution for a petty theft from one of our ships, or the sating of his men's lust on little girls because they were unwilling to take the time to seek out their older sisters, I could not help but feel that there is something to be said in favor of our sort of decadence.

During these three days and nights of steady reading of the journals I saw no one, neither Spiculo nor the Caesar nor any of the women with whom I have allayed the boredom of my years in Sicilia. I read on and on and on, until my head began to swim, and I could not stop, horrified though I often was.

Now that the empty part of the Pacificus was behind them, one island after another appeared, not only the myriad Augustines, but others farther to the west and south, multitudes of them; for although there is no continent in this ocean, there are long chains of islands, many of them far larger than our Britannia and Sicilia. Over and over I was told of the boats ornamented with gold and peacock feathers bearing island chieftains offering rich gifts, or of horned fish and oysters the size of sheep and trees whose leaves, when they fall to the ground, will rise on little feet and go crawling away, and kings called rajahs who could not be addressed face-to-face, but only through speaking tubes in the walls of their palaces. Isles of spices, isles of gold, isles of pearls—marvel after marvel, and all of them now seized and claimed by the invincible Roman Emperor in the name of eternal Roma.

Then, finally, these strange island realms gave way to familiar territory: for now Asia was in sight, the shores of Khitai. Trajan made landfall there, exchanged gifts with the Khitaian sovereign, and acquired from him those Khitaian experts in the arts of printing and gunpowder-making and the manufacture of fine porcelains whose skills, brought back by him to Roma, gave such impetus to this new era of prosperity and growth that we call the Renaissance.

He went on to India and Arabia afterward, loading his ships with treasure there as well, and down one side of Africa and up the other. It was the same route as all our previous far voyages, but done this time in reverse.

Trajan knew once he had rounded Africa's southernmost cape that the spanning of the globe had been achieved, and he hastened onward toward Europa, coming first to Lusitania's southwestern tip, then coasting along southern Hispania until he returned with his five ships and their surviving crew to the mouth of the River Baetis and, soon after, to the starting point at Sevilla. "These are mariners who surely merit an eternal fame," he concluded, "more justly than the

Argonauts of old who sailed with Jason in search of the golden fleece. For these our wonderful vessels, sailing southwards through the Ocean Sea toward the Antarctic Pole, and then turning west, followed that course so long that, passing round, we came into the east, and thence again into the west, not by sailing back, but by proceeding constantly forward: so compassing about the globe of the world, until we marvelously regained our native land of Hispania, and the port from which we departed, Sevilla."

There was one curious postscript. Trajan had made an entry in his journal for each day of the voyage. By his reckoning, the date of his return to Sevilla was the ninth day of Januarius in 2282; but when he went ashore, he was told that the day was Januarius 10. By sailing continuously westward around the world, they had lost a day somewhere. This remained a mystery until the astronomer Macrobius of Alexandria pointed out that the time of sunrise varies by four minutes for each degree of longitude, and so the variation for a complete global circuit of three hundred sixty degrees would be 1,440 minutes, or one full day. It was the clearest proof, if anyone had dared to doubt Trajan's word, that the fleet had sailed entirely around the world to reach the strange new isles of that unknown sea. And by so doing had unlocked a treasure chest of wonders that the great Emperor would fully exploit in the two decades of absolute power that remained to him before his death at the age of eighty.

And did I, having gained access at last to the key document of the reign of Trajan VII, set immediately about the task of finishing my account of his extraordinary life?

No. No. And this is why.

Within four days of my finishing my reading of the journal, and while my head was still throbbing with all I had discovered therein, a messenger came from Italia with news that the Emperor Lodovicus Augustus had died in Roma of an apoplexy, and his son the Caesar Demetrius had succeeded to the throne as Demetrius II Augustus.

It happened that I was with the Caesar when this message arrived. He showed neither grief over his father's passing nor jubilation over his own ascent to the highest power. He simply smiled a small smile, the merest quirking of the corner of his mouth, and said to me, "Well, Draco, it looks as if we must pack for another trip, and so soon after our last one, too."

I had not wanted to believe—none of us did—that Demetrius would ever become Emperor. We had all hoped that Lodovicus would find some way around the necessity of it: would discover, perhaps, some hitherto unknown illegitimate son, dwelling in Babylon or Londin all these years, who could be brought forth and given preference. It was Lodovicus, after all, who had cared so little to witness the antics of his son and heir that he had packed Demetrius off to Sicilia these three years past and forbidden him to set foot on the mainland, though he would be free to indulge whatever whim he fancied in his island exile.

But that exile now was ended. And in that same instant also was ended all the Caesar's scheme to beautify Sicilia.

It was as though those plans had never been. "You will sit among my high ministers, Draco," the new Emperor told me. "I will make you Consul, I think, in my first year. I will have the other Consulship myself. And you will also have the portfolio of the Ministry of Public Works; for the capital beyond all doubt is in need of beautification. I have a design for a new palace for myself in mind, and then perhaps we can do something about improving the shabby old Capitol, and there are some interesting foreign gods, I think, who would appreciate having temples erected in their honor, and then—"

If I had been Trajan Draco, I would perhaps have assassinated our crazy Demetrius in that moment and taken the throne for myself, both for the Empire's sake and my own. But I am only Tiberius Ulpius Draco, not Trajan of the same cognomen, and Demetrius has become Emperor and you know the rest.

And as for my book on Trajan the Dragon: well, perhaps I will complete it someday, when the Emperor has run short of projects for me to design. But I doubt that he ever will, and even if he does, I am not sure that it is a book I still want to give to the public, now that I have read Trajan's journal of the circumnavigation. If I were to tell the story of my ancestor's towering achievement, would I dare to tell the whole of it? I think not. And so I feel only relief at allowing my incomplete draft of the book to gather dust in its box. It was my aim, in this research of mine, to discover the inner nature of my great royal kinsman the Dragon; but I delved too deeply, it seems, and came to know him a little too well.

THE HYPERION CANTOS

Dan Simmons

Hyperion (1989)
The Fall of Hyperion (1990)
Endymion (1996)
The Rise of Endymion (1997)

The four *Hyperion* books cover more than thirteen centuries in time, tens of thousands of light-years in space, more than three thousand pages of the reader's time, the rise and fall of at least two major interstellar civilizations, and more ideas than the author could shake an epistemological stick at. They are, in other words, space opera.

As the reviewer for the *New York Times* said of the last book in the series, "Yet *The Rise of Endymion,* like its three predecessors, is also a full-blooded action novel, replete with personal combats and battles in space that are distinguished from the formulaic space opera by the magnitude of what is at stake—which is nothing less than the salvation of the human soul."

The salvation of the human soul—in the sense of finding the essence of what makes and keeps us human—is indeed the binding theme through all of these space battles, dark ages, new societies, and the coming of a new messiah.

Hyperion introduces us to seven pilgrims crossing the WorldWeb of the Hegemony of Man on their way to the Valley of the Time Tombs on the planet Hyperion. In true Chaucerian form, six of the pilgrims (one doesn't survive long enough) tell each other their personal stories and reasons for coming on the pilgrimage as they cross The Sea of Grass and other obstacles to reach the Shrike—the fabled killing creature of the Time Tombs, part machine, part time-traveling god, part avenging angel, and all sharp thorns, spikes, claws, and teeth. The idea is that one of the pilgrims will have his or her request granted by the Shrike; the others will die. Through their stories we learn of the TechnoCore—a hidden and manipulative group of Autonomous Intelligences escaped from human control—of the destroyed (or perhaps just kidnapped) Old Earth; of the fake war between the Hegemony and the space-adapted, human-evolved Ousters; and of one Jesuit's discovery—and rejection—of a cross-shaped symbiote called the cruciform which can bring about physical resurrection. The story ends with the pilgrims' arrival at the Valley of the Time Tombs.

The Fall of Hyperion picks up exactly where *Hyperion* left off but utilizes totally different narrative techniques and structures to pursue John Keats's themes of individuals—and species—not happily surrendering their place in the scheme of things when evolution tells them it is time to go. The pilgrims from the first book find that their fates are not as simple as they had thought: the Time Tombs open, mysterious messages and messengers from the future show that the struggle for the human soul continues on for many centuries, the Shrike wreaks havoc but does not kill all, nor does it grant requests, and the complex interstellar society of the Hegemony of Man with its WorldWeb farcaster system is kicked apart like an ant hill by interstellar war—although whether the war is between Hegemony and Ousters, or Humanity and the TechnoCore, is not clear. Of the pilgrims, one named Brawne Lamia is pregnant by her lover—the John Keats cybrid created by the Core—and it is rumored that her child will be The One Who Teaches, humanity's next Messiah. Another, soldier Fedmahn Kassad, travels to the future to meet his fate in combat with the Shrike. A third, Sol Weintraub, has stopped his daughter from aging backward to nonexistence, but now has to travel with her through a Time Tomb to their own complicated part in the mosaic of the future. The fourth pilgrim, the Hegemony Consul, takes an ancient spacecraft whose AI is inhabited with the essence of the dead John Keats cybrid and returns to explore the ruins of the Hegemony. The fifth pilgrim, a priest, dies and is reborn through the cruciform as the Jesuit whose tale he told—now the pope of a reborn Catholic Church. The final living pilgrim—the seven-hundred-year-old poet, Martin Silenus, who has been telling all this tale—remains as obscene and crotchety as ever.

Endymion opens 274 years after the Fall of the Farcasters. Things have gone to hell—which is usually the case in so-called Dark Ages between empires—but the Pax, the civil-military arm of the reinvigorated Catholic Church, now extends its dominion to most of the former worlds of the Hegemony. The Church—and the Pax—control its citizens through its monopoly of resurrection. Unknown to most, the Church has entered into a

Faustian bargain with the now-hidden TechnoCore and utilizes the cruciform symbiotes to bring its followers back to life and into obedience. Suddenly, an eleven-year-old messiah-to-be named Aenea appears on the scene. Aenea is Brawne Lamia's daughter, and she has fled across almost three centuries through the Time Tombs only to find the Pax authorities searching for her, and with both the Church and the Core acting on an absolute need to destroy her. The still alive, still obscene, still cranky poet, Martin Silenus, assigns a young soldier and escaped murderer—Raul Endymion—to rescue the girl and to transport her wherever she wants to go on the now-dead Consul's returned ship. Most of *Endymion* is a massive chase across human space with the Pax in close pursuit, as Raul, Aenea, and the blue android A. Bettik run for their lives and perhaps the future of humanity. Created by the Core, unleashed by the Church, is a female monstrosity named Rhadamanth Nemes who makes the killing-creature Shrike look like a Sunday-school teacher. At the end of *Endymion,* Raul, Aenea, and a wounded A. Bettik make it to Old Earth—not destroyed after all, just transported to the Lesser Magellanic Clouds by aliens known only as the Lions and Tigers and Bears. Our trio settles in at Frank Lloyd Wright's Taliesin West while young Aenea trains to be an architect.

The Rise of Endymion picks up four years after the events of *Endymion.* Aenea, now sixteen, knows that she must return to Pax-dominated space to carry out her role as The One Who Teaches. Raul, her protector and friend, has no wish to go. The idea of martyrdom—especially his beloved Aenea's martyrdom—appalls him. Aenea sends Raul "ahead" by farcaster, but actually his few weeks of traveling allow Aenea to age five years, thanks to the miracle of time dilation and time-debt during Raul's interstellar travels in the old Consul's ship. When they meet again, Aenea is a woman and well along in her role of The One Who Teaches. The Pax is still after her. The Church still needs her dead. The creature Nemes has now been joined by three equally impossibly powerful and destructive siblings. And amidst all this, on the mountaintop-and-cloud world of T'ien Shan, Aenea and Raul become lovers. This makes Raul, our narrator through the two books, even less happy at the thought of his beloved's becoming the messiah so many have predicted. Raul is not the smartest character in these books, but he is absolutely loyal, absolutely in love, and he is smart enough to know the fate of most messiahs.

The Rise of Endymion ends with tragedy, torture, death, and separation, followed—not miraculously but inevitably—by great enlightenment and the reunion of Raul and Aenea. The Pax has murdered her—thus unwittingly bringing about their own downfall through Aenea's Shared Moment, wherein every human being on every world glimpses the truth behind the Pax, the Church, the cruciform, and the parasitic TechnoCore—but during her "absent five years" while Raul was traveling, she had come ahead in time with the help of the Shrike to spend one year, eleven months, one week, and six hours with Raul on Old Earth. Earth has been emptied, cleansed, renewed, and returned to its proper place in the solar system by the Lions and Tigers and Bears.

Martin Silenus, the poet and constant character through all the books, dies shortly after Raul and Aenea are wed. Some of the poet's final words were to the Consul's ship, which has also come through a thousand years and four fat books—"See you in hell, Ship."

As *The Rise of Endymion* ends, the still-mysterious Shrike stands vigil over Martin Silenus's grave on Old Earth; thanks to Aenea's sacrifice, humanity has been freed to "learn the language of the dead" by tapping into the empathic fabric underlying the universe—and also by now being able to freecast, that is, personally teleport anywhere; and Raul and Aenea fly off on their ancient hawking mat to celebrate their honeymoon on the empty, virginal Old Earth—". . . our new playground, our ancient world . . . our new world . . . our first and future and finest world."

—*Dan Simmons*

Orphans of the Helix

by

Dan Simmons

THE GREAT SPINSHIP TRANSLATED DOWN FROM HAWKING SPACE INTO THE RED-and-white double light of a close binary. While the 684,300 people of the Amoiete Spectrum Helix dreamt on in deep cryogenic sleep, the five AIs in charge of the ship conferred. They had encountered an unusual phenomenon and while four of the five had agreed it important enough to bring the huge spinship out of C-plus Hawking space, there was a lively debate—continuing for several microseconds—about what to do next.

The spinship itself looked beautiful in the distant light of the two stars, white and red light bathing its kilometer-long skin, the starlight flashing on the three thousand environmental deep-sleep pods, the groups of thirty pods on each of the one hundred spin hubs spinning past so quickly that the swing arms were like the blur of great, over-lapping fan blades, while the three thousand pods themselves appeared to be a single, flashing gem blazing with red and white light. The Aeneans had adapted the ship so that the hubs of the spinwheels along the long, central shaft of the ship were slanted—the first thirty spin arms angled back, the second hub angling its longer thirty-pod arms forward, so that the deep-sleep pods themselves passed between each other with only microseconds of separation, coalescing into a solid blur that made the ship under full spin resemble exactly what its name implied—*Helix*. An observer watching from some hundreds of kilometers away would see what looked to be a rotating human double DNA helix catching the light from the paired suns.

All five of the AIs decided that it would be best to call in the spin pods. First the great hubs changed their orientation until the gleaming helix became a series of three thousand slowing carbon-carbon spin arms, each with an ovoid pod visible at its tip through the slow-ing blur of speed. Then the pod arms stopped and retracted against the long ship, each deep-sleep pod fitting into a concave nesting cusp in the hull like an egg being set carefully into a container.

The *Helix*, no longer resembling its name now so much as a long, slender arrow with command centers at the bulbous, triangular head, and the Hawking drive and larger fusion engines bulking at the stern, morphed eight layers of covering over the nested spin arms and pods. All of the AIs voted to decelerate toward the G8 white star under a conservative four hundred gravities and to extend the containment field to class twenty. There was no visible threat in either system of the binary, but the red giant in the more distant system was—as it should be—expelling vast amounts of dust and stellar debris. The AI who took the greatest pride in its navigational skills and caution warned that the entry trajectory toward the G8 star should steer very clear of the L_1 Roche lobe point because of the massive heliosphere shock waves there, and all five AIs began charting a deceleration course into the G8 system that would avoid the worst of the helio-sphere turmoil. The radiation shock waves there could be dealt with easily using even a class-three containment field, but with 684,300 human souls aboard and under their care, none of the AIs would take the slightest chance.

Their next decision was unanimous and inevitable. Given the rea-son for the deviation and deceleration into the G8 system, they would have to awaken humans. Saigyō, AI in charge of personnel lists, duty rosters, psychology profiles, and who had made it its business to meet and know each of the 684,300 men, women, and children, took several seconds to review the list before deciding on the nine people to awaken.

Dem Lia awoke with none of the dull hangover feel of the old-fashioned cryogenic fugue units. She felt rested and fit as she sat up in her deep-sleep crèche, the unit arm offering her the traditional glass of orange juice.

"Emergency?" she said, her voice no more thick or dull than it would have been after a good night's sleep.

"Nothing threatening the ship or the mission," said Saigyō, the AI. "An anomaly of interest. An old radio transmission from a system which may be a possible source of resupply. There are no problems whatsoever with ship function or life support. Everyone is well. The ship is in no danger."

"How far are we from the last system we checked?" said Dem Lia, finishing her orange juice and donning her shipsuit with its emerald green stripe on the left arm and turban. Her people had traditionally worn desert robes, each robe the color of the Amoiete Spectrum that the different families had chosen to honor, but robes were impractical for spinship travel where zero g was a frequent environment.

"Six thousand three hundred light-years," said Saigyō.

Dem Lia stopped herself from blinking. "How many years since last awakening?" she said softly. "How many years' total voyage ship time? How many years' total voyage time-debt?"

"Nine ship years and one hundred two time-debt years since last awakening," said Saigyō. "Total voyage ship time, thirty-six years. Total voyage time-debt relative to human space, four hundred and one years, three months, one week, five days."

Dem Lia rubbed her neck. "How many of us are you awakening?"

"Nine."

Dem Lia nodded, quit wasting time chatting with the AI, glanced around only once at the two-hundred-some sealed sarcophagi where her family and friends continued sleeping, and took the main shipline people mover to the command deck, where the other eight would be gathering.

The Aeneans had followed the Amoiete Spectrum Helix people's request to construct the command deck like the bridge of an ancient torchship or some Old Earth, pre-Hegira seagoing vessel. The deck was oriented one direction to down and Dem Lia was pleased to notice on the ride to the command deck that the ship's containment field held at a steady one gee. The bridge itself was about twenty-five meters across and held command-nexus stations for the various specialists, as well as a central table—round, of course—where the awakened were gathering, sipping coffee and making the usual soft jokes about cryogenic deep-sleep dreams. All around the great hemisphere of the command deck, broad windows opened onto space: Dem Lia stood a minute looking at the strange arrangement of the stars, the view back along the seemingly infinite length of the *Helix* itself where heavy filters dimmed the brilliance of the fusion-flame tail that now reached back eight kilometers toward their destination—and the binary system itself, one small white star and one red giant, both clearly visible. The windows were not actual windows, of course; their holo pickups could be changed and zoomed or opaqued in an instant, but for now the illusion was perfect.

Dem Lia turned her attention to the eight people at the table. She had met all of them during the two years of ship training with the Aeneans, but knew none of these individuals well. All had been in the select group of fewer than a thousand chosen for possible awakening during transit. She checked their color-band stripes as they made introductions over coffee.

Four men, five women. One of the other women was also an emerald green, which meant that Dem Lia did not know if command would fall to her or the younger woman. Of course, consensus would determine that at any rate, but since the emerald green band of the Amoiete Spectrum Helix poem and society stood for resonance with nature, ability to command, comfort with technology, and the preservation of endangered life-forms—and all 684,300 of the Amoiete refugees could be considered endangered life-forms this far from human space—it was assumed that in unusual awakenings the greens would be voted into overall command.

In addition to the other green—a young, redheaded woman named Res Sandre—there was: a red-band male, Patek Georg Dem Mio; a young, white-band female named Den Soa whom Dem Lia knew from the diplomacy simulations; an ebony-band male named Jon Mikail Dem Alem; an older yellow-band woman named Oam Rai whom Dem Lia remembered as having excelled at ship system's operations; a white-haired blue-band male named Peter Delen Dem Tae whose primary training would be in psychology; an attractive female violet-band—almost surely chosen for astronomy—named Kem Loi; and an orange male—their medic, whom Dem Lia had spoken to on several occasions—Samel Ria Kem Ali, known to everyone as Dr. Sam.

After introductions there was a silence. The group looked out the windows at the binary system, the G8 white star almost lost in the glare of the *Helix*'s formidable fusion tail.

Finally the red, Patek Georg, said, "All right, ship. Explain."

Saigyō's calm voice came over the omnipresent speakers. "We were nearing time to begin a search for earthlike worlds when sensors and astronomy became interested in this system."

"A *binary* system?" said Kem Loi, the violet. "Certainly not in the red giant system?" The Amoiete Spectrum Helix people had been very specific about the world they wanted their ship to find for them—G2 sun, earthlike world at least a 9 on the old Solmev Scale, blue oceans, pleasant temperatures—paradise, in other words. They had tens of thousands of light-years and thousands of years to hunt. They fully expected to find it.

"There are no worlds left in the red-giant system," agreed Saigyō the AI affably enough. "We estimate that the system was a G2 yellow-white dwarf star . . ."

"Sol," muttered Peter Delen, the blue, sitting at Dem Lia's right.

"Yes," said Saigyō. "Much like the Old Earth's sun. We estimate that it became unstable on the main sequence hydrogen-burning stage about three and one half million standard years ago and then expanded to its red giant phase and swallowed any planets that had been in system."

"How many AUs out does the giant extend?" asked Res Sandre, the other green.

"Approximately one-point-three," said the AI.

"And no outer planets?" asked Kem Loi. Violets in the *Helix* were dedicated to complex structures, chess, the love of the more complex aspects of human relationships, and astronomy. "It would seem that there would be some gas giants or rocky worlds left if it only expanded a bit beyond what would have been Old Earth's or Hyperion's orbit."

"Maybe the outer worlds were very small planetoids driven away by the constant outgassing of heavy particles," said Patek Georg, the red-band pragmatist.

"Perhaps no worlds formed here," said Den Soa, the white-band diplomat. Her voice was sad. "At least in that case no life was destroyed when the sun went red giant."

"Saigyō," said Dem Lia, "why are we decelerating in toward this white star? May we see the specs on it, please?"

Images, trajectories, and data columns appeared over the table.

"What is that?" said the older yellow-band woman, Oam Rai.

"An Ouster forest ring," said Jon Mikail Dem Alem. "All this way. All these years. And some ancient Ouster Hegira seedship beat us to it."

"Beat us to what?" asked Res Sandre, the other green. "There are no planets in this system are there, Saigyō?"

"No, ma'am," said the AI.

"Were you thinking of restocking on their forest ring?" said Dem Lia. The plan had been to avoid any Aenean, Pax, or Ouster worlds or strongholds found along their long voyage away from human space.

"This orbital forest ring is exceptionally bountiful," said Saigyō the AI, "but our real reason for awakening you and beginning the in-system deceleration is that someone living on or near the ring is transmitting a distress signal on an early Hegemony code band. It is very weak, but we have been picking it up for two hundred and twenty-eight light-years."

This gave them all pause. The *Helix* had been launched some eighty years after the Aenean Shared Moment, that pivotal event in human history which had marked the beginning of a new era for most of the human race. Previous to the Shared Moment, the Church-manipulated Pax society had ruled human space for three hundred years. These Ousters would have missed all of Pax history and probably most of the thousand years of Hegemony history that preceded the Pax. In addition to that, the *Helix*'s time-debt added more than four hundred years of travel. If these Ousters had been part of the original Hegira from Old Earth or from the Old Neighborhood Systems in the earliest days of the Hegemony, they may well have been out of touch with the rest of the human race for fifteen hundred standard years or more.

"Interesting," said Peter Delen Dem Tae, whose blue-band training included profound immersion in psychology and anthropology.

"Saigyō, play the distress signal, please," said Dem Lia.

There came a series of static hisses, pops, and whistles with what might have been two words electronically filtered out. The accent was early Hegemony Web English.

"What does it say?" said Dem Lia. "I can't quite make it out."

"Help us," said Saigyō. The AI's voice was tinted with an Asian accent and usually sounded slightly amused, but his tone was flat and serious now.

The nine around the table looked at one another again in silence. Their goal had been to leave human and posthuman Aenean space far behind them, allowing their people, the Amoiete Spectrum Helix culture, to pursue their own goals, to find their own destiny free of Aenean intervention. But Ousters were just another branch of human stock, attempting to determine their own evolutionary path by adapting to space, their Templar allies traveling with them, using their genetic secrets to grow orbital forest rings and even spherical startrees completely surrounding their suns.

"How many Ousters do you estimate live on the orbital forest ring?" asked Den Soa, who with her white training would probably be their diplomat if and when they made contact.

"Seven hundred million on the thirty-degree arc we can resolve on this side of the sun," said the AI. "If they have migrated to all or most of the ring, obviously we can estimate a population of several billion."

"Any sign of Akerataeli or the zeplens?" asked Patek Georg. All of the great forest rings and startree spheres had been collaborative efforts with these two alien races, which had joined forces with the Ousters and Templars during the Fall of the Hegemony.

"None," said Saigyō. "But you might notice this remote view of the ring itself in the center window. We are still sixty-three AUs out from the ring . . . this is amplified ten thousand times."

They all turned to look at the front window where the forest ring seemed only thousands of kilometers away, its green leaves and yellow and brown branches and braided main trunk curving away out of sight, the G8 star blazing beyond.

"It looks wrong," said Dem Lia.

"This is the anomaly that added to the urgency of the distress signal and decided us to bring you out of deep sleep," said Saigyō, his voice sounding slightly bemused again. "This orbital forest ring is not of Ouster or Templar bioconstruction."

Doctor Samel Ria Kem Ali whistled softly. "An alien-built forest ring. But with human-descended Ousters living on it."

"And there is something else we have found since entering the system," said Saigyō. Suddenly the left window was filled with a view of a machine—a spacecraft—so huge and ungainly that it almost defied description. An image of the *Helix* was superimposed at the bottom of the screen to give scale. The *Helix* was a kilometer long. The base of this other spacecraft was at least a thousand times as long. The monster was huge and broad, bulbous and ugly, carbon black and insectoidal, bearing the worst features of both organic evolution and industrial manufacture. Centered in the front of it was what appeared to be a steel-toothed maw, a rough opening lined with a seemingly endless series of mandibles and shredding blades and razor-sharp rotors.

"It looks like God's razor," said Patek Georg Dem Mio, the cool irony undercut slightly by a just-perceptible quaver in his voice.

"God's razor my ass," said Jon Mikail Dem Alem softly. As an ebony, life support was one of his specialties, and he had grown up tending the huge farms on Vitus-Gray-Balianus B. "That's a threshing machine from hell."

"Where is it?" Dem Lia started to ask, but already Saigyō had thrown the plot on the holo showing their deceleration trajectory in toward the forest ring. The obscene machine-ship was coming in from above the ecliptic, was some twenty-eight AUs ahead of them, was decelerating rapidly but not nearly as aggressively as the *Helix,* and was headed directly for the Ouster forest ring. The trajectory plot was clear—at its current rate of deceleration, the machine would directly intercept the ring in nine standard days.

"This may be the cause of their distress signal," the other green, Res Sandre, said dryly.

"If it were coming at me or my world, I'd scream so loudly that you'd hear me two hundred and twenty-eight light-years away without a radio," said the young white-band, Den Soa.

"If we started picking up this weak signal some two hundred twenty-eight light-years ago," said Patek Georg, "it means that either that thing has been decelerating in-system *very* slowly, or . . ."

"It's been here before," said Dem Lia. She ordered the AI to opaque the windows and to dismiss itself from their company. "Shall we assign roles, duties, priorities, and make initial decisions?" she said softly.

The other eight around the table nodded soberly.

To a stranger, to someone outside the Spectrum Helix culture, the next five minutes would have been very hard to follow. Total consensus was reached within the first two minutes, but only a small part of the discussion was through talk. The combination of hand gestures, body language, shorthand phrases, and silent nods that had evolved through four centuries of a culture determined to make decisions through consensus worked well here. These people's parents and grandparents knew the necessity of command structure and discipline—half a million of their people had died in the short but nasty war with the Pax remnant on Vitus-Gray-Balianus B, and then another hundred thousand when the fleeing Pax vandals came looting through their system some thirty years later. But they were determined to elect command through consensus and thereafter make as many decisions as possible through the same means.

In the first two minutes, assignments were settled and the subtleties around the duties dealt with.

Dem Lia was to be in command. Her single vote could override consensus when necessary. The other green, Res Sandre, preferred to monitor propulsion and engineering, working with the reticent AI named Basho to use this time out of Hawking space to good advantage in taking stock.

The red-band male, Patek Georg, to no one's surprise, accepted the position of chief security officer—both for the ship's formidable defenses and during any contact with the Ousters. Only Dem Lia could override his decisions on use of ship weaponry.

The young white-band woman, Den Soa, was to be in charge of communications and diplomacy, but she requested and Peter Delen Dem Tae agreed to share the responsibility with her. Peter's training in psychology had included theoretical exobiopsychology.

Dr. Sam would monitor the health of everyone aboard and study the evolutionary biology of the Ousters and Templars if it came to contact.

Their ebony-band male, Jon Mikail Dem Alem, assumed command of life support—both in reviewing and controlling systems in the *Helix* along with the appropriate AI, but also arranging for necessary environments if they met with the Ousters aboard ship.

Oam Rai, the oldest of the nine and the ship's chess master, agreed to coordinate general ship systems and to be Dem Lia's principal advisor as events unfolded.

Kem Loi, the astronomer, accepted responsibility for all long-range sensing, but was obviously eager to use her spare time to study the binary system. "Did anyone notice what old friend our white star ahead resembles?" she asked.

"Tau Ceti," said Res Sandre without hesitation.

Kem Loi nodded. "And we saw the anomaly in the placing of the forest ring."

Everyone had. The Ousters preferred G2-type stars, where they could grow their orbital forests at about one AU from the sun. This ring circled its star at only 0.36 AUs.

"Almost the same distance as Tau Ceti Center from its sun," mused Patek Georg. TC^2, as it had been known for more than a thousand years, had once been the central world and capital of the Hegemony. Then it had become a backwater world under the Pax until a Church cardinal on that world attempted a coup against the beleaguered pope during the final days of the Pax. Most of the rebuilt cities had been leveled then. When the *Helix* had left human space eighty years after that war, the Aeneans were repopulating and repopularizing the ancient capital, rebuilding beautiful, classical structures on broad estates and essentially turning the lance-lashed ruins into an Arcadia. For Aeneans.

Assignments given and accepted, the group discussed the option of awakening their immediate family members from cryogenic sleep. Since Spectrum Helix families consisted of triune marriages—either one male and two females or vice versa—and since most had children aboard, this was a complicated subject. Jon Mikail discussed the life-support considerations—which were minor—but everyone agreed that it would complicate decision-making with family awake only as passengers. It was agreed to leave them in deep sleep, with the one exception of Den Soa's husband and wife. The young white-band diplomat admitted that she would feel insecure without her two loved ones with her, and the group allowed this exception to their decision with the gentle suggestion that the reawakened mates would stay off the command deck unless there was compelling reason for them to be there. Den Soa agreed at once. Saigyō was summoned and immediately began awakening Den Soa's bond pair. They had no children.

Then the most central issue was discussed.

"Are we actually going to decelerate to this ring and involve ourselves in these Ousters' problems?" asked Patek Georg. "Assuming that their distress signal is still relevant."

"They're still broadcasting on the old bandwidths," said Den Soa, who had jacksensed into the ship's communications system. The young woman with blond hair looked at something in her virtual vision. "And that monster machine is still headed their way."

"But we have to remember," said the red-band male, "that our goal was to avoid contact with possibly troublesome human outposts on our way out of known space."

Res Sandre, the green now in charge of engineering, smiled. "I believe that we made that general plan about avoiding Pax or Ouster or Aenean elements without considering that we would meet up with humans—or former humans—some eight thousand light-years outside the known sphere of human space."

"It could still mean trouble for everyone," said Patek Georg.

They all understood the real meaning of the red-band security chief's statement. Reds in the Spectrum Helix devoted themselves to physical courage, political convictions, and passion for art, but they also were deeply trained in compassion for other living things. The other eight understood that when he said the contact might mean trouble for "everyone," he meant not only the 684,291 sleeping souls aboard the ship, but also the Ousters and Templars themselves. These orphans of Old Earth, this band of self-evolving human stock, had been beyond history and the human pale for at least a millennium, perhaps much longer. Even the briefest contact could cause problems for the Ouster culture as well.

"We're going to go in and see if we can help . . . and replenish fresh provisions at the same time, if that's possible," said Dem Lia, her tone friendly but final. "Saigyō, at our greatest deceleration figure consistent with not stressing the internal containment fields, how long will it take us to a rendezvous point about five thousand klicks from the forest ring?"

"Thirty-seven hours," said the AI.

"Which gets us there seven days and a bit before that ugly machine," said Oam Rai.

"Hell," said Dr. Sam, "that machine could be something the Ousters built to ferry themselves through the heliosphere shock fields to the red-giant system. A sort of ugly trolley."

"I don't think so," said young Den Soa, missing the older man's irony.

"Well, the Ousters have noticed us," said Patek Georg, who was jacksensed into his system's nexus. "Saigyō, bring up the windows again, please. Same magnification as before."

Suddenly the room was filled with starlight and sunlight and the reflected light from the braided orbital forest ring that looked like nothing so much as Jack and the Giant's beanstalk, curving out of sight around the bright, white star. Only now something else had been added to the picture.

"This is real time?" whispered Dem Lia.

"Yes," said Saigyō. "The Ousters have obviously been watching our fusion tail as we've entered the system. Now they're coming out to greet us."

Thousands—tens of thousands—of fluttering bands of light had left the forest ring and were moving like brilliant fireflies or radiant gossamers away from the braid of huge leaves, bark, and atmosphere. The thousands of motes of light were headed out-system, toward the *Helix*.

"Could you please amplify that image a bit more?" said Dem Lia.

She had been speaking to Saigyō, but it was Kem Loi, who was already wired into the ship's optic net, who acted.

Butterflies of light. Wings a hundred, two hundred, five hundred kilometers across catching the solar wind and riding the magnetic-field lines pouring out of the small, bright star. But not just tens of thousands of winged angels or demons of light, hundreds of thousands. At the very minimum, hundreds of thousands.

"Let's hope they're friendly," said Patek Georg.

"Let's hope we can still communicate with them," whispered young Den Soa. "I mean . . . they could have forced their own evolution any direction in the last fifteen hundred years."

Dem Lia set her hand softly on the table, but hard enough to be heard. "I suggest that we quit speculating and hoping for the moment and get ready for this rendezvous in . . ." She paused.

"Twenty-seven hours eight minutes if the Ousters continue sailing out-system to meet us," said Saigyō on cue.

"Res Sandre," Dem Lia said softly, "why don't you and your propulsion AI begin work now on making sure that our last bit of deceleration is mild enough that it isn't going to fry a few tens of thousands of these Ousters coming to greet us. That would be a bad overture to diplomatic contact."

"If they *are* coming out with hostile intent," said Patek Georg, "the fusion drive would be one of our most potent weapons against . . ."

Dem Lia interrupted. Her voice was soft but brooked no argument. "No discussion of war with this Ouster civilization until their motives become clear. Patek, you can review all ship defensive systems, but let us have no further group discussion of offensive action until you and I talk about it privately."

Patek Georg bowed his head.

"Are there any other questions or comments?" asked Dem Lia. There were none.

The nine people rose from the table and went about their business.

A largely sleepless twenty-four-plus hours later, Dem Lia stood alone and god-sized in the white star's system, the G8 blazing away only a few yards from her shoulder. The braided worldtree was so close that she could have reached out and touched it, wrapped her god-sized hand around it, while at the level of her chest the hundreds of thousands of shimmering wings of light converged on the *Helix*, whose deceleration fusion tail had dwindled to nothing. Dem Lia stood on nothing, her feet planted steadily on black space, the alien forest ring roughly at her belt line, the stars a huge sphere of constellations and foggy galactic scatterings far above, around, and beyond her.

Suddenly Saigyō joined her. The tenth-century monk assumed his usual virreal pose: cross-legged, floating easily just above the plane of the ecliptic a few respectful yards from Dem Lia. He was shirtless and barefoot, and his round belly added to the sense of good feeling that emanated from the round face, squinted eyes, and ruddy cheeks.

"The Ousters fly the solar winds so beautifully," muttered Dem Lia.

Saigyō nodded. "You notice, though, that they're really surfing the shock waves riding out along the magnetic-field lines. That gives them those astounding bursts of speed."

"I've been told that, but not seen it," said Dem Lia. "Could you . . ."

Instantly the solar system in which they stood became a maze of magnetic-field lines pouring from the G8 white star, curving at first and then becoming as straight and evenly spaced as a barrage of laser lances. The display showed this elaborate pattern of magnetic-field lines in red. Blue lines showed the uncountable paths of cosmic rays flowing into the system from all over the galaxy, aligning themselves with the magnetic-field lines and trying to corkscrew their way up the field lines like swirling salmon fighting their way upstream to spawn in the belly of the star. Dem Lia noticed that magnetic-field lines pouring from both the north and south poles of the sun were kinked and folded around themselves, thus deflecting even more cosmic waves that should otherwise have had an easy trip up smooth polar-field lines. Dem Lia changed metaphors, thinking of sperm fighting their way toward a blazing egg, and being cast aside by vicious solar winds and surges of magnetic waves, blasted away by shock waves that whipped out along the field lines as if someone had forcefully shaken a wire or snapped a bullwhip.

"It's stormy," said Dem Lia, seeing the flight path of so many of the Ousters now rolling and sliding and surging along these shock fronts of ions, magnetic fields, and cosmic rays, holding their positions with wings of glowing forcefield energy as the solar wind propagated first forward and then backward along the magnetic-field lines, and finally surfing the shock waves forward again as speedier bursts of solar winds crashed into more sluggish waves ahead of them, creating temporary tsunami that rolled out-system and then flowed backward like a heavy surf rolling back in toward the blazing beach of the G8 sun.

The Ousters handled this confusion of geometries, red lines of magnetic-field lines, yellow lines of ions, blue lines of cosmic rays, and rolling spectra of crashing shock fronts with seeming ease. Dem Lia glanced once out to where the surging heliosphere of the red giant met the seething heliosphere of this bright G8 star and the storm of light and colors there reminded her of a multihued, phosphorescent ocean crashing against the cliffs of an equally colorful and powerful continent of broiling energy. A rough place.

"Let's return to the regular display," said Dem Lia, and instantly the stars and forest ring and fluttering Ousters and slowing *Helix* were back—the last two items quite out of scale to show them clearly.

"Saigyō," said Dem Lia, "please invite all of the other AIs here now."

The smiling monk raised thin eyebrows. "All of them here at once?"

"Yes."

They appeared soon, but not instantly, one figure solidifying into virtual presence a second or two before the next.

First came Lady Murasaki, shorter even than the diminutive Dem Lia, the style of her three-thousand-year-old robe and kimono taking

223

the acting commander's breath away. *What beauty Old Earth had taken for granted,* thought Dem Lia. Lady Murasaki bowed politely and slid her small hands in the sleeves of her robe. Her face was painted almost white, her lips and eyes were heavily outlined, and her long, black hair was done up so elaborately that Dem Lia—who had worn short hair most of her life—could not even imagine the work of pinning, clasping, combing, braiding, shaping and washing such a mass.

Ikkyū stepped confidently across the empty space on the other side of the virtual *Helix* a second later. This AI had chosen the older persona of the long-dead Zen Poet: Ikkyū looked to be about seventy, taller than most Japanese, quite bald, with wrinkles of concern on his forehead and lines of laughter around his bright eyes. Before the flight had begun, Dem Lia had used the ship's history banks to read about the fifteenth-century monk, poet, musician, and calligrapher: it seemed that when the historical, living Ikkyū had turned seventy, he had fallen in love with a blind singer just forty years his junior and scandalized the younger monks when he moved his love into the temple to live with him. Dem Lia liked Ikkyū.

Basho appeared next. The great *haiku* expert chose to appear as a gangly seventeenth-century Japanese farmer, wearing the coned hat and clog shoes of his profession. His fingernails always had some soil under them.

Ryōkan stepped gracefully into the circle. He was wearing beautiful robes of an astounding blue with gold trim. His hair was long and tied in a queue.

"I've asked you all here at once because of the complicated nature of this rendezvous with the Ousters," Dem Lia said firmly. "I understand from the log that one of you was opposed to translating down from Hawking space to respond to this distress call."

"I was," said Basho, his speech in modern post-Pax English but his voice gravel-rough and as guttural as a Samurai's grunt.

"Why?" said Dem Lia.

Basho made a gesture with his gangly hand. "The programming priorities to which we agreed did not cover this specific event. I felt it offered too great a potential for danger and too little benefit in our true goal of finding a colony world."

Dem Lia gestured toward the swarms of Ousters closing on the ship. They were only a few thousand kilometers away now. They had been broadcasting their peaceful intentions across the old radio bandwidths for more than a standard day. "Do you still feel that it's too risky?" she asked the tall AI.

"Yes," said Basho.

Dem Lia nodded, frowning slightly. It was always disturbing when the AIs disagreed on an important issue, but that was why the Aeneans had left them Autonomous after the breakup of the TechnoCore. And that was why there were five to vote.

"The rest of you obviously saw the risk as acceptable?"

Lady Murasaki answered in her low, demure voice, almost a whisper. "We saw it as an excellent possibility to restock new foodstuffs and water, while the cultural implications were more for you to ponder and act on than for us to decide. Of course, we had not detected the huge spacecraft in the system before we translated out of Hawking space. It might have affected our decision."

"This is a human-Ouster culture, almost certainly with a sizable Templar population, that may not have had contact with the outside human universe since the earliest Hegemony days, if then," said Ikkyū with great enthusiasm. "They may well be the farthest-flung outpost of the ancient Hegira. Of all humankind. A wonderful learning opportunity."

Dem Lia nodded impatiently. "We close to rendezvous within a few hours. You've heard their radio contact—they say they wish to greet us and talk, and we've been polite in return. Our dialects are not so diverse that the translator beads can't handle them in face-to-face conversations. But how can we know if they actually come in peace?"

Ryōkan cleared his throat. "It should be remembered that for more than a thousand years, the so-called Wars with the Ousters were provoked—first by the Hegemony and then by the Pax. The original Ouster deep-space settlements were peaceful places and this most-distant colony would have experienced none of the conflict."

Saigyō chuckled from his comfortable perch on nothing. "It should also be remembered that during the actual Pax wars with the Ousters, to defend themselves, these peaceful, space-adapted humans learned to build and use torchships, modified Hawking drive warships, plasma weapons, and even some captured Pax Gideon drive weapons." He waved his bare arm. "We've scanned every one of these advancing Ousters, and none carry a weapon—not so much as a wooden spear."

Dem Lia nodded. "Kem Loi has shown me astronomical evidence which suggests that their moored seedship was torn away from the ring at an early date—possibly only years or months after they arrived. This system is devoid of asteroids, and the Oort cloud has been scattered far beyond their reach. It is conceivable that they have neither metal nor an industrial capacity."

"Ma'am," said Basho, his countenance concerned, "how can we

know that? Ousters have modified their bodies sufficiently to generate forcefield wings that can extend for hundreds of kilometers. If they approach the ship closely enough, they could theoretically use the combined plasma effect of those wings to attempt to breach the containment fields and attack the ship."

"Beaten to death by angels' wings," Dem Lia mused softly. "An ironic way to die."

The AIs said nothing.

"Who is working most directly with Patek Georg Dem Mio on defense strategies?" Dem Lia asked into the silence.

"I am," said Ryōkan.

Dem Lia had known that, but she still thought, *Thank God it's not Basho.* Patek Georg was paranoid enough for the AI-human interface team on this specialty.

"What are Patek's recommendations going to be when we humans meet in a few minutes?" Dem Lia bluntly demanded from Ryōkan.

The AI hesitated only the slightest of perceptible instants. AIs understood both discretion and loyalty to the human working with them in their specialty, but they also understood the imperatives of the elected commander's role on the ship.

"Patek Georg is going to recommend a hundred-kilometer extension of the class-twenty external containment field," said Ryōkan softly. "With all energy weapons on standby and pre-targeted on the three hundred nine thousand, two hundred and five approaching Ousters."

Dem Lia's eyebrows rose a trifle. "And how long would it take our systems to lance more than three hundred thousand such targets?" she asked softly.

"Two-point-six seconds," said Ryōkan.

Dem Lia shook her head. "Ryōkan, please tell Patek Georg that you and I have spoken and that I want the containment field not at a hundred-klick distance, but maintained at a steady one kilometer from the ship. It may remain a class-twenty field—the Ousters can actually see the strength of it, and that's good. But the ship's weapons systems will not target the Ousters at this time. Presumably, they can see our targeting scans as well. Ryōkan, you and Patek Georg can run as many simulations of the combat encounter as you need to feel secure, but divert no power to the energy weapons and allow no targeting until I give the command."

Ryōkan bowed. Basho shuffled his virtual clogs but said nothing.

Lady Murasaki fluttered a fan half in front of her face. "You trust," she said softly.

Dem Lia did not smile. "Not totally. Never totally. Ryōkan, I want you and Patek Georg to work out the containment-field system so that if even one Ouster attempts to breach the containment field with focused plasma from his or her solar wings, the containment field should go to emergency class thirty-five and instantly expand to five hundred klicks."

Ryōkan nodded. Ikkyū smiled slightly and said, "That will be one very quick ride for a great mass of Ousters, Ma'am. Their personal energy systems might not be up to containing their own life support under that much of a shock, and it's certain that they wouldn't decelerate for half an AU or more."

Dem Lia nodded. "That's their problem. I don't think it will come to that. Thank you all for talking to me."

All six human figures winked out of existence.

Rendezvous was peaceful and efficient.

The first question the Ousters had radioed the *Helix* twenty hours earlier was, "Are you Pax?"

This had startled Dem Lia and the others at first. Their assumption was that these people had been out of touch with human space since long before the rise of the Pax. Then the ebony, Jon Mikail Dem Alem, said, "The Shared Moment. It has to have been the Shared Moment."

The nine looked at each other in silence at this. Everyone understood that Aenea's "Shared Moment" during her torture and murder by the Pax and TechnoCore had been shared by every human being in human space—a gestalt resonance along the Void Which Binds that had transmitted the dying young woman's thoughts and memories and knowledge along those threads in the quantum fabric of the universe which existed to resonate empathy, briefly uniting everyone originating from Old Earth human stock. But out here? So many thousands of light-years away?

Dem Lia suddenly realized how silly that thought was. Aenea's Shared Moment of almost five centuries ago must have propagated everywhere in the universe along the quantum fabric of the Void Which Binds, touching alien races and cultures so distant as to be unreachable by any technology of human travel or communication while adding the first self-aware human voice to the empathic conversation that had been going on between sentient and sensitive species for almost twelve billion years. Most of those species had long since become extinct or evolved beyond their original form, the Aeneans had told Dem Lia, but their empathic memories still resonated in the Void Which Binds.

Of course the Ousters had experienced the Shared Moment five hundred years ago.

"No, we are not Pax," the *Helix* had radioed back to the three-hundred-some thousand approaching Ousters. "The Pax was essentially destroyed four hundred standard years ago."

"Do you have followers of Aenea aboard?" came the next Ouster message.

Dem Lia and the others had sighed. Perhaps these Ousters had been desperately waiting for an Aenean messenger, a prophet, someone to bring the sacrament of Aenea's DNA to them so that they could also become Aeneans.

"No," the *Helix* had radioed back. "No followers of Aenea." They then tried to explain the Amoiete Spectrum Helix and how the Aeneans had helped them build and adapt this ship for their long voyage.

After some silence, the Ousters had radioed, "Is there anyone aboard who has met Aenea or her beloved, Raul Endymion?"

Again the nine had looked blankly at each other. Saigyō, who had been sitting cross-legged on the floor some distance from the conference table, spoke up. "No one on board met Aenea," he said softly. "Of the Spectrum family who hid and helped Raul Endymion when he was ill on Vitus-Gray-Balianus B, two of the marriage partners were killed in the war with the Pax there—one of the mothers, Dem Ria, and the biological father, Alem Mikail Dem Alem. Their son by that triune—a boy named Bin Ria Dem Loa Alem—was also killed in the Pax bombing. Alem Mikail's daughter by a previous triune marriage was missing and presumed dead. The surviving female of the triune, Dem Loa, took the sacrament and became an Aenean not many weeks after the Shared Moment. She farcast away from Vitus-Gray-Balianus B and never returned."

Dem Lia and the others waited, knowing that the AI wouldn't have gone on at such length if there were not more to the story.

Saigyō nodded. "It turns out that the teenage daughter, Ces Ambre, presumed killed in the Pax Base Bombasino massacre of Spectrum Helix civilians, had actually been shipped offworld with more than a thousand other children and young adults. They were to be raised on the final Pax stronghold world of St. Theresa as born-again Pax Christians. Ces Ambre received the cruciform and was overseen by a cadre of religious guards there for nine years before that world was liberated by the Aeneans and Dem Loa learned that her daughter was still alive."

"Did they reunite?" asked young Den Soa, the attractive diplomat. There were tears in her eyes. "Did Ces Ambre free herself of the cruciform?"

"There was a reunion," said Saigyō. "Dem Loa freecast there as soon as she learned that her daughter was alive. Ces Ambre chose to have the Aeneans remove the cruciform, but she reported that she did not accept Aenea's DNA sacrament from her triune stepmother to become Aenean herself. Her dossier says that she wanted to return to Vitus-Gray-Balianus B to see the remnants of the culture from which she had been kidnapped. She continued living and working there as a teacher for almost sixty standard years. She adopted her former family's band of blue."

"She suffered the cruciform but chose not to become Aenean," muttered Kem Loi, the astronomer, as if it were impossible to believe.

Dem Lia said, "She's aboard in deep sleep."

"Yes," said Saigyō.

"How old was she when we embarked?" asked Patek Georg.

"Ninety-five standard years," said the AI. He smiled. "But as with all of us, she had the benefit of Aenean medicine in the years before departure. Her physical appearance and mental capabilities are of a woman in her early sixties."

Dem Lia rubbed her cheek. "Saigyō, please awaken Citizen Ces Ambre. Den Soa, could you be there when she awakens and explain the situation to her before the Ousters join us? They seem more interested in someone who knew Aenea's husband than in learning about the Spectrum Helix."

"Future husband at that point in time," corrected the ebony, Jon Mikail, who was a bit of a pedant. "Raul Endymion was not yet married to Aenea at the time of his short stay on Vitus-Gray-Balianus B."

"I'd feel privileged to stay with Ces Ambre until we meet the Ousters," said Den Soa with a bright smile.

While the great mass of Ousters kept their distance—five hundred klicks—the three ambassadors were brought aboard. It had been worked out by radio that the three could take one-tenth normal gravity without discomfort, so the lovely solarium bubble just aft and above the command deck had its containment field set at that level and the proper chairs and lighting adapted. All of the *Helix* people thought it would be easier conversing with at least some sense of up and down. Den Soa added that the Ousters might feel at home amongst all the greenery there. The ship easily morphed an airlock onto the top of the great solarium bubble, and those waiting watched the slow approach of two winged Ousters and one smaller form being towed in a transparent spacesuit. The Ousters who breathed air on the ring, breathed 100 percent oxygen so the ship had taken care to accommodate them in the solarium. Dem Lia realized that she felt slightly euphoric as the Ouster guests entered and were shown to their specially tailored chairs, and she wondered if it was the pure O_2 or just the novelty of the circumstances.

Once settled in their chairs, the Ousters seemed to be studying their five Spectrum Helix counterparts—Dem Lia, Den Soa, Patek Georg, the psychologist Peter Delen Dem Tae, and Ces Ambre, an attractive woman with short, white hair, her hands now folded neatly on her lap. The former teacher had insisted on dressing in her full robe and cowl of blue, but a few tabs of stiktite sewn at strategic places kept the garment from billowing at each movement or ballooning up off the floor.

The Ouster delegation was an interesting assortment of types. On the left, in the most elaborately constructed low-g chair, was a true space-adapted Ouster. Introduced as Far Rider, he was almost four meters tall—making Dem Lia feel even shorter than she was, the Spectrum Helix people always having been generally short and stocky, not through centuries on high-g planets, just because of the genetics of their founders—and the space-adapted Ouster looked far from human in many other ways. Arms and legs were mere long, spidery attachments to the thin torso. The man's fingers must have been twenty centimeters long. Every square centimeter of his body—appearing almost naked under the skintight sweat-coolant, compression layer—was covered with a self-generated forcefield, actually an enhancement of the usual human body aura, which kept him alive in hard vacuum. The ridges above and beneath his shoulders were permanent arrays for extending his forcefield wings to catch the solar wind and magnetic fields. Far Rider's face had been genetically altered far from basic human stock: the eyes were black slits behind bulbous, nictitating membranes; he had no ears but a gridwork on the side of his head that suggested the radio receiver; his mouth was the narrowest of slits, lipless—he communicated through radio-transmitting glands in his neck.

The Spectrum Helix delegation had been aware of this Ouster adaptation and each was wearing a subtle hearplug, which, in addition to picking up Far Rider's radio transmissions, allowed them to communicate with their AIs on a secure tightband.

The second Ouster was partially adapted to space, but clearly more human. Three meters tall, he was thin and spidery, but the permanent field of forcefield ectoplasmic skin was missing, his eyes and face were thin and boldly structured, he had no hair—and he spoke early Web English with very little accent. He was introduced as Chief Branchman and historian Keel Redt, and it was obvious that he was the chosen speaker for the group, if not its actual leader.

To the Chief Branchman's left was a Templar—a young woman with the hairless skull, fine bone structure, vaguely Asian features, and large eyes common to Templars everywhere—wearing the traditional brown robe and hood. She introduced herself as the True Voice of the Tree Reta Kasteen, and her voice was soft and strangely musical.

When the Helix Spectrum contingent had introduced themselves, Dem Lia noticed the two Ousters and the Templar staring at Ces Ambre, who smiled back pleasantly.

"How is it that you have come so far in such a ship?" asked Chief Branchman Keel Redt.

Dem Lia explained their decision to start a new colony of the Amoiete Spectrum Helix far from Aenean and human space. There was the inevitable question about the origins of the Amoiete Spectrum Helix culture, and Dem Lia told the story as succinctly as possible.

"So if I understand you correctly," said True Voice of the Tree Reta Kasteen, the Templar, "your entire social structure is based upon an opera—a work of entertainment—that was performed only once, more than six hundred standard years ago."

"Not the *entire* social structure," Den Soa responded to her Templar counterpart. "Cultures grow and adapt themselves to changing conditions and imperatives, of course. But the basic philosophical bedrock and structure of our culture was contained in that one performance by the philosopher-composer-poet–holistic artist, Halpul Amoiete."

"And what did this . . . poet . . . think of a society being built around his single multimedia opera?" asked the Chief Branchman.

It was a delicate question, but Dem Lia just smiled and said, "We'll never know. Citizen Amoiete died in a mountain-climbing accident just a month after the opera was performed. The first Spectrum Helix communities did not appear for another twenty standard years."

"Do you worship this man?" asked Chief Branchman Keel Redt.

Ces Ambre answered. "No. None of the Spectrum Helix people have ever deified Halpul Amoiete, even though we have taken his name as part of our society's. We do, however, respect and try to live up to the values and goals for human potential which he communicated in his art through that single, extraordinary Spectrum Helix performance."

The Chief Branchman nodded as if satisfied.

Saigyō's soft voice whispered in Dem Lia's ear. "They are broadcasting both visual and audio on a very tight coherent band which is being picked up by the Ousters outside and being rebroadcast to the forest ring."

Dem Lia looked at the three sitting across from her, finally resting her gaze on Far Rider, the completely space-adapted Ouster. His human eyes were essentially invisible behind the gogglelike, polarized, and nictitating membranes that made him look almost insectoid. Saigyō had tracked Dem Lia's gaze, and his voice whispered in her ear again. "Yes. He is the one broadcasting."

Dem Lia steepled her fingers and touched her lips, better to conceal the subvocalizing. "You've tapped into their tightbeam?"

"Yes, of course," said Saigyō. "Very primitive. They're broadcasting just the video and audio of this meeting, no data subchannels or return broadcasts from either the Ousters near us or from the forest ring."

Dem Lia nodded ever so slightly. Since the *Helix* was also carrying out complete holocoverage of this meeting, including infrared study, magnetic-resonance analysis of brain function, and a dozen other hidden but intrusive observations, she could hardly blame the Ousters for recording the meeting. Suddenly her cheeks reddened. Infrared. Tightbeam physical scans. Remote neuro-MRI. Certainly the fully space-adapted Ouster could *see* these probes—the man, if man he still was, lived in an environment where he could see the solar wind, sense the magnetic-field lines, and follow individual ions and even cosmic rays as they flowed over and under and through him in hard vacuum. Dem Lia subvocalized, "Shut down all of our solarium sensors except the holocameras."

Saigyō's silence was his assent.

Dem Lia noticed Far Rider suddenly blinking as if someone had shut off blazing lights that had been shining in his eyes. The Ouster then looked at Dem Lia and nodded slightly. The strange gap of a mouth, sealed away from the world by the layer of forcefield and clear ectodermal skin plasma, twitched in what the Spectrum woman thought might be a smile.

It was the young Templar, Reta Kasteen, who had been speaking. ". . . so you see we passed through what was becoming the Worldweb and left human space about the time the Hegemony was establishing itself. We had departed the Centauri system some time after the original Hegira had ended. Periodically, our seedship would drop into real space—the Templars joined us from God's Grove on our way out—

so we had fatline news and occasional firsthand information of what the interstellar Worldweb society was becoming. We continued outbound."

"Why so far?" asked Patek Georg.

The Chief Branchman answered, "Quite simply, the ship malfunctioned. It kept us in deep cryogenic fugue for centuries while its programming ignored potential systems for an orbital worldtree. Eventually, as the ship realized its mistake—twelve hundred of us had already died in fugue crèches never designed for such a lengthy voyage—the ship panicked and began dropping out of Hawking space at every system, finding the usual assortment of stars that could not support our Templar-grown tree ring or that would have been deadly to Ousters. We know from the ship's records that it almost settled us in a binary system consisting of a black hole that was gorging on its close red-giant neighbor."

"The accretion disk would have been pretty to watch," said Den Soa with a weak smile.

The Chief Branchman showed his own thin-lipped smile. "Yes, in the weeks or months we would have had before it killed us. Instead, working on the last of its reasoning power, the ship made one more jump and found the perfect solution—this double system, with the white-star heliosphere we Ousters could thrive in, and a tree ring already constructed."

"How long ago was that?" asked Dem Lia.

"Twelve-hundred-and-thirty-some standard years," broadcast Far Rider.

The Templar woman leaned forward and continued the story. "The first thing we discovered was that this forest ring had nothing to do with the biogenetics we had developed on God's Grove to build our own beautiful, secret startrees. This DNA was so alien in its alignment and function that to tamper with it might have killed the entire forest ring."

"You could have started your own forest ring growing in and around the alien one," said Ces Ambre. "Or attempted a startree sphere as other Ousters have done."

The True Voice of the Tree Reta Kasteen nodded. "We had just begun attempting that—and diversifying the protogene growth centers just a few hundred kilometers from where we had parked the seedship in the leaves and branches of the alien ring, when . . ." She paused as if searching for the right words.

"The Destroyer came," broadcast Far Rider.

"The Destroyer being the ship we observe approaching your ring now?" asked Patek Georg.

"Same ship," broadcast Far Rider. The two syllables seemed to have been spat out.

"Same monster from hell," added the Chief Branchman.

"It destroyed your seedship," said Dem Lia. So that was why the Ousters seemed to have no metal and why there was no Templar-grown forest ring braiding this alien one.

Far Rider shook his head. "It *devoured* the seedship, along with more than twenty-eight thousand kilometers of the tree ring itself— every leaf, fruit, oxygen pod, water tendril—even our protogene growth centers."

"There were far fewer purely space-adapted Ousters in those days," said Reta Kasteen. "The adapted ones attempted to save the others, but many thousands died on that first visit of the Destroyer . . . the Devourer . . . the Machine. We obviously have many names for it."

"Ship from hell," said the Chief Branchman, and Dem Lia realized that he was almost certainly speaking literally, as if a religion had grown up based upon hating this machine.

"How often does it come?" asked Den Soa.

"Every fifty-seven years," said the Templar. "Exactly."

"From the red giant system?" asked Den Soa.

"Yes," broadcast Far Rider. "From the hell star."

"If you know its trajectory," said Dem Lia, "can't you know far ahead of time the sections of your forest ring it will . . . devastate, devour? Couldn't you just not colonize, or at the very least evacuate, those areas? After all, most of the tree ring has to be unpopulated . . . the ring's surface area has to be equal to more than half a million Old Earths or Hyperions."

Chief Branchman Keel Redt showed his thin smile again. "About now—some seven or eight standard days out—the Destroyer, for all its mass, not only completes its deceleration cycle, but carries out complicated maneuvers that will take it to some populated part of the ring. Always a populated area. A hundred and four years ago, its final trajectory took it to a massing of O_2 pods where more than twenty million of our non–fully space-adapted Ousters had made their homes, complete with travel tubes, bridges, towers, city-sized platforms and artificially grown life-support pods that had been under slow construction for more than six hundred standard years."

"All destroyed," said True Voice of the Tree Reta Kasteen with sorrow in her voice. "Devoured. Harvested."

"Was there much loss of life?" asked Dem Lia, her voice quiet.

Far Rider shook his head and broadcast, "Millions of fully space-adapted Ousters rallied to evacuate the oxygen breathers. Fewer than a hundred died."

"Have you tried to communicate with the . . . machine?" asked Peter Delem Dem Tae.

"For centuries," said Reta Kasteen, her voice shaking with emotion. "We've used radio, tightbeam, maser, the few holo transmitters we still have, Far Rider's people have even used their wingfields—by the thousands—to flash messages in simple, mathematical code."

The five Amoiete Spectrum Helix people waited.

"Nothing," said the Chief Branchman in a flat voice. "It comes, it chooses its populated section of the ring, and it devours. We have never had a reply."

"We believe that it is completely automated and very ancient," said Reta Kasteen. "Perhaps millions of years old. Still operating on programming developed when the alien ring was built. It harvests these huge sections of the ring, limbs, branches, tubules with millions of gallons of tree-ring manufactured water . . . then returns to the red-star system and, after a pause, returns our way again."

"We used to believe that there was a world left in that red-giant system," broadcast Far Rider. "A planet which remains permanently hidden from us on the far side of that evil sun. A world which built this ring as its food source, probably before their G2 sun went giant, and which continues to harvest in spite of the misery it causes us. No longer. There is no such planet. We now believe that the Destroyer acts alone, out of ancient, blind programming, harvesting sections of the ring and destroying our settlements for no reason. Whatever or whoever lived in that red giant system has long since fled."

Dem Lia wished that Kem Loi, their astronomer, was there. She knew that she was on the command deck watching. "We saw no planets during our approach to this binary system," said the green-banded commander. "It seems highly unlikely that any world that could support life would have survived the transition of the G2 star to the red giant."

"Nonetheless, the Destroyer passes very close to that terrible red star on each of its voyages," said the Ouster Chief Branchman. "Perhaps some sort of artificial environment remains—a space habitat—hollowed-out asteroids. An environment which requires this plant ring for its inhabitants to survive. But it does not excuse the carnage."

"If they had the ability to build this machine, they could have simply fled their system when the G2 sun went critical," mused Patek

Georg. The red-band looked at Far Rider. "Have you tried to destroy the machine?"

The lipless smile beneath the ectofield twitched lizard-wide on Far Rider's strange face. "Many times. Scores of thousands of true Ousters have died. The machine has an energy defense that lances us to ash at approximately one hundred thousand klicks."

"That could be a simple meteor defense," said Dem Lia.

Far Rider's smile broadened so that it was very terrible. "If so, it suffices as a very efficient killing device. My father died in the last attack attempt."

"Have you tried traveling to the red giant system?" asked Peter Delem.

"We have no spacecraft left," answered the Templar.

"On your own solar wings then?" asked Peter, obviously doing the math in his head on the time such a round trip would take. Years—decades at solar sailing velocities—but well within an Ouster's life span.

Far Rider moved his hand with its elongated fingers in a horizontal chop. "The heliosphere turbulence is too great. Yet we have tried hundreds of times—expeditions upon which scores depart and none or only a few return. My brother died on such an attempt six of your standard years ago."

"And Far Rider himself was terribly hurt," said Reta Kasteen softly. "Sixty-eight of the best deep spacers left—two returned. It took all of what remains of our medical science to save Far Rider's life, and that meant two years in recovery pod nutrient for him."

Dem Lia cleared her throat. "What do you want us to do?"

The two Ousters and the Templar leaned forward. Chief Branchman Keel Redt spoke for all of them. "If, as you believe, as we have become convinced, there is no inhabited world left in the red giant system, kill the Destroyer now. Annihilate the harvesting machine. Save us from this mindless, obsolete, and endless scourge. We will reward you as handsomely as we can—foods, fruits, as much water as you need for your voyage, advanced genetic techniques, our knowledge of nearby systems, anything."

The Spectrum Helix people glanced at one another. Finally Dem Lia said, "If you are comfortable here, four of us would like to excuse ourselves for a short time to discuss this. Ces Ambre would be delighted to stay with you and talk if you so wish."

The Chief Branchman made a gesture with both long arms and huge hands. "We are completely comfortable. And we are more than delighted to have this chance to talk to the venerable M. Ambre—the woman who saw the husband of Aenea."

Dem Lia noticed that the young Templar, Reta Kasteen, looked visibly thrilled at the prospect.

"And then you will bring us your decision, yes?" radioed Far Rider, his waxy body, huge eyeshields, and alien physiology giving Dem Lia a slight chill. This was a creature that fed on light, tapped enough energy to deploy electromagnetic solar wings hundreds of kilometers wide, recycled his own air, waste, and water, and lived in an environment of absolute cold, heat, radiation, and hard vacuum. Humankind had come a long way from the early hominids in Africa on Old Earth.

And if we say no, thought Dem Lia, *three-hundred-thousand-some angry space-adapted Ousters just like him might descend on our spinship like the angry Hawaiians venting their wrath on Captain James Cook when he caught them pulling the nails from the hull of his ship. The good captain ended up not only being killed horribly, but having his body eviscerated, burned, and boiled into small chunks.* As soon as she thought this, Dem Lia knew better. These Ousters would not attack the *Helix.* All of her intuition told her that. *And if they do,* she thought, *our weaponry will vaporize the lot of them in two-point-six seconds.* She felt guilty and slightly nauseated at her own thoughts as she made her farewells and took the lift down to the command deck with the other three.

"You saw him," said True Voice of the Tree Reta Kasteen a little breathlessly. "Aenea's husband?"

Ces Ambre smiled. "I was fourteen standard years old. It was a long time ago. He was traveling from world to world via farcaster and stayed a few days in my second triune parents' home because he was ill—a kidney stone—and then the Pax troopers kept him under arrest until they could send someone to interrogate him. My parents helped him escape. It was a very few days a very many years ago." She smiled again. "And he was not Aenea's husband at that time, remember. He had not taken the sacrament of her DNA, nor even grown aware of what her blood and teachings could do for the human race."

"But you *saw* him," pressed Chief Branchman Keel Redt.

"Yes. He was in delirium and pain much of the time and hand-cuffed to my parents' bed by the Pax troopers."

Reta Kasteen leaned closer. "Did he have any sort of . . . *aura* . . . about him?"

"Oh, yes," said Ces Ambre with a chuckle. "Until my parents gave him a sponge bath. He had been traveling hard for many days."

The two Ousters and the Templar seemed to sit back in disappointment.

Ces Ambre leaned forward and touched the Templar woman's knee. "I apologize for being flippant—I know the important role that Raul Endymion played in all of our history—but it was long ago, there was much confusion, and at that time on Vitus-Gray-Balianus B I was a rebellious teenager who wanted to leave my community of the Spectrum and accept the cruciform in some nearby Pax city."

The other three visibly leaned back now. The two faces that were readable registered shock. "You *wanted* to accept that . . . that . . . *parasite* into your body?"

As part of Aenea's Shared Moment, every human everywhere had seen—had known—had felt the full *gestalt*—of the reality behind the "immortality cruciform"—a parasitic mass of AI nodes creating a TechnoCore in real space, using the neurons and synapses of each host body in any way it wished, often using it in more creative ways by *killing* the human host and using the linked neuronic web when it was at its most creative—during those final seconds of neural dissolution before death. Then the Church would use TechnoCore technology to resurrect the human body with the Core cruciform parasite growing stronger and more networked at each death and resurrection.

Ces Ambre shrugged. "It represented immortality at the time. And a chance to get away from our dusty little village and join the real world—the Pax."

The three Ouster diplomats could only stare.

Ces Ambre raised her hands to her robe and slipped it open enough to show them the base of her throat and the beginning of a scar where the cruciform had been removed by the Aeneans. "I was kidnapped to one of the remaining Pax worlds and put under the cruciform for nine years," she said so softly that her voice barely carried to the three diplomats. "And most of this time was *after* Aenea's shared moment—after the absolute revelation of the Core's plan to enslave us with those despicable things."

The True Voice of the Tree Reta Kasteen took Ces Ambre's older hand in hers. "Yet you refused to become Aenean when you were liberated. You joined what was left of your old culture."

Ces Ambre smiled. There were tears in her eyes, and those eyes suddenly looked much older. "Yes. I felt I owed my people that—for deserting them at the time of crisis. Someone had to carry on the Spectrum Helix culture. We had lost so many in the wars. We lost even more when the Aeneans gave us the option of joining them. It is hard to refuse to become something like a god."

Far Rider made a grunt that sounded like heavy static. "This is our greatest fear next to the Destroyer. No one is now alive on the forest ring who experienced the Shared Moment, but the details of it—the glorious insights into empathy and the binding powers of the Void Which Binds, Aenea's knowledge that many of the Aeneans would be able to farcast—freecast—anywhere in the universe. Well, the Church of Aenea has grown here until at least a fourth of our population would give up their Ouster or Templar heritage and become Aenean in a second."

Ces Ambre rubbed her cheek and smiled again. "Then it's obvious that no Aeneans have visited this system. And you have to remember that Aenea insisted that there be no 'Church of Aenea,' no veneration or beatification or adoration. That was paramount in her thoughts during the Shared Moment."

"We know," said Reta Kasteen. "But in the absence of choice and knowledge, cultures often turn to religion. And the possibility of an Aenean being aboard with you was one reason we greeted the arrival of your great ship with such enthusiasm and trepidation."

"Aeneans do not arrive by spacecraft," Ces Ambre said softly.

The three nodded. "When and if the day ever comes," broadcast Far Rider, "it will be up to the individual conscience of each Ouster and Templar to decide. As for me, I will always ride the great waves of the solar wind."

Dem Lia and the other three returned.

"We've decided to help," she said. "But we must hurry."

There was no way in the universe that Dem Lia or any of the other eight humans or any of the five AIs would risk the *Helix* in a direct confrontation with the Destroyer or the Harvester or whatever the hell the Ousters wanted to call their nemesis. It was not just by engineering happenstance that the three thousand life-support pods carrying the 684,300 Spectrum Helix pioneers in deep cryogenic sleep were egg-shaped. This culture had all their eggs in one basket—literally—and they were not about to send that basket into battle. Already Basho and several of the other AIs were brooding about the proximity to the oncoming harvesting ship. Space battles could easily be fought across twenty-eight AUs of distance—while traditional lasers, or lances, or charged particle–beam weapons would take more than a hundred and ninety-six minutes to creep that distance—Hegemony, Pax, and Ouster ships had all developed hyperkinetic missiles able to leap into and out of Hawking space. Ships could be destroyed before radar could announce the presence of the incoming missile. Since this "harvester" crept around its appointed rounds at sublight speed, it seemed unlikely that it would carry C-plus weaponry, but "unlikely" is a word that has undone the planning and fates of warriors since time immemorial.

At the Spectrum Helix engineers' request, the Aeneans had rebuilt the *Helix* to be truly modular. When it reached its utopian planet around its perfect star, sections would free themselves to become probes and aircraft and landers and submersibles and space stations. Each of the three thousand individual life pods could land and begin a colony on its own, although the plans were to cluster the landing sites carefully after much study of the new world. By the time the *Helix* was finished deploying and landing its pods and modules and probes and shuttles and command deck and central fusion core, little would be left in orbit except the huge Hawking drive units with maintenance programs and robots to keep them in perfect condition for centuries, if not millennia.

"We'll take the system exploratory probe to investigate this Destroyer," said Dem Lia. It was one of the smaller modules, adapted more to pure vacuum than to atmospheric entry, although it was capable of some morphing. But compared to most of the *Helix*'s peaceful subcomponents the probe was armed to the teeth.

"May we accompany you?" said Chief Branchman Keel Redt. "None of our race has come closer than a hundred thousand kilometers to the machine and lived."

"By all means," said Dem Lia. "The probe's large enough to hold thirty or forty of us, and only three are going from our ship. We will keep the internal containment field at one-tenth gee and adapt the seating accordingly."

The probe was more like one of the old combat torchships than anything else, and it accelerated out toward the advancing machine under 250 gravities, internal containment fields on infinite redundancy, external fields raised to their maximum of class twelve. Dem Lia was piloting. Den Soa was attempting to communicate with the gigantic ship via every means available, sending messages of peace on every band from primitive radio to modulated tachyon bursts. There was no response. Patek Georg Dem Mio was meshed into the defense/counterattack virtual umbilicals of his couch. The passengers sat at the rear of the probe's compact command deck and watched. Saigyō had decided to accompany them, and his massive holo sat bare-chested and cross-legged on a counter near the main viewport. Dem Lia made sure to keep their trajectory aimed *not* directly at the monstrosity, in the probability that it had simple meteor defenses: if they kept traveling toward their current coordinates, they would miss the ship by tens of thousands of kilometers above the plane of the ecliptic.

"Its radar has begun tracking us," said Patek Georg when they were six hundred thousand klicks away and decelerating nicely. "Passive radar. No weapons acquisition. It doesn't seem to be probing us with anything except simple radar. It will have no idea if life-forms are aboard our probe or not."

Dem Lia nodded. "Saigyō," she said softly, "at two hundred thousand klicks, please bring our coordinates around so that we will be on intercept course with the thing." The chubby monk nodded.

Somewhat later, the probe's thrusters and main engines changed tune, the starfield rotated, and the image of the huge machine filled the main window. The view was magnified as if they were only five hundred klicks from the spacecraft. The thing was indescribably ungainly, built only for vacuum, fronted with metal teeth and rotating blades built into mandible-like housings, the rest looking like the wreckage of an old space habitat that had been mindlessly added onto for millennium after millennium and then covered with warts, wattles, bulbous sacs, tumors, and filaments.

"Distance, one hundred eighty-three thousand klicks and closing," said Patek Georg.

"Look how blackened it is," whispered Den Soa.

"And worn," radioed Far Rider. "None of our people have ever seen it from this close. Look at the layers of cratering through the heavy carbon deposits. It is like an ancient, black moon that has been struck again and again by tiny meteorites."

"Repaired, though," commented the Chief Branchman gruffly. "It operates."

"Distance one hundred twenty thousand klicks and closing," said Patek Georg. "Search radar has just been joined by acquisition radar."

"Defensive measures?" said Dem Lia, her voice quiet.

Saigyō answered. "Class-twelve field in place and infinitely redundant. CPB deflectors activated. Hyperkinetic countermissiles ready. Plasma shields on maximum. Countermissiles armed and under positive control." This meant simply that both Dem Lia and Patek Georg would have to give the command to launch them, or—if the human passengers were killed—Saigyō would do so.

"Distance one hundred five thousand klicks and closing," said Patek Georg. "Relative delta-v dropping to one hundred meters per second. Three more acquisition radars have locked on."

"Any other transmissions?" asked Dem Lia, her voice tight.

"Negative," said Den Soa at her virtual console. "The machine seems blind and dumb except for the primitive radar. Absolutely no signs of life aboard. Internal communications show that it has . . . intelligence . . . but not true AI. Computers more likely. Many series of physical computers."

"*Physical* computers!" said Dem Lia, shocked. "You mean silicon . . . chips . . . stone axe–level technology?"

"Or just above," confirmed Den Soa at her console. "We're picking up magnetic bubble-memory readings, but nothing higher."

"One hundred thousand klicks . . ." began Patek Georg, and then interrupted himself. "The machine is firing on us."

The outer containment fields flashed for less than a second.

"A dozen CPBs and two crude laser lances," said Patek Georg from his virreal point of view. "Very weak. A class-one field could have countered them easily."

The containment field flickered again.

"Same combination," reported Patek. "Slightly lower energy settings."

Another flicker.

"Lower settings again," said Patek. "I think it's giving us all it's got and using up its power doing it. Almost certainly just a meteor defense."

"Let's not get overconfident," said Dem Lia. "But let's see all of its defenses."

Den Soa looked shocked. "You're going to *attack* it?"

"We're going to see if we *can* attack it," said Dem Lia. "Patek, Saigyō, please target one lance on the top corner of that protuberance there . . ." She pointed her laser stylus at a blackened, cratered, fin-shaped projection that might have been a radiator two klicks high. ". . . and one hyperkinetic missile . . ."

"*Commander!*" protested Den Soa.

Dem Lia looked at the younger woman and raised her finger to her lips. "One hyperkinetic with plasma warhead removed, targeted at the front lower leading edge of the machine, right where the lip of that aperture is."

Patek Georg repeated the command to the AI. Actual target coordinates were displayed and confirmed.

The CPB struck almost instantly, vaporizing a seventy-meter hole in the radiator fin.

"It raised a class-point-six field," reported Patek Georg. "That seems to be its top limit of defense."

The hyperkinetic missile penetrated the containment field like a bullet through butter and struck an instant later, blasting through sixty meters of blackened metal and tearing out through the front feeding-orifice of the harvesting machine. Everyone aboard watched the silent impact and the almost mesmerizing tumble of vaporized metal expanding away from the impact site and the spray of debris from the exit wound. The huge machine did not respond.

"If we had left the warhead on," murmured Dem Lia, "and aimed for its belly, we would have a thousand kilometers of exploding harvest machine right now."

Chief Branchman Keel Redt leaned forward in his couch. Despite the one-tenth g field, all of the couches had restraint systems. His was activated now.

"Please," said the Ouster, struggling slightly against the harnesses and airbags. "Kill it now. Stop it now."

Dem Lia shifted to look at the two Ousters and the Templar. "Not yet," she said. "First we have to return to the *Helix*."

"We will lose more valuable time," broadcast Far Rider, his tone unreadable.

"Yes," said Dem Lia. "But we still have more than six standard days before it begins harvesting."

The probe accelerated away from the blackened, cratered, and newly scarred monster.

"You will not destroy it, then?" demanded the Chief Branchman as the probe hurried back to the *Helix*.

"Not now," responded Dem Lia. "It might still be serving a purpose for the race that built it."

The young Templar seemed to be close to tears. "Yet your own instruments—far more sophisticated than our telescopes—told you that there are no worlds in the red giant system."

Dem Lia nodded. "Yet you yourselves have mentioned the possibility of space habitats, can cities, hollowed-out asteroids . . . our survey was neither careful nor complete. Our ship was intent upon entering your star system with maximum safety, not carrying out a careful survey of the red giant system."

"For such a small probability," said the Chief Branchman Ouster in a flat, hard voice, "you are willing to risk so many of our people?"

Saigyō's voice whispered quietly in Dem Lia's subaudio circuit. "The AIs have been analyzing scenarios of several million Ousters using their solar wings in a concentrated attack on the *Helix*."

Dem Lia waited, still looking at the Chief Branchman.

"The ship could defeat them," finished the AI, "but there is some real probability of damage."

To the Chief Branchman, Dem Lia said, "We're going to take the *Helix* to the red giant system. The three of you are welcome to accompany us."

"How long will the round trip last?" demanded Far Rider.

Dem Lia looked to Saigyō. "Nine days under maximum fusion boost," said the AI. "And that would be a powered perihelion maneuver with no time to linger in the system to search every asteroid or debris field for life-forms."

The two Ousters were shaking their heads. Reta Kasteen drew her hood lower, covering her eyes.

"There's another possibility," said Dem Lia. To Saigyō, she pointed toward the *Helix*, now filling the main viewscreen. Thousands of energy-winged Ousters parted as the probe decelerated gently through the ship's containment field and aligned itself for docking.

They gathered in the solarium to decide. All ten of the humans—Den Soa's wife and husband had been invited to join in the vote but had decided to stay below in the crew's quarters—all five of the AIs, and the three representatives of the forest-ring people. Far Rider's tightbeam continued to carry the video and audio to the three hundred thousand nearby Ousters and the billions waiting on the great curve of tree ring beyond.

"Here is the situation," said Dem Lia. The silence in the solarium was very thick. "You know that the *Helix*, our ship, contains an Aenean-modified Hawking drive. Our faster-than-light passage does harm the fabric of the Void Which Binds, but thousands of times less than the old Hegemony or Pax ships. The Aeneans allowed us this voyage." The short woman with the green band around her turban paused and looked at both Ousters and the Templar woman before continuing. "We could reach the red giant system in . . ."

"Four hours to spin up to relativistic velocities, then the jump," said Res Sandre. "About six hours to decelerate into the red giant system. Two days to investigate for life. Same ten-hour return time."

"Which, even with some delays, would bring the *Helix* back almost two days before the Destroyer begins its harvesting. If there is no life in the red-giant system, we will use the probe to destroy the robot harvester."

"But . . ." said Chief Branchman Keel Redt with an all-too-human ironic smile. His face was grim.

"*But* it is too dangerous to use the Hawking drive in such a tight binary system," said Dem Lia, voice level. "Such short-distance jumps are incredibly tricky anyway, but given the gas and debris the red giant is pouring out . . ."

"You are correct. It would be folly." It was Far Rider broadcasting on his radio band. "My clan has passed down the engineering from generation to generation. No commander of any Ouster seedship would make a jump in this binary system."

True Voice of the Tree Reta Kasteen was looking from face to face. "But you have these powerful fusion engines . . ."

Dem Lia nodded. "Basho, how long to survey the red-giant system using maximum thrust with our fusion engines?"

"Three and one-half days transit time to the other system," said the hollow-cheeked AI. "Two days to investigate. Three and one-half days back."

"There is no way we could shorten that?" said Oam Rai, the yellow. "Cut safety margins? Drive the fusion engines harder?"

Saigyō answered. "The nine-day round-trip is posited upon ignoring all safety margins and driving the fusion engines at one hundred twelve percent of their capacity." He sadly shook his bald head. "No, it cannot be done."

"But the Hawking drive . . ." said Dem Lia, and everyone in the room appeared to cease breathing except for Far Rider, who had never been breathing in the traditional sense. The appointed Spectrum Helix commander turned to the AIs. "What are the probabilities of disaster if we try this?"

Lady Murasaki stepped forward. "Both translations—into and out of Hawking space—will be far too close to the binary system's Roche lobe. We estimate probability of total destruction of the *Helix* at two percent, of damage to some aspect of ship's systems at eight percent, and specifically damage to the pod life-support network at six percent."

Dem Lia looked at the Ousters and the Templar. "A six percent chance of losing hundreds—thousands—of our sleeping relatives and friends. Those we have sworn to protect until arrival at our destination. A two percent chance that our entire culture will die in the attempt."

Far Rider nodded sadly. "I do not know what wonders your Aenean friends have added to your equipment," he broadcast, "but I would find those figures understated. It is an impossible binary system for a Hawking drive jump."

Silence stretched. Finally Dem Lia said, "Our options are to destroy the harvesting machine for you without knowing if there is life—perhaps an entire species—depending upon it in the red giant system, however improbable. And we cannot do that. Our moral code prevents it."

Reta Kasteen's voice was very small. "We understand."

Dem Lia continued, "We could travel by conventional means and survey the system. This means you will have to suffer the ravages of this Destroyer a final time, but if there is no life in the red giant system, we will destroy the machine when we return on fusion drive."

"Little comfort to the thousands or millions who will lose their homes during this final visit of the Destroyer," said Chief Branchman Keel Redt.

"No comfort at all," agreed Dem Lia.

Far Rider stood to his full four-meter height, floating slightly in the one-tenth gravity. "This is not your problem," he broadcast. "There is no reason for you to risk any of your people. We thank you for considering . . ."

Dem Lia raised a hand to stop him in mid-broadcast. "We're going to vote now. We're voting whether to jump to the red giant system via Hawking drive and get back here before your Destroyer begins destroying. If there is an alien race over there, perhaps we can communicate in the two days we will have in-system. Perhaps they can reprogram their machine. We have all agreed that the odds against it accidentally 'eating' your seedship on its first pass after you landed are infinitesimal. The fact that it constantly harvests areas on which you've colonized—on a tree ring with the surface area equal to half a million Hyperions—suggests that it is programmed to do so, as if eliminating abnormal growths or pests."

The three diplomats nodded.

"When we vote," said Dem Lia, "the decision will have to be unanimous. One 'no' vote means that we will not use the Hawking drive."

Saigyō had been sitting cross-legged on the table, but now he moved next to the other four AIs who were standing. "Just for the record," said the fat little monk, "the AIs have voted five to zero against attempting a Hawking drive maneuver."

Dem Lia nodded. "Noted," she said. "But just for the record, for this sort of decision, the AIs' vote does not count. Only the Amoiete Spectrum Helix people or their representatives can determine their own fate." She turned back to the other nine humans. "To use the Hawking drive or not? Yes or no? We ten will account to the thousands of others for the consequences. Ces Ambre?"

"Yes." The woman in the blue robe appeared as calm as her startlingly clear and gentle eyes.

"Jon Mikail Dem Alem?"

"Yes," said the ebony life-support specialist in a thick voice. "Yes."

"Oam Rai?"

The yellow-band woman hesitated. No one on board knew the risks to the ship's systems better than this person. A two percent chance of destruction must seem an obscene gamble to her. She touched her lips with her fingers. "There are two civilizations we are deciding for here," she said, obviously musing to herself. "Possibly three."

"Oam Rai?" repeated Dem Lia.

"Yes," said Oam Rai.

"Kem Loi?" said Dem Lia to the astronomer.

"Yes." The young woman's voice quavered slightly.

"Patek Georg Dem Mio?"

The red-band security specialist grinned. "Yes. As the ancient saying goes, no guts, no glory."

Dem Lia was irritated. "You're speaking for 684,288 sleeping people who might not be so devil-may-care."

Patek Georg's grin stayed in place. "My vote is yes."

"Dr. Samel Ria Kem Ali?"

The medic looked as troubled as Patek had brazen. "I must say . . . there are so many unknowns . . ." He looked around. "Yes," he said. "We must be sure."

"Peter Delem Dem Tae?" Dem Lia asked the blue-banded psychologist.

The older man had been chewing on a pencil. He looked at it, smiled, and set it on the table. "Yes."

"Res Sandre?"

For a second the other green-band woman's eyes seemed to show defiance, almost anger. Dem Lia steeled herself for the veto and the lecture that would follow.

"Yes," said Res Sandre. "I believe it's a moral imperative."

That left the youngest in the group.

"Den Soa?" said Dem Lia.

The young woman had to clear her throat before speaking. "Yes. Let's go look."

All eyes turned to the appointed commander.

"I vote yes," said Dem Lia. "Saigyō, prepare for maximum acceleration toward the translation point to Hawking drive. Kem Loi, you and Res Sandre and Oam Rai work on the optimum inbound translation point for a systemwide search for life. Chief Branchman Redt, Far Rider, True Voice of the Tree Kasteen, if you would prefer to wait behind, we will prepare the airlock now. If you three wish to come, we must leave immediately."

The Chief Branchman spoke without consulting the others. "We wish to accompany you, Citizen Dem Lia."

She nodded. "Far Rider, tell your people to clear a wide wake. We'll angle above the plane of the ecliptic outward bound, but our fusion tail is going to be fierce as a dragon's breath."

The fully space-adapted Ouster broadcast, "I have already done so. Many are looking forward to the spectacle."

Dem Lia grunted softly. "Let's hope it's not more of a spectacle than we've all bargained for," she said.

The *Helix* made the jump safely, with only minor upset to a few of the ship's subsystems. At a distance of three AUs from the surface of the red giant, they surveyed the system. They had estimated two days, but the survey was done in less than twenty-four hours.

There were no hidden planets, no planetoids, no hollowed-out asteroids, no converted comets, no artificial space habitats—no sign of life whatsoever. When the G2 star had finished its evolution into a red giant at least three million years earlier, its helium nuclei began burning its own ash in a high-temperature second round of fusion reactions at the star's core while the original hydrogen fusion continued in a thin shell far from that core, the whole process creating carbon and oxygen atoms that added to the reaction and . . . presto . . . the short-lived rebirth of the star as a red giant. It was obvious that there had been no outer planets, no gas giants, no rocky worlds beyond the new red sun's reach. Any inner planets had been swallowed whole by the expanding star. Outgassing of dust and heavy radiation had all but cleared the solar system of anything larger than nickel-iron meteorites.

"So," said Patek Georg, "that's that."

"Shall I authorize the AIs to begin full acceleration toward the return translation point?" said Res Sandre.

The Ouster diplomats had been moved to the command deck with their specialized couches. No one minded the one-tenth gravity on the bridge because each of the Amoiete Spectrum specialists—with the exception of Ces Ambre—was enmeshed in a control couch and in touch with the ship on a variety of levels. The Ouster diplomats had been silent during most of the search, and they remained silent now as they turned to look at Dem Lia at her center console.

The elected commander tapped her lower lip with her knuckle. "Not quite yet." Their searches had brought them all around the red giant, and now they were less than one AU from its broiling surface. "Saigyō, have you looked inside the star?"

"Just enough to sample it," came the AI's affable voice. "Typical for a red giant at this stage. Solar luminosity is about two thousand times that of its G8 companion. We sampled the core—no surprises. The helium nuclei there are obviously engaged despite their mutual electrical repulsion."

"What is its surface temperature?" asked Dem Lia.

"Approximately three thousand degrees Kelvin," came Saigyō's voice. "About half of what the surface temperature had been when it was a G2 sun."

"Oh, my God," whispered the violet-band Kem Loi from her couch in the astronomy station nexus. "Are you thinking . . ."

"Deep-radar the star, please," said Dem Lia.

The graphics holos appeared less than twenty minutes later as the star turned and they orbited it. Saigyō said, "A single rocky world. Still in orbit. Approximately four-fifths Old Earth's size. Radar evidence of ocean bottoms and former riverbeds."

Dr. Samel said, "It was probably earthlike until its expanding sun boiled away its seas and evaporated its atmosphere. God help whoever or whatever lived there."

"How deep in the sun's troposphere is it?" asked Dem Lia.

"Less than a hundred and fifty thousand kilometers," said Saigyō.

Dem Lia nodded. "Raise the containment fields to maximum," she said softly. "Let's go visit them."

It's like swimming under the surface of a red sea, Dem Lia thought as they approached the rocky world. Above them, the outer atmosphere of the star swirled and spiraled, tornadoes of magnetic fields rose from the depths and dissipated, and the containment field was already glowing despite the thirty micromonofilament cables they had trailed out a hundred and sixty thousand klicks behind them to act as radiators.

For an hour the *Helix* stood off less than twenty thousand kilometers from what was left of what could once have been Old Earth or Hyperion. Various sensors showed the rocky world through the swirling red murk.

"A cinder," said Jon Mikail Dem Alem.

"A cinder filled with life," said Kem Loi at the primary sensing nexus. She brought up the deep-radar holo. "Absolutely honeycombed.

Internal oceans of water. At least three billion sentient entities. I have no idea if they're humanoid, but they have machines, transport mechanisms, and citylike hives. You can even see the docking port where their harvester puts in every fifty-seven years."

"But still no understandable contact?" asked Dem Lia. The *Helix* had been broadcasting basic mathematical overtures on every bandwidth, spectrum, and communications technology the ship had—from radio maser to modulated tachyons. There had been a return broadcast of sorts.

"Modulated gravity waves," explained Ikkyū. "But not responding to our mathematical or geometrical overtures. They are picking up our electromagnetic signals but not understanding them, and we can't decipher their gravitonic pulses."

"How long to study the modulations until we can find a common alphabet?" demanded Dem Lia.

Ikkyū's lined face looked pained. "Weeks, at least. Months more likely. Possibly years." The AI returned the disappointed gaze of the humans, Ousters and Templar. "I am sorry," he said, opening his hands. "Humankind has only contacted two sentient alien races before, and *they* both found ways to communicate with *us*. These . . . beings . . . are truly alien. There are too few common referents."

"We can't stay here much longer," said Res Sandre at her engineering nexus. "Powerful magnetic storms are coming up from the core. And we just can't dissipate the heat quickly enough. We have to leave."

Suddenly Ces Ambre, who had a couch but no station or duties, stood, floated a meter above the deck in the one-tenth g, moaned, and slowly floated to the deck in a dead faint.

Dr. Sam reached her a second before Dem Lia and Den Soa. "Everyone else stay at your stations," said Dem Lia.

Ces Ambre opened her startlingly blue eyes. "They are so *different*. Not human at all . . . oxygen breathers but not like the Seneschai empaths . . . modular . . . multiple minds . . . so fibrous . . ."

Dem Lia held the older woman. "Can you communicate with *them?*" she said urgently. "Send *them* images?"

Ces Ambre nodded weakly.

"Send them the image of their harvesting machine and the Ousters," said Dem Lia sternly. "Show them the damage their machine does to the Ouster city clusters. Show them that the Ousters are . . . human . . . sentient. Squatters, but not harming the forest ring."

Ces Ambre nodded again and closed her eyes. A moment later she began weeping. "They . . . are . . . so . . . *sorry*," she whispered. "The machine brings back no . . . pictures . . . only the food and air and water. It is programmed . . . as you suggested, Dem Lia . . . to eliminate infestations. They are . . . so . . . so . . . *sorry* for the loss of Ouster life. They offer the suicide of . . . of their species . . . if it would atone for the destruction."

"No, no, no," said Dem Lia, squeezing the crying woman's hands. "Tell them that won't be necessary." She took the older woman by the shoulders. "This will be difficult, Ces Ambre, but you have to ask them if the harvester can be reprogrammed. Taught to stay away from the Ouster settlements."

Ces Ambre closed her eyes for several minutes. At one point it looked as if she had stopped breathing. Then those lovely eyes opened wide. "It can. They are sending the reprogramming data."

"We are receiving modulated graviton pulses," said Saigyō. "Still no translation possible."

"We don't need a translation," said Dem Lia, breathing deeply. She lifted Ces Ambre and helped her back to her couch. "We just have to record it and repeat it to the Destroyer when we get back." She squeezed Ces Ambre's hand again. "Can you communicate our thanks and farewell?"

The woman smiled. "I have done so. As best I can."

"Saigyō," said Dem Lia. "Get us the hell out of here and accelerate full speed to the translation point."

The *Helix* survived the Hawking space jump back into the G8 system with no damage. The Destroyer had already altered its trajectory toward populated regions of the forest ring, but Den Soa broadcast the modulated graviton recordings while they were still decelerating, and the giant harvester responded with an indecipherable gravitonic rumble of its own and dutifully changed course toward a remote and unpopulated section of the ring. Far Rider used his tight-beam equipment to show them a holo of the rejoicing on the ring cities, platforms, pods, branches, and towers, then he shut down his broadcast equipment.

They had gathered in the solarium. None of the AIs was present or listening, but the humans, Ousters, and Templar sat in a circle. All eyes were on Ces Ambre. That woman's eyes were closed.

Den Soa said very quietly, "The beings . . . on that world . . . they had to build the tree ring before their star expanded. They built the harvesting spacecraft. Why didn't they just . . . leave?"

"The planet was . . . is . . . home," whispered Ces Ambre, her eyes still shut tight. "Like children . . . not wanting to leave home . . .

because it's dark out there. Very dark . . . empty. They love . . . *home.*" The older woman opened her eyes and smiled wanly.

"Why didn't you tell us that you were Aenean?" Dem Lia said softly.

Ces Ambre's jaw set in resolve. "I am *not* Aenean. My mother, Dem Loa, gave me the sacrament of Aenea's blood—through her own, of course—after rescuing me from the hell of St. Theresa. But I decided *not* to use the Aenean abilities. I chose *not* to follow the others, but to remain with the Amoiete."

"But you communicated telepathically with . . ." began Patek Georg.

Ces Ambre shook her head and interrupted quickly. "It is *not* telepathy. It is . . . being connected . . . to the Void Which Binds. It is hearing the language of the dead and of the living across time and space through pure empathy. Memories not one's own." The ninety-five-year-old woman who looked middle-aged put her hand on her brow. "It is *so* tiring. I fought for so many years not to pay attention to the voices . . . to join in the memories. That is why the cryogenic deep sleep is so . . . restful."

"And the other Aenean abilities?" Dem Lia asked, her voice still very soft. "Have you freecast?"

Ces Ambre shook her head, with her hand still shielding her eyes. "I did not want to *learn* the Aenean secrets," she said. Her voice sounded very tired.

"But you could if you wanted to," said Den Soa, her voice awestruck. "You could take one step—freecast—and be back on Vitus-Gray-Balianus B or Hyperion or Tau Ceti Center or Old Earth in a second, couldn't you?"

Ces Ambre lowered her hand and looked fiercely at the young woman. "But I *won't.*"

"Are you continuing with us in deep sleep to our destination?" asked the other green-band, Res Sandre. "To our final Spectrum Helix colony?"

"Yes," said Ces Ambre. The single word was a declaration and a challenge.

"How will we tell the others?" asked Jon Mikail Dem Alem. "Having an Aenean . . . a potential Aenean . . . in the colony will change . . . everything."

Dem Lia stood. "In my final moments as your consensus-elected commander, I could make this an order, Citizens. Instead, I ask for a vote. I feel that Ces Ambre and only Ces Ambre should make the decision as to whether or not to tell our fellow Spectrum Helix family about her . . . gift. At any time after we reach our destination." She looked directly at Ces Ambre. "Or never, if you so choose."

Dem Lia turned to look at each of the other eight. "And we shall never reveal the secret. Only Ces Ambre has the right to tell the others. Those in favor of this, say aye."

It was unanimous.

Dem Lia turned to the standing Ousters and Templar. "Saigyō assures me that none of this was broadcast on your tightbeam."

Far Rider nodded.

"And your recording of Ces Ambres's contact with the aliens through the Void Which Binds?"

"Destroyed," broadcast the four-meter Ouster.

Ces Ambre stepped closer to the Ousters. "But you still want some of my blood . . . some of Aenea's sacramental DNA. You still want the choice."

Chief Branchman Keel Redt's long hands were shaking. "It would not be for us to decide to release the information or allow the sacrament to be distributed . . . the Seven Councils would have to meet in secret . . . the Church of Aenea would be consulted . . . or . . ." Obviously the Ouster was in pain at the thought of millions or billions of his fellow Ousters leaving the forest ring forever, freecasting away to human-Aenean space or elsewhere. Their universe would never be the same. "But the three of us do not have the right to reject it for everyone."

"But we hesitate to ask . . ." began the True Voice of the Tree Reta Kasteen.

Ces Ambre shook her head and motioned to Dr. Samel. The medic handed the Templar a small quantity of blood in a shockproof vial. "We drew it just a while ago," said the doctor.

"You must decide," said Ces Ambre. "That is always the way. That is always the curse."

Chief Branchman Keel Redt stared at the vial for a long moment before he took it in his still-shaking hands and carefully set it away in a secure pouch on his Ouster forcefield armor. "It will be interesting to see what happens," said the Ouster.

Dem Lia smiled. "That's an ancient Old Earth curse, you know. Chinese. 'May you live in interesting times.' "

Saigyō morphed the airlock and the Ouster diplomats were gone, sailing back to the forest ring with the hundreds of thousands of other beings of light, tacking against the solar wind, following magnetic lines of force like vessels of light carried by swift currents.

"If you all don't mind," said Ces Ambre, smiling, "I'm going to return to my deep-sleep crèche and turn in. It's been a long couple of days."

The originally awakened nine waited until the *Helix* had successfully translated into Hawking space before returning to deep sleep. When they were still in the G8 system, accelerating up and away from the ecliptic and the beautiful forest ring which now eclipsed the small, white sun, Oam Rai pointed to the stern window, and said, "Look at that."

The Ousters had turned out to say good-bye. Several billion wings of pure energy caught the sunlight.

A day into Hawking space while conferring with the AIs was enough to establish that the ship was in perfect form, the spin arms and deep-sleep pods functioning as they should, that they had returned to course, and that all was well. One by one, they returned to their crèches—first Den Soa and her mates, then the others. Finally only Dem Lia remained awake, sitting up in her crèche in the seconds before it was to be closed.

"Saigyō," she said, and it was obvious from her voice that it was a summons.

The short, fat, Buddhist monk appeared.

"Did you know that Ces Ambre was Aenean, Saigyō?"

"No, Dem Lia."

"How could you not? The ship has complete genetic and med profiles on every one of us. You must have known."

"No, Dem Lia, I assure you that Citizen Ces Ambre's med profiles were within normal Spectrum Helix limits. There was no sign of posthumanity Aenean DNA. Nor clues in her psych profiles."

Dem Lia frowned at the hologram for a moment. Then she said, "Forged bio records then? Ces Ambre or her mother could have done that."

"Yes, Dem Lia."

Still propped on one elbow, Dem Lia said, "To your knowledge—to any of the AIs' knowledge—are there other Aeneans aboard the *Helix*, Saigyō?"

"To our knowledge, no," said the plump monk, his face earnest.

Dem Lia smiled. "Aenea taught that evolution had a direction and determination," she said softly, more to herself than to the listening AI. "She spoke of a day when all the universe would be green with life. Diversity, she taught, is one of evolution's best strategies."

Saigyō nodded and said nothing.

Dem Lia lay back on her pillow. "We thought the Aeneans so

generous in helping us preserve our culture—this ship—the distant colony. I bet the Aeneans have helped a thousand small cultures cast off from human space into the unknown. They want the diversity—the Ousters, the others. They want many of us to pass up their gift of godhood."

She looked at the AI, but the Buddhist monk's face showed only his usual slight smile. "Good night, Saigyō. Take good care of the ship while we sleep." She pulled the top of the crèche shut and the unit began cycling her into deep cryogenic sleep.

"Yes, Dem Lia," said the monk to the now-sleeping woman.

The *Helix* continued its great arc through Hawking space. The spin arms and life pods wove their complex double helix against the flood of false colors and four-dimensional pulsations which had replaced the stars.

Inside the ship, the AIs had turned off the containment-field gravity and the atmosphere and the lights. The ship moved on in darkness.

Then, one day, about three months after leaving the binary system, the ventilators hummed, the lights flickered on, and the containment-field gravity activated. All 684,300 of the colonists slept on.

Suddenly three figures appeared in the main walkway halfway between the command-center bridge and the access portals to the first ring of life-pod arms. The central figure was more than three meters tall, spiked and armored, four-armed, and bound about with chrome razorwire. Its faceted eyes gleamed red. It remained motionless where it had suddenly appeared.

The figure on the left was a man in early middle age, with curly, graying hair, dark eyes, and pleasant features. He was very tan and wore a soft blue cotton shirt, green shorts, and sandals. He nodded at the woman and began walking toward the command center.

The woman was older, visibly old even despite Aenean medical techniques, and she wore a simple gown of flawless blue. She walked to the access portal, took the lift up the third spin arm, and followed the walkway down into the one-g environment of the life pod. Pausing by one of the crèches, she brushed ice and condensation from the clear faceplate of the umbilically monitored sarcophagus.

"Ces Ambre," muttered Dem Loa, her fingers on the chilled plastic centimeters above her triune stepdaughter's lined cheek. "Sleep well, my darling. Sleep well."

On the command deck, the tall man was standing among the virtual AIs.

"Welcome, Petyr, son of Aenea and Endymion," said Saigyō with a slight bow.

"Thank you, Saigyō. How are you all?"

They told him in terms beyond language or mathematics. Petyr nodded, frowned slightly, and touched Basho's shoulder. "There are too many conflicts in you, Basho? You wished them reconciled?"

The tall man in the coned hat and muddy clogs said, "Yes, please, Petyr."

The human squeezed the AI's shoulder in a friendly embrace. Both closed their eyes for an instant.

When Petyr released him, the saturnine Basho smiled broadly. "Thank you, Petyr."

The human sat on the edge of the table, and said, "Let's see where we're headed."

A holocube four meters by four meters appeared in front of them. The stars were recognizable. The *Helix*'s long voyage out from human-Aenean space was traced in red. Its projected trajectory proceeded ahead in blue dashes—blue dashes extending toward the center of the galaxy.

Petyr stood, reached into the holo cube, and touched a small star just to the right of the projected path of the *Helix*. Instantly that section magnified.

"This might be an interesting system to check out," said the man with a comfortable smile. "Nice G2 star. The fourth planet is about a seven-point-six on the old Solmev Scale. It would be higher, but it has evolved some very nasty viruses and some very fierce animals. Very fierce."

"Six hundred eighty-five light-years," noted Saigyō. "Plus forty-three light-years course correction. Soon."

Petyr nodded.

Lady Murasaki moved her fan in front of her painted face. Her smile was provocative. "And when we arrive, Petyr-san, will the nasty viruses somehow be gone?"

The tall man shrugged. "Most of them, my Lady. Most of them." He grinned. "But the fierce animals will still be there." He shook hands with each of the AIs. "Stay safe, my friends. And keep our friends safe."

Petyr trotted back to the three-meter chrome-and-bladed nightmare in the main walkway just as Dem Loa's soft gown swished across the carpeted deckplates to join him.

"All set?" asked Petyr.

Dem Loa nodded.

The son of Aenea and Raul Endymion set his hand against the monster standing between them, laying his palm flat next to a fifteen-centimeter curved thorn. The three disappeared without a sound.

The *Helix* shut off its containment-field gravity, stored its air, turned off its interior lights, and continued on in silence, making the tiniest of course corrections as it did so.

THE SLEEPLESS

Nancy Kress

Beggars in Spain (1993)
Beggars and Choosers (1994)
Beggars Ride (1996)

In the early twenty-first century, genetic engineering for such traits as appearance, intelligence, and health is well established. A Chicago biotech company has just developed a new "genemod" trait: sleeplessness. The nineteen beta-test babies don't sleep at all, ever, thus gaining eight more hours in their waking days. In addition, the removal of sleep, with its concomitant need to dream, seems to result in dispositions that are more stable and adaptable than average.

In *Beggars in Spain,* Roger Camden, billionaire, has his daughter Leisha engineered for sleeplessness. But when the embryo is implanted in Camden's wife, a second naturally fertilized egg also takes root in the uterine wall. Leisha is born with a twin sister who has none of her genemod advantages.

While the girls are maturing, a discovery changes both Leisha's world and the country's attitude toward sleeplessness. Sleepless tissue regenerates naturally. Leisha and her fellows, by now numbering in the thousands, may live indefinitely. It's one advantage too many. A great many "norms" react with jealousy, fear, distaste, or anger that the evolutionary race has been rigged against them and their children. As the Sleepless grow up to be successful, rich, and powerful, the country polarizes, a situation made worse by the establishment by the Sleepless of Sanctuary, a defended enclave in New York State where they feel safe.

The rest of the novel explores the implications of this split between the haves and the have-nots. The Sleepless, led by the widowed Jennifer Sharifi, move through more and more elaborate safety measures to ensure their own isolation, and practice genetic engineering of their own offspring. Sanctuary, now located on an orbital, decides to secede from the United States. Only Leisha and a few other holdouts, including her sister Alice, try to convince the world that there is still just one human species, not two.

Beggars and Choosers opens a few years after *Beggars in Spain*. It follows three characters as they try to find ways to live in the tripartite society that the United States has become. Billy Washington is a poor and uneducated "norm," nearing the end of a hard life, who has finally found a family to love. Diana Covington is a "have," genemod for every attribute except sleeplessness, but aimless and disillusioned. Drew Arlen is an artist of unusual powers who is also the lover of the Sleepless Miranda Sharifi, granddaughter of Jennifer Sharifi. Miranda plans to give the "beggars" of the country freedom and independence by forcibly altering the very biology of the human body. She does so, while Diana and the rest of the Genetic Standards Enforcement Agency try to stop her. The results, however, are not what anybody—including Miranda—expected. Only Billy sees the real answer to the novel's central question, "Who should control radical new technology: scientists, the government, or the people it will affect?"

Beggars Ride, the conclusion of the trilogy, occurs a generation later. The United States is more balkanized than ever. Most people live in nomadic, self-sufficient tribes that need nothing from anyone else, not even food, thanks to the biological alterations made available by the Sleepless, who have all left Earth. The genemod rich stay in their defended enclaves, increasingly purposeless. The country itself is on the verge of ceasing to exist as a political, cultural, or economic entity.

But babies keep being born, and the supply of biology-altering drugs left by the Sleepless is running out.

Jackson Aranow, a doctor totally unneeded by any patients, and his mentally fragile sister, Theresa, are preoccupied with personal concerns. But they get drawn into a struggle between Jennifer Sharifi, released from prison after serving twenty-seven years for treason, and her granddaughter Miranda Sharifi. The war includes engineered viruses that attack not the human body but the mind. At stake is Jennifer's concept of "safety" for her people versus Miranda's concept of "progress" for humanity. Neither Jackson nor Theresa possesses the ruthless certainty of the Sharifi women. Yet the Aranows are the ones who find the next tentative step for a country so changed that not even its most basic tenets any longer apply to daily life, and must be "engineered" anew from a new reality.

—*Nancy Kress*

Sleeping Dogs

by

Nancy Kress

"The new technologies will be dangerous as well as liberating. But in the long run, social constraints must bend to new technologies."
—Freeman Dyson

"THIS IS GOING TO MAKE ALL THE DIFFERENCE IN THE WORLD TO US," DADDY says when the truck pulls into our yard. "All the difference in the world."

I pull my sweater tighter around me. Cool spring air comes in at my elbow, where the sweater has a hole. The truck, which is covered with mud from its trip up the mountain, bumps into a ditch in our driveway and then out of it again. Behind his glass window the driver makes a face like he's cursing, but I can't hear him. What I can hear is Precious crying in the house. We don't have any more oatmeal left, and only a little milk. We surely need *something* to make all the difference in the world.

"Closer, closer . . . hold it!" Daddy yells. The driver ignores him. He stops the truck where he chooses, and the back door springs open. In the pens our dogs are going crazy. I walk around the back of the truck and look in.

Inside, there's nothing to see except a metal cage, the kind everybody uses to ship dogs. In the cage a bitch lies on her side. She's no special kind of dog, maybe some Lab, for sure some German shepherd, probably something else to give her that skinny tail. Her eyes are brown, soft as Precious's. She's very pregnant.

"Don't touch her, Carol Ann, stay off the truck, you don't know her disposition," Donna says, pushing me aside. There's no point in listening to Donna; she doesn't even listen to herself. She climbs into the truck she told me to stay out of and puts her hand into the cage, petting the bitch and crooning at it. "Hey there, sweetie, you old sweetie you, you're going to be lucky for us yes you are . . ."

Donna believes anything Daddy tells her.

262

I go around to the front of the truck, which has big orange letters saying STANLEY EXPRESS, in time to see the Arrowgene scientist get out. He has to be the scientist; nobody would hire him to be a trucker. He's the shortest man I've ever seen, slightly over five feet tall, and one of the skinniest, too. He's all dressed up in a business suit with a formal vest and commpin. I don't like his looks—he's staring at Daddy like Daddy's some kind of oaf—but I'm interested. You'd think genemod scientists would make their own kids taller. Or maybe he's the first one in his family to be a scientist, and his parents were like us, regular people. That might explain why he's so rude to Daddy.

". . . understand that there is no way you can reach us, ever, for technical support. So ask any questions you might have right now."

"I don't have no questions," Daddy says, which is true. He never has questions about anything, just goes ahead and gets all enthusiastic about it and sails on like a high cloud on a March day, sunny and blue-sky right up until the second the storm starts. And Donna's the same way.

"You're sure you have no questions?" the scientist asks, and his voice curls over on itself.

"No, sir," Daddy says.

"*I* have questions," I say.

The Arrowgene scientist looks at me like he's surprised I'm old enough to talk, even though I'm as tall as he is. I'm seventeen but look a whole lot younger. Daddy says, "Carol Ann, I hear Precious crying. Shouldn't you—"

"It's Donna's turn," I say, which is a laugh because Donna never tends to Precious, even though Donna's two years older than I am and should do more work. It isn't that Donna doesn't love Precious, she just doesn't hear the baby cry. Donna doesn't hear anything she doesn't want to hear. She's like Daddy that way.

I say, "What if the litter the bitch is carrying turns out not to be genemod for what you say, after all? If we can't ever find you again for technical support, we can't ever find you again to get our money back."

He's amused, damn him. "That's true, young lady. Your father and I have been all over this, however. And I assure you that the puppies will have exactly the genetic modifications you requested."

"Big? Strong? All male?"

"Yes."

"And they won't ever sleep? Ever?"

"No more than Leisha Camden, Jennifer Sharifi, or Tony Indivino."

He's named three of the most famous Sleepless people in the world, two rich girls and a loudmouth man. The vid reporters follow them around, bothering them. They're all just a few years older than Donna, but they seem much older than that. The women are both beautiful and super-rich. The man, Tony Indivino, calls himself an activist, spouting about "discrimination borne of jealousy and fear" and the "self-assisted evolution of the human race." He's pretty obnoxious, but maybe he's right. I don't know. I never thought much about sleeplessness before, not until Daddy got this business idea that's going to make all the difference to us.

I say to the Arrowgene scientist, "The bitch you implanted the embryos into isn't a purebred. Are the embryos?"

"No."

"Why not? Purebred puppies sell for more money."

"Easier to trace. Your father requested as much anonymity as possible." He scowls. He doesn't like being questioned.

"If animals that don't sleep are going to make such good profits, how come everybody doesn't try to raise and market them?"

He probably wouldn't answer me at all—I'm just another stupid hick to him—except that just then Donna comes around from the back of the truck, leading the bitch on one of our old leashes. The scientist perks up. Donna looks like Mama looked, only maybe even prettier. I remember every line of Mama's face. Of course I do; it wasn't that long since she died. Precious isn't even two. Donna shakes all that red hair, smiles, and walks up to us. The toxic midget scientist gets very sparkly.

"No, young lady, it's true that sleepless animals have not proved a market boon. Why should they? Why would you want a cow or chicken that doesn't sleep, and just eats more from an increased metabolism without a correspondingly steeper increase in meat or milk? Of course, a few researchers went ahead anyway, intrigued to see if the complete elimination of sleep-inducing neurotransmitters had the same side effects in other vertebrates as in humans, which is to say—"

He goes on, talking directly to Donna, who's beaming at him like he's the most fascinating man in the world. She doesn't understand a word. Daddy's not listening, either, rocking back on his heels like he always does when he's pleased about a new business, sure this one'll make us rich. He's already planned his slogan, underground of course since this is all illegal until the FDA approves: BENSON'S GENEMOD GUARD DOGS. THEY NEVER SLEEP, SO YOU CAN. In the house Precious is still wailing, and in their pens the two dogs left over from the previous, legal business (BENSON'S GENEMOD LAPDOGS. CUTER THAN HELL) are barking their heads off. They smell the new bitch.

I go in to Precious. Our house is falling apart: paint peeling, floorboards saggy, water stains from the leaky roof Daddy never gets around to fixing. But at least it's warm inside. Y-energy cones are much cheaper than food. Precious stands up in her crib, screaming, but the minute she sees me she stops and smiles, even though I know she's hungry. She's as sunny as Daddy and Donna, and as pretty. I'm the only plain one. I scoop Precious up in my arms and hug her tight, and she squeals and hugs me back. I sniff that baby smell at the back of her neck, and I wonder what's left to eat that I can fix for her. There has to be something that Daddy didn't give to the dogs because he felt sorry for them, genemod bluish big-eyed collies that nobody in their right mind would want in the same room with them. They don't even look like real dogs.

I find some rice in the back of a cupboard, and heat it with a sliced dried apple. While I feed Precious, I watch the Stanley Express truck drive away and disappear into the mountains.

Donna names the bitch Leisha, after the rich Sleepless woman with the bright gold hair and green eyes. This makes no sense, but we all follow along and call the dog Leisha. She whelps in my bed in the middle of the night. I wake up Daddy and Donna. Daddy moves Leisha to the kitchen. Donna brings her own blankets to put under the panting dog, who has a hard time delivering.

"Here comes the second one . . . *finally* . . . look, there's the head . . . another male!"

Daddy puffs as hard as Leisha. He's as happy as I've ever seen him. It looks like I'm the only one who thinks about Mama, dying right while she was doing this same thing. Two more pups emerge, and they're both males, too. At least the Arrowgene scientist hasn't lied so far. All the pups are big, maybe part Doberman or even Great Dane. It's hard to tell, so young.

One more pup squeezes out, and then the afterbirth. Leisha's almost too tired to eat it. Two pups are brown and black, two are black, and one is a sort of gray color like spoiled yogurt. Their eyes are all closed.

Donna cries, "Aren't they beautiful!"

"They look like slimy rats," I say. She gives me a look. Leisha whimpers and shifts on the spoiled blanket.

Donna says, "Wait till Precious sees them!"

"Now, princess, we can't let Precious get too attached to these pups," Daddy says. "These here aren't our pets." He looks at Donna and me, head tipped to one side like he's making a critical judgment. But his eyes are shining.

"These here are our fortune."

We don't have a terminal. We did, once, but Daddy sold it after Mama died. He did a lot of things then that didn't make too much sense. His grief ran hard but not too long. Then he got interested in life again. I wouldn't want him any different—at least, most of the time.

The library at Kellsville has a public terminal. Once a month a good friend of Daddy's, Denny Patterson, takes one of us girls down the mountain to town to shop. Only two people can fit in the cab of Denny's truck. This month it's my turn.

PROPERTY OF THE STATE OF PENNSYLVANIA comes up when I log on to the Net. REQUEST, PLEASE. A poor county like ours doesn't get voice-interacts.

I can use the Net pretty well. I finished all the high-school software by fifteen and so I was legally done, which is lucky because somebody had to look after Precious. Donna never did finish. I type my request in the only format the public terminals accept:

- PERSONAL SEARCH
- WANTED: BASIC OVERVIEW, MOST RECENT
- LENGTH: 2,000 WORDS
- LEVEL: COLLEGE FRESHMAN
- SUBJECT: SLEEPLESSNESS IN DOGS

I read the answer off the screen. Printouts cost money. It doesn't tell me much, mostly that research on sleeplessness in dogs came after sleeplessness in people, because monkeys had served as both the basic lab animals and the primary beta-test subjects. What is known about sleeplessness in canines "indicates that its mechanisms are similar to those in humans. The same side effects were reported as those observed in sleepless people—sleepless dogs were physiologically calmer, ate more, never slept, displayed increased resistance to disease." The dogs used in the research had been various breeds, but mostly small because it was easier to house and exercise them. All had been destroyed. There is no FDA approval for genemod canine sleeplessness and it isn't legal to take the sleeplessness dogs out of laboratories. There's been no applications to fund the FDA approval process, since "no one has identified significant market opportunity."

Nothing I don't already know. Nothing I want to know. I type another request.

- PERSONAL SEARCH
- WANTED: BASIC INFORMATION, MOST RECENT
- LENGTH: 2,000 WORDS
- LEVEL: COLLEGE FRESHMAN
- SUBJECT: MARKET OPPORTUNITY FOR GUARD DOGS IN PENNSYLVANIA

The terminal searches the Net a longish time. NO INFORMATION AVAILABLE. Great. What good is it?

I pick up our food credits at the government office. At the store I spend a long time choosing. If I'm careful, I'll have enough credits left to get new overalls for Precious, the synth kind that dirt slides off of, and that doesn't ever tear. I also try to choose foodstuffs that will stretch: rice, oatmeal, soy, synthmeat. Trouble is, dogs like all those things, too.

The same side effects were reported as those observed in sleepless people—sleepless dogs were physiologically calmer, ate more, never slept, displayed increased resistance to disease. "Ate more": that was the problem. I figure out where to hide some of the food so there will actually be some left for us by the end of the month. No matter what Daddy and Donna think, Precious comes before Leisha and her pups. Dogs aren't people.

They're cute, though. I have to admit that. Their names, until they're sold anyway, are Tony, Kevin, Richard, Jack, and Bill. Donna named them after the sleepless she sees on the news. Tony Indivino, the loudmouth who thinks Sleepless should live in their own separate guarded city, away from norms. Kevin Baker, the first Sleepless ever engineered. Richard Keller, Leisha Camden's boyfriend. Jack Bellingham, a rich investor. William Thaine, a supersmart Harvard lawyer. I imagine how these people might feel if they knew illegal mutts are named after them.

By the time August turns into a hot September, the pups are huge. They chew everything in the house, day and night. Finally Daddy moves them outside during the day, to an empty pen. Donna starts to train them. She's very good at animal training. But the pups don't seem to learn.

"I don't get it," she says to me. "They're smart enough. Watch them remember where I hide food. And they aren't overdistractible, not like some I've trained."

"Well, then, what is it?" I say, but the truth is I don't really care. I'm losing faith in BENSON'S GENEMOD GUARD DOGS as a way of making all the difference in the world. It's near the end of the month, and there's only a little rice and canned beans left, and Precious is teething. She fusses all the time. She needs the medicine you put on baby's gums, and a regular bed now that she's outgrowing her crib, and new clothes. I sit in the yard, in the shade of a sugar maple, feeling out of sorts. The air is hot and heavy. A thunderstorm is brewing, but there's no guarantee it'll relieve either the heat or the humidity. Mosquitoes whine everywhere. I hold Precious while she twists to get down into a patch of sumac she's allergic to, and I think that I don't care if Tony, Kevin, Richard, Jack, and Bill never learn to guard anything.

Donna says, "I just don't know what it *is* about them pups. They're smart enough to learn."

"You said that." Precious rocks and slobbers against my shoulder: hyenh hyenh hyenh.

"They just don't obey. They just don't seem like no dogs I trained before. They're more like . . . like cats."

"Donna, that doesn't make sense."

"I know it don't. But maybe that cute little scientist used cat genes somewhere in there."

"That's not possible. You can't just mix—Precious, stop it! Let go!" She's pulling on my hair, hard. I reach up and try to get my hair loose from her little fist. Precious lets out a wail and bites my shoulder.

I jerk her loose and shake her. She screams for real, screwing up her eyes and turning red. It's five whole minutes before I can get her calmed down, and when I do I turn on Donna.

"I don't care if those dogs are acting like cats or like elephants. All I care about is they aren't bringing in any money. We need all kinds of things just to live, and we can't afford them. The bathroom roof leaks worse than ever. The house is full of dog poop because Daddy won't let the pups out at night in case anybody realizes they never sleep. *Who,* for fucking sake? Except for Denny and his last girlfriend, we haven't seen another human being in a month!"

Donna stares. "What's got into you, Carol Ann? You used to be so patient and helpful but—"

"I'm sick of being patient and helpful! I'm sick of dogs pooping and barking and chewing things up twenty-four hours a day!"

"—since you turned eighteen you just turned into a fucking bitch."

Eighteen. I had a birthday last week. I forgot all about it. And so, until this very minute I'd bet, did everybody else. Except to tell me that it's turned me into a bitch.

I shove Precious at Donna, so hard that Precious starts crying again. Donna looks at me with wide, hurt eyes, innocent as flowers. I hate her. I hate all of it, the dogs and the poorness and my birthday and everything else. Nothing works right, and all I want to do is get away from all of it. I stumble across the yard, so worked up I can't see straight, and so I miss the aircar land. I don't even know it's there until Donna says soft, like it's a prayer, "O fucking crazy hellfire god."

I've never seen an aircar for real, only on vid. This one is small, built for two people. Maybe only one. The Y-energy cones on the sleek sides are painted a different shade of gray from the body. In our yard it looks like a bullet on a torn-up and rotted body. A man gets out, and Donna gasps. "Tony Indivino!"

It really is. Even I recognize him from vid. He's medium height, a little stocky, not particularly good-looking. His family couldn't afford any genemods except sleeplessness, according to the vid. He starts across the yard toward us, and Donna and I stand up. She thrusts Precious back at me and smoothes her skirt. Precious looks wide-eyed at the car that just dropped out of the sky, and all at once she stops fussing. There, that's what we need: an aircar to land every five minutes to distract her from her aching teeth.

"Hello. May I please speak with David Benson?"

Donna smiles, and I see his reaction in his eyes. He doesn't like reacting, but he reacts anyway. A Sleepless man is still a male.

"David Benson's not here right this minute. I'm his daughter, Donna. Can I help you, Mr. Indivino?"

I say, "You're here because of the dogs."

"Carol Ann!" Donna says. "Where're your manners?"

Tony Indivino hesitates, but only for a second. "That's right. I want to talk to your father about the dogs."

I push. "You want to buy one."

He looks at me then, hard. His eyes are gray, with little flecks of brown in them. I say again, just so there's no mistake. "You want to buy a dog. That's the only reason my father talks about them to anybody."

He finally smiles, amused. "Okay. Sure. I want to buy one."

Donna cries, "But they aren't even trained yet!"

She doesn't have a glimmer. Tony Indivino needs a trained guard dog like he needs a third foot. The Sleepless must have all kinds of Y-shields, bodyguards, secret weapons to protect themselves. Nobody's going to hurt Tony Indivino. He'll buy this dog so his scientist buddies can take it apart in some lab, see how it's different from other dogs. All I care is how much he'll pay for it. Maybe I can get a grand out of him. He's one of the "poor" Sleepless (yeah, right), but his girl-friend is supposed to be Jennifer Sharifi. The daughter of an Arab oil prince and an American holo star, she's the richest woman in the entire world.

Maybe two grand. A bed for Precious, a terminal, some new clothes . . .

Donna says, "Well, I suppose you could buy the dog now and then come back for it later, after I done finish its guard training." She likes this idea.

Indivino says, "How is the training going?"

"Fine," I say, real fast. I'm not going to give him an excuse to pay less. I stare at Donna, who finally nods.

"Really?" Indivino says.

"Why *wouldn't* the training go good?" Donna says.

His voice turns serious. "No specific reason that I know of. But that's what I wanted to talk to your father about."

"Then you can talk to me. Daddy's gone for two–three days, hunting in the mountains," I lie. "But I can repeat to him any information you like."

He doesn't even hesitate. Probably Sleepless are used to young people accepting responsibility, even better than the adults around them. The oldest Sleepless is only twenty-seven.

He says, "What I wanted to tell your father isn't hard data. It's more a principle, but a very important one. It's this: advanced biologic systems are very complex. They're past that critical point beyond which behavior is complicated but predictable, and into the realm where behavior becomes chaotic, and more sensitive to small differences in initial conditions. Do you know what that means?"

"No." Donna says, and smiles.

"Sort of," I say, because I had this in the high-school software. He simplifies it for me anyway.

"It means that genemod changes that worked one way in humans might not work the same way in dogs. Or they might work the same way in most dogs but not in your dogs. Or in some of your dogs but not in others from the same litter but with different genetic makeup, or different *in vitro* conditions, or different environmental conditions."

Donna says, "But our dogs are sleepless just exactly like you sleepless humans are, Mr. Indivino. Come see!"

He looks at me. I say, "It means we should be careful."

"Yes," he says, "there isn't that much research on canine sleeplessness to guide you."

No applications to fund the FDA approval process, since no one has identified significant market opportunity. But, come to think of it, how had Tony Indivino heard of this particular market opportunity? Daddy isn't advertising yet. He doesn't have anything to advertise with: no terminal, no money. I feel a prickle on my spine, and Precious squirms in my arms. I put her down. She toddles toward the aircar.

Donna's saying, "You've got to come choose your pup, Mr. Indivino. Wait till you see them, they're so cute you—"

"How'd you hear about us?" I demand. "Who told you?"

He doesn't answer.

"Are you going to report Daddy to the law?" Amazingly, this only occurs to me now. Sleepless generally keep inside the law, the vids all say. Maybe there's too many eyes on them not to.

"No, I'm not going to report to the law. I'm here only to warn you to be careful."

"Why? What's it to you if our business fails?" I almost say "like our others," but I catch myself in time. I don't want him feeling sorry for us.

"Your business is nothing to me personally," he says coolly. "But we Sleepless like to keep an eye on genetic research. I'm sure you can see why. Even underground research. How we do that really isn't your concern. I'm here only to tell you what I have. And maybe a little out of curiosity."

Donna says brightly, "Then you're curious to see the pups and choose your very own!"

She takes him by the hand and leads him away, toward the house. Precious is trying to climb the smooth, rounded side of the aircar, which of course she can't do. In a minute she'll be on her little ass in the dirt. I start toward her and leave Tony Indivino to Donna and the sleepless pups. It doesn't matter which pup he picks, or if he ever actually comes back for it. It only matters that he pays before he leaves.

Which he does. Two and a half thousand dollars, and in certified preloaded credit chips, not just transfers. I hold the chips in my hand while Donna dances and cheers around the kitchen, setting the dogs to barking, and Precious stands up in her high chair and crows. It's chaos. For once, I don't care. This money is going to make all the difference in the world to us.

Three weeks later, everything ends.

"Come look at this here," Daddy calls through the screen door. He's sitting at the kitchen table in front of our new terminal, researching what he calls "ad futures" on the Subnet. His friend Denny, with the truck, showed him how. Daddy won't tell me how Denny learned, or what Denny's buying or selling that he needs underground ads. But I know the Subnet's not easy to ride. It isn't all that hard to log onto, but after that it has a way of melting away unless you know all the key underground code words and procedures, which keep changing all the time. "The shadow economy," vidnews calls it, or sometimes "the ghost market." Supposedly you can get anything there, if you know how.

"Carol Ann!" Daddy calls again, louder. "Come see this."

"I'm busy," I call back from the yard. I'm watching Precious dig a hole with a kitchen fork. She sits in the slanting fall sunshine, covered with sweat and dirt, happy as day. Somewhere in the woods I hear Donna yelling at dogs. They still aren't training properly. She's having a terrible time with them.

"I said come here, Carol Ann, and I mean come here!" Daddy yells. Reluctantly I get myself up and go into the house.

It's funny about getting a little money. All last winter and spring, when I was scrounging for rice and beans enough for us, and Daddy was working his ass off to get the money to buy the genemod embryos implanted in Leisha, and Donna had just one dress—all that long cold winter everybody was in a good mood. Sunny, hopeful. We were nice to each other. But since we got Tony Indivino's credit chips, everybody's been tense and snappy. Maybe I'm always that way, but Donna and Daddy aren't. Or weren't.

The stakes are higher now. Daddy has to figure out the right places to buy ads: Subnet sites that will be profitable, as well as safe from the law. We can't afford to make mistakes. And the news is full of the feds closing illegal genemod labs, and the pups won't listen to Donna unless she's right there with a piece of meat—that's what she meant when she said they're like cats, they only do what you want them to if you're standing right there with a prize or a poke. Everybody's nervous.

For once, we have something to lose.

"Tell me what this means," Daddy growls, and I bend over the screen. It's an FDA recommendation to Congress about making genemod animals. The sentences are long and difficult, with a lot of scientific words I don't understand.

"It's about what a new law should allow in genetic engineering," I say. "The summary says 'No genemods that alter external appearance or basic internal functioning such that a creature deviates significantly from other members of not only its genus and species but also its breed.' "

"I can read!" Daddy snaps. After a minute he says, "I'm sorry, Carol Ann. But I need to know what every bit of it means. You explain it. One sentence at a time."

"Daddy, I can't—"

"Sure you can. You're the smartest one of us, and don't think I don't know you know it."

"But—"

"Please, baby. Help me understand."

So I do. One sentence at a time, guessing at words, groping around to lay my hands on the meaning. It takes a long time. Right up until the minute I hear Precious start screaming.

We're out the door in half a second. But I can't see her anywhere. And then the screaming stops.

Donna comes running from the woods, yelling "Richard! Richard!" and it takes me a minute to realize she's yelling for the dog. Her eyes are crazy. We all stop like the air holds us, only our heads swiveling. I can't see Precious. I can't see her. And then Donna, who's got hearing almost as good as the dogs', tears off into the woods to the left of the house.

I hear the snapping before I see Richard. His jaws are working over a piece of meat that Donna must have given him, a piece of reward meat. He lies down peacefully eating it, the shifting of his head and body on the fallen leaves making little rustling noises. I hear the rustles, because suddenly these woods are the quietest things I ever heard. The quietest things I ever will hear again.

Precious lies about eight feet away, down a little hill with a stream at the bottom. Her neck is broken. Her hands are smeared with beef juice, from the steak she tried to take away from Richard. Maybe she wanted a bite. Or maybe she thought it was a game: tug-of-war. But Richard wasn't playing. He tossed Precious away—the bite marks are clear on her little arm—and Precious fell down the hill and landed wrong. She hit her head, or twisted her neck, or something. Later on the coroner would say it was a freak accident. Except for her arm, she isn't bruised at all, or wet from the stream. She lies there in her new dirt-resistant pink overalls like she's asleep.

Daddy shatters the quiet with a howl like hell breaking open. I run to Precious and pick her up. I hardly even hear the rifle going off not ten yards from me. The other shots—four more, and then a last, senseless one for Leisha—I don't hear at all. Not an echo, not a whimper. Nothing.

I don't know what makes people stay glued together inside, or not. Maybe it's like Tony Indivino said: Behavior is just chaotic, mostly sensitive to small differences in initial conditions. I don't know. Anything.

Daddy doesn't stay glued together. He starts drinking right after the funeral, and he doesn't ever stop. He doesn't get mean or weepy. He doesn't explain why he could ride out Mama's death but not Precious's. Maybe he doesn't know. He just sits at the kitchen table, night after night, and quietly empties one bottle after another. During the day, he waits for night. Pretty soon, I think, he won't bother to wait.

Donna doesn't stick around to find out. She cries all the time for a few months. She wants to talk on and on about Precious, and I can't listen. I can't. Eventually she finds someone who will, a government counselor in Kellsville, who also finds her a job waiting on customers in a fancy restaurant. Customers like her. Bit by bit Donna stops crying. She makes some friends, then a boyfriend. I don't see her much. And when I do, it's hard to look straight into each other's eyes.

And me. I don't know if I stayed glued together or not. I'm too mad to know.

"You're Dave's girl," Denny says, just like he hasn't taken me back and forth from Kellsville in his truck for years. He's one of those men terrified of female scenes. "What can I do for you, uh . . ."

"Carol. You can let me stay here and keep house for you."

He looks like I could be rabid. "Well, uh, Carol, I don't know about that, I thought you were keeping house for your father, he sure needs you since, uh—"

"He doesn't need anybody," I said. "And you do." I looked around me. Denny's wife left him, finally, last month. Denny had one girl too many. Since she moved, Denny hasn't washed a dish or a sheet or a tabletop. His girlfriends, who he mostly meets at the Road Nest Bar, aren't the type given to housekeeping. The two cats stopped using their litter box. Denny's got all the windows open to control the smell, which it doesn't, even though it's pouring outside and rain is blowing in sideways on what's left of his cat-piss-soaked couch. Everybody's got a limit how much reeking mess they can tolerate. Denny's must be pretty high, but I'm still betting he's got one.

"I'm a good housekeeper," I say. "And I can cook. Daddy says he'd take it as a favor if you let me live here. He knows I need to get away from the memories in our house."

Denny nods slowly. It makes him feel better to think that he's helping Daddy. But he still has doubts.

"The thing is, Carol, you know how folks are. They talk. And you ain't a kid no more. I don't want nobody to think—"

"The only one that matters is Daddy, and he knows better. Besides, if you go on having lady-friend company, the ladies will tell them I sleep in the spare room and that you treat me like a daughter for my daddy's sake."

Again Denny nods. He likes the idea of having lady-friend company and a clean house, too. "But I can't, uh, pay you nothing, Carol, things are tight right now. Maybe later when—"

"I don't want any money, Denny. All I want is for you to teach me how to use the Subnet. On your terminal, same as you taught Daddy. For two hours a day, at least in the beginning."

He doesn't like that. Too much time. But just then one of the cats squats and shits on the table, into a plate of rice so congealed the rice grains are hard as kitty-litter pellets.

"Okay," Denny says.

All winter I work like hell. I throw out Denny's couch and everything else I can't boil. I scrub and pound and make a new couch out of boards and blankets. I cook and launder and shop with Denny's dole credits. Twice a week I walk over to Daddy's to do the same for him. And half the night I practice what Denny teaches me, until I'm tired enough to sleep. A lot of days my eyes ache from the constant reading, and not only on the Subnet, either. I spend hours in the science sections of the Net. When one of Denny's girlfriends complains that I "talk snooty," I realize that my vocabulary has changed. Well, why not . . . everything else has.

By the time crocuses push up through the snow, Denny can't teach me any more. Actually, I know much more than Denny's taught me, because I found other people on the Subnet who also taught me things. There's an entire class of Subnet riders—mostly young, mostly with little to lose personally—who like nothing better than showing off what they know. I've learned how to let such people impress me.

However, that sort of petty rider only knows so much. So does Denny. And I have nothing to trade. So far I haven't been able to get the Subnet to tell me the one thing I want to know the most. And I'm not going to find it out by staying here.

I write notes to Denny and Daddy, and I walk down the mountain to the highway.

The Red Goldfish Trucking Company is guarded by dogs.

There's a fence, too, of course, a single strand of token wire to mark the Y-energy-alarmed barrier surrounding the facility. I push against the invisible field with one hand, and it feels solid as brick. But any power-generated security system has to be turned on, and that means it can be turned off. Dogs are harder to turn off, unless you kill them, and it's hard to get anything like a bullet or a slab of poisoned meat through most Y-energy security fields without setting off the alarm. There's a Subnet rumor that the Sleepless have developed a missile to penetrate Y-barriers, plus a field that will stop that same missile and anything else, including air. But it's only a rumor. Sleepless do not sell weapons. They're too smart to arm their enemies.

I stand a few inches outside the fence and gaze in at the Red Goldfish Trucking Company. It's a windowless foamcast building standing in the middle of rows of white trucks, each with a red goldfish painted on both sides. Before the goldfish, those trucks bore flowing blue script that said *Pennsylvania Shipping*. Before that, they had the blue daisies of Flower Delivery Systems. Before that, the orange lettering of Stanley Express. It was a Stanley Express truck that delivered Leisha the pregnant dog to Daddy's new business.

No record exists on-line of that transaction. It's hard enough to track the company itself on the Subnet, let alone its customers. Or its owner.

I watch through the fence for two nights, very carefully, until I'm sure about the dogs. There are three dogs, all German shepherds, all unneutered males. They're probably genemod for strength and hearing. They're superbly trained, much better than poor Donna could have done. They sleep in shifts. They are not genemod for intelligence.

You can do certain things to the genetic makeup of dogs and they remain functioning dogs. Other things you can't do. You can't really boost a dog's intelligence much. If you do, you end up with a pattern of neural connections too complex for the hindbrain to handle. It's like a cable jammed with too much information. The signal breaks down. The pups just sit in one place and shiver and whimper. They can't be fixed, and eventually you have to kill them. Some scientists at Harvard published a paper about this on the Net. Some underground labs in Ohio and Florida already knew it. They advertised HIGH

IQ DOGS! on the Subnet. Until they didn't anymore. Somebody's looking for them, too, although I don't think it's an angry customer. I think it's the cops.

The cops are the main link between the Net and the Subnet. But they're not the only link.

Red Goldfish Trucking's dogs patrol the entire fence every six minutes. They're efficient, alert, and dedicated. But they're still dogs.

Just before one of them passes my place outside the fence, I roll over on my back. I'm wearing perfume: a scent genetically created as a wolf attractant for use in Consolidated Wilderness Areas. It was developed at the University of California at La Jolla, which holds the patent. It was also developed at underground labs in Idaho and Minnesota. You can order it at Subnet 784jKevinMart, access route 43ICE7946, through JemalTown, Cash Drop Described Elsewhere.

The guard dog smells me. His gait falters. His gaze shoots sideways to me, on my back on the ground, all fours in the air, the posture of submission in wolf packs. And dog packs. But I'm outside the fence. After that brief falter, he resumes his normal pace and trots on.

Six minutes later, I'm still there.

At midnight the dogs change shifts; I don't know on what conditioned signal. The new dog goes through the same reaction to me: faltering, then going on. I roll slightly, wiggling, my limbs in the air. At 3:00 A.M., I go home. Workers show up here every day at four.

I'm back the next night. And the next. During the day I work for a housecleaning company that sends out maids to rich houses. Very quickly I become popular with their customers. I'm skillful at using the special bots for each job, and I'm especially good at cleaning up disasters left by other, malfunctioning bots.

On the twentieth night, the 4-P.M.-to-midnight dog stops on his side of the fence, reaches through the Y-energy with one paw, and cuffs me roughly on the butt. He's the alpha male, the biggest of the guard dogs, the one who carries his tail the highest and his ears pricked forward the farthest. He tears a gash in my padded trousers and then trots away on his regular patrol.

I lie still, waiting for him to return. Six minutes later he does, cuffs me again, and moves on.

By the end of the month, half his body juts through the Y-fence, which from the inside he doesn't know is there, while he rolls me around on the ground. Sometimes he's rough, sometimes just playful. I have deep scratches on my neck and hands. I try to keep him away from my face, and when I fail, I wear heavy makeup at work. When the dog's on top of me, snapping and fake-growling, I try to never remember Precious.

It's not the dog's fault. His brain is hard-wired. All the dogs in a pack pick on one dog. That's the function of the omega dog, the last and lowest: to give all the other dogs something to pick on and exploit. The pack needs that outlet to work off tension they might otherwise use fighting each other. The omega dog is in their genes.

Sometimes, when Alpha takes my arm in his jaws and shakes it, I put my hand on his neck. I can feel the beeper, just under his skin. It's transmitting the electronic signal that lets him penetrate the fence if he happens to brush up against it without setting off alarms. And anything attached to him would also penetrate: you don't want the alarms going off just because your guard dog's tail brushed a Y-field and that tail just happens to have a burr stuck on it.

On the thirty-third day, I roll through the fence, smelling like a female wolf, my arms wrapped around the Alpha guard dog. Inside, he cuffs me sharply on the shoulder and leaves me there. He's been trained never to let a stranger inside. But I'm a member of his pack filling a necessary position. It makes all the difference.

The Subnet claims, over and over, that it keeps no records. But the Subnet itself is a record, endlessly downloaded. If there's one, there'll be others. Nobody can remember every business deal without help. Especially if you need to know who you had better not try to deal with a second time.

Nothing inside Red Goldfish Trucking is locked. But nothing gives me what I want, either. The windowless building is mostly used for storing cargo and fixing trucks, with a tiny, filthy office walled off in one corner. There's a terminal, although I know better than to think I'll find anything on that. It's free-standing, but the government has new microwave equipment that can lift data off even free-standing terminals, as long as the terminal's switched on. The Subnet says it also has that equipment for sale. I don't believe it. I don't believe anything on the Subnet unless I try it out for myself, like I did the dog attractant. However, I know the Red Goldfish records won't be electronic.

They're plastic, written by hand on stiff blue cards stored in a blue box in the back of the closet. And they're in code.

Beta dog comes into the office. He's off duty. I have to let him knock me around for a few minutes before he curls up in the corner and goes to sleep.

I take the whole box with me, ride Alpha back through the fence, and catch the next bus out. On the bus I fall into the deepest sleep of my life. It feels like a reward.

There are five blue plastic cards, headed 1, 2, 3, 4, 5. That could mean chronological order, or groupings of different kinds of trucking jobs, or almost anything else. Each card is densely covered in small neat handwriting, row after row of it, letters and numbers and symbols with no breaks between. Card 5 is covered only two-thirds of the way down.

Donna stares as I walk with my suitcase into the Kellsville restaurant where she works. It's not a cheap table-delivered soysynth place; it has real food and human servers, including Donna. She wears a black uniform with a blue apron. Her red hair is piled on top of her head. She looks like Mama.

"Carol! What on God's green earth . . . Daddy said you went clean over into Ohio to work!"

"I did. I'm back. Can I stay with you a bit?"

" 'Course you can, honey! And I want you to meet my boyfriend Jim, he's a real sweetie and I just know you two'll—"

"Is there a housecleaning firm in town? I've been working as a maid."

Donna laughs. "In Kellsville? You got to be kidding. But in the city, maybe . . . there's a gravtrain goes back and forth every day now, they just started it. But honey, you look terrible. You all right?"

I look at her. It's like looking at Mama: just as dead to me, just as far away. Donna's put Precious clean out of her mind. She doesn't know anything about deep black places you can fall into and never get out. She just doesn't know.

"I'm fine," I say. "Tell me your address and give me your key. You have a terminal, Donna?"

"One came with the apartment," she says proudly. "Though I don't use it much except for vid. You're welcome to it, honey. You're welcome to anything you find there, except Jim."

She laughs, and I try to smile, and then I go to her place and get to work cleaning it up.

The next three months I work as fiendishly as I did at Denny's. Every day I take the new gravtrain to the city and work my cleaning job. They're glad to have me; I'm experienced with every kind of maintenance bot they have. Every night I sit at the terminal in the ten-by-ten living room of Donna's apartment, trying not to hear Donna and Jim making love in the ten-by-ten bedroom.

I start with free code programs off the Net. I feed in all the data from the five blue plastic cards and run the programs. None of them makes any sense out of the data.

After a month I've saved up enough credits to download programs that cost money. None of them works either.

"What're you doing on that terminal all night every night, honey?" Donna asks. "You're getting circles under your pretty eyes. Don't you want to come out dancing with us and have a little fun? Jim's got some pretty peccy friends!"

"No, thank you," I say. "You seen Daddy lately?"

Her face goes flat. "Tomorrow. You know I go every Tuesday. You want to come with me?"

I shake my head and go back to the terminal. Donna doesn't say anything more. After she leaves, I can still smell her perfume, flimsy and sweet, in the stale air.

The best code breakers aren't programs you can buy. They're net-sites that take your data and run it through their own decryption algorithms. All are very expensive, although you can negotiate with them. They're on the Subnet, of course. From what I read, some of them use programs stolen from the government. The best ones might even be stolen from the military. Maybe.

The problem is guessing which ones might be best. Housemaids don't make a lot of money, not even when they're called cleaning bot technicians.

Finally I contract with a Subnet site called Bent. They seem to do business in Pennsylvania, New York, and Ohio. It's a heavily shielded transaction, although it uses regular credit, not a cash drop. I give them the data off the blue plastic cards, and they empty my bank account. Afterwards I close the account and open a new one with a different e-bank.

That night, for the first time ever, I dream about Precious. She's sitting in her high chair, dressed in pink overalls, laughing. Whatever she's laughing at is behind me, and when I try to turn around, I'm frozen in place. Frantically I twist my body, but no muscles will move. Precious goes on laughing.

Donna and Jim bring home a chair. They've been saving to buy it. It's bright screaming green, and it gives off eight different scents, including sex pheromones. They spend ten minutes trying to decide where to put it.

"In this corner, sweetie," Donna says.

"In the bedroom would be better." Jim leers.

"Carol Ann, what do you think?"

I think it's the ugliest piece of furniture I've ever seen. "I don't care."

"About anything," Jim says under his breath. I pretend not to hear him. He's getting a little impatient with me living here so long. But he won't say anything, because it's what Donna wants.

Donna says, "Okay, the bedroom," and she and Jim look at each other in a way that says I should leave the apartment for an hour or so.

I leave for three, walking the streets more or less aimlessly. When Bent tells me who the bastards are who sold Daddy the sleepless dogs . . . Daddy's gun is one thing he hasn't sold for whiskey. I know because I buried it before I left, well oiled, behind the place the dog pens used to be. Ammunition doesn't cost that much. It can be ordered off the Subnet, no questions asked, no records kept. (Right.)

I would recognize the Arrowgene scientist anywhere. His appearance, his voice, his supercilious manner with people who are ignorant. Scientists aren't cops. They don't go around armed. They don't walk wary. I'm not a good shot, but with this gun, I don't need to be.

It's not what I'd prefer, of course. I'd prefer to get him somewhere isolated, tie him up, smear him with blood from a freshly killed rabbit. Let loose a pack of dogs that have been starved for a week . . .

These imaginings fill up three hours. They've filled up whole nights, weeks, months. I walk until the sun starts to set, and then I go back to Donna's apartment building. Outside sit two police aircars. A stretcher bot rolls out beside an orderly.

"Jim! What—"

But his stretcher rolls on past. A cop moves in beside me. "Who are you, miss?"

"I live here! He's . . . *where's my sister?*"

Donna isn't inside. She's already gone to work. The cop tells me they've sent for her, she's on her way, she's safe.

"Jim . . ."

"The medic says he'll be all right. Just roughed up some. Now you tell me, miss. Is anything missing?"

I look around Donna's apartment. Drawers have been pulled out, furniture turned over, the bed flung apart. I pretend to study the mess, but I already know. Everything's still here except five blue plastic cards, and the next time I try to find Bent on the Subnet, it'll be gone.

Arrowgene must not've been a small underground lab after all. It must've been part of a bigger organization, with terminal-trace programs. With enforcers. With the idea of protecting their truckers and scientists and anonymity.

"Miss?"

There was no way I could fight that sort of organization. Nobody could, not even the government, or the FBI would have shut it down by now. Nobody with enough power and information . . . except maybe one other organization.

"Miss, I *asked* you if you notice anything missing."

"No," I say. "Everything here is just the way it always was."

Tony Indivino was already living in Sanctuary when he visited us last spring. We didn't know that then. We didn't care, then.

Sanctuary is nearly completed by the time I arrive there. It's huge, half of a rural New York State county circled by a Y-field. Most of the Sleepless in the United States are moving inside, where they feel safe. They trade with the rest of the world, information and inventions and money deals I don't understand. Mostly they trade data, but you can also find a few tangible Sleepless products on the Net. The ones on the Subnet are fakes.

I stand at the front gate of Sanctuary in a crowd of tourists who've gotten off bus after bus. They mutter and glare.

"Walling themselves in, and us out."

"They better stay the fuck in there if they know what's good for them."

"A monument to genemod narcissism."

I look at the man who says that. He looks genemod himself, handsome and well dressed, but apparently not a Sleepless. And just as resentful as the rest of the haters who still spent their good money to travel here to a place full of people they're jealous of. Go figure.

On the front of the gate is a big screen with the Sleepless, Inc. logo on it: an open eye. Some kids throw rocks at it, big ones, but the screen doesn't waver. Protected by a Y-field. It says quietly, over and over, "To leave a message for Sanctuary, Incorporated, or for any individual inside, please speak clearly into one of the five recorders below. Thank you. To leave a message for Sanctuary, Incorporated—"

People are lined up to leave messages, mostly nasty. I can guess how this works. A smart system sorts through the messages, flagging them by key word, choosing the ones that actually get delivered. If any do. People with real business with Sanctuary don't use this channel.

Except that I have real business with Sanctuary.

When it's my turn, I speak quietly, so the jerks behind me can't hear.

"This is a message for Tony Indivino, from Carol Benson. You came to our house in Forager County, Pennsylvania, last March to warn us about the genemod dogs my Daddy bought on the Subnet. They were Sleepless embryos implanted in a mongrel bitch, bought from a company called Arrowgene. You were right about the dogs, and now I need to talk with you. Just for a minute. Please see me." And then, after I could get the words up my throat, "My baby sister was killed by one of those sleepless dogs."

I wait. Nothing happens. The man in line behind me finally says, "I think it's *my* turn now." When he repeats it, I step aside.

How long does the smart program take? And what if Tony Indivino isn't inside Sanctuary? He must leave sometime; he came to us.

Five minutes later the large screen flashes a different icon: my name. It says, "Will Ms. Carol Benson please step into the elevator." And there it is, a sudden dimple in the gate like a small elevator, complete with wood-paneled walls. Before the surprised people around me can react, I dart inside. The "door" closes. I touch it, and the walls, too; they're pure force field, with holos of wooden paneling. The whole thing doesn't move at all. It just "opens" on the other side, into a real room with white foamcast walls, clean-lined white sofas, and a wall screen which says, "Please wait, Ms. Benson, a few minutes longer."

I want to try the door at the far end of the room, to see if it's real. To see if it's locked. To see if I can really go into Sanctuary, where sleepers aren't allowed. But I don't dare. I'm a beggar here.

The door opens and a woman walks in, alone. Tall, with long black hair, dressed in jeans and sweater. She is more beautiful, and more exotic, for real than on vid.

"Ms. Benson, I'm Jennifer Sharifi, Tony Indivino's associate. Tony cannot come himself. Please tell me what happened with the sleepless dogs."

She's nothing like Tony Indivino. He was friendly. She's cold, like some queen talking to a grubby peasant. But there's a weird nervousness to her, too. She keeps pushing back that long black hair, even when it's not in her face. I don't like her. But I need her.

I say, "My father ordered the embryos on the Subnet, from Arrowgene. The dogs were engineered to not—"

"I know all that," Jennifer Sharifi interrupts. "Tony told me about his visit to you. What happened subsequently?"

Does she remember everything "Tony" ever told her? Maybe she does. She's genemod for every ability possible. Suddenly I remember a story Mama read to Donna and me when we were small. "Sleeping Beauty." Fairy-blessed at her christening with beauty, intelligence, grace, talent, fortune . . .

"How did your sister die?" Jennifer Sharifi asks, and pushes back her long hair. "Did a Sleepless dog kill her?"

"Yes. No. Not deliberately. Precious—she was two—was bothering the dog while it ate, and it just cuffed her and she fell and she hit the ground at an angle where her neck . . ." I can't finish.

"Had the dogs been acting out of character before that?"

"Yes. My sister—my other sister—couldn't get them trained right. She said they were more like cats. They just didn't . . . want to be trained."

She was silent so long I finally said, "Ms. Sharifi, I came here to—"

"Biological systems are very complex," she says. "And species are not identical in their neural inheritance, even when structures seem completely analogous. A dog is not a human being, and sleeplessness doesn't affect both equally."

"I already know that!" I snap. It's what Tony Indivino said last March, in easier words. "Tell me now what killed my sister! If you know!"

"We know," she says, precisely. But her hand goes again to her long dark hair. "We keep track of all research worldwide on sleeplessness, even that not yet published on the Net. A Danish institute is doing work on canine sleeplessness. The key is dreaming."

"Dreaming?" I don't expect this.

"Yes. Let me try to explain it in terms you can understand." She thinks a minute, and I see she doesn't know how she sounds. Or else she doesn't care.

"One facet of the human brain is its ability to imagine different realities. Today I don't have a cake. I picture the cake I want, and tomorrow I construct it. Or a house, or a concerto, or a city. That's one way the brain uses its ability to imagine alternate realities. Another way is to think up fantasies that never will or could be, like stories about magic. Another way is through dreaming, asleep at night. Are you following me?"

I'm not stupid. But all I say is, " Yes."

"We Sleepless don't dream, obviously. But we do all the other methods of imagining alternate reality. Better, in fact, than you do. So the basic ability gets ample exercise.

"Now consider canine species. They evolved from wolves, but they're not wolves. They've been domesticated by humans for at least twenty thousand years. During that time—did you hear something?"

"No," I say. Her eyes dart toward the door, then the wallscreen. She pushes her hair back.

She's waiting for something, and jumpy as a cat. But she goes on.

"During the time the dog was domesticated, it developed the ability to do as humans do, and visualize an altered reality. To some undefined extent, anyway. A dog doesn't just remember its master. And it doesn't just respond to Pavlovian conditioning, either. There's evidence from advanced neurological imagining that parts of a dog's brain activate when the animal interacts with humans. When, for instance, a human pets a dog, the dog actually pictures itself in an alternate reality with the human. Maybe at home in front of a fire. Maybe rolling around on the ground playing. There's no way to deduce specifics, but the chemical, electromagnetic, and cerebral imaging evidence is all quite strong."

I nod, listening hard, making sure I understand it all.

"And there's one more piece of research that's relevant here. These same brain functions go on during REM sleep, when dogs dream. That, too, is an imaging of alternate reality, as I already said."

She looks at me like she thinks I don't remember. I nod, hating her, to show I do. Tony Indivino wasn't like this.

"Here is the crucial piece. In sleepless canines, there's no REM sleep. When that's removed, so is dreaming. And when dogs don't dream, the alternate-reality imagining slowly disappears from their brain scans. The function is still there when they're born, but over the next several months it fades. Without reinforcement from dreaming, imagination— as humans know the term—disappears. Without imagination, the bond with man weakens and the older limbic behavior takes over. Dreaming made all the difference. Its absence is what killed your sister."

I struggle to understand. "You mean . . . because the dog couldn't imagine people and dogs together in ways that weren't happening at just that minute . . . it wouldn't take its training and it didn't care about Precious? She died because Leisha's pup couldn't *dream*—"

"What?" Jennifer says sharply. "Who couldn't dream?"

I remember that she and Leisha Camden, who Donna named the pup after, are enemies. They have different dreams for the Sleepless.

Jennifer wants them all in Sanctuary; Leisha wants them to live outside in the real world with us, the inferior animals.

"The dog," I stumble on, "my sister named the pups, my other sister, not me—"

"That's all I have to tell you, Ms. Benson," Jennifer Sharifi says. She stands crisply. "I hope the information explains what happened. Sanctuary is sorry for your loss. If you'll step back into the security elevator—"

"No, wait! You didn't tell me what I have to know!"

"I've told you all I can. Good-bye."

"But I need to know the name and location of the company that sold Daddy the embryos! They were called Arrowgene then, but now I can't track them on the Subnet, they've changed their name or shut down . . . but I have their truckers' business records! Only they're in code and I don't know anybody else who could figure out—"

"I can't give you that information. Good-bye, Ms. Benson."

I spring toward her. It's a mistake. I hit an invisible barrier that's apparently been there the whole time, unseen. It doesn't hurt me, but I can't move any farther toward Jennifer Sharifi.

She turns. "If you don't get into the elevator, Ms. Benson, the field will carefully push you into it. And don't bother leaving any more messages for Tony. He's not here, and if he were, he would tell you that Sanctuary is about survival. Not revenge."

She leaves. The Y-field pushes me into the security box and then opens on the other side, and I'm back in the Allegheny hills.

Later that day, on a bus going home, I hear on vid that Sleepless activist Tony Indivino has been arrested. The FBI linked him to a kidnapping four years earlier. He abducted a four-year-old boy named Timmy DeMarzo, a Sleepless child whose normal parents had beaten him for disturbing them in the middle of the night nearly every night. Tony Indivino had hidden the kid with people who had taken much better care of him. But now he's been caught and arraigned, and is being held without bail in the Conewango County jail.

There must be other ways beside the Subnet to find an underground genemod lab. But I don't know what they are. I've done everything I can think of to do. But how can I give up the search for Precious's killer? If I give up the search . . .

Outside the bus windows, the road climbs higher into the mountains. Already it's June. The woods are in full leaf, although they're not yet deep green but instead that tender yellow-green you see only a week or ten days every year. The sunny roadside bursts with daisies and buttercups and Queen Anne's lace. Creeks rush; streams burble.

If I lose my anger, there won't be anything of me left.

For just a second I look into a black place so deep and cold that my breath freezes. Then it's gone and the bus keeps on climbing the mountain road.

It lets me off in Kellsville and I walk the rest of the way up the mountain, which takes until sunset. Daddy's yard looks just the same. Straggly grass, deep ruts, sagging porch. But it's not Daddy sitting on the porch. It's Donna.

"I thought you'd come here," she says, not standing up. "Or did you go by my place first?"

"No." In the shadows I can't see her face.

"Did you go by the hospital to see how Jim's doing?"

"No."

" 'No.' 'Course not. He don't concern you, does he?"

I ignore this. "Where's Daddy?"

"Asleep. No—passed out. Let's be honest for once, okay, Carol Ann?"

But it was always Donna who wasn't honest. Who insisted on being sunny in a world where the sun only really shines on the rich. I don't say this.

She continues, "You're the reason Jim got hurt, aren't you? And the reason my place got trashed. You're doing something you shouldn't be doing, and somebody important don't like it."

"It's none of your business, Donna."

" 'None of my business.' " She stands up then, in the porch shadows. " 'None of my business!' Who the fuck do you think you are to tell me what's my business and what isn't? How much more family do you think I got to lose?"

This isn't Donna. This is somebody else. I climb the porch steps and turn her face toward the sunset. She hasn't been crying, but in the red light she starts to shake all over with a fury I never in a million years thought she was capable of.

"You stupid fuck—what do you think you're *doing*? You got Jim hurt and you're going to get yourself hurt next, or Daddy, or me! Whatever you're doing, it isn't going to bring Precious back, and it isn't going to get even because there isn't no 'even.' Don't you even know that? You can't beat those people; all you can do is try and stay away from them, and when you do brush up against them you get out quick and forget anything you learned or they'll wreck whatever you got left of your life!"

"Donna, you don't know—"

"No, it's you who don't know! You don't know nothing about how the world works! You're supposed to be the smart one, and I'm supposed to be dumb as a bucket of hair, poor old dumb Donna, but I know you can't fight them and win. You can only lose more'n you already did and I'm not going to do that—I'm not going to lose everything else I got left. And you're not going to lose it for me neither, Carol Ann. Promise me right here and now, on Precious's grave, that you'll leave this alone."

"I can't."

"Promise me."

"I said I can't!"

We stare at each other in the dying light, and I see that we're never going to agree, never going to understand each other. We're made too different. She lives in a world where when you get slammed hard, you pick yourself up and go on. I don't live in that world. I don't want to. That's what makes all the difference.

But it's her that crumbles first. "All right, Carol," she says wearily, not meaning it. "All right."

"I'm sorry," I say, not meaning it either.

We don't say anything more. The sun goes down, and somewhere down the mountain, a dog barks.

I move back to the city, and go back to work at my old housecleaning company. Whenever I can I sign up for double shifts, houses in the day and offices at night. It makes me tired enough to sleep. Donna visits me once. I cook her dinner, we go to a vid, she takes the gravtrain back the next day. The whole time, she chats and laughs and hugs me. The guy in the apartment next door watches her like she's a vid star.

I'm hanging on. Trying not to think. Not to feel. Waiting, although I don't know for what. The days are frozen and the nights dreamless.

It's not that way for the rest of the country. Every day something else happens. A Sleepless teenager dies in a car crash in Seattle, and doctors take apart his body and brain. They find that every bit of tissue is perfect. Not just in good shape—he's only seventeen—but perfect. Sleepless tissue regenerates. The Sleepless won't age. An unexpected side effect, the scientists say.

A county in New York says Sleepless can't serve on juries because they aren't "peers" of everybody else.

A scientist in Illinois publishes a study on sparrows made to be sleepless. Their metabolism is so high they can't eat enough to keep themselves alive. They die, eating and eating, of starvation.

Pollux, Pennsylvania, votes a law that Sleepless can be refused apartment rentals. They're awake too much, which would run up landlords' utility bills.

Some institute in Boston proves that sleepless mice are unable to contract or carry hantoviruses.

A vid preacher declares Jennifer Sharifi the Antichrist, sent to Earth to represent ultimate evil just before the final Armageddon.

The *New York Times* prints an editorial that says, essentially, that everybody should take a deep breath and calm down about sleeplessness.

And in July, the inmates of the Conewango County Jail kill Tony Indivino in the recreation yard. They beat him to death with a lead pipe.

I learn this on the eleven o'clock news, drinking a beer and cleaning my own apartment. The terminal is a cheap standard wallscreen, rimmed in black plastic. The news has no pictures of the death.

". . . promised a full investigation of the incident, which occurred at twelve-twenty this afternoon Eastern Standard Time. The inspector general of the New York State Correctional System—"

If they knew the exact time the "incident" was occurring, why didn't somebody stop it?

I stand there, staring at the screen, a glass of beer in one hand and a cleaning rag in the other. The red message light on the side of the terminal blinks. These cheap systems can't split the screen. I choose the message, and the Sanctuary logo fills the black rim.

"Message for Carol A. Benson," says a pleasant computer voice, "from Jennifer Sharifi of Sanctuary, Incorporated, New York State. This message is shielded to Class One-A. It will not record on any system and will repeat only once. The message is: Arrowgene operating as Mountview Bionetics, Sarahela, Pennsylvania. Chief scientist is Dr. Tyler Robert Wells, 419 Harpercrest Lane. End message."

The screen blanks.

If Tony Indivino were here, he would tell you that Sanctuary is about survival. Not revenge.

Not anymore.

I fiddle with the terminal for half an hour, but the computer voice was accurate. The message hasn't been recorded. There's no trace of it anywhere, in my system or in the retrievables off the parent system. I'm the only one who will ever hear it.

*   *   *

Daddy's gun is where I left it, and in the same condition. So is he.

"Hey, Daddy."

It takes him a minute to focus. "Carol Ann."

"It's me."

"Welcome home." Suddenly he smiles, and I see a flash of what he was, the old cheerful sweetness, before it sinks under the heavy smell of whiskey. "You here? Long?"

"No," I say. "Just overnight."

"Well, 'night. Sleep tight." It's seven o'clock in the evening.

"Sure, Daddy. You, too."

"Gonna sit up. Little longer."

"You do that."

The next morning, I'm gone by five. The gun comes apart, and it's in my duffel bag. I wear jeans and good shoes. By seven I'm in Kellsville. The bus south leaves at eight. I drink a cup of coffee and watch the headlines circle the news kiosk.

NO SUSPECTS IDENTIFIED IN INDIVINO MURDER.

"NO ONE IS TALKING," SAYS CONEWANGO WARDEN (STORY 1—click here)

FBI RECEIVES ANON CALL TO BOMB SANCTUARY (STORY 2)

INDIVINO DEATH CALLED NATIONAL DISGRACE (STORY 3)

RAIN PUMMELS SOUTHEAST (STORY 4)

FRANCE CALLS FOR MAJOR EUROCREDIT REFORM (STORY 5)

SCIENTISTS CREATE GENEMOD ALGAE. POTENTIAL FOR FEEDING THE WORLD IS ENORMOUS, SAYS NOBELIST (STORY 6)

I put in a credit chip and press button six. The flimsy prints out, but there's not time to read it before my bus leaves. I shove the flimsy in my duffel and sleep all the way to Sarahela, Pennsylvania.

Four-nineteen Harpercrest Lane is in a shielded community. From beyond the gate I can see streets running down to a river park. The houses are tall, narrow, and stuck together in fours and fives. There are trees, small playgrounds, beds of perfect genemod flowers. The river, which I don't know the name of, sparkles blue.

It's the kind of community that cooperates, that relies on word of mouth. A single day of loitering outside the gate gives me the name of the most commonly used residential cleaning company: Silver's Polish. The next day I'm hired. They're glad to have such an experienced cleaning tech.

The Dr. Tyler Wellses have a tech come every Thursday. On my second week I trade shifts with another worker, two for one, telling him I need Wednesday off to see a doctor. By eight o'clock I'm in the house. I set the vacuuming bot to snuffling around the kitchen floor and spray the sink with organic-molecule-eating foam. Four littered places on the breakfast table. I go through the rest of the house.

Two kids' rooms, toys and small clothing. They've already left for school.

A woman singing in the master-bedroom shower.

Nobody else is home. I go back down the stairs. Halfway down, on a landing with a sculpture of a Greek wrestler below a cool blue-tinted window, I see him come out of a backyard shed, carrying a trowel and wearing gloves. Short, skinny, slightly balding. Dr. Tyler Robert Wells, scientist, gardens by hand, without bots.

I slip the gun from my cleaning kit, push the parts together, and raise it to the window. Once he's in the crosshair, I tell the chip to take over, keeping centered on his head. It's in his head, the knowledge that genemods animals to kill other people's children. I sit the gun on the wide polished windowsill, where it follows Wells's every move on its all-directional swivel. I programmed it to my voice, within a five-foot radius. All I have to do is say "Fire."

"Don't," a voice says.

I look up, expecting to see the woman from the shower standing above me. But she's still singing in a distant room. The female voice is below, a much older woman dressed like a bodyguard. Her gun is the handheld kind. "Carol, don't say it. Listen first."

A bodyguard shouldn't know my name. And I shouldn't take time to listen. She's too late to stop my verbal command to my gun, and that's all that matters. It never mattered whether or not I got out.

"Don't say your gun codeword because we're going to get him anyway. The government is. Yes, we know who you are, ever since you tried to use Bent to decode Red Goldfish Trucking. We went back and put it together then. We'll get Wells, I promise you. But if you kill him now, there's a lot of information we won't get. Don't say the codeword. Just come down the stairs and I'll deprogram the gun."

"No."

"Carol, if you kill him we'll prosecute you. We'll have to. But if you leave, I'll get immunity for you. And your father, too, about the sleepless dog embryos. Come down."

"No."

"I know about your little sister. But our chances of getting the right evidence against Wells are stronger if we have more time with him. It will make all the difference to our case."

"Fire," I say to the gun, and close my eyes.

Nothing happens.

My eyes fly open. The gun still sits on the windowsill, swiveling to follow the back of Wells's head. The FBI agent has climbed the stairs between us. She puts a hand on my arm. I feel the biometal joints augmenting her grip. Her eyes are sad. "I gave you the chance to get out. Now please come quietly."

"What . . . how . . ."

"We have counterfields you couldn't possibly know about. Don't you realize you're way over your head? Weapons get more complex every day. And you're not even a pro."

I let her lead me quietly out of the house, into an aircar marked BLAISEDELL BODYGUARDS, INCORPORATED. Nobody pays any attention to us. As we lift above Harpercrest Lane, the last two things I notice are Wells, bent happily over his garden, and a dog, a collie, lying on the bright green genemod grass on somebody's front lawn, asleep.

The FBI agent turns out not to be an FBI agent after all. She works for something called the United States Genetic Standards Enforcement Agency, something new, something created because of the eruption of genemod, legal and illegal. The GSEA is going to prosecute me. They have to, my new lawyer says. But they'll do it slowly, to give themselves more time to nail Wells and Mountview Bionetics and Bent and all the other companies woven together with underground labs. The government will get Wells eventually, my lawyer says. The GSEA agent was right about that.

But she was wrong about something else. Every day I sit in my cell, on the edge of my cot, and think about how wrong she was.

Nothing makes all the difference. To anything. The systems are too complex. You genemod dogs for sleeplessness and you destroy their imagination. You genemod people for sleeplessness and you get super-people, who can imagine everything and invent anything. But Tony Indivino was killed by the lowest scum there is, and Jennifer Sharifi is taking Sanctuary from purposes of safety to purposes of revenge. Donna chooses to deny anything that makes her unhappy, but the deep black frozen place is in her just as much as in me. Daddy survives his wife's death but breaks down at his daughter's. Sleepless mice have great immune systems; sleepless sparrows starve to death; Sleepless humans regenerate tissue. Genemod algae will end world hunger. Dogs genemod for IQ go catatonic, and guard dogs with the best training in the world will revert to pack pecking order if the omega animal smells right.

No one factor can make all the difference. There are too many different factors, now. Maybe there always were.

So I'll let my lawyer, who is a Sleepless named Irving Lewis, defend me. He wants the case for what he calls "the eventual chance to set significant Constitutional precedents." Except for court appearances, he does most of his work inside Sanctuary.

Maybe he can get me off, maybe he can't. Either way, I don't know what will happen next. Not to me, not to anything. I can only try to make things come out my way: get a job, make up with Donna, go to college. Someday I'd like to work for the GSEA. That wouldn't make up for Precious, or for anything else. But maybe it might make a small, slight, necessary difference.

TALES OF THE HEECHEE

Frederik Pohl

Gateway (1977)
Beyond the Blue Event Horizon (1980)
Heechee Rendezvous (1984)
The Annals of the Heechee (1987)
The Gateway Trip (1990)

When the first human colonists arrived on the planet Venus (as described in the novelette, "The Merchants of Venus," included in the book *The Gateway Trip*), they discovered its surface was honeycombed by tunnels, the work of some ancient alien visitors from space they called the Heechees. Apart from a few cryptic artifacts, the tunnels were empty. Who the Heechees were, why they had come to Venus, and where they had gone, everyone wondered and no one could say. (A prankster published a book of several hundred pages called *All We Know About the Heechee*. Every page was blank.) In their exploration of our solar system, the Heechee had not stopped with Venus. They had come to Earth as well, but the closest they found to intelligent creatures at that time were the short, hairy, small-brained primates now called *Australopithecus robustus*.

The Heechee did one more thing before they left. They established a sort of spaceship base in an asteroid. When it was found by human beings, quite by accident, it too was riddled with tunnels. The corridors were stripped as clean as those of Venus, but the Heechee had not left the asteroid entirely bare. Its surface was pocked with launch pods for spacecraft; hundreds of the ships were still there; and they worked.

The Heechee spaceships had many wondrous virtues, and one severe flaw. They could travel far faster than light. They were fitted with automatic navigation systems, so that they went to specific parts of the Galaxy, presumably those that had interested the Heechee enough to explore. But no one knew how to choose one course over another; once you got in and started the ship's drive you were on your way—but to where, you could not say until you got there. Abandoned Heechee base, supernova remnant, planet stripped bare by some other intelligent race—the destination could be anything at all.

But sometimes—not often—the end of the long flight was a place where the Heechee had left other examples of their machines and instruments. They were products of technological skills far more advanced than humankind's, and consequently of incalculable value.

To seek out this treasure trove, the governments of Earth established the Gateway Corporation, and (as described in the novel *Gateway* and its sequels) invited the daring ones to come to the Gateway asteroid and try their luck—and their courage. For the courses set hundreds of thousand of years ago by the Heechee did not any longer wind up in places where fragile human beings could survive.

When published in 1977 *Gateway* won nearly all the annual awards for best science-fiction novel, including the Hugo, the Nebula, the Campbell Memorial Award, and the national prizes of France and Yugoslavia. It has been translated into some thirty languages, was made into two video games, and is currently under development as a motion picture.

—Frederik Pohl

The Boy Who Would Live Forever

by

Frederik Pohl

• I •

ON STAN'S SEVENTEENTH BIRTHDAY THE WRATH OF GOD CAME AGAIN, AS IT DID
every six weeks or so. Stan was alone in the apartment, cutting up
vegetables for his birthday dinner, when he felt that familiar, sudden,
overwhelming, disorienting, *horny* rush of vertigo that everybody
called the Wrath and nobody understood. Screams and sirens from
outside the building told him that everybody else was feeling it, too.
When it hit, Stan managed to drop the paring knife to the floor so
he wouldn't cut himself and staggered to a kitchen chair to sweat
it out.

People said the Wrath was a terrible thing. Well, it was. Whatever
it was, it struck everyone in the world at once—and not just the
people on Earth, either; ships in space, the colonies on Mars and
Venus, they all were caught up in it at the same moment, and its
costs in accidents and disasters were enormous. Personally, Stan
didn't mind it all that much. It felt like suddenly being overwhelmed
by a vast, lonely, erotic nightmare. Like, Stan thought, probably what
it would be like to get good and drunk. The erotic part was not very
different from some of the yearnings Stan himself felt from time to
time, and when the Wrath was over there was no hangover.

When it had passed, Stan shook himself, picked up the things he
had knocked to the floor and turned on the local TV news to see how
bad it had been this time. It had been bad enough. Fires. Car
smashes—Istanbul's aggressive drivers relied on their split-second re-
flexes to avert disaster, and when the Wrath took away their skill the
crashes came fast. The worst thing that happened this time was an

oil tanker that had been coming into the Golden Horn. With everyone on both the tugs and the tanker's own bridge suddenly incapacitated, it had plowed, dead slow and irresistible, into one of the cruise-ship docks on the Old City side and there exploded into flame.

Like any teenager, Stan had a high tolerance for other people's misfortunes. He just hoped the commotion wouldn't make his father too late getting back with the saffron and mussels for the stew. When he finished with the vegetables and put them in a pot of cold water he put a couple of his precious old discs on to play—this time it was Dizzy Gillespie, Jack Teagarden, and the Firehouse Five Plus Three—and sat down to wait, thumbing through some of his comics and wondering if, for once, his father would have stayed sober long enough to get him some kind of a present for his birthday.

That was when the polis came to the door.

There were two of them, male and female, and they looked around the shabby apartment suspiciously. "Is this where the American citizen, Walter Avery, lived?" the woman demanded, and the past tense of the verb told the whole story.

The rest of the facts were quickly told. The Wrath had made a statistic of Stan's father. Overcome, he had fallen while crossing the street and a spellbound taksi driver had run right over him. There was no hope of holding the driver responsible, the woman said at once; the Wrath, you know. Anyway, the driver had long disappeared. And, besides, witnesses said that Stan's father had of course been drunk at the time. Of course.

The male polis took pity on Stan's wretched stare. "At least he didn't suffer," he said gruffly. "Died right away."

The woman was impatient. "So you've been notified," she said. "You'll have to come to the morgue to collect the body before midnight, otherwise there'll be a charge for holding it an extra day. Good-bye."

And they left.

* II *

Since there would be neither mussels nor saffron for his birthday meal, Stan found a few scraps of leftover ham and tossed them into the pot with the vegetables. When he had put them on to simmer he sat down with his head in his hands, to think about what it meant to be an American—well, half-American—orphan, alone in the city of Istanbul.

Two facts presented themselves at once. First, that long-dreamed-of day when his father would sober up, take him back to America and there make a new life for the two of them—that day wasn't going to come. From that fact it followed that, second, there was never going to be the money to pay for his college, much less to indulge his dream of flying to the Gateway asteroid and wondrous adventure. Therefore he wasn't ever going to have the chance to become one of those colorful and heroic Gateway prospectors who flew to strange parts of the Galaxy. He wasn't going to discover a hoard of priceless artifacts left by the vanished old race of Heechee. And so he wasn't going to become both famous and rich.

Neither of these new facts was a total surprise to Stan. His faith in either had been steadily eroding since he reached the age of the first dawn of skepticism at twelve. Still, they had seemed at least theoretically *possible*. Now, nothing seemed possible at all.

That was when Stan at last allowed himself to begin to cry.

While Stan was drearily cleaning up the kitchen after his flavorless birthday meal, Mr. Ozden knocked on the door.

Mr. Ozden was probably around seventy years old. To Stan he might just as easily have been a hundred—a shriveled, ugly old man, hairless on the top of his head, but with his mustache still black and bristly. He was the richest man Stan had ever met. He owned the ramshackle tenement where Stan lived, and the two others that flanked it, as well as the brothel that took up two floors of one of them. Mr. Ozden was a deeply religious man, so devout in his observances that he did not allow alcohol on his premises anywhere except in the brothel, and there only for the use of non-Islamic tourists. "My deepest sympathies to you on your loss, young Stanley," he boomed in his surprisingly loud voice, automatically scanning everything in sight for traces of a forbidden bottle of whiskey. (But he never found any; Stan's father had been clever about that.) "It is a terrible tragedy, but we may not question the ways of God. What are your plans, may I ask?"

Stan was already serving him tea, as his father always did. "I don't exactly know yet, Mr. Ozden. I guess I'll have to get a job."

"Yes, that is so," Mr. Ozden agreed. He nibbled at a crumb of the macaroon Stan had put on a saucer for him, eyeing the boy. "Perhaps working at the consulate of the Americans, like your father?"

"Perhaps." Stan knew that wasn't going to happen, though. It had already been discussed. The Americans weren't going to hire any translator under the age of twenty-one.

"That would be excellent," Mr. Ozden announced. "Especially if it were to happen quickly. As you know, the rent is due tomorrow, in addition to last week's, which has not been paid, as well as the week's before. Would they pay you well at the consulate, do you think?"

"As God wills," Stan said, as piously as though he meant it. The old man nodded, studying Stan in a way that made the boy uneasy.

"Or," he said, with a smile that revealed his expensive teeth, "I could speak to my cousin for you, if you like."

Stan sat up straight; Mr. Ozden's cousin was also his brothel-keeper. "You mean to work for him? Doing what?"

"Doing what pays well," Mr. Ozden said severely. "You are young, and I believe in good health? You could have the luck to earn a considerable sum, I think."

Something was churning, not pleasantly, in Stan's belly and groin. From time to time he had seen the whores in Mr. Ozden's cousin's employ sunning themselves on the rooftop when business was slow, often with one or two boys among them. The boys were generally even younger than himself, mostly Kurds or hill-country Anatolians, when they weren't from Algeria or Morocco. The boys didn't seem to last long. Stan and his friend Tan had enjoyed calling insults at them from a distance, and none of them had seemed very lucky.

Before Stan could speak Mr. Ozden was going on. "My cousin's clients are not only men, you know. Often women come to him, sometimes wealthy widows, tourists from Europe or the East, who are very grateful to a young man who can give them the pleasures their husbands can no longer supply. There are frequently large tips, of which my cousin allows his people to keep nearly half—in addition to providing his people with Term Medical as long as they are in his employ, as well as quite fine accommodations and meals, at reasonable rates. Quite often the women clients are not unattractive, also. Of course," he added, his voice speeding up and diminishing in volume, "naturally there would be men as well." He stood up, most of his tea and macaroon untouched. "But perhaps the consulate will make you a better offer. You should telephone them at once in any case, to let them know of your father's sad accident. It may even be that he has some uncollected salary still to his account which you can apply to the rent. I will come again in the morning."

When Stan called the consulate Mr. Goodpastor wasn't in, but his elderly secretary was touched by the news. "Oh, Stanley! This terrible

Wrath thing! How awful for you! Your father was a, uh, a very nice man." That part was only conditionally true, Stan knew. His father had been a sweet-natured, generous, unreliable drunk, and the only reason the consulate had given him any work at all was that he was an American who would work for the wages of a Turk. And when Stan asked diffidently if there was any chance of uncollected salary she was all tact. "I'm afraid not, Stanley. I handle all the vouchers for Mr. Goodpastor, you know. I'm sure there's nothing there. Actually," she added, sounding embarrassed, "I'm afraid it's more likely to be a little bit the other way. You see, your father had received several salary advances lately, so his account is somewhat overdrawn. But don't worry about that, dear. I'm sure no one will press a claim."

The news was nothing Stan hadn't expected, because he knew how chronically short of money they had always been. All the same, it sharpened his problem. The Americans might not demand money from him, but Mr. Ozden certainly would. And had. And would do his best to collect. The last time someone had been evicted from one of his tenements Mr. Ozden had seized every stick of their possessions to sell for the rent owed.

Which made Stan look appraisingly around their tiny flat. The major furnishings didn't matter, since they belonged to Mr. Ozden in the first place. Even the bed linens and the kitchenware. His father's skimpy wardrobe would certainly be taken. Stan's decrepit music player and his stacks of ancient American jazz recordings; his collection of space adventures, both animé and morphed; his schoolbooks; the small amount of food on the shelves—put them all together and they would barely cover the rent. The only other things of measurable value were the musical instruments, his battered trumpet and the drums. Of course Mr. Ozden had no proper claim to the drums, since they weren't Stan's. They'd been brought there and left by his friend Tan, when Tan's parents refused to have any more music-making in their house.

That Stan could do something about. When he phoned it was Tan's mother who answered, and she began weeping as soon as she heard the news. It was a while before Mrs. Kusmeroglu could manage to tell Stan that Oltan wasn't home. He was at work, but she would get the sad message to him at once, and if there was anything they could do . . .

When he got off the phone with Mrs. Kusmeroglu Stan looked at the clock. He had plenty of time before he had to get to the morgue, so he opened up the couch he slept on—he wasn't quite ready to move into his father's bed—and lay down in case he needed to cry some more.

He didn't, though. He fell asleep instantly, which was even better for him. What woke him, hours later, was Tan Kusmeroglu standing over him. Stan could hear the braying of the muezzin, calling the faithful to prayer from the little mosque around the corner, almost drowned out by Tan's excited voice as he shook Stan awake. "Come on, Stan, wake up! The old fart's at prayer now and I borrowed my boss's van. You'll never have a better time to get your stuff out!"

That meant they had ten minutes at most. Stan didn't argue. It took less than that to load the drums, the trumpet, the precious music discs and player and a handful of other things into the van. They were already driving away before Stan remembered. "I have to go to the morgue," he said.

Tan took his eyes from the tour bus before them and the delivery truck that was trying to cut in from the side long enough to glance at Stan. His expression was peculiar—almost unTanly sympathetic, a little bit flushed in the way he always looked when about to propose some new escapade. "I have been thinking about that," he announced. "You don't want to go there."

"But they want me to identify my father's body, so I have to."

"No, you don't. What's going to happen if you do? They're going to want you to pay for a funeral, and how are you going to do that? No. You stay out of sight."

Stan asked simply, "Where?"

"With us, stupid! You can share my room. Or," he added, grinning, "you can share my sister's if you'd rather, only you would have to marry her first."

· III ·

Everybody in the Kusmeroglu family worked. Mr. Kusmeroglu was a junior accountant in the factory that made Korean-brand cars for export. Tan delivered household appliances for a hardware store. His sixteen-year-old sister, Naslan, worked in the patisserie of one of the big hotels along the Bosphorus. Even Mrs. Kusmeroglu worked at home, assembling beads into bracelets that spelled out verses from the Koran for the tourist trade—when she wasn't cleaning or cooking or mending the family's clothes. Even so, Stan knew without being told, they were barely making ends meet, with only the sketchiest of

Basic Medical and a constant fear of the future. Finishing school was now as out of the question for Stan as it had been for Tan. So was sponging off the Kusmeroglus for any length of time. He had to find a way to make money.

That wasn't easy. Stan couldn't get a regular job, even if there was one to be got, because under Turkish law he was now an unregistered nonperson. He wasn't the only one of that sort, of course. There were millions like him in poverty-stricken Istanbul. It wasn't likely the authorities would spend much effort in trying to track him down—unless he made the mistake of turning up on some official record.

The good part was that the season was spring, well on the way to becoming summer. That meant that the city's normal population of twenty-five million, largely destitute, was being enriched each week by two or three million, maybe even five million, tourists. These were people who, by definition, had money and nothing better to spend it on than Istanbul's sights, meals, curios, and inhabitants. "You can become a guide," Mr. Kusmeroglu pronounced at dinner. "You speak both Turkish and English without flaw, Stanley. You will do well."

"A guide," Stan repeated, looking as though he thought it a good idea out of courtesy to his host, but very far from convinced.

"Of course a guide," Tan said reprovingly. "Father is right. You have learned all you need to know about Istanbul already—you remember all those dull history classes when we were at school together. Simply subtract the Ottoman period and concentrate on those crazy empresses in the Byzantine, which is what tourists want to hear about anyway. Also we can get guidebooks from the library for you to study."

Stan went right to the heart of the matter. "But I can't get a guide's license! The polis—"

"Will not bother you," Tan's mother said firmly. "You simply linger around Topkapi, perhaps, or the Grand Bazaar. When you see some Americans who are not with a tour group you merely offer information to them in a friendly way. Tell them you are an American student here—that is almost true, isn't it? And if any polis should ask you any questions, speak to them only in English, tell them you are looking for your parents, who have your papers. Fair-haired, with those blue eyes, you will not be doubted."

"He doesn't have any American clothes, though," Naslan put in.

Her mother pursed her lips for a moment, then smiled. "That can be dealt with. You and I will make him some, Naslan. It is time you learned more about sewing anyway."

*　　*　　*

The endless resources of the Lost & Found at Naslan's hotel provided the raw material, the Kusmeroglu women made it fit. Stan became a model American college student on tour: flared slacks that looked like designer pants, but weren't, spring-soled running shoes, a Dallas Dodgers baseball cap and a T-shirt that said, "Gateway or Bust," on the front, and on the back, "I busted." The crowds of tourists were as milkable as imagined. No, more so. The Americans on whom he concentrated all seemed to have more money than they knew what to do with. Like the elderly couple from Riverdale, New York, so confused by the hyperinflated Turkish currency that they pressed a billion New Lira banknote on Stan as a tip for helping them find clean toilets when a million or two would have been generous. And then, when he pointed out the error, insisted that he keep the billion as a reward for his honesty. So in his first week Stan brought back more than Tan earned at his job and almost as much as Naslan. He tried to give it all to Mrs. Kusmeroglu, but she would take only half. "A little capital is a good thing for a young man to have."

And her daughter added, "After all, someday soon you may want to get married."

Of course, Stan had no such plans, although Naslan certainly was pretty enough in the perky pillbox hat and miniskirt that was her uniform in the patisserie. She smelled good, too. That was by courtesy of the nearly empty leftover bits of perfume and cosmetics the women guests of the hotel discarded in the ladies' room, which it was part of her duties to keep spotless, but it had its effect on Stan. Sometimes, when she sat close to him as the family watched TV together in the evenings, he hoped no one was noticing the embarrassing swelling in his groin. It was natural enough. He was, after all, a male, and seventeen.

But he was also thoroughly taken up by his new status as an earner of significant income. He was diligent in memorizing whole pages from the guidebooks, and he supplemented them by lurking about to listen in on the professional guides as they lectured to their tour groups. The best places for that were in places like the Grand Mosque or Hagia Sofia, where all the little clusters of a dozen or a score tourists were crowded together, with six or eight guides all talking at once, in half a dozen languages. Their gossip was usually more interesting than anything in the books, and a lot more scurrilous.

That was not without risk, though. In the narrow alleyway outside the great kitchens of Topkapi Palace he saw a couple of the licensed guides looking at him in a way he didn't like as they waited for their tour groups to trickle out of the displays. When both of them began talking on their pocket phones, still looking at him, he quickly removed himself from the scene.

Actually, he was less afraid of the guides, or the polis, than he was of Mr. Ozden finding him. What the old man could do if that happened Stan didn't know. In a pinch, he supposed he could actually pay off the overdue rent out of the wads of lira that were accumulating under his side of the mattress he shared with Tan. But who knew what law he had broken by his furtive departure? Mr. Ozden would know all about that, all right, and so Stan stayed far away from his old tenements.

It wasn't all work for Stan. If he got home in time, he helped Mrs. Kusmeroglu with the dinner—she affected to be amazed by his fairly rudimentary cooking skills—and then sometimes they would all watch TV together. Mrs. Kusmeroglu liked the weighty talk shows, pundits discussing the meaning of such bizarre events as that inexplicable Wrath of God that visited them from time to time, or what to do about the Cyprus question. Mr. Kusmeroglu preferred music—not the kind the boys could play, though. Both Tan and Stan voted for programs about space or sports. But then it seldom came to a vote, because what Naslan liked was American sitcoms—on the English-language channels, so she could practice her English—happy groups of wealthy, handsome people enjoying life in Las Vegas or Malibu or the Hamptons, and Naslan talked faster than anyone else. It didn't matter. What they did was to share things as a family. A real *family*. And that was in some ways the best part of all for Stan, who had only the faintest memories of what living in a family was like.

Although the Kusmeroglus were all unfailingly kind to Stan, their tolerance did not extend to getting out the drums and trumpet in the house. So once or twice Stan and Tan lugged their instruments to the school gym, where the nighttime guard was a cousin and nobody cared how much noise you made when school was out.

It wasn't the same, of course. When they were twelve-year-olds in school they had a plan. With the Kurdish boy on the bass fiddle and the plain little girl from the form below theirs on keyboard, they were going to be a group. The four of them argued for days, and finally picked out a winner of a name: "Stan, Tan and the Gang." The plan was to start small, with birthday parties and maybe weddings. Go on to the clubs as soon as they were old enough. Get a recording contract. Make it big. . . . But then the Kurdish boy got expelled because his father was found to be contributing money to the underground

Kurdistan movement, and the little girl's mother didn't want her spending so much time with older boys anyway.

It wasn't too much of a blow. By then Stan and Tan had a larger dream to work on. *Space.* The endless frontier. Where the sky was no limit to a young man's ambitions.

If they could only somehow get their hands on enough money to pay their way, they were determined to go there, to Gateway, or maybe to one of the planetary outposts. Stan liked Mars, where the colonists were making an almost Earthlike habitat under their plastic domes. Tan preferred the idea of roaming the ancient Heechee catacombs on Venus, where, who knew?, there might still be some old artifacts to discover that might make them almost as rich as any Gateway prospector. The insuperable problem was the money to get to any of those places. Still, maybe you didn't need money, because there were other chances. Robinette Broadhead, for instance, was rich beyond avarice with his Gateway earnings, and he was always funding space missions. Like the one that even now was gradually climbing its years-long way toward the Oort cloud, where some fabulous Heechee object was known to exist but no one had found a way to get to other than a slow, human rocket ship. Broadhead had paid the way for volunteers to make that dreary quest; he might pay for others. When Tan and Stan were old enough. If by then everything hadn't already been explored.

Of course, those were childish dreams. Stan no longer hoped they could become real. But he still dreamed them.

Meanwhile there was his work as a guide and his life with the Kusmeroglu family, and those weren't bad, either. In his first month he had accumulated more money than he had ever seen before. He made the mistake of letting Naslan catch him counting it, and she immediately said, "Why, you're loaded, Stanley! Don't you think it's about time you spent some of it?"

He gave her a guarded look. "On what?"

"On some decent clothes, for God's sake! Look, Friday's my day off. Dad won't let me skip morning prayers, but afterward how about if I take you shopping?"

So the first thing that Friday morning Stan and Naslan were on a bus to the big supersouks and Stan was accumulating his first grown-up wardrobe. Everything seemed to cost far more than Stan wanted to pay, but Naslan was good at sniffing out bargains. Of course, she made him try on six different versions of everything before letting him buy any. And then, when they had all the bundles they could carry and half his bankroll was gone, they were waiting for a bus when a car pulled up in front of them. "Hey, you!" a man's voice called.

It was a consulate car, with the logo of the United States of America in gold on its immaculate black door, and the driver was leaning out, gesturing urgently to Stan. "Aren't you Stan Avery, Walter Avery's son? Sure you are. Listen, Mr. Goodpastor's been looking all over hell and gone for you. Where've you been hiding yourself, for God's sake?"

Stan gave Naslan a trapped look. "I, uh, I've been staying with friends."

Behind the stopped car half a dozen others were stuck, and they were all blowing their horns. The driver flipped them an obscene gesture, then barked at Stan, "I can't stay here. Look, Mr. Goodpastor's got something for you. Have you at least got an address?"

While Stan was trying to think of an answer, Naslan cut in smoothly. "But you're not sure of what your address will be, are you, Stan? He's getting ready to move into his own place," she informed the driver. "Why don't you send whatever it is to where he works? That's the Eklek Linen Supply Company. It's in Zincirlikuyu, Kaya Aldero Sok, Number 34/18. Here, I'll write it down for you." And when the driver at last unplugged the street and was gone, she said sweetly, "Who knows what it might be, Stan? Maybe they want money for something or other, maybe your father's funeral? Anyway, there's a foreman at the linen supply who likes me. He'll see that I get whatever it is, and he won't tell anybody where it went."

But when Naslan brought the envelope home, thick with consular seals, it wasn't a bill. There was a testy note from Mr. Goodpastor:

Dear Stanley:

When we checked the files it turned out your father still held a life-insurance policy, with you as beneficiary. The face amount is indexed, so it amounts to quite a sum. I hope it will help you make a proper life for yourself.

Stan held the note in one hand, the envelope it was attached to in the other, looking perplexedly at Mr. Kusmeroglu. "What does 'indexed' mean?"

"It means the face value of the policy is tied to the cost of living, so the amount goes up with inflation. Open it, Stanley. It might be quite a lot of money."

But when Stan plucked the green US government voucher out of its envelope the numbers were a cruel disappointment. "Well," he said, trying to smile as he displayed it to the family, "what shall we do with it? Buy a pizza all around?"

But Naslan's eyes were sharper than his. She snatched it from his hand. "You stupid boy," she scolded, half-laughing, "don't you see? It isn't lira, it is in American *dollars*! You're rich now, Stan! You can do what you like. Buy yourself Full Medical. Marry. Start a business. Even go to a whole new life in America!"

"Or," Tan put in, "you can pay your way to the Gateway asteroid, Stan."

Stan blinked at him, then at the voucher. It was true. There was plenty of money there for the fare, indeed much more than enough.

He didn't stop to think it over. His voice trembled as he said, "Actually, we can both go, Tan. Shall we do it?"

· **IV** ·

The first thing that struck Stan about the Gateway asteroid was that, since he weighed next to nothing at all there, the place had no solid *up*. His body had only one way of dealing with this unprecedented state of affairs; it responded by becoming violently ill. This sudden *mal d'espace* took Stan completely by surprise because he had never had any experience of being seasick or airsick—well, had never been on either a ship or a plane at all until now. He was thrown by the sudden dizzying vertigo as much as by his quick and copious fountaining that followed. The guards at Reception weren't surprised. "New meat," one sighed to another, who quickly produced a paper sack for Stan to finish puking into.

Mercifully, Stan wasn't the only one affected. Both of the other two strange men in his group were hurling as violently as he. The one woman, sallow, frail, and young—and with something very wrong about the way her face was put together, so that the left side seemed shorter than the right—was in obvious distress, too, but she refused the sick bag. Tan was the only one spared. So he was the one who collected their belongings—drums, trumpet, music, and not much else—and got him and Stan through the formalities of registering. Then he managed to haul Stan, baggage and all, through the labyrinthine corridors and drops of Gateway to their assigned cubicle. Stan found the strength to hitch himself into his sleeping sack, miserably closed his eyes, and was gone.

When he woke Tan was looming over him, one hand on a holdfast, the other carrying a rubbery pouch of coffee. "Don't spill," he cautioned. "It is weak, but it is coffee. Do you think you can keep it down?"

Stan could. In fact, he was suddenly hungry. Nor was the twisting, falling feeling as bad, though there were enough remnant feelings to make him uncomfortable.

Tan seemed immune. "While you slept I have been busy, old Stan," he announced affectionately. "I have found where we eat, and where we can go for pleasure. There do not seem to be any people from Istanbul on Gateway, but I have met another Moslem here. Tarsheesh. He is a Shiite from Iran, but seems a good enough fellow. He checked and told me that we have funds enough to stay for eighteen days, while we select a mission. Unfortunately there are not very many missions scheduled for some reason, but we'll find something. We have to. If our funds run out before that they will simply deport us again." Then he grinned. "I also spoke with the young woman who came up with us. One could get used to the way her face looks, I think. With luck, soon I will know her quite well."

"Congratulations," Stan said. Experimentally he released himself from the sleep sack, grabbing a holdfast. Weightlessness was not permanently unbearable, he discovered, but there was another problem. "Have you also discovered a place where I can pee?" he asked.

"Of course. I'll show you the way. Then we can start studying the list of available missions, because there's no sense hanging around here when we could be making our fortunes."

Time was, Stan knew, when any brave or desperate volunteer who got to Gateway could have his choice of a score of the cryptic Heechee ships. You got into the one you picked. You set the funny-looking control wheels any which way you liked, because nobody had a clue which ways were "right." You squeezed the go-teat. And then—traveling faster than light, though no one knew how that was done—you were on your way to adventure and fortune. Or to disappointment and frustration, when the chance-set destination held nothing worthwhile. Or, frequently enough, to a horrible death . . . but that was the risk you had to take when the rewards were so great.

That was then. It was different now. Over the years, nearly two hundred of the ships that had bravely set off had never come back. Another few dozen of those that remained—particularly the larger ships, the Fives and a few Threes—were now set aside for transport duty, ferrying colonists to newly discovered livable worlds like Valhalla or Peggy's Planet, or to exploit the other cache of usable ships that had been found on Gateway Two. When the boys checked the listings they were disappointed. Three or four missions were open, but every one of them was in a One—no use at all to two young men who were determined to ship out together.

They didn't stop at watching the postings on the screen. They went to see the dispatcher himself, a fat and surly Brazilian named Hector Montefiore. To get to Montefiore's office you had to go all the way to Gateway's outermost shell, where the ships nestled in their pods, waiting for a mission. Some of the pods were empty, the outer port closed against the vacuum of space; those were where their ships were actually Out. When they had looked their fill they shook the curtain of Montefiore's office and went in.

The dispatcher was idly watching an entertainment screen, eating something that had not come out of the Gateway mess hall. He listened to them for a moment, then shook his head. "Fuck off, you guys," he advised. "I can't help you. I don't assign the missions, that's the big domes that do that. When they decide on a flight the computer puts it up on the board and I just take the names of the volunteers. Next big one? How the hell do I know?"

Stan was disposed to argue. Tan pulled him away. In the corridor outside Stan snarled at his friend. "He's bound to know *something*, isn't he?"

"Maybe so, but he isn't going to tell us, is he? We could try bribing him—"

Stan laughed sourly. "With what?"

"With nothing, right. Exactly, Stan. So let's get out of here."

They retired to the common space in Gateway's central spindle, the place they called the Blue Hell, to consider their options over cups of Gateway's expensive and watery coffee. Coffee was not all you could buy in the Blue Hell. There was fine food, if you could pay the price, and liquor of all sorts, and the gambling that gave the place its name. The boys jealously smelled the great steaks, and watched the magnetized roulette ball spin around, and then Stan took a deep breath.

He poked Tan in the shoulder. "Hey, man! We're on *Gateway*! Let's at least look around the joint!"

They did, almost forgetting that their money was going and the mission they had come for did not appear. They went to Central Park, where fruit trees and berry bushes grew—but were not to be picked unless you paid their price. They looked at Gateway's great water reservoir, curling up with the shape of the asteroid but reminiscent of the big underground lakes of Istanbul. And they went, reverently, to Gateway's museum.

Everything they saw was halfway familiar to Stan from the Gateway stories he had devoured in his youth, but nothing matched actually being in the museum itself. It was filled with Heechee artifacts, brought back from one mission or another: prayer fans, fire pearls, gadgets of all kinds. There were holos of planets that had been visited; they admired Peggy's Planet, with its broad, cultivated fields and handsome woods; they shivered at Valhalla—habitable, the Gateway authorities had pronounced, but more like Siberia than Paradise.

Most interesting, in a practical way, were the holos of the various models of Heechee ships, Ones, Threes, and Fives. Some of them had fittings that didn't seem to do anything, particularly the few that contained a Heechee-metal dome that no one had dared try to open. Many were armored, particularly the Threes and Fives. Nearly all had human-installed external sensors and cameras, as well as racks of food, tanks of oxygen, rebreathers, all the things that made it possible for a prospector to stay alive while he flew, though if the Heechee had had anything of the sort it was long gone.

While they were puzzling over how the Heechee had survived they heard a cough from behind. When they turned it was the girl with the lopsided face who had come up from Earth with them, Estrella Pancorbo. She seemed a lot less pale, and a lot more lively. Surprised, Stan said, "You're looking, uh, well." Meaning, apart from the fact that your face looks as though someone sat on it.

She gave him a searching look, but bobbed her head to acknowledge the compliment. "Better every day, thank you. I fooled them," she added cryptically, but didn't say who the "them" was. She didn't want to continue the conversation, either; had studying to do, she said, and immediately began running through the ship holos and taking notes.

The boys lingered for a while, but then they left because it was clear she preferred to be alone—but not without having had her effect on Stan, who had not been near a girl of anything like his own age since Naslan.

On the way out Tan mused, "I wonder how the folks are getting along back home."

Stan nodded. He recognized homesickness when he saw it. He even felt a little of it himself, though he hadn't had much experience of having a real home. "We could write them a letter," he offered.

Tan shook himself, and gave Stan a grin. "And pay transmission costs? Not me, Stan. I'm not much for writing letters anyway. Let's get some more coffee."

• V •

That day passed. So did another day. A couple of Ones appeared on the screen, but nothing better, and even those were snapped up. The boys spent more and more of their time hanging around the Blue Hell, wondering, but not willing to ask each other, what they were going to do when their money ran out.

They did not lack for advice. Old Gateway hands, many of them wearing the wrist-bracelets that showed that they had been Out, were often willing to share their lore. The friendliest was a spry, middle-aged Englishwoman with a drawn face and unshakable views on what missions to take. "Do you know what the Heechee control wheels look like? What you want are settings that show two bands in the red on the first wheel and none in the yellow on the second," she lectured.

"Why?" Tan asked, hanging on every word.

"Because they are safe settings! No mission with those settings has ever been lost. Trust me on this, I know." And when she had finished the coffee she had cadged from them and left, Tan pursed his lips.

"She may have something there," he said.

"She has *nothing* there," Stan scoffed. "Did you count her bangles? Nine of them! She has been Out nine times and hasn't earned the price of a cup of coffee. No, Tan. We want something that might be less safe, but would be more profitable."

Tan shrugged, conceding the point. "In any case," he said philosophically, "if any of them did know what to do, they would be doing it instead of telling us about it. So let us go eat."

"All right," Stan said, and then shook his head, struck with a thought. "The hell with that. I'm not hungry. Besides, I've got a better idea. We lugged those instruments with us, why not jam a little?"

Tan blinked at him. "Here? They'd throw us out."

"Maybe. Or maybe not, if we practiced a little first—there's not much entertainment here, is there? We could go somewhere where nobody would be bothered for practice. Maybe Central Park?"

Stan was right, there was nobody there. They picked a corner with plenty of holdfasts and set up to play.

Stan had no problem with his trumpet, once he was securely hooked to a wall bracket. Tan's drums were another matter. He had to lash them to each other and to a pair of holdfasts, and then he complained that the sticks wouldn't bounce properly without solid gravity. All the same they managed "When the Saints Come Marching In," after a fashion, and did better on "A String of Pearls." Stan was riffing on "Saint James Infirmary Blues" when Tan stopped drumming and caught his arm. "Look there!"

Tarsheesh was hurtling toward them around the rim of the lake. As soon as he came close, Tan called, "Are we making too much noise?"

Tarsheesh grabbed a bracket and stopped himself, painting in excitement. "Noise? No! It is the news that just came! You haven't heard? The Herter-Hall party has reached the object in the Oort, and it is big, and it is Heechee, and it is *still working!*"

There hadn't been that much excitement in Gateway in years—a whole working Heechee orbiter, the size of an ocean liner, of a kind never seen before. The thing manufactured *food!* CHON-food, they called it, made out of the basic elements that were in the comets of the Oort cloud: carbon, hydrogen, oxygen, nitrogen. And the old Heechee machine was still doing it, after all those hundreds of thousands of years. And if they could bring it to a near-Earth orbit, as the Herter-Hall people were trying to do, and if they could feed it with comets as they entered the lower solar system, why, hunger for the human race was over!

They speculated enviously on what that could be worth to the Herter-Hall family and to Robinette Broadhead himself, as backer of the expedition. "Billions," Stan said profoundly, and Tan gave him a look of scorn.

"Only billions? For a thing like that?"

"Billions of American dollars, you cow. Many billions for all of them, so Robinette Broadhead can add more billions to the billions he already owns. So you see, old Tan, what one lucky find can do?"

Tan did see. So did everybody else. When they checked the listings every one of the few missions offered had been snapped up. "Not even a One left! Nothing at all," Tan complained. "And yet they take money out of our balance every day, even when there is nothing for us to sign up for."

So they did. And kept on doing it, one day, and then another day, and then another. The boys followed the mission listings obsessively, but without much luck. A One showed up, then two more—both of them also Ones, and taken as soon as they appeared. Tan groaned when he saw the notice that the third ship was filled, because the name on the roster was his friend Tarsheesh. "I was hoping the three of us could ship together," he said, angry. "He wouldn't wait!"

Stan couldn't blame him. He even toyed with the thought of taking a One himself, leaving Tan behind. But then no more Ones showed up, so he didn't have to deal with that strain on his conscience.

There was a little traffic in the other direction. Two or three ships straggled back from their missions. All Ones, and mostly duds of one kind or another. And then a lordly Five made it back, and this one had had success. Well, *some* success. Not the dazzling kind, but not bad. They had reached an airless moon of a gas-giant planet they couldn't identify. It had Heechee artifacts, all right. They could see a domed Heechee-metal structure, and things that looked sort of like tractors nearby, but they could only look. They couldn't touch. Their ship had no equipment to let them maneuver in vacuum. The pictures they did come back with earned them enough of a bonus to retire to, respectively, Cincinnati, Johannesburg, Madrid, Nice, and Mexico City, and their Five was thus open for anyone who cared to take it.

Not right away, of course. The elderly Englishwoman with the nine Out bangles caught Tan and Stan as they were leaving the mess hall, giddy with excitement. "There's your best bet, ducks! They'll clean it up and put in fresh stores, and then they'll send it right back to make the finds—this time with space suits and handling equipment aboard. Oh, it'll take a while. A fortnight or so, I imagine, but wait for it! Good color, too—but we don't want everyone to know, so, remember, softly-softly-catchee-monkey!" and hurried happily off to tell her secret to anyone else with the price of a cup of coffee.

Of course, the secret wasn't worth much more than that, especially to two young men who didn't have a fortnight or so to spare.

Then, without warning, a Five did appear on the list. It didn't do Stan and Tan any good, though. The listing appeared while they were asleep, and by the time they saw it the crew roster was long filled.

What made it worse was that every day, *every* day of those few remaining days, there were fresh bulletins from the people who were making it really big, the Herter-Hall party on the Food Factory in the Oort. The Herter-Halls were strapping ion rockets onto the object to nudge it out of orbit and back toward Earth. Then further news: the object wouldn't be nudged. Somehow it counteracted the force applied, they couldn't say how. Then they found indications that there was someone else aboard. Then—oh, miraculous happening!—they met that someone. And he was a human boy! And he seemed to have a Heechee ship of his own that he used to commute between the Food Factory and some even larger, more complex Heechee vessel. A vast one, stuffed with Heechee machines of all kinds, and still working!

Tan was surly with envy, Stan little better. Snapping at each other, they parked themselves in front of the mission screen, taking turns to pee, refusing sleep. "The very next one," Tan vowed. "Three or Five, we will be on it!"

Stan concurred. "Damn right we will! We may not make trillions, like these people, or even billions, but we'll make something out of it, and we won't let anything get us away from this screen—"

But then something did.

Stan stopped in the middle of his vow, suddenly stricken. His eyes burned. His throat was suddenly agonizingly raw. His head pounded, and he could hardly breathe.

It was the Wrath of God again. Not exactly the same as before. Worse. Stan felt his whole body burning with fever. He was *sick*. Tan was in equal distress. Sobbing, his hands to his temples and curled up like a baby in the womb, he was floating away, the holdfast forgotten. It wasn't just sickness, either. Under the malaise was the familiar desperate sexual yearning, the loneliness, the unfocused, bitter anger. . . .

And it went on, and on . . .

And then, without warning, it was over.

Stan reached out to catch Tan's flailing arm and dragged him back to a holdfast. *"Jesus,"* he said, and Tan agreed.

"That was a pisser." And then, urgently, "Stan! Look!"

He was staring at the mission monitor. Gateway's computers, unaffected by whatever it was that drove every human momentarily mad, had been carrying out its programmed routine. Something new was posted on the screen:

Mission 2402
Armored Three, immediate departure

"Let's take it!" Tan yelled.

"Of course," Stan said, already logging in. In a moment their names appeared on the roster:

Mission 2402
Armored Three, immediate departure
Stanley Avery
Oltan Kusmeroglu

Rapturously the two boys pounded each other's arms and backs. "We made it!" Tan shouted.

"And just in time," Stan said, pointing. "Look at that!" Only seconds later another name had appeared:

Mission 2402
Armored Three, immediate departure
Stanley Avery
Oltan Kusmeroglu
Estrella Pancarbo
Roster complete

• VI •

The dream had come true. Stanley Avery was actually in an actual Heechee ship, actually following in the footsteps of those immortal Gateway heroes who braved the perils of star travel and came back to wealth unimaginable and fame that would go down through the ages. . . .

"Or," Tan growled, when Stan ventured to say as much to him, "to some very unpleasant death. I do not care for this shit-struck little ship. Why is it armored?"

Across the cabin, Estrella Pancorbo looked up from her task of stowing her possessions. "If this trip is to be bearable at all," she said, "it would be better if you spoke only English when I am present."

Tan's lips compressed. "And, in this closet we are to live in, when will you not be?" he demanded, but Stan spoke quickly.

"She is right," he told Tan. And, to the woman, "We'll try to remember. He was only wondering why our ship is so heavily armored."

"Because it accepts some destinations which would damage a ship that wasn't, of course. Don't be afraid. Such destinations are rare; this particular Three has been Out four times, but not to any such dangerous place. Didn't you familiarize yourself with its specifications? All the data for every working ship was on file," she said.

The reproof didn't improve Tan's mood. "I'm not *afraid,* Estrella," he snapped, wounded, and cast about for something hurtful to say in return. He found it. "Why does your face look like that?" he demanded.

She gave him a long stare. Her left eyelid, Stan noticed, hung lower than the other. "Because a bull stepped on it," she said at last, and added, "I think this is going to be a very long cruise."

How long the trip was going to take was a question always in their minds. Estrella's researches had given them some information. "This Three has never gone more than eighteen days in each direction," she informed them. "We have supplies for more than sixty. Of course," she added, "they can't always read the colors right, but it shouldn't be more than that. We'll know at the halfway point."

They would. Stan knew that much, as everybody did. Gateway prospectors always kept their eye on that funny-looking drive coil every waking minute, because it held the secret of life or death. When it changed color they were at the halfway point; the gentle micro-G that tugged them toward the stern of the craft would change so that then they would drift gently toward the bow. That was the time for doing arithmetic. If they had then used up less than a quarter of their air, water, and stores, that meant they had enough to last them for the remainder of their outbound leg and for the return. If they hadn't, they didn't.

The three of them lived, ate, and slept in the same tiny space, no bigger than Stan's very small bathroom in Mr. Ozden's tenement. Being so intimately close with a girl of more or less his own age was a disturbing experience for Stan, and they were very intimate. They couldn't help it. When Tan was in the toilet Stan averted his eyes from Estrella's, because the sound of his urination was loud and clear. All three of them had to get used to each other's smells, too, of which there were many. There were not many opportunities for exercise in a Three, and so the diet the Gateway authorities provided for them was high in fibers. Stan tried to break wind inconspicuously; Tan didn't, grinning widely every time he farted. Estrella succeeded in paying no attention.

The funny thing was that the more time Stan spent with Estrella's damaged face seldom out of his sight, the less damaged it looked. Tan was affected, too. Once or twice, when Estrella was momentarily more or less out of earshot—in the crapper, or asleep—he muttered something dark and lecherous in Stan's ear. In Turkish, of course. There wasn't any place in the Three that was really out of hearing range except for the lander, tucked in its bay in the bottom of the vessel and not comfortable enough for anyone to stay in it for very long.

Estrella spent most of her time reading from a little pocket screen, but after the third day she allowed herself to be persuaded into a card game with the boys. When Tan had lost his third big pot to her he gave her a suspicious look. "I thought you said you didn't know how to play poker," he growled.

"I didn't. It's a very simple game," she said carelessly, and then realized she had hurt his feelings. She tried to be complimentary. "I meant to tell you that I was surprised at your command of English, Tan. You speak it very well."

He shrugged. "Why should I not? I went to the English-language school from the age of six until I had to leave to go to work, at fourteen." But he was mollified. More cheerfully, he went on. "It is where I met Stan. We became friends quickly, because we were interested in the same things. Even as small boys, in recess we would run out to the teeter-totter and climb on, bouncing each other up and down and pretending we were on a Gateway ship like this one."

"And no one more surprised than I that we are finally here," Stan added, grinning. "What was your life like, Estrella?"

She picked up the cards and shuffled for a moment without answering. Then she said briefly, "I was a butcher. Whose deal is it now?"

By the seventh day the three of them were having trouble keeping their eyes off the coil. It didn't change. "Well," Estrella said brightly, "I guess this Three is setting a new record for itself. Still, we have a good margin in supplies, and anyway it will probably change tomorrow."

It didn't, though, not on the eighth day and not on the ninth. On the eleventh day Tan sighed, pushed the cards away, and said, "Now we must face the facts. We may go on forever in this flying rathole."

Estrella patted his arm. "You give up too easily, Tan."

He glowered at her. "What do you know? Such things have happened before! Haven't you heard the story of, I forget his name, the old prospector who only got home because he ate his shipmates?"

"Don't quarrel," Stan begged.

But Estrella's temper was up. "Why did I sign on with two Turks—well, a Turk and a half—who are willing to be cannibals? I suppose you have already decided which of us you will eat first, Tan. Me? Because you are both strong, and I am the smallest? Well, let me tell you—"

Her voice trailed off. Her damaged face looked startled, then seraphic. Stan felt it, too, as *down* in the little ship slipped gently to *up* and the coil brightened.

It was the halfway point at last. So they were not going to die, after all, or at least not in that particular way.

Since they were to live, the atmosphere became more relaxed. Tan gave Estrella a great smile, and to Stan he muttered, in Turkish, "Perhaps we will eat this one after all, but in a more friendly way."

Estrella heard, and even in the rapture of the moment her expression froze. "Tan," she said, "I do not understand Turkish, but I understand fully the way you look when you speak it. You have pricks sticking out of your eyes, Tan. Save them for someone else. I am a virgin. I have remained so when it was more difficult than it is here, and will go on as a virgin until I marry."

"Hell and devils," Tan groaned. "I thought it was only Moslem girls who kept their knees locked so, not free-spirited Americans."

She chose to be friendly. "So you have learned something new about American women. Some of them, at least. Now shall we play cards again, or maybe get some sleep?"

• VII •

For most of a day Tan was glumly quiet, but his good nature came back. After all, they were on their way to a great adventure together. Stan could see him revising his attitude toward Estrella. All right, she was not to be a lover. A sister, then, and Tan had long practice at living with a sister.

The thing at which Tan had had no practice at all was being confined in a tiny space with nothing to do. "I wish we had at least brought our damn instruments," he growled to Stan, who shrugged.

"No room," he said.

Estrella looked up from her plate. "We could play a few hands of poker," she offered. Tan, his lips pressed tightly together, shook his head. "Or," she added, "we could just talk. There is so much I don't know about you guys. Oltan? What was your life like in Istanbul?"

He declined to be cheered up. "I drove a van for a living," he said sourly. "I lived with my mother and father and my kid sister, Naslan, and I had five, actually five, regular girlfriends, who were very fond of me and extremely obliging. What else is there to tell?"

She nodded as though that were a pleasing answer and turned to Stan. "How about you?"

Stan did his best to cooperate. "My father was a code clerk at the American consulate, a very well-paid job, when he met my mother. She was Turkish, but Christian—a Methodist, like him. I was born in the hospital at the embassy in Ankara, which was American soil so I would be born as an American, like you."

That made her smile. "Not much like me."

"You mean the well-paid part? I guess not, but that was only when I was little. My mother died when I was seven, and after that—" He shrugged without finishing the sentence, not willing to tell her about his father's steady decline to drink.

Tan, listening without patience, straightened up and pushed himself away. "I have to pee," he said.

Stan looked after him, then back to Estrella. "And you?" he said, over the plashing sounds from the crapper. "You said you were a butcher?"

She reached up to stroke her left, off-center cheekbone. "Until the accident, yes. In Montana. I'm a mixture, too, Stan. My father was Basque, mostly. My mother was Navajo, with a little Hopi, but a big woman, and strong. There was no work around the Four Corners, so they managed to get up to Montana to work in the corrals. You know the bison ranches in America?"

"Oh, yes. Well, sort of. I read stories when I was little. Before I thought of Gateway I thought it would be great to be a cowboy, sitting around the campfire at night, herding the bison across the prairies."

That time she laughed out loud. "You don't herd bison, Stan. They won't let you. You let them run free, because the prairie grasses are all they need to eat anyway. Then, when they're old enough for slaughter, you lay a trail of something they like to eat even better than the prairie grasses. That takes them right into the corrals, that have a three-meter steel-plate fence all around them, because the bison can jump right over anything smaller. They can run fast, too, a hundred kilometers an hour. And then, one by one, the handlers like my parents let them into the chutes to the slaughterhouse. And then the pistoliers shoot them in the head with a big gun that has a kind of a piston, goes right into the brain and comes out again, ready for the next one. When they're dead the belt carries them to me, to slit their throats. Then I clamp on the irons from the overhead tracks and they're picked up so the blood can drain, and taken to the coolers before they're cut into steaks and roasts. Each bison has nearly fifty liters of blood, which goes into the tank below—what doesn't go onto me."

Tan had come out of the head, fastening his clothes as he listened. "Yes, Estrella," he said argumentatively, "but you said a bull stepped on you and broke your head. How does a dead bison step on you?"

"It wasn't a dead one," she said shortly.

"But if the pistolier shot it in the head—"

"This time he shot it only in the shoulder. It was very alive when it came to me, and very angry."

"It sounds like a nasty accident," Stan offered.

"No. It wasn't an accident. He did it on purpose. He was a man with pricks in his eyes, too, Tan, and when I would not go to bed with him he taught me a lesson."

Twentieth day. Twenty-first day. They didn't play cards much anymore, because they couldn't concentrate. They didn't even talk much. They had already said everything they could say about their hopes to each other, and none of them wanted to speak their fears out loud. Their nerves were taut with the itch of a gambler with a ticket on a long shot that is coming up fast in the stretch, but maybe not quite fast enough. Finally, Estrella said firmly, "There is no use fidgeting around. We should sleep as much as we can."

Stan knew that was wise. They would need all their strength and alertness to do whatever there was to be done when they were—there. Wherever "there" turned out to be.

The wise advice was hard to follow, though. Hard as it was for Stan to make himself fall asleep, it was even harder for him to make himself stay that way. He woke frequently, counting the time by minutes as the twenty-first day passed and the twenty-second began.

Then none of them could sleep at all. Looking at the time every few seconds. Arguing fiercely about at what hour and what minute turnaround had come, and thus at what minute and hour they would arrive. . . .

And then they did arrive. They knew it when the coil winked out.

And, at once, every instrument on the ship went wild.

The readings were preposterous. They said their Three was immersed in a tenuous plasma, hotter than the Sun, drenched with death-dealing radiation of all kinds, and then Stan understood why their Three was armored.

This was no planet to make them rich with its abandoned trove of Heechee treasures. There wasn't even a star close enough to matter. "Get us the hell out of here!" Tan was bellowing, and Estrella shrilled:

"No, take readings first! Pictures! Make observations!"

But there was nothing to observe beyond what the instruments had told them already. When Stan closed his hand on the go-teat Estrella didn't object any more, but only wept.

The flight back was no longer than the flight out, but it didn't seem that way. It seemed interminable. They could not wait for it to be over, and then, when it was, the bad news began.

The ancient Oriental woman who climbed aboard their Three as soon as it docked listened to their story with half an ear. It was the instrument readings that interested her, but she absently answered a few questions. "Yes," she said, nodding, "you entered a supernova remnant. The Heechee were very interested in stars that were about to explode; many courses led to observe one. But in the time since, of course, some of those stars have actually exploded. Like yours. And all that is left is a nebula of superheated gases; it is a good thing for you that your Three was armored."

Estrella was biting her lower lip. "Do you think there will be a science bonus, at least?"

The old woman considered. "Perhaps. You would have to ask Hector Montefiore. Nothing very big, though. There is already a large body of data about such objects."

The three looked at each other in silence. Then Stan managed a grin. "Well, guys," he said, "it's like my father used to say. If you fall off a horse, you want to get right back on again."

The woman peered at them. "Horses?"

"He means," Estrella explained, "we will all ship out on another mission the first chance we get."

"Oh," the old woman said, looking surprised, "you were out when it happened, weren't you? You didn't hear. They've solved the guidance problem. There are no more missions. The Gateway exploration program has been terminated."

• VIII •

Terminated! Gateway terminated? No more missions? No more of those scared, valiant Gateway prospectors daring everything to fly out on mystery missions to pick over the tantalizing scraps the long-ago Heechee had left behind when they went away—whenever they went, and wherever it was they went to?

It was all Robinette Broadhead's doing again. While Estrella and the boys were Out, things had gone crazy at the Food Factory and some other fabulous Heechee ship nearby. Broadhead had flown there solo to straighten it out. And had succeeded. And in the process had not only elevated his already sky-high fortune to incalculable heights, with this fabulous new cache of Heechee wonders, but in the process had learned the secret of controlling Heechee spacecraft.

The other thing he had done was to turn Gateway itself into a backwater. There would be no more random flying to God knew where. There would be no more flying to anywhere at all until the big brains who planned Gateway missions decided how to use all this new data. Meanwhile, nothing. Everything was on hold. The scores of would-be explorers had nothing to do but to grit their teeth and practice patience.

In the mess hall Tan nibbled at his meal, glowering. "So what's our plan supposed to be now?" he demanded.

Stan swallowed his mouthful of vegetarian lasagna. "We wait. What else can we do? But this can't last forever. The ships are still there! Sooner or later they'll start up again, and then maybe we'll have a chance at going on a different kind of mission. Better! Knowing where we're going before we start! Maybe even knowing that we'll live to come back!"

Tan gazed around the mess hall, where a couple of dozen other would-be adventurers were as subdued as themselves. "Maybe," he said.

"At least we're not using up capital," Stan pointed out. The Gateway Corporation had elected to show that it had a heart. No per diems would be charged until further notice, so at least their clocks were not running out.

"The bastards can afford it," Tan grumbled.

Of course the bastards could afford it. The bastards were the Gateway Corporation, and they owned a piece of every discovered piece of Heechee treasure. The Corporation was owned in consortium by the world's governments—on paper—but it was just about as true to say that they owned the world's governments. And, after due deliberation, the Corporation decided it could even afford a little something for Tan, Stan, and Estrella.

They found out about it when, for lack of anything better to do, Tan and Stan were nursing their weak, but more or less drinkable, coffees in the Blue Hell, watching the other prospectors gamble away their no longer needed per diems. Estrella was perched beside them, as always studying something or other from her pocket plate. This time, Stan saw wonderingly, what she was studying was music, and she fingered the air as she read. "Do you play?" he asked, surprised.

She flushed. "A little. The flute," she said.

"Well, why didn't you say so? Maybe the three of us can play together sometime. What do you think, Tan?"

Tan wasn't listening. He nudged Stan. "Here come the big shots," he said as Hector Montefiore sailed in, along with two or three others of the permanent party. They were obviously looking for action, and Stan was not pleased to see that Montefiore was coming in their direction. He did not care for Hector Montefiore. He liked him even less when the man slapped his shoulder and patted Estrella on the rump. "Congratulations," he boomed. "Getting ready to celebrate, are you?"

"Celebrate what?" Tan demanded.

The fat man gave him a look of surprise. "Your science bonus, of course. Didn't you know? Well, check it out, for Christ's sake! Who knows, then you might loosen up and buy me a drink!"

He didn't wait for it, though; went off, chuckling, while the three of them bent over Estrella's plate as she switched to the status reports.

And, yes, their names were there. "Not bad," Tan said, when he saw the amount.

Estrella shook her head. "Divided among the three of us, not all that good, either," she said practically. "Are you willing to settle for a *little* money?"

"A little money would be enough for me to go home and buy my own van, so I could go into business for myself," Tan said stiffly.

"If that is what you wish. It isn't, for me. I didn't come all this way to spend the rest of my life struggling to stay alive in a one-room condo with Basic Medical and no future. Anyway, Hector says there will surely be more missions soon."

Stan gave her a thoughtful look. "How do you know what Hector says?" he asked, surprising himself by the tone of his own voice. He almost sounded *jealous*.

Estrella shrugged. "He likes me," she said, as though that explained everything.

"He likes everybody," Tan sneered. "Boys, girls, he doesn't care, as long as it has a hole he can get into."

Estrella gazed at him for a moment in silence. "He has not got into any of mine," she said finally. "Let's talk sensibly. What do you want to do? Take your share and go home? Or wait for something worthwhile?"

*   *   *

They waited. While they waited they watched the unfolding story of what Robinette Broadhead had discovered on the news.

And what had he not! Strange, semihuman creatures that at first everyone thought, heart-stoppingly, might actually be Heechee, but were not. (Were, it seemed, relatives of primitive humanity, captured by the Heechee on Earth millennia ago and transported to one of their space outposts for study.) There were a clutch of surviving—well, sort of surviving—lost Gateway prospectors, taken to this place by the luck of the draw and unable to leave. Now they were more or less dead, but also more or less still alive, preserved in some bizarre sort of Heechee machinery. There was the half-wild living human boy named Wan, descendant of other Gateway castaways and now, somehow, through some Heechee wizardry that broadcast his yearnings and hates to the entire solar system, the source of the Wrath of God. And—the final secret Broadhead had learned—now he even knew where the Heechee had fled to! They had holed up in the Galaxy's Core, and they were still there, all of them!

It was one wonder after another. Everyone was talking about it—well, everyone but Estrella, it seemed to Stan. For whatever reason, she was spending more and more time with the permanent party and less with her old shipmates. Stan didn't approve. "She shouldn't do that," he told Tan seriously. "They mean her no good."

Tan laughed coarsely. "Depends on what you think 'good' is. Montefiore has his own ideas about that. But don't worry about Estrella," he advised. "That one'll take good care of her maidenhead."

Stan did worry, though. He told himself that what Estrella did was none of his business, but he thought about her a lot as the days passed.

The nine-bangle Englishwoman came back, having earned not only a tenth bangle but, at last, a stake. She had roamed a tunnel on a world not much kindlier than Mercury, wearing a spacesuit that kept her in air but didn't keep out the blazing heat that radiated from the tunnel walls. Pushed to the limit she had scoured the empty corridors until she found—something; no one was sure what. Possibly it was a game, something like a 3-D version of Go; at any rate her bonus was enough to pay her way back to a decent retirement in the little village in Sussex she had come from. She even bought coffees for the boys before she left, listening to them tell her about all the amazing things that had happened while she was gone. "Heigh-ho," she said, grinning the grin of someone who no longer had to worry about such things, "sounds like fun and games, doesn't it? Well, good luck to you! Don't give up. You never know, you might hit a good one yet."

Tan looked sourly after her as she made the payback rounds, buying drinks for everyone who had bought them for her. "I doubt it," he said, half under his breath.

"You've been doubting it ever since we got here," Stan said in irritation, though the fact was that he was beginning to doubt it, too. It might have turned into a really serious argument, but that was when Estrella appeared in the entrance, looking around for them.

Estrella didn't hesitate. As soon as she saw the two of them she launched herself in their direction with a great, accurate kick against the doorframe. Tan caught her as she came in range, but she grabbed a holdfast and freed herself. Her twisted face looked grim, but the news she brought was great. She looked around, then whispered: "There's a mission coming up. A big one."

Stan's heart leaped, but Tan was unresponsive. "One of these guaranteed new ones, where the Corporation will keep most of the profits?"

"Yes," she said, "and no. They know the destination, but that's all they know. They don't know how long it will take, so it will be in an armored Five, one of the ones with the special fittings no one understands—but Broadhead says they're essential for this trip. They will load it with supplies and material, enough for a very long flight, so it will be able to carry only two people. I'll be one. There's room for another."

She was looking from one to the other of them, but mostly at Stan. But Tan spoke up. "Not me," he declared. "I don't want any more mystery bus rides."

Stan ignored him. "You said they knew the destination?"

Estrella took a deep breath. "It will go to where the Heechee have gone. Where they have been hiding all this time, in the Core of the Galaxy."

Stan swallowed convulsively. You came to Gateway hoping for a big score—but *this* big? Not nibbling at bits and pieces the Heechee had left behind, but going straight to those vanished supercreatures themselves?

And what sort of reward might there be for *that*?

He didn't think. He heard himself saying, "I'll go!" almost before he realized he had made the decision. Then he turned to Tan. "Look. There's only room for two, so you take my share of our bonus, too.

Go home and have a good life. Buy Naslan the prettiest wedding dress she can find." And then he added, "But tell her not to wait for me."

IX

A Heechee Five was supposed to be much bigger than a Three. Not this one, though. One whole corner of its space was taken up with the peculiar, unexplained device that—Broadhead had said—was necessary for them to enter the Core. Another couple of cubic meters were filled with the goods they were told to deliver to the Heechee—records of Gateway explorations and Heechee finds, background material on the human race, all sorts of odds and ends along with a recorded Message to the Heechee that was meant to explain just who human beings were. Add in their year's worth of supplies for themselves, and there wasn't much room for Stan and Estrella to get around in.

As far as Estrella was concerned, not much room was needed. She didn't move around much. She didn't talk much to Stan, either. She went directly to her sleep sack as soon as they took off and stayed there, coming out only to eat or excrete, and uninterested in conversation in either case. When Stan asked her if something was wrong, she said only, "Yes." When he asked her if there was anything he could do, she shook her head and said, "I have to work through this myself." When he asked her what "this" was, all she would say was, "I have to find a way to like myself again." Then she went back to her sleep shelf again, and stayed there. For three whole days, while Stan wondered and stewed.

Then, on the fourth day, Stan woke up and found Estrella studying him. She was perched on the uncomfortable forked Heechee pilots' seat, and she seemed to have been there for a long time. Experimentally, he said, "Hello?" with a question mark at the end.

She gazed at him thoughtfully for a moment longer, then sighed. "Excuse me," she said, and disappeared into the head again.

She was in there for quite a while. When she came out it appeared that she had spent the time fixing herself up. She had washed her hair and brushed it still damp, and she was wearing fresh shorts and top. She gave him another of those long, unexplained looks.

Then she said, "Stan. I have something to say to you. We will be together for a long time, I think, and it would be better if there were no tensions between us. Do you want to make love to me?"

Startled, Stan said the first thing that came into his head. Which was, "I've never made love to a virgin before."

She laughed, not joyously. "That is not a problem, Stan. I'm not a virgin anymore. How do you think I got us on this mission?"

Stan's only previous coupling, when he had painfully saved up enough to afford one of Mr. Ozden's cousin's less expensive girls, had not taught him much about the arts of love. Estrella didn't know much more than he did, but inexperience wasn't their only problem. A Heechee Five wasn't designed for fucking. They tended to float away from the hold-ons the first time he tried to enter her.

But experimenting was enjoyable enough on its own, and they finally found what worked best was for him to come to her from behind, with Estrella curling her ankles over his while he gripped her waist with both hands. Then it was quick enough.

Then, still naked, they hung together, arms wrapped around each other, without speaking. Stan found it very comfortable. His cheek was pressed against her ear, his nose in her still-damp and sweet-smelling hair. After a bit, without moving away, she asked, "Are we going to be friends, Stan?"

"Oh, yes," he said. And they were.

Now that they were friends, especially friends who fucked, their Five didn't seem so crowded anymore. They touched often, and in all kinds of ways—affectionate pats, casual rubs in passing, quick kisses, sweet strokings that, often, turned into more fucking. Estrella seemed to like it well enough, Stan very much.

They talked, too. About what the Core might be like. About the Heechee who might (or might not) still be there. About what it would be like when they came back and collected the unquestionably huge bonus due the first humans to visit the Heechee—"It'll be *billions*!" Stan gloated. "Enough to have a waterfront estate like Robinette Broadhead's, with servants, and a good life—and we'll have plenty of time to enjoy, too, because we'll have Full Medical."

"Full Medical," Estrella whispered, sharing his dream.

"Absolutely! We won't be old at forty and dead at fifty-five. We'll live a long, long time, and"—he swallowed, aware that he was getting into a commitment—"and we'll live it together, Estrella." Which naturally led to more tender kissing, and to not-so-tender sex.

They had much to talk about, including the chapters in their earlier lives that had been omitted in their previous telegraphic summaries. When Stan talked about his mother's death and what it had done to his father, Estrella took his hand in hers and kissed it. When he told her about life in Istanbul she was interested, and more so when he talked about the city itself—about its centuries as the mighty Christian city of Constantinople, about the Christian Crusaders who looted it, about Justinian and Theodora and the—well—the Byzantine court of Byzantium. All that fascinated her. She knew nothing of the Byzantine Empire, little enough of Rome itself, its Caesars, its conquests, its centuries of world rule. To her it was all exciting myths and legends, all the better because they were true. Or as true, anyway, as Stan's memory allowed.

While Stan, of course, knew even less of the America of the Native Americans, before their subjugation by the white man and since. It was not the American history of school or his father's stories. Her own people, Estrella told him—the ones on her mother's side—had a history of their own. Sometimes they had even built great cities like Machu Picchu and the immense Mayan structures in the south, and the mysterious works of the Anasazi. But that, she said, sounding both wistful and proud, was only until the Europeans arrived and took their lands away, and often enough their lives as well, and pushed them into harsher lives in reservations, and endless, retreating battles, and finally defeat. "There isn't much left, Stan," she said. "The only good thing—well, it isn't really good, is it?—is that now most of the Yankees are as poor as we."

Which reminded Stan of an unsolved puzzle. "But you weren't all that poor, were you? I mean, personally. Like when you had your, uh, accident. If that had happened to Tan, or almost anybody else I knew, there wouldn't have been any big payoff to finance your going to Gateway. Did you have Full Medical or something?"

She laughed, surprised. "We had *no* medical. What I had was my brother." Who, she said, let it be known that he was going to kill the pistolier. Whose sister's husband was a clerk in the slaughterhouse's accounts department. Who had juggled the books to pay them off, just to save his brother-in-law's worthless life. "It was supposed to be a death benefit, but I double-crossed them. I lived. Then, when I was well enough to travel, I took the rest of the money and used it for Gateway."

She looked so sad when she was telling about it that Stan couldn't help kissing her, which before long led to more of that pleasurable lovemaking. And why not? After all, they were really on a sort of honeymoon cruise, weren't they?

The days passed, ten, twelve, twenty. They slept holding each other tight, and never seemed to tire of it. It was a little cramped, to be sure. But the one-size-fits-all sleep sacks were constructed to be long enough for a string-bean Maasai or a corpulent Bengali, and skinny Stan and slim Estrella could fit inside well enough for lovers. Sometimes they played music together, weird combinations of Stan's trumpet and the flute Estrella produced from her bags. Sometimes they talked. Sometimes they played cards or read or just sat companionably together in silence. And sometimes Stan pulled out the recorded Message to the Heechee—the reason they were on this trip in the first place—and they played it and wondered what the Heechee (if any) would make of it.

The Message had been cobbled together in a hurry by God knew who—some of the big brains in Gateway Corp, no doubt, and no doubt with Robinette Broadhead leaning over their shoulder. It didn't have any narration. No point of that, since the Heechee were not likely to understand any human language. Its only sound was music, first Tchaikovsky's somber *Pathétique* in its entirety, then, to show that humans had more than one musical mood, Prokofiev's jokey, perky *Classical Symphony*.

But mostly the Message was pictures. The empty Heechee tunnels on Venus. The nearly equally empty corridors on Gateway, when human beings first got there. A crew of prospectors warily climbing into an early Five. Another crew, travel-stained, coming out of a Three bearing prayer fans and other Heechee gadgets. A picture of the pinwheel of the Galaxy, seen from above, with an arrow showing Earth's position in the Orion Arm. A slowly spinning globe of the Earth itself. Quick flashes of human cities—New York, Tokyo, London, Rome. Shots of people doing things: painting landscapes, running a tractor, peering through a telescope, masked around a hospital birthing bed where a new baby was coming into the world. Then things that neither Estrella nor Stan had ever seen before. There was a series of pictures of an enormous floating object, then of a huge spindle-shaped chamber, blue Heechee-metal walls and a strange, huge machine squatting on tractor treads in the middle of it. "The Food Factory and that other thing," Estrella guessed. Then internal passageways and a couple of—they both caught their breaths—queer, hairy creatures that looked almost human, and had to be the primitives Broadhead had discovered there. And, at the last, the shot of the Galaxy again, with a tiny image of a Heechee Five that was probably meant to be their own craft, slowly moving from the Orion Arm to the Core.

When it was over—for the fourth or fifth time—Stan was thoughtfully rubbing the place where his wispy mustache had been until Estrella teased him into shaving it off. They had been watching with their arms around each other. He yawned, which made her yawn, too, because they had both been getting sleepy. She moved slightly for a better fit, but not away, as she saw that he was staring at their stacked piles of supplies.

"What is it, Stan?" she asked.

He said pensively, "It looks like a long flight. I don't know if anybody's gone this far before."

She tried to reassure him. "Sometimes short flights take a long time, and the other way around, too. With Heechee ships you never can tell."

"I guess," he said, turning his head to kiss her ear in the way she liked. She wriggled companiably and put up her lips, and that was better than reassurance.

For Stan was happy with Estrella. He thought about it drowsily. He had never been happier in his life than he was this minute. So why worry about how long the trip would take when he didn't want it to end at all, would have been content if it had lasted a very long time indeed. . . .

But it didn't.

It ended that day, almost at that very moment, when kissing had turned to caressing but before they began to take each other's clothes off, and it ended in a startling way.

The great drive coil gave them no warning. It was that other thing, the squat, domed gadget whose purpose had never been explained to them in any terms that made sense. It began to mutter and glow, then growl, then begin to scream on a rising pitch until they could hear it no more, as the glow brightened. Then at last the drive coil got into the act, beginning to glow and brightening to an eye-hurting incandescent white, with revolving barber-pole stripes of hot red and chrome yellow. It began to shudder. Or the ship did. Stan couldn't tell which because he was shaking, too, in a way that was frighteningly unlike anything he had felt before. He wasn't sleepy anymore as they clung to each other. . . .

Then, without warning, everything stopped.

Estrella pulled herself free and turned on the outside eyes. Behind them was a scary spread of mottled pale blue. Before them, a sky of unbelievable stars, so many of them, so bright, and, very near, a large metallic dodecahedron, twelve symmetrical sides, each with a little dimple in its center. Their ship plunged with breakneck speed into one of the dimples and nestled there. Before Stan or Estrella could move, the port was opened from outside.

Something that looked like a furry, animated skeleton was glaring in at them. "I think it must be a Heechee," Estrella whispered numbly.

And, of course, it was. And that was the beginning of the longest, the unbelievably longest, day in Stan's life.

• X •

Nothing in Stan's seventeen years of life had taught him how to greet an alien creature from another planet. He fell back on the fictions of his childhood. He raised his hands above his head, and declaimed, "We come in peace."

In those old fictions that had seemed to work. In the real world it didn't. The Heechee fell back in obvious panic. A low, hooting moan came from its queerly shaped mouth, and it turned and ran away. "Shit," Stan said dismally, staring after it. Estrella clutched his arm.

"We frightened the thing," she said.

"I bet we did. It frightened the hell out of me!"

"Yes, but we have to show him we're friendly. Maybe we should start playing the Message for them?"

That sounded like a good idea. At least Stan didn't have a better one, but while they were trying to start the playback the Heechee came running back. This time he had all his friends with him. There were half a dozen of the creatures, dressed in smocks with curious pod-shaped objects hanging between their legs—king-size jockstraps? Heavy-duty? Stan couldn't guess. The creatures were jabbering agitatedly among themselves as they hurried in, and they wasted no time. One of them slapped Estrella's hand away from the playback machine while a couple of the others grabbed Stan. They were surprisingly strong. They were armed. More or less armed, at least; several of them were carrying an assortment of knives—bright blue metal or gold, some curved like a scalpel, all of them looking dangerous. Especially when one of the Heechee held a knife with its extremely sharp point almost touching Stan's right eyeball and tugged him toward the exit. "Don't fight them!" Estrella cried, herself captive in the same way.

He didn't. He let himself be dragged unresisting into a larger chamber—red-veined blue-metal walls, unidentifiable machines and furnishings scattered around. As they crossed the threshold Stan stumbled, taken unaware by the sudden return of weight; they were in gravity again, not as strong as Earth's, maybe, but enough to make him totter against his captor. He jerked his head back from the blade just in time to avoid losing an eye. The Heechee with the knife screeched a warning, but Stan wasn't trying to give him any trouble. Not even when he and Estrella were dragged against a wall and chained, spread-eagled, to what might have been coatracks. Or statuary. Or anything at all, but were solid enough to hold them.

Things were coming to a boil. More Heechee were arriving on the run, all of them chattering agitatedly at the top of their voices. As one batch of them disappeared into the Five, others began to use those knives to cut away the captives' clothing. "What the hell do you think you're doing?" Stan squawked, but the Heechee didn't try to understand. They didn't stop doing what they were doing, either. As each scrap of garment was cut away, right down to their underwear, it was searched and sniffed and carried away somewhere for study.

Halfway through the process Estrella yelped in sudden shock as one of those knives nicked her thigh. The Heechee wielding it jumped back, startled. "Be careful with her!" Stan shouted, but they didn't even look at him. The one with the knife screeched an order; another produced a little metal cup and caught a drop of the blood that was oozing from the cut. "Are you all right?" Stan called, suddenly more angry and solicitous than afraid.

"It's only a scratch," she said, then added uncomfortably, "But I have to pee."

There didn't seem to be any way to communicate that urgency to their captors. Assuming the Heechee would have cared if there had; but they didn't seem interested in any needs or desires of their prisoners. More and more of the Heechee were crowding into the room, yammering to each other without stop. When one appeared who wore a fancier tunic than the rest, gold-streaked and silky, there was a momentary hush, then they all began talking to him at once. The new one had a sort of frazzled look, the way a man might appear if he had just been wakened from sleep with very unwelcome news. The newcomer listened for just a moment before waving for silence. He snapped what sounded like a command, then raised one skeletal hand to his narrow lips and began to speak into what looked like a large finger ring.

Heechee were beginning to come out of the Five carrying things— spare clothes, packets of food, and, very gingerly, Stan's trumpet. There was a babble over that as they presented it to the one with the ring microphone. He considered for a moment, then issued more orders. Another Heechee bustled forward with what looked like a stethoscope and touched it to the trumpet, here, there, all over, listening worriedly and reporting to the leader.

A moment later there was a sudden squawking from inside the Five, and Stan heard the familiar blare of the opening bars of Tchaikovsky's Sixth Symphony. "Listen, Stan, they've turned on the Message!" Estrella cried gladly. "Maybe it'll be all right now!"

But it wasn't all right. It didn't get any better at all. If the Heechee made any sense of the Message, which did not seem likely, it did not appear to reassure them.

How long the two of them hung there, poked and palped and examined, Stan could not know. It seemed to be a very long time. He worried about himself, but worried more about Estrella. Now and then he called empty reassurances to her. She spoke bravely back. "It'll work out, Stan," she said, and then, in a different tone, "Oh, *damn* it."

Stan saw the problem. Though she had been squeezing her knees together as hard as she could, her bladder would not be denied. Urine was running down her legs. Among the Heechee that produced a new flurry of excitement, as one of them ran for another cup to catch a few drops for study.

What Stan felt was shame—for his lover's embarrassment—and a sudden hot flash of rage at these coarse and uncaring Heechee who had caused it; and that was the end of the first hour of Stan's long, long day.

Then, for no reason that Stan could see, things did improve, and they improved very fast.

The Heechee in the gold-embroidered robe had gone off to do whatever Heechee bosses had to do. Now he returned, puffing importantly as he issued orders in all directions. When he marched up close to Estrella Stan strained against his chains, expecting some new deviltry. That didn't happen. The Heechee reached up with one wide, splay-fingered hand and patted her cheek.

Was that meant as reassurance of some kind? It evidently was, Stan saw, because other Heechee were hurrying toward them to remove their chains, the boss Heechee chattering at them all the while. Stan didn't listen. Staggering slightly—the chains had cut off circulation, and he weighed less than he expected here—he reached out for Estrella. Naked as they were, they hugged each other while the Heechee stared at them in benign fascination.

"Now what?" Stan asked the air. He didn't expect an answer. And got none, unless there was an answer in what happened next. A couple of Heechee hustled toward them, one bearing a few scraps of their ruined clothes, as though to apologize or explain, the other with a couple of Heechee smocks as replacements, gesturing that they might put them on.

The garments didn't fit them all that well. Human beings were a lot thicker front to back than the squashed frames of the Heechee. All the same, having their nakedness covered before these weird beings made Stan feel better.

What it didn't do for Stan was make him understand just what was going on. That wasn't because the Heechee weren't doing their best to explain. They were chirping, gesturing, trying to make something understood, but without a language in common they weren't getting very far.

"At least we're not trussed up like a Christmas pig anymore," Estrella offered hopefully, holding Stan's hand. They weren't. They were allowed to roam freely around the chamber, the busy Heechee dodging around them on their errands.

"I wonder if they'll let us go back in the ship," Stan said, peering inside. A couple of Heechee were playing the Message again, holding what might have been a camera to record what it showed. Another patted Stan's shoulder encouragingly as he stood at the entrance.

He took it for permission. "Let's try it," he said, leading the way. No one interfered, but Estrella gasped when she saw what had been done to their Five. Most of the movables had been taken away, and two Heechee were puzzling over the fixtures in the head.

Estrella asserted herself. "Get out!" she ordered, flapping her arms to show what she meant. The Heechee jabbered at each other for a moment, then complied.

That made a difference. The toilet had been partly disassembled, but it still worked. A little cleaner, a lot more comfortable, Stan and Estrella took care of their next needs: they were hungry. It was impossible to use the food-preparation equipment, because that was already in fragments, but among the odds and ends that had been hauled out of the Five they found a packet of biscuits that could be eaten as they were, and water. Every move they made was watched by the Heechee with interest and approval.

Then the boss Heechee came back, trundling a gadget that looked like a portable video screen. One of the Heechee touched something, and a picture appeared.

They were looking at a Heechee male who was talking to them excitedly—and, of course, incomprehensibly to the humans. Behind him was the interior of a Heechee ship, but not any ship Stan had ever seen before. It was much larger than even a Five, and the only familiar item in it was one of those dome-shaped machineries that had got them into the Core.

Then the Heechee in the scene gestured. The scene widened, and they saw something else that was familiar.

"Mother of God," Estrella whispered. "Isn't that Robinette Broadhead?"

It was Broadhead. He was grinning widely, and he was touching the Heechee in the screen, offering a handshake, which the Heechee clumsily accepted.

Beside Stan, the boss Heechee was patting his shoulder enthusiastically with his splayed hand. It seemed to be a gesture of apology, and hesitantly Stan returned it. The Heechee's shoulder was warm but bony, and he seemed to be smiling.

"Well," Estrella said wonderingly. "It looks like we're all friends together now." And that was the end of the second hour in this longest of days.

It was good to be friends, better to have had a chance to eat and drink and relieve themselves, best of all to be free. What Stan really wanted was some sleep, but there didn't seem much chance of that. The Heechee kept trying to tell them things by sign language; they kept not understanding. When the boss Heechee approached, bearing Stan's horn inquiringly, he got that message right away. "It's a trumpet," he informed them. He repeated the name a couple of times, touching the instrument, then gave up. "Here, let me show you." And he blew a scale, and then a couple of bars of the Cab Calloway version of the "St. Louis Blues." All the Heechee jumped back, then made gestures urging him to play more.

That was as far as Stan was prepared to go. He shook his head. "We're *tired*," he said, demonstrating by closing his eyes and resting his check on his folded hands. "*Sleep*. We need *rest*."

Estrella took a hand. Beckoning to the nearest Heechee, she led him to the entrance to the Five, pointing to their sleep shelves, now bare. After more jabbering, the Heechee seemed to get the idea. A couple of them raced away, and the boss Heechee beckoned to them to follow. They left the big chamber that had been all they had seen of the worlds of the Heechee and followed the leader down a short corridor. Its walls, Stan saw, seemed to be Heechee-metal still, but a veined rose pink instead of the familiar blue. They paused at a chamber. A waiting Heechee showed them the ruins of their own sleep sacks, then pointed hopefully inside. There were two heaps of something side by side on the floor. Beds? Evidently so. The Heechee closed the door on them, and Estrella immediately stretched out on one. When Stan followed her example it was more like burrowing into a pile of dried leaves than any bed he had ever had. But it wasn't uncomfortable, and best of all it was flat and horizontal, and no one was jabbering at him.

Thankfully he stretched out and closed his eyes. . . .

But only for a moment.

Almost at once he was awakened as the door opened again. It was the boss Heechee, jabbering in excitement but beckoning insistently.

"Oh, hell," Stan muttered. Things happened pretty fast in this place; but the two of them got up and followed. Farther, this time, along the rose pink corridor and then a gold-colored one. They stopped in a chamber like the one they had first entered, where half a dozen Heechee were jabbering and pointing at the lock.

"I think they're trying to tell us that another ship's coming in," Estrella said.

"Fine," Stan grumbled. "They could've let us sleep a little bit, though."

They didn't have long to wait. There was a faint sound of metal against metal from outside the door. One of the Heechee, watching a display of color from something beside the door, waited just a moment, then opened it. A pair of Heechee came in, talking excitedly to the equally excited ones meeting them, and then a pair of human beings.

Human beings! They were talking, too, but the people they were talking to were the Heechee. In their own Heechee language. And then one of the human arrivals caught sight of Stan and Estrella. His eyes went wide. "Jesus," he said unbelievingly. "Who the hell are you?"

Who the hell the man himself was was somebody named Lon Alvarez, one of Robinette Broadhead's personal assistants, and as soon as Stan told him their names he snapped his fingers. "The kids who took off from Gateway right after the discovery, sure. I guess everybody thought you were dead."

"Well, we're not," Estrella said, "just dead tired."

But Stan had a sudden sense of guilt. Everybody thought they were dead? And so they'd be telling Tan so, and Naslan. "Is there some way you can communicate with Gateway? Because if there is, I'd better get a message off to them right away."

Puzzlingly, Lon Alvarez gave Stan a doubtful look. "A message to who?"

"To the Gateway authorities, of course," Stan snapped. "They'll be waiting to hear from us."

Alvarez glanced at the Heechee, then back at Stan. "I don't think they're exactly waiting, Mr. Avery. You know you're in a black hole, don't you?"

"A black *hole*?" Stan blinked at the man, and heard Estrella gasp beside him.

"That's right. That's what the Core is, you know. A big black hole, where the Heechee went to hide long ago, and inside a black hole there's time dilation." He looked at Stan to see if he was following this, but Stan's muddled stare wasn't reassuring. Alvarez sighed. "That means things go slower in a black hole. In this one, the dilation comes to about forty thousand to one, you see, so a lot of time has passed outside while you were here. How much? Well, when we left it would have been about, let's see, about eleven years."

• XI •

When Stan and Estrella could take no more they staggered back to those queer Heechee beds. They didn't talk; there was too frighteningly much that needed to be talked about, and no good place for them to begin.

Estrella dropped off at once, but not Stan. His head was too full of arithmetic, and all the sums were scary. The man had said forty thousand to one! Why, that meant that every minute that passed here in the Heechee's Core was more than a *month* in the outside world! An hour was five *years*! A day would be over a century, a week would be—

But then fatigue would no longer be denied. He fell into an uneasy sleep, but it didn't last. There was too much haunting his dreams. But when he woke enough to reach out for Estrella her bunk was empty, and she was gone.

Stan staggered to his feet and went in search of her. It was urgent that he find her. Even more urgently, he wanted the two of them to get right back in their Five, if it would still work after everything the Heechee had done to it, and head for home . . . before everyone they knew was dead and gone.

Estrella wasn't in the hallway, though there were voices coming from somewhere, lots of them. She wasn't in the room they had entered in, either, though there were plenty of Heechee there looking very busy, about what Stan could not say. One of the Heechee took pity on him. He led Stan, chattering cheerfully, with plenty of those reassuring shoulder-pats, to still another entrance chamber. It was the biggest yet, and the most crowded, with a constant stream of Heechee going in and out of the port to a docked ship. The guide led Stan to the door and gently nudged him inside.

The ship was the biggest he'd ever seen, and it was full of people, both human and Heechee. When one of the humans looked up he saw that it was Estrella, and she was talking—yes, apparently talking—to a Heechee. She beckoned Stan over, holding up a flask of something brown. "It's coffee, Stan," she said with pleasure. "They've got a great kitchen on the immigrant ship. Want some?"

"Sure," he said absently, staring at the Heechee. Incongruously, the creature was wearing a Texas sombrero, a sweatshirt that bore the legend Welcome to Houston, and what looked like cowboy boots. He stuck out an affable hand to Stan.

"Great seeing you again, Mr. Avery," he said—in English! "What, you don't remember me? I'm Doorwatcher. I was in charge of the entry lock when you and Ms. Pancorbo arrived." And added proudly, "I went with the first party of ours to go Outside, as soon as we saw what was happening."

"Nice to see you again," Stan said faintly. "You, ah, speak English very well."

Doorwatcher made a deprecating gesture with those skeletal hands. "I spent four years on your planet, so I had plenty of time to learn. Then when this ship of immigrants was leaving I came home." Someone was chattering urgently to him in the Heechee language. He replied briefly, then sighed. "I'd better get back to work. All these new people! My second-in-command is really swamped. And I'm anxious to see my family, too. It's been a long time for me . . . though they don't even know I was gone!"

· XII ·

When Stan tried to remember that very long day, that forty-thousand-days-in-a-day day, its events and discoveries flew wildly around in his mind like angry bees when the hive is attacked. The surprises were too many and too great. The new ship was a *human*-built ship, though using Heechee drive technology. The humans on it were *immigrants,* come to the Core to visit the Heechee for a few days or weeks (or centuries!), and that same ship was going to go right back for more. The Door—the floating dock they had come to—was swarming with other humans from previous ships, waiting for transportation to take them to one of the Heechee planets to go on display. Some of them were dignitaries from Gateway Corp or one of the nations of Earth, there to open embassies from the human race to the Heechee. Some were simply people who hadn't liked the lives they had on Earth, and jumped at the chance for new ones in the Core. "Like us, Stan," Estrella told him as he blearily tried to take it all in. "Like everybody who came to Gateway, and they're going to get what they want here. The Heechee are wild to meet us, Stan. Every human being who gets here is going to live like a king." And then she added worriedly, "Drink your coffee, hon. I think they put something in it to wake us up. You'll need it."

They had. It did. When Stan had swallowed his second flask of the stuff fatigue was banished, and his mind was racing. "What do you mean, live like a king?" he demanded.

"What I said, Stan," she said patiently—or not all that patiently; she was on overdrive, too, her eyes sparkling in a way Stan had never seen before. "They're *welcoming* us, Stan. They want to hear *everything* about the human race. They're fascinated by the idea that we have different countries and cultures and all. When I told Doorwatcher about herding bison he begged me to come to his own planet and talk about it—seems he'd missed that when he was on Earth. He says they'll give us our own home, and a *wonderful* home, too, and . . . and I don't think they know anything about Istanbul, either, or human history, and they'll want to hear it all from you—"

But Stan was shaking his head. "We won't have time," he announced.

Estrella stopped short, peering at him from under her dragging eyelid. "Why won't we?" she asked, suddenly shot down from her enthusiasm.

"Because we've got to be on that ship when it goes back, Estrella. We have to get there while we're still news, the first people to come back from the Core. Can you imagine what that will be worth? Not just the bonus—I bet that'll be *huge*—but we'll be famous! And rich, Full Medical and all!" He ran out of steam then, peering at Estrella's face, trying to read her expression. "Don't you see what we're missing, Estrella?"

She said contemplatively, "Full Medical. Long, rich lives."

He nodded with vigor. "Exactly! And time is passing us by. We have to go back!"

Estrella took his hand and pressed it to her cheek. She asked simply, "Why?"

He blinked at her. "What do you mean, why?"

"Well, Stan," she said reasonably, "there's no real hurry, is there? What have we got to go back to that we won't have right here?"

"Our friends—" he began, but she shook her head. She kissed his hand before she released it, and spoke.

"Have you looked at the time, dear? Our friends are getting old, may even have died by now. You wanted to live a long, long time. Now we're doing it." She took pity on the look on his face and hugged him tightly. "Besides," she said persuasively, "we've come all this way. As long as we're here, we might as well see what the place looks like."

Stan found words at last. "How long?"

"Not long, if that's what you want. A week or two—"

"Estrella! That'll be—what? A thousand years or more!"

She nodded. "And by then maybe it'll be worth going back to."

THE GALACTIC CENTER SERIES

Gregory Benford

In the Ocean of Night (1977)
Across the Sea of Suns (1984)
Great Sky River (1987)
Tides of Light (1989)
Furious Gulf (1994)
Sailing Bright Eternity (1995)

The series comprises six novels, composed over a twenty-five-year span. The events stretch from the early 2000s to A.D. 37518, an immense scope imposed because its central focus, our galactic center, is 28,000 light-years away, and characters had to get there to take part in the galaxy's larger games.

But as well, I wanted to convey the huge scales of both time and distance that a galaxy implies. We are mayflies on the stage lit by the stars, and science fiction should remember that.

In the Ocean of Night, published in 1977, explored our discovery that computer-based life seemed dominant throughout the galaxy. A British astronaut in NASA's space program, Nigel Walmsley, had uncovered the implication that "evolved adding machines," as he put it, had inherited the ruins of earlier, naturally derived alien societies. We realized this by finding wrecked craft on the moon, and because a roving machine from an ancient interstellar society enters the solar system to study it.

Across the Sea of Suns follows Walmsley on the first manned interstellar expedition. Drawn by curiosity, humans want to know more about nearby stars, where there are aliens of very strange properties. There Walmsley finds that Naturals—organic beings like us— have been annihilated or at least greatly hampered by the galaxy's pervasive machine societies.

During this flight Earth is invaded by an ocean-living species, as a method the machine-based civilizations use to disrupt any advanced Natural society. As soon as others know of our presence, they seek to wipe us out, as feared Natural rivals. The novel concludes with a few remaining people, including Walmsley, capturing a sophisticated interstellar ship. They head for the galactic center, to find out what's going on.

In our galactic core, within a few light-years of the exact center, there are a *million* stars within a single light-year. Imagine having several stars so close they outshine the moon!

Worse, the galactic center was the obvious place for machines to seek. Virulent gamma rays, hot clouds, and enormously energetic processes dominate the crackling activity.

Great Sky River opens on this landscape; the title refers to the ancient American Indian name for the Milky Way. Its central figure is a man named Kileen, who flees with his Family Bishop across a ruined landscape. Its sky is dominated by the black hole at True Center, which his people call the Eater of All Things—though they don't quite know why.

In this ravaged panorama humans have fallen from grace. Though the Walmsley-led expedition reached the Center and did well there, building a considerable civilization, they could not evade the superiority of machines. Pursuing them is an enigmatic mech, or machine, the Mantis, who views humans as an endangered species, their extinction inevitable. It wishes to record what it finds worthy in the few remaining societies. Not since humans lived in immense space stations called Chandeliers have they been on even terms with the mechs.

The Bishops flee their home world, Snowglade, in hopes of finding refuge and a solution to their many riddles about the true nature of mechs closer to the black hole. In the fourth novel, *Tides of Light,* they reach another planet and form an alliance with another organic species, one also endangered by the relentless mechs. We meet other kinds of mechs, too. Machines which can reproduce themselves would inevitably fall under the laws of natural selection, and would specialize to use local resources. The entire panoply of biology would recapitulate: parasites, predators, prey.

The Bishops deal with this while trying to fathom enigmatic messages from an intelligence lodged in the magnetic strands that loom throughout the Center. It tells of a place, the Wedge, where humans might find refuge and perhaps discover the legendary Galactic Library, which comprises a history of the entire galaxy.

In the fifth novel, *Furious Gulf,* we enter the gulf around the powerful black hole, and see another kind of gulf, that between intelligences born of different realms. Our human concern with mortality and individualism as a feature of biological creatures is unnecessary among intelligences that never had to pass through our Darwinnowing filter.

If we can copy ourselves indefinitely, why worry about a particular copy? What kind of society would emerge from such origins? What would it think of us—us Naturals, still hobbled by our biological destiny?

A slowly emerging theme in these novels, then, is how intelligence depends on the "substrate," whether in evolved humans or adaptive machines—both embodying intelligence, but with wildly different styles.

Since the second novel we had not seen Nigel Walmsley, though there are hints that he was active near True Center much earlier. Much history echoes in ruins and enigmatic messages. Finding and entering the Wedge finally brings signs of humans who have sustained themselves against the mechs, though in a bewildering folded space-time (the s-t, or esty).

Sailing Bright Eternity, book six, finished in 1995, pulls all the series' major characters together. In the Wedge they find that humans themselves have been carrying information they did not know they had, data crucial to stopping the mechs from erasing all Natural life.

It had been twenty-five years since I started on *In the Ocean of Night,* and our view of the galactic center had changed enormously. Some parts of the first two books, especially, are not representative of current thinking. Error goes with the territory.

The themes of the series resolve in favor of humanity as unique and worth saving, even in as hostile a galaxy as I envisioned. But I suspect that if natural life is as foolish and vulnerable as we seem to be, quite possibly machines may inherit the galaxy, and thus sit bemused, watching us with cool indifference from afar.

This added story deals with an essential question asked of humans at the beginning of their decline, about A.D. 36000. It also reveals several aspects of the dreaded Mantis I never found room for in the novels.

—*Gregory Benford*

⁙

A Hunger for the Infinite

by

Gregory Benford

DEATH CAME IN ON SIXTEEN LEGS.

If it is possible to look composed while something angular and ominous is hauling you up out of your hiding place, a thing barbed and hard and with a gun-leg jammed snug against your throat—then Ahmihi was composed.

He had been the Exec of the Noachian 'Sembly for decades and knew this corner of Chandelier Rook the way his tongue knew his mouth. Or more aptly, for the Chandelier was great and vast, the way winds know a world. But he did not know this thing of sleek, somber metal that towered over him.

He felt himself lifted, wrenched. A burnt-yellow pain burst in his sensorium, the merged body/electronic feeling-sphere that enveloped him. Behind this colored agony came a ringing message, not spoken so much as implanted into his floating sense of the world around him:

I wish to "talk"—to convey linear meaning.

"Yeasay, and you be—?" He tried to make it nonchalant and failed, voice guttering out in a dry gasp.

I am an anthology intelligence. I collapse my holographic speech to your serial inputs.

"Damn nice of you."

The gun-leg spun him around lazily like a dangling ornament, and he saw three of his people lying dead on the decking below. He had to look away from them, to once-glorious beauties that were now a battered panorama. This section of the Citadel favored turrets, galleries, gilded columns, iron wrought into lattices of byzantine stillness. It was over a millennium old, grown by biotech foundries, unplanned beauty by mistake. The battle—now quite over, he saw—

had not been kind. Elliptical scabs of orange rust told of his people, fried into sheets and splashed over walls. White waste of disemboweled bodies clogged corners like false snow. An image-amp wall played endlessly, trying to entertain the dead. Rough-welded steel showed ancient repairs beneath the fresh scars of bolt weaponry that had sliced men and women into bloody chunks.

I broke off this attack and intervened to spare you.

"How many of my people . . . are left?"

I count 453—no, 452; one died two xens ago.

"If you'll let them go—"

That shall be your reward, should you comply with my desire for a conversation. You may even go with them.

He let a glimmer of hope kindle in him.

This final mech invasion of Chandelier Rook had plundered the remaining defenses. His Noachian Assembly had carried out the fighting retreat while other families fled. Mote disassemblers had breached the Chandelier's kinetic-energy weapons, microtermites gnawing everywhere. Other 'Semblies had escaped while the Noachians hung on. Now the last act was playing out.

Rook was a plum for the mechs. It orbited near the accretion disk of the black hole, the Chandelier's induction nets harvesting energy from infalling masses and stretched space-time.

In the long struggle between humans and mechs, pure physical resources became the pivot for many battles. It had been risky, even in the early, glory days after mankind reached the Galactic Center, to build a radiant, massive Chandelier so close to the virulent energies and sleeting particle hail near the black hole itself: mech territory. But mankind had swaggered then, ripe and unruly from the long voyage from Earth system.

Now, six millennia since those glory days, Ahmihi felt himself hoisted up before a bank of scanners. His sensorium told of probings in the microwave and infrared spectra. Cool, thin fingers slid into his own cerebral layers. He braced himself for death.

I wish you to view my work. Here:

Something seized Ahmihi's sensorium like a man palming a mouse, squeezed—and he was elsewhere, a flat broad obsidian plain. Upon which stood . . . things.

They had all been human, once. Now the strange wrenched works were festooned with contorted limbs, plant growths, shafts of metal and living flesh. Some sang as winds rubbed them. A laughing mouth of green teeth cackled, a cube sprayed tart vapors, a blood-red liquid did a trembling dance.

At first he thought the woman was a statue. But then breath whistled from her wrenched mouth. Beneath her translucent white skin pulsed furious blue-black energies. He could see *through* her paper-thin skin, sensing the thick fibers that bound muscle and bone, gristle and yellow tendons, like thongs binding a jerky, angular being . . . which began to walk. Her head swiveled, ratcheting, her huge pink eyes finding him. The inky patch between her legs buzzed and stirred with a liquid life, a strong stench of her swarmed up into his nostrils, she smiled invitingly—

"No!" He jerked away and felt the entire place telescope away. He was suddenly back, dangling from the gun-leg. "What *is* this place?"

The Hall of Humans. An exhibition of art. Modesty compels me to add that these are early works, and I hope to achieve much more. You are a difficult medium.

"Using . . . us?"

For example, I attempted in this artwork to express a coupling I perceive in the human world-sum, a parallel: often fear induces lust shortly after, an obvious evolutionary trigger function. Fear summons up your mortality, so lust answers with its fleeting sense of durability, immortality.

Ahmihi knew this Mantis was of some higher order, beyond anything his 'Sembly had seen. To it, their lives were fragmented events curved into . . . what? So the Mantis thought of itself as an artist, studying human trajectories with ballistic precision.

He thought rapidly. The Mantis had some cold and bloodless passion for diseased art. Accept that and move on. How could he use this?

You share with others (who came from primordial forces) a grave limitation: you cannot redesign yourselves at will. True, you carry some dignity, since you express the underlying First Laws. Still, you express in hardware what properly belongs in software. An unfortunate inheritance. Still, it provides ground for aesthetic truths.

"If your kind would just leave us alone—"

Surely you know that competition for resources, here at the most energetic realm of the galaxy, must be . . . significant. My kind too suffers from its own drive to persist, to expand.

"If you'd showed up when we had full Chandelier strength, you'd be lying in pieces by now."

I would not be so foolish. In any case, you cannot destroy an anthology intelligence. My true seat of intelligence is dispersed. My aesthetic sense, primary in this immediate manifestation, still lodges strongly in the Hall of Humans that I have constructed light-years away. You visited it just now.

"Where?" He had to keep this angular thing of ceramic and carbon steel occupied. His people could still slip away—

Quite near the True Center and its Disk Engine. You shall visit it again in due time if you are fortunate and I select you for preservation.

"As suredead?"

I find you primates an entrancing medium.

"Why don't you just keep us alive and talk to us?"

He was sorry he had asked the question, for instantly, from the floor below, the Mantis made a corpse rise. It was Leona, a mother of three who had fought with the men, and now had a trembling, bony body blackened by Borer weaponry.

You are a fragile medium—pay witness. I do know how to express through you, though it is a noise-thickened method. Inevitably you die of it. But if you prefer—

She teetered on broken legs and peered up at him. Her mouth shaped words that whistled out on separate exhalations, like a bellows worked by an unseen hand.

"I find this . . . overly hard-wired . . . medium is . . . constrained sufficiently . . . to yield . . . fresh insights."

"My God, kill her." He thrashed against the pincers that held him aloft.

"I am . . . dead as . . . a human . . . But I remain . . . a medium."

He looked away from Leona. "Don't you have any sense of what she's going through?"

My level does not perceive pain as you know it. At best, we feel irreducible contradiction of internal states.

"Wow, that must be tough."

Working her like a ventriloquist's dummy, the Mantis made Leona cavort below, singing and dancing at a hideous heel-drumming pace, her shattered bones poking through legs caked with dried brown blood. Fluids leaked from the punctured chest.

"Damn it, just talk through my sensorium. Let her go!"

My communicative mode is part of the craft I create. Patterns of fear, of hatred; your flood of electrical impulses and brain chemicals that signifies hopelessness or rebellion: all part of the virtuosity of the passing mortal moment.

"Sorry I can't seem to appreciate it. Leona . . . she's suredead?"

"Yes . . . This one . . . has been . . . fully recorded . . ." Leona wheezed, "I have . . . harvested her . . . joyously."

"This way . . . she's hideous."

As this revived form, I can see your point. But with suitable reworking, hidden elements may emerge. Perhaps after my culling among the harvested, I shall add her to my collected ones. She has thematic possibilities.

Ahmihi shook his head to clear it. His muscles trembled from being held suspended and from something more, a strange sick fear. "She doesn't deserve this."

Yet I feel something missing in my compositions, those you saw in the Hall of Humans. What do you think of them?

He fought down the impulse to laugh, then wondered if he was close to hysteria. "Those were artworks? You want art criticism from me? *Now?*"

Leona gasped, "I sense . . . I have . . . missed essentials . . . The beauty . . . is seeping . . . from my . . . works."

"Beauty's not the sort of thing that gets used up."

"Even through . . . the tiny . . . grimed window . . . of your sensorium . . . you sense . . . a world-set . . . I do not. Apparently . . . there is . . . something gained . . . by such . . . blunt . . . limitations."

Which way was this going? He had a faint glimmering. "What's the problem?"

"I sense . . . far more . . . yet do not . . . share your . . . filters."

"You know too much?" He wondered if he could get a shot at Leona, stop this. No human tech could salvage a mind that was sure-dead, "harvested" by the mechs—though *why* mechs wanted human minds, no one knew. Until now. Ahmihi had heard legends of the Mantis and its interest in humans, but not of any Hall of Humans.

"I have . . . invaded nervous . . . systems . . . driven them to . . . insanity, suicide." Leona twitched, stumbled, sprawled. Her eyes goggled at the vault above, drifted to peer into Ahmihi's. "Not the . . . whole canvas . . . something . . . missing."

He tried to reach a beam tube and failed. The Chandelier's phosphor lights were dimming, shadowing Leona.

With obvious pain she struggled to her feet. "I tried . . . Ephemerals . . . so difficult . . . to grasp."

Ahmihi thought desperately. "Look, you have to *be* us."

For the first time in this eerie discussion the Mantis paused. It let Leona crumple on the floor below, a rag doll tossed aside.

That is a useful suggestion. To truncate my selves into one narrow compass, unable to escape. Yes.

Ahmihi felt a sudden pressure, like a wall of flinty resolve, course through his sensorium. He had no hope that he would live more than a few moments longer, but still, the hard dry coldness of it filled him with despair.

THE HARVESTED

>I had come around the corner and there it was, more like a piece of furniture than a mech, and it poked something at me.

>The last thing I saw was a 'bot we used for ore hauling, tumbling over and over like something had blown it, and I thought, I'm okay because I'm behind this stressed glass.

>I still got the memory of something hard and blue in my line of sight, a color I'd never seen before.

>She fell down and I stooped to help her up and saw she had no head and the thing that was holding her head on the floor jumped up at me, too.

>It had a kind of ceramic tread that came around on me when I thought it was dead, booby-trapped some way, I guess, and it caught me in the side like a conveyor belt.

The Noachian 'Sembly fled the mech plunder of their Chandelier. Their Exec, Ahmihi, had emerged from his capture by the Mantis with a sensorium that howled with discord. Each neurological node of his body vibrated in a different pattern. His voice rang like a stone in a bucket. It was as if the symphony of his body had a deranged conductor.

But within hours he recovered. He would never speak of the experience with the Mantis. He led his 'Sembly into craft damaged but serviceable. The mechs did not attack as over three hundred escaped the drifting hulk their once-glorious spin-city had become.

This was one of the last routs of the Chandelier Age. After these defeats, humanity fled deep space for the nostalgic refuge of planets. This was in the end foolish, for the Galactic Center is unkind to the making and tending of worlds. There, within a single cubic light-year, a million suns glow. Glancing near-collisions between stars can strip the planets from a star within a few million years. Only worlds carefully stabilized can persist. Even then, they suffer weathering unknown in the calm outer precincts of the great spiral galaxy.

The Noachian 'Sembly used a gravitational whip around the black hole to escape pursuit. This cost lives and baked their ships until they could barely limp on to a marginally habitable world, named Isis by some other 'Sembly, which a millennium before had departed for greener planets, farther out from True Center. Isis was dry and wind-swept, but apparently of little interest to mechs. This was enough; the Noachians spiraled in and began to live again. But much had happened on the way.

Mech weaponry can be insidious, particularly their biological tricks. A 'Sembly platitude was all too true. *You may get better after getting hit, but you do not get well.*

A year into their voyage, Ahmihi lay dying. As he gasped hideously, lungs slowly eaten by the nano-seekers the mechs had carried, his wife came near to say goodbye. The 'Sembly folk were afraid to record Ahmihi's personality into an Aspect, since he was plainly mech-damaged, perhaps mentally. In his fever he spoke of some bargain he had struck with the near-mythical Mantis, and no one could fathom the terms. He had been tampered with in some profound way, perhaps so that the story he told could give away nothing vital.

But they did have his archived recording from the year before; not everything would be lost. In a desperate era, skills and knowledge had to be preserved into the chips which rode at the nape of the neck of each 'Sembly member. These carried the legacy of many ancient personalities, rendered into Aspects or the lesser Faces or Profiles. Ahmihi would survive in fractional form, his expertise available to his descendants.

No one noticed when a small insectlike entity crawled from the dying Ahmihi's mouth. It whirred softly toward his wife, Jalia, and stung her. She slapped it away, thinking it no different from the other vermin released from the hydro sections.

The flier implanted in Jalia a packet of nanodevices that quickly recoded one of her ova. Then it dissolved to avoid detection. The Noachian 'Sembly burned Ahmihi's body to prevent any possible dese-cration by mechs, especially if nanos were alive in the ship.

Their prayers were answered; apparently the small band of fleeing humans were not worth mech time or effort to pursue.

Jalia gave birth to a son, a treasure in an era when human num-bers were falling. Gene scanners found nothing out of the ordinary. She called the boy Paris, in the tradition of the Noachian 'Sembly, to use city names from Earth—Akron, Kiev, Fairhope—though Earth itself was now a mere legend, doubted by many.

When he was five his intensive education began. He had been an ordinary boy until then, playing happily in the dry fields from which skimpy crops came. He was wiry, athletic, and seldom spoke.

When Paris began learning, he made a discovery. Others did not sense the world as he did.

Every second, many millions of bits of information flooded through his senses. But he could consciously discern only about forty bits per second of this cataract. He could read documents faster than he could write, or than people could speak, but the stream was still torpid.

Whether the information was going in or out, his body was designed for roughly the same torpid flow speed. All serial ways of taking in information were painfully sluggish. His awareness was like a spotlight gliding across a darkened stage, lighting an actor's face dramatically, leaving all else in the blackness. Consciousness stood on a mountain of discarded information.

Even thinking about this fact was slow. It took him much longer to explain to himself what he was thinking than it did to think it. His brain channeled ten billion bits per second, far more than he took in from his surroundings.

There were as many incoming signals from his sensorium as there were outgoing commands to his body. But nearly none of this could he *tell* anyone about. His sensibility, his speech—all were hopelessly serial logjams. Everybody else was the same; humans were not alone in their serial solitude.

He had already learned how important *story* was to them—and to him. Plots, heroes and villains, for and against, minor roles and major ones, action and wisdom, tension and release—as fundamental as the human linear mouth-gut-anus tube, for story was the key to *mental* digestion.

And without knowing it, each of them told their own stories, in every moment. Their bodies gave them away with myriad expressions, grunts, shrugs, unconscious gestures. Big chunks of their personalities came through outside their conscious control, as the unconscious spoke for itself through the body, a speech unheard by the discerning driver, hidden from it.

For a young boy this was a shock. Others knew more about him than he knew about himself. By sensing the megabits that leaked through the body, they could read him.

This was enormously embarrassing. Such a silent language must have come early in human evolution, Paris guessed, when it was more vital to know what strangers meant than what they said, using some crude protolanguage.

And laughter—the wine of speech, he learned—was the consciousness's admission of its own paucity. He laughed often, after realizing that.

Soon, even while scampering in madcap joy over the hard-packed dirt of the playground, he felt a part of him stand apart. What he experienced—all those billions of bits per second—was a *simulation* of what he sensed. This he *felt* as a gut-level truth.

Worse, the simulation lagged half a second behind the world outside. He tested this by seeing how fast his body reacted to pain or pleasure. Sure enough, he jerked away from a needle before he consciously knew it was poking him in the calf.

His sensorium was ripe with tricks. His vision had a blind spot, which he deduced must emerge from the site where nerves entered the back of the eye. An abandoned, ruined Chandelier seemed larger when it hung in its forlorn orbit just above the Isis horizon than when it arched high in the sky. When he ran across the crinkled plains and stopped to admire filmy clouds overhead, his eyes told him for a while that the clouds were rushing by—a kinesthetic memory of running, translated by his mind into an observed fact.

All because evolution shaped the eye-brain system to regard things high up as farther away, more unattainable, and so made people perceive them as smaller. And retained the sensation of running, unable to discard the mind's pattern-frame right away.

He sat in class and regarded his giggling classmates. How *odd* they seemed. Understanding himself had helped in dealing with them. He was popular, with a natural manner that some mistook for leadership. It was something decidedly different, something never seen in human society before. He felt this but could not name it. Indeed, there was no word.

Gradually Paris saw that their—and his—world was meaning-filled, before they became aware of it. Scents, rubs, flavors—all carried the freight of origins many millennia and countless light-years away.

So he came to make his next discovery: the unconscious ruled. He learned this when he noticed that he was happiest when he was not in control—when consciousness did not command. Ecstasy, joy, even simple gladness—these were the fruit of acting without thinking.

"I am more than my *I*," he said wonderingly. "I am my *Me*."

When his work went well—and everyone worked, even children—his Me was engaged. When things went well, they just *went*, zinging along. He ran 'facturing 'bots, tilled fields, prepared spicy meals—all in the flow, immersed.

Even when he used his Faces or Profiles for craft labors, he could manifest their outlined selves without conscious management. These ancient sliced segments of real people used some of his perception-processing space, so that when working he lost Isis's crisp savannah scent, wind-whispers, and prickly rubs. The Faces particularly needed to siphon off these sensory stimuli, to prevent them from becoming husklike embodiments, mere arid digital textbooks. He could feel them sitting behind his eyes, eagerly supping snippets of the world, relishing in scattershot cries. As he slept, he enabled them to raise his eyelids and catch glimpses that fed them gratifying slivers. Listening through his eardrums, they could keep watch—a safety precaution. Of such thin gruel they made their experience. This also isolated him, ensuring deep sleep.

But there was something more, as well.

Something shadowy sat within him, a Me beyond sensing except as specter. It seemed to watch while eluding his inner gaze. Yet he could feel this brooding blankness informing his own sense of self.

This frightened him. He cast about for reassurance. There were sport and sex and spectacle, all unsatisfying. He probed deeper.

The 'Sembly's religion—its teachings so varied as to be contradictory—somehow summoned forth that state of free *going*, while the conscious mind was deflected by prayers, liturgy, hymns, rituals, numbing repetition. One day in Chapel, bored to distraction, Paris tried engaging the skimpy bandwidth of language with a chant, cycling it endlessly in his mind. He found his Me set free; thus he invented meditation.

In adolescence he found a genuine talent for art. But his work was strange, transitory: ice carvings that melted, sand-sculptures held together by decaying electrostatic fields. He would write poetry with a stylus on pounded plant material, using vegetable pigments . . . and then rapturously watch them burn in a fire.

"Poignancy, immediacy," he replied, when asked about his work. "That is the essence I seek."

Few understood, but many flocked to see his strange works pass through the moments he allowed them to have.

Art seemed utterly *natural* to him. After all, he reasoned, far back in human history, on mythical Earth, there must have been some primate ancestor who saw in the stone's flight a simple and graceful parabola, and so had a better chance of predicting where it would fall. That cousin would eat more often and presumably reproduce more as well. Neural wiring could reinforce this behavior by instilling a sense of genuine pleasure at the sight of an artful parabola.

He descended from that appreciative cousin. Though living 28,000 light-years from the dusty plains where art had emerged in genes, he was building on mental processing machinery finely tuned to that ancient place. While he shared a sense for the beauty of simplicity, though, something in him felt the poignancy of each passing moment. That was human, too, but something else in him felt this sense of the sliding moment as a contrast. He did not know why, but he did know that this set him apart.

This was his first fame, but not his last.

Quickly he saw that while the Me acted, society held the I accountable. The human social vow was *I agree to take responsibility for my Me.* On this he brooded.

He found love, as a young man, and felt it as an agreement: *Lover, my Me accepts you.* So as well did spirituality come from *I know my Me,* just as true courage came from *I trust my Me.*

Consciousness—bit-starved, ill-informed—was the brain's model of itself, a simulation of a much more ornate under-Self.

To experience the world directly, with no editing—what a grail! He attained that state only now and then, and when in it, felt the shocking fullness of the true world. Language evaporated like a drop of water beneath the sun's full glare. All he could do was point a finger and mutter, *"That."*

Still riding behind his eyes was that phantom, the watcher who could not be watched. Yet it did not control. He felt it riding in him, and learned to ignore it.

Or rather, his *I* agreed abstractly to accept the watcher. His Me never did. But there was no way it could control a shadowy vacancy.

In dreams, his *I* could not control. In everyday life, he learned that his body could not lie; its bandwidth was too high, sending out data from his Me in an unconscious torrent. Conversely, with its small bit rate, the *I* could lie easily—in fact, could hardly avoid lying, at least by omission. But not his Me.

This made him into the leader he had no real desire to become. He was too busy learning more than anyone had ever known about what it meant to be human.

One evening, as he stood guard in a distant precinct at the outer edge of their holdings, he caught a mouse and tried to talk to it. Since they were both of flesh and had sprung from similar origins— this was an Earth rodent, imported by the original expeditions for reasons best known to themselves—he thought he should be able to commune with it. The mouse studied his face across an abyss of processing ability, and Paris could get nothing whatever from the creature on his sensorium.

Yet somehow he knew that within that tiny head lay deep similarities. Why could a communion not come from a mech? He wondered.

Amid such puzzles, life pressed upon him. The mechs had returned to Isis.

He met a Rattler while playing with some young men. They were chasing each other, carrying a ball, a game that called forth the hunting joys buried in the primordial past. So immersed they were that the Rattler got within a few hundred meters.

They were playing near the ruins of a huge Kubla left by the people who had claimed Isis millennia before, then left. Its pleasure dome still offered vibrant illusions if stimulated, and Paris thought the Rattler must be one of these when he first saw it—moving slinky-quick, armatures pivoting to focus upon the men.

The Rattler cut down six of them before Paris could reach his weapon, a long-bore kinetic rifle. It was hopelessly antique, but that was all they had to give the young men in training. He fired at the Rattler and even hit it but then a friend fell nearby and that distracted him. He had seen death, but not this way. He hesitated and by pure luck the Rattler did not kill him. A bolt from two others stilled the coiled thing. Paris knew he was of no use then and resolved to do better. The emotions that wrenched him as he helped carry the bodies away were like a fever, an illness that did not soon abate.

That was the beginning. You start out thinking that other people get killed, but not you, of course. The first time you are badly wounded the worst shock of it is not the physical one, but the sudden realization that death can come so easily, and to you.

It had taken a long time after that to know that nothing could happen to him that had not already happened to every generation before. They had done it and so could he. In a way, dying was the easiest of the hard things.

There was an inscription above the archway of a broad public plaza, one crowned with a transparent dome through which the whole mad swirl of the Galactic Center constantly churned, and he had written it down to keep it, for the strange joy it brought when he understood it:

By my troth, I care not: a man can die but once; we owe God a death . . . and let it go which way it will, he that dies this year is quit for the next.

After a while he came to know that nothing happens until it actually comes to you, and you live your life up until then to get the most out of it. To live well, you had to live in each gliding moment. Cowardice—the real thing, not momentary panic—came from inability to stop the imagination from working on each approaching possibility. To halt your imagining and live in the very moving second, with no past and no future, was the vital secret. With it you could get through each second and on to the next without needless pain.

The Me learned this and the I accepted it.

THE HARVESTED

>They threw me in this pit of mech-waste, stuff like greasy packing fluff and I figured, sure as hell I can climb out of this.

>All around these mechs were gathered like it was a ritual and they hanged me upside down first, shooting me through the belly and watching the blood run out and down over my breasts and into my face so I could taste it, warm in the cold air.

>A whistling sharp by me and then a smack.

>Must of been some nanos in the bread I ate before this hot sour taste rose up in my throat and I started choking real bad.

>It stabbed me with an antenna, a big surprise because I thought it was one of those mechs that only used microwave pulsers.

>It was at the very end of the campaign and I was tired out and lay down to catch a few snores and this slow thing came by, I didn't pay it any mind.

>We were going real fast to get away.

>She went first and made the jump clean as you like and I did too but my leggings busted out and I lost my Goddamn balance.

Riding in his upper spine he carried an advisor Aspect of great antiquity named Arthur.

By then Paris was listened to in 'Sembly gatherings, though he was still fairly young. Arthur always urged moderation in diplomacy with the mechs and gave examples from ancient human history. When Paris questioned the hardships Arthur related from the Olden Times when humans had first come to Galactic Center, Arthur huffily replied,

Let us say it was not precisely tea with the Queen.

Every now and then Arthur would use these archaic expressions from the Old Time and nobody knew what they meant, but Arthur never seemed to notice. He had others, such as

Warts and all—some big enough to hang a hat on.

When plasma discharges sent burnt-gold lattices across the entire sector of the night sky, Arthur observed

Any sufficiently advanced technology at the Center will appear to be a natural phenomenon.

He was right, of course. Mech constructions swam in gossamer profusion within a few light-years. No one knew what the mechs were doing at Galactic Center, beyond the obvious point that here the raw energies and particle fluxes favored their kind. Not only were they less vulnerable to the cutting climate, they seemed to have a larger purpose.

Arthur regaled Paris with tales of how grand the earlier human eras had been, one of his more irritating habits. Still, his Aspect-stilted advice was useful in dealing with the roving mechs who now pestered the 'Sembly's days.

Mechs were moving in and they made arrogant displays of their contempt for mere mongrel humans. Dried-up carcasses of animals and humans alike—for to mechs they were alike—dangled on rubbery ties from some mechs' legs, so that they bounced and swayed with walking or just in the wind. Some thought this was just another way to terrorize humans, but Paris sensed in it the mech sense of humor, or something like it, for none of it of course was funny to humans.

So the mechs came: Snouts, Lancers, Scrabblers, Stalkers, Rattlers, Baba Yagas, Zappers, Dusters, Luggos. Humanity had paid a high price for each name, each word calling up in a sensorium an instant, resonant, precise catalog of traits and vulnerabilities the mech had, facets won by many deaths.

Beneath a smoldering sky where there was never truly a night—for dozens of nearby stars brimmed with furious glows, giving a simmering, nebula-lit sense of spreading immensity—mech ships descended like locusts.

Paris fought in the sprawling, terrible, year-long battle that destroyed the principal mech units on Isis. In that year he wore a wolfish grin, all sharp edges and strung wire. He distinguished himself beneath the Walmsley statue, an ancient shaped mountain. There was a small village and some shacks built into the foot of the memorial monument; that's how big it was. There Paris deduced the mech maneuverings before they could execute them, and so won the way.

Not that the men serving under him found him warm. By then his increasing distance had become legendary. "Tight bastard, couldn't fart without a shoehorn," he overheard, and took it as a term of respect.

By then he saw that a machine was a man turned inside out. It could describe all the details but in its flood of data it missed the sum of it all, the experience plucked from the endless stream. A vital secret of humans lay in their filters, what they chose to ignore.

He did not feel degrees Kelvin or liters per second or kilograms; he felt heat or cold, flows, heaviness. He knew love and hate, fear and hunger—all beyond measure. Beyond the realm of digits.

Their defeat of the mechs on Isis was surely only temporary. Everyone knew it.

So the 'Sembly—grown to many millions now by immigration and fast-breeding—convened to celebrate the continuity they honored. It might be the last chance they had to do so.

In a communal linkage the entire 'Sembly resurrected the Ole Bros—Personae so complete that some interpreted their very twilight existence as evidence for an afterlife. The Ole Bros advised that the 'Sembly strike back at the mechs in deep space, where they dwelled. Only by taking the fight to them could humans hope to survive.

Paris believed this. *Plan on being surprised,* the Ole Bros said, and then unaccountably laughed. Paris took up their cause. He had many followers by this time, and women came to him easily, but he was not distracted. Something in the dire situation of his time called to him. He used the 'Sembly's reverence for the Ole Bros to sway them, while not for a moment believing the theology surrounding the 'Sembly's reverence for digital resurrections, for the implied afterlife in some remote analytical heaven.

This turned Paris to a question many had asked in adversity. Of what use to humanity was religion?

He knew this was not how the others of 'Sembly Noachian saw the world. But part of him insisted: *Bare a benefit, explain the behavior.* Why he thought automatically in terms of this rule he did not know, but he felt the shadow-self move in himself.

For the 'Sembly, religion was a social cement. In its extreme form it could even get the believer to go off on crusades. Was it all based on a theory and solution to the greatest human problem, death? The power of theology among people around him then seemed to come from that shared, looming menace. He could see how this notion would spread readily, since in himself he, too, felt the hunger to resolve the anxiety brought on by the fear of death.

But religion had no apparent feedback from the world; God did not answer his mail. Miracles are few and not reproducible. So why does religion persist, even grow?

His mechanistic explanations, cutting and skeptical as a young man's can be, did not seem to capture the essence of religion. There were big questions about the origins of the universe and of natural law. These science gripped only tentatively, converging on the grand riddle: why was there something, with all its order, rather than nothing? Chaos seemed as likely an outcome as the scrupulous, singing harmonies revealed by science.

If Mind brought humans forth from Matter, enabling the universe to comprehend itself—to do its own homework—then religion manifested this underlying purpose, this evolution. But then, why did the mechs have no religion?

To Paris, such abstract ways of envisioning the deep, devout impulse in humanity did not quite capture the heart-thumping urgency of faith. Something was missing.

This, more than rituals and the 'Sembly's celebrations of human triumphs over mechs, formed for Paris the convoluted condition of being human.

THE COLLECTED

>First thing I knew was, I was here and been turned into some kind of flowerpot.

>I was in pieces all over but still able to think in little short pieces like this.

>The *pain* that was it, and then they made less of it and I could stand it for longer but my arm was still on backwards.

>It had written my name on my face which I thought was for identification until I saw the hologram of me standing right next door with my dick in the middle of the back of my head and hard all the time even though I couldn't feel it at all when this thing like a woman climbed onto my neck.

>The suet wasn't so bad but drowning in mucus was and when I coughed and it came out through my mouth tasting like something that rotted down there in me.

>After my skin blistered up black and brown and peeled back the chill set in on the skin below it and ran like scorching oil all over me.

>I screamed but this thing with lots of legs would not stop.

*   *   *

He met the Mantis while on patrol, alone.

It was a glimmering thing, a play upon the planes of rock against a distant hillside. To see it meant looking past the illusions it projected. He could taste and smell it better than see it. Since he was on a routine transport job, alone with some simple 'bots, he was not well armed.

Paris stood absolutely still and felt it glide closer. No point in running.

Clan legend told of such a seldom-seen mech class, striding down through a corridor of ruin, broken lives and widespread suredeath, with tales of phantoms glimpsed as many-legged silhouettes scrambling across shadowy horizons, a tradition bequeathed to all the human Families and 'Semblies of horror, ghostly and undeniable, millennia of desiccated Aspect memories and encounters which few survived.

I ask entrance. You echo of some essence I fathom from a far past. Do you recognize me?

"No." Though something buzzed and stirred at the back of his mind, his fear froze it. Then his training asserted itself and he felt rising in his chest a cold anger. He estimated how easily he might damage this thing. It refracted his sensorium's interrogations, sending back to him hard claps and images of refracted icy layers.

You have a quick and savory life, here in the wild. Your primate form is sculpted from a longer logic than I customarily encounter.

Paris caught a fragment of a many-legged image moving rapidly at the base of distant hills. Carefully he calibrated the distance.

Your phylum of laughing, dreaming vertebrates is capable of manifold surprises. You are an especially complex example of this; you have harvested many of these facets. I look forward to reaping and reviewing them.

"From me?"

Of course. You . . . do not know?

"Know what?" The Mantis had paused, which in an entity of such vast computing power implied much.

I see. We, who propagate forward forever, though in mixed forms, do not share your concern for artifacts. Though they seem permanent to you, I have already outlasted mountain ranges. Artifacts are passing tools, soon to be rubbish.

"Just like me?"

In your way, yes. So you do intuit . . . ?

Paris felt in the Mantis's slow question some hint, but abruptly a part of him swerved from that line of thought. No, he would not go that way.

Instead he locked his sole weapon on the last vector-signature of the Mantis and fired off a swift burst. The Mantis flickered and was gone.

We shall merge in time, vessel.

Seconds ticked by. Not a sign wrinkled his sensorium. No retaliation.

The rattle of the salvo had soaked through him, enormously gratifying. His heart pounded. Something in him loved the release of action, while another seethed with unease. He felt an exhilaration at having veered away from a confusion his Me did not wish to confront. And what had the Mantis meant by that last transmission?

He moved away quickly, fear and pride somehow eclipsing the moment, and he seldom thought of it ever again.

Other Families and 'Semblies had come to Isis, strengthening this planetary redoubt. But in the fast pace of events at Galactic Center, great changes came even over the comparatively tiny life span of three centuries enjoyed by humans. Mechs lasted millennia and planned accordingly. Nanomechs still harried the people of Isis. Their Citadels were hard-hammered by the drawing dry climate of prickly dust storms, laden with nanos borne on the restless winds.

Against the salting of the Isis atmosphere they mounted considerable space-based defenses. No mech could drop an asteroid on Isis, no ship could easily penetrate its magnetosphere. Paris volunteered for training in these military arts. He loved weightless glee, the play of hard dynamics, of Newtonian glides in a friction-free void.

Isis beckoned with its dry beauties. At the dawn line, arid valleys lay sunk in darkness while snowy mountains gleamed above, crowned by clouds that glowed red-orange like live coals. Mountaintops cleaved the sheets of clouds, leaving a wake like that of a ship. Brooding thunderheads, lit by lightning flashes, recalled the blooming buds of white roses.

The glories of humanity were just as striking. The shining constellations of Citadels at night lay enmeshed in a glittering web of highways. His heart filled with pride at human accomplishments—beaten down, perhaps, but still casting spacious designs upon whole planets. So much done, in the mere century of his life! He had helped shape artificial seas and elliptical water basins, great squared plains of cultivated fields, immaculate order hard-won from dry valleys.

By then he had found a wife who loved him despite his strangeness, his need for solitude and silence. He had children of his own, but they showed no interest in art. Their children had children, and Paris sensed their continuity with him. Yet something rode in him he could not name, for it seethed on the billion-bit flow beneath the well-lit theatre of his conscious mind.

He helped the burgeoning space fleet secure a wormhole for their sun-system. This one had been discovered in a murky molecular cloud that came coasting by the Isis star many centuries before. Hauling it closer consumed two decades of Paris's life, but he gave them freely. A wormhole mouth opened to humanity a fresh grasp. Until then, only mechs had employed them.

His labors were well timed.

After many decades of the full experience of the 'Sembly, after creating an amazing body of his strange short-lived artwork, the skies blazed once more with constructs the size of moons.

More vast mechs arrived, ready to break down all seven planets in this solar system, all for raw materials to aid their great Constructions. A faction urged diplomacy. Some other 'Sembly members struggled to complete a vessel to take them away, before the mechs got around to disassembling their planet out from under them.

Paris opposed this. Instead, he urged the 'Sembly to strike back. "Destroy something *they* value!" he shouted. "Only then will they respect us enough to listen."

But even as he said it, he knew that something different brewed in him.

The shadowy presence that had sat beyond view of his inner self now moved with sluggish purpose. Into his mind flashed the coordinates and routes necessary to take a desperate band of pilots within reach of the great accretion disk at True Center. The data-flow was a torrent, thick and fast and coming from a source he could not clearly sense. Perhaps a deep-carried Aspect? But no, another portion of himself denied it. What, then?

He chuckled ruefully to release the tension such thoughts brought, and for a darting moment saw himself down a long telescoping tunnel of immense perspective, glimpsing himself as a member of a phylum—that of the laughing, dreaming vertebrates.

THE COLLECTED

>The thing with plenty legs, it said I was a monument to my kind.

>There was a team of five of the little ones and a big one with funny legs and they cut me up slowly to see.

>My mother was there with parts of animals growing out of her and when I tried to get to her they did that to me, too.

>I was kept in my fighting suit like being laid to rest only there were these maggots that kept bursting out from puckers in my skin and crawling all over me.

>They said I would not feel the things that went in through my eyes but they lied.

>I think they forgot all about me and let me lie there on the floor while they worked on the others and finally decided to just use me for parts.

>I could see pretty well but looked down and there was no body, just my head on a pike they carried around with them, I figure to scare other members of my 'Sembly in battle, with me pleading and screaming most of the time but without lungs.

The Galactic Center was a collection of debris swirling at the bottom of a gravitational pothole. Its howling, riotous inner precincts were by this time well guarded by mech fleets.

But worms made it traversable. The first human expeditions through the wormhole mouth had been successful. It opened upon a site nearer to True Center. Paris himself had flown through it, darting in and back like a mouse dashing anxiously from its hole. And so they were—pests in the walls.

They flew through in order, then met on convergent asymptotes. Paris demanded and got a role in the assault. He was an accomplished pilot, easily able to angle in on the wormhole at high speeds, with a nudge here and a twist there.

Wormholes were fossils of the first split second of the universe. They were held open by onionskin layers of negative energy, sheets of anti-pressure made in that primordial convulsion. As natural resources, they had been gathered—by whom?—billions of years before and brought here, to serve as a transport nexus.

Quantum froth fizzed at the worm-mouth rim, a gaudy spray of burnt hues. These "struts" were of unimaginable density, but danger lurked only at the rim, where stresses would tear ordinary matter into virulent plasma. To hit the walls of the constantly shifting, oblong target, would be fatal, as several pilots had inadvertently proved.

The mouth was now an ellipsoid rimmed in quantum fire. He flew a pencil-thin ship, its insulation slight, safety buffers minimal. Yet he somehow felt no fear, only a serene certainty. Tidal stresses wrenched squeals from his ship as lightning curled in snakes of violet and gold—

—and he was tumbling out the other end, in a worm complex over a hundred light-years away.

A blue-green star majestically greeted the human fleet with a coronal plume. Nearby orbited a mech complex; picket craft policed it. With quick swerves the tiny human ships angled into a traffic-train headed for a large wormhole mouth. Fifty men and eighty-six women had died learning the route they would follow, gaining the override codes to pass through the mech complexes. But their disguises would withstand only a moment's inspection; dally and they were dead.

Their second transit was through a spacious wormhole that left them racing in low orbit over a smoldering red dwarf. They could use their hard-won code-status perhaps a few more times before the mech complexes would catch on. They had to take whatever wormhole mouths they could get.

Wormholes could take traffic only one way at a time. High-velocity ships plowed down the wormhole throats, which could vary from a finger's length to a planet's diameter. A jump through could leave one near mysteriously useless solar systems, or in virulent places that would fry a human in seconds.

Long before, presumably by brute-force interstellar hauling, someone—perhaps those who had made the earliest mechs?—had built an elaborate system at Galactic Center. Smaller worm mouths, massing perhaps as much as a mountain range, allowed only thin-ships to pass. These Paris and the other eighteen volunteers chose when they popped out in a mech complex. They never slowed; each network site was well policed, and speed was their only defense.

Shoot through a worm mouth, aim for a small worm mouth nearby, *go*. The snaky, shiny worm-walls zoomed by as Paris lay watching his displays and trying not to think of what was coming.

The tapering gray sheen of the throat flexed. Each worm mouth kept the other "informed" of what it had just eaten, the information flowing as a surge in the tension of the wormhole itself. Stress waves sent clenching oscillations, making the throat ripple like sausage links. If a sausage neck met him, tightened too fast, he would emerge as a rosy plume of ionized gas at the exit mouth.

From an elaborate wormhole calculus human theorists had worked out the route to follow. Between Isis and the space near True Center were a dozen wormhole jumps. Worse, some wormholes had multiple mouths, so the sleek throat split into choices—selections they had to make at immense speed.

Suns and planets of great, luminous beauty floated in the distant blackness when they emerged. Behind the resplendent nebulae loomed the radiant promise of True Center. It seemed a strange contrast, to leap about the vast distances while boxed into a casket-sized container.

Blink-quick, they jumped and dodged and jumped again.

Subtlety was wasted here; when a mech craft approached on a routine check, they destroyed it with kinetic energy bolts. Mechs never used such crude methods, so they were leaving behind clear signs that "vermin" had passed that way.

They emerged amid an eerie halo of white-dwarf stars, arranged in a hexagonal. Paris wondered why mechs would arrange such a pattern, which from simple orbital mechanics could not last. But like so many mech traits, this had no explanation, even in Arthur's huge memory stores, nor any likelihood of one.

Ahead, the galactic disk stretched in luminous splendor. Lanes of clotted dust framed stars azure and crimson and emerald. This wormhole intersection afforded five branches: three black spheres orbited like circling lethal leopards, while two cubes blared bright with quantum rim radiation.

Their pencil ships thrust directly into a flat face of a cubic worm. The negative-energy-density struts that held the wormhole open were in the edges, so the faces were free of tidal forces. A flicker, a stomach-twisting wrench—and they were near True Center.

The inner disk glowed with fermenting scarlets and mean purples. Great funnels of magnetic field sucked and drew in interstellar dust clouds. Sullen cyclones narrowed toward the brilliant accretion disk.

Mech contrivance orbited everywhere here, filling a bowl of sky alive with activity. Vast gleaming grids and reflectors caught radiation from the friction and infalling of the great disk. This crop of raw photon energy was flushed into the waiting maws of wormholes, apparently moving the flux to distant worlds in need of cutting lances of light. For what—mech planet-shaping, world-raking, moon-carving?

They flitted into yet another wormhole mouth—

—and the spectacle made him hold his breath.

Magnetic filaments towered, so large the eye could not take them in. Through them shot immense luminous corridors alive with wriggling energies. These arches yawned over tens of light-years, their immense curves descending toward the white-hot True Center. There matter frothed and fumed and burst into dazzling fountains.

At True Center, three million suns had died to feed gravity's gullet. The arches were plainly artificial, orderly arrays of radiance a light-year across. Yet they sustained themselves along hundreds of light-years, as gauzy as a young girl's hair as they churned with airy intricacy.

Could intelligence dwell here? There had been ancient stories, never confirmed. Emerald threads laced among tangled ruby spindles. He had a powerful impression of layers, of labyrinthine order ascending beyond his view, beyond simple understanding.

Hard acceleration rammed him back into his flow-couch. From behind, a torrent of malignant light.

They have detonated the worm! came a cry over comm.

Braking hard, veering left into a debris cloud—

Evidently mechs knew how to trigger the negative-energy-density struts inside a worm mouth—and would do so to catch vermin. Now their line of retreat was gone.

They fled to a huge blot that beckoned with the promise of sullen shelter. They were close to the edge of the black hole's accretion disk. Around them churned the deaths of stars, all orchestrated by the magnetic filaments. Which in turn, Paris was quite sure, worked to the command of something he did not care to contemplate. Did mechs govern here, or had he ventured into a realm where even they were vermin?

Here stars were ripped open by processes he could not fathom—spilled, smelted down into fusing globs. They lit up the dark, orbiting masses of debris like tiny crimson match heads flaring in a filthy coal-sack.

Amid this swam the strangest stars of all. Each was half-covered by a hanging hemispherical mask. This shroud gave off infrared, a strange screen hanging at a fixed distance from each star. It hovered on light, gravity just balancing the outward light pressure. The mask reflected half the star's flux back on it, turning up the heat on the cooker, sending virulent arcs jetting from the corona.

Light escaped freely on one side while the mask bottled it up on the other. This pushed the star toward the mask, but the mask was bound to the star by gravitation. It adjusted and kept the right distance. The forlorn star was able to eject light in only one direction, so it recoiled oppositely.

The filaments were herding these stars: sluggish, but effective. Herded toward the accretion disk, stoking the black hole's appetite.

Paris and the others hung in a narrow gulf overlooking the splendor below. Blackness dwelled at the core, but friction heated the infalling gas and dust. Storms worried these great banks; white-hot tornadoes whirled. A virulent glow hammered outward, shoving incessantly at the crowded masses jostling in their doomed orbits. Gravity's gullet forced the streams into a disk, churning ever inward.

Amid this deadly torrent, life persisted. Of a sort.

He peered through the gaudy view, seeking the machine-beasts who ate and dwelled and died here. Records millennia old told of these. *There.*

Suffering the press of hot photons, a grazer basked. To these photovores, the great grinding disk was a source of food. Above the searing accretion disk, in hovering clouds, gossamer herds fed.

Vector that way, came the command. This way led to their target, but already mechs were moving toward the spindly human ships.

Sheets of the photovores billowed in the electromagnetic winds, luxuriating in the acrid sting. Some seemed tuned to soak up particular slices of the electromagnetic spectrum, each species with a characteristic polish and shape. They deployed great flat receptor planes to maintain orbit and angle in the eternal brimming day.

The human ships slipped among great wings of high-gloss moly-sheet. The photovore herds skated on winds and magnetic torques in a complex dynamical sum. They were machines, of course, presumably descended from robot craft which had explored this center billions of years before. More complex machines, evolved in this richness, prowled the darker lanes farther out.

A bolt seared through the dust and struck a human ship. Another lanced through some photovores, which burst open in flares.

They hugged the shadow and waited. Moments tiptoed by.

A contorted shape emerged from a filmy dust bank, baroquely elegant in a shape no human mind could have conceived, ornate and glowing with purpose, spiraling lazily down the gravitational gradients. Paris saw a spindly radiance below the photovore sheets. A magnetic filament, he guessed. His Arthur Aspect broke in,

> *I was here once, in my Aspect manifestation, during the glorious era when we were allowed this close. I advise that you shelter there, for the guardian ship approaching is lethal beyond even my comprehension.*

"Your memory is that good?"

> *This was merely 3,437 years ago. I have suffered some copying errors, true, but fear is still the most potent stabilizer of recall. I was quite terrified during my carrier's incursion here. She was one of three who survived that, out of over a thousand.*

"I don't know . . ."

His intuition failed him. The other human pencil ships zoomed all around, sending panicked transmissions that he could scarcely filter. The ornate mech craft lumbered down toward them, many hundreds of kilometers away but still close, close, in the scales of space battle.

We are surely doomed if we stay here. If you are losing at a game, change the game.

Paris nodded and sent a compressed signal to the others. At full power he slipped below the shiny sheets of photovores, their outstretched wings banking gracefully on the photon breeze. Storms worried the flocks. White-hot tornadoes whirled and sucked, spun off from the disk below. When fire-flowers blossomed in the disk, a chorus arose from the feeding layers. Against the wrathful weather, position-keeping telemetry flitted between the herd sheets. They sang luminously to each other in the timeless glare.

Paris watched one herd fail. Vast shimmering sheets peeled away. Many were cast into the shrouded masses of molecular clouds, which were themselves soon to boil away. Others followed a helpless descending gyre. Long before they could strike the brilliant disk, the hard glare dissolved their lattices. They flared with fatal energies.

He felt, in the ship's bubble-sensorium, fresh attention focused on him. Lenses swiveled to follow: prey?

Here a pack of photovores had clumped, caught in a magnetic flux tube that eased down along the axis of the galaxy itself. Among them glided steel-blue gammavores, feeders on the harder gamma-ray emission from the accretion disk. Arthur said,

These sometimes fly this far above the disk, as I recall, to hunt the silicate-creatures who dwell in the darker dust clouds. Much of the ecology here was unknown in my time, and humans were banished from such territories before we could well explore. We sought the Wedge, the place where the earliest humans had taken shelter, including the legendary Walmsley. We wished to find there the rumored Galactic Library, a wealth which could have aided—

"Fine, stick to business."

He stopped the Aspect's idle musing with an internal block. Time to move. Where? Into the magnetic tube. But could they draw down some concealing cover?

He swooped with the others toward the filament. This also angled them toward a huge sailcraft photovore. It sighted them, pursued.

Here navigation was simple. Far below them, funneling away to an infinite well, lay the rotational pole of the Eater of All Things, the black hole of three million stellar masses: a pinprick of absolute black at the center of a slowly revolving, incandescent disk.

The metallivore descended after them, through thin planes of burnt-gold light seekers. The pencil ships scattered, firing ineffectually at it. They had speed, it had durability.

"How the hell do we deal with *that?*"

The metallivore prunes less efficient photovores. Its ancient codes, sharpened over time by natural selection, prefer the weak. Those who have slipped into unproductive orbits are easier to catch. It also prefers the savor of those who have allowed their receptor planes to tarnish with succulent trace elements, spewed up by the hot accretion disk below. The metallivore spots these by their mottled, dusky hue. Each frying instant, millions of such small deaths shape the mechsphere.

"We need something to zap it!"

I shall ponder. Meanwhile, be fleet of foot.

He veered and sheered, letting his feel for the craft take over. Others were not so swift; he heard the dying cries of three people nearby.

These placid conduits all lived to ingest light and excrete microwave beams, but some—like the one gliding after the tiny human ships—had developed a taste for metals: a metallivore. It folded its mirror wings, became angular and swift, accelerating.

The higher phyla are noticing us.

"Coming damned fast, too."

Plants harness only one percent of the energy falling upon them. Here photovoltaics capture ten percent, and evolution acting upon the mechs has improved even that. Admirable, in a way, I suppose—

"Give it to me compressed, not true-voice." An Aspect always tried to expand his airing time.

Arthur sent a squirt of compacted ancient lore—Fusion fires, he said, inside the photovores digested the ruined carcasses of other machines. Exquisitely tuned, their innards yielded pure ingots of any alloy desired.

The ultimate resources here were mass and light. The photovores lived for light, and the sleek metallivore lived to eat them—or even better, the human ships, an exotic variant. It now gave gigahertz cries of joy as it plunged after them into the magnetic fields of the filament.

"These magnetic entities are intelligent?" he asked.

Yes, though not in the sense we short-term thinkers recognize. They are more like fitfully sleeping libraries. I have an idea. Their thinking processes are vulnerable.

"How?"

They trigger their thinking with electrodynamic potentials. We are irritating them, I am sure.

He saw the metallivore closing fast. Beyond it came the convoluted mech guardian ship, closing remorselessly.

The remaining human ships executed evasions—banks, swoops, all amid the pressing radiance from the disk-glare. Around them magnetic strands glowed like smoldering ivory.

The metal-seeker would ingest them with relish, but with its lightwings spread to bank it could not maneuver as swiftly as their sleek ships. Deftly they zoomed through magnetic entrails. The mech ship followed.

"How soon will these magnetic beings react?"

Soon, if experience is a guide. I advise that we clasp the metallivore now. Quickly!

"But don't let him *quite* grab us?"

Arthur gave a staccato *yes,* its panic seeping into Paris's mind. Accurate simulations had to fear for their lives.

The steel-gray metallivore skirted over them. Predators always had parasites, scavengers. Here and there on the metallivore's polished skin were things like limpets and barnacles, lumps of orange-brown and soiled yellow that fed on chance debris, purging the metallivore of unwanted elements—wreckage and dust which could jam even the most robust mechanisms, given time.

It banked, trying to reach them along the magnetic strands, but the rubbery pressure of the field lines blunted its momentum.

He let it get closer, trying to judge the waltz of creatures in this bizarre ballroom of the sky: a dance to the pressure of photons. Light was the fluid here, spilling up from the blistering storms far below in the great grinding disk. This rich harvest supported the great spherical volume of hundreds of cubic light-years, a vast, vicious veldt.

He began receiving electrodynamic static. The buzzing washed out his comm with the other human ships, distant motes. The metallivore loomed. Pincers flexed forth from it.

The crackling jolt. Slow lightning arced along the magnetic filament, crisp lemony annihilation riding down.

"It'll fry us!" Paris cried out. Arthur recovered some calm, saying, *We are minor players here. Larger conductors will draw this crackling fire.*

Another jarring jolt. But then the metallivore arced and writhed and died in dancing, flaxen fire.

The magnetic filaments were slow to act, but muscular. Induction was sluggish but inescapable. Suddenly Paris saw Arthur's idea.

As soon as the discharge had abated on the metallivore, the potentials sought another conducting surface, that with the greatest latent difference. The laws of electrodynamics applied to the bigger conductor, closing in—the guardian ship.

The guardian ship drew flashes of discharge, their jagged fingers dancing ruby-red and bile-green.

Calls of joy from the pencil-ships. The ornate shape coasted, dead. The larger surface areas of both metallivore and starship had intercepted the electrical circuitry of the filaments.

"I . . . you really did know what you were doing," he said weakly.

Not actually. I was following my archived knowledge, but theory makes a dull blade. Though perhaps some scrap of my intuition does remain . . .

Paris could sense the Aspect's wan pride. The human ships accelerated now, out of the gossamer filaments; there might be more bolts of high voltage.

Near the rim of the garish disk, oblivious to the lashing weather there, whirled a curious blotchy gray cylinder.

There. Clearly a mech construct.

"The Hall of Humans," he said, wondering how he knew.

THE COLLECTED

>I had this terrible dream and I woke up and it was real.

>Thousands of us there must be, all in this black flat place only it curves around above, I can see up there with my one eye, and the ceiling is filled with us, too, all planted in place.

>I'm all veins, big fat blue ones, no mouth but I want to eat all the time.

>My mother is here just a few meters away but I know her only by the sobbing, sounds just like her, and none of the rest of that thing is.

>I got my hand free and poked one of my eyes out so I didn't have to look at it but they fixed the eyes, said it was part of the expressiveness of me, and now I have to look all the time, no eyelids and they never turn out the lights.

>It is not hot but it is Hell and we whisper to each other about that and about it being forever and ever, hallowed be thy Name, amen.

It was a place of chalk and blood, of diamond eyes and strident songs.

Paris and the eleven other survivors found the lock, broke in, and prowled the vast interior of the rotating cylinder. He passed by things he could not watch for long, searching for sense.

Plumes of scent, muddy voices, words like fevered birdcalls.

Some of them were no longer remotely human, but rather coiled tubes of waxy flesh. Others resembled moving lumps of buttery bile. A man stood on one hand, his belly an accordion-pleated bulge, and as he moved oval fissures opened all over him, wheezing forth a fine yellow mist, long words moaning out: "I . . . am . . . a . . . holy . . . contri . . . vance . . ." and then a throttled gasp and "Help . . . me . . . be . . . what . . . I . . . am . . ."

A sewer smell came swarming up from nearby. A woman gazed directly back into his eyes. She said nothing but her skin ran with tinkling streams of urine. Nearby a little girl was a concert of ropy pink cords, red-rimmed where they all tried to speak.

The twelve spread out in a daze. Some recognized warped versions of people they had known. There were people here from far antiquity and places no one knew.

Paris found an entire aisle of shivering couples, entwined in sexual acts made possible by organs designed in ways nature never had allowed: sockets filled by slithering rods, beings which palped and stroked themselves to a hastening pace that rose to a jellied frenzy, shrieked from fresh mouths, and then abated, only to begin again with a building rhythm.

An Isis man was vomiting nearby. "We've got to save them," he said when Paris went to help him.

"Yeasay," a woman pilot agreed. The survivors were drifting back together, pressed by the enveloping horror.

A wretched nearby sculpture of guts that sprouted leaves managed to get out three words, "No . . . don't . . . want . . ."

Paris felt the fear and excitement of the last few hours ebbing from him, replaced by a rising, firm feeling he could not force out through his throat. He shook his head. The woman started to argue, saying that they could take the cases that had been deformed the least, try to free them from the alterations.

Paris found his voice. "They want to *go*. Listen."

From the long axis that tapered away to infinity there rose a muttered, moaning, corpuscular symphony of anguish and defeat that in its accents and slurred cadences called forth the long corridor of ruin and affliction that was the lot of humanity here at Galactic Center, down through millennia.

He stood listening. Parts of his mind rustled—moving uneasily, understanding.

The Mantis sculptures got the most important facets profoundly wrong. The Mantis had tried to slice human sliding moments from the robed minds of the suredead, but it could not surecopy them: their essence lay in what was discarded from the billion-bit/second stream. In the mere passing twist and twinge of a second, humans truncated their universe with electrochemical knives.

Hot-hearted, to humans death was the mother of beauty. Their gods were, in the end, refracted ways of bearing the precarious gait of the mortal.

To Paris as a boy the compact equation $e^{i\pi}+1=0$ had comprised a glimpse of the eternal music of reason, linking the most important constants in the whole of mathematical analysis, $0, 1, e, \pi,$ and i. To Paris the simple line was beautiful.

To a digitally filtered intelligence the analog glide of this relation would be different, not a glimpse of a vast and various landscape. Not better or worse, but irreducibly different.

That he could never convey to the Mantis.

Nor could he express his blood-deep rage, how deeply he hated the shadow that had dogged his life.

But his fury was wise in a way that mere anger is not. He surprised himself: he breathed slowly, easily, feeling nothing but a granite resolve.

Paris began killing the sculptures systematically. The others stood numbly and watched him, but their silence did not matter to him. He moved quickly, executing them with bolts, the work fixing him totally in the moment of it.

He did not notice the sobbing.

After a time he could not measure he saw that the others were doing the same, without discussion. No one talked at all.

The wails of the sculptured people reverberated, moist glad cries as they saw what was coming.

It took a long time.

The Mantis was waiting outside the Hall of Humans, as Paris had felt it would be.

I was unable to predict what you and the others did.

"Good." His pencil ship lifted away from the long gray cylinder, now a mausoleum to madness.

I allowed it because those are finished pieces. Whereas you are a work in progress, perhaps my best.

"I've always had a weakness for compliments."

He could feel his very blood changing, modulating oxygen and glucose from his body to feed his changing brain. The accretion disk churned below, a great lurid pinwheel grinding to an audience of densely packed stars.

Humor is another facet I have mastered.

"There's a surprise." Vectoring down, the boost pressing him back. "Very human, too. Everybody thinks he's got a good sense of humor."

I expect to learn much from you.

"Now?"

You are ripe. Your fresh, thoroughly human reactions to my art will be invaluable.

"If you let me live, you'll get one or two centuries more experience when I finally die."

That is true, for yours has been an enticingly rich one, so far. There are reasons to envy the human limitations.

"And now that I've seen your art, my life will be changed."

Truly? It is that affective with you, a member of its own medium? How?

He had to handle this just right. "Work of such impact, it will take time for me to digest it."

You use a chemical-processing metaphor. Precisely a human touch, incorporating the most inefficient portions of your being. Nonetheless, you point to a possible major benefit for me if you are allowed to live.

"I need time to absorb all this."

He could feel his body's energy reserve sacrificing itself in preparation for the uploading process. He had come to understand himself for the first time as he killed the others. Some part of him, the Me, knew it all now. The I spoke haltingly. "I think you have truly failed to understand."

I can remedy that now.

"No, that's exactly what you won't. You can't know us this way."

I had a similar conversation with your father. He suggested that I invest myself in you.

"But you won't get it just by slicing and dicing us."

There is ample reason to believe that digital intelligences can fathom analog ones to any desired degree of accuracy.

"The thing about aliens is, they're alien."

He felt intruding into him the sliding fingers of a vast, cool intellect, a dissolving sea. Soon he would be an empty shell. Paris would become part of the Mantis in the blending across representations, in their hologram logics. He could feel his neuronal wiring transfiguring itself. And accelerated.

Art is everywhere in the cosmos. I particularly liked your ice sculptures, melting in the heat while audiences applauded. Your tapestry of dim senses and sharp pains and incomprehensible, nagging, emotional tones—I wish to attain that. An emergent property, quite impossible to predict.

"Never happen. You could understand this if you would allow me to fill out my natural life span."

That is a telling point. I shall take a moment to ponder it. Meanwhile, cease your descent toward the accretion disk.

Here was the chance. The Mantis would withdraw to consult all portions, as an anthology intelligence. That would give him seconds to act. He accelerated powerfully down. "Take your time."

For long moments he was alone with the hum of his tormented ship and the unfolding geysers outside, each storm bigger than a world.

I have returned. I have decided, and shall harvest you now.

"Sorry to hear that," he said cheerfully. Dead men could afford pleasantries.

I wish you could tell me why you desired to end all my works. But then, shortly, I shall know.

"I don't think you'll ever understand."

Paris took his ship down toward the disk, through harrowing, hissing plumes of plasma.

His I sensed great movements deep within his Me and despite the climbing tones of alarms in his ship, he relaxed.

Pressed hard by his climbing acceleration, he remembered all that he had seen and been, and bade it farewell.

You err in your trajectory.

"Nope."

You had to live in each gliding moment. This mantra had worked for him and he needed it more now. Cowardice—the real thing, not momentary panic—came from inability to stop the imagination from working on each approaching possibility. To halt your imagining and live in the very moving second, with no past and no future—with that he knew he could get through each second and on to the next without needless pain.

Correct course! Your craft does not have the ability to endure the curvatures required, flying so near the disk. Your present path will take you too close—

"To the end, I know. Whatever that means."

His Arthur Aspect was shouting. He poked it back into its niche, calmed it, cut off its sensor link. No need to be cruel.

Then Arthur spoke with a thin cry, echoing something Paris had thought long ago. The Aspect's last salute:

> *If Mind brought humans forth from Matter, enabling the universe to comprehend itself—to do its own homework—*

"Then maybe that's why we're here," Paris whispered to himself.

The only way to deprive the Mantis of knowledge no human should ever give up, was to erase that interior self, keep it from the consuming digital.

He skimmed along the whipped skin of doomed incandescence. Ahead lay the one place from which even the Mantis could not retrieve him, the most awful of all abysses, a sullen dot beckoning from far across the spreading expanse of golden luminance. Not even the Mantis could extract him from there.

Paris smiled and said good-bye to it all and accelerated hard, hard.

THE SHIP WHO SANG

Anne McCaffrey

The Ship Who Sang (1970)
The Partnership (with Margaret Ball) (1992)
The Ship Who Searched (with Mercedes Lackey) (1992)
The City Who Fought (with S.M. Stirling) (1993)
The Ship Who Won (with Jody Lynn Nye) (1994)

"**S**he was born a thing and as such would have been condemned if she failed to pass the encephalograph test required of all newborn babies. There was always the possibility that though the limbs were twisted, the mind was not; that though the ears would hear only dimly, the eyes see vaguely, the mind behind them was receptive and alert.

"The electro-encephalogram was entirely favorable, unexpectedly so, and the news was brought to the waiting, grieving parents. There was the final, harsh decision: to give their child euthanasia or permit it to become an encapsulated 'brain,' a guiding mechanism in any one of a number of curious professions. As such, their offspring would suffer no pain, live a comfortable existence in a metal shell for several centuries, performing unusual services to Central Worlds.

"She lived and was given a name, Helva."

Those are the opening paragraphs of the first Helva novel, *The Ship Who Sang*, which tells the story of how Helva becomes the mind behind the operation of a stargoing spaceship, and how her first ship-partner, Jennan Sahir Silan, dies tragically when he and Helva have to rescue a religious group from a planet soon to be reduced to a cinder as its primary goes nova. The rest of the first novel tells of Helva's journey out of the intense grief she suffered on Jennan's death and her attempts to find another partner who would be as compatible. Niall Parollan, clever, sharp, outrageously nonconformist, and a womanizer, becomes her "brawn" and they go off together to seek adventures, which have been chronicled in a number of later novels done in collaboration with other writers.

—*Anne McCaffrey*

The Ship That Returned

by

Anne McCaffrey

HELVA HAD BEEN PROWLING THROUGH HER EXTENSIVE MUSIC FILES, TRYING TO find something really special to listen to, when her exterior sensors attracted her attention. She focused on the alert. Dead ahead of her were the ion trails of a large group of small, medium and heavy vessels. They had passed several days ago but she could still "smell" the stink of the dirty emissions. She could certainly analyze their signatures. Instantly setting her range to maximum, she caught only the merest blips to the port side, almost beyond sensor range.

"Bit off regular shipping routes," she murmured.

"So they are," replied Niall.

She smiled fondly. The holograph program had really improved since that last tweaking she'd done. There was Niall Parollan in the pilot's chair, one compact hand spread beside the pressure plate, the left dangling from his wrist on the armrest. He was dressed in the black shipsuit he preferred to wear, vain man that he'd been: "because black's better now that my hair's turned." He would brush back the thick shock of silvery hair and preen slightly in her direction.

"Where exactly are we, Niall? I haven't been paying much attention."

"Ha! Off in cloud-cuckoo land again . . ."

"Wherever that is," she replied amiably. It was such a comfort to hear his voice.

"I do believe . . ." and there was a pause as the program accessed her present coordinates, "we are in the Cepheus Three region."

"Why, so we are. Why would a large flotilla be out here? This is a fairly empty volume of space."

"I'll bring up the atlas," Niall replied, responding as programmed.

It was bizarre of her to have a hologram of a man dead two months but it was a lot better—psychologically—for her to have the comfort of such a reanimation. The "company" would dam up her grief until she could return her dead brawn to Regulus Base. And discover if there were any new "brawns" she could tolerate as a mobile partner. Seventy-eight years, five months and twenty days with Niall Parollan's vivid personality was a lot of time to suddenly delete. Since she had the technology to keep him "alive"—in a fashion, she had done so. She certainly had enough memory of their usual interchanges with which to program this charade. She would soon have to let him go but she'd only do that when she no longer needed his presence to keep mourning at bay. Not that she hadn't had enough exposure to that emotion in her life—what with losing her first brawn partner, Jennan, only a few years into what should have been a lifelong association.

In that era, Niall Parollan had been her contact with Central Worlds Brain and Brawn Ship Administration at Regulus Base. After a series of relatively short and only minimally successful longer-term partnerships with other brawns, she had gladly taken Niall as her mobile half. Together they had been roaming the galaxy. Since Niall had ingeniously managed to pay off her early childhood and educational indebtedness to Central Worlds, they had been free agents, able to take jobs that interested them, not compulsory assignments. They had not gone to the Horsehead Nebula as she had once whimsically suggested to Jennan. The NH-834 had had quite enough adventures and work in this one not to have to go outside it for excitement.

"Let's see if we can get a closer fix on them, shall we, Niall?"

"Wouldn't be a bad idea on an otherwise dull day, would it?" Though his fingers flashed across the pressure plates of the pilot's console, it was she who did the actual mechanics of altering their direction. But then, she would have done that anyway. Niall didn't really need to, but it pleased her to give him tasks to do. He'd often railed at her for finding him the sort of work he didn't *want* to do. And she'd snap back that a little *hard* work never hurt anyone. Of course, as he began to fail physically, this became lip service to that old argument. Niall had been in his mid-forties when he became her brawn and she the NH-834, so he had had a good long life for a softshell person.

"Good healthy stock I am," the hologram said, surprising her.

Was she thinking out loud? She must have been for the program to respond.

"With careful treatment, you'll last centuries," she replied, as she often had.

She executed the ninety-degree course change that the control panel had plotted.

"Don't dawdle, girl," Niall said, swiveling in the chair to face the panel behind which her titanium shell resided.

She thought about going into his "routine," but decided she'd better find out a little more about the "invasion."

"Why do you call it an invasion?" Niall asked.

"That many ships, all heading in one direction? What else could it be? Freighters don't run in convoys. Not out here, at any rate. And nomads have definite routes they stick to in the more settled sectors. And if I've read their KPS rightly . . ."

". . . Which, inevitably, you do, my fine lady friend . . ."

"Those ships have been juiced up beyond freighter specifications and they're spreading dirty stuff all over space. Shouldn't be allowed."

"Can't have space mucked up, can we?" The holo's right eyebrow cocked, imitating an habitual trait of Niall's. "And juiced-up engines as well. Should we warn anyone?"

Helva had found the Atlas entries for this sector of space. "Only the one habitable planet in the system they seem to be heading straight for. Ravel . . ." Sudden surprise caught at her heart at that name. "Of all places."

"Ravel?" A pretty good program to search and find that long-ago reference so quickly. She inwardly winced at the holo's predictable response. "Ravel was the name of the star that went nova and killed your Jennan brawn, wasn't it?" Niall said, knowing the fact perfectly well.

"I didn't need the reminder," she said sourly.

"Biggest rival I have," Niall said brightly as he always did, and pushed the command chair around in a circle, grinning at her unrepentantly as he let the chair swing 360 degrees and back to the console.

"Nonsense. He's been dead nearly a century . . ."

"Dead but not forgotten . . ."

Helva paused, knowing Niall was right, as he always was, in spite of being dead, too. Maybe this wasn't a good idea, having him able to talk back to her. But it was only what he would have said in life anyhow, and had done often enough or it wouldn't be in the program.

She wished that the diagnostics had shown her one specific cause for his general debilitation so she could have forestalled his death. Some way, somehow.

"I'm wearing out, lover," he'd told her fatalistically in one of their conversations when he could no longer deny increasing weakness. "What can you expect from a life-form that degenerates? I'm lucky to have lived as long as I have. Thanks to you fussing at me for the last seventy years."

"Seventy-eight," she corrected him then.

"I'll be sorry to leave you alone, dear heart," he'd said, coming and laying his cheek on the panel behind which she was immured. "Of all the women in my life, you've been the best."

"Only because I was the one you *couldn't have,*" she replied.

"Not that I didn't try," the hologram responded with a characteristic snort.

Helva echoed it. Reminiscing and talking out loud were not a good idea. Soon she wouldn't know what was memory and what was programming.

WHY hadn't she used the prosthetic body that Niall had purchased for her—reducing their credit balance perilously close to zero and coming close to causing an irreparable breach between them? He *had* desperately wanted the physical contact, ersatz as she had argued it would be. The prosthesis would have been *her* in Niall's eyes, and arms, since she would have motivated it. And he'd tried so hard to *have* her. He had supplied Sorg Prosthetics with the hologram statue he'd had made long before he became her brawn, using genetic information from her medical history and holos of her parents and siblings. Until he'd told her, she hadn't known that there had been other, physically normal children of her parents' issue. But then, shell-people were not encouraged to be curious about their families: they were shell-people, and ineffably different. He swore blind that he hadn't maximized her potential appearance—the hologram was of a strikingly good-looking woman—when he'd had a hologram made of her from that genetic information. He'd even produced his research materials for her inspection.

"You may not like it, kid," he'd said in his usual irreverent tone, "but you are a blond, blue-eyed female and would have grown tall and lissome. Just like I like 'em. Your dad was good-lookin' and I made you take after him, since daughters so often tend to resemble good ol' dad. Not that your ma wasn't a good-looking broad. Your siblings all are, so I didn't engineer anything but a valid extrapolation."

"You just prefer blondes, don't tell me otherwise!"

"I never do, do I?" responded the hologram and Helva brought herself sharply to the present—and the fact she tried to avoid—that the Niall Parollan she had loved was dead. Really truly dead. The husk of what he called his "mortal coil" was in stasis in his quarters. He had died peacefully—not as he had lived, with fuss and fury and fine histrionics. One moment her sensors read his slowly fading life signs—the next second, the thin line of "nothing" as the essence of the personality that had been Niall Parollan departed—to wherever souls or a spiritual essence went.

She who could not weep was shattered. Later she realized that she had hung in space for days, coming to grips with his passing. She had said over and over that they had had a good, long time together: that these circumstances differed from her loss of Jennan after just a few very short years. Jennan had never had a chance to live a full, long, productive life. Niall had. Surely she shouldn't be greedy for just a little more, especially when for the last decade he had been unable to enjoy the lifestyle that he had followed so vibrantly, so fully, in such a raucous nonconformist spirit. Surely she had learned to cope with grief in her last hundred years. That was when she realized that she couldn't face the long silent trip back to Regulus Base. He'd insisted that he had a right to be buried with other heroes of the Service since he'd had to put up so much with them and especially her, all these decades. They had been a lot closer to Regulus at the time that subject had come up. But she was determined to grant that request.

There were no other brain ships anywhere in her spatial vicinity to contact and act as escort. She and Niall had been on a primary scouting sweep of unexplored star systems. She might have resented that first escort back from Ravel with Jennan's body. Not that there was much chance of her suiciding this time. She'd passed that test on the first funereal return to Regulus Base. Which is when the notion to program a facsimile had occurred to her. So it was a way to delay acceptance? Surely she could be allowed this aberration—if aberration it was. She didn't have to mention the matter to Regulus. They'd be glad enough to have her ready to take another partner. Experienced B&B ships were always in demand for delicate assignments. She was one of their best, her ship-self redesigned and crammed with all the new technology that had been developed for brain ships, and stations. Like that damned spare body Niall had bought and which she had never used. She couldn't. She simply couldn't inhabit the Sorg prosthesis. Oh, she knew that Tia did and the girl was glad of the ability to "leave" the shell and ambulate. Lovely word, "ambulate." She and Niall had had some roaring arguments over the whole notion of prosthesis.

"You'd fit me out with a false arm or leg, if I lost one, wouldn't you?" had been one of Niall's rebuttals.

"So you could walk or use the hand, yes, but this is different."

"Because you know what I'd be using on you, don't you?" He was so close to her panel that his face had been an angry blur. He'd been spitting at her intransigence. "And you don't want any part of my short arm, do you?"

"At least they can't replace *that* in prosthesis," she'd snarled.

"Wanna bet?" He'd whirled away, back to his command chair, sprawling into it, glaring at her panel. "Trouble is, with you, girl, you're aged in the keg. Set in plascrete. You don't know what you're missing!" And he was snarling with bitterness.

Since she considered herself tolerant and forward thinking, that accusation had burned. It still did. Maybe, after all, she was too old in her head to contemplate physical freedom. But she could not make use of that empty body-shell as something she, Helva, could manipulate. Not all the brain ships she had spoken to about the Sorg prosthesis had found it a substitute for immolation in a shell. And some of them had been just commissioned, too. Of course, Tia—Alex/Hypatia AH-1033—had once *been* a walking, unshelled person as a child. Maybe, as Niall had vociferously bellowed at the top of his lungs at her, Helva needed to have her conditioning altered: a moral update. For a brain ship, she wasn't that old, after all. Why couldn't she have accepted the prosthesis when he wanted so desperately for her to use it? She and Niall had been partnered a long time, so how could it have altered their special relationship to have added to it that final surrender of self? She really hadn't thought of herself as a technological vestal virgin, one of the epithets Niall had flung at her. She wasn't prudish. She'd just been *conditioned* to accept herself, as she was, so thoroughly that to be "unshelled" was the worst imaginable fate. Using the prosthetic body was not at all the same thing as being unshelled, he had shouted back at her. While she *had* been sensorily deprived once, she hadn't also been *out* of her shell. Nearly out of her mind, yes, but not out of the shell. But she couldn't, simply could *not*, oblige. Oblige? No, she couldn't oblige Niall in that way. A weak word to define a response to his unreasonable, but oh-so-much masculine request. Well, she had refused. Now she wished she hadn't. But if Niall were still living, would she have relented? Not likely, since it was his death that had now prompted remorse for that omission.

"Preferably before I became impotent, my girl," and this was the holo speaking.

"If you knew how sorry I am, Niall . . ." she murmured.

Information started to chatter in from her sensors. She didn't quite recall having asked for a spectrographic analysis of the ion trail. Such an action was so much a part of her standard operating procedure that she supposed, in between self-castigation and listening to her Niall program, that she had automatically instigated it.

"Well, well, armed and loaded for bear, huh?"

"Yeah," Niall in holo replied, "but what sort of bear?"

"Those religious fanatics on Chloe had used fur rugs to keep warm . . . so the analogy is accurate enough," she replied, amused to have been so accurate. "I remember they went merrily off to . . ."

"Merrily?" Niall's voice cracked in dismay. "That lot never heard the word. So what's hunting bear in this volume of space?" he asked.

"Well, now hear this, dear friend. They're on that habitable planet which, being the gluttons for punishment they seemed to be when I first met them, they have named Ravel."

"No doubt a penitential derived gimmick to remind them of their sins," Niall said in a dour tone.

Helva analyzed the report. "Got an ID on the visitors. Pirates," she said, for her data files had been able to match the emissions with those of Kolnari raiders. Small—yachts more likely—and some medium-sized spaceships, probably freighters, gutted and refitted for piratical practices and two heavier but older cruiser-sized vessels.

The Niall holo whipped the chair round, staring at her. (Mind you, the program was very good to get this sort of reaction so quickly.) "Kolnari? The bastards that attacked your space-station friend, Simeon?"

"The very same. Not all of those fanatics got captured when Central World's Navy tried to round all of them up."

"Wily fiends, those Kolnari." And the holo's expression was dead serious. "Last info from Regulus suggested that two groups, possibly four, had escaped completely. Even one group's more than enough bear-hunters to ravage Ravel with their modus operandi." The holo slammed both hands on the armrests in frustration.

"I wonder that there are any still alive. After all, the virus that Dr. Chaundra let loose on them was one of the most virulent ever discovered." She gave a sigh. "The Kolnari were dying in droves."

The Kolnari—a dissident splinter group that had so adapted to the conditions of their harsh home planet that they were considered a human subspecies—were known to have an incredible ability to adapt to and survive otherwise fatal diseases, viruses and punishing planetary conditions. They had a short life span, maturing when other male human types were only hitting puberty, but the short generations were dangerous despite the limitation. They raided wherever they could, planets, space platforms or freighter convoys, using the human populations or crews as slaves and refitting the captured vessels to their uses—piracy. After their nearly successful raid on Space Station 900, Central Worlds Navy was reasonably certain they had destroyed the main body of peripatetic Kolnari units. They were on alert to locate, and destroy on sight, any other units.

"Huh!" Niall snorted. "Adapting to that particular virus would be just the sort of thing the Kolnari *would* be able to do, given their perverse nature and crazy metabolism."

"I'm afraid you could be right. Who else would be insane enough to run ships in that condition? Even nomads don't get that sloppy about emissions," Helva said.

"Not if they wish to continue their nomadic existence if they're leaving a system on the sly. Are you being wise to go after Kolnari?" Niall asked, a trace of anxiety in his tone. "You'd constitute a real prize."

Helva did a mental shudder, all too vividly reminded of what the Kolnari leader, Belazir t'Marid, had nearly done to the space-station brain, Simeon. Odd that Niall would remind her of that. She knew she'd done a good program but . . . Could she rationally believe in the transmigration of souls? Or that the holo was the ghost of the real Niall?

"I can no more leave those Ravel idiots to the Kolnari than I could to the damned nova. And it is sort of poetic justice," she said with a sigh. "Let's see. It's nearly a hundred years since I had to transport them off their planet before their sun fried it. It took time for Central Worlds to find such a suitably remote star system where they would be safe from both nova stars and any profanity from the evils that beset mere men. Let's hope that they have some sort of modern equipment protecting them. If not against novas, at least against predators. Ah! The Atlas says the sun's stable. And there is, or was, a space facility for incoming converts."

"Ha!" The holo gave a bark of disgust. "Any satellite systems?"

"None mentioned. No contact in the past forty years, in fact. Well, I'm about to break into their meditations or whatever it is they do down there. There's nothing but females on that planet. I can't let Kolnari get their hands on all those innocent pious virgins, now can I?"

"It'd be fun to watch, though," said a totally unrepentant Niall.

"Shut up, you prurient sadist," she said as firmly as possible. Maybe she should also shut the program down. No, she *needed* him, one way or the other, because embedded in that program was the distillation of seventy-eight years of experience . . . his and hers.

"I was never a sadist, my dear Helva," he said haughtily, and then grinned wickedly. "I'll admit to hedonism but none of my women ever minded my attention . . . bar you! Have you considered a pulse to any listening Central Worlds units of the imminent unRaveling disaster?"

"I am and"—she paused as she put the final URGENT ALL EYES tag on the beam—"and it's away."

For the first time she experienced a touch of relief that she could approach the group without defiling it by the presence of a male. She'd pause the program—since Niall seemed to talk without any cues from her. Quite likely she wouldn't have as much trouble this time persuading them to seek whatever hidden shelters the planet might provide. Possibly the fact that she had saved them once before would weigh in their obedience to her urgings to make themselves as scarce as possible when the Kolnari arrived. Whatever! She wouldn't let them be victims to Kolnari rape and brutality. And Ravel was only a minor detour from the way to Regulus. She not only felt better to have something useful to do after going into a fugue over Niall's death but also was revived by the need. As she had been needed at Ravel, as Jennan's father had been at Parsaea. True tragedy occurred when those who could have helped were not *there* when needed. She was here. She was needed. Vigor flowed through the tubes that supplied her nutrient fluids.

"Feeling on form, are you?" the holo asked brightly. "Thatta girl! We gotta do what we gotta do. Data suggests that there'll be a lot of small settlements, cloisters they call 'em. They've increased their population from the Chloe figures." He sighed. "There isn't enough of the geo-ecological survey to show possible refuges. Planet's high on vegetation though."

"Lots of forests and lots of mountains and valleys. Plenty of cover if they separate. Make it that much harder for the Kolnari to tag 'em even from the air. That is, if they keep their wits about them," Helva said, charged with hope. "They need only lie doggo until the Fleet arrives."

"That is"—and the holo's tone was cynical—"if the Fleet has any squadrons near enough to send in timely fashion or decides such a splinter group is worth saving. I've never heard of their type of Faith . . . the Inner Marian Circle. Who's this Marian they worship?"

"In this case, 'marian' is an adjective and refers to Mary, mother of Jesus."

"Oh . . . and what's an inner circle then?"

"I don't know and it scarcely matters, does it? We have to warn them."

"Maybe there isn't anyone left to warn," Niall suggested. "Hey, did you just say they've increased their population from the Chloe figures? How does a celibate religious order perpetuate its membership?"

"Converts," she suggested. She often had wondered how such minorities did manage to continue to practice a faith that rejected procreation as a sin. "There was a new shipment forty years ago."

"Ach!" and Niall dismissed that. "Even if they converted preteens, how could the present inhabitants run fast enough at fifty-odd years to escape galloping Kolnari?"

"Parthenogenesis?" she suggested.

"That is, at least, virgin birth." And he snickered.

"That would go with the theories about Mary."

Niall snorted. "That was just the first recorded case of exogenesis."

"Possibly, but it doesn't detract from the Messiah's effect on man . . . and woman . . . kind."

"I'll allow that."

"Big of you."

"To the realities, woman," he said, stirring forward in his chair. "First we have to find out if there's anyone to rescue. AND if there's any safe place to send them so the Kolnari don't get 'em until the Fleet heaves into sight. I wouldn't wish that bunch on my worst enemy . . . Even my second-worst enemy."

Helva had been scanning the file on the Kolnari. "They might be looking for a new home base. Central Worlds sterilized their planet of origin."

"Then let's not let them have this Ravel, which seems to be a nice planet. Wouldn't want the neighborhood to go to such dogs . . ."

"They have an indigenous sort of canine on Ravel. Have you been speed-reading ahead of me again?" she asked, surprised because the list of local fauna was just coming up for her to peruse.

"*Most* of the M-type planets we've been on have some sort of critter in the canine slot. Cats don't always make it." And he shot a snide glance at her. He was a dog person but she had long ago decided she liked the independence of felines. They could argue the merits of the two species quite happily on their journeys between star systems. "Planet does have predators. Furthermore, our Inner Circle does not have any weaponry and does not hunt. They're vegetarians." He grinned around at her again.

"So it's all organic material?" Helva asked at her most innocent, playing on the theme.

"Just the kind of organic virgin material the Kolnari adore." The holo rubbed its hands together and leered.

She ignored that. "Temperate climate, too. Makes a change from Chloe, which was frozen most of the time."

"What! No harsh temperatures to mortify the body and soul?"

"No! And a good basic ecology, which they don't interfere with. Haven't even domesticated any of the indigenous beasts for use, but then, this entry is forty years old, dating from the last landfall. They live in harmony with their environment, it says here, and do not plunder it."

"Which sure does leave them wide-open to being plundered themselves. Which is about to happen. Though, when all's said and done, I wouldn't like to see them plundered or deflowered among their vegetable patches by the Kolnari."

"Nor will we permit it," Helva said fiercely, although she devoutly hoped that she wouldn't meet with the incredulity and pious fatalism that she'd encountered the first time and which, obliquely, had caused Jennan's death.

"Frankly, my dear, I don't know what I could do to help you. You know my reputation with women . . ." the holo began.

"I'll do the talking," she said, firmly interrupting him.

He leaned back in his chair, idly swinging it on the gimbals. "I wonder if they added you to their Inner Circle as a savior."

"Nonsense. None of the original group would be still alive. They didn't believe in artificially prolonging life . . ."

"All cures provided by prayer?"

"Avoiding all impure substances. Like Kolnari."

Niall cocked his head at her. "Maybe they'll welcome the Kolnari as a trial sent by whatever Universal Diety they revere . . ." He paused, scowling. "Mary was never a god, was she? Goddess, I mean? Any rate, would they consider the Kolnari have been sent to test their faith?"

"I'm hoping not. What do we have left of the tapes Simeon recorded?"

"I opine that you would be referring to the rape scene? My favorite of them all," Niall said, and his fingers tapped a sequence. "You wouldn't actually dare to play that back at those innocents . . ."

"A picture is worth a thousand words," she quoted at him. "If we have to tour as much of the planet as Jennan and I had to on Chloe, I'm going to need to use a sharp, fast lesson. I can rig a hologram for them to see," she added, since she was pleased with the way she handled holographic programming.

"If you do half as well with that program as you have with mine, it'll work, honey."

That remark startled Helva and she activated a magnification of his holographic image. But it was the hologram . . . one could see just the faintest hint of the light source. How could Niall *know* that he was a holo? Then she remembered the one they had done together at Astrada III when he had had to replay an historical event to prove a point to a skeptical audience. Surely that was his reference.

"I can't find any indication of how large the population is," she added, having replayed the entry on Ravel several times.

"Might be they don't keep an accurate census. Do they even *have* a space facility?"

"No, but they DO have a satellite with a proximity alarm!" she cried in triumph.

"And how far away is the nearest inhabited system that'd hear it, much less act?" Niall wanted to know. "Probably contains no more than the usual silly warning . . ." And he chanted in the lifeless tones of an automated messager, ". . . This . . . Is . . . An . . . Interdicted Planet. You . . . Will Not . . . Proceed Further." He abandoned that tone and, in a pious falsetto, added, "Or you'll get a spanking when the Fleet comes."

Helva gave him the brief chuckle he would have expected. "Our message will prompt action. No one ignores a B&B ship message."

"And rightly so," Niall said, loyally fierce, pounding one fist for emphasis on the desk.

There was no sound attached to that action. She'd have to work on that facet . . . when she'd managed to preserve the Chloists, or Chloe-ites or Inner Marian Circle Ravellians from the imminent arrival of the Kolnari. She'd have to be sure they knew just how dangerous and bloody-minded the Kolnari were so they'd make themselves as scarce as possible.

Helva was now speeding along the ion trail, its dirty elements all the more pronounced as she reduced the distance separating them. She'd overtake the flotilla within twenty hours. And arrive at Ravel four or five days ahead of them. She'd have to start decelerating once she passed the heliopause, but so would the Kolnari.

"Don't forget to cloak," Niall said, rising from his chair. He stretched until she was sure she could hear the sinews popping: which, she reminded herself, is why she hadn't added more than vocal sound to the holo. Stretching he was allowed, but not the awful noise he'd make popping his knucklebones. "I'd better get some shut-eye before the party begins."

"Good idea. I'll work on the hologram while you're resting and call you for a critique."

Niall the holo walked across the main compartment and to the aisle and down to Niall's quarters. Did it never realize that it melded with Niall's stasis-held body on the bunk?

She'd almost forgotten the cloaking mechanism that bent light and sensory equipment around the ship itself. She'd only used that device once and had held that up to Niall as a *really* unnecessary piece of technology for a B&B ship to waste credit on. So, it was coming in handy again. B&B ships had no weaponry with which to defend themselves and vanishing provided a much more effective evasion than the tightest, most impervious shielding.

As she judiciously edited the tapes from the Kolnari occupation of Space Station 900, she mulled over the first encounter with the Chloe-ites. At least this time her brawn couldn't be killed, however unintentional Jennan's death had been. She also had more tricks in her arsenal than she had had as that raw young brain ship.

She sped along and, well before any sensors the Kolnari might have could track her approach, she went into cloak. Of course, *they* became spots on her sensors, rather than three-dimensional ships. Still, by the size of the signals as she passed them, she learned a good deal about them. To begin with, there were more than she had anticipated, even taking into consideration all the dirty emissions. None of this lot matched the signatures of any of those that had attacked her friend, Simeon: not that that provided her with any consolation.

The Kolnari fleet was an incredible mixture of yachts, large and small, prizes of other Kolnari attacks—a round dozen of them, stuffed far above the optimum capacity with bodies: some evidently stashed in escape pods as last-resort accommodation. The conditions on board those ships would have been desperate even if the life-support systems managed to cope with such overloading. Three medium-sized freighters, equally jam-packed with little and large Kolnaris. Two destroyer types, quite elderly, but these were loaded with missiles and other armaments. Two of the freighters were hauling drones, five apiece, which cut down on the speed at which the entire convoy could travel. Four drones contained nothing but ammunition, missiles and spare parts: the fifth probably food as she got no metallic signals from it. Nineteen ships. A veritable armada and certainly able to overwhelm the inhabitants of Ravel. Which was undoubtedly why that luckless planet had been picked.

She pulsed an update of her earlier message with these details to the nearest Fleet facility—a good ten days away even by the speed of a pulse. The Admiralty had sworn blind that they intended to wipe Kolnari pirates out of space forever. So here was a chance for an ambitious picket commander to make that clean sweep and get a promotion. A small, modern force could easily overwhelm this shag-bag-rag-bag of barely spaceworthy vehicles. On the other hand, the Kolnari would fight to the last male child able to wield a weapon or fire a missile . . . and they had rather a few of those. Even Kolnari females were vicious fighters. Reviewing what was known of their lifestyle, it was likely a great many of the women were slaves, captured and forced to breed up more Kolnari offspring.

She sped on, wishing she had more information on the Chloes. Living close to nature on another planet was fine in theory, but practice was another thing altogether. As the original religious group had found out the hard way on Daphnis and Chloe a hundred years ago.

She had completed a holographic account of the less palatable habits of the Kolnari, including the modus operandi of their invasion of the peaceful planet, Bethel. The Tri-D coverage had been found in the space wreckage and used in the trial against those that had been captured at SS900. She was delighted to have found the one that showed vividly how the Kolnari dealt with anyone who defied them. That was the short sharp lesson she needed to project. She edited it, added some voice-over, and then programmed the exterior vid systems to play it.

That ought to cut down the waste of time spent arguing. She wanted every single female resident of Ravel safely hidden away when the Kolnari arrived.

She didn't rouse Niall—why bother him when he was sleeping like the dead—or rather the holo of him. He had always been hard to wake, though once roused, he altered from sleepy to alert in seconds. She had the time, so she did a leisurely spin-in, quartering the globe from darkside to daylight and identifying congregates of life signs . . . all too many. She'd never make it to every settlement. How could these piously celibate folk have increased almost fourfold from the numbers of the registered settlers? "Multiply and be fruitful" might be a Biblical injunction but, if the last bunch had come four decades before, there were a great many more than there ought to be. Rabbits might multiply so. But virgin rabbits? Well, she'd get to as many . . . what had they called themselves—ah, cloisters—as she could. Maybe they had some form of communication between the settlements, widespread as they were on the sprawling main continent. She'd simply have to ignore the island groups and concentrate on the larger, juicier targets that the Kolnari would be likely to attack first.

Smack-dab in the middle of the main continent, she easily identified what had been the landing field—well, a few square acres of burnt-out ground, a flimsy concrete-covered grid where ships or shuttles had landed to off-load people and supplies. Rows of temporary barracks, weathered and in need of maintenance, bordered two sides of the field to show that humans had once been accommodated there for however brief a time. There was a low-power source discernible and vegetation had not grown back over the landing area, though in forty-some years there should have been some weeds regaining a root hold. A blocky tower, now tilting sideways, held the corner position of the two barrack rows. From her aerial advantage, she could also see four roads, each going away from the deserted landing place: north, south, east and west. She could see where auxiliary lanes had split off from the main ones, smaller arteries leading to probably smaller settlements. Though none appeared to be more than dirt tracks, the vigorous growths had not reclaimed the track, leaving a clear margin on both sides. Some sort of chemical must have been used to discourage succession.

"I wonder how they decided who went in which direction," she murmured, forgetting that oddity in the press of more important concerns.

"Probably by divine intervention," Niall said, and there he was, seated at the pilot's console.

She hadn't put a voice-operated command in the program, but there he was, and she was rather pleased to hear another voice after the silent days of inward travel.

"Makes it easier to have just four main directions to search in."

"Those tracks were made over a period of years or they wouldn't be quite so visible since the last time they were used forty years ago."

"True. So, eeny, meeny, miny, moe . . . which track will we follow now? East is east and west is west and never the twain shall meet," he said in one of his whimsical moods.

"Nothing for north and south?"

"Well, we could go this way?" And he crossed his arms, pointing in two separate directions, neither of which was a cardinal compass point.

"North, I think, and then swing round . . ." Helva decided.

"In ever-increasing circles?" His tone was so caustically bright!

"Mountains, too. That's good."

" 'Purple mountains' majesty, above the fruited plain' . . ." he quoted.

"That doesn't sound right."

"I've forgot how it goes," he said, frowning.

"They do say that memory is the first thing that aging affects . . ."

"Thanks! I'll remember that."

Cloaked and at low altitude, she followed the northern track, noting the offshoots and realizing she had bit off quite a lot to chew if she was going to warn even half the inhabitants. She refused to allow the fact to discourage her from her chosen task. And night was falling on the continent.

"Ah-ha!" Niall pointed urgently at the view port. "Fires. Port three degrees."

"And far too much forest for me to land in."

"I don't mind backtracking when you can find a landing spot . . . Oh, no, I can't, can I?"

"No, you can't, but I appreciate your willingness to offer. Especially since I need to show my little vid to stir them to action."

"You *could* use the prosthesis," he said in a wheedling tone, grinning at her.

She said nothing—pointedly—and he chuckled. She might have to at that if daylight didn't show her settlements she could reach. She could hover . . . but she'd need something to project the vid on to for maximum effectiveness.

"I'll just use the darkness for reconnaissance and find out how many places I'm going to have to visit."

"Good thinking. I'll make a list of the coordinates. You might need them if the Fleet does come to our aid and comfort."

By morning his list of settlements, in all directions, had reached the three hundred mark. Some were small in the forested areas, but the plains or rolling hill country had many with several hundred inhabitants. All were ringed with walls, and these seemed to exude the power that showed up at every settlement, as well as a land-dike that Niall called a margin of no-woman's-land. The largest congregation was sited at the confluence of two rivers.

"If they have such a thing as an administrative center, that is likely it," she said. "We'll go there first thing in the morning. When I've had a quick look at that island complex."

"Whatever you say, love," Niall remarked with unusual compliance.

So she—they—arrived bright and early as the sun rose over the cup of the mountains that surrounded the largest congregation of Ravel's Chloe-ites.

"Rather impressive, wouldn't you say?" Niall remarked. "Orderly, neat. Everyone must have a private domicile. Thought you said they were a cloistered order."

The arrangement of the town, small city, did surprise Helva. Streets laid out in the center while garden plots and some large fields were positioned all around but within the customary low surrounding wall. There were main gates at each of the cardinal points of the compass but they weren't substantial: a Kolnari war axe would have reduced them to splinters with the first blow. A power source was visible on her sensors but it seemed to power the wall. What could they be keeping out that wasn't very tall or large or strong? Odd. Larger buildings set in the midst of fenced fields suggested either storage or barn shelters. She saw nothing grazing, though the season looked to be spring, to judge by the delicate green of cultivated fields, all within the walled boundary.

All four of the major avenues leading from the gates, for they were broad enough to be dignified with that title, tree-lined as well, led toward a large building which dominated the center. Part of it looked like a church, with an ample plaza in front of it for assemblies. Behind the church were low lines of buildings, possibly administration. This was a far-better-organized place than the original Chloe had been. Maybe they had learned something in the last century. She could hope.

"Hey, get that, Helva," Niall said suddenly, pointing to a slim structure atop the front of the building. "Not a steeple after all—no bells in it—but it's got something atop it."

Their approach had now been sighted, for the avenues as well as the smaller lanes between the individual housing units were filling with figures, faces upturned. Most were racing towards the square in front of the church, or whatever the big building was.

"Early risers . . ." Helva remarked.

"Early to bed—that power source is limited to the wall, not any electricity—and early to rise, you know," Niall said in a revoltingly jocular tone of voice. Then he altered to a practical tone, "And there's just about enough space for you to land in front of that church."

"So there is. But it's also full," she said, for they had arrived at the back end of the building and now that she had swung round, she could see that the plaza was filled with kneeling bodies. No one was working the fields.

"The more you squash the fewer we'll have to save from the Kolnari," Niall said.

"Oh, be quiet."

"It's over and out to you, Helva love. Sock it to them."

The devout knelt with upturned faces. She could see their mouths open with dark O's of surprise. But not fear. At some unseen signal, the kneelers rose and quickly, but without panic, moved back, out of the plaza.

"Be not afraid," Helva said gently, using her exterior sound system and ignoring the rich chuckle of amusement from Niall.

"They're not. Maybe you better alter your program, dear heart."

"I need to speak with you."

"Why don't you just hover?"

She made sure she was on interior sound only before she said sharply, "Will you shut up and let me handle this, Niall?"

"Remind them that you saved them from the hellfire of Chloe, dear," suggested Niall.

"That's my next line," she said in a caustic aside. "I am called Helva."

"Hey, Helva, that's you they've got mounted on that building."

In her careful vertical descent, she was now level with the spire. Which wasn't a spire but a replica of her earlier ship-self, vanes and all.

"Well, how's that for being canonized!" Niall said, but she could hear a note of pride in his voice. "You may be able to pull this off after all, love."

Rather more shaken by the artifact than she'd ever let him know, she completed her landing. One of the improvements on her ship body was the vertical cabin and a ramp directly to it, rather than the old and inconvenient lift from the stern.

"You even have a reception party of one," Niall remarked, as a tall figure became visible on the starboard viewers. All around the square the others turned towards that figure, heads bowing in a brief obeisance.

"How else are you called, Ship Helva?" said the tall woman, the hood falling back and revealing the serene face of an older woman.

"Not bad at all," Niall murmured. "She'd look even better in something feminine."

Indeed, Helva agreed with him since the woman had the most amazingly attractive face. A pity she had taken up religion instead of a man and a family. The long cassock robe she wore was one of those amorphous affairs, probably woven or pounded out of indigenous fibers and strictly utilitarian.

"I am Ship NH-834, who was once also the JH-834."

The woman nodded and inclined forward from her waist in a deep bow.

"Bingo!" said Niall.

"We have sent eternal prayers for the repose of the soul of Jennan," the woman said in a richly melodious voice, and from the onlookers rose a murmur of "Praise ever to his name."

"His memory is honored," Helva replied sincerely. "May I ask your name?"

"I am the Helvana," the woman replied, again with a reverent bow of her head.

"Oh, my God, Helva, you made it to sainthood," Niall said with complete irreverence and rolled with laughter in the pilot's chair. "With your own priestess caste system. Wow!"

Somehow his reaction annoyed her so much she almost erased his program. But common sense reasserted itself. If she was indeed some sort of saint to these people, she needed his irreverence more than ever—to keep her balance.

"You lead your people?"

"I am she who has been chosen," the woman said. "For many decades, we have hoped that you would honor us with your appearance . . ."

"Once more I come to you with bad tidings," Helva said quickly before she could be inundated with sanctimonious sentiments or perorations.

"That you have come is enough. What is your bidding, Ship Who Sings?"

"They have you pegged, my dear," Niall murmured, grinning like an idiot.

"An enemy approaches this planet . . . ah . . . Helvana." Helva had a bit of trouble getting that name/title out. "I have sent for assistance but it will not arrive in time to prevent the landing, nor the brutality with which these people—they are called the Kolnari—overwhelm an unprotected population."

A chuckle, rich and throaty, surprised Helva. She also caught smiles from those around the square.

"It's no laughing matter, Helvana. I have documentation of how they overwhelm resistance. How they . . . abuse the population." She couldn't quite say "rape" in the presence of girls who looked to be in their teens. "I must ask that you retreat to whatever safety the forests and mountains can provide until the Fleet arrives. Having warned you here in this fine city, I must spread the alarm to all that I can, to protect as many as I can."

The woman named Helvana raised one hand, a polite interruption. "Bird-keepers, send the flocks to warn our sisters. Ship Who Sings, would you know how soon they will land?"

"I'm no more than four days ahead of them," Helva said, wondering at her calmness. With relief, she did see quite a few women disappearing from the perimeter and doing whatever duties the bird-keepers might have. "You must gather what belongings you cherish and make for forest and mountain."

"Four days is plenty of time to set all in motion, Ship Who Sings."

This Helvana sounded not the least bit alarmed, as she bloody well should have been.

"You don't understand, Hel . . . Helvana. These men are pirates, vicious. They have no mercy on their victims . . ."

"Show them the tape," Niall said.

"This is what they did on the planet Bethel," she said, and activated the exterior display, using the whitewashed façade of the imposing main building as a screen.

"That will not be necessary," Helvana said. "Turn it off now. Please!" And, since some of the captive audience looked decidedly unnerved by the first scene of battle-armored Kolnari making mighty jumps towards screaming and panicking Bethelites, Helva found herself obeying. "There is absolutely no need to terrify. NO need at all."

"But there is, Helvana. Those men . . ."

"May I speak to you in private, Ship Who Sings?"

"I wouldn't like to go against that one," Niall said. "She's tough."

"Yes, of course," Helva said to the Helvana. And then to Niall, "Get lost!"

"Immediately," Niall said, rising and skittering off to his quarters.

The Helvana was tall enough to have to duck her head to clear the lintel of the opening and stood for a moment, looking calmly around her, a little smile flickering at the corners of her mouth. Then, to Helva's surprise, she bowed with great reverence toward the central panel behind which Helva's titanium shell was situated.

"I have dreamed of being granted such a moment, Ship Who Sings," she said, her voice vibrant with exultation.

"Please be seated in the lounge on your right," Helva said.

The Helvana took a second look at the raised bridge area that had been Niall's favorite place and turned to the lounge area. With considerable grace, the heavy folds of her cassock flowing around her feet and her heavy boots grating on the metal part of the deck, she reached the first of the sectional couches. With another bow, she seated herself facing Helva's panel.

"I must tell you, Ship Who Sings, that the pitiful colony of the religious you rescued from Ravel's nova learned from that basic mistake."

"I am pleased to hear that," Helva began, "but you must . . ."

The graceful hand raised from the deep-cuffed sleeve. "There was much to be learned if the Inner Marian Circle would survive the science of your civilization."

"Really?" Helva decided that this was a time to listen.

"The satellite will have sent its preprogrammed message even as I am certain you sent messages?" Her voice ended on an upward querying note.

"Several, with such details of the invading force as I was able to glean. But, really, Helvana, they're going . . ."

The hand raised and Helva subsided. She did have four days in hand.

"My grandmother . . ."

Well, that was unexpected.

". . . Was one of those whom you yourself rescued. A wise but older Christian sisterhood succored her and the other younger members of that community until a new planet could be found for our Order. And they acquired much wisdom during their waiting."

"Not, however, how to combat bloodthir . . ."

The hand went up and Helva subsided again.

"We had been children on Chloe, ignorant and kept in ignorance when knowledge would have saved us, and the Blessed Jennan. My grandmother studied much, as did her intimate circle. With prayer and research, we found that this planet was available. A stable primary was our first consideration, of course," she said with a graceful wave of her hand. "Surveys of Ravel proved it would be adequate for our needs and our preferred style of life once we overcame its . . . nature. The planet has inherent dangers. Indeed we were required to devise a means whereby we could safely land the first colony expedition." Her expression became distant with memories, but she pulled herself back to the present with a little shake of her head. "We were averse to the use of technology, but that, in the end, was what we required and what we still employ. We have maintained the landing site out of respect for the achievement of technology over rampant nature. The touch of a switch will deter any unwelcome . . . visitors."

She was talking a great deal more rationally than that rabid idiot Mother Superior at Chloe had. But defending the broad open plains of this Ravel would be the task of an army. A much-better-equipped one than these people could possibly mount.

"We have cultivated not only the land, but the resources of the vegetation and wildlife. There are predators on Ravel . . ."

"Not anything that could overcome a battle-armed Kolnari . . ."

The Helvana smiled.

"How many are in this Kolnari battle armor?"

Well, that was the first sensible question.

"I'd estimate five, maybe six regiments."

Her well-shaped eyebrows arched in surprise. "How many are in a regiment?"

Helva told her.

"That many?"

"Yes, that many, and impregnable in that battle armor, too. Unless you happen to have armor-piercing missiles hidden in your fields."

"Nothing to pierce armor," the Helvana said blithely, with a light emphasis on "pierce." "But we will defend ourselves well."

"Don't even consider hand-to-hand combat, Helvana," Helva said.

"Oh"—and there was a lovely rippling contralto laugh—"we wouldn't consider attacking anyone."

"Then HOW do you plan to deal with the Kolnari?"

"May I surprise you?"

"If it doesn't lead immediately to your death and the slaughter of all those innocents out there."

"It won't."

"Which reminds me, Helvana, I saw young children out there, and teenage girls as well as matrons your age and older."

Helva had been reviewing her tapes, because something had puzzled her about the composition of those calm observers.

"Ah, yes," the Helvana said, smiling graciously. "My grandmother also decided that our community must propagate . . ."

"Parthenogenesis?"

"Oh, no, that would have been against our precepts. We brought with us sufficient fertilized female ova, removed from our Faithful, to supply us with the necessary diverse genetic balance to ensure that our community will last for centuries."

"Clever," Helva said.

"Not the least of our . . . cleverness, Ship Who Sings."

Just then Helva's outside sensors picked up a little cough and she became aware that a covey of girls was standing just outside the hatch.

"I think they wish to speak to you, Helvana," the ship said. "Come on in, girls."

Their faces either red with embarrassment or white with exultation, the young women entered, bowing with varying degrees of grace as the Helvana had done, towards Helva's panel. Did the whole damned planet know where *she* lived?

"The birds have flown, Helvana. And some nearby have responded."

Helvana nodded, pleased. "Enter the responses and report back when all have answered."

The girls left in a flurry, but not before a second obeisance to Helva.

"You've trained avians as messengers?"

"It seemed wise since there are such distances between our communities and decisions must be circulated when necessary."

"Does every community have a . . . Helvana?"

"No, I am the one so honored by my peers."

"How long will you serve, if that is the correct phrase?"

"It is you I serve," the Helvana said with great dignity. "When I know myself too old to continue intelligent administration, my successor will be installed, chosen from among those who are diligent in learning the canon and tradition of our Circle."

"Well, yes, but let's get to the point. DO you have some safe refuge where you can't be found until the Fleet arrives?"

"Ravel supplies our defense," Helvana said, again with the confident smile.

"Enlighten me, then, because I have every reason to fear for your safety."

"You must look more closely at Ravel."

"Don't tell me you've trained the predators to defend you?"

"No, the planet itself will."

"Well, if your defense is classified, I assure you I won't disclose your methods but the Kolnari are the most effective and ruthless fighting force of all humanoids. They . . ."

"Against other humans, quite likely . . ."

"They have weaponry"—and Helva was getting a bit tired of this woman's self-confident denial of any threat—"that could turn this settlement into a cinder . . ."

"From the air?" And there was just a touch of fear in this Helvana's voice.

"You're lucky," Helva said dryly, "the Kolnari strategy is based more on overwhelming their target with ground forces. Of course, your satellite warning system'll be blasted out of space as soon as they spot it, but the bunch that's headed here don't have any assault ships, unless they've modified some of the bigger yachts. And all of *them* seem so full of bodies that I doubt they are armed with space-to-surface missiles, too. Though," Helva added thoughtfully, "they could be. However, they think they have total surprise as an advantage to a quick rout."

The Helvana crossed her arms and said, not quite smugly, "Then we shall not be harmed."

"Look, their ships are crammed with bodies, bodies which intend to take over *this* planet for their purposes which, I assure you, you won't like. You have no armament . . ."

"We need none . . ."

"So you say, but you've never seen the Kolnari take over a planet. Let me just show you how they conquered . . ."

Helvana held up her hand. "God forfend."

"He's not in a position to forfend anything. Look, you've got to take precautions."

"They are already in place."

"What?"

"The planet itself."

"And round and round we go," Helva said, irked. "This is Chloe all over again with a slightly different scenario," she said, allowing her irritation to show in her voice. "You won't be fried by the sun this time but by . . ."

"No." And Helvana held up a hand with such authority that Helva broke off. "You will have noticed that our settlements, large and small, are walled . . ."

"Not much good against Kolnari battle-armored troops . . ."

"Who will not get close enough to our walls . . . Nor do we go beyond them very often, for it is the vegetation of Ravel that is danger-ous to all. Even the predators venture out only on cold nights when the planet sleeps."

"Come again?"

Helvana's smile just missed being a smirk and she cocked her head slightly at Helva. "How much would these Kolnari know about our planet?"

"Only what is in the Galactic Atlas."

"May I see that entry?"

Helva brought it up on the main-lounge screen and the Helvana read it swiftly, smiling her smile as she finished.

"There have been no additions. As promised."

"I do wish I could be as confident as you are," Helva said.

The Helvana rose. "The last time it was the primary which would destroy us. This time the planet will work for us. One question: since the entry indicates a spaceport, will the Kolnari land there first? To organize their invasion?"

Helva thought of that battered collection of ships. "They use whatever's available. They've enough ships to use all the space the landing field offers. Though, in my judgment," she added grimly, "some of them may not make a controlled landing." She paused, wondering if in those dilapidated buildings there were any emergency vehicles or equipment. Then she ruthlessly decided that a few Kolnari would not be missed. "Some are barely spaceworthy, and one was leaking oxygen. You must realize that this is the Kolnari's last-gasp attempt to resettle. They'll fight whatever you have in mind to put against them. They must know this planet is a walkover."

"Not . . ." Helvana paused with an inscrutable twist to her lips. ". . . an easy walkover. Not by any means."

"They do have arsenals of some pretty sophisticated weapons," Helva reminded her guest. "Don't discount the possibility of an air-to-surface barrage to soften you up."

Helvana actually chuckled. "What? Bomb our fields and settlements? If their object is to settle here, they wouldn't destroy available housing or crops."

"You don't know the Kolnari as I do, Helvana. Don't treat this lightly."

"I assure you I do not," the woman said, and her face assumed a concerned and serious expression. "Our fields, our homes would be targeted?"

"Very likely, although it is equally likely that, fearing no resistance, they may just land and march . . ."

"Oh, I do hope so," said the Helvana, one moment her face brightening with something akin to triumph, instantly fading to self-recrimination. "We do not take pleasure in destruction of any kind on Ravel."

"Even to save your lives?"

"Your presence, and your warning, is sufficient." The Helvana rose.

"I have no weapons, no way to defend you," Helva said, unable to keep the frustration and anger out of her voice.

The woman turned, inclining her head. "That is known, so you must seek safety yourself. I know little of what transpires in other sections of the Universe, and your pictures showed us it is not a safe place in which to reside, so you are at risk. You have warned us. We are advised. We shall be safe. Go you to be safe, too, Ship Who Sings."

"I can't JUST LEAVE YOU!" Helva's voice rose and she could hear it resounding outside, causing some of the women still gathered in groups in the plaza to turn around.

"As you cannot defend yourself," Helvana said in a tone that implied Helva was indeed more at risk than her adherents were, "you must depart. I have much to organize."

"Well, I'm glad to hear that," Helva said in a caustic tone.

The woman turned at the airlock, made a deep and respectful obeisance, and strode down the ramp. Immediately she began issuing commands that had all the onlookers scurrying to obey. In moments the plaza was empty and the Helvana had reentered the church or administration building or whatever it was.

"Well, well." And Niall peered around the edge of the corridor that led to his quarters. "That one has style!"

"She's no smarter than that rabid, ranting ascetic on Chloe!" Helva's voice crackled with anger. "As if I'm the one who's vulnerable."

"What was that about the vegetation?" Niall asked. "And close the hatch, love. I don't want someone peering in and catching sight of a MAAAALE . . ." He jiggled his hands in clownish antic and dragged out the last word.

"What about the vegetation?" Helva demanded irritably as she retracted the ramp and shut off access.

"I'd say it's dangerous and the power to the walls is to keep it at bay. Remember the roads here? All with neat margins . . . and haven't been used . . . and they employ birds to carry messages? Doesn't that suggest to you they don't wander much from the walls of their cloisters?"

Helva thought about that possibility. "As a weapon against the Kolnari?" she demanded with trenchant incredulity.

"We can cloak and watch," Niall said, cocking his head slightly at something he had perceived that eluded her. "That lady seemed far too certain of their . . . indigenous . . . protections. And we haven't seen everything on this world yet, now have we?"

Helva had been scanning with her exterior sensors, and except for birds coming in to land on what she had initially thought to be multiple chimneys but were rooftop aviaries, she reconsidered the situation.

"I'm going to try another of their settlements," she said, and, making sure there were no bodies anywhere near her, lifted slowly.

The plaza was so hard-packed from much usage that only little swirls of dust marked her ascent.

She tried nine settlements, medium, small and another large one, but each time the head woman of the group, while respectful in all other ways, replied that there was no need this time for The Ship Who Sings to worry about Ravellians. But it was good of her to appear to warn them that a time of trial was coming. Helva tried to show the hologram and, after the first horrified glances, everyone turned their backs, squeezing their eyes closed against the proof she tried to exhibit.

"I don't think it's a case of your losing your touch," Niall said kindly, drumming silent fingers on the armrest. "They honestly believe they're safe. Not that the mere odor of sanctity ever saved a saint and certainly won't save these sisters from the Kolnari. But, in case you've been fretting too much to notice, every single one of the walls around these cloisters is on full power."

"Where're the sources? That's something the Kolnari will spot if they make even the most routine scan or aerial reconnaissance." And Helva was more afraid than ever. On the previous occasion, the expanding sun itself had provided proof positive of danger to the doubting religious. What would it take to prove it this time? And why was she stuck with this gullible lot again?

She kept trying and kept getting the same responses from all ninety-seven cloisters she visited. On the way to the ninety-eighth, they saw the spark of bright light in the sky that indicated the Kolnari had just demolished the satellite.

"Nice of them to give us fair warning. Now's the time to cloak, Helva," Niall remarked, his fingers in their restless dance on the armrests.

"I have been while I was flying between these damnable stubborn towns," she replied curtly, and headed towards the pathetic landing field. Since it was there, and nothing else on this vegetating world offered any other large cleared space as a come-on to the Kolnari, she figured that would be where the invaders would land.

At dawn, she and Niall arrived close enough to the landing site, hovering just behind the nearest of the hills that surrounded the facility.

"Ah-ha," Niall said in a thoughtful drawl, as he leaned across the control board to peer at the forward view screen. He flipped on each of the exterior viewers, reducing them to a patchwork that made Helva almost dizzy until she spotted what had alerted him.

The landing field, once unpatterned, level soil, had sprouted the most obscene-looking ground cover, greasy, slimy, a sort of pus yellow and mold green. No more than a few centimeters high. Undoubtedly it gave a smooth, even appearance to anyone above.

"Those are not my favorite colors for a solid footing, Helva," Niall said in a low ominous tone. "Let's just hover and shelter in our cloak."

"Excellent notion," she said, noticing on the port sensor near the prow of her ship that tendrils thrust up towards her, lashing in their attempt to snare the ship. She put more distance between herself and the ground. "Very interesting indeed. Malevolent vegetation."

Niall began rubbing his hands, an unholy expression on his face. "Serves the bastards right. Though let's hope their disintegrating metabolism doesn't affect the stuff. They're mean enough to poison anything that doesn't poison them first."

"They may have met their match," she replied, willing to be convinced.

The first two Kolnari ships to land were two of the heavier, armed cruisers. They landed smack-dab in the middle of the greasy sward and instantly deployed their armored infantry units while gunners started setting up their portable projectile units. They didn't, as Helva half expected them to, take out the rickety old buildings, which were now covered with viler chartreusey green vines. Not that the Kolnari were apt to be color-conscious. Much less suspicious. Their home world was noted for its offputting appearance.

The troops marched off the landing field, kicking their metallic booted feet at now calf-high shrubs and bushes that impeded their progress, ignorant of the fact that the growths were brand-new additions on the field. They had split into four sections and each started off up one of the main tracks. Three more of the larger ships landed at one edge of the field, crowded with additional troops, who set off after the vanguard, smaller units turning off at each arterial lane. In quick succession, the yacht-sized spacecraft zoomed in, one or two making such rough landings that they plowed their noses into the ground. They were instantly covered with tendrils and twigs that shortly turned into thick branches, wrapping about the ships, tethering them to the field. Had these not been Kolnari whose prime intent was capture and enslavement of the Ravellians, Helva might have been tempted to warn those unarmed, unsuited people who swarmed out of the ships, coughing, falling to the ground, raising arms upward as if they had just been saved. From dying of asphyxia they had. But Ravel's indigenous vegetation vigorously began to engulf them . . . consuming their still-living forms . . . to judge by the frantic green-covered contortions and the screams, shrieks and tortured calls. The seeking vines penetrated the open hatches, cutting off the escape of any who saw what was happening and thought of seeking safety inside.

There was undoubtedly not even time for one of the more intelligent captains to warn off the rest of the armada, which continued to touch down wherever they could. Remaining aloft did not seem to have been an option. Every passenger was in too much of a hurry to disembark to notice what had been happening to the earlier arrivals.

"Truly a just retribution has been meted out to them," Niall muttered. "A planet fighting back!" The verdure kept moving, probing, twining, inserting itself everywhere, bursting the seams of some of the oldest and most fragile vessels. "After all the violence they have dealt out to unsuspecting and innocent populations . . ." His voice trailed off and he snapped off the screen displays of the chartreuse catastrophe.

Without a word, Helva lifted and started up the nearest track, actually the one that headed towards the main settlement, to see what the flora of Ravel was doing to the armored infantry units. The demise of the ground troops—none of which reached even the nearest and smallest of the cloisters—only took a little longer, though they didn't penetrate even within howling distance of any of the cloisters.

"The weeds must exude some really corrosive kind of acid. Look at the pockmarks—holes even—in some of that armor where the vine tips have lashed it," Niall said, shaking his head in amazement. "How do the girls manage that stuff if it can do that to spaceworthy body armor?"

"I do not care so long as it is as effective as it seems to be."

Belatedly realizing the danger they were in, the bold Kolnari were, of course, turning their weapons on the demon flora that was smothering them. Perhaps someone on the space field had lasted long enough to send out a message. But on this field of battle the Kolnari weapons increased, rather than decreased, the foe. Blasting or flaming the vegetable matter only caused it to fragment, each part then expanding and multiplying into more attackers. Kolnari warriors in their heavy boots were being tripped up and, once down, became greeny yellow mounds of writhing shrubbery. Their power packs would have been infiltrated by vine tips, their equipment shorted out. Safe now from Kolnari weapons, Helva uncloaked and recorded the Kolnari defeat, focusing occasionally on what happened when flora was fragmented. She stayed high enough above the carnage . . . or did she mean "vernage" . . . to avoid any contact. She thought—only briefly—of trying to acquire a leaf or twig to preserve—at maximum botanical security—for later analysis in the High Risk laboratories at Central Worlds.

"I've never seen anything like it," Niall said, shaking his head. "We do know that there are inimical planetary surfaces, but one which can be contained, tamed, and used in emergencies? One more for the files!" Then he leaned back in the chair, locking his fingers and rubbing his palms together with the great satisfaction he enjoyed at this totally unexpected Kolnari defeat. "Those lassies learned a thing or two, didn't they, about passive resistance."

"Passive wasn't what we just witnessed," Helva said drolly. "They simply let the nature of the planet take its course. Mind you, somewhere in the ethics of their Marian religiosity there must be a shibboleth about taking human lives . . ."

"Ha! I never considered the Kolnari as humans," was Niall's response. "Besides which, the religious have as much right to protect themselves as any other life-form."

"THEY aren't doing anything. The planet is. That's the beauty part."

"Ah, yes." And Niall's tone turned sanctimonious. "Suffer the meek for they shall inherit the earth . . . of Ravel, in this case. Well-done, ladies, well-done." He brought his hands together in a silent applause. "We should extend our felicities. Or you should."

"I think the outcome was not only taken for granted but has been observed," Helva said, and activated a long-range screen that showed little flocks of avians circling here and there, before darting off so quickly not even Helva could have plotted so many different course directions.

When Helva touched down again in the plaza, the Helvana and a group of about fourteen awaited her. They wore long black scarves and tight-fitting black caps.

"'We come to mourn Caesar not to praise him,'" Niall quoted.

"Get thee hence, Marc Antony," she replied warningly.

"I'm going. I'm going. I'll not attend this wake in mournful array."

"You're already arrayed appropriately," she called after his disappearing figure, then opened her airlock and extended the ramp.

The deputation entered, making obeisance to her until all had filed into the lounge, their expression somber if respectful, though some were red-eyed with weeping. There would be some tender hearts among such a group. Why they'd spend their tears on the Kolnari, when they knew what would have been their fate, defeated Helva's understanding. But then, she was not religious. She spoke first, not wishing to be embroiled in specious gratitude for this second inadvertent "deliverance" in which she had been only a passive spectator, not the rescue vehicle.

"I apologize, Helvana, for doubting your efficiency and ingenuity. The meek have indeed inherited this earth."

Helva devoutly hoped that no one else heard the scoffing snort from the passageway.

"We all deeply regret that we had to prove our invulnerability on Ravel," the Helvana said in a slow, sad tone. "We shall pray for their departed souls."

"I sincerely doubt they had any," Helva said, an acid remark that occasioned gasps of surprise from some of the younger women. "Uncharitable of me, I know, but I have seen their form of conquest at firsthand. I do not regret their destruction. Nor should any here shed any more remorseful tears or rue the incident. The Universe is now considerably safer. After all, none of you . . ." She paused briefly. ". . . did anything. Your planet is well able to take care of unwanted visitors and has done so."

There was a brief awkward pause, while the faithful dealt with the unexpected candor of their "savior." To fill in the silence, Helva went on.

"How long will it take you to repair the damage to the space field and the tracks?"

"We may not," the Helvana said after glancing at her companions. "We keep in touch with the other cloisters and there is really no need for all to assemble at the same time. Each community is self-sufficient and there is no longer any need for the space field."

"But you'll keep the walls functioning."

A little smile tugged at the Helvana's lips. "Yes." She inclined her head. "They are required to keep the flora of Ravel in its place."

"But surely those plant forms that have had such . . ." Helva hesitated, not wishing to upset the tenderhearted with the word "fertilizing." ". . . unexpected freedom will wish to retain it?"

"What needs to be restored will be. It is a long and painstaking process and we have much to occupy ourselves in the normal course of our daily routine," the Helvana said.

One of her escort pulled at her sleeve.

"Yes, of course, and our eternal gratitude to you should have been spoken of first," Helvana said kindly to the woman. "We are once again in your debt, Ship Who Sings, and once again have no way to repay your watchful guardianship."

"If I said I only happened to be in the neighborhood, would you believe me?" Helva asked gently.

There was just a hint of a sparkle in the Helvana's eyes as she caught the irony.

"Let us then hope that we have not caused you an unnecessary delay," the Helvana said.

"No, you have not," Helva replied more graciously. Perversely, she really didn't want to destroy her reputation among the cloisters. "I will not be late arriving at my destination." Since she wasn't expected at Regulus, that was no lie. More worldly remarks must be made however. "I shall apprise the Fleet that they may stand down from the alert I sent out. I shall report the demise . . ."

That rattled them all but the Helvana raised her hand and the startled expressions of dismay were silenced.

"Let not death be part of the message. Merely that the . . . emergency has been dealt with," the Helvana said with great dignity.

"So it shall be said," Helva replied solemnly, though she was in honor bound to inform the Fleet that the Kolnari were well and truly annihilated. "If I may suggest it, I would feel better if you let me have the satellite beacon replaced: the one that the . . . recent visitors blasted from your skies so you will not be further interrupted." Once the fate dealt the Kolnari invaders was known, no one would dare land on Ravel. "May I attend to that detail for you?"

"There is a small group of our Marian Circle on Vega III," the Helvana said. "If you would be good enough to inform them that . . . a replacement satellite is required, they will attend to the expense and installation. You need not be troubled with such a detail."

"It would not trouble me," Helva said. "But I will inform your sisters in religion of the need and your continued safety. No debt exists between us, wise and good Helvana. I was here when I was needed as I was at Chloe. That is enough."

"So be it," the Helvana said, bowing her head in acceptance while the others murmured the same response. Then, with firm gestures, she led the delegation to the airlock, standing to one side as each made proper obeisance to Helva's column. This took long enough so that Helva was getting fidgety. She adjusted her nutrient flow to account for the recent stress.

The Helvana hesitated after she made her deep bow.

"We shall pray for your lost partner," she said, and inclined her head in the direction of Niall's cabin. "May you be comforted in his loss by another as worthy to hold his position as Niall Parollan."

She was gone, leaving Helva so stunned that she couldn't speak.

"Pray for me, indeed!" snapped Niall's crisp voice as he strode into the main cabin.

Helva closed the airlock with a clang.

"How did she know that piece of gossip?" Niall went on, "And let's get off this planet. Gives me the creeps, all those women weeping over Kolnari. Much less me."

Somehow Helva went through the necessary routines to lift her ship-self as adroitly as possible. The plaza was clear of all save the Helvana and her delegation, backed up against the main building, forming an orderly triangle on the steps, with the Helvana at the apex. From her stern sensors, Helva saw the upturned faces as the faithful watched the sight of *their* Ship ascending once again into the heavens from which she had come to succor them.

"They never will believe you were 'just in the neighborhood,' you know," Niall said, but there was an odd quirk to his lips. "At least that wise one won't."

"We were," Helva replied, more involved with figuring out how the Helvana had known of Niall's death when the woman had been no farther inside the ship than the airlock and the lounge. What astonished her even more was that the Helvana's blessing *did* comfort her.

Once clear of the system, Helva sent out an All-Points saying that the emergency was over and that she could report the extermination of the remnants of the Kolnari fleet; full details would be presented at Regulus on her arrival there. She did not give an estimated time, though she encountered several picket forces making all possible speed in obedience to her summons. She knew they were disappointed about losing a chance to gain fame and promotion fighting the last remnants of the Kolnari but she advised them that the Ravellians were not people interested in having quests. Ever. She could, and did, patch across the tapes she had taken of the disastrous Kolnari defeat. Obliquely she kept her word to the Helvana while still satisfying Fleet Intelligence. What she didn't realize was that her reticence only added to the glamour surrounding her living legend.

She met up with the escort five days out of the Regulus system, two squadrons no less. And with a Commodore on board the Nova Class flagship.

"Commodore Halliman reporting, ma'am, as escort for yourself and Niall Parollan," was the initial message and there was the happily grinning Commodore, in full-dress uniform, on the bridge of the battle cruiser. He glanced around, expecting to see Helva's brawn.

"I bring back the body of my scout, Niall Parollan, Commodore," she said more calmly than she expected she could. The Helvana's prayers were working?

"I hadn't known . . ." The Commodore was patently shocked, and she could hear a murmur run around the bridge at such news. "My condolences and apologies. You have sustained a great loss. Was he a casualty of the Kolnari action?"

"Niall Parollan died quietly in his sleep. The diagnosis was total systems failure caused by extreme age," she said. She went on before she'd be asked the time and place of death. Stasis provided no clues. "He requested the ceremonies due his rank and service, Commodore," she went on, smiling inwardly at Niall's idea of a reward for putting up with her for so many years.

"Only his just due, ma'am. We shall proceed with the arrangements immediately . . . if that is your wish."

"It is," she said with a gentle sigh. Actually, that program hadn't been such a bad idea at all. It *had* given her time to become accustomed to the fact of Niall's death. *Death, Death, where is thy sting? Grave thy victory?*

"Our deepest sympathies," said the Commodore, and saluted with solemn precision. Behind him she saw others come smartly to attention and salute. "The NH-834 made inestimable contributions to the Service."

"Niall was a paragon of partners," she replied. "You'll forgive me if I resume my silence." She really didn't mean to misrepresent any facet of her recent history, but there were certain details she intended to keep hidden in her head.

"Don't think that's going to get you off the hook of explaining the Kolnari defeat, my pet," Niall said. He had been propping up a wall just beyond the view of the one screen she had activated to receive the Commodore's call. "And will I have performed my part there in true heroic form?"

"What else? I'll not have you go to your grave without every bit of honor due you. And you did perform your designated role on Ravel. You stayed out of sight."

"Not entirely, evidently," Niall said with a wicked grin, waggling a finger at her.

"If you mean that Helvana woman's little surprise remark, forget that. A lucky guess, since she would have known I'd have to have had a brawn with me somewhere."

"She knew me by name."

"Maybe she can talk to the dead. And you are dead, you know. Can't you stay down?"

"Why should I? Miss my own obsequies? How can you ask that of me?" He pressed one hand against his chest in dismay.

She laughed. "I should have known you'd pull a Tom Sawyer."

He laughed, too. "Why not, since you have provided me the ability to watch? I've always wanted to hear what people thought of me."

"You won't hear any candor at your funeral. It's not good manners to speak ill of the dead, you know. Besides which, I do NOT want Psych checking my synapses for fear I've blown a few by concocting your holo program."

"No one will see me, my love, I assure you," he said.

She had intended to delete the program totally, even the petabytes that had once stored it, when she reached Regulus Base. Now she changed her mind. He had the right to see the ceremony: all of it from the slow march with his bier, the atmosphere planes doing their wing-tipping salute, the volley of rifles, the whole nine yards of changeless requiem for the honored dead. This time, she was not mourning the sudden, unnecessary death of a beloved partner: she was celebrating the long and fruitful life of a dear friend whom she would also never forget.

When the burial detail came to collect the mortal husk, the stasis in the coffin replaced that in which she had held his body intact during her long journey home. Regulus officialdom turned out in force, from the Central Worlds' current Administrative Chief with every one of his aides in formal-dress parade uniforms to the planetary Governor in her very elegant black dress and fashionable hat, to the parade of mixed armed services as well as whatever brawns were on the Base, and all the brawn trainees. The service was just long enough. A little longer and she'd have believed the fulsome eulogies about the man they mourned, who was sitting in the pilot's chair and watching the entire show with the greatest of satisfaction. She'd remember that as the best part of the whole show.

"I wouldn't have missed this for the damned Horsehead Nebula we never did get to," he exclaimed several times. As Helva was parked where her cabin could not be seen from those either on the ground or on the raised platform for the dignitaries, he could peer about, wisecracking and reminiscing as he chose.

She did, as she had done before and as it was expected of Helva, the ship who sings, let the heavens resound with the poignant strains of the service song of evening and requiem. But this time her tone was triumphant, and as her last note died away across the cemetery and all the bowed heads, she deleted Niall's holographic program.

They left her alone until she had decided she'd had enough solitude. She ought to have held off deleting Niall a few days longer, but there was a time to end things, and his funeral had been it. Then she contacted Headquarters.

"This is the XH-834 requesting a new brawn," she said, "and you'd better arrange a time for the Fleet to query me on that Ravel incident. I want it down on the records straight. I want a top priority message to the Marian Circle Cloister on Vega III that Ravel needs to have its warning satellite replaced. The Kolnari blew the old one out of space."

"New brawn?" repeated the woman who had responded to her call. Her brain had gone into neutral at being unexpectedly contacted by the XH-834.

"Yes, a new brawn." Helva then repeated her other requests. "Got them? Good. Please expedite. And, as soon as you've informed the brawn barracks of my availability, patch me over whatever missions are currently available for a brain ship with my experience."

"Yes, indeed, XH-834, yes indeed." There was a pause through which Helva heard only sharp excited words clipped off before she quite caught any of the agitated sentences. Surprise always gives you an advantage.

She laughed with pure vindictive satisfaction as the brawn barracks erupted with people hastily flinging on tunics or fixing their hair or adjusting buttons. The scene brought back fond memories as the young men and women, all determined to win this prize of prizes, raced to be first aboard her.

They had not quite reached the ramp when she suddenly became aware of a hazy object. The outlines were misty, but it was Niall Parollan, striding to her column, laying his cheek once more against the panel that covered her.

"Don't give the next one any more grief than you gave me, will you, love?" He started to turn away, his outline noticeably fading. "And if you ever use that Sorg Prosthesis with anyone else but me, I'll kill him! Got that?"

She thought she muttered something as she watched his image

drift to the hull by the forward screen, not towards the airlock. Just as she heard the stampede of the brawns outside, he disappeared altogether with one last wave of a hand that seemed to flow into the metal of her ship-self.

"Permission to come aboard, ma'am?" a breathless voice asked.

THE WAY

Greg Bear

Eon (1985)
Eternity (1988)
Legacy (1995)

Once upon a very long extension, not precisely time nor any space we know, there existed an endless hollow thread of adventure and commerce called the Way, introduced in Eon. The Way, an artificial universe fifty kilometers in diameter and infinitely long, was created by the human inhabitants of an asteroid starship called Thistledown. They had become bored with their seemingly endless journey between the stars; the Way, with its potential of openings to other times and other universes, made reaching their destination unnecessary.

That the Way was destroyed (in *Eternity*) is known; that it never ends in any human space or time is less obvious.

Even before its creators completed their project, the Way was discovered and invaded by the very non-human Jarts, who sought to announce themselves to Deity, what they called Descendant Mind, by absorbing and understanding everything, everywhere. The Jarts nearly destroyed the Way's creators, but were held at bay for a time, and for a price.

Yet there were stranger encounters. The plexus of universes is beyond the mind of any individual, human or Jart.

One traveler experienced more of this adventure than any other. His name was Olmy Ap Sennen. In his centuries of life, he lived to see himself become a living myth, be forgotten, rediscovered, and made myth again. So many stories have been told of Olmy that history and myth intertwine.

This story is set early in his life. Olmy has experienced only one reincarnation (*Legacy*). In fee for his memories, he has been rewarded with a longing to return to death everlasting.

—*Greg Bear*

The Way of All Ghosts
A Myth from Thistledown

by

Greg Bear

For William Hope Hodgson

"Probabilities fluctuated wildly, but always passed through zero, and gate openers, their equipment, and all associated personnel within a few hundred meters of the gate, were swallowed by a null that can only be described in terms of mathematics. It became difficult to remember that they had ever existed; records of their histories were corrupted or altered, even though they lay millions of kilometers from the incident. We had tapped into the geometric blood of the gods. But we knew we had to continue. We were compelled."

—

Testimony of Master Gate Opener Ry Ornis, Secret Hearings Conducted by the Infinite Hexamon Nexus, "On the Advisability of Opening Gates into Chaos and Order"

The ghost of his last lover found Olmy Ap Sennen in the oldest columbarium of Alexandria, within the second chamber of Thistledown.

Olmy stood in the middle of the hall, surrounded by stacked tiers of hundreds of small golden spheres. The spheres were urns, most of them containing only a sample of ashes. They rose to the glassed-in ceiling, held within columns of gentle yellow suspension fields. He reached out to touch a blank silver plate at the base of one column. The names of the dead appeared as if suddenly engraved, one after another.

He removed his hand when the names reached *Ilmo, Paul Yan*. This is where the soldiers from his childhood neighborhood were honored; in this column, five names, all familiar to him from days in school, all killed in a single skirmish with the Jarts near 3 ex 9, three billion kilometers down the Way. All had been obliterated without trace. These urns were empty.

He did not know the details. He did not need to. These dead had served Thistledown as faithfully as Olmy, but they would never return.

Olmy had spent seventy-three years stranded on the planet Lamarckia, in the service of the Hexamon, cut off from Thistledown and the Way that stretched beyond the asteroid's seventh chamber. On Lamarckia, he had raised children, loved and buried wives . . . lived a long and memorable life in primitive conditions on an extraordinary world. His rescue and return to the Way, converted within days from an old and dying man to a fresh-bodied youth, had been a shock worse than the return of any real and ancient ghost.

Axis City, slung on the singularity that occupied the geodesic center of the Way, had been completed during those tumultuous years before Olmy's rescue and resurrection. It had moved four hundred thousand kilometers "north," down the Way, far from the seventh chamber cap. Within the Geshel precincts of Axis City, the mental patterns of many who died were now transferred to City Memory, a technological afterlife not very different from the ancient dream of heaven. Using similar technology, temporary partial personalities could be created to help an individual multi-task. These were sometimes called ghosts. Olmy had heard of partials, sent to do the bidding of their originals, with most of their mental faculties duplicated, but limited power to make decisions. He had never actually met one, however.

The ghost appeared just to his right and announced its nature by flickering slightly, growing translucent, then briefly turning into a negative. This display lasted only a few seconds. After, the simulacrum seemed perfectly solid and real. Olmy jumped, disoriented, then surveyed the ghost's features. He shook his head and smiled wryly.

"It will give my original joy to find you well," the partial said. "You seem lost, Ser Olmy."

Olmy did not quite know what form of speech to use with the partial. Should he address it with respect due to the original, a corprep and a woman of influence . . . The last woman he had tried to be in love with . . . Or as he might address a servant?

"I come here often. Old acquaintances."

The image looked concerned. "Poor Olmy. Still don't belong anywhere?"

Olmy ignored this. He looked for the ghost's source. It was projected from a fist-sized flier hovering several meters away.

"I'm here on behalf of my original, corporeal representative Neya Taur Rinn. You realize . . . I am not her?"

"I'm not ignorant," Olmy said sharply, finding himself once more at a disadvantage with this woman.

The ghost fixed her gaze on him. The image, of course, was not actually doing the seeing. "The Presiding Minister of the Way, Yanosh Ap Kesler, instructed me to find you. My original was reluctant. I hope you understand."

Olmy folded his hands behind his back as the partial picted a series of ID symbols: Office of the Presiding Minister, Hexamon Nexus Office of Way Defense, Office of Way Maintenance. Quite a stack of bureaucracies, Olmy thought, Way Maintenance currently being perhaps the most powerful and arrogant of them all.

"What does Yanosh want with me?" he asked bluntly.

The ghost lifted her hands and pointed her index finger into her palm, tapping with each point. "You supported him in his bid to become Presiding Minister of the Seventh Chamber and the Way. You've become a symbol for the advance of Geshel interests."

"Against my will," Olmy said. Yanosh, a fervent progressive and Geshel, had sent Olmy to Lamarckia—and had also brought him back and arranged for his new body. Olmy for his own part had never known quite which camp he belonged to: conservative Naderites, grimly opposed to the extraordinary advances of the last century, or the enthusiastically progressive Geshels.

Neya Taur Rinn's people were Geshels of an ancient radical faction, among the first to move into Axis City. "Ser Kesler has won reelection as presiding minister of the Way and now also serves as mayor of three precincts in Axis City."

"I'm aware of that."

"Of course. The Presiding Minister extends his greetings and hopes you are agreeable."

"I am very agreeable," Olmy said mildly. "I stay out of politics and disagree with nobody. I can't pay back Yanosh for all he has done—but then, I have rendered him due service as well." He did not like being baited—and could not understand why Yanosh would send Neya to fetch him. The Presiding Minister knew enough about Olmy's private life—probably too much. "Yanosh knows I've put myself on permanent leave." Olmy could not restrain himself. "Pardon me for boldness, but I'm curious. How do you feel? Do you actually *think* you are Neya Taur Rinn?"

The partial smiled. "I am a high-level partial given subordinate authority by my original," it said. *She* said . . . Olmy decided he would not cut such fine distinctions.

"Yes, but what does it *feel* like?" he asked.

"At least you're still alive enough to be curious," the partial said.

"Your original regarded my curiosity as a kind of perversity," Olmy said.

"A morbid curiosity," the partial returned, clearly uncomfortable. "I couldn't stand maintaining a relationship with a man who wanted to be *dead.*"

"You rode my fame until I bored you," Olmy rejoined, then regretted the words. He used old training to damp his sharper emotions.

"To answer your question, I *feel* everything my original would feel. And my original would hate to see you here. What do *you* feel like, Ser Olmy?" The ghost's arm swung out to take in the urns, the columbarium. "Coming here, walking among the dead, that's pretty melodramatic."

That a ghost could remember their time together, could carry tales of this meeting to her original, to a woman he had admired with all that he had left of his heart, both irritated and intrigued him. "You were attracted to me because of my history."

"I was attracted to you because of your strength," she said. "It hurt me that you were so intent on living in your memories."

"I clung to you."

"And to nobody else . . ."

"I don't come here often," Olmy said. He shook his hands out by his side and stepped back. "All my finest memories are on a world I can never go back to. Real loves . . . real life. Not like Thistledown now." He squinted at the image. The image's focus was precise; still, there was something false about it, a glossiness, a prim neatness unlike Neya. "You didn't help."

The partial's expression softened. "I don't take the blame entirely, but your distress doesn't please me. My original."

"I didn't say I was in distress. I feel a curious peace in fact. Why did Yanosh send you? Why did you agree to come?"

The ghost reached out to him. Her hand passed through his arm. She apologized for this breach of etiquette. "For your sake, to get you involved, and for the sake of my original, please, at least speak to our staff. The Presiding Minister needs you to join an expedition." She seemed to consider for a moment, then screw up her courage. "There's trouble at the Redoubt."

Olmy felt a sting of shock at the mention of that name. The

conversation had suddenly become more than a little risky. He shook his head vigorously. "I do not acknowledge even knowing of such a place," he said.

"You know more than I do," the partial said. "I've been assured that it's real. Way Defense tells the Office of Way Maintenance that it now threatens us all."

"I'm not comfortable holding this conversation in a public place," Olmy protested.

This seemed to embolden the partial, and she projected her image closer. "This area is quiet and clean. No one listens."

Olmy stared up at the high glass ceiling.

"We are not being observed," the partial insisted. "The Nexus and Way Defense are concerned that the Jarts are closing in on that sector of the Way. I am told that if they occupy it, gain control of the Redoubt, Thistledown might as well be ground to dust and the Way set on fire like a piece of string. That scares my original. It scares *me* as I am now. Does it bother you in the least, Olmy?"

Olmy looked along the rows of urns . . . Centuries of Thistledown history, lost memory, now turned to pinches of ash, or less.

"Yanosh says he's positive you can help," the partial said with a strong lilt of emotion. "It's a way to rejoin the living and make a new place for yourself."

"Why should that matter to you? To your original?" Olmy asked.

"Because my original still regards you as a hero. I still hope to emulate your service to the Hexamon."

Olmy smiled wryly. "Better to find a living model," he said. "I don't belong out there. I'm rusted over."

"That is not true," the partial said. "You have been given a new body. You are youthful and strong, and very experienced . . ." She seemed about to say more, but hesitated, rippled again, and faded abruptly. Her voice faded as well, and he heard only "Yanosh says he's never lost faith in you—"

The floor of the columbarium trembled. The solidity of Thistledown seemed to be threatened; a quake through the asteroid material, an impact from outside . . . or something occurring within the Way. Olmy reached out to brace himself against a pillar. The golden spheres vibrated in their suspensions, jangling like hundreds of small bells.

From far away, sirens began to wail.

The partial reappeared. "I have lost contact with my original," it said, its features blandly stiff. "Something has broken my link with City Memory."

Olmy watched Neya's image with fascination as yet untouched by any visceral response.

"I do not know when or if there will be a recovery," she said. "There's a failure in Axis City." Suddenly the image appeared puzzled, then stricken. She held out her phantom arms. "My original . . ." As if she were made of solid flesh, her face crinkled with fear. "She's died. I've *died*. Oh my God, Olmy!"

Olmy tried to understand what this might mean, under the radical new rules of life and death for Geshels such as Neya. "What's happened? What can we do?"

The image flickered wildly. "My body is *gone*. There's been a complete system failure. I don't have any legal existence."

"What about the whole-life records? Connect with them." Olmy walked around the unsteady image, as if he might capture it, stop it from fading.

"I kept putting it off . . . So stupid! I haven't put myself in City Memory yet."

He tried to touch her and of course could not. He could not believe what she was saying, yet the sirens still wailed, and another small shudder rang through the asteroid.

"I have no place to go. Olmy, please! Don't let me just *stop!*" The ghost of Neya Taur Rinn drew herself up, tried to compose herself. "I have only a few seconds before . . ."

Olmy felt a sudden and intense attraction to the shimmering image. He wanted to know what actual death, final death, could possibly feel like. He reached out again, as if to embrace her.

She shook her head. The flickering increased. "It feels so strange—losing—"

Before she could finish, the image vanished completely. Olmy's arms hung around silent and empty air.

The sirens continued to wail, audible throughout Alexandria. He slowly dropped his arms, all too aware of being alone. The projector flew in a small circle, emitting small *wheep*ing sounds. Without instructions from its source, it could not decide what to do.

For a moment, he shivered and his neck hair pricked—a sense of almost religious awe he had not experienced since his time on Lamarckia.

Olmy had started walking toward the end of the hall before he consciously knew what to do. He turned right to exit through the large steel doors and looked up through the thin clouds enwrapping the second chamber, through the glow of the flux tube to the axis borehole on the southern cap. His eyes were warm and wet. He wiped them with the back of his hand and his breath hitched.

Emergency beacons had switched on around the flux tube, forming a bright ring two-thirds of the way up the cap.

His shivering continued, and it angered him. He had died once already, yet this new body was afraid of dying, and its wash of emotions had taken charge of his senses.

Deeper still and even more disturbing was a scrap of the old loyalty . . . To his people, to the vessel that bore them between the stars, that served as the open chalice of the infinite Way. A loyalty to the woman who had found him too painful to be with. "Neya!" he moaned. Perhaps she had been wrong. A partial might not have access to all information; perhaps things weren't as bad as they seemed.

But he knew that they were. He had never felt Thistledown shake so.

Olmy hurried to the rail terminal three city squares away, accompanied by throngs of curious and alarmed citizens. Barricades had been set across the entrances to the northern cap elevators; all interchamber travel was temporarily restricted. No news was available.

Olmy showed the ID marks on his wrist to a cap guard, who scanned them quickly and transmitted them to her commanders. She let him pass, and he entered the elevator and rode swiftly to the borehole.

Within the workrooms surrounding the borehole waited an arrowhead-shaped official transport, as the Presiding Minister's office had requested. None of the soldiers or guards he questioned knew what had happened. There were still no official pronouncements on any of the citizen nets. Olmy rode the transport, accompanied by five other officials, through the vacuum above the atmospheres of the next four chambers, threading the boreholes of each of the massive concave walls that separated them. None of the chambers showed any sign of damage.

In the southern cap borehole of the sixth chamber, Olmy transferred from the transport to a tuberider, designed to run along the singularity that formed the core of the Way. On this most unusual railway, he sped at many thousands of miles per hour toward the Axis City at 4 ex 5—four hundred thousand kilometers north of Thistledown.

A few minutes from Axis City, the tuberider slowed and the forward viewing port darkened. There was heavy radiation in the vicinity, the pilot reported. Something had come down the Way at relativistic velocity and struck the northern precincts of Axis City.

Olmy had little trouble guessing the source.

• 2 •

A day passed before Olmy could see the Presiding Minister. Emergency repairs on Axis City had rendered only one precinct, Central City, habitable; the rest, including Axis Prime, were being evacuated. Axis Prime had taken the brunt of the impact. Tens of thousands had lost their lives, both Geshels and Naderites. Naderites by and large did not participate in the practice of storing their body patterns and recent memories as insurance against such a calamity.

Some Geshels would receive their second incarnation—many thousands more would not. City Memory itself had been damaged. Even had Neya taken the time to make her whole-life record, store her patterns, she might still have died.

The last functioning precinct, Central City, now contained the combined offices of Presiding Minister of the Way and the Axis City government, and it was here that Yanosh met with Olmy.

"Her name was Deirdre Enoch," the Presiding Minister said, floating over the transparent external wall of the new office. His body was wrapped below the chest in a shining blue medical support suit; the impact had broken both of his legs and caused severe internal injuries. For the time being, the Presiding Minister was a functioning cyborg, until new organs could be grown and placed. "She opened a gate illegally at three ex nine, fifty years ago. Just beyond the point where we last repulsed the Jarts. She was helped by a master gate opener who deliberately disobeyed Nexus and guild orders. We learned about the breach six months after she had smuggled eighty of her colleagues—or maybe a hundred and twenty, we aren't sure how many—into a small research center—and just days after the gate was opened. There was nothing we could do to stop it."

Olmy gripped a rail that ran around the perimeter of the office, watching Kesler without expression. The irony was too obvious. "I've only heard rumors. Way Maintenance—"

Kesler was hit by a wave of pain, quickly damped by the suit. He continued, his face drawn. "Damn Way Maintenance. Damn the infighting and politics." He forced a smile. "Last time it was a Naderite renegade on Lamarckia."

Olmy nodded.

"This time—Geshel. Even worse—a member of the Openers Guild. I never imagined running this damned starship would ever be so complicated. Makes me almost understand why you long for Lamarckia."

"It wasn't any easier there," Olmy said.

"Yes—but there were fewer people." Yanosh rotated his support suit and crossed the chamber. "We don't know precisely what happened. Something disturbed the immediate geometry around the gate. The conflicts between Way physics and the universe Enoch accessed were too great. The gate became a lesion, impossible to close. By that time, most of Enoch's scientists had retreated to the main station, a protective pyramid—what she called the Redoubt."

"She tapped into chaos?" Olmy asked. Some universes accessed through the Way were empty voids, dead, useless but relatively harmless; others were virulent, filled with a bubbling stew of unstable "constants" that reduced the reality of an observer or instrumentality. Only two such gates had ever been opened in the Way; the single fortunate aspect of these disasters had been that the gates themselves had quickly closed and could not be reopened.

"Not chaos," Kesler said, swallowing and bowing his head at more discomfort. "This damn suit . . . could be doing a better job."

"You should be resting," Olmy said.

"No time. The Openers Guild tells me Enoch was looking for a domain of enhanced structure, hyperorder. What she found was more dangerous than any chaos. Her gate may have opened into a universe of endless fecundity. Not just order: creativity. Every universe is in a sense a plexus, its parts connected by information links; but Enoch's universe contained no limits to the propagation of information. No finite speed of light, no separation between anything analogous to the Bell continuum . . . and other physicality."

Olmy frowned, trying to make sense of this. "My knowledge of Way physics is shaky . . ."

"Ask your beloved Konrad Korzenowski," Kesler snapped.

Olmy did not react to this provocation.

Kesler apologized under his breath. He floated slowly back across the chamber, his face a mask of pain, a pathetic parody of restlessness. "We lost three expeditions trying to save her people and close the gate. The last was six months ago. Something like life-forms had grown up around the main station, fueled by the lesion. They've become *huge,* unimaginably bizarre. No one can make sense of them. What was left of our last expedition managed to build a barrier about a thousand kilometers south of the lesion. We thought that would give us the luxury of a few years to decide what to do next. But that barrier has been destroyed. We've not been able to get close enough since to discover what's happened. We have defenses in that sector, key defenses that keep the flaw from being used against us." He looked down through the transparent floor at the segment of the Way twenty-four kilometers below.

"The Jarts were able to send a relativistic projectile along the flaw, hardly more than a gram of rest mass. We couldn't stop it. It struck Axis City at twelve hundred hours yesterday."

Olmy had been told the details of the attack: a pellet less than a millimeter in diameter, traveling very close to the speed of light. Only the safety and control mechanisms of the sixth chamber machinery had kept the entire Axis City from disintegrating. The original of Neya Taur Rinn had been conducting business on behalf of her boss, Yanosh, in Axis Prime while her partial had visited Olmy.

"We're moving the city south as fast as we can and still keep up the evacuation," Kesler said. "The Jarts are drawing close to the lesion now. We're not sure what they can do with it. Maybe nothing—but we can't afford to take the chance."

Olmy shook his head in puzzlement. "You've just told me nothing can be done. Why call me here when we're helpless?"

"I didn't say *nothing* could be done," Kesler responded, eyes glittering. "Some of our gate openers think they can build a cirque, a ring gate, and seal off the lesion."

"That would cut us off from the rest of the Way," Olmy said.

"Worse. In a few days or weeks it would destroy the Way completely, seal us off in Thistledown forever. Until now, we've never been that desperate." He smiled, lips twisted by pain. "Frankly, you were not my choice. I'm no longer sure that you can be relied upon, and this matter is far too complicated to allow anyone to act alone."

Neya had not told him the truth, then. "Who chose me?" Olmy asked.

"A gate opener. You made an impression on him when he escorted you down the Way some decades ago. He was the one who opened the gate to Lamarckia."

"Frederik Ry Ornis?"

Kesler nodded. "From what I'm told, he's become the most powerful opener in the guild. A senior master."

Olmy took a deep breath. "I'm not what I appear to be, Yanosh. I'm an old man who's seen women and his friends die. I miss my sons. You should have left me on Lamarckia."

Kesler closed his eyes. The blue jacket around his lower body adjusted slightly, and his face tightened. "The Olmy I knew would never have turned down a chance like this."

"I've seen too many things already," Olmy said.

Yanosh moved forward. "We both have. This . . . is beyond me," he said quietly. "The lesion . . . The gate openers tell me it's the strangest place in creation. All the boundaries of physics have collapsed. Time and causality have new meanings. Heaven and hell have married. Only those in the Redoubt have seen all that's happened there—if they still exist in any way we can understand. They haven't communicated with us since the lesion formed."

Olmy listened intently, something slowly stirring to life, a small speck of ember glowing brighter.

"It may be over, Olmy," Yanosh said. "The whole grand experiment may be at an end. We're ready to close off the Way, pinch it, seal the lesion within its own small bubble . . . dispose of it."

"Tell me more," Olmy said, folding his arms.

"Three citizens escaped from the Redoubt, from Enoch's small colony, before the lesion became too large. One died, his mind scrambled beyond retrieval. The second has been confined for study, as best we're able. What afflicts him—or *it*—is something we can never cure. The third survived relatively unharmed. She's become . . . unconventional, more than a little obsessed by the mystical, but I'm told she's still rational. If you accept, she will accompany you." Yanosh's tone indicated he was not going to allow Olmy to decline. "We have two other volunteers, both apprentice gate openers, both failed by the guild. All have been chosen by Frederik Ry Ornis. He will explain why."

Olmy shook his head. "A mystic, failed openers . . . What would I do with such a team?"

Yanosh smiled grimly. "Kill them if it goes wrong. And kill yourself. If you can't close off the Way, and if the lesion remains, you will not be allowed to come back. The third expedition I sent never even reached the Redoubt. But they were absorbed by the lesion." Another grimace of pain. "Do you believe in ghosts, Olmy?"

"What kind?"

"Real ghosts?"

"No," Olmy said.

"I think I do. Some members of our rescue expeditions came back. Several versions of them. We *think* we destroyed them."

"Versions?"

"Copies of some sort. They were sent back—echoed—along their own world-lines in a way no one understands. They returned to their loved ones, their relatives, their friends. If more return, everything we call real could be in jeopardy. It's been very difficult keeping this secret."

Olmy raised an eyebrow skeptically. He wondered if Yanosh was himself still rational. "I've served my time. More than my time. Why should I go active?"

"Damn it, Olmy, if not for love of Thistledown—if you're beyond that, then because you *want to die.*" Kesler grunted, his face betraying quiet disgust behind the pain. "You've wanted to die since I brought you back from Lamarckia. This time, if you make it to the Redoubt, you're likely to have your wish granted.

"Think of it as a gift from me to you, or to what you once were."

• 3 •

"If you were enhanced, this would go a lot faster," Jarr Flynch said, pointing to Olmy's head. Frederik Ry Ornis smiled. The three of them walked side by side down a long, empty hall, approaching a secure room deep in the old Thistledown Defense Tactical College building in Alexandria.

Ry Ornis had aged not at all physically. In appearance he was still the same long-limbed, mantislike figure, but his gawkiness had been replaced by an eerie grace, and his youthful, eccentric volubility by a wry spareness of language.

Olmy dismissed Flynch's comment with a wave of his hand. "I've gone through the important files," he said. "I think I know them well enough. I have questions about the choice of people to go with me. The apprentice gate openers . . . They've been rejected by the guild. Why?"

Flynch smiled. "They're flamboyant."

Olmy glanced at the master opener. "Ry Ornis was as flamboyant as they come."

"The guild has changed," Ry Ornis said. "It demands more now."

Flynch agreed. "In the time since I've been a teacher in the guild, that's certainly true. They tolerate very little . . . creativity. The defection of Enoch's pupils scared them. The lesion terrified all of us. Rasp and Karn are young, innovative. Nobody denies they're brilliant, but they've refused to settle in and play their roles. So . . . the guild denied them final certification."

"Why choose them for this job?" Olmy asked.

"Ry Ornis did the choosing," Flynch said.

"We've discussed this," Ry Ornis said.

"Not to my satisfaction. When do I meet them?"

"No meeting has been authorized with Rasp and Karn until you're on the flawship. They're still in emergency conditioning." Flynch glanced at Ry Ornis. "The training has been a little rough on them."

Olmy felt less and less sure that he wanted anything to do with the guild, or with Ry Ornis's chosen openers. "The files only tell half a story," he said. "Deirdre Enoch never became an opener—she never even tried to qualify. She was just a teacher. How could she become so important to the guild?"

Flynch shook his head. "Like me, she was never qualified to be an opener, but also like me, as a teacher, she was considered one of the best. She became a leader to some apprentice openers. Philosopher."

"Prophet," Ry Ornis said softly.

"Training for the guild is grueling," Flynch continued. "Some say it's become torture. The mathematical conditioning alone is enough to produce a dropout rate of over ninety percent. Deirdre Enoch worked as a counselor in mental balance, compensation, and she was good . . . In the last twenty years, she worked with many who went on to become very powerful in Way Maintenance. She kept up her contacts. She convinced a lot of her students—"

"That human nature is corrupt," Olmy ventured sourly.

Flynch shook his head. "That the laws of our universe are inadequate. Incomplete. That there is a way to become better human beings, and of course, better openers. Disorder, competition, and death corrupt us, she thought."

"She knew high-level theory, speculations circulated privately among master openers," Ry Ornis said. "She heard about domains where the rules were very different."

"She heard about a gate into complete order?"

"It had been discussed, on a theoretical basis. None had ever been attempted. No limits have been found to the variety of domains—of universes. She speculated that a well-tuned gate could access almost any domain a good opener could conceive of."

Olmy scowled. "She expected order to balance out competition and death? Order versus disorder, a fight to the finish?"

Ry Ornis made a small noise, and Flynch nodded. "There's a reason none of this is in the files," Flynch said. "No opener will talk about it, or admit they knew anybody involved in making the decision.

It's been very embarrassing to the guild. I'm impressed that you know what questions to ask. But it's better that you ask Ry Ornis—"

Olmy focused on Flynch. "You say you and Enoch occupied similar positions. I'd rather ask you."

Flynch gestured for them to turn to the left. The lights came on before them, and at the end of a much shorter hall, a door stood open. "Deirdre Enoch read extensively in the old religious texts. As did her followers. I believe they lost themselves in a dream," he said. "They thought that anyone who bathed in a stream of pure order, as it were—in a domain of unbridled creation without destruction—would be enhanced. Armored. Annealed. That's my opinion . . . what they might have been thinking. She might have told them such things."

"A fountain of youth?" Olmy ventured, still scowling.

"Openers don't much care about temporal immortality," Ry Ornis said. "When we open a gate—we glimpse eternity. A hundred gates, a hundred different eternities. Coming back is just an interlude between forevers. Those who listened to Enoch thought they would end up more skilled, more brilliant. Less corrupted by competitive evolution." He smiled, a remarkably unpleasant expression on his skeletal face. "Free of original sin."

Olmy's scowl faded. He glanced at Flynch, who had turned away from Ry Ornis. Something between them, a coolness. "All right. I can see that."

"Really?" Flynch shook his head dubiously.

Perhaps the master opener could tell even more. But it did not seem wise at this point to push the matter.

A bell chimed and they entered the conference room.

Already seated within was the only surviving and whole escapee from the Redoubt: Lissa Plass. As a radical Geshel, she had designed her own body and appearance decades ago, opting for a solid frame, close to her natural physique. Her face she had tuned to show strength as well as classic beauty, but she had allowed it to age, and the experience of her time with the expedition, the trauma at the lesion, had not been erased. Olmy noted that she carried a small book with her, an antique printed on paper—a Bible.

Flynch made introductions. Plass looked proud and more than a little confused. They sat around the table.

"Let's start with what we know," Flynch said. He ordered up visual records made by the retreating flawship that had carried Plass.

Olmy looked at the images hovering over the table: the great pipeline of the Way, sheets of field fluorescing brilliantly as they were breached, debris caught in whirling clouds along the circumference, the flaw itself, running along the center of the Way like a wire heated to blinding blue-white.

Plass did not look. Olmy watched her reaction closely. For a moment, something seemed to swirl around her, a wisp of shadow, smoothly transparent, like a small slice of twilight. The others did not see or ignored what they saw, but Plass's eyes locked on Olmy's, and her lips tightened.

"I'm pleased you've both agreed to come," Ry Ornis said, as the images came to an end.

Plass looked at the opener, and then back at Olmy. She studied Olmy's face closely. "I can't stay here. That's why I'm going back. I don't belong in Thistledown."

"Ser Plass is haunted," Flynch said. "Ser Olmy has been told about some of these visitors."

"My husband," she said, swallowing. "Just my husband, so far. Nobody else."

"Is he still there?" Olmy asked. "In the Redoubt?"

Bitterly, she said, "They haven't told you much that's useful, have they? As if they want us to fail."

"He's dead?"

"He's not in the Redoubt and I don't know if you could call it death," Plass said. "May I tell you what this really means? What we've actually done?" She stared around the table, eyes wide.

Ry Ornis lifted his hand tolerantly.

"I have diaries from before the launch of Thistledown, from my family," she said. "As far back as my ancestors can remember, my family was special . . . They had access to the world of the spiritual. They all saw ghosts. The old-fashioned kind, not the ones we use now for servants. Some described the ghosts in their journals." She reached up and pinched her lower lip, released it, pinched it again. "I think some of the ghosts were my husband. I recognize that now. Everyone on my world-line, back to before I was born, haunted by the same figure. My husband. Now I see him, too."

"I have a hard time visualizing this sort of ghost," Olmy said.

Plass looked up at the ceiling and clutched her Bible. "Whatever it is that we tapped into—a domain of pure order, something else clever—it's *suffused* into the Way, into Thistledown. It's like a caterpillar crawling up our lives, grabbing hold of events and . . . crawling, spreading backward, maybe even forward in time. They try to keep us quiet. I cooperate . . . but my husband tells me things when he returns. Do the others hear . . . reports? Messages from the Redoubt?"

Ry Ornis shook his head, but Olmy doubted this meant simple denial.

"What happened when the gate became a lesion?" Olmy asked.

Plass grew pale. "My husband was at the gate with Enoch's master opener, Tom Issa Danna."

"One of our finest," Ry Ornis said.

"Enoch's gate into order was the second they had opened. The first was a well to an established supply world where we could bring up raw materials."

"Standard practice for all far-flung stations," Flynch said.

"I wasn't there when they opened the second gate," Plass continued, her eyes darting between Flynch and Olmy. She seemed to have little sympathy for either. "I was at a support facility about a kilometer from the gate, and two kilometers from the Redoubt. There was already an atmospheric envelope and a cushion of sand and soil around the site. My husband and I had started a quick-growth garden. An orchard. We heard they had opened the second gate. My husband was with Issa Danna. Ser Enoch came by on a tractor and said it was a complete success. We were celebrating, a small group of researchers, opening bottles of champagne. We got reports of something going wrong two hours later. We came out of our bungalows—a scout from the main flawship was just landing. Enoch had returned to the new gate to join Issa Danna. My husband must have been right there with them."

"What did you see?"

"Nothing at first. We watched them on the monitors inside the bungalows. Issa Danna and his assistants were working, talking, laughing. Issa Danna was so confident. He radiated his genius. The second gate looked normal—a well, a cupola. But in a little while, a few hours, we saw that the people around the new gate sounded drunk. All of them. Something had come out of the gate, something intoxicating. They spoke about a shadow."

She looked up at Olmy, and Olmy realized that before this experience, she must have been a very lovely woman. Some of that beauty still shone through.

"We saw that some kind of veil covered the gate. Then the assistant openers in the bungalows, students of Issa Danna, said that the gate was out of control. They were feeling it in their clavicles, slaved to the master's clavicle."

Clavicles were devices used by gate openers to create the portals that gave access to other times, other universes, "outside" the Way. Typically, they were shaped like handlebars attached to a small sphere.

"How many openers were there?" Olmy asked.

"Two masters and seven apprentices," Plass said.

Olmy turned to Ry Ornis. He held up his hand, urging patience.

"A small truck came out of the gate site. Its tires wobbled, and all the people clinging to it were shouting and laughing. Then everyone around the truck—the bungalows were almost empty now—began to shout, and an assistant grabbed me—I was the closest to her—and said we had to get onto the scout and return to the flawship. She—her name was Jara—said she had never felt anything like this. She said they must have made a mistake and opened a gate into chaos. I had never heard about such a thing—but she seemed to think if we didn't leave now, we'd all die. Four people. Two men and me and Jara. We were the only ones who made it into the scout ship. Shadows covered everything around us. Everybody was drunk, laughing, screaming."

Plass stopped and took several breaths to calm herself. "We flew up to the flawship. The rest is on the record. The Redoubt was the last thing I saw, surrounded by something like ink in water, swirling. A storm."

Flynch started to speak, but Plass cut him off. "Two of the others on the flawship, the men, were afflicted. They came out of the veil around the truck and Jara helped them get into the scout. As for Jara . . . Nobody remembers her but me."

Flynch waited a moment, then said, "There were only two people aboard the scout when it reached the flawship. You, and the figure we haven't identified. There was no other man, and there has never been an assistant opener named Jara."

"They were real."

"It doesn't matter," Ry Ornis said impatiently. "Issa Danna knew better than to open a gate into chaos. He knew the signs and never would have completed the opening. But—in the linkage, the slaving, qualities can be reversed if the opener loses control."

"A gate into order—but the slaved clavicles behaving as if they were associated with chaos?" Olmy asked, trying to grasp the complexities.

Ry Ornis seemed reluctant to go into more detail. "They no longer exist in our world-line," he said. "Ser Plass remembers that one hundred and twenty people accompanied Enoch and Issa Danna. She remembers two master openers and seven assistants. Here on Thistledown, we have records, life-histories, of only eighty, with one master and two assistants."

"I survived. You remember me," Plass said, her expression desperate.

"You're in our records. You survived," Ry Ornis confirmed. "We don't know why or how."

"What about the other survivor?" Olmy said.

"We don't know who he or she was," Ry Ornis said.

"Show him the other," Plass said. "Show him Number 2, show him what happens when you survive, but you *don't* return."

"That's next," Ry Ornis said. "If you're ready, Ser Olmy."

"I may never be *ready*, Ser Ry Ornis," Olmy said.

• 4 •

The flawship cradled in the borehole dock was sleek and new and very fast. Olmy tracted along the flank of the ship, resisting the urge to run his fingers along the featureless reflecting surface.

He was still pondering the meeting with the figure called Number 2.

Around the ship's dock, the borehole between the sixth and seventh chamber glowed with a violet haze, a cup-shaped field erected to receive the southernmost extensors of Axis City, gripping the remaining precincts during their evacuation and repair. Olmy swiveled to face the axis and the flaw's blunt conclusion and watch the workers and robots guiding power grids and huge steel beams to act as buffers.

The dock manager, a small man with boyish features and no hair, his scalp decorated with an intricate green and brown Celtic braid, pulled himself toward Olmy and extended a paper certificate.

"We're going to vacuum in an hour," he said. "I hope everybody's here before then. I'd like to seal the ship and check its integrity."

Olmy applied his sigil to the document, transferring its command from borehole management and the construction guild to Way Defense.

"Two others were here earlier," the dock manager said. "Twins, young women. They carried the smallest clavicles I've ever seen."

Olmy looked back along the dock and saw three figures tracting toward them. "Looks like we're all here," he said.

"No send-off?" the manager asked.

Olmy smiled. "Everyone's much too busy," he said.

"Don't I know it," the manager said.

As a rule, gate openers had a certain look and feel that defined them, sometimes subtle, usually not. Rasp and Karn were little more than children, born (perhaps *made* was a better word) fifteen years ago in Thistledown City. They were of radical Geshel ancestry, and their four parent-sponsors were also gate openers.

They tracted to the flawship and introduced themselves to Olmy. Androgynous, ivory white, slender, with long fingers and small heads covered with a fine silvery fur, they spoke with identical resonant tenor voices. Karn had black eyes, Rasp green. Otherwise, they were identical. To Olmy, neither had the air of authority he had seen in experienced gate openers.

The dock manager picked a coded symbol and dilated the flawship entrance, a glowing green circle in the hull. The twins solemnly entered the ship.

Plass arrived several minutes later. She wore a formal blue suit and seemed to have been crying. As she greeted Olmy, her voice sounded harsh. She addressed him as if they had not met before. "You're the soldier?"

"I've worked in Way Defense," he said.

Gray eyes small and wary, surrounded by puffy pale flesh, face broad and sympathetic, hair dark and cut short, Plass today reminded Olmy of any of a dozen matrons he had known as a child: polite but hardly hesitant.

"Ser Flynch tells me you're the one who died on Lamarckia. I heard about that. By birth, a Naderite."

"By birth," Olmy said.

"Such adventures we have," she said with a sniff. "Because of Ser Korzenowski's cleverness." She glanced away, then fastened her eyes on him and leaned her head to one side. "I'm not looking forward to this. Have they told you I'm a little broken, that my thoughts take odd paths?"

"They said your studies and experiences have influenced you," Olmy said, a little uncomfortable at having to reestablish an acquaintance already made.

Rasp and Karn watched from the flawship hatch.

"She's broken, we're young and inexperienced," Rasp said. Karn laughed, a surprising watery tinkle, very sweet. "And you've died once already, Ser Olmy. What a crew!"

"I presume everyone knows what they're doing," Plass said.

"Presume nothing," Olmy said.

Olmy guided Plass into the ship. The dock manager watched this with dubious interest. Olmy swung around fields to face him.

"I take charge of this vessel now. Thanks for your attention and care."

"Our duty," the dock manager said. "She was delivered just yesterday. No one has taken her out yet—she's a virgin, Ser Olmy. She doesn't even have a name."

"Call her the *Lark!*" Rasp trilled from inside.

Olmy shook hands firmly with the manager and climbed into the ship. The entrance sealed with a small beep behind him.

The flawship's interior was cool and quiet. With intertial control, there were no special couches or nets or fields; they would experience only simulated motion, for psychological effect, on their journey: at most a mild sense of acceleration and deceleration.

Plass introduced herself to Karn and Rasp. Since she wore no pictor, only words were exchanged. This suited Olmy.

"Ser Olmy," Plass said, "I assume we are in privacy now. No one outside can hear?"

"No one," Olmy said.

"Good. Then we can speak our minds. This trip is useless." She turned on the twins, who floated like casual accent marks on some unseen word. "They've chosen you because you're inexperienced."

"Unmarked," Rasp said brightly. "Open to the new."

Karn smiled and nodded. "And not afraid of spooks."

This seemed to leave Plass at a loss, but only for a second. She was obviously determined to establish herself as a Cassandra. "You won't be disappointed."

"We visited with Number 2," Rasp said, and Karn nodded. "Ser Ry Ornis insisted we study it."

Olmy remembered his own encounter with the vividly glowing figure in the comfortably appointed darkened room. It was not terribly misshapen, as he had anticipated before the meeting, but certainly far from normal. Its skin had burned with the tiny firefly deaths of stray metal atoms in the darkened room's air. It had stood out against the shadows like a nebula in the vastness beyond Thistledown's walls. Its hands alone had remained dark, ascribing arcs against its starry body as it tried to speak.

It lived in a twisted kind of time, neither backward nor forward, and its words had required special translation. It had spoken of things that would happen in the room after Olmy left. It had told him the Way would soon end, "in the blink of a bird's eye." The translator relayed this clearly enough, but could not translate other words; it seemed the unknown figure was inventing or accessing new languages, some clearly not of human origin.

Plass said, "It'll be a mercy if all that happens is we end up like *him.*"

"How interesting," Rasp said.

"We are fiends for novelty," Karn added with a smile.

"Monsters are *made,*" Plass said with a grimace, clasping her Bible, "not born."

"Thank you," Karn said, and produced a forced, fixed smile, accompanied by a glassy stare. Rasp was obviously thinking furiously to come up with a more witty riposte.

Olmy decided enough was more than enough. "If we're going to die, or worse, we should at least be civil." The three stared at him, each surprised in a different way. This gave Olmy a bare minimum of satisfaction. "Let's go through our orders and manifest, and learn how to work together."

"A man who wants only to die again—" Karn began, still irritated, her stare still glazed, but her twin interrupted.

"Shut up," Rasp said. "As he says. Time to work." Karn shrugged and her anger dissolved instantly.

At speed, the flawship's forward view of the Way became a twisted lens. Stray atoms and ions of gas within the Way piled up before them into a distorting, white-hot atmosphere. Rays of many colors writhed from a skewed vertex of milky brightness; the flaw, itself a slender geometric distortion, now resembled a white-hot piston.

Stray atoms of gas in the Way were becoming a problem, the result of so many gates being opened to bring in raw materials from the first exploited worlds.

The flawship's status appeared before Olmy in steady reassuring symbols of blue and green. Their speed: three percent of c', the speed of light in the Way, slightly less than c in the outside universe. They were now accelerating at more than six g's, down from the maximum they had hit at 4 ex 5. None of this could be felt inside the hull.

The display showed their position as 1 ex 7, ten million kilometers beyond the cap of the seventh chamber, still almost three billion kilometers from the Redoubt.

Olmy had a dreamlike sense of dissociation, as always when traveling in a flawship. The interior had been divided by its occupants into three private compartments, a common area, and the pilot's position. Olmy was spending most of his time at the pilot's position. The others kept to their compartments and said little to each other.

The first direct intimation of the strangeness of their mission came on the second day, halfway through their journey. Olmy was studying what little was known about the Redoubt, from a complete and highly secret file. He was deep into the biography of Deirdre Enoch when a voice called him from behind.

He turned and saw a young woman floating three meters aft, her head nearer to him than her feet, precessing slightly about her own axis. "I've felt you calling us," she said. "I've felt you studying us. What do you want to know?"

Olmy checked to make sure this was not some product of the files, of the data projectors. It was not; no simulations were being projected. Behind the image he saw the sisters and Plass emerging from their quarters. The sisters appeared interested, Plass bore an expression of shocked sadness.

"I don't recognize her," Plass said.

Olmy judged this was not a prank. "I'm glad you're decided to visit us," he said to the woman, with a touch of wry perversity. "How is the situation at the Redoubt?"

"The same, ever the same," the young woman answered. Her face was difficult to discern. As she spoke, her features blurred and re-formed, subtly different.

"Are you well?" Olmy asked. Rasp and Karn sidled forward around the image, which ignored them.

"I am nothing," the image said. "Ask another question. It's amusing to see if I can manage any sensible answers."

Rasp and Karn joined Olmy. "She's real?" Rasp asked. The twins were both pale, their faces locked in dread fascination.

"I don't know," Olmy said. "I don't think so."

"Then she's used her position on the Redoubt's timeline to climb back to us," Rasp said. "Some of us at least do indeed get to where we're going!"

Karn smiled with her usual fixed contentment and glazed eyes. Olmy was beginning not to like this hyperintelligent twin.

Plass moved forward, hands clenched as if she would hit the figure. "I don't recognize you," she said. "Who are you?"

"I see only one of you clearly." The young woman pointed at Olmy. "The others are like clouds of insects."

"Have the Jarts taken over the Redoubt?" Rasp asked. The image did not answer, so Olmy echoed the question.

"They are alone in the Redoubt. That is sufficient. I can describe the situation as it will be when you arrive. There is a large groove or valley in the Way, with the Redoubt forming a series of bands of intensely ranked probabilities within the groove. The Redoubt has grown to immense proportions, in time, all possibilities realized. My prior self has lived more than any cardinal number of lives. Still lives them. It sheds us as you shed skin."

"Tell us about the gate," Karn requested, sidling closer to the visitor. "What's happened? What state is it in?" Again, Olmy relayed the question. The woman watched him with discomforting intensity.

"It has become those who opened it. There is an immense head of Issa Danna on the western boundary of the gate, watching over the land. We do not know what it does, what it means."

Plass made a small choking sound and covered her mouth with her hand, eyes wide.

"Some tried to escape. It made them into living mountains, carpeted with fingers, or forests filled with fog and clinging blue shadow. Some waft through the air as vapors that change whoever encounters them. We've learned. We don't go outside, none for thousands of years . . ."

Rasp and Karn flanked the visitor, studying her with catlike focus.

"Then how can you leave, return to us?" Olmy asked.

The young woman frowned and held up her hands. "It doesn't speak. It doesn't know. I am so lonely."

Plass, Rasp and Karn, and Olmy stood facing each other through clear air.

Olmy started, suddenly drawn back to the last time he had seen a ghost vanish—the partial of Neya Taur Rinn.

Plass let out her breath with a shudder. "It is always the same," she said. "My husband says he's lonely. He's going to find a place where he won't be lonely. But there are no such places!"

Karn turned to Rasp. "A false vision, a deception?" she asked her twin.

"There are no deceptions where we are going," Plass said, and relaxed her hands, rubbed them.

Karn made a face out of her sight.

"No one knows what happened to the gate opened at the Redoubt," Rasp said, turning away from her own session with the records. Since the appearance of the female specter, they had spent most of their time in the pilot cabin. Olmy's presence seemed to afford them some comfort. "None of the masters can even guess."

Karn sighed, whether in sympathy or shame, Olmy could not tell.

"Can either of you make a guess?" Olmy asked.

Plass floated at the front of the common space, just around the pale violet bulkhead, arms folded, looking not very hopeful.

"A gate is opened on the floor of the Way," Rasp said flatly, as if reciting an elementary lesson. "That is a constraint in the local continuum of the Way. Four point gates are possible in each ring position. When four are opened, they are supposed to always cling to the wall of the Way. In practice, however, small gates have been known to rise above the floor. They are always closed immediately."

"What's that got to do with my question?" Olmy asked.

"Oh, nothing, really!" Rasp said, waving her hand in exasperation.

"Perhaps it does," Karn said, playing the role of thoughtful one for the moment. "Perhaps it's deeply connected."

"Oh, all right, then," Rasp said, and squinched up her face. "What I might have been implying is this: if Issa Danna's gate somehow lifted free of the floor, the wall of the Way, then its constraints would have changed. A free gate can adversely affect local world-lines. Something can enter and leave from any angle. In conditioning we are made to understand that the world-lines of all transported objects passing through such a free gate actually shiver for several years backward. Waves of probability retrograde."

"How many actually went through the gate?" Olmy asked.

"My husband never did," Plass said, pulling herself into the hatchway. "Issa Danna and his entourage. Maybe others, after the lesion formed . . . against their will."

"But you didn't recognize this woman," Olmy said.

"No," Plass said.

"Was she extinguished when the gate became a lesion?" Olmy continued. "Was her world-line wiped clean in our domain?"

"My head hurts," Rasp said.

"I think you might be right," Karn said thoughtfully. "It makes sense, in a frightening sort of way. She is suspended . . . We have no record of her existence."

"But the line still exists," Rasp said. "It echoes back in time even in places where her record has ended."

"No," Plass said, shaking her head.

"Why?" Rasp asked.

"She mentioned an *allthing*."

"I didn't hear that," Rasp said.

"Neither did I," Olmy said.

Plass gripped her elbow and squeezed her arms tight around her, pulling her shoulder forward. "We heard different words." She pointed at Olmy. "He's the only one she really saw."

"It looked at you, too," Rasp said. "Just once."

"An allthing was an ancient Nordic governmental meeting," Olmy

said, reading from the flawship command entry display, where he had
called for a definition.

"That's not what she meant," Plass said. "My husband used another phrase in the same way. He referred to the Final Mind of the
domain. Maybe they mean the same thing."

"It was just an echo," Rasp said. "We all heard it differently. We
all interacted with it differently depending on . . . Whatever. That
means more than likely it carried random information from a future
we'll never reach. It's a ghost that babbles . . . like your husband,
perhaps."

Plass stared at the twins, then grabbed for the hatch frame. She
stubbornly shook her head. "We're going to hear more about this
allthing," she said. "Deirdre Enoch is still working. Something is still
happening there. The Redoubt still exists."

"Your husband told you this?" Rasp asked with a taunting smile.
Olmy frowned at her, but she ignored him.

"We'll know when we see our own ghosts," Plass said, with a kick
that sent her flying back to her cabin.

Plass calmly read her Bible in the common area as the ship prepared a meal for her. The twins ate on their own schedule, but Olmy
matched his meals to Plass's, for the simple reason that he liked to
talk to the woman and did not feel comfortable around the twins.

There was about Plass the air of a spent force, something falling
near the end of its arc from a truly high and noble trajectory. Plass
seemed to enjoy his company, but did not comment on it. She asked
about his experiences on Lamarckia.

"It was a beautiful world," he said. "The most beautiful I've ever
seen."

"It no longer exists, does it?" Plass said.

"Not as I knew it. It adapted the way of chlorophyll. Now it's
something quite different, and at any rate, the gate there has
collapsed . . . No one in the Way will ever go there again."

"A shame," Plass said. "It seems a great tragedy of being mortal
that we can't go back. My husband, on the other hand . . . has visited
me seven times since I left the Redoubt." She smiled. "Is it wrong
for me to take pleasure in his visits? He isn't happy—but I'm happier
when I can see him, listen to him." She looked away, hunched her
shoulders as if expecting a blow. "He doesn't, can't, listen to me."

Olmy nodded. What did not make sense could at least be politely
acknowledged.

"In the Redoubt, he says, nothing is lost. I wonder how he knows?

Is he there? Does he watch over them? The tragedy of uncontrolled order is that the past is revised—and revisited—as easily as the future. The last time he returned, he was in great pain. He said a new God had cursed him for being a counterrevolutionary. The Final Mind. He told me that the Eye of the Watcher tracked him throughout all eternity, on all world-lines, and whenever he tried to stand still, he was tortured, made into something different." Plass's face took on a shiny, almost sensual expectancy and she watched Olmy's reaction closely.

"You denied what the twins were saying," Olmy reminded her. "About echoes along world-lines."

"They aren't just *echoes*. We *are* our world-lines, Ser Olmy. These ghosts . . . are really just altered versions of the originals. They have blurred origins. They come from many different futures. But they have a reality, an independence. I feel this . . . when he speaks to me."

Olmy frowned. "I can't visualize all this. Order is supposed to be simplicity and peace . . . Not torture and distortion and coercion. Surely a universe of complete order would be more like heaven, in the Christian sense." He pointed to the antique book resting lightly in her lap. Plass shifted and the Bible rose into the air a few centimeters. She reached out to grasp it, hold it close again.

"Heaven has no change, no death," she said. "Mortals find that attractive, but they are mistaken. No good thing lasts forever. It becomes unbearable. Now imagine a force that demands that something last forever, yet become even more the essence of what it was, a force that will accept nothing less than compliance, but *can't communicate.*"

Olmy shook his head. "I can't."

"I can't, either, but that is what my husband describes."

Several seconds. Plass tapped the book lightly with her finger.

"How long since he last visited you?" Olmy asked.

"Three weeks. Maybe longer. Things seemed quiet just before they told me I could return to the Redoubt." She closed her eyes and held her hands to her cheeks. "I believed what Enoch believed, that order ascends. That it ascends forever. I believed that we are made with flaws, in a universe that was itself born flawed. I thought we would be so much more beautiful when—"

Karn and Rasp tracked forward and hovered beside Plass, who fell quiet and greeted them with a small shiver.

"We have ventured a possible answer to this dilemma," Karn said.

"Our birth geometry, outside the Way, is determined by a vacuum of infinite potential," Rasp said, nodding with something like glee.

"We are forbidden from tapping that energy, so in our domain, space has a shape, and time has direction and a velocity. In the universe Enoch tapped, the energy of the vacuum is available at all times. Time and space and this energy, this potential, are bunched in a tight little knot of incredible density. That is what your husband must call the Final Mind. That our visitor renamed the allthing."

Plass shook her head indifferently.

"How amazing that must be!" Karn said. "A universe where order took hold in the first few nanoseconds after creation, controlling all the fires of the initial expansion, all the shape and constants of existence . . ."

"I wonder what Enoch would have done with such a domain, if she could have controlled it," Rasp said, hovering over Plass, peering down on her. Plass made as if to swat a fly, and Rasp tracked out of reach with a broad smile. "Ours is a pale candle indeed by comparison."

"Everything must tend toward a Final Mind. This force blossoms at the end of the Time like a flower pushed up from all events, all lives, all thought. It is the ancestor not just of living creatures, but of all the interactions of matter, space, and time, for all things tend toward this blossom."

Olmy had often thought about this quote from the notes of Korzenowski. The designer of the Way had put together quite an original cosmology, which he had never tried to spread among his fellows. The original was in Korzenowski's library, kept as a Public Treasure, but few visited there now.

Olmy visited Rasp and Karn in their cabin while Plass read her Bible in the common area. The twins had arranged projections of geometric art and mathematical figures around the space, brightly colored and disorienting. He asked them whether they believed such an allthing, a perfectly ordered mind, could exist.

"Goodness, no!" Karn said, giggling.

"You mean, *Godness*, no!" Rasp added. "Not even if we believed in it, which we don't. Energy and impulse, yes; final, perhaps. Mind, no!"

"Whatever you call it—in the lesion, it may already exist, and it's different?"

"Of course it would exist! Not as a mind, that's all. Mind is impossible without neural qualities—communication between separate nodes that either contradict or confirm. If we think correctly, a domain of order would reach completion within the first few seconds of existence, freezing everything. It would grasp and control all the energy of its beginning moment, work through all possible variations in an instant—become a monobloc, still and perfected, timeless. Not eternal—eviternal, frozen forever. Timeless."

"Our universe, our domain, could spin on for many billions or even trillions more years," Karn continued. "In our universe, there could very well be a Final Mind, the summing up of all neural processes throughout all time. But Deirdre Enoch found an abomination. If it were a mind, think of it! Instantly creating all things, never being contradicted, never *knowing*. Nothing has ever frustrated it, stopped it, trained or tamed it. It would be as immature as a newborn baby, and as sophisticated—"

"And ingenious," Rasp chimed in.

"—As the very devil," Karn finished.

"Please," Rasp finished, her voice suddenly quiet. "Even if such a thing is possible, let it not be a mind."

For the past million kilometers, they had passed over a scourged, scrubbed segment of the Way. In driving back the Jarts from their strongholds, tens of thousands of Way defenders had died. The Way had been altered by the released energies of the battle and still glowed slightly, shot through with pulsing curls and rays, while the flaw in this region transported them with a barely noticeable roughness. The flawship could compensate some, but even with this compensation, they had reduced their speed to a few thousand kilometers an hour.

The Redoubt lay less than ten thousand kilometers ahead.

Rasp and Karn removed their clavicles from their boxes and tried as best they could to interpret the state of the Way as they came closer to the Redoubt.

Five thousand kilometers from the Redoubt, evidence of immense constructions lined the wall of the Way: highways, bands connecting what might have been linked gates; yet there were no gates. The constructions had been leveled to narrow lanes of rubble, like lines of powder.

Olmy shook his head, dismayed. "Nothing is the way it was reported to be just a few weeks ago."

"I detect something unusual, too," Rasp said. Karn agreed. "Something related to the Jart offensive . . ."

"Something we weren't told about?" Plass wondered. "A colony that failed?"

"Ours, or Jart?" Olmy asked.

"Neither," Karn said, looking up from her clavicle. She lifted the device, a fist-sized sphere mounted on two handles, and rotated the display for Olmy and Plass to see. Olmy had watched gate openers perform before, and knew the workings of the display well enough— though he could never operate a clavicle. "There have never been gates opened here. This is all sham."

"A decoy," Plass said.

"Worse," Rasp said. "The gate at the Redoubt is twisting probabilities, sweeping world-lines within the Way to such an extreme . . . The residue of realities that never were are being deposited."

"Murmurs in the Way's sleep, nightmares in our unhistory," Karn said. For once, the twins seemed completely subdued, even disturbed. "I don't see how we can function if we're incorporated into such a sweep."

"So what is this?" Olmy asked, pointing to the smears of destroyed highways, cities, bands between the ghosts of gates.

"A future," Karn said. "Maybe what will happen if we fail . . ."

"But these patterns aren't like human construction," Plass observed. "No human city planner would lay out those roadways. Nor does it match anything we know about the Jarts."

Olmy looked more closely, frowned in concentration. "If someone else had created the Way," he said, "maybe this would be their ruins, the rubble of their failure."

Karn gave a nervous laugh. "Wonderful!" she said. "All we could have hoped for! If we open a gate here, what could possibly happen?"

Plass grabbed Olmy's arm. "Put it in our transmitted record. Tell the Hexamon this part of the Way must be forbidden. *No gates should be opened here, ever!*"

"Why not?" Karn said. "Think what could be learned. The new domains."

"I agree with Ser Plass," Rasp said. "It's possible there are worse alternatives than finding a universe of pure order." She let go of her clavicle and grabbed her head. "Even touching our instruments here causes pain. We are useless . . . any gate we open would consume us more quickly than the gate at the Redoubt! You *must* agree, sister!"

Karn was stubborn. "I don't see it," she said. "I simply don't. I think this could be very interesting. Fascinating, even."

Plass sighed. "This is the box that Konrad Korzenowski has opened for us," she said for Olmy's benefit. "Spoiled genius children drawn to evil like insects to a corpse."

"I thought evil was related to disorder," Olmy said.

"Already, you know better," Plass rejoined.

Rasp turned her eyes on Olmy and Plass, eyes narrow and full of uncomfortable speculation.

Olmy reached out and grasped Rasp's clavicle to keep it from bumping into the flawship bulkheads. Karn took charge of the instrument indignantly and thrust it back at her sister. "You forget your responsibility," she chided. "We can fear this mission, or we can engage it with joy and spirit," she said. "Cowering does none of us any good."

"You're right, sister, about that at least," Rasp said. She returned her clavicle to its box and straightened her clothing, then used a cloth to wipe her face. "We are, after all, going to a place where we have always gone, always will go."

"It's what happens when we get there that is always changing," Karn said.

Plass's face went white. "My husband never returns the same way, in the same condition," she said. "How many hells does he experience?"

"One for each of him," Rasp said. "Only one. It is different husbands who return."

Though there had never been such this far along the way, Olmy saw the scattered wreckage of Jart fortifications, demolished, dead and empty. Beyond them lay a region where the Way was covered with winding black and red bands of sand, an immense serpentine desert, also unknown. Olmy felt a spark of something reviving, if not a wish for life, then an appreciation of what extraordinary sights his life had brought him.

On Lamarckia, he had seen the most extraordinary variations on biology. Here, near the Redoubt, it was reality itself subject to its own flux, its own denial.

Plass was transfixed. "The next visitors, if any, will see something completely different," she said. "We've been caught up in a sweeping world-line of the Way, not necessarily our own."

"I would never have believed it possible," Rasp said, and Karn reluctantly agreed. "This is not the physics we were taught."

"It can make any physics it wishes," Plass said. "Any reality. It has all the energy it needs. It has human minds to teach it our variations."

"It knows only unity," Karn said, taking hold of Plass's shoulder.

The older woman did not seem to mind. "It knows no will stronger than its own," she said. "Yet it may divide its will into illusory units. It is a tyrant . . ." Plass pointed to the winding sands, stretching for thousands of kilometers beneath them. "This is a moment of calm, of steady concentration. If my memories are correct, if what my husband's returning self . . . selves . . . tell me, is correct, it is usually much more frantic. Much more inventive."

Karn made a face and placed her hands on the bars of her clavicle. She rubbed the grips and her face became tight with concentration. "I feel it. There is still a lesion . . ."

Rasp took hold of her own instrument and went into her own state. "It's still there," she agreed. "It's bad. It floats above the Way, very near the flaw. From below, it must look like some sort of bale star . . ."

They passed through a fine bluish mist that rose from the northern end of the desert. The flawship made a faint belling sound. The mist passed behind.

"There," Plass said. "No mistaking it!"

The gate pushed through the Way by Issa Danna had expanded and risen above the floor, just as Rasp and Karn had felt in their instruments. Now, at a distance of a hundred kilometers, they could see the spherical lesion clearly. It did indeed resemble a dark sun, or a chancre. A glow of pigeon's blood flicked around it, the red of rubies and enchantment. The black center, less than the width of a fingertip at this distance, perversely seemed to fill Olmy's field of vision.

His young body decided it was time to be very reluctant to proceed. He swallowed and brought this fear under control, biting his cheek until blood flowed.

The flawship lurched. Its voice told Olmy, "We have received an instructional beacon. There is a place held by humans less than ten kilometers away. They say they will guide us to safety."

"It's still there!" Plass said.

They all looked down through the flawship's transparent nose, away from the lurid pink of the flaw, through layers of blue and green haze wrapped around the Way, down twenty-five kilometers to a single dark, gleaming steel point in the center of a rough, rolling land.

The Redoubt lay in the shadow of the lesion, surrounded by a penumbral twilight suffused with the flickering red of the lesion's halo.

"I can feel the whipping hairs of other world-lines," Karn and Rasp said together. Olmy glanced back and saw their clavicles touching sphere to sphere. The spheres crackled and clacked. Karn twisted her instrument toward Olmy so that he could see the display. A long list of domain "constants"—pi, Planck's constant, others—varied with a regular humming in the flawship hull. "Nothing is stable out there!"

Olmy glanced at the message sent from the Redoubt. It provided navigation instructions for their flawship's landing craft: how to disengage from the flawship, descend, undergo examination, and be taken into the pyramid. The message concluded, "We will determine whether you are illusions or aberrations. If you are from our origin, we will welcome you. It is too late to return now. Abandon your flawship before it approaches any closer to the allthing. Whoever sent you has committed you to our own endless imprisonment."

"Cheerful enough," Olmy said. The ghastly light cast a fitful, abbatoir glow on their faces.

"We have always gone there," Rasp said quietly.

"We have to agree," Plass said. "We have no other place to go."

They tracted aft to the lander's hatch and climbed into the small, arrowhead-shaped craft. Its interior welcomed them by fitting to their forms, providing couches, instruments, tailored to their bodies. Plass sat beside Olmy in the cockpit, Rasp and Karn directly behind them.

Olmy disengaged from the flawship and locked the lander onto the pyramid's beacon. They dropped from the flawship. The landscape steadily grew in the broad cockpit window.

Plass's face crumpled, like a child about to break into tears. "Star, Fate, and Pneuma, be kind. I see the opener's head. There!" She pointed in helpless dread, equally horrified and fascinated by something so inconceivable.

On a low, broad rise in the shadowed land surrounding the Redoubt, a huge dark head rose like an upright mountain, its skin like gray stone, one eye turned toward the south, the other watching over the territory before the nearest face of the pyramid. This watchful eye was easily a hundred meters wide, and glowed a dismal sea green, throwing a long beam through the thick twisted ropes of mist. Plass's voice became shrill. "Oh Star and Fate . . ."

The landscape around the Redoubt rippled beneath the swirling rays of rotating world-lines, spreading like hair from the black center of the lesion, changing the land a little with each pass, moving the bizarre landmarks a few dozen meters this way or that, increasing them in size, reducing them.

Olmy could never have imagined such a place. The Redoubt sat within a child's nightmare of disembodied human limbs, painted over the hills like trees, their fingers grasping and releasing spasmodically. At the top of one hill stood a kind of castle made of blocks of green glass, with a single huge door and window. Within the door stood a figure—a statue, perhaps—several hundred meters high, vaguely human, nodding steadily, idiotically, as the lander passed over. Hundreds of much smaller figures, gigantic nevertheless, milled in a kind of yard before the castle, their red and black shadows flowing like capes in the lee of the constant wind of changing probabilities. Olmy thought they might be huge dogs, or tailless lizards, but Plass pointed, and said, "My husband told me about an assistant to Issa Danna named Ram Chako . . . Duplicated, forced to run on all fours."

The giant in the castle door slowly raised its huge hand, and the massive lizards scrambled over each other to run from an open portal in the yard. They leaped up as the lander passed overhead, as if they would snap it out of the air with hideous jaws.

Olmy's head throbbed. He could not bring himself out of a conviction that none of this could be real; indeed, there was no necessity for it to *be* real in any sense his body understood. For their part, Rasp and Karn had lost all their earlier bravado and clung to each other, their clavicles floating on tethers wrapped around their wrists.

The lurid glare of the halo flowed like blood into the cabin as the lander rotated to present points of contact for traction fields from the Redoubt. Olmy instructed the ship to present a wide-angle view of the Redoubt and the land, and this view revolved slowly around them, filling the lander's cramped interior.

The perverse variety seemed never to end. Something had dissected not only a human body, or many bodies, and wreaked hideous distortions on its parts, but had done the same with human thoughts and desires, planting the results over the region with no obvious design.

Within the low valley—as described by the female visitant—a large blue-skinned woman, the equal of the figure in the doorway of the castle, crouched near a cradle within which churned hundreds of naked humans. She slowly dropped her hand into the cauldron of flesh and stirred, and her hair sprayed out from her head with a sullen cometary glow, casting everything in a syrupy, heavy green luminosity.

"Mother of geometries," Karn muttered, and hid her eyes.

Olmy could not turn away, but everything in him wanted to go to sleep, to die, rather than to acknowledge what they were seeing.

Plass saw his distress. Somehow she took strength from the incomprehensible view. "It does not need to make sense," she said with the tone of a chiding schoolteacher. "It's supported by infinite energy and a monolithic, mindless will. There is nothing new here, nothing—"

"I'm not asking that it make sense," Olmy said. "I need to know what's behind it."

"A sufficient force, channeled properly, can create anything a mind can imagine—" Karn began.

"More than any mind will imagine. Not a mind like our minds," Rasp restated. "A unity, not a *mind* at all."

For a moment, Olmy's anger lashed and he wanted to shout his frustration, but he took a deep breath, folded his arms where he floated in tracting restraints, and said to Plass, "A mind that has no goals? If there's pure order here—"

Karn broke in, her voice high and sweet, singing. "Think of the dimensions of order. There is mere arrangement, the lowest form of order, without motive or direction. Next comes self-making, when order can convert resources into more of itself, propagating order. Then comes creation, self-making reshaping matter into something new. But when creation stalls, when there is no mind, just force, it becomes mere elaboration, an endless spiral of rearrangement of what has been created. What do we see down there? Empty elaboration. Nothing new. No understanding."

"She shows some wisdom," Plass acknowledged grudgingly. "But the allthing still must exist."

"And all this . . . elaboration?" Olmy asked.

"Spoiled by deathlessness," Plass said, "by never-ending supplies of resources. Never freshened by the new, at its core. Order without death, art without critic or renewal, the final mind of a universe where only riches exist, only joy is possible, never knowing disappointment."

The lander shuddered again and again as they dropped toward the pyramid. Its inertial control systems could not cope with the sweeping rays of different world-lines.

"Sounds like a spoiled child," Olmy said.

"Far worse," Karn said. *"We're* like spoiled children, Rasp and I. Willful and maybe a little silly. Humans are silly, childish, always learning, full of failure. Out there—beyond the lesion, reaching through it . . . ."

"Perpetual success," Rasp mocked. "Ultimate and mature. It cannot learn. Only rearrange."

"Deirdre Enoch was never content with limitations," Plass said, looking to Olmy for sympathy. "She went searching for what heaven would really be." Her eyes glittered with her emotion—exaltation brought on by too much fear and dismay.

"Maybe she found it," Karn said.

• 5 •

"I can't welcome you," Deirdre Enoch said, walking heavily toward them. Behind Olmy, within a chamber high in the Redoubt, near the tip of the steel pyramid, the lander sighed and settled into its cradle.

Olmy tried to compare this old woman with the portraits of Enoch in the records. Her voice was much the same, though deeper, and almost without emotion.

Rasp, Karn, and Plass stood beside Olmy as Enoch approached. Behind Enoch, in the lambency of soft amber lights spaced around the base of the chamber, wavered a line of ten other men and women, all of them old, all dressed in black, with silver ribbons hanging from the tops of their white-haired heads. "You've come to a place of waiting where nothing is resolved. Why come at all?"

Before Olmy could answer, Enoch smiled, her deeply wrinkled face seeming to crack with the unfamiliar expression. "We assume you are here because you think the Jarts could become involved."

"I don't know what to think," Olmy said, his voice hoarse. "I recognize you, but none of the others . . ."

"We survived the first night after the lesion. We formed an expedition to make an escape attempt. There were sixty of us that first time. We managed to return to the Redoubt before the Night Land could change us too much, play with us too drastically. We aged. Some of us were taken and . . . You see them out there. There was no second expedition."

"My husband," Plass said. "Where is he?"

"Yes . . . I know you. You are so much the same it hurts. You escaped at the very beginning."

"I was the only one," Plass said.

"You called it the Night Land," Rasp said, holding up her hands, the case with her clavicle. "How appropriate."

"No sun, no hope, only *order*," Enoch said, as if the word were a curse. "Did you send yourselves, or were you sent by other fools?"

"Fools, I'm afraid," Plass said.

"And you . . . You came back, knowing what you'd find?"

"It wasn't like this when I left. My husband sent ghosts to visit me. They told me a little of what's happened here . . . or might have happened."

"Ghosts try to come into the Redoubt and talk," Enoch said, her many legs shifting restlessly. "We refuse them. Your husband was caught outside that first night. He hasn't been changed much. He stands near the Watcher, frozen in the eyebeam."

Plass sobbed and hid her face.

Enoch continued, heedless. "The only thing left in his control— to shed ghosts like dead skin. And never the same . . . are they? He's allowed to take temporary twists of space-time and shape them in his own image. The allthing finds this sufficiently amusing. Needless to say, we don't let the ghosts bother us. We have too much else to do, just to keep our place secure, and in repair."

"Repair," Karn said with a beatific smile, and Olmy turned to her, startled by a reaction similar to his own. Karn did a small dance. "Disorder has its place here, then. You have to *work* to *fix things*?"

"Precisely," Enoch said. "I worship rust and age. But we're only allowed so much of it and no more. Now that you're here, perhaps you'll join us for some tea?" She smiled. "Blessedly, our tea cools quickly in the Redoubt. Our bones grow frail, our skin wrinkles. Tea cools. Hurry!"

"Don't be deceived by our bodies," Deirdre Enoch said as she poured steaming tea into cups for all her guests. "They are distorted, but they are sufficient. The allthing can only perfect and elaborate; it knows nothing of real destruction."

Olmy watched something ripple through the old woman, a shudder of slight change. She seemed not as old and wrinkled now, as if some force had turned back a clock.

"I'm not clear about perfection," Olmy said, lifting the cup without enthusiasm. "I'm not even clear on how you come to look old."

"We're not unhappy," Enoch said. "That isn't within our power. We know we can never return to Thistledown. We know we can never escape."

"You haven't answered Ser Olmy's question," Plass said gently. "Are you independent here?"

"That wasn't his question, Ser Lissa Plass," Enoch said, an edge in her voice. "What you ask is not a *polite* question. I said, we were caught trying to escape. Some of us are out there in the Night Land now. Those of us who returned to the pyramid . . . did not escape the enthusiasm of the allthing. But its influence here is limited. To answer one question at least: we have some independence." Enoch nodded as if falling asleep, her head dropping briefly to an angle with her shoulders . . . an uncomfortable angle, Olmy would have thought. She raised it again with a jerk. "The universe I discovered . . . there is nothing else. It is all."

"The Final Mind of the domain," Plass said.

"I gather it regards the Way and the humans it finds here as objects of curiosity," Olmy said. Rasp and Karn fidgeted but did not object to this line of discussion.

"Objects to be recombined and distorted," Enoch said. "We are materials for the ultimate in decadent art. The allthing is beyond our knowing." She leaned forward on her cushion, where she had gracefully folded her legs into an agile lotus, and rubbed her nose reflectively with the back of one hand. "We are allowed to resist, I suspect, because we are antithesis."

"The allthing has only known thesis," Rasp said with a small giggle.

"Exa-a-a-ctly," Enoch said, drawing out the word with pleasure. Struck by another sensation of unreality, Olmy looked around the group sitting with Enoch and himself: Plass, the twins, and, behind Enoch, a small woman with a questing, feline expression who had said nothing. She carried the teapot around again and refilled their cups.

The tea was cold.

Olmy turned on his sitting pillow to observe the other elderly followers, arrayed around the circular room, still, subservient. Their faces had changed since his arrival, yet no one had left, no one had entered.

It had been observed for a dozen generations that Thistledown's environment and culture bred followers with proportionally fewer leaders, often assigned much greater power. Efforts were being made to remedy that—to reduce the extreme schisms of rogues such as Deirdre Enoch. Too late for these, he thought. Does this allthing want followers?

He could not get his bearings long enough to plan his course of action. He felt drugged, but knew he wasn't.

"Can it tolerate otherness?" Karn asked, her voice high and sweet once more, like a child's.

"No," Enoch said. "Its nature is to absorb and disguise all otherness in mutation, change without goal."

"Like the Jarts?" Rasp asked, chewing on her thumb with a coyness and insecurity that was at once studied and completely convincing.

"Not like the Jarts. The Jarts met the allthing and it gave them their own Night Land. I fear it won't be long until ours is merged with theirs, and we are both mingled and subjected to useless change."

"How long?" Olmy asked.

"Another few years, perhaps."

"Not so soon, then," he said.

"Soon enough," Enoch said with a sniff. She rubbed her nose again. "We've been here already for well over a thousand centuries."

Olmy tried to understand this. "Truly?" he asked, expecting her to break into laughter.

"Truly. I've had millions of different followers here. Look around you." She leaned over the table to whisper to Olmy, "Waves in a sea. I've lived a thousand centuries in a thousand infinitesimally different universes. It plays with all world-lines, not just the tracks of individuals. Only I am relatively the same with each tide. I appear to be the real nexus in this part of the Way."

"Tea cools . . . skin wrinkles . . . But you experience such a length of time?"

"Ten thousand lengths cut up and bundled and rotated." She took a scarf from around her thin neck and stretched it between her fists. "Twisted. Knotted. You were sent here to correct the reckless madness of a renegade . . . weren't you?"

"A Geshel visionary," Olmy said.

Enoch was not mollified. She drew herself up and returned her scarf to her neck, tying it with a conscious flourish. "I was appointed by the Office of Way Maintenance. By Ry Ornis himself. They gave me two of the best gate openers in the guild, and they instructed me, specifically, to find a gate into total order. I wasn't told why. I can guess now, however."

"I remember two openers," Plass said. "They don't."

"They hoped you would find me transformed or dead," Enoch said. "Well, I'm different, but I've survived, and after a few thousands of centuries, one's personality becomes rather rigid. I've become more like that Watcher and its huge gaping eye outside. I don't know how to lie anymore. I've seen too much. I've fought against what I found, and I've endured atrocities beyond what any human has ever had to face. Believe me, I would rather have died before my mission began than see what I've seen."

"Where is the other opener?" Olmy asked.

"In the Night Land," Enoch said. "Issa Danna was the first to encounter the allthing. He and his partner, master Tolby Kin, took the brunt of its first efforts at elaboration."

Rasp walked over to Olmy and whispered in his ear. "There never was a master opener named Tolby Kin."

"Can anybody else confirm your story?" Olmy asked.

"Would you believe anyone here? No," Enoch said.

"Not that it matters," Plass said fatalistically. "The end result is the same."

"Not at all," Enoch said. "We couldn't close down the lesion now even if we had it in our power. Ry Ornis was correct. The rift had to be opened. The infection is not finished. If we don't wait for completion, our universe will never quicken. It'll be born dead." Enoch shook her head and laughed softly. "And no human in our history will ever see a ghost. A haunted world is a living world, Ser Olmy."

Olmy touched his teacup with his finger. The tea was hot again.

The living quarters made available were spare and cold. Most of the Redoubt's energy went to keeping the occupants of the Night Land at bay; that energy was derived from the wall of the Way, an ingenious arrangement set up by Issa Danna before he was caught up in the lesion; sufficient, but not a surfeit by any means.

For the first time in days, Olmy had a few moments alone. He cleared a window looking south, toward the lesion and across about fifty kilometers of the Night Land. Enoch had provided him with a pair of ray-tracing binoculars.

Beyond a tracting grid stretched to its limits, and a glowing demarcation of complete nuclear destruction, through which nothing made of matter could hope to cross, less than a thousand meters from the pyramid, lay the peculiar vivid darkness and the fitful nightmare glows of the allthing's victims.

Olmy swung the lightweight binoculars in a slow, steady arc. What looked like hills or low mountains were constructions attended by hundreds of pale figures, human-sized but only vaguely human in shape. They seemed to spend much of their time fighting, waving their limbs about like insect antennae. Others carried loads of glowing dust in baskets, dumping them at the top of a hill, then stumbling and sliding down to begin again.

The giant head modeled after the opener stood a little to the west of the Green Glass Castle. Olmy could not tell whether the head was actually organic material—human flesh—or not. It looked more like stone, though the eye was very expressive.

From this angle, he could not see the huge figure standing in the door of the castle; that side was turned away from the Redoubt. Nothing that he saw contradicted what Plass and Enoch had told him. He could not share the cheerful nihilism of the twins. Nevertheless, nothing that he saw could be fit into any philosophy or web of physical laws he had ever encountered. If there was a mind here, it was incomprehensibly different—perhaps no mind at all.

459

Still, he tried to find some pattern, some plan to the Night Land. A rationale. He could not.

Just before the tallest hills stood growths like the tangled roots of upended trees, leafless, barren, dozens of meters high and stretching in ugly, twisted forests several kilometers across. A kind of pathway reached from the northern wall of the Redoubt, through the demarcation, into a tortured terrain of what looked like huge strands of melted and drawn glass, and to the east of the castle. It dropped over a closer hill and he could not see where it terminated.

The atmosphere around the Redoubt was remarkably clear, though columns of twisted mist rose around the Night Land. Before a wall of blue haze at some fifty kilometers distance, everything stood out with complete clarity.

Olmy turned away at a knock on his door. Plass entered, wearing a look of contentment that seemed ready to burst into enthusiasm. "Now do you doubt me?"

"I doubt everything," Olmy said. "I'd just as soon believe we've been captured and are being fed delusions."

"Do you think that's what's happened?" Plass asked, eyes narrowing as if she had been insulted.

"No," Olmy said. "I've experienced some pretty good delusions in training. This is real, whatever that means."

"I must admit the little twins are busy," Plass said, sitting on a small chair near the table. These and a small mattress on the floor were the only items of furniture in the room. "They're talking to anybody who knows anything about Enoch's gate openers. I don't think you can talk to the same person twice here in an hour—unless it's Enoch."

Olmy nodded. He was still digesting Enoch's claim that the Office of Way Maintenance had sent an expedition with secret orders . . . In collusion with the Openers Guild.

Perhaps the twins knew more than he did, or Plass. "Did you know anything about an official mission?" he asked.

Plass did not answer for a moment. "Not in so many words. Not 'official.' But perhaps not without . . . support from Way Maintenance. We did not think we were outlaws."

"You've both talked about completion. Was that mentioned when you joined the group?"

"Only in passing. A theory."

Olmy turned back to the window. "There's a camera obscura near the top of the pyramid. I'd like to look over everything around us, try to make sense of our position."

"Useless," Plass said. "I'd wait for a visitation first."

"More ghosts?"

Plass shrugged her shoulders and stretched out her legs, rubbing her knees.

"I haven't been visited," Olmy said.

"It will happen," Plass said flatly. She appeared to be hiding something, something that worried her. "I wouldn't look forward to it. But then, there's nothing you can do to prepare."

Olmy laughed, but the laugh sounded hollow. He felt as if he were slowly coming unraveled, like Enoch's bundle of relived world-lines. "How would I know if I've seen a ghost?" he asked. "Maybe I have— on Thistledown. Maybe they're around us all the time, but don't reveal themselves."

Plass looked to one side, then said, with an effort, her voice half-choking, "I've met my own ghost."

"You didn't mention that before."

"It came to visit me the night after we left Thistledown. It told me we would reach the pyramid."

Olmy held back another laugh, afraid it might get loose and never stop. "I've never seen a ghost of myself."

"We do things differently, then. I seemed to be working backward from some experience with the allthing. A ghost lets you remember the future, or some alternate of the future. Maybe in time I'll be told what the allthing will do to me. Its elaborations."

Olmy considered this in silence. Plass's somber gray eyes focused on him, clear, childlike in their perfect gravity. Now he saw the resemblance, the reason why he felt a tug of liking for her. She reminded him of Sheila Ap Nam, his first wife on Lamarckia.

"Your loved ones, friends, colleagues . . . They will see you, versions of you, if you meet the allthing," Plass said. "A kind of immortality. Remembrance." She looked down and clutched her arms. "No other intelligent species we've encountered has a history of myths about spirits. No experience with ghosts. You know that? We're unique. Alone. Except perhaps the Jarts . . . and we don't know much about them, do we?"

He nodded, wanting to get rid of the topic. "What are the twins planning?"

"They seem to regard this as a challenging game. Who knows? They're working. It's even possible they'll think of something."

Olmy aimed the binoculars toward the Watcher, its single glowing eye forever turned toward the Redoubt. He felt a bone-deep revulsion and hatred, mixed with a desiccating chill. His tongue seemed frosted.

Perversely, the flesh behind his eyes felt hot and moist. His neck hair pricked.

"There's—" he began, but then flinched and blinked. A curtain of shadow passed through the few centimeters between him and the window. He backed off with a groan and tried to push something away, but the curtain would not be touched. It whirled around him, passed before Plass, who tracked it calmly, and then seemed to press against and slip through the opposite wall.

The warmth behind his eyes felt hot as steam.

"I *knew* it!" he said hoarsely. "I could feel it coming! Something about to happen." His hands trembled. He had never reacted so drastically to physical danger.

"That was nothing," Plass said. "I've seen them many times, more since I first came here."

Olmy's reaction angered him. "What is it?"

"Not a ghost, not any other version of ourselves, that's for sure," she said. "A parasite, maybe, like some sort of flea darting around our world-lines. Harmless, as far as I know. But much more visible here than back on Thistledown."

Trying to control himself was backfiring. All his instincts rejected what he was experiencing. "I don't accept any of this!" he shouted. His hands spasmed into fists. "None of it makes sense!"

"I agree," Plass said, her voice low. "Pity we're stuck with it. Pity you're stuck with me. But more pity that I'm stuck with you. It seems you try to be a rational man, Ser Olmy. My husband was exceptionally rational. The allthing adores rational men."

• 6 •

Rasp and Karn walked with Olmy on the parapet near the peak of the Redoubt. Their work seemed to have sobered them. They still walked like youngsters, Karn or Rasp lagging to peer at something in the Night Land and then scurrying to catch up; but their voices were steady, serious, even a little sad.

"We've never experienced anything like the lesion," Karn said. The huge dark disk, rimmed in bands and flares of red, blotted out the opposite side of the Way. "It's much more than just a failed gate. It doesn't stop here, you know."

"How do you mean?" Olmy asked.

"Something like this influences the entire Way. When the gate got out of control—"

Rasp took Karn's hand and tugged it in warning.

"What does it matter?" Karn asked, and shook her twin loose. "There can't be secrets here. If we don't agree to do something, the allthing will get us soon anyway, and then we'll be planted out there . . . bits and pieces of us, like lost toys."

Rasp dropped back a few steps, folded her arms in pique. Karn continued. "When the lesion formed, gate openers felt it in every new gate. Threads trying to get through, like spidersilk. We can see the world-lines being twirled here . . . But they bunch up and wind around the Way even where we can't see them. Master Ry Ornis thought—"

"Enough!" Rasp said, rushing to catch up.

Karn stopped with tears in her eyes and glared over the parapet wall.

"I can guess a few things," Olmy said. "What Deirdre Enoch says leaves little enough to imagine. You aren't failed apprentices, are you?"

Rasp stared at him defiantly.

"No," Karn said.

Her twin turned and lifted a hand as if to strike her, then dropped it by her side. She drew a short breath, said, "We act like children because of the mathematical conditioning. Too fast. Ry Ornis told us we were needed. He accelerated training. We were the best, but we *are* too young. It holds us down."

A sound like hundreds of voices in a bizarre chorus floated over the Night Land, through the field that protected the Redoubt's atmosphere. The chorus alternately rose and sank through scales, hooting forlornly like apes in a zoo.

"Ry Ornis thought the lesion was bending world-lines even beyond Thistledown," Karn said. Rasp nodded and held her sister's hand. "Climbing back along the Thistledown's world-line . . . where all our lives bunch together with the lives of our ancestors. Using us as a ladder."

"Not just us," Rasp added. The hooting chorus now came from all around the Redoubt. From this side of the pyramid, they could see a slender obelisk the colors of bright moon on an oil slick rising within an immense scaffold made of parts of bodies, arms and legs strapped together with cords. These limbs were monstrous, however, fully dozens of meters long, and the obelisk had climbed within its scaffolding to at least a kilometer in height, twice as tall as the Redoubt.

The region around the construction crawled with pale tubular bodies, like insect larvae, and Olmy decided it was these bodies that were doing most of the singing and hooting.

"Right," Karn agreed. "Not just us. Using the branching lines of all the matter, all the particles in Thistledown and the Way."

"Who knows how far it's reached?" Rasp asked.

"What can it do?" Olmy asked.

"We don't know," Karn said.

"What can *we* do?"

"Oh, we can close down the lesion, if we act quickly," Rasp said with a broken smile. "That shouldn't be too difficult."

"It's actually growing smaller," Karn said. "We can create a ring gate from here . . . A cirque. Cinch off the Way. The Way will shrink back toward the source, the maintenance machinery in the sixth chamber, very quickly—a million kilometers a day. We might even be able to escape along the flaw, but—"

"The flaw will act weird if we make a cinch," Rasp finished.

"Very weird," Karn agreed. "So we probably don't get home. We knew that. Ry Ornis prepared us. He told us that much."

"Besides, if we did go back to Thistledown, who would want us now, the way we are?" Rasp asked. "We're pretty broken inside."

The twins paused on the parapet. Olmy watched as they clasped hands and began to hum softly to each other. Their clavicles hung from their shoulders, and the cases tapped as they swayed. Rasp glanced at Olmy, primming her lips.

"Enoch spoke of a plan by the Office of Way Maintenance," Olmy said. "She claims she was sent here secretly."

"We know nothing about that," Karn said guilelessly. "But that might not mean much. I don't think they would have trusted us."

"She also said that the allthing has some larger purpose in our own universe," Olmy continued. "Something that has to be completed, or our existence will be impossible."

Karn considered this quietly, finger to her nostril, then shook her head. "We heard her, but I don't see it," she said. "Maybe she's trying to justify herself."

"*We* do that all the time," Rasp said. "We understand that sort of thing."

They had reached the bottom of the stairs leading up to the peak and the camera obscura. Karn climbed two steps at a time, her robe swinging around her ankles, and Rasp followed with more dignity. Olmy stayed near the bottom. Rasp turned and looked down on him.

"Come on," she said, waving.

Olmy shook his head. "I've seen enough. I can't make sense out of anything out there. I think it's random—just nonsense."

"Not at all!" Rasp said, and descended a few steps, beseeching him to join her. "We have to see what happened to the openers' clavicles. What sort of elaboration there might be. It could be very important."

Olmy hunched his shoulders, shook his head like a bull trying to build courage. He followed her up the steps.

The camera obscura was a spherical all-focal lens, its principle not unlike that of the ray-tracing binoculars. Mounted on a tripod on the flat platform at the peak of the pyramid, it projected and magnified the Night Land for anyone standing on the platform. Approaching the tripod increased magnification in logarithmic steps, with precise quickness; distances of a few tens of a centimeter could make objects zoom to alarming proportions. Monitors on the peripheral circle, small spheres on steel poles, rolled in and out with slow grace, tracking the developments in the Night Land and sending their results down to Enoch and the others inside.

Olmy deftly avoided the monitors and walked slowly, with great concentration, around the circle. Karn and Rasp made their own surveys.

Olmy stopped and drew back to take in the Watcher's immense eye. The angle of the hairless brow, the droop of the upper lid, gave it a corpselike and sad lassitude, but the eye still moved in small arcs, and from this perspective, there was no doubt it was observing the Redoubt. Olmy felt that it saw him, knew him; had he ever met the opener, before his mission to Lamarckia, perhaps by accident? Was there some residual memory of Olmy in that immense head? Olmy thought such a connection might be very dangerous.

"The Night Land changes every hour, sometimes small changes, sometimes massive," Enoch said, walking slowly and deliberately up the steps behind them. She stopped outside the camera's circle. "It tracks our every particle. It's patient."

"Does it fear us?" Olmy asked.

"No fear. We haven't even begun to be played with."

"That out there is not elaboration—it's pointless madness."

"I thought so myself," Enoch said. "Now I see a pattern. The longer I'm here, the more I sympathize with the allthing. Do you understand what I told you earlier? It *recognizes* us, Ser Olmy. It sees its own work in us, a cycle waiting to be completed."

Rasp held a spot within the circle and motioned for Karn to join her. Together, they peered at something in complete absorption, ignoring Enoch.

Olmy could not ignore her, however. He needed to resolve this question. "The Office of Way Maintenance sent you here to confirm that?"

"Not in so many words, but . . . Yes. We know that our own domain, our home universe outside the Way, should have been born barren, empty. Something quickened it, fed it with the necessary geometric nutrients. Some of us thought that would only be possible if the early universe made a connection with a domain of very different properties. I told Ry Ornis that such a quickening need not have happened at the beginning. We could do it now. We had the Way . . . We could perform the completion. There was such a feeling of power and justification within the guild. I encouraged it. The connection has been made . . . And all that, the Night Land, is just a side effect. Pure order flowing back through the Way, through Thistledown, back through time to the beginning. Was it worth it? Did we do what we had planned? I'll never know conclusively, because we can't reverse it now . . . and cease to be."

"You weren't sure. You knew this could be dangerous, harm the Way, fatal if the Jarts gained an advantage?"

Enoch stared at him for a few seconds, eyes moving from his eyes to his lips, his chest, as if she would measure him. "Yes," she said. "I knew. Ry Ornis knew. The others did not."

"They suffered for what you've learned," Olmy said. Enoch's gaze steadied, and her jaw clenched.

"I've suffered, too. I've learned very little, Ser Olmy. What I learn repeats itself over and over again, and it has more to do with arrogance than metaphysics."

"We've found one!" Karn shouted. "There's a clavicle mounted on top of the green castle. We can pinpoint it!"

Olmy stood where Rasp indicated. At the top of the squat, massive green castle stood a cube, half-hidden behind a mass of rootlike growth. On top of the cube, a black pillar about the height of a man supported the unmistakable sphere-and-handles of a clavicle. The sphere was dark, dormant; nothing moved around the pillar or anywhere on the castle roof.

"There's only one, and it appears to be inactive," Rasp said. "The lesion is independent."

Karn spread her arms, wiggling her fingers. A wide smile lit up her face. "We can make a cirque!"

"We can't do it from here," Rasp said. "We have to go out there."

Enoch's face tensed into a rigid mask. "We haven't finished," she said. "The work isn't done!"

Olmy shook his head. He'd made his decision. "Whoever started this, and for whatever reason, it has to end now. The Nexus orders it."

"They don't know!" Enoch cried out.

"We know enough," Olmy said.

Rasp and Karn held each other's hands and descended the stairs. Rasp stuck her tongue out at the old woman.

Enoch laughed and lightly slapped her hands on her thighs. "They're only children! They won't succeed. What have I to fear from failed apprentices?"

The Night Land's atmosphere was a thin haze of primordial hydrogen, mixed with carbon dioxide and some small trace of oxygen from the original envelope surrounding the gate. At seven hundred millibars of pressure, and with a temperature just above freezing, they could venture out of the Redoubt in the most basic pressurized worksuits.

Enoch and her remaining, ever-changing people would not help them. Olmy preferred it that way. He walked through the empty corridors of the pyramid's ground floor and found a small wheeled vehicle that at one time had been used to reach the garden outside the Redoubt—a garden that now lay beyond the demarcation.

Plass showed him how the open vehicle worked. "It has its own pilot, makes a field around the passenger compartment."

"It looks familiar enough," Olmy said.

Plass sat next to Olmy and placed her hand on a control bar. "My husband and I used to tend our plot out there . . . flowers, herbs, vegetables. We'd drive one of these for a few hundred meters, outside the work zone, to where the materials team had spread soil brought through the first gate."

Olmy sat in the vehicle. It announced it was drawing a charge in case it would be needed. It added, in a thin voice, "Will this journey last more than a few hours? I can arrange with the stationmaster for—"

"No," Olmy said. "No need." He turned to Plass. "Time to put on a suit."

Plass stepped out of the car and nervously smoothed her hands down her hips. "I'm staying here. I can't bring myself to go out there again."

"I understand."

"I don't see how you'll survive."

"It looks very chancy," Olmy admitted.

"Why can't they open a ring gate from here?"

"Rasp and Karn say they have to be within five hundred meters of the lesion. About where the other clavicle is now."

"Do you know what my husband was, professionally? Before we came here?"

"No."

"A neurologist. He came along to study the effects of our experiment on the researchers. There was some thought our minds would be enhanced by contact with the ordered domain. They were all very optimistic." She put her hand on Olmy's shoulder. "We had faith. Enoch still believes what they told her, doesn't she?"

Olmy nodded. "May I make one last request?"

"Of course," Plass said.

"Enoch promised us she would open a way through the demarcation and let us through. She claimed we couldn't do anything out there but be taken in by the allthing, anyway . . ."

Plass smiled. "I'll watch her, make sure the fields are open long enough for you to go through. The guild was very clever, sending you and the twins, you know."

"Why?"

"You're all very deceptive. You all seem to be failures." Plass clenched his shoulder.

She turned and left as Rasp and Karn entered the storage chamber. The twins watched her go in silence. They carried their clavicles and had already put on their pressure suits, which had adjusted to their small frames and made a precise fit.

"We've always made her uncomfortable," Rasp said. "Maybe I don't blame her."

Karn regarded Olmy with deep black eyes. "You haven't met a ghost of yourself, have you?"

"I haven't," Olmy said.

"Neither have we. And that's significant. We're never going to reach the allthing. It's never going to get us."

Olmy remembered what Plass had said. She had seen her own ghost . . .

• **7** •

They cursed the opening of the Way and the change of the Thistledown's mission. They assassinated the Way's creator, Konrad Korzenowski. For centuries they maintained a fierce opposition, largely underground, but with connections to the Naderites in power. In any given year there might be only four or five active members of this most radical sect, the rest presuming to lead normal lives; but the chain was maintained. All this because their original leader had a vision of the Way as an easy route to infinite hells.

—

Lives of the Opposition, Anonymous,
Journey Year 475

The three rode the tiny wheeled vehicle over a stretch of bare Way floor, a deeply tarnished copper-bronze–colored surface of no substance whatsoever, and no friction at this point. They kept their course with little jets of air expelled from the sides of the car, until they reached a broad low island of glassy materials, just before the boundary markers that warned they were coming to the demarcation.

As agreed, the traction lines switched to low power, and an opening appeared directly ahead of them, a clarified darkness in the pale green field. This relieved Olmy somewhat; he had had some doubts that Enoch would cooperate, or that Plass could compel her. The vehicle rolled through. They crossed the defenses. Behind them, the fields went up again.

Now the floor of the Way was covered with sandy soil. The autopilot switched off the air jets and let the vehicle roll for another twenty meters.

The pressure suits were already becoming uncomfortable; they were old, and while they did their best to fit, their workings were in less than ideal condition. Still, they would last several weeks, recycling gases and liquids and complex molecules, rehydrating the body through arterial inserts and in the same fashion providing a minimal diet.

Olmy doubted the suits would be needed for more than a few more hours.

The twins ignored their discomfort and focused their attention on the lesion. Outside the pyramid, the lesion seemed to fill the sky, and in a few kilometers, it would be almost directly overhead. From this angle, the hairlike swirls of spinning world-lines already took on a shimmering reflective quality, like bands sliced from a wind-ruffled lake; their passage sang in Olmy's skull, more through his teeth than through his ears.

The full character of the Night Land came on gradually, beginning with a black, gritty, loose scrabble beneath the tires of the vehicle. Olmy's suit readout, shining directly into his left eye, showed a decrease in air pressure of a few millibars beyond the demarcation. The temperature remained steady, just above zero degrees Celsius.

469

They turned west, to their left as they faced north down the Way, and came upon the path Olmy had seen from the peak of the pyramid. Plass had identified it as the road used by vehicles carrying material from the first gate Enoch had opened. It had also been the path to Plass's garden, the one she had shared with her husband. Within a few minutes, about three kilometers from the Redoubt, passing over the rise that had blocked his view, they came across the garden's remains.

The relief here was very low, but the rise of some fifty meters had been sufficient to hide what must have been among the earliest attempts at elaboration. Olmy was not yet sure he believed in the all-thing, but what had happened in the garden, and in the rest of the Night Land, made any disagreement moot. The trees in the southwest corner of a small rapid-growth orchard had spread out low to the ground, and glowed now like the body of Number 2. Those few trees left standing flickered like frames in a child's flipbook. The rest of the orchard had simply turned to sparkling ash. In the center, however, rose a mound of gnarled brown shot through with vivid reds and greens, and in the middle of this mound, facing almost due south, not looking at anything in particular, was a face some three meters in height, its skin the color of green wood, cracks running from crown to chin. The face did not move or exhibit any sign of life.

Puffs of dust rose from the ash, tiny little explosions from within this mixture of realities. The ash re-formed to obliterate the newly formed craters. It seemed to have some purpose of its own, as did everything else in the garden but the face.

Ruin and elaboration; one form of life extinguished, another imbued.

"Early," Karn said, looking to their right at a sprawl of shining dark green leaves, stretched, expanded, and braided into eye-twisting knots. "Didn't know what it was dealing with."

"Doesn't look like it ever did," Olmy said, realizing she was speaking as if some central director actually did exist.

Rasp set her sister straight. "We've seen textbook studies of gates gone wrong. Geometry is the living tissue of reality. Mix constants and you get a—"

"We've sworn not to discuss the failures," Karn said, but without any strength.

"We are being driven through the worst failure of all," Rasp said. "Mixed constants and skewed metrics explain all of this."

Karn shrugged. Olmy thought that perhaps it did not matter; perhaps Rasp and Karn and Plass did not really disagree, merely described the same thing in different ways. What they were seeing up close was not random rearrangement; it had a demented, even a vicious quality, that suggested purpose.

Above the rows of flipbook trees and the living layers of ash stretched a dead and twisted sky. From the hideous chancre of dead blackness, with its sullen ring of congealed red, depended curtains of rushing darkness that swept the Night Land like rain beneath a moving front.

"Mother's hair," Karn said, and clutched her clavicle tightly in white-knuckled hands.

"She's playing with us," Rasp said. "Bending over us, waving her hair over our crib. We reach up to grab, and she pulls away."

"She laughs," Karn said.

"Then she gives us to the—"

Rasp did not have time to finish. The vehicle swerved abruptly with a small squeak before a sudden chasm that had not been there an instant before. Out of the chasm leaped white shapes, humanlike but fungal, doughy and featureless. They seemed to be expelled and to climb out equally, and they lay on the sandy black-streaked ground for a moment, as if recovering from their birth. Then they rose to loose and wobbling feet and ran with speed and even grace over the irregular landscape to the trees, which they began to uproot.

These were the laborers Olmy had seen from the pyramid. They paid no attention to the intruders. The chasm closed, and Olmy instructed the car to continue.

"Is that what we'll become?" Karn asked.

"Each of us will become *many* of them," Rasp said.

"Such a relief to know!" Karn said sardonically.

The rotating shadows ahead gave the ground a blurred and frantic aspect, like unfocused time-lapse photography. Only the major landmarks stood unchanged in the sweeps of metaphysical revision: the Watcher, pale beam still glowing from its unblinking eye; the Castle with its unseen giant occupant; and the obelisk with its scaffold and hordes of white figures working directly beneath the lesion.

Olmy ordered the vehicle to stop, but Rasp grabbed his hand. "Farther," she said. "We can't do anything here."

Olmy grinned and threw back his head, then grimaced like a monkey in the oldest forest of all, baring his teeth at this measureless madness.

"Farther!" Karn insisted. The car rolled on, jolting with the regular ridges some powerful force had pushed up in the sand.

Above the constant sizzle of rearranged world-lines, like a symphony of scrubbing and tapping brooms, came more sounds. If a burning forest could sing its pain, Olmy thought, it would be like the rising wail that came from the tower and the Castle. Thousands of the white figures made thousands of different sounds, as if trying to talk to each other, but not succeeding. Mock speech, singsong pidgin nonsense, attempts to communicate emotions and thoughts they could not truly have; protests at being jabbed and pulled and jiggled along the scaffolding of the tower, over the uneven ground, like puppets directed by something trying to mock a process of construction.

Olmy's body had up to that moment sent him a steady bloodwash of fear. He had controlled this emotion as well as he could, but never ignored it; that would have been senseless and wrong, for fear was what told him he came from a world that made sense, that held together and was consistent, that *worked*.

Yet fear was not enough, could not be an adequate response to what they were seeing. This was a threat beyond anything the body had been designed to experience. Had he allowed himself to scream, he could not have screamed loudly enough.

The Death we all know, Olmy told himself, is an end to something real; death here would be worse than nightmare, worse than the hell one imagines for one's enemies and unbelievers.

"I know," Karn said, and her hands shook on the clavicle.

"What do you know?" Rasp asked.

"Every meter, every second, every dimension, has its own mind here," Karn said. "Space and time are arguing, fighting."

Rasp disagreed violently. "No mind, no minds at all!" she insisted shrilly.

Light itself began to waver and change as they came closer to the tower. Olmy could see the face of oncoming events before they occurred, like waves on a beach, rushing over the land, impatient to reach their destinations, their observers, before all surprise had been lost.

They now entered the fringes of shadow. The revisions of their surroundings felt like deep drumming pulses. Caught directly in a shadow, Olmy felt a sudden rub of excitement. He saw flashes of colors, felt a spectrum of unfamiliar emotions that threatened to cancel out his fear. He looked to his left, into the counterclockwise sweep, anticipating each front of darkness, leaning toward it. Ecstasy, followed by a buzz of exhilaration, suddenly a spasm of brilliance, all the while the back of his head crisping and glowing and sparking. He could see into the back of his brain, down to the working foundations of every thought—where symbols with no present meaning are painted and arrayed on long tables, then jerked and jostled until they become emotions and memories and words.

"Like opening a gate!" Karn shouted, seeing Olmy's expression.

"Much worse. Dangerous! Very dangerous!"

"Don't ignore it, don't suppress," Rasp told him. "Just pay attention to what's in front! That's what they teach us when we open a gate!"

"These aren't gates!" Olmy shouted above the hideous symphony of brooms. The twins' heads jerked and vibrated as he spoke.

"They are!" Rasp said. "Little gates into directly adjacent worlds. They're trying to escape their neighboring realities, to split away, but the lesion gathers them, holds them. They flow back behind us, along our world-lines."

"Back to the beginning!" Karn said.

"Back to our birth!" Rasp said.

"Here!" Karn said, and Olmy brought the car to a stop. The two assistants, little more than girls, with pale faces and wide eyes and serious expressions climbed down from the open cab and marched resolutely across the rippled sand, leaning into the pressure of other streams of reality. Their clothes changed color, their hair changed its arrangement, even their skin changed color, but they marched until the clavicles seemed to lift of their own will.

Rasp and Karn faced each other.

Olmy told himself, with whatever was left of his mind, that they were now going to attempt a cirque, a ring gate, that would bring all this to a meeting with the flaw. Within the flaw lay the peace of incommensurable contradictions, pure and purifying. Within the flaw this madness would burn to less than nothing, to paradoxes that would cancel and expunge.

He did not think they would have time to escape, even if the shrinking of the Way was less than instantaneous.

He stood on the seat of the car for a moment, watching the twins, admiring them. *Enoch underestimates them. As have I. This is what Ry Ornis wanted, why he chose them.*

He hunched his shoulders: something coming. Before he could duck or jump aside, Olmy was caught between two folds of shadow, like a bug snatched between fingers, and lifted bodily from the car. He twisted his neck and looked back to see a fuzzy image of the car, the twins lifting their clavicles, the rippled and streaked sand. The car seemed to vibrate, the tire tracks rippling behind it like snakes; and for a long moment, the twins and the car were not visible at all, as if they had never been.

Olmy's thoughts raced and his body shrieked with joy. Every nerve shivered, and all his memories stood out together in sharp relief, with different selves viewing them all at once. He could not distinguish between present and future; all were just parts of different memories. His reference point had blurred to where his life was a flat field, and within that field swam a myriad of possibilities. What would happen, what had happened, became indistinguishable from the unchosen and unlived moments that *could* happen.

This blurring of his world-line rushed backward. He felt he could sidle across fates into what was fixed and unfix it, free his past to be all possible, all potential, once more. But the diffusion, the smearing and blending of the chalked line of his life, came up against the moment of his resurrection, the abrupt shift from Lamarckia—

And could not go any farther. Dammed, the tide of his life spilled out in all directions. He cried out in surprise and a kind of pain he had never known before.

Olmy hung suspended beneath the dark eye, spinning slowly, all things above and below magnified or made minute depending on his angle. The pain passed. Perhaps it had never been. He felt as if his head had become a tiny but all-seeing camera obscura.

There was a past in which Ry Ornis accompanied the twins; he saw them working together near a very different vehicle, tractor rather than small car, to make the cirque. Already they had forced the Way to extrude a well through the sand. A cupola floated over the well, brazen and smooth, reflecting in golden hues the flaw, the lesion.

Olmy turned his head a fraction of a centimeter and once more saw only the twins, but this time dead, lying mangled beside the car, their clavicles flaring and burning. Another degree or two, and they were resurrected, still working. Ry Ornis was with them again.

A memory: Ry Ornis had traveled with them in the flawship. How could he have lost this fact?

Olmy rotated again, this time in a new and unfamiliar dimension, and felt the Way simply cease to exist and his own life with it. From this dark and soundless eventuality, he turned with a bitter, acrid wrench and found a very narrow course through the gripping shadows, a course illuminated by half-forgotten emotions that had been plucked like flowers, arranged like silent speech.

He had been carried to the other side of the lesion, looking north down the endless throat of the Way.

The gripping baleen of shadow from the whale's mouth of the lesion, the driving cilia wisking him between world-lines, drove him under and over a complex surface through which he could see a deep mountainous valley, its floor smooth and vitreous like obsidian.

Black glass, reflecting the lesion, the flaw behind the lesion, scudding layers of mist. The cilia that controlled Olmy's orientation let him drop to a few meters above the vitreous black floor.

Motion stopped. His thoughts slowed. He felt only one body, one existence. All his lines clumped back into one flow.

He tried to close his eyes, to not see, but that was impossible. He faced down and saw his reflection in the mirror-shiny valley floor, a small still man floating beneath the red-rimmed eye like an intruding mote.

On either side of the valley rose jagged glassy peaks, mountain ranges like shreds of pulled taffy. A few hundred meters ahead of him—or perhaps a few kilometers—mounted in the middle of the valley, lay something he recognized: a Jart defensive emplacement, white as ivory, jagged spikes thrusting like a sea urchin's spines from a squat discus. Shaded cilia played around the spikes, but the spikes did not track, did not move.

The emplacement was dead.

Olmy held his hands in front of his face. He could see them, see through them, with equal clarity. Nothing was obscured, nothing neglected by his new vision.

He tried to speak, or perhaps to pray, to whatever it was that held him, directed his motion. He asked first if anything was there, listening. No answer.

He remembered Plass's comments about the allthing: that in its domain it was unique, had never learned the arts of communication, was *one* without other and controlled all by *being all*. No separation between mind and matter, observed and observer. Such a being could neither listen nor answer. Nor could it change.

He thought of the emotions arrayed along the path that had guided him here. Pain, disappointment, fear. Weariness. Had the allthing learned this method of communication after its time in the Way? Had it dissected and rearranged enough human elements to change its nature this much?

Why pain? Olmy asked, spoken but unheard in the stillness.

He moved north down the center of the valley, over the dead Jart emplacement. His reflection shimmered in the uneven black mirror of the floor. He looked east and west, up the long curves of the Way beyond the jagged mountain, and saw more Jart emplacements, the spiral and beaded walls of what looked like Jart settlements, all abandoned, all spotted with large, distorted shapes he could not begin to comprehend.

Olmy thought, *It's made a Night Land for the Jarts. It does not know any difference between us.*

As if growing used to the extraordinary pressure of the shadow cilia gripping him, his body once more sent signals of fear, then simple, childlike wonder, and finally its own exhaustion. Olmy's head rolled on his shoulders and he felt his body sleep, but his mind remained alert. All his muscles tingled as they went off-line and would not respond to his tentative urgings.

How much time passed, if it were possible for time to pass, he could not judge. The tingling stopped and control returned. He lifted his head and saw a different valley, this one lined with huge figures. If the scale he had assumed at the beginning of his journey was still valid, these monolithic sculptures or shapes or beings—whatever they might be—were fully two or three kilometers distant, and therefore hundreds of meters in height. They were so strange he found himself looking at them in his peripheral vision, to avoid the confusion of placing them at the points of his visual focus. While vaguely organic in design—compound curves, folds of what might have been a semblance of tissue weighted by gravity, a kind of multilateral symmetry—the figures simply refused to be analyzed.

Olmy had many times experienced a lapse of visual judgment, when he would look at something in his living quarters and not remember it right away, and because of dim lighting or an unfamiliar angle, be unable to judge what it was. Under those conditions, he could feel his mind making hypotheses, trying desperately to compare them with what he was looking directly at, to reach some valid conclusion, and so actually *see* the object. This had occurred to him many times on Lamarckia, especially with regard to objects unique to that planet.

Here, he had no prior experience, no memory, no physical training or familiarity whatsoever with what he looked at, so he saw *nothing* sensible, nameable, to which he could begin to relate. Slowly, it dawned on Olmy that these might be more trophies of the allthing's encounters with Jarts.

He was drifting down a rogue's gallery of failed models, failed attempts to duplicate and understand, much like the gallery of objects and conditions around the Redoubt that made up the Night Land.

Humans had approached from the south, Jarts from the north. The allthing had applied similar awkward tools to both, either to unify them into its being, or to find some new way to experience their otherness. Both had been incomprehensibly alien to the allthing.

Pain. One of the emotions borrowed from Olmy's mind and arrayed along the pathway. A sense of disunification, unwanted change. The allthing had been disturbed by this entry; there was no evil, no enthusiastic destruction, in the Night Land. Olmy suddenly saw what Enoch had been trying to communicate to him, and went beyond her own understanding.

A monobloc of pure order had been invaded by a domain whose main character was that of disunity and contradiction. That must have been very painful indeed. And this quality of order was being sucked backward, like gas into a vacuum, into their domain.

Enoch and the guild of gate openers had manufactured the tip of a tooth. They had thrust into this other domain the bloody predatorial tooth of a hungry universe seeking quickening, a completion at its own beginning.

But this hypothesis did not instantly open any floodgate of comprehension or communication. Olmy did not find himself suddenly analyzing the raw emotional outbursts of another mind, godlike or otherwise; the allthing was not a mind in any sense he could understand. It was simply a pure and necessary set of qualities. It gripped him, controlled him, but literally had no use for him. Like everything else here, it could neither analyze nor absorb him. It could not even spread back along his world-line, for Olmy's existence had begun over with this new body, with his resurrection.

That was why he had not met any ghosts of himself. Physically, he had almost no past. The allthing, if such existed, had flung him along this valley of waste and failure, another piece of detritus, even more frustrating than most.

He squirmed, his body struggling to break free like an animal in a cage. Panic overwhelmed him despite his best efforts. Olmy could not locate any point of reference within; not even a self was clearly defined.

Everything blurred, became confused, as if he had been smudged by an enormous finger and no outline remained. *I am no where, no here, no name, moving, no future.*

He twisted, convulsed, trying to find his center. The figures mounted on the ranges of mountains to either side seemed interested in this effort. He could feel their attention and did not welcome it. He fancied they moved, however slowly, advancing toward him across astronomical time.

If this lump of conflicting order and chaos could define himself anew, perhaps these incomprehensible monoliths, these unworshiped gods and unrealized mockeries, could establish a presence as well.

The panic stopped. Signals stopped.

He had come to an end. That minimum condition he had wished for was now upon him. He cared nothing for past or future, had lost nothing, gained nothing.

I am or was a part of a society really no part of any
This name is Olmy Ap Sennen
Lover of many loved and loving by few
Contact nothing without
Without contact nothing
Uprooted tree

The lesion's inflamed rim began to brighten. The suspended and aimless figure in its gripping cilia of probabilities maintained enough structure and drive to be interested in this, and noted that, compared to past memory, the lesion was much smaller, much darker, and the flaring rim much broader. It resembled an immense solar eclipse with a bloody corona.

Loyalties and loves uprooted

Language itself faded until the aimless figure saw only images, the lushness of another world out of reach, closed off, the faces of old humans, once loved, once reassuringly close, now dead and without ghosts.

Can't even be haunted by a past uprooted

The figure's motion down the valley slowed. No time passed. Eternity, endless now. Naked, skinless, fleshless, boneless. Consumed, integrated.

Experiences stillness.

Mark this in an endless column: *experiences*

Experiences stillness
stillness
stillness

No divisions. A tiny place no bigger than a fist, a womb. Tiny place of infinite peace at the heart of a frozen geometry. All elabora-

tion, variation, permutation, long since exhausted; infinite access to unbounded energy contained in oneness.
You/I/We no difference. See?
See. Vidya. All seeing. Eye of Buddha. Nerveless kalpas of some body. Nerve vanity.
This oneness consumed. Many nows, peace past.
At peace in the past. Loved women, raised children, lived a long life on a world to which there is no returning.
Nothing one at peace in no past all completed no returning.
Point.
One makes possible all.
I see. Buddha, do not leave your student bound.
The eye is shrinking, closing, its gorgeous bloody flare dimming. It is pierced by a white needle visible behind the small dark center.

Small large no matter no time
Do not go. Take us with
Am your father/mother/food
loved raised living longing no return
my own ghost

∘ 8 ∘

Ry Ornis, the tall insect-thin master, smiled down on him. Olmy saw many of the master opener, like an avatar of an ancient god. All the different masters merged.

They were surrounded by a glassy tent and a slow breeze cooled his face. Ry Ornis had wrapped him in a rescue field where he fell, carrying safe cool air to replenish what his worksuit could no longer provide.

Olmy rediscovered scattered rivers of memory and bathed his ancient feet there. He swallowed once. The eye, the lesion, had shut forever. "It's gone," he said.

Ry Ornis nodded. "It's done."

"I can never tell anybody," Olmy realized out loud.

"You can never tell anybody."

"We robbed and ate to live. To be born."

Ry Ornis held his fingers to his lips, his face spectral in a new light from the south. A huge grin was spreading around half the Way,

479

a gorgeous brilliant electric light. "The ring gate. A cirque," the gate opener said, glancing over his shoulder. "Rasp and Karn, my students, have done well. We've done what we came here to do, and we saved the Way, as well. Not bad, eh, Ser Olmy?"

Olmy reached up to grab the gate opener, perhaps to strangle him. Ry Ornis had moved, however.

Olmy turned away, swallowed a second time against a competing dryness. There had been no need to complete the ring gate. The unfinished cirque had done its job and drained the final wasted remnants of the lesion, forcing a closure.

As they watched, the cirque shrank. The grin became a smile, became an all-knowing serene curve, then collapsed to a point, and the point dimmed on distant rippled sands.

"I think the twins are a little disappointed they can't finish the cirque. But it's wonderful," Ry Ornis enthused, and performed a small dance on the black obsidian of the valley floor. "They are truly master now! When I am tried and convicted, they will take my place!"

The Way remained. Rolling his head to one side, Olmy could not see the Redoubt.

"Where's the pyramid?" he asked hoarsely.

"Enoch has her wish," Ry Ornis said, and shaded his eyes with one hand.

Plass, Enoch, the allthing.

Plass had seen her own ghost.

To east and west, the ruined mountains and their statues remained, rejected, discarded. No dream, no hallucination.

He had been used again. No matter. For an endless instant, like any gate opener, only more so, he had merged with the eye of the Buddha.

· 9 ·

"The Infinite Hexamon Nexus does not approve of risky experiments that cannot be documented or explained. How many were deceived, Master Ry Ornis?"

"All, myself included."

"Yet you maintain this was done out of necessity?"

"All of it. The utmost necessity."

"Will this ever be necessary again? Answer honestly; the trust between us has worn very thin!"

"Never again."

"How do you explain that one universe, one domain, must feed on another in order to be born?"

"I don't. We were compelled. That is all I know."

"Could it have gone badly?"

"Of course. As it is, in our clumsiness and ignorance, we have condemned all our ancestors to live with unexplainable presences, ghosts of past and future. A kind of afterbirth."

"You are smiling, Master Gate Opener. This is intolerable!"

"It is all I can do, Sers."

. . .

"For your disobedience and arrogance, what punishment do you choose, Master Ry Ornis?"

"Sers of the Nexus. This I swear. I will put down my clavicle from this time forward, and never know the grace again."

— Sentencing Phase of Secret Hearings Conducted by the Infinite Hexamon Nexus, "On the Advisability of Opening Gates into Chaos and Order"

Tracting through the weightless forest of the Wald in the rebuilt Axis Nader, reaching out to the trees to push or grab roots and branches, half-flying and half-climbing, in his mind's river-wide eye, Olmy Ap Sennen returned to Lamarckia, where he had once nearly died of old age, and retrieved a package he had left there, tied in neat pieces of mat-paper. His wives and children had kept it safe for him, and now they returned it. There was much smiling and laughter, then saying of farewells, last of all a farewell to his sons, whom he had left behind Occupants of a different land, another life.

As they faded, in his mind's eye, he opened the package they had given to him and greedily swallowed the wonderful contents.

His soul.

Copyright Acknowledgments